Ohio

*The Young Buckeye State Blossoms with Love
and Adventure in Four Complete Novels*

DIANNE CHRISTNER

BARBOUR
PUBLISHING

Cover photo: © GettyOne, Inc.

ISBN 1-58660-555-0

All Scripture quotations are taken from the King James Version of the Bible.

Published by Barbour Publishing, Inc., P.O. Box 719, Uhrichsville, Ohio 44683, www.barbourbooks.com.

ᏂᏓ Member of the
Evangelical Christian
Publishers Association

Printed in the United States of America.
5 4 3

DIANNE CHRISTNER

Dianne and her husband make their home in Scottsdale, Arizona, enjoying the beauty of the desert. However, it is fond memories of her childhood spent in Ohio that inspired this book. After years of working as an executive secretary, she is happy to be able to spend her time at home writing or traveling and researching. If you enjoyed this book, she invites you to visit her website www.diannechristner.com so that you can meet her and her family members and follow her latest writing endeavors.

Proper Intentions

Dedicated with devotion to my husband, Jim, whose love inspires me, and in memory of my grandmother Mattie.

Chapter 1

Yoo-hoo, Kate!" The familiar voice grated on Kate's nerves like squeaky chalk. Melanie Whitfield stood across Beaver Creek's main thoroughfare waving her arms. Kate regarded Melanie as a meddler and gossipmonger. However, she was inclined to be kind toward all folks, so she started across the street.

The roadway was uneven and marred with ruts and rocks. Her foot slipped into a pothole, and the ladylike Miss Carson transformed straightway into a reeling drunkard. The next few seconds seemed like an eternity.

The earth tilted. The toe of her boot caught the hem of her long calico dress. *I can't fall in front of Melanie and the whole town,* she thought as she toppled forward with arms flailing.

Sprawled headfirst in the dirt road, Kate felt the sting of tiny pebbles embedded in her palms and a burning sensation in her knees. Grit caked her teeth, and her nose ached. She lay unbelieving and dazed until she heard Melanie's scream. "Look out, Kate!"

In a feeble attempt to shield herself from a thundering team of horses, Kate closed her eyes and threw up her arms. The driver of the rig strained to turn his animals. Jaws clenched, he braced his feet against the floorboards of the wagon. His heart did cartwheels when he spotted a young man charging toward the frightened woman. He breathed a prayer for them and yanked back on the reins.

Kate's rescuer plucked her from the ground and dove to safety as the huge beasts lunged past. When the dust cleared, Kate blinked and looked into a pair of familiar blue eyes that mirrored her own fright.

"Tanner!" she sputtered through a mouthful of grit.

"Are you hurt?"

Kate wiggled her ankle, which felt fine, and brushed off her hands and gown. "No, I don't think so."

Tanner supported her as she tested wobbly legs. "What a scare!" he groaned. Then he pulled her close.

Meanwhile, the driver of the wagon pulled his team to a standstill. Pitching the reins to his companion, he leaped to the ground and shouted, "Are you all right, Ma'am?"

Folks nearby stopped what they were doing when they heard the racket. A trapper in buckskin breeches turned to see what was causing all the commotion. Kate felt their curious stares and jerked away from Tanner's embrace. She raised a trembling hand and brushed at the black ringlets that clung tenaciously to her forehead. "Yes, just a bit shaken."

Melanie flung herself into Kate's arms and wailed, "I thought you were doomed." Then she folded her hanky and dabbed at Kate's dirt-smeared face.

The driver of the wagon spoke. "My apologies for the scare, Ma'am. I'm sure glad you're all right. The potholes in this road are big enough to swallow man, woman, or beast."

Kate felt concern in his scolding. She studied the young man with the ruddy complexion. "I don't believe we've met."

"Just moved to the valley, Ma'am. My name is Ben—Ben Wheeler."

"Pleased to meet you. I'm Kate Carson. This is Melanie Whitfield and Tanner Matthews."

Melanie hastened to greet the newcomer. "Welcome to Beaver Creek, Mr. Wheeler." Freckles spotted his face, and sky blue eyes gazed out beneath brown bangs and a droopy hat.

Wheeler warmed under the enthusiasm of the blond, frizzy-haired girl, but he quickly focused on Tanner who offered his hand. Ben gripped it tightly.

"Oh, and that's my brother Luke in the wagon." The siblings had similar features. The obvious difference was Luke's straw-colored hair. "I'd better be getting back to my rig. My apologies again, Miss Carson. I'm sorry about your dress."

Kate looked down at the tattered hem of her blue calico. "It can be fixed." She managed a smile in Ben's behalf. "Please don't give it another thought."

Ben gave his floppy hat a tug. "It was nice meeting you folks."

"We'll be seeing you around, Mr. Wheeler," Melanie called.

Tanner quickly took charge. "Let's get you ladies out of the middle of the road." They crossed the street. "Where are you headed?"

"Cooper's General Store to pick up the mail." Embarrassed from the incident, Kate stole a glance at Tanner and marveled that such a dashing young man was courting her. He was tall, lean, and blond. His eyes were blue and penetrating, his smile dimpled.

At the General Store Tanner turned toward Kate, studying the petite creature that disarmed him so.

Kate's china-doll appearance often misled those who did not know her. She was neither fragile nor weak, but steady and strong in character. Tanner knew her strength stemmed from a faith in God. His gaze rested on the angelic face with its creamy complexion and soft brown eyes. Silky black tresses curled about her face, cascading far past her shoulders. Her lips were two delicate rose petals. He knew they were pure and untouched. Kate was very proper, and today was the first time she had been in his arms.

Kate shifted under his intense scrutiny. Often she felt uneasy around Tanner and did not know why.

Tanner grinned. "Take care, Darlin'. No more stepping in front of wagons. See you Friday night?"

Kate nodded. "Thank you, Tanner."

"At your service, Milady."

The instant he was out of hearing, Melanie whirled to face Kate. "Well! He's a Prince Charming, isn't he?"

"Tanner?" Kate hesitated. "Perhaps."

"Too obliging if you ask me, and bold as brass calling you darlin' in broad daylight."

"That's just the way Tanner talks. It doesn't mean anything. I saw the way you looked at that new fellow."

Melanie replied, "You certainly were clever, throwing yourself in front of his wagon. Let's see. Ben Wheeler." She rolled the words around on her tongue. "Yes, I do like the sound of that. Did you see his brother?"

"I did not throw myself in front of that wagon!"

"Ah-hum. Can I help ya, ladies?" Mr. Cooper interrupted. Propping his broom against the wall, he wiped his hands on his apron and waited on the girls.

"Oh, yes. We're here for the mail. How are you today, Mr. Cooper?"

Elias Cooper mopped the brow of his high forehead. A shiny bald head shone through brown hair combed straight back and styled long at the neck. His beard bobbed up and down when he spoke. "Fine, fine."

They followed him into the store, and he continued, "Over here. I'll git it for ya. It jest came in yesterday. Here ya are. Two letters for Miss Whitfield, and one for Mattie Tucker, which I'll be givin' you, Miss Carson. That reminds me, I've got some seed packets and a large parcel filled with items that Mattie wanted."

The girls parted, and Kate headed home, shifting the large parcel from arm to arm. She clutched the letter and seed packets. *Mattie will be tickled to see these,* she thought. Mattie Tucker had been a mother to her for many years—ever since the Indian raid that orphaned Kate and her two sisters, Annabelle and Claire.

The thoughts of the eighteen-year-old girl wandered here and there and finally settled on Melanie. *I didn't find out what Melanie wanted. Just as well, I suppose.* Then she remembered Melanie's warning about Tanner. She sighed. *Prince Charming is calling on Friday.*

Chapter 2

Kate thumbed through her Bible. The fragile pages fanned through her fingers and then lay open in the thirty-first chapter of Proverbs, where the words jumped off the page at her. "Favour is deceitful, and beauty is vain: but a woman that feareth the LORD, she shall be praised." She reread it, trying to take in the meaning.

Weeks at a time she would ponder over a single verse, for Beaver Creek had no church or parson to question. There was not a soul at Tucker House with whom Kate could discuss the Bible. Mattie was not a believer, but Kate's parents had introduced her to the Lord when she was a small child. Her faith was a link to her past that she adhered to with strong sentiments.

Kate mulled over the verse. *What does it mean to fear the Lord?* she wondered. *This verse is addressed to women. Don't men struggle with vanity? Especially capable men, handsome men. . . .Tanner! Why he'll be here in less than an hour!* She reverently placed her feather bookmark in the page and fled to get ready.

Tanner Matthews's cattle ranch was a small jaunt away—five miles south of Beaver Creek. He entered the town riding his black stallion, Pistol. Tucker House, his destination, perched on the northern fringe of the settlement. On impulse, he reined in his horse at Green's Mill where Jake Hamilton worked. It was quitting time, and Tanner scanned the premises, hoping to have a word with Jake.

A drifter from Kentucky, Hamilton had hired on temporarily at the Matthews's spread two years earlier. Tanner had admired his reckless, worldly wise manner, and they became fast friends.

"You look scrubbed to a shine," Jake said in his lazy Southern drawl.

"On my way to Kate's."

"When you gonna figure out you're jest wastin' your time?"

"What makes you think that, Jake?"

"She's not your type. What about the gals in Dayton?"

"Don't worry, Jake. I'll still be making trips to Dayton with you."

"I think you ought to jest forget her."

"Can't do that, Jake." Tanner reached out to steady Pistol, patting the beast's quivering neck. "It's too late. She's sweet on me. I got her melting like butter on a summer's day."

10

Jake shook his head and smirked. "Sure, Tanner. Maybe you can tell me about it later. There's gonna be a game tonight. Are you in?"

"I'll be there."

"Leave ya to your dreamin' then." Jake turned to walk away.

"Yeah, so long." Tanner spurred his horse into motion. His mouth curled up in a lopsided grin. No girl was unattainable.

Kate's sisters were sitting on the front porch steps when Tanner arrived at Tucker House. Annabelle was a mixture of mischief and delight, having a neverending source of energy. At thirteen, she teetered between womanhood and childhood. Her chestnut tresses bobbed up and down with wisps of cinnamon fluff framing her face. Claire was the baby of the family, which made her seem even younger than her tender twelve years. Atop golden plaited hair, her bonnet was askew, bouncing on her shoulders with ribbons streaming through the air like a kite tail.

"Evening," Annabelle said sweetly. "He's sure a beautiful horse."

"Got him for my sixteenth birthday."

"Can we pet him?"

"Sure. Look here, fella. Two pretty ladies want to meet you."

Pistol nodded his head as if he agreed, and the girls giggled.

Claire's blue eyes danced as she quipped, "Are you here to see Kate again?"

"As a matter of fact, I am." He winked. "Is she home?"

Mattie was just coming out of the kitchen when they entered the sitting room. She smoothed back her hair. "Mr. Matthews, good to see ya. Won't ya have a seat? I'm sure Kate will be down in a minute."

"Thank you, Miss Tucker."

Tanner had a few minutes to wait until Kate appeared followed close at the skirts by Claire. "Hello, Tanner." She seated herself in a wooden rocker.

"You shouldn't keep a fellow waiting, Kate, with Tucker House packed full of lovely ladies."

"This is too soppy! Come on, Annabelle." Claire left the room, leading her sister by the arm.

Mattie laughed and busied her hands, hemming a gown. "It's a lovely evenin'," she said.

"It is. Would you mind if I took Kate for a walk, Miss Tucker?"

"Of course not. Enjoy yourselves."

Once they were outside, he directed Kate around the back of the house toward the creek. It was a lovely spot, thick with springtime growth. Wild lilac bushes lined the path, and small trees congregated in clumps along the creek bank. Crickets chirped in harmony with hoarse frogs. Occasionally a hungry trout flipped out of the water, producing elaborate rings of silver that drifted away with the current.

"Are you fully recovered? Any scrapes or bruises?"

Kate answered pertly, "I think it is very rude of you to bring up such an embarrassing incident." She smiled. "I feel fine—except for my pride."

They watched the sun set from a hill that overlooked the countryside. When it slipped behind the trees, Tanner led Kate to a crude bench beneath the hickory tree that spread its limbs wide over the house. "Sit here awhile and watch the moon come out?" he asked.

Kate nodded. As the first shade of night fell, the air turned cool. Kate shivered, and Tanner moved closer. "Cold?"

"I'm fine. The night is lovely, but the sounds are eerie."

"Animals. They just killed a big panther at the mill this week. You're not scared, are you? I'm handy with this, you know." Tanner patted his pistol, which hung strapped to his hip. He continued, "I've scared off plenty of wild beasts. I was in a gunfight once in Dayton."

"A gunfight! How awful. What happened?"

Tanner hesitated a moment as he mentally pieced his story together, summing up the parts he would leave out. "Not so terrible. I caught a man cheating in cards. He went for his gun, and I shot him in the arm."

"I've heard those kinds of things happen often when men gamble."

"You don't approve?"

"Does any woman?"

Tanner thought about the painted Stella at the Six Star Saloon in Dayton. She approved of anything he did. He grinned sheepishly and lied, "I guess not, Kate. Then there was the time we caught Indians stealing our cattle."

Kate stiffened. "Indians killed my folks, you know."

"No, I didn't."

Kate shuddered. She still had vivid dreams about it. Tanner seized the opportunity and drew her closer, slipping his arm around her.

"I was only six. Annabelle was one and Claire just a baby. We lived at Big Bottom on the Ohio River. Father hid us in the root cellar, but I could hear the shots, the screams—and smell the smoke. It was awful."

"Oh, poor darlin'." In a practiced motion, he tilted her chin and kissed her. Kate did not feel the joy that she imagined her first kiss would hold. As he pulled her into a passionate embrace, she firmly pushed him away.

"Darlin'?"

Kate replied breathlessly, "You stole that kiss! I meant to save it for my betrothed."

"Ah, Kate, it was just a kiss, and a very sweet one. I've no regrets."

Kate blushed. "I see. You are presumptuous then."

He jerked his arm away. "Am I? Perhaps you're a bit prudish." Kate's chin quivered, and she blinked back tears. "I should not have said that. I'm sorry. Look, I'm not one to play games. You stir me, Kate, and that kiss was an honest reaction. Obviously, you do not feel the same way about me."

"Of course I'm attracted to you, but I'm a Christian."

"What has that got to do with anything?"

"I believe that when a man and woman love each other, they wed and remain faithful to each other."

"So do I, Darlin'. But marriage is a big step, Kate. I don't recall. . ."

"I also believe in being pure until marriage, to save my kisses for the man I choose to live with for the rest of my life."

"I see. Well, I ain't never heard that one before. That's quite a notion— one that will take a bit to get used to."

They sat still, watching the fireflies flicker. Finally Tanner spoke. "Do you know why I noticed you?" Kate shook her head. "I've always had girls chasing me, trying to latch on to my money, I suppose."

Kate smiled. She knew that was not the only reason women sought Tanner. He could stand on good looks alone.

"You were special, like a rose in a daisy patch. Who wouldn't choose the rare flower over all the others?"

"I don't understand. Why was I different?"

"You were hard to get, Darlin', and now I'm trying to change you. Don't know what came over me. Will you forgive me?" Kate studied his handsome face. When she did not respond immediately, Tanner added softly, "Please."

Tears welled up in Kate's eyes, and a lump formed in her throat.

Tanner reached out for her hand. "Aw, don't cry, Darlin'. Let me make it up to you. How about a picnic next Saturday?"

Kate smiled, "All right."

Chapter 3

Sheriff Buck Larson knocked at the door, right on time. He was treating the Tucker House ladies to dinner at the town's new tavern. Buck styled his salt-and-pepper hair slicked back at the sides, and his bushy white sideburns and black mustache provided a striking contrast against his weathered face.

Mattie's eyes lit up when she saw him. "Buck! Good to see ya. Come in." Mattie pointed to a chair in the sitting room and led the way with Buck towering over her, a massive man at six foot one and powerfully built.

Huge creases lined his face, marking him as a man who often smiled. She knew that beneath his calm demeanor he was a man of principle. Stubborn as a mule and stable as the ground beneath his feet, he was not afraid to take any action necessary to keep the law and order in Beaver Creek.

The girls entered the room and found their longtime friend chatting with Mattie. Kate thought, *I wonder why they've never married? Mattie doesn't seem to have any interest in marrying. Maybe she thinks sheriffing is too dangerous.* Romance and marriage intrigued her now that Tanner had entered her life.

"Hello, Sheriff. Sorry to keep you waiting."

"Not at all. My time is yours today." His nod included them all.

"Perhaps," Mattie said with a grin. She knew that if any trouble crossed their paths Buck would lend a hand, for he was not one to shirk a duty.

Buck led them to the wagon, and they rode the mile and a half into town. They could have easily walked, but the sheriff liked to pamper Mattie. Minutes later, he pointed to the valley's newest structure. "There she is: The Lone Wolf."

A wooden sign creaked and groaned between two iron posts where a crude image of the creature's head was etched into the grain. They burst into laughter at the name. Everyone in Beaver Creek knew that there was no lone wolf. The animals were so plentiful that a bounty of fifty cents was offered for each wolf killed in the county.

When they entered the tavern's spacious dining room, Kate's gaze rested on a slight girl with brown hair carrying a pewter water pitcher. The young woman approached and greeted them cheerfully. "Sheriff Larson, nice to see ya. What can I be doin' for ya?"

Buck called her by name. "Elizabeth, this is Mattie Tucker and her daughters, Kate, Annabelle, and Claire. I'll be buying their dinner."

She led them to a small table with four chairs, and Buck pulled up another to make room for the five of them. The inn was pleasant, with two curtained windows facing the street. A shaft of light shot across the room, highlighting an open hearth.

The proprietor's daughter walked with a spring to her step, bringing piping hot roast beef, turnips, and potatoes on pewter plates. A wooden bowl filled with biscuits soon appeared, along with a small platter of butter.

"This is luxury, bein' waited on and such," Mattie said to the sheriff. "Thank ya for givin' us sech a special treat, Buck."

"It's my pleasure."

The heavy door creaked open, and Rose Whitfield and her daughter Melanie entered the room with great commotion. Rose maneuvered across the room, easing her large body between chairs and tables.

"Mattie Tucker! Imagine meeting you here the first time we dropped in, and with the sheriff, too."

"Please join us," Mattie offered. The sheriff shot Mattie a look of disapproval that she disregarded.

"Oh, no! Well, maybe jest to chat a bit." Rose wheezed as she plopped down in a chair that Melanie had pulled up beside the others. The sheriff stretched out his long legs, preparing for a lengthy discourse. Admiring Mattie for her hospitality, he did not interfere.

Melanie began a lengthy narrative involving Kate, something about a pothole and Tanner rescuing her. Annabelle poked Claire, and they burst into a fit of giggles as they watched their older sister squirm.

"Kate, you'll never guess! Ma found out all about Ben Wheeler. Emmett Wheeler is a widower. He has two unmarried sons, Ben and Luke." Melanie cocked her blond curly head to the side and waited for Kate's reply.

Kate smiled. "It's good to have new folks moving into the valley."

Rose interrupted, "My Melanie might even set her cap for one of them. Right handsome they are, the whole lot of them. After she takes her pick, there would be one left over for you, Kate." Rose cackled like an old hen at her own joke, her heavy bosom heaving until she quieted down.

"Kate already has a beau," Annabelle piped up.

"She does now? Who might that be?"

"Mother, I told you Tanner Matthews was courting Kate," Melanie added.

"Oh, that's right. Now that's a man I'm not so sure about. There's rumors going around about those trips he takes to Dayton. Word has it that he gambles and chases women."

"Mother!"

"Like I said, it's jest hearsay, but perhaps it'd be worth checking into. About those Wheeler boys, Annabelle's getting to be about the right age for. . ."

"Rose, please," interrupted Mattie. "There's plenty of time for that." Mattie's stern look dissipated Rose's rambling.

"Very well then."

Kate pitied the Wheeler boys. Ben had seemed like a nice young man to her. She wondered how long it would be until Melanie had her cat claws in him. She shuddered at her own evil thoughts. Anyway, she had her hands full worrying about Tanner.

"I've met the Wheelers. They seem to be a fine family." The sheriff straightened up in his chair as he spoke.

But the matter was dropped when Lillian Denton, the proprietor, came to their table. She had met the sheriff already, and he quickly introduced her to the group. She welcomed them to The Lone Wolf.

"I hope you find Beaver Creek to your likin'," Mattie said.

"I'm sure we will. Everyone is quite agreeable."

"You did sech a wonderful job with the inn. It is very modern." Rose's eyes darted about as she spoke.

"Why thank ya. Now, what kind of pie would ya like for dessert?" She turned toward Rose. "We'll be gettin' your order right away, Ma'am."

Mattie and the girls declined pie, and Buck was soon leading them out of the tavern. "Would you mind if we stroll over to the office just to check things?"

"We'd be delighted," Mattie said, taking his arm while Kate and her sisters followed. As they approached the center of town, they could see Green's Mill, which was situated on the Little Miami close to the juncture of the Beaver Creek. The entire area was humming with the activity of a main thoroughfare. The oldest building was the blockhouse, modified into a jailhouse. Cabins converted into shops lined either side, one of which served as the sheriff's home and office.

"Look! A flatboat!" Claire exclaimed.

"Sure enough!" Buck agreed. "Wonder where they're headed?" They all watched the barge drift close, piled high with barrels of merchandise. One of the passengers waved, and Buck shouted, "What's your cargo?"

The traveler hollered, "Pork, flour, bacon, and whiskey."

"Where you headed?"

"Downriver ta Cincinnati."

A canoe glided by the slow-moving craft, stealing Kate's attention. Two Indians paddled to shore and climbed out. Kate cringed, and her heart beat wildly in her breast.

"The one on the right is Tecumseh," Buck whispered. "He's a Shawnee chief. James Galloway says he speaks good English. His brother, The Prophet, has a mission near Greenville."

The Indians passed with a brisk, elastic step. Tecumseh walked erect and proud, measuring about five feet nine inches.

Annabelle gasped. "Why, he's good looking!"

Kate gave her sister a disgusted sidelong glance, then riveted her gaze on the Shawnee chief. He wore tanned buckskins and a perfectly fitting hunting frock trimmed in leather fringe. A silver tomahawk hung strapped to his muscular body. It was quite some time before Kate could concentrate on anything except the red-skinned men they had just encountered.

That night Kate's eyes fluttered as she drifted into a fitful slumber and dreamed of childhood days. Six years old again, she was playing in the barn and watching the newborn calf. Caressing her pillow, she rubbed his pink nose, soft as the velvet in Mattie's sewing box. His tongue was rough as sandpaper when he slipped it out to lick her hand. "So long," she murmured. "I gotta go help Ma now."

While Kate dreamed, a storm brewed, and branches squeaked outside her bedroom window. In her vision it was the barn door creaking. She pushed it open and looked around. The wind inflated her bedroom curtains, but she dreamed that her ma's wash was blowing in the breeze with her Sunday dress lying in the mud. "Ma!" Kate called with concern, but her mother was nowhere to be found.

Thunder cracked, then she heard a door slam and saw her pa running out of the house. He had his rifle across one arm, toting Annabelle and Claire with the other. "Pa! Why are you runnin'?" Fear gripped her body.

"Take your sisters!" he yelled. "Quick! Get down in the root cellar!"

"What's a-matter, Pa?" she cried, grabbing Annabelle and Claire. Her father shoved her into the dark cellar despite her protests, kissed the top of her head, and shut the trapdoor.

Another crack of thunder ripped through the night, and she heard her pa's rifle. Kate put her hand over her ears, but she could still hear the dreadful howling of the Indians.

"No! No!" Kate bolted upright in her bed, shaking and drenched in sweat. She looked around the room. "It was just a dream." She slowly climbed out of bed. Shivering, she stood before her window and watched the rain pelting the earth. Tears tracked her cheeks, and she pulled the window closed with a fierceness that emanated from the terror and hatred that stirred her anew.

Chapter 4

Kate opened her eyes but quickly closed them as bright ribbons of sunshine splashed across her face. The sensation was warm and pleasant. Mercifully, the nightmare of the past evening eluded her. Snuggled under the fluffy comforter, she rolled over and savored the moment. *It must be late—the sun is high*. She blinked and took a quick peek. Chatter from below drifted into her room. In a determined motion, she bolted out of bed and pulled on her clothes.

"Morning, Mattie, girls. Glad it's not my turn to fix breakfast or you'd all be starving."

"I'll say," Annabelle grumbled. "We need our nourishment to do all our chores. Why do I have to pull weeds? I'd rather do the cooking."

Mattie shook her finger at Annabelle. "Grab patience by the tail, Child, and hang on with all your might. You'll get your turn ta cook. We all need ta do our share. That's what makes us a family, pullin' together."

"Oh, I know," Annabelle murmured. "I'm sorry."

Kate poured herself a cup of steaming coffee and sat down. She ran her finger around the rim absentmindedly as her thoughts wandered to the recent warnings about Tanner.

Mattie noticed her faraway look. "Thinkin' hard on somethin'?"

"Tanner asked me to go on a picnic Saturday."

"I see. Do ya plan to go?"

Kate nodded and then continued, "I was wondering what you know about him. Do you think there's any truth to Rose's comments at The Lone Wolf?"

"As I recollect, the girls have always chased him. I asked Buck about his trips to Dayton. Tanner goes on business for his pa. Word is out that he had a girl there, but nothin' came of it. All hearsay, mind ya. How do you feel about him, Honey?"

"I'm not sure. He is spoiled and self-centered, but so attractive." Kate giggled. "Those blue eyes and big dimples are hard to resist when he turns on the charm."

"Yes, he is a very good-lookin' lad. Sometimes ya have ta be even more careful with those, Kate. Don't let your heart rule your mind. Ya have to do what ya know is right, even with them blue eyes tellin' ya different."

Mattie wondered if she should tell Kate about her own painful past.

She had never planned to share her secret. *Would it keep Kate from making the same mistakes?* Mattie looked around the table and realized that Claire and Annabelle were quietly listening. She decided to wait and see what developed.

Bored with the turn of the discussion, Claire piped up, "I'll go collect the eggs and get started on my chores. Little chicks should be hatching soon." She headed toward the porch for the egg basket.

"I'll help clear the table," Annabelle offered.

Kate and Mattie looked at each other, puzzled. It was natural for Claire to get right at her chores, but not Annabelle. In truth, Annabelle thought she might hear a little more about the charming Tanner Matthews if she stayed in the kitchen. However, the topic was closed.

The week passed quickly, with Annabelle and Claire easily fitting into the summer routine of more chores and free time. Claire checked daily on the setting hens, waiting for those new chicks. Annabelle liked to explore the banks along the creek and watch the beavers at work. The sisters were inseparable. Annabelle provided sparks of creativity to their days while it was usually Claire who managed to keep them out of trouble.

Mattie and Kate went about their chores quietly, in reflection. Mattie worried about Kate's acquaintance with Tanner. Kate looked forward to the picnic but was plagued with a growing sense of uneasiness as well.

On the day of the picnic, Mattie put nervous energy to good use and baked a pie. *Don't know why I'm providin' extra bait for the catch. There he is now, knockin' at the door!* She wiped the wrinkles out of her apron and went to the door, where Tanner stood on the porch. "Come in, Mr. Matthews. I'll be gettin' Kate."

"Thank ya, Miss Tucker." Hat in hand, he waited just inside the door.

Soon Kate, carrying a pie, greeted Tanner. He offered her his arm, and they made their way to his buggy. "Here, let's put that in this basket my mother packed. Looks delicious. Did you bake it?"

"No, I didn't." Kate smiled. "It does look good."

Tanner helped Kate into the buggy, then climbed up and took the reins.

"I hope it doesn't rain again today," said Kate.

"Me, too. I wouldn't miss this picnic, rain or shine."

Kate looked at him warmly. "Where are we going, Tanner?"

"You just wait till you see it, the loveliest spot in Beaver Creek. It's on my property—a small meadow down by the creek with lots of wildflowers and very secluded." He glanced over and noticed Kate's blush. "Don't let that worry you any," he added with one of his most fetching smiles and continued to point out the spring attractions as they rode along.

"Here we are," said Tanner at last. "We have to leave the buggy here and walk the rest of the way." He jumped down and eagerly dashed around the side of the buggy to take Kate by the waist and assist her to the ground. "Just be patient, Darlin', while I tie up the horses."

Kate watched Tanner as he worked. He appeared self-assured. She closed her eyes for just a moment and wished herself to be calm.

Then Tanner grabbed the picnic basket and was back at Kate's side. He offered her his hand, and they walked toward the creek through a wooded thicket. A narrow footpath indicated that the area was visited frequently. The path sloped downward to the creek, and Kate had to watch her footing so she would not slip.

A breeze kicked up, and she let go of Tanner's hand to fasten her bonnet more securely. In that instant, Kate slid on the steep trail, toppling forward with a shriek. Tanner quickly dropped his basket and reached out to steady her. He held her closely and gazed at her intently.

"Are you all right, Kate?"

Kate laughed nervously. "Yes, I'm fine. Thank you, Tanner."

"Better just let that bonnet fly next time; I'd like to see your hair blowing free anyway." Tanner released her and picked up his basket. "We're almost there. Look!"

"Why, it's lovely! It is the most beautiful place in Beaver Creek! Is all this land yours?"

"Yep. My land and Father's join, making a sizeable spread. This meadow is on the edge of our property. The creek is the boundary line. It's good grazing land."

They spread a blanket on the ground, but the cloth billowed and flapped like a sail at sea. Tanner picked up a couple of rocks and secured the corners. They both ignored the warning signs of an angry sky, behaving as if the day were fine for a picnic. However, the wind got more fierce by the minute.

Tanner managed to secure Kate's hand and started to speak a word of endearment, "Kate, Darlin'. . ." But lightning shot across the sky, followed by a loud crack of thunder that startled them both. They looked up and saw huge, black buffalo clouds rolling in behind them.

Kate smiled. "I think it's going to rain after all. Looks like a storm, too."

"You're right. I don't think we'll have time to take shelter at the house. If we can make it to the buggy, I know of an empty cabin. We could take the horses and wait it out inside."

Quickly, they gathered the picnic fixings. Kate tied her bonnet ribbons securely this time. They started back up the hill, and the return trip proved slower than coming had been. As they reached the buggy and horses, great drops of rain fell, making tiny dimples in the road.

Tanner shoved the basket under the seat and yelled for Kate to throw the blanket over her head. He took the horses, and together they ran toward the deserted cabin, the wind howling and blowing on their backs. Tanner tethered the horses on the protected side of the building and entered the shelter breathlessly.

"Sorry, Darlin', you're all soaked. I reckon we should have cancelled the picnic, but I wanted to see you so much." He gently pulled the blanket down from around Kate and reached up to untie her bonnet. "This is all wet. Better just take it off so you can dry out." He moved his hand to the back of her hair, loosening it to fall freely down her back. Pulling her into a tight embrace, Tanner kissed her passionately.

Kate struggled and pushed him away. "Don't, Tanner! Stop it! I thought you understood. Y—you promised!" He continued to grip her tightly by the arms, angered by her Puritan attitude. "Tanner, you're hurting me!"

"I adore you. I don't want to hurt you." He leaned close, and she turned her face aside. His breath was hot against her cheek.

"Let me go this instant!"

With most women, he just saw what he wanted and took it. A battle raged within him as he struggled to control his frustration, then slowly he released her. "I'm sorry, Kate." The lies slipped smooth as oil off his tongue. "It's just that I'm falling head over heels in love with you." Remembering her convictions, Tanner dramatized by dropping to the floor on his knees. "Marry me, Kate," he pleaded.

"Please get up. The storm is passing, and I'd like to go home."

"Okay, Kate, if that's what you want. But tell me first, I didn't hurt you, did I? Will you forgive me?"

"I'm all right. I just need to think."

"As soon as the storm is over, we'll go. First, listen to what I have to say. I love you and want to marry you."

Half an hour later they headed to Tucker House.

When they arrived, Tanner helped Kate out of his buggy and held her hand a moment longer. "Think about what I said."

Once inside, Kate tried to act calm. She told Mattie that she got caught in the storm and needed to change into dry clothes. Alone in her room, she leaned against the closed door and searched her heart.

Chapter 5

Claire and Annabelle were in the henhouse admiring the newly hatched chicks, now two days old. Keeping constant vigil, the hen cackled at the girls and swept her chicks to safety beneath her plump body. They tired easily and slept huddled together looking lifeless. When awake, however, they scrambled about until the anxious hen gathered them safely under her wings. It was an endless routine. The girls were so captivated that they lost track of time.

Claire cooed, "Aren't they just the cutest little things, so soft. I could watch them all day."

Annabelle stretched and yawned. "I think we have."

"Oh, my!" Claire jumped up. "It's getting late! We'd better do the milking and get to the house for supper."

"I hope it's not chicken tonight!" The girls laughed.

Half an hour later they entered the kitchen, where a pleasant aroma greeted them. "Mm, cornbread and beans," said Annabelle, winking at her sister.

Later that evening they sat around the fireplace enjoying each other's company. The June nights were cool, and the fire took off the chill. Mattie was busy sewing lace on a dress for a neighbor. Kate was occupied cleaning out the sewing box and arranging threads and notions. They were listening to Claire and Annabelle's chatter as they played checkers on the board Buck had made for them. The night seemed ordinary enough until a rap at the door startled them.

Mattie placed her sewing aside and moved toward the door. She unlocked the latch and pulled it open.

"Why, Mr. Matthews. . .hello," she said. "Come on in."

"Good evenin', Miss Tucker," said Tanner. "Is Kate here?"

"Yes, come in the sittin' room and pull up a chair. We're jest enjoyin' the fire."

"Yes, the nights are still a bit chilly. Hello, Kate." He gave her a big grin. "Hello, girls." Then he pulled up a chair beside Kate.

"Hello, Tanner," Kate replied softly. She had not found the courage to confide in Mattie about Tanner's behavior. She had been praying for direction; however, she felt confused and uncomfortable in his presence.

"I just got back from a trip to Dayton." Tanner did not realize that was not the best thing he could have said.

"I see," answered Kate sharply. "On a pleasure trip?"

"Why no, Darlin', on business—and a hard trip it was, too."

Mattie interrupted, "What's it like in Dayton now, Mr. Matthews? It's a long while since I've been there."

"Please, call me Tanner. Lively, very lively. All sorts of merchants are setting up shop, and there's all kinds of folks coming in on the Miami from the Ohio River. Folks are moving west in hordes with all their belongings on flatboats." He motioned vigorously with his hands as he spoke. "Others are trading and moving their goods down the river. There's several new inns in town." He blushed and then continued, "And a variety of merchandise. Anything you could be wanting."

"Sounds like a beehive of activity," Mattie said.

"You're right, that's just what it's like." Tanner nodded enthusiastically.

"And the queen bee?" Kate asked.

"Darlin'?" Tanner replied, wondering if he had heard Kate quite right.

"Sounds excitin'," Mattie sighed. "Perhaps we'll take a trip ta Dayton sometime, girls. Would ya like that?"

"Yes! When?" chimed Claire and Annabelle.

"Well, not tonight." Mattie laughed. "It's gettin' ta be your bedtimes. You girls shoo on up to bed. Don't dawdle now! As for me, I think I'll do some readin' in my room. Will ya tend to the fire, Kate, and put out the candles?"

"Yes, Mattie. Good night." The girls made their good nights, and soon all was quiet in the sitting room except for the crackling fire.

"I feel you're upset, Kate," said Tanner, moving his chair closer to her and searching her eyes for his answer. "Is it because I didn't call sooner? I should have sent word that I had to leave town."

"No, Tanner. It isn't that at all," insisted Kate.

"Kate, please look at me." Tanner gently tilted her chin upwards.

A shiver ran through Kate. She quickly moved to the fire, rubbing her arms as if she were cold. Slowly she turned around. Then taking a deep breath, she ventured, "Tanner, you said once that you don't like to play games, so I'd like to be very honest with you if I may."

"That's right, Kate. Go ahead."

"I hear a lot of rumors about your trips to Dayton. I did not want to believe what I heard, but your actions tend to confirm. . ."

Tanner jumped up and stood before her. "What? That I gamble now and then?"

"That you are a womanizer."

Tanner studied Kate before he answered. "I'll admit there may have been some truth to that at one time, but not anymore. I swear it. You're just what I'm needing to become a proper husband. Believe me, Kate, I had good intentions of. . ."

"No!" Kate interrupted him. "I could forgive if you could change, but I don't think you can. You are too practiced."

"I cannot believe that you would hold what's already past against me."

"It's not just that. I don't want to be encouraging you when I don't even know what I'm feeling. You'd better just look somewhere else."

"You think I could just forget you? No! I love you, and my offer of marriage still stands." Kate shook her head sadly, but he continued. "Give me a chance to prove I can change."

"Tanner. . ."

"No. Don't say anything more tonight. Just think about it." He walked to the door, then stopped and looked at Kate with determination. "This isn't good-bye, Darlin'. It's just the beginning." His deep blue eyes spoke words more tender than any that had ever escaped his lips.

"Good night," she said. She wanted to believe him. After the door closed, Kate put out the fire, blew out the candles, and headed upstairs. After much struggling, she fell into a deep sleep.

A few hours later, a terrible ruckus woke Mattie. Jumping out of bed, she ran for the rifle, loaded it, and stole to the front porch to see what was causing the trouble. Something was in the henhouse.

She proceeded cautiously, toting the rifle. Sheriff Larson had taught her to shoot several years back. She was not a very good shot but could scare whatever animal was out there. *If it's a bear*. . . She shuddered to think such a thing. Raising the rifle to her shoulder to take aim, she eyed the culprit. It was just a fox, so she lowered the rifle. Her heart was drumming, rising to the call of battle. She forced herself to relax a moment, and then she made an issue of stomping loudly to the henhouse with her arms swinging wildly like a windmill on wheels. The fox ran off, dragging the old hen with him, and disappeared in the weeds down by the creek.

Mattie peeked inside. It was not a pretty sight. Tomorrow she would deal with it. Now she latched the door and leaned against it for support. Claire and Annabelle would be upset.

Mattie was up at daybreak removing the evidence of the previous night's raid. Feathers were everywhere. She wiped her damp brow with her arm, feeling a little queasy. She knew the trouble was not over. That old fox probably would come sneaking back the first chance he got. Finally, she headed to the kitchen as the house came alive with morning activities.

"Good morning, Mattie. Morning, Kate," Annabelle said as she and Claire entered the kitchen. They sat down and scooted their bench closer to the table.

Kate glanced at Mattie and knew right away that something was wrong. "Mattie, are you feeling all right? What's wrong?"

"Girls, a fox got into the henhouse last night."

"Oh no!" cried Claire. "Are the baby chicks all right?"

"I'm sorry." Mattie shook her head. "They're all dead. When I got out there, it was too late. He took the mother hen and ran off towards the creek."

"Why did he have to kill them? Why not that mean old rooster?"

"I reckon the mother hen put up a ruckus protectin' her chicks and attracted his attention all the more. The chicks were easy pickin's. I guess the hen must've put up a fight."

Claire started sobbing. Annabelle reached to hug her and helplessly looked up at Mattie. That expression broke open the floodgates for Mattie. She joined them in a cry until a knock came at the front door.

Kate jumped up and said, "I'll go." She slipped out and closed the door behind her to provide privacy for her family. There stood James and Frank Potter.

"Hello, boys," said Kate.

"Howdy, Miss Carson. Our ma sent us for the milk. We couldn't get away yesterday."

"That's all right, boys. Let's go down to the springhouse." Kate liked these little fellas. Frank was eleven and James, twelve. Their pa had died a year back, and times were getting real hard for them. They had had to get rid of their milk cows and were one of the families who got their milk at Tucker House. Kate wondered how long they would be able to stay at Beaver Creek. She expected them to move to Dayton, where the boys could earn a living at an early age and support their ma.

"Bye, boys. Tell your ma hello."

"Yes, Miss Carson. Thank ya," said James.

Inside, breakfast was eaten slowly without the usual lively conversation. Kate could hear the scraping of Claire's fork, pushing her food.

Please, Lord, Kate prayed silently, *help us through this morning. Give Claire something good to think about. Help us catch that old fox before he can steal more chickens. May I be an encourager around this house today, Lord.* Then the words of Philippians 4:19 ran through her mind. *"But my God shall supply all your need according to his riches in glory by Christ Jesus."* She smiled. *Thank you, Jesus.*

Chapter 6

The icy creek felt so good! The mud oozed up between Claire's toes. *Folks say wading is for boys,* she thought. *But why should girls miss such a pleasure?* She had stripped off her shoes and socks and hiked her skirts, draping them over her arm. *I guess I should have told Annabelle where I was headed.* Her sister loved wading, but Claire wanted to be alone to do some thinking. Plunk! Swish!

"Hey! I didn't see you there, Miss. Did I get you all wet?"

Claire laughed. "Well, I am wet, but it's not your fault." She waded to the edge of the creek and climbed the grassy, sloped bank.

The intruder had a pleasant-sounding voice.

"My name is Ben—Ben Wheeler." He held out his huge, tanned hand and shook her tiny, soft one.

"Nice to meet you. I'm Claire and I live at Tucker House with Mattie Tucker and Annabelle and Kate, who are my sisters. We've all been living together since my folks died."

Ben's heart went out to the little girl. "Oh, I see. I live with my brother, Luke, and my pa. We just moved here a few weeks ago."

"So you're the new neighbor we heard about at The Lone Wolf. Melanie said you almost ran over Kate, and Melanie's ma told her to set her cap for you."

Ben's eyebrows raised in surprise and trepidation at this last remark. Then he chuckled at her innocent expression. "I think I'll like it here if everyone is as friendly as you are, Claire." His eyes wandered far away, taking in the lay of the land. "It's beautiful country."

"Sometimes." A little sob rose in her throat as she recalled the morning's calamity.

"Why do you say that?"

"A fox killed my baby chicks and their mother last night. The fox probably will come back tonight." Claire was trying very hard not to cry, but her mouth twitched uncontrollably, and a tear rolled down her cheek.

"Is there anyone who could catch that fox for you?"

"Catch him? No, we're all afraid. Mattie can shoot, but she was crying this morning. Could you catch him?"

"Perhaps I can. Whoa! Looks like I got what I came for!"

"What's that?"

Plop! Splash! "My supper." He grinned.

Claire wiped away her tears and smiled at the huge shirtless young man. He was tan and muscular. His blue eyes twinkled, and she felt like she could trust him. Something about his freckles made him appealing.

"Here, help me pull him in," Ben offered.

When the fish was safely on shore, Claire giggled. "That was fun! I never fished before."

Ben look astonished. "You mean to tell me that you live here and never fished before? You're pulling my leg."

"No, I'm not. It's menfolk's work and there's no men in our family. We hardly ever have fish for supper, only when Sheriff Larson brings us some."

"Perhaps I could stop by and share my catch after I'm done here and check on that fox for you."

"That would be great!" She proceeded to explain which house was theirs, and Ben assured her he could find his way.

Claire thought she'd better get home before she was missed, so she followed the bank until she came to the place where she had left her socks and shoes. She brushed off her feet, pulled them on without lacing, and hurried home with her news.

That evening, after dinner and before dark, there was a rap on the door.

"I'll get it!" Claire ran to the door. "It's probably him." She flung it open and asked, "You been fishing all this time?"

Ben smiled at the girl with the long blond braids. "No. As a matter of fact, I've been home, cleaned my fish, and had my supper already."

"Well, you sure smell good!"

Ben laughed. "Thank you, Claire."

Mattie came to the door. "Claire, invite our guest in and introduce him."

"Come on in, Ben. This is Mattie."

Mattie reached out and shook his hand. "I'm Mattie Tucker. This is Kate and her sister Annabelle."

"Pleased to meet you all. The name is Ben Wheeler, but please call me Ben, as Claire and I are already on a first-name basis." Ben turned a rosy shade as he continued, "I believe we've met before, Kate."

She smiled, but before she could answer, Claire piped up, "Didn't you bring us any fish?"

Ben's face reddened even further, and Mattie corrected her daughter. "Claire! Where are your manners, Child?"

Ben quickly said, "Oh, that's all right." Then he addressed Claire, "I thought I should check with Miss Tucker before I came with a pail of smelly fish. Would you like some fish the next time I have a catch?"

"Why, that would be very nice, Ben. We certainly would. We don't fish ourselves, and it would be a real treat."

"Great! It's a promise then."

Claire interrupted. "Kate?"

"Yes," Kate answered.

"I told you he was nice; I like him better than your beau."

Ben looked at Kate, and they blushed as their eyes met. Then Ben burst out in hearty laughter. "It's good to be around children," he said, adding, "You see, my ma died when I was twelve. My brother, Luke, and Pa and I live alone. Luke is eighteen. So we don't have any women or children's chatter at our place."

Kate relaxed. He had such an openness about him, and his sincerity touched her. *Yes, Claire, I like him better, too,* she thought. But she said, "Ben, I'll bet you would enjoy a piece of Mattie's cherry pie then."

"I sure would."

"Me, too," said Annabelle.

Their appetites led them into the kitchen. As they seated themselves around the table, Mattie noticed Kate was stealing glances at their new neighbor, whose back was turned. Ben had brown hair, a ruddy complexion, and the kindest blue eyes. Kate was thinking, *There is something different about his eyes. . . .* He was very tall, even taller than Tanner, with broad shoulders and large hands. He seemed to be genuinely enjoying himself. As Kate sat down to join them at the table, she thought, *I wonder who bakes their bread if it's all menfolk at their place?*

Meanwhile Ben was thinking, *It's good you led me to that fishing hole, Lord. I think these ladies are needing a man's help, and I'd be honored to be your means of helping them.* As he finished his pie, he said, "I thank you for your hospitality. I'm glad to meet my neighbors. The real reason I stopped in was to see if I could help you trap a fox."

"Fox?" Kate asked. "Oh yes! But how?"

"Luke and I will ride back and keep watch. If he doesn't show up tonight, we can set a trap tomorrow."

"Oh, my!" Mattie said. "That's too much trouble for ya, Ben."

"Not at all; I'd really like to help."

"Well, I have been worried all day," admitted Mattie. "It seems that things have a way of workin' themselves out."

"The Lord provides for His people, Mattie," said Ben.

Kate's head shot up, and a warm sensation rose in her bosom. Did this man know her Lord? *Yes! That's it! I knew there was something special about him,* she thought while gazing into his kind eyes.

Chapter 7

Ben was pleased with the choice they had made to move to Ohio. He was delighted that the soil was rich and black, even more fertile than he had imagined. He was contemplating what would make the farm prosper as he trotted along on his horse, Pepper, taking in the lay of the land. Headed home from Beaver Creek, he had picked up supplies they needed for the farm along with the trap for Tucker House. He thought he would drop by now and set the trap.

Reaching Tucker House, he dismounted and secured Pepper to a tree. He intended to go on back to the henhouse and set the trap up right away. Later he would drop by the house and warn the women. As he headed toward the henhouse, a low voice startled him.

He stood still, then ventured a little closer and stopped again. There was Kate, sitting on a bench beneath a big hickory tree. Her head was bowed. Was she crying? He moved forward to approach her, but when he heard her words, he froze in his tracks.

"Today I shall see him again. I dreamed about him last night. He's every inch a man, with a heart as big as all outdoors. . .handsome, and a tower of strength. But best of all, he belongs to You, Lord. Thank you for showing me there are honorable men after all, men worth trusting. Amen."

Ben swallowed hard; now what was he to do? Not meaning to eavesdrop, he had caught her praying about her beau. He quietly backed away. A flood of disappointment washed over him. He sounded nice enough. What was wrong then? He always wanted the best for folks. Why did he feel so low? Maybe he felt ashamed of himself for invading her privacy. *That must be it*, he decided.

Just then, a bloodcurdling scream ripped through the air, stirring him from his reverie. It came from the direction of the creek. Dropping the trap, he raced back to the hickory tree where Kate was rising.

"It's coming from the creek; it's Annabelle!" she shouted. Ben flew by her. The yard sloped downward, past the other buildings to the creek. He ran toward the water. Kate picked up her skirts and followed close behind.

"Head for the water!" screamed Ben. The sight was awful. Annabelle was covered with bees, which were swarming everywhere. He swooped Annabelle up into his strong arms and, swatting at the bees, charged ahead for the creek. "Come on, get in the water," he yelled to Kate. Bees were stinging both of them by now. The buzzing was horrendous. Ben dunked Annabelle several times. "Dip under," he yelled to Kate. She plunged under. Each time she came up gasping, the bees landed on her head. They stormed madly, a small winged army.

Finally, the bees were avenged. They slowly dispersed, flying in bands back to the tree that held their honeycomb. Annabelle was choking and crying hysterically. Ben held her close, speaking soothingly, "It's all right now, Annabelle. They're all gone." He carried her to Kate, who stood in the water totally soaked, her dress clinging to her, and her hair drenched and dripping in little ringlets. "Are you all right, Kate?" he asked.

"Yes," she said. "Is Annabelle?"

"Her eyes are swelling shut. We'd better get some mud packs on these welts on her face right away." He gently laid her down on the bank, but she clung tightly to his drenched shirt, sobbing. Ben went to work, quickly scooping handfuls of mud and patting it onto the welts. "The ones on her face are covered. It will draw out the poison. Run to the house and tell Mattie, Kate. Then come back and we'll take care of the stings you got."

Kate jumped up and raced for the house. "Mattie! Mattie!" she screamed as she approached.

Mattie came running out of the house and beheld Kate's soaked clothes and dripping hair. "What's the matter?" she asked.

"Annabelle got into a beehive," Kate gasped. "Ben has her down at the creek. He's putting mud on the welts."

"Oh no!" Mattie exclaimed. They both ran back to the creek. By this time, Annabelle had calmed down. The mud felt cool and had eased the pain. Mattie rushed to tend her.

Ben went over to Kate. "Come on, let's get some mud on your welts." By the time they finished plastering themselves, they looked like two mud pies.

"Thank you, Ben." Kate shivered. "Come up to the house; let's see if we can find some dry clothes for you."

"You don't have in mind to put me in a dress, do you?" he teased.

"I was thinking more in the line of a blanket." She blushed.

"Well, I don't know about that."

Minutes later he sat at the kitchen table wrapped in a quilt while Mattie brewed coffee. She had left Annabelle resting comfortably in her bed, sipping hot tea and receiving sympathy from Claire. Kate was changing into dry clothes.

When Kate came down the stairs and entered the kitchen, she heard Ben say, "We got here too late to plant; the land had to be cleared and prepared. So we started on our cabin and barn first. With the shelter built now, we've started to work the land."

"Sounds like hard work," said Mattie. "I hate to have ya bothered with our problems, too."

"It's really no bother. Pa says helping folks is the most important part of living. People in Virginia chipped in and helped us when our ma died."

"I'm sure your pa is a very decent man; we'd like ta meet him and your brother. We're having some neighbors for dinner Sunday. Would ya like ta come and bring your family?"

"Sure thing! Never turn down home cooking."

Kate looked at his huge hands. She could not imagine him stirring a pot of stew or pouring coffee, but she could imagine him chopping wood, felling trees, and clearing land. Then she realized they were staring at her and had asked her a question. She blushed. "I'm sorry. What did you say?"

"You feeling all right, Kate?" Ben asked.

"Fine." She nodded.

When Ben's clothes were dry enough to wear, he prepared to leave. He still had to set the trap. "Don't forget the bread I baked for you," Kate reminded him. "See you on Sunday."

"I probably won't be stopping in before then unless I catch the fox. I'll let you know if we get him."

"Hmm," Mattie muttered as she listened to the sound of his horse riding away.

Kate glanced her way. "What's wrong, Mattie?" She rubbed a welt on her shoulder.

"It's a tricky situation," Mattie replied. "They're a family of menfolk, and we're a bunch of womenfolk. We could be helpin' each other, but we don't want them to think we're chasin' them; and we don't want people ta start talkin'. I invited them to dinner."

"Well, let's invite others, too. I know! Let's invite the sheriff."

Mattie laughed. "That doesn't fix it; that still makes all menfolks."

"I know," Kate said. "Let's invite the Potters—James, Frank, and their ma."

"Hmm." Mattie studied a moment and then replied, "I guess that would be fittin'. Well then, it's settled. Now, I'd better go check Annabelle." Mattie started to walk away. She glanced back, and there stood Kate, rubbing a painful welt on her neck with a sweet smile on her lips.

Chapter 8

Sunday morning Tucker House teemed with activity and excitement in anticipation of the company coming that day. Perfect pies waited on the table. Mattie fried chicken, and already prepared were freshly baked bread and butter. There were greens from the garden, deviled eggs, potatoes and gravy, beans and hominy, and strawberries and cream.

Annabelle and Claire finished setting the table and perched on the porch like two little sparrows, waiting for the folks to arrive. Both girls were now admirers of Ben. He had won Claire's heart when he taught her to fish and Annabelle's when he rescued her.

The first buggy approached, and James, Frank, and Mrs. Potter arrived. The boys seated themselves beside the girls on the porch. Annabelle captivated them immediately, telling of her horrible adventure with the bees and proudly pointing to the spots on her face. Mrs. Potter bustled past them into the house, carrying a bowl of rice pudding.

The sheriff and the Wheelers arrived at the same time and made their own introductions. Then Mattie came out and invited everybody inside, where they sat down to the delicious meal.

"What, no honey?" teased Ben as he winked at Annabelle.

"That's what I was doing," she exclaimed. "Looking for their honey."

"I thought so." He smiled. "You're looking very good, considering what an ordeal you've been through."

After the tale had been told about the bees, Sheriff Larson said he had big news to share. "We'll be getting some important visitors around Independence Day."

"Really, who?" Mattie looked at the sheriff with admiration as she posed her question.

"Ohio's Gov. Edward Tiffin. He will be speaking at the Independence Day doin's in Dayton and spending the night in Beaver Creek on his way. I reckon there will be celebrating in Dayton. The militia will parade with fifes and drums and fire a volley followed by a blast from a cannon. The governor will speak. There will be a hog roast and drinking and toasting, then a dance in the evening."

"It's a wondrous thing we have, this freedom of ours," said Mr. Wheeler.

"Yes, and Ohio's future looks bright since we finally have our statehood," the sheriff added.

"What have you heard of Jeremiah Morrow?" Emmett Wheeler asked while he scratched his chin. "Is he a man to be trusted?"

"Oh, yes," the sheriff quickly answered. "Why, he'll make a fine representative for Ohio. He already has done so much. . . ."

Claire interrupted the sheriff as he stopped to take a sip of water. "Will we celebrate here in Beaver Creek, or will we go to Dayton?"

Mattie turned to the sheriff, and he replied, "I guess we should have our own celebration, Claire, for those folks who can't go to Dayton."

"Yeah! Yeah!" the children all cheered.

Buck thought aloud, "The Coopers of the General Store, and the Bennetts and Dentons who own the inns ought to be in charge. I'll talk to them about it."

Luke asked about the merchants in Beaver Creek, and the sheriff was proud to give him information on his little town. Kate was listening and dreaming. *Luke looks a lot like Ben. I wouldn't know he was the youngest. Ben is twenty and Luke eighteen. They have the same broad shoulders and freckles, only Luke's hair is blond while Ben's is brown.* Emmett Wheeler had white hair, so she could not tell if Ben favored his pa or ma. Now Mr. Wheeler was talking.

"We lived in Virginia, where I preached while I raised my family. The state got overcrowded, and the prices kept going up. Farms gave way to plantations. Folks mostly wanted to raise tobacco. Ben was interested in farming and heard about the sale of land in Ohio. A man could buy a hundred sixty acres for a dollar an acre and pay it off in four years. Well, the long and the short of it is, we came west."

"So you're a Virginian," exclaimed the sheriff. "A lot of good men come from Virginia."

"I suppose you're referring to President Jefferson. Yes, a good man indeed," Mr. Wheeler answered.

"Well, the Federalists probably wouldn't agree with us," said Sheriff Larson.

"No, that they wouldn't!" Emmett Wheeler laughed. "But Jefferson's got good principles. He tries to keep tyranny from seeping into the government, and he stands behind the farmers. He promotes education, hopes to better inform folks and let the intellectual govern rather than the rich."

Buck nodded. "Yes, but he rides the fence when it comes to states' rights."

"I think he just sees both sides and tries to do what is best for the country and the states," answered Mr. Wheeler. "I suppose we should change the subject before you ladies throw us out," he added with a chuckle.

"What happened to your church when you left?" Mary Potter asked.

"There was plenty of time for folks to get another preacher. I think I'll let Luke do the preaching in this family from now on, unless God changes my mind."

"Luke?" she asked.

"Yes, Luke plans to help us get our farm going, and then go back East for more schooling. He wants to preach, and Ben and I will farm."

Luke blushed. "Yes, that's what I want to do. Don't know another man whose tracks I'd rather follow than my father's."

Sheriff Larson said, "I heard there is a new university in Athens, Ohio."

"I'll check into that, Sir."

After dinner the children took a jaunt to the creek, and the men visited in the sitting room while the ladies cleared the table and did the dishes. By the time the women finished, the sheriff and the Wheelers seemed very comfortable sharing together. As the ladies entered the sitting room, Ben was thinking, *I'm surprised Kate didn't have her beau here today.* Then he heard his pa saying, "Do you know of someone who would want to cook, wash, and clean for a bunch of menfolk a couple days a week?"

Mary Potter piped up, "I'd be willin' to work at your place a couple days a week. Since the boys' pa died, it's been hard to make ends meet. I've been wonderin' how long it would be before we'd have to move to the city so the boys could get some work."

"It'd be hard work at our place," Mr. Wheeler warned with a smile.

"I'm used to hard work," she said anxiously.

"Very well, Mrs. Potter, it's a deal then." Mr. Wheeler stood up and held out his hand. She smiled, and they shook on it.

On the way home that evening, Mr. Wheeler was telling his sons how faithful God was in finding them a widow to help around the place.

"It sure will be nice," agreed Luke.

"That Kate sure is a pretty one, boys."

"Oh, Father," Luke spoke, "you know I won't be settling down for a long time with schooling ahead."

"She already has a beau," added Ben thoughtfully.

"Strange he wasn't there today." Mr. Wheeler glanced sidelong at Ben, whose wrinkled forehead gave him the impression of being disturbed about something. Mr. Wheeler had observed Ben's quiet side all day. As he pondered on the meaning of it, he said quietly, "We still got chores to do before dark, boys."

Back at Tucker House, darkness swallowed up the light where Mattie and the sheriff sat on the porch visiting.

Chapter 9

June passed without a fuss to make way for the pomp and splendor of July, whose gown of golden glory was woven with threads of independence, honor, and liberty. She touched hearts with the message of freedom and stirred the townsfolk into action. They prepared for the Independence Day celebration with great anticipation.

During this time, Tanner continued to drop in occasionally at Tucker House, and Kate endeavored to discourage him, but in vain. She turned down his invitation to the Independence Day picnic but promised to see him there.

Gov. Edward Tiffin arrived at Beaver Creek on schedule. Much ado was made. All the townsfolk gave him a hearty welcome. He gave a short speech, a portion of the one that he would be delivering in Dayton on the following day. The menfolk gathered around and listened hungrily, lapping up every morsel of political news.

The next morning, his departure ushered in the long-awaited Independence Day. There would be a picnic at noon by the creek and games in the afternoon. Toward nightfall, everyone would gather on the main street in Beaver Creek for speeches, more celebrating, and dancing.

Sheriff Larson stopped by to pick up the ladies at eleven o'clock, right on time. Spirits were high with expectation as they climbed into his wagon. Mattie perched on the front seat with the sheriff, and the girls climbed into the back.

Kate picked a few pieces of straw off her skirt and flicked them over the side while watching the ground, parched and dusty, passing by beneath her. The girls at Tucker House dressed nicer than most with Mattie's trade being such as it was. Kate had on a new blue dress capped with a round white collar. Her shiny, black hair hung to her waist and curled at the ends. A few short strands worked free and curled about her face. Blue ribbons intertwined her hair and fashioned a bow in the back. Her white bonnet sat on her lap like a cloud spewing showers of blue ribbons.

Soon they heard the sound of laughter and chatter emanating from the folks gathered along the banks of the Beaver Creek. Then the site of the fete came into view, a small grassy meadow that glimmered in the sun. It was surrounded on three sides by shady glades fringed in forest, and a shady creek bank on the fourth. The area brimmed with activity.

The Wheelers had just arrived and came to greet them as their wagon rolled to a stop. Mr. Wheeler chatted with Mattie and Buck as Ben rushed to help Annabelle and Claire off the wagon. Luke reached up to offer Kate a hand, and then grabbed her by the waist, whirling her to the ground. She felt light as a feather in his iron arms.

Annabelle and Claire dashed off to find the friends that they had not seen since school. "That'll be the last we see of them until it's dinner time," Kate said laughingly.

"They make a lively pair," said Ben warmly.

"You know they're both crazy about you."

"Yes, and I love the attention."

Ben and Luke helped Kate carry pies, potatoes, and strawberries to the tables. "What did you fellas make?" she teased.

"Why, Mrs. Potter will be bringing our share," Ben offered.

"Are you happy with your arrangement?"

"Happy as a lark!" Ben said.

"I'll say," agreed Luke. "She's a great cook, and the place is starting to seem like a home."

"I'm glad," Kate said. "How is your farmland coming along?"

"Fine. I believe we'll be ready to plant next spring for sure," said Luke.

"If Luke would just do his share," teased Ben. They playfully punched at each other.

As they walked on, Kate introduced them to friends. Blankets and quilts were being spread; children were running and laughing, dodging in and out of the crowd of adults where folks shared the latest bits of gossip.

As usual, Sheriff Larson was the one in charge of speaking. He climbed onto a wagon and tried to get folks' attention. Some of the older boys came to his aid with whistles, loud and shrill. Finally the crowd settled down, and he spoke. "Good morning, friends and neighbors! It's good to get together and celebrate the freedom and birth of our country, the United States of America!" There was clapping and hooting all around the crowd.

"Three cheers for Ohio!" someone shouted. "Hurray for statehood!" another yelled.

When it finally grew quieter, the sheriff said, "Emmett Wheeler will pray, and then everyone help themselves. There's water on the wagon at the end of the last table and don't forget to get some of that tasty pork so generously donated by the Bennetts." Everyone clapped and some whistled, then all quieted down as Mr. Wheeler prayed.

"Shall we get in line?" Kate asked.

Ben nodded. "Sure, Kate. Come on, Luke. Looks like a real feast."

This is going to be a fine day, Kate thought. She was enjoying the

Wheeler brothers' company and easy ways. Just as the line moved again and they started to fill their plates, she felt a hand on her elbow. She turned, and there stood Tanner.

"H–hello, Tanner," Kate stammered. She blushed scarlet.

"Hello, Darlin'," he said.

Kate stiffened. Ben thought she looked embarrassed. "You remember the Wheelers, don't you, Tanner?"

"Of course, Darlin'." Tanner reached out to shake their hands. His charming smile was intact, but his handshake told a different story. It was stiff and unfriendly.

As they made their way through the tables laden with all the good foods, Kate hardly knew what she was dipping onto her plate. Tanner had squeezed between Kate and the Wheelers and was whispering something in her ear. Then he said loudly, "May I talk to ya a minute, Darlin'?"

Ben quickly said, "Excuse us," and nodded a good-bye to Kate.

Tanner led her the opposite direction and stopped under a tree. "Is this why you wouldn't come to the picnic with me?"

"What do you mean?"

"Got your eye on one of them Wheelers?"

Across the meadow, Ben and Luke observed the scene. Luke said with a sheepish grin, "It looks like we got Kate into an argument with her beau."

"I feel mighty bad about that," sighed Ben sadly.

"Don't worry, Ben. They'll make up soon enough."

As soon as the food had a little time to settle, groups started gathering here and there, preparing for the games. First came the children's games—various relays and races for all ages. Then some of the older men went down to the creek for a fishing contest. Ben wanted to ask the sheriff about the shooting match but thought he should stay clear of Kate. He did not want to cause trouble; it was the Wheelers' way to try to live peaceably with all folks.

Sheriff Larson told Mattie that he would not be able to hold up his head in town unless he participated in the shooting match. She encouraged him to enter and moved her blanket close to watch. Ben and Luke spied Buck, and they all entered together.

The first shot was Sheriff Larson's, and he was a little low and to the right of the bull's-eye. Ben and Luke were not nearly as close. Carl Hawkes hit the bull's-eye right on.

During the applause Tanner handed Kate a posy. She clutched it in surprise. Then he marched up to the Wheelers with a threat. "Stay away from Kate," he said straightway.

"We're just neighbors; there's nothing for you to worry about," Ben replied.

"Look, you'll be sorry if I catch you together again," Tanner warned. Then he took his shot. It was close, but too high. Tanner's strutting took the pleasure out of the contest for Ben.

When the target looked like a sieve and all was done, Sheriff Larson won by getting the last two shots into the bull's-eye. Carl Hawkes piped up, "If somebody had to beat me, I'm glad it's the sheriff we got protectin' the town!" But he was interrupted by screams coming from the creek.

Everyone looked, and a crowd gathered. Kate got there just as twelve-year-old Sammy Hawkes dove into the middle of the creek. "What? Why, that's my Sammy! What's goin' on?" Carl Hawkes yelled.

"It's little Zach, the Greens' baby boy," a lady nearby sobbed. "He's disappeared under the water."

Mr. Hawkes was just about to dive into the water when Sammy emerged, gasping. "I–I f–found h–him," he stuttered.

Mr. Hawkes lifted the small boy from his son and hurried to the bank, where he quickly worked over him. Sammy and the Greens gathered around with a crowd of friends pressing in behind them.

The baby kicked and sputtered. After a moment Carl handed him to his ma. "He's breathin'! Oh, my baby's breathin'! Thank the Lord," Rose Green sobbed as she cradled her son in her arms and rocked him back and forth.

David Green turned to Sammy and his pa. Deeply moved, he embraced them each in turn and thanked them for saving the boy. Sammy was smiling from ear to ear.

Kate saw Claire standing not too far away with teary eyes and went to her. "I'm so happy," Claire said, "for baby Zach, but most of all for Sammy!" Claire felt compassion for her friend Sammy. She had often brought stories home from school about his stuttering problem. The older boys teased him, and it saddened her.

"Yes, he's a real hero," Kate agreed.

After that, the afternoon seemed to wind down, and before long, everyone was packing up to head home. Tanner led Kate to the sheriff's wagon and made her promise to dance with him later in the evening. As she watched him walk away, she noticed Ben and Luke were not lacking for friends.

They stood in a group of folks, laughing and talking. Melanie Whitfield whispered in Ben's ear, and he nodded and grinned. She recalled what Mrs. Whitfield had predicted about Melanie setting her cap for one of the Wheeler boys.

As the wagon rolled down the shady road again, it seemed to hit every rut and bump in the road. With each bump, Kate grew angrier.

Chapter 10

Late that same afternoon, the Tucker House ladies walked into Beaver Creek to take part in the street festivities. The road was hot and dusty, and they wore their best clothes with shawls draped over their arms. As they entered the outskirts of town where all the buggies and wagons were left, they heard a loud bong. Their excitement mounted.

On Main Street, they were met by the familiar smells of beaver pelts and tanned leather goods, mixed with the repugnant odors of livestock, sweating men, and cigar smoke. Occasionally the ladies' sweet smell of lavender lingered.

The bong was a huge drum. A wooden platform was erected in front of Cooper's General Store. Various merchants and townsfolk gave speeches on freedom and liberty. The people addressed the political events that Gov. Edward Tiffin had introduced. They discussed Ohio's statehood and plans for their town. There was even talk of locks and canals on the Ohio River.

By six o'clock the speeches were concluded. Drums sounded and men fired rifles into the air. They grabbed their women and swung them around and around, like colorful twirling tops. There was hooting and hollering, and it all ended with rounds of applause.

Kate noticed several men gathering around the big bonfire site to ignite the fires for light and warmth when the evening chill set in. Various shopkeepers set out candles and hung oil lamps from rafters. As darkness fell, they created an enchanting setting.

The fiddlers consisted of two farmers, one shopkeeper, and a half-grown youngster. As they started warming up, Kate stopped to watch.

Kate noticed Ben Wheeler asking Melanie Whitfield to dance. Disappointed, she quickly looked away. Luke saw her moping. He glanced around, and Tanner was not in view, so he asked her to dance. Colorful dresses made a beautiful sight, full and swaying like a myriad of flowers floating in a pond. When the dance was over, Luke thanked her and politely excused himself.

Kate watched Mattie dance with the sheriff. She hummed and tapped her feet to the music. Claire, Annabelle, and Dorie Cooper were sitting on the porch in front of Cooper's General Store, enjoying themselves and watching the crowd and the dancing. She waved to them.

Then Tanner asked her to dance. He held her possessively and whispered in her ear, "You look beautiful tonight, Darlin'."

Ben danced a set each with Annabelle and Claire. Kate was studying his graceful moves with her sister when suddenly he turned and caught her gazing his way. He gave her a wink and a smile. Kate reddened and quickly looked up at Tanner. The gesture had escaped his notice for his attention focused on Elizabeth Denton across the way. Kate noticed that his eyes were red and realized that he had been drinking.

"Are you as thirsty as I am?" Tanner asked.

Kate nodded, seeing her chance to get out of his grip. "I could use a drink." Tanner led her to the edge of the crowd, and they strolled along the wooden walkway that ran in front of the shops.

"Wait here, Darlin'. I'll be right back."

Meanwhile, Ben and Luke happened on each other and stopped to talk. "Having a good time?" asked Luke.

"Who wouldn't?" his brother replied.

"A lot of pretty girls," Luke drawled, smiling.

"Now remember your goals," Ben chided.

"Sometimes it's hard," Luke admitted. "Say, look over there! Tanner is deserting Kate."

Ben winced. "He's drunk, the scoundrel! Think he'd carry his threat through?"

"Are you afraid of him?"

"Of course not!"

"Well, what are you waiting for? I've had a dance with Kate myself."

That was all the prodding Ben needed. He headed toward Kate, who stood in a small gathering of young folks. "Hello, Ben! Have you met everyone here?"

"Yes, I believe I have." He nodded to the others and smiled. Then he added, "Would you like to dance, Kate?"

The question roused a tingling sensation like teeny, tiny soldiers marching up and down her spine. She heard herself reply ever so softly, "Yes." Then she was in his arms, gliding as if on air to the movements of the dance.

"Enjoying yourself, Ben?"

"Yep. Folks are friendly and know how to have a good time."

"I noticed you are making many friends," she said. Suddenly, she was too hot and feeling dizzy. "Could we walk a spell?" she asked.

"Sure, Kate." He led her toward the walkway. "Do you want to tell me about it?" he asked. "I don't want to push you, Kate. But you know I'm your friend, and I can tell something's bothering you."

The words were barely out of his mouth when they turned the corner and came upon a sight that shocked them completely. There was Tanner with another woman in his arms.

Kate gasped and Tanner released the young lady he was kissing. "Tanner! E–Elizabeth!" Kate stammered. She did not wait for an answer but turned on her heels and fled, with Ben following close behind.

"Wait, Kate!" Tanner hollered. He saw it was no use. He'd best let her cool off. He turned to Elizabeth with a sheepish grin. "Dance?"

Ben caught up with Kate and grabbed her arm. "Kate!" Ashamed, she turned toward him with her eyes glued to the ground. "I know it hurts," he said.

"No, not really." She laughed a hollow laugh. "I was trying to break it off for weeks anyway."

"You don't care for him then?"

"No. At first I was attracted to him. . .but I soon realized what he was like, and now I cannot tolerate him."

Ben tenderly wiped Kate's tear away from her cheek. "Tanner may be a fool, but I'm not. May I escort my good friend for the rest of the evening?"

Kate smiled. "I guess we didn't finish our dance, did we?" Ben led her through the crowd and took her in his arms, moving to the rhythm of the music. The fiddler started to play some familiar tunes, and the people clapped and sang along.

All of a sudden, Ben was stumbling awkwardly, falling against some ladies who moved out of the way screaming and shrieking. Kate gasped and looked at Ben questioningly, and then in an instant she realized that Tanner had pushed him.

Ben soon had his balance and turned to face Tanner. A crowd gathered around, and the fiddlers stopped playing. "I thought I told ya to keep away from my girl!" Tanner yelled in a drunken drawl.

"She's not your girl, Tanner," Ben said firmly.

Tanner took a wild swing at Ben, and Ben grabbed his arm in midair and held it for an instant. Jake Hamilton was standing nearby and shouted to his friend, "Aw, come on, Tanner. Let it be!"

Tanner struggled free and lurched at Ben again, swinging wildly and hitting Ben with several punches. His eyes were red with fury and whiskey, and he looked like a mad bull. Ben stood tall, letting Tanner hammer away at him until Tanner hit him with a blow to the stomach. Just as Ben hunched over, struggling for air, the sheriff intervened, hitting Tanner in the temple and sending him sprawling to the ground.

"I hate to hit a man when he's drunk," the sheriff said. "Take him home, Jake."

Then the sheriff turned to Ben. "Are you all right?" he asked, watching

Ben and wondering why he had not defended himself.

"I'll be fine," Ben said.

After the fight was over, the fiddlers started playing again. Slowly the people dispersed, but Kate just stood there, the horror of the scene besetting her like a big, dark cloud. "I'm so sorry, Ben," she cried.

"It's all right, Kate. It's not your fault."

The throng of lively dancers was fast closing in on them. "If you'd like to walk me home, we can clean up your cuts," Kate suggested. "Your face is bleeding."

Ben took her hand, leading her through the crowd. Melanie was watching as they walked away. "So much for Tanner Matthews and Kate Carson," she mumbled and marched away in a huff.

When they reached the dirt road that led to Tucker House, Kate broke the silence. "Ben?"

"Yeah?"

"Why did you let him hit you without striking back?"

"Why, Kate, fighting is not my way; I'm not a violent man," he said softly.

"I thought all men had to be tough to survive today. . .out here in the West, I mean."

"I reckon it ain't any different today than any other time, when it comes to living," Ben mused. Then he grinned. "I didn't say I wasn't tough, did I?"

Kate didn't respond as she was taking it all in, trying to understand the meaning of it.

"A man shows strength in restraint," Ben said simply.

"I don't understand. What do you mean?"

"It's the way I believe. It's part of my faith. Jesus instructs in His Word, 'Ye have heard that it hath been said, An eye for an eye, and a tooth for a tooth: But I say unto you, That ye resist not evil: but whosoever shall smite thee on thy right cheek, turn to him the other also.' That's not an easy thing to do, Kate."

Kate looked up at him with wonder in her eyes. Although it was too dark to see him clearly, she understood. With this new insight, she saw him clear as a bell, this huge strong man with the freckled bleeding face and tender heart. He had said he was her friend. She realized this was indeed a precious thing.

Walking on in the dim moonlight, his presence by her side seemed comfortable, and she felt very safe beside this man who practiced nonresistance. As they walked on in silence, Kate wondered why this was. Then she realized it was because he was a man of God and she trusted God.

At the same time, Ben was considering, *She couldn't have been praying about Tanner that day. I wonder who it was then?*

Chapter 11

Mattie and Kate did their washing outside under the trees with their tub near the springhouse so they did not have to carry the water so far. A clothesline hung close by. They took turns scrubbing with lye soap and hanging the clothes on the line or over bushes to dry. There was plenty to do today. Whenever there was a special event, it meant extra wash. However, sharing each other's company always made their work seem lighter. Kate was pondering on this when familiar words ran through her mind.

"Come unto me, all ye that labour and are heavy laden, and I will give you rest. Take my yoke upon you, and learn of me; for I am meek and lowly in heart: and ye shall find rest unto your souls. For my yoke is easy, and my burden is light."

"Mattie?"

"Yes, Kate?"

"When do you think we'll have a church in Beaver Creek?"

"Why, I don't know, Kate. You'd really like that, wouldn't ya?"

"Yes, I would. I read my Bible, and sometimes the words I've read go running through my mind, and I don't fully understand them. I wish there was someone to explain them to me. Mattie?"

"Yes?"

"Don't you believe in God?"

"Well, sure I do, Kate. It's jest that. . .I have some painful memories, and I don't feel like He ever cared much about me. But if it's important to you, why don't ya talk to Emmett Wheeler about it? It's a shame ta have his talents wastin'. I suppose there are others who feel the same way you do, Kate."

"Really? I wonder if he'd consider preaching? I'm sure we could find someplace to meet. Oh, Mattie, thanks for the idea! I will talk to him! Perhaps I'll talk to Ben first."

"Now there's a fine fella," Mattie said. "By the way, what were him and Tanner fightin' about last night?"

Kate blushed. "I didn't want to worry you, Mattie, but Tanner is a womanizer. The day of the picnic when it rained, he took me into a deserted cabin. And, well. . .he tried for my affections. But I refused him, and he was rough with me."

"Oh, no!" Mattie let the wet clothes slip from her hands into the tub of water. Her face turned white with fear, and her hands clenched. "I've failed ya, Kate," she cried.

"Oh, no, Mattie! It's not your fault at all!"

"Yes. Yes, it is. I should have shared somethin' with ya the day you asked me about Tanner. I'm so sorry, Kate." Mattie's shoulders shook, and she started to weep.

Kate rushed to her and knelt at her side. "He didn't hurt me, Mattie," she quickly explained.

"Are. . .are you sure?" Mattie asked.

"I believe Jesus protected me because Tanner was strong enough to do what he wanted."

"Thank God!" Mattie moaned. "I feel so guilty." The words poured out. "I should have told ya what. . .what happened to me."

"Tell me, Mattie," Kate urged.

Mattie was silent for a long moment as Kate waited patiently. Then she painfully and slowly began to share some of the secret from deep within. "There was no one I could talk ta. Ya see, my father was a preacher. He was very strict. My mother was a very quiet and shy person, totally controlled by my father. She didn't tell me anythin' about fellas and havin' babies and what to watch for. When I went to her with questions, she jest brushed me off, tellin' me not ta think of such things!"

Mattie paused a moment, and then continued. "There was a young man who lived nearby, and he started ta come around. My father ran him off. I didn't know why. I think my father knew what he was like, but he didn't explain it to me or anythin'. Instead he yelled at me and accused me of not bein' the proper, chaste young lady I was to be.

Well, the young man and I had secret meetin's. It wasn't too hard, since he lived close. We met in the woods nearby, or after dark he'd come over, and I'd go out ta the barn to be with him. He made me feel loved, which I never felt from my family. He talked of elopin' and havin' a place of our own. I didn't know he was lyin' to me. I–I b–became p–pregnant."

Mattie sobbed uncontrollably now, and Kate held her. "Oh, Mattie, you poor thing," she said. "What happened?"

"I told him." Mattie sighed. "He said we'd get married and not ta worry, but he left town, and I never saw him or heard from him again. I never even knew where he'd gone."

"What did you do?"

"I told my parents about the baby. My father was furious. He said I was a harlot, and he didn't want anythin' ta do with me. I was to get out of his house. My mother took me aside and said that I should go and stay with my sister. So I went to Big Bottom where Beth lived. She took me in."

"Big Bottom!" Kate exclaimed. "Then that's how you found us?"

"I reckon so. . . ." Again Mattie paused, wondering how much to share.

She quickly concluded, "After I had the baby, my sister raised her because she didn't have any children of her own. She was good ta me."

"What happened to your baby?" Kate interrupted.

"The Indians that killed your folks. . ." Mattie could not finish, and Kate, thinking that she understood, did not ask any more about it. She had her own memories of that Indian raid. Both women were kneeling on the ground, holding each other and reliving that time.

Finally Kate said, "I'm so sorry, Mattie. You've been such a good mother to me."

"Kate, I jest want ta spare ya the mistakes I made. If a young man really loves ya, he'll have proper intentions. He'll save his advances for your weddin' night. He'll respect and honor ya."

"Like Ben. He's that kind of man."

"Ya like him?"

"When I'm around him, my heart pounds as if it's going to explode. I'm afraid he's going to discover. . . I don't want to lose him as a friend."

"Jest give it time, Kate. Ben is a good man. He won't go rushin' into anythin'. Did ya tell Ben about Tanner?"

"Just that I wanted to break it off with him. That was after we happened upon Tanner with Elizabeth Denton in his arms."

"Oh, Kate! I'm sorry!"

Kate shrugged. "Tanner attacked Ben because he was jealous. Ben told him to leave me alone. Tanner was so drunk. I don't know if he even remembers or if he understood. I don't know if he'll stay away."

"Well, I won't let him in the next time he comes around here! The scoundrel!"

"With everyone protecting me, I guess it'll be all right. Ben said he'd keep him away, too. He said that he was my friend and I could trust him."

"It's good ta have someone to trust. That's the way I feel with Sheriff Larson."

"There's someone else you can trust, too, Mattie."

"Yeah? Who's that?"

"God. I understand now why you don't want to have anything to do with Him, because of your father. But that wasn't God's fault. Your father was in the wrong. Look at people like the Wheelers; then you get a better picture of what God's like. Sometimes it's best not to look at anyone except God Himself. We're all just human after all."

"How do ya know what God's like, Kate?"

"Well, since I was little, He's always been there for me. My parents were Christians, and they taught me to pray. Even as a little girl, when I prayed I knew He heard me, and I knew He cared for me. During that Indian raid, I felt His presence in such a real way. I felt His hand on my shoulder. I never told anybody that but I knew it was Jesus. I even said, 'Jesus, is that you?' And he said, 'Lo, I am with you always, Child.' He's my best friend, Mattie. He's been faithful to me. I wish Annabelle knew Him. She was just too little at the time, I guess. But if we had a church. . .if she could know him, and Claire, and you, Mattie. . ."

"Well, I guess if God wants me to know Him, He'll have ta make the first move. Maybe He will, Kate."

"One good thing that's happened out of all this is He brought us together," said Kate.

"That is a good thing," choked Mattie.

"Mattie?"

"Yes?"

"What about Sheriff Larson?"

"What about him?" Mattie asked.

"Why haven't you ever married him?" asked Kate.

"I guess I never had the strength ta tell him about my past, and I feel like I'd be cheatin' him."

"Has he asked you?"

"Yeah, he used ta ask me all the time, and now I guess he's resigned to bein' single and to us bein' good friends."

"You know, Mattie, when Jesus comes into your heart, He makes everything new and clean."

"Does He now? I look at this brand-new dress ya wore to the picnic, Kate, and know that after it gets washed, it'll never be as nice and new as it was that first time. So how can He make somethin' old and used, like me, new and clean?"

"I don't know how He does it, Mattie, but I read it in the Bible. It says, 'Therefore if any man be in Christ, he is a new creature: old things are passed away; behold, all things are become new.' "

"Well, Kate, that would be somethin' all right! Maybe I'll do some thinkin' on that, but in the meantime, we'd better get back ta this washin'!"

"Oh, my!" exclaimed Kate. "You're right!"

Both women were quiet as they worked, reflecting on what had been shared. Mattie felt a smoldering fire of shame searing her soul as she pondered on the strange things Kate had told her about getting a clean heart.

Inside Kate, a fountain of joy bubbled up. She knew God was doing a work. She would ask Ben about that church. "Please, Jesus," she prayed, "be changing Mattie's heart. Amen."

Chapter 12

A few days later Ben stopped in at Tucker House. Kate happened to be coming in from the henhouse when she saw him ride up. Her heart felt like a giant hammer in her breast. Her emotions were always in a tumult when Ben was around, but today the feelings intensified because she wanted to talk to him about starting a church. She headed toward the house to greet him.

Ben noticed a sparkle in her eyes as she approached. She looked so radiant, so beautiful. He hated to tell her!

"Hello, Ben."

"Hello, Kate."

"Come on in."

"Could we just sit here on the porch a spell, Kate?"

"Sure." Kate saw concern in Ben's expression. "Something wrong?"

"Well, something is troubling me. I hate to worry you about it, but I must tell you."

"Go ahead, Ben," Kate urged. A sense of helplessness constricted her throat.

"We had some visitors last night."

"What kind of visitors?"

"Troublesome ones. They rode through our farm shooting holes into the barn."

"Was anyone hurt?"

He nodded sadly. "They killed our dog," he said.

"Oh no!" Kate cried. "I'm so sorry, Ben." Tears welled up in her eyes. She remembered once again the Indian raid of her childhood. "But who would do such a thing?" Terrified, she asked, "I—Indians?"

"There were two riders. We got a glimpse from behind, and they weren't Indians."

"But who then?"

Ben sat still, considering how to tell her. His impulse was to take her in his arms and protect her, but he refrained. As she returned his gaze, she read his expression of concern and then she knew!

"You think it was Tanner?"

"He's the only one I can think of with something against us. From behind it looked like Tanner and Jake. I just got back from talking to the sheriff so he

47

will keep an eye out for Tucker House."

"You think he'd take revenge on me?"

Ben reached over and took her hand for a moment. "I don't know, Kate, but I'm real fond of you and your family. I don't want to take any chances."

"Oh! This is terrible! I am so ashamed!"

"Please don't blame yourself, Kate. It's not your fault."

"What if he does something else to you, or Luke, or your pa? What he already did is just awful. I'm so sorry, Ben!"

"We're on alert now so don't fret about us. It's you I'm worried about."

"Ben?"

"Yes?"

"C–could we pray?"

"Well, sure, Kate." Ben looked both astonished and very pleased. "Kate, I thought you were a Christian," he said softly.

"Yes, I am. I've known the Lord since I was a little girl. When I first heard you talking about God, I was thrilled. You see, Mattie and the girls aren't Christians. Not yet. They will be someday, though, because I'm praying for them."

Ben leaned forward, elbows resting on his knees, his head turned toward Kate, listening as she explained. A river of warmth flooded over him, washing him with God's love. He did not understand what God was doing just yet, but he recognized His presence.

"Ben?" Kate trembled.

"Yes?"

"Would your pa consider starting a church here at Beaver Creek? The need is so great! I read my Bible, but there are parts I could use some help with. . .parts that need explaining. I'd like to learn hymns, too."

"Haven't you ever gone to church?" he asked tenderly.

"No."

"It's a miracle how God has kept you all these years, Kate, with no church and no one to share with."

"He is faithful. Maybe sometime I'll share some of my experiences with you."

"I'd like that."

There was silence as they sat on the porch, thinking about their Lord. It felt so good for them to share in this way. "I know!" said Ben. "Would you like me to pick you up tomorrow in our buggy and bring you to the farm? You've never been there. You could talk to Pa yourself. I don't know how he can resist you with those big, brown, pleading eyes of yours, but that's not to say that he'll agree to it."

"Oh, yes!"

"Now, let's pray together," suggested Ben. "Would you like to hold my hand while we pray, like we're in agreement?"

"Sure, Ben. That would be nice. I—I've never prayed with anyone before."

Ben took her hand and prayed out loud. "Dear Father, I thank You for bringing Kate into my life. I thank You that she has a hunger for You. I pray that You will make it clear as a bell so Pa can make the right decision about preaching. You know what Kate wants, Lord, but we ask that Your will be done in this matter.

"Lord, I pray for Your protection on Kate and those at Tucker House. We pray for Tanner. May Your grace turn him away from revenge. Please send someone to witness to him in Your name so he can become a Christian. Amen."

"But I didn't get to pray!"

"Okay, go ahead."

"Dear Jesus, I thank You for Your hand guiding me and protecting me. You have so many times in the past that I trust you to continue to do so. Please protect Ben and his family, and help them to know how to deal with Tanner. Lord, You know how Beaver Creek is needing a church. Please help Ben's pa to say yes." At this point she opened her eyes and sneaked a peek at Ben. His eyes were closed, but he was smiling. She continued, "Thank You for bringing the Wheelers to Beaver Creek. Amen."

Ben gave Kate's hand a squeeze.

"Thank you, Ben," she said. "Won't you come inside for awhile?"

"No, I think I'd best be getting home. The sheriff will be by tonight to check the house. Be sure to bolt the door. I'll be by tomorrow about one o'clock."

"Great! Good-bye, Ben."

"Good-bye, Kate."

Kate went inside with the basket of eggs that she had brought an hour before from the henhouse. Mattie said, "I see your friend was visiting," and emphasized the *friend* part. Then she gave Kate a smile and a hug.

Kate sighed. "Yes, but he came to give me some bad news." She told Mattie all that Ben had said and concluded with words of assurance. "The sheriff will check on us. I prayed with Ben, and he is taking me to his farm tomorrow to talk with Mr. Wheeler about preaching." Even though she tried, Kate could not pass on to Mattie the peace that she herself felt inside. Mattie did not know Jesus, the source of the peace.

Mattie felt miserable. She was thinking, *If God wants ta work in my life, now's a good time to start, with all these troubles.*

Chapter 13

Kate was dressed and eager for Ben to arrive, though fidgety. She rubbed her sweaty hands on the skirt of her light blue calico dress and arranged the ribbons on her plain blue bonnet. Pacing to the window, she gazed out and then returned to her chair, where she had laid some hand sewing for Mattie.

"Goin' ta the window won't make him come any sooner," Mattie said.

Kate blushed, but then she heard his buggy approaching. "Well, seems like it did after all," she piped up smugly, but with a grin.

"I hope it works out for ya, Kate."

"Thanks, Mattie. Don't wait supper for me; I forgot to ask when I'd be back."

She laid the sewing aside and rushed to the door, giving Ben a warm welcome.

"Well, that's nice. I didn't even have to knock," he teased.

"You did tell me to expect you, remember?" she said blushing.

As they rode along the winding dirt road that led to the Wheelers' place, Kate asked on impulse, "What did you tell your pa about inviting me to the farm?"

Now it was Ben's turn to blush. "Shucks, I was so excited about your idea that I didn't even think about appearances. I just told him I was bringing you over for the afternoon. No wonder he grinned at me that way."

"In what way, Ben?"

"Why, he probably thinks I'm courting you," he said, getting redder by the minute. "I hope that doesn't embarrass you, Kate. I'll set him straight first chance I get."

Kate felt a lump forming in her throat. "Of course," she said numbly just as they approached the farm.

"Well, this is it," Ben said proudly. He pulled the buggy up to the barn and helped Kate down. "I'll unhitch the team, and then I'll show you around."

Kate watched him as he worked. She remembered her first impression of him, how she'd respected him for not embarrassing her with pretty words like Tanner. Yet she found herself longing to hear just such words rolling off his tongue. Sweet as honey they would be coming from Ben. Instead, he said painful things like, "I'll set him straight first chance I get."

"All set," Ben said, bringing Kate out of her reverie.

"Great."

"Over there is the ground we've been clearing," Ben said, pointing. "That's where we'll be planting the corn next spring."

"I can't believe how much you've done in the short time you've been here!"

"I love working the land, Kate. It's what I want to do with my life and is about as natural as breathing to me. Well, here we are." Ben held the door open as Kate went inside.

"Hello, Mrs. Potter."

"Hello, Kate, good to see ya! Would you two be likin' some tea or some coffee?"

"Coffee would be great," Ben said as he walked over to Mrs. Potter and patted her arm affectionately. "Thank you, Mary. Kate, I don't know what we'd do without this lady. She's a wonder. Her sons are fine lads, too, and hard workers!"

Kate was glad it had worked out for them, but she felt a pang of jealousy as she watched her working in Ben's kitchen and wondered what it would be like to cook for Ben and his family. The coffee was soon ready. As they sat and chatted, Kate noticed that everything in the cabin was in perfect order. She wondered if it was always like that, or if it was just because Mrs. Potter had been there that morning. It was, undoubtedly, a bachelor's home; the touch of a woman was missing.

Soon Ben was saying, "Pa's working on the fence along with James and Frank. Let's go and have our talk with him, Kate." Mrs. Potter looked in wonder, and then with understanding. It sounded like a proposal plan to her. Kate and Ben both understood at once.

"Oh, no, Mrs. Potter. It's not what it sounded like," Ben said earnestly.

"Wasn't thinkin' nothin', Ben," she replied smiling. "If it was somethin', I'd be hearin' it sooner or later anyway. Here, take this pitcher of cool water to your pa and the boys." Her eyes crinkled from smiling.

Ben shrugged and said, "Kate?"

She quickly followed Ben out-of-doors. They headed past the barn, where Kate saw a newly turned mound. Ben's gaze rested on it, and then he quickly looked away.

Probably his dog, she thought sadly. Then she spotted Mr. Wheeler and the boys building a rail fence out of timber they had cut to clear the land. Mr. Wheeler dropped the piece he held, rubbed his arm across his brow, and ran his fingers through his thick snowy hair. His eyes were dancing with mischief.

"Howdy," he said.

"Pa." Ben nodded.

"Hello, Mr. Wheeler, James, Frank," said Kate. "You've done so much with your place," she added, turning to Emmett.

"That we have, Miss. Got a long way to go yet, too."

"Here's a drink Mrs. Potter sent for you."

Mr. Wheeler and the boys drank deeply until satisfied. "Mm, that hits the spot. Boys, take a short break. Run in and see if your ma needs anything first. Sure is getting hot these days!"

"Yes, we could use a good rain," Kate said. "Where's Luke?"

"He's clearing the land to the east." Then straight to the point, he added, "Ben doesn't usually ask for the afternoon off so I didn't press him for his reasons. Figured it was something important." He gave Kate a wink.

"Mr. Wheeler," Kate said, "as a matter of fact it is important to me. I'm a Christian and. . ."

"Well, glory be! That's real good news, Kate!" Mr. Wheeler exclaimed.

"Well, yes," she said, stealing a glance at Ben. He nodded his encouragement, and she continued, "But Mattie, Claire, and Annabelle, and lots of other folks around here aren't."

"Sad to hear that," Mr. Wheeler said.

"All I've learned has been straight from the Bible with no one to teach me."

"Nothing wrong with that. The Holy Spirit is the best teacher you could have, Kate."

"Yes, but I have so many questions, and I sure wish there was a church so others could learn about Jesus."

"Hmm, I see." Mr. Wheeler leaned on the fence and scratched his chin.

"Mr. Wheeler, would you consider starting a church in Beaver Creek?" Her eyes searched and pleaded.

"Well now, that certainly wasn't what I was expecting to hear this afternoon." Mr. Wheeler cleared his throat, studied Ben a moment, and then continued. "Can't say it comes as a great surprise though. Two things already happened to prepare me for this question."

"What's that, Pa?" asked Ben.

"First, when we were coming west along the Ohio River, I met a man at camp one night. His name was John Chapman. Appleseed, people called him." He stopped his story to chuckle.

Kate asked, "Appleseed?" while Ben listened. He'd met the man also but didn't know what his pa was going to share.

"Yep. Appleseed. A nice fella. He's planting apple seeds across Ohio and selling seedlings. Actually, he gives half of them away. Got a couple myself. They're planted right over there behind the cabin." He pointed toward the cabin. "Anyway, he's a man of God, and I had a good chat with him that night by the campfire. I'd shared our plans to farm so he knew I wasn't coming west to preach. The next day as we fixed to leave, he gave me those seedlings. He said, 'Plant these, and someday I'll come check on them. When I do, I'll come to your church and hear ya preach.' I guess that was the first word the Lord sent me."

"What was the other, Mr. Wheeler?"

"A dream. It was the night we supped with you at Tucker House. I dreamed I was walking in a field of corn when a wind came from the north and swept me up. It set me down on the edge of the field where sheep fed on a green pasture. They drank water from a brook. A voice said, 'Feed my flock.'

"As I watched the sheep grazing, a lamb came romping through the cornfield. Everywhere he leaped, the corn was trodden and destroyed. 'Go away,' I shouted. 'Get out of my corn.' Then I heard the voice again. It said, 'Feed my flock.' So I allowed the lamb to come across the field and enter the pasture. As he did, other lambs followed. I looked back at the cornfield and all the corn sprung up, unharmed. It was a vivid dream and I knew it held a special meaning. I stored it in my heart."

"Pa! You've been keeping this all inside, and it seemed so right to bring Kate here. I didn't even think about the implications. The Lord must be leading you to do this then."

"It seems so, Son, but we need to have a family meeting and talk it over with Luke. Let us pray about it and talk it over as a family, and then I'll give you my answer, Kate."

"Thank you, Mr. Wheeler." Kate grabbed his hands and pumped them up and down. Tears flowed down her cheeks.

"Don't cry, Kate," Ben said.

"It's just so beautiful how Jesus leads us. He's so good!" she said wiping her tears on her sleeve.

"That He is! That He is!" exclaimed Mr. Wheeler nodding.

"Well, Pa, I'll take Kate home."

"Enjoy yourself, Son; you may not get another day off so easily!" Ben laughed. "Bye, Kate, and thank you for coming today."

"Bye, Mr. Wheeler," Kate shouted.

Later that night three men sat around a small wooden table, heads bowed as the father prayed. "Thank You, God, for sending Your Son, Jesus, to die on the cross so our sins can be forgiven. Guide and direct us as I do what we believe is Your will, feeding the flock here at Beaver Creek. Amen."

Chapter 14

Kate wiped her damp brow with the back of her sleeve. Limp hair was twisted into a knot and secured with a white scarf, except for a few unruly strands tickling the nape of her neck. Her old brown dress was frayed and worn through in places, but comfortable and suitable for the day's chores.

It was another hot day, and the windows gaped open in protest. Mercifully, a gentle breeze stirred the curtains while the sweet melody of robins drifted through the open window.

She scrubbed the wooden floor, thinking about the terrible mess the girls had made when they prepared the bread that rose in pans waiting to be baked. They were gone now, at Cooper's General Store with the eggs and visiting their friend, Dorie, whose father owned the store.

When she heard a knock at the door, she plopped the rag into the bucket and dried her hands on her apron as she stood to her feet. "Oh, dear. What a sight I must be!" She tiptoed to the door and pulled it open, trying not to track up the freshly cleaned floor.

"Good morning, Kate."

"Morning, Sheriff Larson!" Kate smiled and motioned toward the wet floor. "I'd invite you in, but the floor's all wet."

"That's all right, Kate. The porch is fine. Is Mattie around?"

"She's out in the garden." Kate nodded.

"Thanks a lot. I'll be heading around the side of the house then." He paused a moment, wondering if he should say what was on his mind, and then continued. "Oh, Kate. I thought you might like to know that Tanner is in Dayton, which means he won't be around for awhile." Buck watched the roses fade from Kate's cheeks as she grew pale.

Kate took a deep breath. "Good," was all she said.

Sheriff Larson turned and left the porch. As he rounded the corner of the house, he spotted Mattie kneeling in the garden and heard her humming sweetly. He sighed, put his hands in his pockets, and headed toward her.

Kate finished her work and carried the heavy bucket of dirty water onto the porch. It had been a week since she had been to the Wheelers, and she still had not heard from them. It did not seem like Ben and Luke to stay away so long. Just then Annabelle and Claire interrupted her thoughts as they bounded up the porch steps to the door.

"Guess what? Guess what?" exclaimed Annabelle excitedly.

"What?" asked Kate.

"Mr. Cooper says next Saturday there will be a barn raising. Some new folks arrived about a week ago." Annabelle talked so rapidly that Kate had to strain to get all the words. "Folks have already helped them start their cabin, but the barn raising is Saturday. And everybody will be there!"

"Good!" replied Kate. "More new folks. That's wonderful. I'll bake some berry pies."

"Oh, can we help?" asked Claire.

"Sure," said Kate. "I'll teach you how to clean up after yourselves while we're at it!"

"Oh, I knew you had a scolding for us!" said Annabelle, pouting.

"Oh, pooh!" Kate laughed. The girls ran outside, and Kate gazed out the window after them. She noticed Mattie and Buck sitting on the bench under the hickory tree.

Claire popped her head back in and announced, "Ben's here! Ben's here!"

"Oh, no!" Kate said. "What a fright I am!" With that she turned her back to the door, lifted her ragged skirt, and bolted for the stair steps. Her intentions of cleaning up were thwarted when she heard the sound of his voice directly behind her.

"Hello, Kate. Claire let me in."

She stopped abruptly, and her hands flew up to brush back her wild hair. Well, she was caught now and must be hospitable. She shrugged and turned to greet him.

Kate did not miss the look of amusement on Ben's face as he caught sight of her. Slowly he looked her over, from head to toe, taking in her disarrayed hair and ragged gown. She burned with embarrassment. "Come in. Sit down," she said, pointing to a chair and trying to direct his attention away from herself.

"Thanks," Ben said as he sat. He grinned as he reflected on the purpose of his visit. He brought good news and would enjoy letting her drag it out of him.

"Would you like something to drink?" Kate asked. She wished he would not gaze at her with that silly grin. She felt so ill at ease.

"That would be real good, Kate."

She poured him some cold water and sat down rigidly across the table from him. Ben sensed her frustration and almost refrained from further teasing. But his sense of humor overpowered him. On impulse, he reached over and touched her cheek with his finger. "A smudge," he said smiling.

She felt the color rising up her neck and face. Flustered, she apologized, "I'm sorry. I'm a terrible mess."

"You should see me at the end of the day," he reassured her. "I look like some poor critter that stumbled into a mud hole."

Kate giggled. "Yes, but it's not even the end of the day yet!" As she spoke, she felt her tension slipping away. *Being with Ben is refreshing and comfortable,* she thought, *like coming home after a long, tiring trip.* Then came the question that had been foremost in her mind the last couple of days. She did not waste another moment.

"Ben, does your pa send me an answer yet?"

"Yes." He grinned at her but said no more.

"Yes?" she asked with trepidation.

"Yes, he sends you an answer."

"Well? What is it?" Kate was frustrated at Ben's teasing mood.

"Yes. The answer is yes." He leaned back, tilting his chair, with satisfaction written all over his face as he watched her eyes light up.

"Oh! Oh! I'm so glad." Kate was up and out of her chair in an instant, rushing to hug Ben. However, a few more steps, and she realized what she was about to do. Appalled at her own improper behavior, she tried to stop herself, tripping in the process, falling and landing right in his lap.

Without a second thought, Ben reached out to catch her. He held her in his arms for just an instant but long enough to know in his heart that it was where she belonged. Her feet dangled, not touching the floor, and she grew frantic. She must get up at once! But time stood still for the moment. Kate heard a creak, then a ripping sound, and in a flash she was part of a pile of twisted body and chair parts, intertwined and deposited in a clump on the kitchen floor.

As the dust settled, she found herself staring directly into Ben's big, blue eyes. They were round with astonishment as he wondered what had happened. His eyebrows raised into a frown, and his face was motionless for a very long moment. Then a smile slowly formed, and he was laughing.

She was such a funny sight! Her little white scarf had been knocked off her head, and her hair knot was working loose. The hair hanging down was swinging wildly and eventually settled over the top of her head and down her forehead. Her expression was one of horror.

"What? What happened?" she asked.

"The chair broke," Ben said, grinning as he released her.

"I'm so sorry. How clumsy of me! I guess I was going to hug you, on a whim. That's what I get for living with a bunch of women who always go around hugging each other."

Ben laughed wildly. She looked comical, but listening to her rationalize was even funnier.

"I'm so sorry, Ben. I'm just so happy!" Kate giggled. They laughed and tried to untangle themselves. Kate rubbed her leg. "I think I'll have a few bruises," she said.

"What are you doing?" Annabelle had just entered the house and stopped dead in her tracks. Claire was right on her heels.

"W—we fell," said Kate.

"The chair broke," added Ben.

Annabelle and Claire just stood gaping as Ben and Kate straightened their clothing and struggled to their feet. Ben slowly bent over and picked up some broken pieces of the chair.

"Looks like I'll have an excuse to come over now," he said. "I—I mean, I'll need to fix that chair for you."

"You can come anytime, Ben," piped up Claire. "Better make that chair stronger next time."

Ben smiled and started to answer, but Kate interrupted him. Remembering the reason for her excitement, she exclaimed, "Ben, where will we meet, and when will we start?"

"Pa wondered if we could use the schoolhouse. Pa will inquire about it. If we can use it, we can spread the word at the barn raising Saturday. Pa thought you could help with that part."

Kate nodded in agreement, and Ben continued, "I would have been over sooner, but I've been at Mary's, fixing up things. James and Frank are pretty young to be keeping up a place."

"You have? That's so thoughtful of you."

"Mary doesn't seem to be the type to take over the farm, either. She's a great lady, strong on the inside, if not on the outside."

"I'm so glad you can help each other."

"That's what friends do, Kate." She wondered if he was stressing the word *friends* for her sake. "Well, I'd better get into town for my supplies and back to the farm before Pa sends Luke looking for me." He looked fondly at Kate.

"Thanks so much for stopping by, Ben. I have so much to look forward to now."

Ben picked up the pieces of chair and asked, "Mind if I take these with me? It'll be easier to fix at home." He winked and walked out the door.

As Ben rode away, he shook his head and laughed. Kate was full of surprises. Then his thoughts sobered as he realized he was falling in love with this girl, another man's girl. *But it felt so right when she was in my arms,* he moaned.

Chapter 15

Folks from all around Beaver Creek gave a hearty welcome to their new neighbors with a barn raising. The men fashioned temporary tables out of wood, and the women loaded them with the sumptuous foods prepared all morning for the noonday meal. Big iron kettles bubbled with beans and hominy. Platters of meat stacked high, golden cornbread, sweet rice pudding, and tempting pies sent their aromas wafting through the summer air.

Kate held a fat, squirmy baby boy. His name was Joey, and he belonged to the new family, the Morgans. The children played a game of Snap the Whip; the heat did not seem to bother them. Claire found friends that she had not seen since Independence Day. Sammy Hawkes eagerly showed the girls his arrowhead collection. He dug in the pockets of his patched and faded overalls to display his many treasures. The girls envisioned painted Indians with bow and arrow, spotted ponies, and tall tepees, as Sammy stuttered his knowledge on the subject. They did not mind his stuttering; he was a hero.

Kate turned to face the barn. The walls were already up. The men used forked poles to raise the center ridgepole higher. She spotted Ben and Luke hauling lumber to the work site, carrying it across their shoulders.

Their muscles bulged through their cotton shirts, rolled up at the sleeves. Sweat dripped down their faces. Yet they looked like they enjoyed the companionship of the other men.

Just then Kate jolted, startled by a sudden cracking noise, like a deer's antlers crashing through a thicket, only louder. Ben and Luke dropped their lumber and raced toward the barn. Kate saw a part of the structure give way. Men catapulted off the top of the barn wall and plummeted to the ground, much like hot cinders spurting skyward out of a burning fire, then extinguishing and falling to the earth. It was a terrible sight. Kate gasped and clung tightly to little Joey.

Dan Whitfield and Jess Bennett rushed to the scene and anxiously bent over Graham Malone, the town doctor, who seemed to be the worst. He moaned and tried to speak. Emmett Wheeler and Sheriff Larson helped those who had fallen. They carefully aided them to their feet, inspecting their bodies for injury. It was soon evident that only the doctor was badly hurt. Mack Tillson, the blacksmith, landed on his side and had a large scrape.

Blood seeped through his shirt, but he motioned the others away, insisting that he was all right. As he rose, he limped stiffly, trying to work out the kinks.

Bennett said, "Doc's leg is badly fractured. It's bleeding, and the bone is exposed."

"We need to make a tourniquet fast," ordered Whitfield.

The doctor's wife ran to his side and placed her hand tenderly on his forehead. Sarah Morgan piped up, "I'll run to the house and be right back with some clean rags." Her skirts flew as she sped past Kate.

"Ma–ma," Joey cried as he got a glimpse of Sarah rushing by. Kate reached up and tenderly patted Joey's cheek, so soft and smooth. She reassured him that his ma would be right back. Kate heard the sound of horses fast approaching and, wondering who it could be at such a time, looked toward the road. To her horror, it was three dark-skinned Indian braves. Kate felt her body tense, frigid with fright. Frozen to the spot, she looked frantically toward the barn, struggling with an intense desire to run to safety. There she saw Ben, standing straight and tall, and drew enough strength from his unruffled composure to whisper soft words of assurance to little Joey.

Sheriff Larson and Carl Hawkes hurried over to the Indians, who were still mounted on their horses. Carl used hand signals and arm motions to communicate with them. Sammy, followed close by Claire, ran breathlessly and stopped to stand beside his father. Kate's heart stopped as she heard Mattie call out sharply, "Claire!"

Mr. Hawkes looked at the children and raised his arm out beside him, motioning for them to remain quiet and still. Then he continued to communicate with the Indian braves. At last he said loudly, "These Wyandot Indians, Little Bear and two braves, are headed to the reservation at Sandusky. They mean no harm. They heard the commotion. Bein' curious, they came to investigate and think they can help. The one called Little Bear seems to know about medicines."

There was muttering along with bits of arguing, and then Bennett said, "No! They're heathens. He's probably a witch doctor."

"Are you going to set the doctor's leg then?" asked Sheriff Larson.

"W–well no, but surely there is someone who can. . .besides these savages. How can we trust them?" argued Bennett.

When Sarah returned with the cloth, she stopped in her tracks. The sheriff nodded, and the Wyandots dismounted off their horses and followed him to the group of men surrounding the doctor. Sarah stepped forward and cautiously handed the cloth to the sheriff, who in turn gave it to Little Bear. Bennett angrily backed away, watching suspiciously as the Indians kneeled down and worked over the doctor.

The doctor moaned again and passed out as Little Bear wound the cloth tightly above the fractured part of the doctor's leg. Little Bear quickly and skillfully set the leg. One of the other Indians handed him a small deerskin pouch, and he removed a bad-smelling ointment, which he plastered generously over the doctor's leg. Then he loosened the tourniquet and bound the leg with more of the cloth that Sarah had provided. Soon the Indians were finished. Bennett quickly moved forward and resumed caring for the doctor. He and Whitfield carried the doctor inside the cabin.

Joe Morgan placed his arm around his wife Sarah and said with a booming voice, "It's almost noon. I thank you folks for all your help today. Perhaps we should call it a day. . .since this accident. But the women worked hard, cooking all morning, and we're all hungry, so let's stop now and eat while we decide what should be done."

Emmett Wheeler said, "I think we should share our lunch with Little Bear and his braves."

There was silence followed by some grumbling, and then Carl Hawkes began with more hand motions. The Wyandots nodded and followed him and the others down to the springhouse to clean up with the buckets of cool water that waited there. They lined up under the oak trees and relaxed as they helped themselves to heaping plates of food.

"Cute little fellow," a voice said over Kate's shoulder. She turned to see Luke standing beside her.

"Luke! Yes, he's a cute little rascal," she said, giving him a tickle. Just then Annabelle appeared at her side.

"Can I hold him, Kate?"

"Sure! Here he is. Keep your eye on him every minute now," she warned as she handed the precious little bundle to Annabelle. She turned to Luke and said, "Sit down, Luke, and rest while you can."

"Sounds good, but only if you'll join me." He eased himself down onto the soft, damp grass while balancing his plate on his knees.

Luke saw the troubled look on Kate's face. He followed her gaze and saw Ben talking to Melanie Whitfield. "Are you all right, Kate?" he asked. "You're looking mighty pale."

"It's just the Indians. They frighten me," she said. Kate did not realize that part of her uneasiness stemmed from the scene taking place between Ben and Melanie. Luke, however, surmised as much.

Across the way, Melanie was detaining Ben. "I'm so frightened of those savages," she whined, clutching his arm.

"Why, you've nothing to be frightened of. There are only three Indians among all of us. I'm sure they won't start trouble."

"You're right, but I'd feel much better if you'd just stay here with me." She clung to his arm.

"As a matter of fact, I was on my way to see what they are up to. Come on, Melanie. Be brave and come with me?" he coaxed.

"Well, I don't know. All right then, but stay right by my side." She clutched his arm tighter.

Ben chuckled as they strolled over to join those gathered around the red-skinned Wyandots. He was curious and wanted to get a closer look at the Indians.

They joined a small circle of children, including Sammy and Claire, who sat on the grass about ten feet away from the braves. Ben saw Indians on their trip west, but nevertheless, he was awed each time anew. He settled down with his plate, able to observe without being noticed because Melanie was close at his side. He watched as Mr. Hawkes carried on a conversation with the natives, consisting of words accompanied by many hand movements.

Two of the Indians wore deerskin loincloths with pouches tied at their waists, embroidered with dyed moose hair. Little Bear had on a deerskin coat as well, trimmed at the cuff and collar with dyed porcupine quills. They wore beads made of shells, and their moccasins were deerskin dyed black and decorated with embroidery.

Sammy poked Ben, and he bent his head down to listen as Sammy whispered, stammering into his ear. "W–why i–is o–one d–different?"

Ben whispered back, "I was wondering the same thing. I'll bet your dad will know. Seems like he's getting a lot of information out of them."

Claire giggled and pointed. "Look at their funny hats!"

"Shh!" Melanie scolded.

"They can't understand me!" she said in a pouty voice.

They wore silly-looking hats made out of beaver skin and adorned with colorful feathers.

Across the yard, Luke finished eating. Kate took his plate and headed toward the tables where the other women stood to serve. Throughout the morning, Kate and the Wheelers spread the word about starting church meetings. There had been a lot of interest, and Kate had held high hopes until just now. As she walked past a group of men, she overheard Bennett saying to Whitfield, "If this is the kind of doin's that comes from having a preacher among us, I ain't so sure I'm for it. I'd just as soon kill them savages as to look at them."

Kate's heart sank in confusion. Whenever she saw Indians, she remembered the massacre at Big Bottom. The Wheelers showed compassion to the savages. These Indians actually helped them! Could she ever forgive? No, she did not think so! She was learning something new about herself. She realized that her heart was filled with hatred as well as fear.

When the meal was finished, the Indians departed unceremoniously.

Soon after, the Bennetts followed the Malone wagon to see them home safely. Doc Malone's wife drove the team. She could best care for him now, with the bone set and the bleeding stopped. The other men decided to continue working on the barn.

About an hour before dark, just as the men finished thatching the roof with bark, lightning flashed, followed by a loud clap of thunder. They had worked hard and steady, determined to get the barn up before the rain fell. Contrary to Kate's fears, no confrontations developed after the Indians left. The men stuck together, letting their resentments, frustrations, and hatred simmer quietly inside, where God looks upon the heart.

Then the rain fell in heavy torrents with more lightning and thunder. The horses grew nervous. Men scurried off the barn and searched for their families. It was time to quit even though the barn was not quite finished. Most of the women had already loaded the wagons, expecting to leave quickly. Some of the women and children took cover in the cabin at the onset of the cloudburst while a few of the children remained outside, running wildly and playing in the rain. Soon the confusion was over, and most of the families headed home.

The dirt road quickly became a ribbon of sticky mud, and wagons made ruts in the road, getting stuck in the potholes. Friends stopped to help each other as needed. Everyone got soaked.

"Guess we should have given up an hour ago," Sheriff Larson said to Mattie as they rode along. "We hoped it would hold off awhile yet."

Claire, Annabelle, and Kate huddled together in the back of the wagon bed with a blanket draped over their heads. "This is fun," exclaimed Claire. "This was the best day I ever had."

"Yes!" agreed Annabelle. "It was a good day. . .and so exciting with the Indians and everything. Don't you think so, Kate?"

"I could do without this rain," admitted Kate, "and without the Indians, too."

"Pooh! I wasn't scared a bit!" piped up Claire. Just then a gush of water rushed under the blanket and onto the back of Claire's neck. "Oooh!" she screamed. Then Annabelle got wet and let out a shriek.

"We're almost there, gals. Just hold on a little longer!" yelled the sheriff from the front of the wagon. "Mattie, I'm so sorry. You doing all right?"

Mattie was drenched through and through and starting to chill, but her smile was as warm as a summer's sun when she answered him.

Just then a wild thought entered Kate's mind. *I wonder where those Indians are right now and if they're getting soaked, too?* And again she asked herself, *Will I ever forgive them?*

Chapter 16

After a week of rain and some exhausting days spent cleaning the schoolhouse that had been boarded up for summer, Sunday finally arrived. Ben observed the calm sky with a sigh of gratitude. "Do you reckon God arranged it special for the sun to shine over Beaver Creek's first church meeting, Luke?"

"It sure seems like it," Luke replied cheerfully. As the brothers chores, they talked. "I'm so glad Father's preaching again," Luke said.

"Me, too; it feels so right."

"Ben? You got special feelings for Kate?"

"W–what?" The question startled Ben.

Luke repeated the question. Still, Ben did not answer. "She really lights up when you come around. I think she's sweet on you."

"Naw, she can't be; she's got a beau already," Ben said sullenly.

"Nonsense! You know Tanner's a scoundrel."

"No, not Tanner. . .someone else."

"What makes you so sure?"

"She said so. I overheard her praying." Ben's face flushed from the memory of it.

"Praying?"

"Yeah. She said that he has a heart as big as all outdoors and he is handsome and strong. She said he's a Christian. . . . She even dreams about him."

"Well, I don't know about the handsome part," Luke teased.

"What?"

"It's as plain as that freckled nose on your face!" Luke grinned at the irony of the situation.

"What do you mean?" Ben demanded.

"It sounds to me like she described you."

"Me?" His mind whirled, reliving that scene again like so many times before. *Could it be?* he wondered.

"Did you ever see her with another fella?" Luke asked.

"Well, no. . .but I can't believe it. You really think so? All this time I've been thinking. . ."

"She acted upset when you sat with Melanie at the barn raising," Luke confided. He reached up and grabbed Ben's hat, giving it a tug. "If I were in your shoes, Brother, I'd go calling."

Ben considered the possibility until Luke brought his head back down out of the clouds. "We better hurry up and finish chores. It's Sunday, remember?"

"Do I!" Ben grinned.

Meanwhile, Sheriff Larson arrived at Tucker House to pick up the ladies for church. "Mattie, I'd like you to meet my nephew, Thaddeas Larson. He's my brother's boy all the way from Boston. He's going to stay with me a spell and try out the West."

"My pleasure," said Thaddeas.

Kate stared foolishly. This was a gentleman dressed in fine Boston clothes. He was built short and sturdy with black, wavy hair and dark, warm eyes.

After the introductions they were on their way in Sheriff Larson's wagon. At the schoolhouse Carl Hawkes and his family pulled up, and Miss Forrester, the school mistress, came from across the meadow.

Inside, Kate waved to the Coopers and stopped to talk to Dr. Malone and his family. He walked with a crutch.

Sheriff Larson followed Mattie to an empty bench. Claire and Annabelle sat beside them. Thaddeas motioned for Kate to go ahead then positioned himself at her side, and they all squeezed together to make room. Kate continued to look around. Not everyone was there, but enough families came to make it all worthwhile. Her face glowed with happiness. Then she spied Ben and Luke sitting in the front row, and she smiled and waved her handkerchief.

Ben returned her smile, noticing how radiant she looked. Then he saw the stranger at her side. Cut to the quick, he took it all in. The stranger definitely came from the East. *It's him, the man of her prayers.* He turned to Luke in panic and saw his own hurt mirrored in his brother's eyes.

But Luke whispered, "Don't give up, Ben."

Heads bowed as their father prayed, "Lord, we give You thanks for allowing us to gather and worship You!" Amens echoed throughout the room.

Kate was surprised as Sarah Morgan led them in singing "The Old Rugged Cross." Her voice was melodious, sweet and high, and the singing was like a taste of heaven to Kate and the others who had waited so long for this moment.

Mr. Wheeler, henceforth called Rev. Wheeler, preached on forgiveness.

Kate fought to gain control of her emotions. Her conscience awoke to truth. She had bitterness in her heart toward Tanner, toward the Indians.

Thaddeas whispered to Kate, pointing behind the Reverend where a skunk boldly pranced across the front of the room.

He grabbed Kate's hand, and they joined a throng of folks squeezing out the back.

Somehow everyone escaped without offending the intruder. As Rev. Wheeler stepped outside he said, "Thank You, Lord, for a sunny day where we can finish worshiping You in this glorious setting fashioned by Your own hands. If we can *forgive* the little creature, we can continue." There was laughter, and he wrapped up his sermon.

When the meeting was over, Sheriff Larson stole Thaddeas away and introduced him to his friends. Luke elbowed his brother. "Go now. See how the land lies." He gave Ben a little push.

He stumbled, shot Luke a disgruntled look, then shuffled forward.

"Ben! It was just like I imagined it would be! It was just glorious. . .even with the skunk."

Her excitement and laughter soon soothed his jitters. "Yes, it was a funny sight, everyone in their Sunday best acting like a bunch of wildcats."

"Your pa was wonderful. He just let the skunk keep the schoolhouse and continued outside. His words were profound."

"It must have been the Lord speaking to you, Kate. Pa's words aren't nothing special. I hear them every day. No harm intended," he added as he grinned. Then the words slipped out without warning. "You look beautiful today, Kate."

Kate blushed. "Thank you," she said softly.

"I'd like you to meet my nephew, Thaddeas," interrupted Sheriff Larson.

Ben's face burned red with anger. Overwhelmed with a strong desire to give the newcomer a swift kick in the pants, instead he shook Thaddeas's hand. Kate gave Ben her sweetest smile and said, "I'm going to go thank your pa, Ben."

"Rev. Wheeler, I'd like to know more about forgiveness." Then with her small white hand in his big rough one, Kate released the bitterness and hatred that had robbed her peace.

Chapter 17

The sun peeked through black clouds that threatened rain again as Kate strolled along the creek with Annabelle and Claire. Its brown, muddy waters rushed high and swift with recent rains. Claire and Annabelle explored the banks, probing and poking under rocks and pebbles at the water's edge with hickory branches that also served as walking sticks.

Claire asked, "Do you suppose the creek could run over and drown folks?"

"I suppose it could, although it doesn't seem likely. But I don't remember it this high before," Kate replied.

"Maybe the beavers have it dammed," Annabelle suggested.

"That's very likely," Kate replied. "You girls about ready to head back?"

"Oh, Kate, do we have to?" Annabelle moaned.

"Look! Look!" screamed Claire pointing. "A snake!"

"Oh! Let's watch him," yelled Annabelle.

"Let him alone, girls," Kate warned as she motioned them to her side.

"Aw, shucks!" Annabelle obeyed but gave the ground a sound kick with her tiny foot.

Moments later, breathless from climbing, they topped the muddy slope. As they approached home, Kate noticed a familiar black stallion tied. Curious, she halted on the edge of the porch, and there stood Tanner! Kate felt the pounding of blood in her temples, followed by a sudden weakness. The three girls stood still, and Tanner spoke. "Kate, could we talk?"

Flustered, Kate considered a moment. Then she said, "Girls, run in the house and tell Mattie that Tanner is here, and I'm talking to him outside."

The girls ran into the house, both talking at once, and relayed Kate's message. Mattie scurried to the kitchen and poked her nose out the window. She could see them, all right, on the bench under the tree! She promptly found some chores to do in the kitchen, keeping her eyes glued to the window.

"You're looking better than you did the last time I saw you," Kate said pertly.

"I'm sorry about that," he said with a sheepish grin. "Were you jealous, Kate?"

"I certainly was not!" she replied angrily.

"Kate, the reason I acted so foolishly was I had too much liquor," he blurted. "I was the jealous one. Please," he pleaded, "give me another chance!"

"I can't."

"Why?"

"Tanner, there are two reasons. First, I don't trust you."

"Aw, Kate, I made a mistake. It'll never happen again." Looking into his heartsick, blue eyes, she was sorely tempted to believe him.

"Go on," he said.

"The other reason is, I love someone else."

Anger raised its ugly head instantaneously, and Tanner shouted, "Wheeler! It's Wheeler, isn't it? Why, I'll fix his wagon!"

"Tanner, please."

His body was rigid, and his voice hard and low. "Kate, a man has a right to be angry when the woman he loves wants another man."

"Don't you see? There is nothing you can do to make me love you. . .if I don't. Harming Ben won't change my mind," she tried to reason.

"But if I can't have you, it would sure make me feel a lot better," he cried.

"Did it? Did it make you feel better when you shot up his farm?"

He looked at her, startled. "Yeah! Yeah, it did!" he shouted.

A tear rolled down Kate's cheek. "Don't you see that it will only make you more miserable if you continue this way? It takes a man to accept things that he can't change. . .to be strong, and move on. That's the kind of man I can respect."

"You think folks don't respect me?"

"Tanner, what about that girl in Dayton?"

"What? What girl?"

"The one you always go to see."

"You don't know nothing, Kate. She ain't respectable, not the marrying kind. That's not why I go to see her."

"I see. Listen to me. You have so much in your favor. You're handsome and smart and charming, downright dazzling. Don't throw it away. Think about your future." Another tear rolled down her cheek. "I really care what happens to you, Tanner."

Tanner's jaw was firmly set, his face hard as flint, and Kate could not read his thoughts. "Thanks for seeing me, Kate," he said simply. He stood up, then reached over and gently wiped her tears away. As he felt the wetness on his hand, he stuffed his fist into his pocket, turned, and walked away.

Kate watched him ride away, and as soon as he was gone, she wept. Mattie was out, posthaste, and at Kate's side. "What did he say? What happened?" She handed Kate a handkerchief and waited.

"Oh, Mattie, I don't know. I just don't know."

Chapter 18

The long, sultry days of August were jam-packed. Mattie's regular sewing customers placed orders for school clothes. Tucker House became a stockpile of dry goods. There were bolts and bolts of colorful calico prints and cottons, threads, and beautiful laces. Mattie savored each piece of fabric, mixing and matching, designing and cutting. She sewed the little girls' dresses with delight and chatted with their customers. Tucker House was alive with all the latest bits of news and gossip.

With Mattie busy at the needle, Kate and her sisters did the canning and harvesting of the garden's abundant crops. Today they canned tomatoes—a gourmet crop, new in the Ohio Valley. They stewed some of the tomatoes and made juice also. Annabelle and Claire picked and washed the large red, ripe tomatoes. Kate plopped them into a huge kettle with a little water from the springhouse. They bubbled and cooked until mushy for the stewed variety. For the juice, she cooked them longer, smashing and stirring them vigorously with a wooden spoon. Annabelle and Claire washed the jars and filled them with the juicy red fruit.

As they cleaned up from their labors, Kate suggested that they make cold sandwiches and entice Mattie to a picnic lunch. Annabelle eagerly sliced the bread while Claire headed out to the springhouse for a jug of milk and the meat. Kate added greens from the garden and large juicy slices of tomato to the sandwiches.

They spread their blanket on the ground where the grass was soft. The breeze felt cool on Kate's wet face. She wiped her forehead with her arm and rubbed the back of her neck. "Oh, this is much better. I didn't even realize there was a breeze today!" she said.

"You girls want to take the eggs in to Cooper's General Store?" Mattie asked. The girls were always eager to abandon their chores around the house and take the short walk into Beaver Creek, especially to see Dorie.

An hour later, the girls left for town while Mattie was in the house preoccupied with her sewing. Kate decided to clean up at the springhouse since the kitchen was sticky and hot. She washed her long, black hair and then relaxed under the hickory tree. It dried quickly. Reluctantly, she headed indoors.

She changed into fresh clothes, humming as she picked up a dress to hem and joined Mattie in the sitting room. The low tones of male voices floated through the open windows, and Mattie hastened to the door to welcome the visitors. It was Sheriff Larson and Thaddeas.

"Come on in," Mattie welcomed them.

Buck declined the invitation, saying, "We just stopped in to get your permission to do some fishing behind the house. I plan to show Thaddeas one of the real pleasures of life!"

"Why, of course! Go right ahead; enjoy yourselves," Mattie replied.

"Smells good in here," Thaddeas said as the aroma tempted him.

"We canned tomatoes this morning." Kate was pleased that someone appreciated her labors.

"If you care to share your catch, you could join us for supper," Mattie suggested.

"That would be great!" the sheriff said eagerly. "We'd better get to it then. We'll be back with plenty."

"Enjoy yourselves," Mattie called as they left. She turned to Kate. "Maybe you could bake one of your famous berry pies for supper tonight."

Kate looked at Mattie helplessly. "I suppose so. I was all settled in for a cool afternoon of stitching."

"I know," Mattie said, "but we should be hospitable."

Kate laid down the dress and headed to the kitchen, taking her apron from a peg on the wall. *Life keeps going in circles,* she thought. *You end up doing the same things over and over.* A smile formed on her face and she shrugged. *Friends make it worthwhile.* Then it faded. *Wish it was Ben coming for supper.*

⇚⇛

Pies cooled under the window, and tossed greens were mixed with cream. Mattie tucked her sewing away and hummed as she dusted with an old cloth. Annabelle and Claire played marbles in the sitting room.

As Kate scanned the kitchen to see if she had forgotten anything, she heard the men coming. They carried a pail. Kate ran to the door and exclaimed, "Wonderful! You caught all those?"

"Yes, the tempting offer inspired us. Actually, Thaddeas was an able pupil." Buck patted his nephew on the back.

"The credit goes to Uncle Buck, an incredible teacher," Thaddeas replied.

"I'm sure you're both to be thanked. Now I'll take those, and you can clean up at the springhouse." Kate took the pail from the sheriff.

When they returned, Claire showed them to the sitting room, and they relaxed a spell and watched the girls play marbles. They could smell the fish frying, and their mouths watered by the time Mattie called them to supper.

"Fresh trout! It is so delicious! Thank ya so much," Mattie said. "We don't get it often enough."

"You need to let me go fishing," Claire piped up. "All I need is the right equipment. Ben showed me how."

"Well, Claire, I didn't know you liked to fish. We should have taken you with us," the sheriff said with surprise.

"How do you like this country life compared ta Boston, Thaddeas?" asked Mattie.

"I love it! It surpasses my expectations. I hope to find work and settle here permanently."

"Good." Mattie nodded.

"What kind of work?" asked Kate.

"I trained in business, and someday I'd like to set up a shop. I don't know much about farming. I'd settle for anything in the meantime."

"Something will show up in town. You'll find yourself a spot," Buck said with assurance.

"That was delicious." Thaddeas thanked his hosts when the meal was finished.

The sheriff offered, "Why don't you take Thaddeas and show him your place, Kate. I'll help Mattie with the dishes. She tells me you've been in the kitchen all day."

"Thank you," Kate replied, "I'd like that."

After they had walked a bit, Kate explained the use of the many buildings, amazed at his ignorance of pioneer life. Then they settled on the porch for a chat. "I wonder if anyone got rid of the skunk in the schoolhouse." Thaddeas chuckled.

"I hope so."

"Could be a real stinky job," Thaddeas continued.

Kate laughed. "Most definitely." Then she grew serious and asked, "Have you gone to church before, back East, I mean?"

"Yes, all my life. It's a lot different there though."

"Really? How?"

"It's the folks who are different. In the East everybody is busy, not as caring and friendly. They seem to forget the meaning of being a Christian later in the week. The singing is good but more formal with a choir and everything."

"Last week was the first time I ever went to church."

"No! I thought sure you were a Christian, Kate."

"Oh, I am. I have been since I was a little girl, and you are, too, I can tell. I like that."

"I do, too, Kate," he said sincerely, "and I like the folks here in the valley. I like them a lot."

Chapter 19

Ben resolved that the only road to travel was the straight one—to win Kate's heart he must be direct and honest, let her know he cared.

"Whoa! You ungrateful cow, stand still now!" Ben hollered as he shoved the pail to the proper spot with a kick of his boot while planning the day's tactics.

I could ask her to go for a ride this afternoon, or I could mention that I might stop in for awhile. Hmm, I hope she's not tied up with old Thaddeas.

"Ben, I'm all through here. Do you need any help?" Luke called to his brother through the open barn door.

"No, I'm nearly finished. Thanks though."

The schoolhouse stood basking in the sunshine, its doors flung open to welcome the families. Ben took his place in the front and scanned the room.

The Whitfields were new this week, and Melanie kept an eye on Ben, reliving in her imagination the times they shared together. Dr. Malone limped in with his family. Mary Potter and her sons found a seat beside the Whitfields. They blocked Melanie's view of Ben, and she squirmed in her seat.

Finally, he spotted the ladies from Tucker House. Ben watched them occupy an empty bench, moving all the way toward the wall. He noted anxiously that a good portion of their bench was vacant and sighed with relief when Mack Tillson, the blacksmith, sat beside them.

What! Ben took a second look. *It's Tanner and his friend Jake. Oh, I hope they're not going to make trouble for Pa,* he fretted as he gave Luke a poke. Ben looked at his pa. The Reverend's head was bent, and Ben thought he must be praying for the congregation.

The service started with singing, and the folks who did not know the songs the previous week started to pick up the tunes. Bursting with joy, Kate sang along with all her heart.

Rev. Wheeler told the folks the sweet story of salvation.

Shivers raced up and down Kate's spine. She twisted the handkerchief on her lap. The reality of Jesus' sacrifice overwhelmed her, and she bowed her head to thank Him.

When Tanner stood to his feet, Kate noticed him for the first time and gasped. Tanner made his way, stumbling, to the front while Jake went out the back door.

"I'd like to be forgiven, to tell Jesus I'm sorry. Would He accept me?" Tanner asked. "I want to change my ways."

Tanner knelt, and the Reverend fervently prayed over him. Eyes grew wet throughout the congregation as Tanner experienced release from a life of sin and exchanged his tattered grave clothes for the clean robe of righteousness.

Tanner took a seat on the front bench while Rev. Wheeler faced the people. He raised his arm toward heaven. "There is joy and celebrating in heaven when one lost lamb is saved. Praise God!" He placed his hand on Tanner's shoulder for a moment, patted his back, and then turned toward the assembly. "I have something else very special to share with you folks." He lingered, savoring the moment. "There's going to be a wedding! Mary Potter and I are going to wed as soon as the circuit preacher comes around. You may now welcome our new brother in the Lord, Tanner Matthews, and congratulate my pretty bride-to-be."

Once people were outside, tongues started wagging with excitement. Everyone was congratulating and backslapping the preacher.

Kate stood among a circle of friends when Tanner appeared. "I'm so happy for you," she said blinking back a tear.

"Aw, you're always crying, Kate. . .every time I'm around."

"That's because I care about you. I told you that before," she said.

He treasured her words in his heart.

"Welcome to the family." Ben held out his hand, and Tanner gripped it firmly.

"Ben? Can I ask you something?"

"Sure, Tanner."

"Why didn't you fight back the night we had our scrap?"

Ben grinned. "The truth is I was aching to."

"Why didn't you?" Tanner probed.

"Because my heart's set to follow Jesus. Let me show you." He thumbed through his Bible until he found Romans 12:18–19. "Here it is, 'If it be possible, as much as lieth in you, live peaceably with all men. Dearly beloved, avenge not yourselves, but rather give place unto wrath: for it is written, Vengeance is mine; I will repay, saith the Lord.' "

"I want to live a decent life, to change, but I don't know if I can. I'll have to get me a Bible."

"Here, take mine. I have another one at home."

Tanner was overcome with emotion. "Thanks, mighty good of you," he mumbled. He felt a firm grip on his shoulder and turned. It was Luke.

"God bless you," he said.

"He already has." Tanner scanned the groups scattered about the school yard. "I guess my friend Jake took off. I sure wish he could experience this."

Luke nodded. "Come on, let's walk a bit and talk about it. There are a few things we can do for him."

They left Ben and Kate standing alone. Glancing around, Ben caught Thaddeas looking their way. *Better move quick,* he thought. "Kate," he asked, "are you busy this afternoon?"

"Why no, Ben. I don't have anything planned," she said.

"Would you mind if I stopped over for a bit?" He did not realize he was digging a deep rut with his foot.

Kate noticed and thought that something must be troubling him. *Maybe he wants to talk about his pa and Mary getting married,* she thought. "I'd love to have you stop in. You know that, Ben," she said warmly. Then she added, "You can tell me all about your pa and Mary."

"Melanie, my dear, you look so pale!" Mrs. Whitfield said with alarm.

"Mama, did you ever see such a tease? First, she toyed with poor Mr. Matthews, and when he walked away from her, she went straightway to entrap Ben. Let me tell you, Ben's no fool. I'm sure he must be nearly bored to death. I must go rescue him. Ben, oh Ben!"

Chapter 20

Ben pushed his food around on his plate with his fork. He could have been chewing on paperboard from Green's Mill for all he cared. Mary Potter had lovingly prepared the meal, and the food was not bad; Ben was just too anxious to enjoy it. Instead he rehearsed what he would say to Kate. *Kate, could I come courting?* or *Kate, you're very special, and I'd like to come calling.*

The Reverend asked him to take Mary and her sons home since he planned to go in that direction. Ben agreed, and now he was biding his time while the meal dragged on and on.

Finally, Mary cleared the table and heated the water in a big black kettle to wash the dirty dishes.

And it was two hours later when they were on their way to the Potter place. Summer's charm captivated Mary. To her right a meadow displayed tall green grasses and a kaleidoscope of wildflowers. To her left passed a lush forest, thick and green, where without warning a doe burst out of a small thicket and dashed wildly in front of the team of horses, then vanished into the forest. It took Ben by surprise, and the horses bolted. The wagon slipped off the edge of the road, careened, and veered into a rut, scraping and bumping wildly behind the horses until it bounced back onto the road.

"Whoa! Whoa!" Ben said as he pulled tightly on the reins. The wagon slowed to a halt and settled in a crazy tilted position. "Just what I was afraid of," Ben said. "We broke a wheel." Disappointed and discouraged from this course of events, he studied what to do. "Will you be all right if I take the team on to your place and come back with your wagon to get you?"

"We'll be fine," Mary assured him. "Take your time, Ben."

"Boys, stay with your ma now, and make sure no harm comes to her!"

"Sure," James and Frank chimed.

Ben unhitched the team and mounted one of his horses bareback, leading the other. The wind whipped under his hat, gently rumpling his hair in disarray, and pushed hard against his shoulders as he rode toward the Potters' place.

Meanwhile back at Tucker House, Kate went to the door, expecting to see Ben. "Hello!" she said cheerfully. Then, "Thaddeas," she added in surprise.

"Good afternoon, Kate," Thaddeas said in his cheerful voice.

"Come in," Kate said.

"Thank you. I was wondering if Claire would like to go fishing?"

"Yes!" cried Claire, who overheard the question. "May I, Mattie?" she begged.

"Of course, that's mighty kind of ya ta be invitin' her, Thaddeas."

"My pleasure," he said sincerely. "Would Annabelle like to come along?" Annabelle heartily agreed.

Then Thaddeas added, "Kate, would you like to join us, too?"

Kate was tempted but declined. "No, not this time, but thank you."

Thaddeas nodded and headed outside to retrieve the fishing pole propped against a tree. A giggling pair of girls followed him.

"You should have gone along, Kate," Mattie said.

"Ben said he was dropping by this afternoon."

"Oh, I see!" Mattie said. "I see, indeed."

❦

Two hours passed. Thaddeas returned with two fatigued but beaming girls and a pail full of cleaned but smelly fish, presented like an offering, plunked down on the porch by Kate's feet. Kate had walked out onto the porch to scan the roadway when the smiling, smelly little group descended upon her.

"What a catch!" she exclaimed. "Are you sure you are a beginner at this, Thaddeas?"

"I caught most of them," Claire piped up, out of breath.

"You did not!" Annabelle shouted.

"Well, I caught three of them, and big ones, too!" Claire said loudly and firmly.

"Yes, you sure did, Peach," Thaddeas said.

They all looked up when a dusty cloud appeared. As it settled, Ben emerged. He pulled his horse, Pepper, to a halt and slid off his back. He straightened his hat, brushed the dust off his clothes, and stomped about a bit before he noticed, embarrassingly, that Kate and Thaddeas stood on the porch.

The rest of the evening developed around Mattie's dinner invitation of fried fish and hush puppies.

Ben was not about to lose any ground to Thaddeas, so he graciously accepted Mattie's invitation. Oblivious to Ben's intentions, Kate sniffed the delicious fish and thought, *How perfect the day has turned out after all.*

Chapter 21

All I'm saying is you don't need to upset the apple cart, Dan. We want to make a good impression on the Reverend," Rose Whitfield warned her husband and pointed her finger sternly.

"Don't go getting your nose out of joint, Rose. I won't muddy the waters as long as the subject don't come up!" Dan Whitfield stuck to his ground.

"Well, I never! You know the subject of savages isn't fit for the supper table anyway. Perhaps you could bring up the Reverend's wedding. It might put a notion in Ben's head. No harm laying the proper groundwork now, is there?" Rose stooped over to eye the side of the table, and then moved her plump body forward, giving the table covering a tug to set it straight.

"More like setting a trap," Dan retorted, shaking his head.

"Now, Dan, you know that none of you fellas would offer for a lady unless properly baited. That's the charm of it." She walked over to give him a playful squeeze.

"They're here!" cried Melanie, peering out the sitting room window.

"All right, Daughter. Act like a lady now. Pa, answer the door."

At supper, Rose seated Melanie beside Ben. He glanced across the table and did not miss the smirk on Luke's face.

"It's mighty good of you to be weddin' the widow Potter," Rose addressed the Reverend and waited to see what he had to say for himself.

"Oh, it's not charity, I assure you! I'm quite fond of Mary and her boys. It will do us bachelors good to have a woman in the house."

"Really! Well, try some of this berry pie, Reverend. My Melanie baked it. I don't like to brag, but she's a wonderful cook. I reckon she'll do a man proud some day," she added, looking directly at Ben and winking.

"Mama, really!" Melanie exclaimed in mock humility. Then she teased, "However, I predict another wedding shortly."

"Whose?" Luke was the first to fall for the bait.

"Kate and Thaddeas!" she announced saucily.

Luke choked on his water, and Ben squirmed in his seat under the steady gaze of Rose Whitfield.

The room became still, and Rose picked up on the comment. "They do make sech a lovely couple. . .as long as Thaddeas knows what he's getting into. From what I hear, Kate breaks hearts like Mattie makes dresses, a new one for every occasion. She likes to toy with men's affections. Probably gets it honest enough. Look how long the sheriff's courted Mattie, and she still refuses to tie the knot. More pie, anyone?"

Ben thought about Sunday, how Thaddeas had ruined his visit. *What a fool I am!* Then the mention of Kate's name snapped him back to the present.

"Kate seems like a real nice girl to me, Rose," the Reverend said sternly. "I think whatever you heard is just the product of someone's active imagination."

"Well, some things just do set tongues a-wagging, Reverend," she retorted.

Later on the ride home, the Reverend said, "I hate to see Mattie and Kate's names darkened, but the Whitfields are teetering on the edge of the totter. I must be careful not to offend them and turn them away from the church when they need Jesus."

Luke spoke angrily, "It appears they come to Sunday meeting with the sole purpose of marrying Melanie to Ben."

Chapter 22

At the Potters', Mary put a pot of coffee on the fire and scrutinized the cabin, planning in her head. She ached to do some heavy work and burn off the restlessness that stemmed from waiting. Movement through the window caught her eye. She rushed out the door and greeted Mattie with a hug. "Come on in and have yourselves some coffee," she invited.

"I thought we came to work," Mattie said, laughing.

"That, too. There's plenty of that! I didn't know how much belongin's we had until I started to rummage through things. We can start in the kitchen. I won't be takin' all my cookin' kettles and such; some we'll just have ta leave."

At the Wheelers', things commenced along the same lines. Ben and Luke rearranged their room to fit both beds and all their belongings into a small space. "Maybe if we hang a few pegs here for your clothes. . . ," Luke suggested. "Aw, shucks, why don't you get married; then we wouldn't have to bunk together," he teased.

"Don't hold your breath a-waiting."

Luke knew Ben was upset since their dinner at the Whitfields. "What you need is more determination." Ben's back was turned, and when he did not respond, Luke continued. "If you care about Kate, you have to go after her."

"I don't believe I asked for your advice, little brother," Ben snapped.

"Aw, simmer down now. I don't want to scrap."

"How are you boys doing in there?" called the Reverend.

"Fine, Pa," Ben said. "Come on in, if you can get in."

"No, I'm headed to Mary's to load up her things. Wanted you to know I was leaving."

The afternoon dragged for Ben, who knew Kate was returning with the wagons. Finally, a cloud of dust appeared in the distance.

"Here they come," Luke said with a tinge of dread. "Things will never be the same as they were."

Everyone pitched in, and the Potters' belongings were soon in place. James and Frank were elated that they would soon be kin to Ben and Luke, whom they idolized.

Kate looked wistfully about the cabin at Mary's belongings lovingly placed here and there. She thought it looked cozy.

Mary planned to stay with Mattie until the wedding. The next day, preparations would take place for the wedding itself, which was to be held at Tucker House.

The Reverend looked at Ben and Luke. "One of you boys want to take the ladies home?"

Ben's face turned pink, but he did not offer. Luke could not believe how stubborn his brother was acting. "I'll go, Father," Luke said.

On the ride home Kate had ample time to sulk. Ben had ignored her all day, and she knew he did it intentionally. Why was he angry? She racked her brain, trying to recall his last visit.

The wagon squeaked to a stop, and Luke helped Mattie and Mary to the ground. Annabelle and Claire jumped off the back when he came around to help Kate. Tired, they made their way toward the house after offering Luke thanks. Luke hesitated a moment and then called out, "Kate!"

She wanted to be left alone, but she turned toward him. "Yes?" She noticed the worried look that set creases in his freckled face and felt ashamed. "Something on your mind, Luke?"

"I may be sticking my nose where it does not belong. . . ."

Kate smiled. "What are you trying to say?"

"Don't be too hard on Ben." Her brows arched in surprise. "He was rude to you today, but he's got a case of green fever."

"I don't understand."

Her look of innocence encouraged him to stick out his neck even further. "Do you care for Thaddeas?" Kate could not believe this conversation was taking place. "As a suitor?" Luke probed.

"No, of course not," Kate replied, shaking her head.

"Ben has the crazy idea that you do. He's sick with jealousy. There, now I've said it, and he would skin me alive if he knew. Good day, Kate."

Kate watched him ride away in disbelief. Ben was jealous. He cared! Lifting her skirts, she ran toward the creek. She felt alive. At the top of the ridge with the water swirling below her, she shouted, "Ben cares! He cares!"

Slowly she dropped to the ground and looked toward heaven. She remembered Ben's sullenness and hurt. "Oh, Father," she prayed, "what shall I do?"

Chapter 23

September 20, the Reverend's wedding day, dawned warm and sweet. The Reverend looked elegant enough in his new gray suit. His snow-white hair was newly cut and topped with a dapper gray hat to match. James and Frank were dressed in new linen shirts, feeling stiff and starched in their buttoned-up collars. Ben and Luke looked handsome in their Sunday best.

Mary wore a pale blue dress that brought out the sky in her eyes. Her fingers lingered as she touched the white lacework that danced circles on her dainty round collar. The material was the prettiest she had ever laid eyes on, soft as a kitten and delightful to the touch. It was a gift from her betrothed. He ordered it from Dayton via Cooper's and hired Mattie to design and sew it, a luxury which Mary would never have afforded herself.

Outside, colorful leaves floated to the earth to carpet the wedding floor. Sheriff Larson and Thaddeas were in charge as folks gathered.

The Reverend shook hands and received blessings as he walked to the big hickory tree where they were to be married. Ben and Luke stood toward the front of the crowd and waited while Mattie, Kate, and the girls took their honored place.

Ben stole a glance and thought Kate looked like an angel in a very pale green dress with a big bow in the back and a full flowing skirt. Her long black hair hung in curls with flowers for adornment.

The crowd turned as Mary approached, escorted by her young sons. A hush fell over the crowd. Mary's face radiated love's bloom, a flower lovely and sweet. Everyone knew the sorrows she had experienced and rejoiced with her in this newfound love and family being created. Everything went just as planned as the circuit preacher gave a short sermon on marriage.

Kate's eyes searched Ben's a few times, but he stared straight ahead. The couple repeated their vows and sealed them with a kiss. Afterward there was a fabulous feast. The fiddlers got out their instruments, and the newlyweds celebrated to the sound of lively music as couples paired off to dance the quadrille.

"Afternoon, Ben." Melanie looked radiant in a yellow gown that complemented her golden hair. "Such a lovely wedding," she sighed. The music boomed too loud for talking, which suited Ben fine.

Tanner approached Kate with a woman on his arm. "You've met Elizabeth?"

"Of course. How lovely you look," Kate replied with a smile.

Tanner took courage and spoke out. "This wedding seems like a good place to announce that we plan to tie the knot soon, too. We just need to talk with the Reverend. Elizabeth gave me her answer last night."

Kate squeezed Tanner's hand. "I'm so happy for you, Tanner." She turned to give Elizabeth a hug to show that all was forgiven.

"Well, how about that!" Melanie exclaimed, watching on. "I guess Thaddeas won't have to worry about Tanner anymore."

"Let's not talk about them," Ben grunted.

"They make such a lovely couple. Look! They're dancing."

"Would you care for something to drink, Melanie?" Ben asked while leading her away from the crowd. He burned with jealousy.

"Kate?" Thaddeas said. "I have a confession to make."

"You do? What is it, Thaddeas?"

"You're very beautiful; in fact, the first time I saw you, I was deeply shook." Kate stiffened. "Buck keeps telling me that I should pursue you."

"Thaddeas!" She must stop this talk at once.

"But my heart is elsewhere."

"What? It is?"

"As much as I come calling, I thought I'd better clear the air. I wouldn't want you to get the wrong idea."

"I see."

"I'm sorry, Kate, but my heart is set on Annabelle."

"What! Annabelle! Why, she's just a child."

"I know, but I have plenty of time to wait."

Ben tried to keep his eye on Kate and Thaddeas, and noticed they were in deep conversation when he was interrupted by Luke.

"Determination, Brother. . .you need more determination."

Melanie's eyes followed their gaze and rested on Kate and Thaddeas. "I wonder what makes a girl behave like that? Anyone can see you're smitten with her, yet she flaunts Thaddeas under your nose. I would never treat you that way, Ben."

"Why, that's sweet of you to say, Melanie, but I think you're too hard on her," Ben said without taking his eyes off the couple.

"How can you defend her?"

Melanie turned in exasperation to glare at Luke, and he just shrugged his shoulders. As she marched off, he muttered under his breath, "That's it, Brother, determination!"

Meanwhile Thaddeas went on, "I have to get established, get started in business, save up some money. I've got plenty of time. She isn't thinking about romance yet, I know, but I'm willing to wait until she's older."

"I–I wish you well, Thaddeas," Kate said, not sure how to reply to this astonishing news.

"You're not upset, are you, Kate?"

"Of course not." *Twice in one day!* she thought. *I've been dumped twice today by men I don't even love.*

"Do you suppose she'd dance with me?"

Kate nodded.

"Mind if I cut in, Thaddeas?" Ben towered over them.

"Not at all." He gave Ben a big grin and nudged his way through the throng to look for Annabelle.

Kate's heart was a wicked beating drum. *I may not get another chance like this.* Her lips trembled. "Ben?"

When he looked into her soft brown eyes, his mind flashed back to the day he had taken her to his farm, and he remembered her excitement about starting a church. He recalled her sweet spirit on that first Sunday. How could he doubt her? She might love Thaddeas, but she was not a heartbreaker.

"Kate, I'm sorry. I've treated you badly."

"No need to apologize. I understand."

"You do?"

She nodded.

"Could I call on you this week?"

On the way home, Luke reflected. "A lot of changes have come our way since we left Virginia."

"Yeah, when we were back on that flatboat crossing the Ohio River, I never dreamed Pa would get married again," Ben replied.

"I'm feeling a bit restless. I think maybe it's time for me to go back to school. . .get ready to start my ministry and all."

"I had a feeling you were going to leave us pretty soon. I'm gonna miss you something terrible!"

Chapter 24

Mattie, Kate, and Annabelle toiled in the garden. Now that the wedding was over, it was time to give it the attention it sorely needed. They turned most everything under except the big round pumpkins still growing on winding vines. The days were cool and brisk, but the hard work still made them thirsty and hot. Mattie sent Annabelle after water. Kate stood and put her fist in the small of her back to work out the kinks as she stretched with one arm and then the other. "On a day like today, it's good to be alive," she said.

"Yes, it is," Mattie replied absentmindedly. "Kate, let's invite company for Annabelle's birthday; she'll soon be fourteen."

"What a good idea! Who shall we invite?"

Just then the door slammed shut; Annabelle approached with a pitcher of cool water. "Think on it; we'll talk later," Mattie said quickly.

Annabelle giggled as she looked at Kate and Mattie. "Do you realize how dirty you two are?"

"I reckon you were just as dirty till ya just now cleaned up, weren't ya?" Mattie teased back.

"Nope, I didn't have a big smudge on my face like that." She scooped a handful of soil and wiped her dirty hands across Kate's face.

"Why, you!" Kate said, grabbing for Annabelle and missing. Annabelle shot off like a cannonball, running to the edge of the garden while Kate picked up a dirt clod and hurled it, hitting her right in the back.

"Ouch! Hey, that's not fair!" Annabelle knelt down to get her own ammunition while another clod buzzed high overhead. She stood up, but instead of pitching it at Kate, she threw it at an unsuspecting target, Mattie.

Smack! "What? Oh, you're in trouble now, Girl," Mattie cried.

Several minutes later they drank the water Annabelle had brought. "Whew! I'm gettin' too old for this," Mattie complained. "I think we've done enough for today. By the time we clean up and get dinner on, it'll be time for Claire ta come home."

"May I go to meet her?" Annabelle begged.

"Yes, that would be fine."

With Annabelle gone, Kate and Mattie talked about Annabelle's birthday. "Let's surprise her!"

"Ya think we could?" Mattie asked. "Pull it off, I mean?"

"It would take some planning, but it would be fun."

"I reckon it could be done; let's do it!" Mattie agreed.

"Who should we invite?"

"The young folks about her age? Maybe we could get Ben and Thaddeas to take a couple of wagons, pick 'em all up, and deliver them home again so their folks don't have ta tote 'em all," Mattie suggested.

"This is going to be such fun; I can hardly wait!" Kate exclaimed.

"Sure. . .they could throw some hay in the wagon and let the kids have fun. Annabelle could get in on the hayride when they take the children home."

When Ben arrived for supper that night, he suggested that they take a walk, and that suited Kate. She grabbed her sweater off the peg in the kitchen and joined him.

"How are things going at your place?" she asked.

"Different, that's for sure!" Ben said. "It's hard to find any quiet. There's usually commotion during dinner with James and Frank horsing around. After dinner Mary and Pa visit. If I go to my room, Luke's in there. If I go to do chores, the boys follow me."

"I know what it's like to be around chatterboxes; it gets pretty lively around Tucker House. But I can always go to my room or sneak off to the creek, or out to the hickory tree. Do they follow you everywhere?" she asked.

"Well, not everywhere; sometimes they follow Luke," he said with a chuckle. Then, "Don't get me wrong; I shouldn't be complaining because they're good boys, and there's lots of love being shared around home. It's a good feeling. It's been a long time since Pa's been happy like this."

"That's good. I'm sure it'll work out in time."

"Luke's going to be leaving for school soon. I guess I'll have a room to myself then. I sure hate to see him go. We've always been close."

They stopped walking then and sat on a large log. As Kate gathered her skirts in her hand and spread them out about her in a perfect circle, she remembered her surprise. "Mattie and I are planning a birthday surprise for Annabelle." She shared the plan, and he volunteered to help.

"Will Thaddeas come?" he ventured.

"We plan to ask him, but we haven't seen him since the wedding. He usually comes over pretty often with the sheriff."

"So I've noticed. Answer a question for me? Does Thaddeas come calling on you? Courting. . .I mean?"

"No. We're only friends. As a matter of fact. . ."

"What?"

"Oh, Ben, I can't tell you. It's a secret."

"Tell me, Kate," Ben pleaded.

"Thaddeas has his heart set on Annabelle."

"Annabelle!" Ben exclaimed in surprise.

"Yes, now hush. Don't tell the world! He knows she's too young and aims to wait for her. Anyway, we're just friends. He needs friends, being from the East, and all."

"Annabelle!" Ben said again, shaking his head in disbelief. "He's looking at Annabelle when you live in the same house. I find that hard to believe."

"Well, believe it! Anyway, I don't care about him like that, even if he were to look my way."

"You don't know how glad I am to hear you say that. Ever since that first Sunday when he came to church with you, I've been crazy with jealousy."

"You have?" Ben nodded and looked at the ground. "Well, whenever Melanie comes around, I turn green," Kate confessed. "She made a special trip to Tucker House to tell me that you had dinner with them and how charming you were."

"Aw-shucks, she ain't nothing to me, Kate. Why does she bother you?"

"I recall you've danced with her more than once."

"You danced with Thaddeas!" With this outburst they broke into hearty laughter.

"I guess we've been a couple of fools," Ben admitted as a wave of contentment settled over him.

"Yes, we have."

"Kate? I wonder if dancing is such a good idea. Sure brings the worst out in people. Remember Tanner on Independence Day? Pa said some folks don't even participate. . .that they think dancing is wrong because it causes many evils."

"I never thought about it before, Ben."

"It sure seemed right when I was holding you," Ben admitted as his freckled face turned pink. "But I don't hold to the thought of you dancing with anyone else."

"I wonder how married folks feel about it?" Kate asked.

"I reckon some don't care, but I know I would!" Ben answered.

"I guess it's one of those things everyone has to decide for themselves."

"Yeah, I reckon so."

"I'm glad you came tonight, Ben."

"Me, too. May I call on you again?"

Kate nodded. "Now," she said, "let's talk about Annabelle's party!"

Chapter 25

October 10 blew in a very cold day. It fell on Friday, which was perfect for the surprises concocted for Annabelle's birthday.

She awoke to the aroma of birthday cake, which was a ploy to keep her off track. She chattered excitedly throughout breakfast, trying to discover what the day held.

Mattie said that she would have to wait until evening to open her gift. In her excitement, evening seemed days away. Mattie laughed at the pathetic expression on Annabelle's face. Then according to plan, Mattie suggested that she spend the day with Dorie Cooper in town. Annabelle was ecstatic. To spend a whole day with Dorie would be splendid indeed! Dorie always knew the latest gossip, the latest fads, and the most up-to-date styles. Sometimes they studied catalogs filled with new merchandise that Mr. Cooper used to purchase supplies. And, of course, they shared secrets and dreams.

Claire was in on the surprise, but put on a convincing act, portraying the disappointed child, going to school while Annabelle had such an entertaining day with Dorie.

With Annabelle finally out the door and Claire off to school, Kate and Mattie hustled to get everything in order for the festivities that evening. The day flew by, and they tried to act as normal as possible when Annabelle returned for supper that evening. They all listened as she told about her day with Dorie and thanked them over and over again for letting her go. They made a big hoopla out of the birthday cake and showered her with hugs and kisses.

Mattie disappeared and came back carrying a brown package. "Happy Birthday!" she said as she presented it to Annabelle. It was small but heavy for its size. She shook it carefully and after lengthy examination tore open the brown paper wrappings.

"Oh!" she exclaimed in delight. "How lovely." It was a small glass dish with flowers boldly painted on the lid, just the right size to store precious trinkets.

After the dishes were washed, Mattie started a fire in the fireplace, and they all gathered in the sitting room, listening to the wind's howl outside. Annabelle rambled on with recollections of the day. All of a sudden, they heard a terrible commotion.

"I wonder what that could be?" Mattie said, and they all moved to the window and jerked the curtains aside to peer out. Two lights bobbed like stars in the darkness. They were the flickering lanterns from two wagons, loaded with folks making a loud racket.

"What in the world?" Mattie exclaimed as the three girls crowded in close to see what was happening. Two already knew, and one was being totally taken in.

As the wagons drew nearer, the young folks yelled wildly, "Annabelle! Annabelle! We want Annabelle!"

Annabelle still did not comprehend, and Claire clapped with delight. One more look at Mattie and Kate and understanding dawned. "Oh! Oh!" Annabelle joined Claire in clapping, and then picked up her skirts and ran outside. The young folks piled out and grabbed and hugged her until she was totally overcome with sentiment.

Ben and Thaddeas worked together and made a fire in spite of the gusty wind. The young folks gathered around them. "Dorie, you scamp! You knew all the time, didn't you? Shame on you for tricking me!" Annabelle scolded.

"I thought sure I'd burst, keeping it inside all day." Dorie giggled.

Mattie brought out corn to pop over the fire and cider for the young folks to drink. There were nine young people, all of Annabelle's favorites. The girls had brought small gifts and demanded that Annabelle open them immediately. The adults kept a special eye out for Bart and Andy, two older boys known for their ornery pranks. Thaddeas noticed that Bart and Andy were not living up to their reputation of roughhousing. Instead they kept their eyes on the girls, especially Annabelle and Dorie. *They must be growing up,* Thaddeas thought.

Thaddeas felt frustrated over the age difference between himself and Annabelle. Sometimes she was a young lady, and other times she was still a child. *At least this birthday makes her one year older,* he thought dismally.

A few hours later, Annabelle and her friends had settled down and gathered around the fire where they chatted quietly. "I hate to break it up, especially now that it's quieted down, but I reckon we should be getting these young people back to their folks," Ben whispered to Kate.

"Yes, I suppose you're right," Kate said dreamily. "It's been a good party."

"I was hoping that you would ride along."

"I'd love to go. Let me get a couple of blankets while you round up everybody. I'll tell Mattie the plan," Kate replied.

Soon they were jostling down the road, hardly able to talk with all of the horseplay and laughter coming from behind. Kate was content, happy that the surprise had worked and Annabelle was having such a fine time. The young folks sang some songs. Then they became quieter, snuggling down in the hay and giggling.

"Are you warm enough, Kate?" Ben asked.

"Yes, warm from the inside out," she replied, hoping that he would understand her intended meaning.

He did, as those in love are apt to cling hopelessly to every real or imagined gesture of endearment.

The wagons pulled to a stop to let Sammy off at the Hawkes' place. The boy jumped off the wagon, gave a wave, and headed for his house. Just then Annabelle noticed he had left his cap lying in the hay. She jumped up to yell after him. At the same time, Thaddeas started the team to pull ahead. The movement caught Annabelle by surprise, and she lost her balance and fell, head first, over the side of the wagon.

What followed was a blur. Someone screamed and yelled, and Thaddeas stopped the team to find the trouble. When he understood, he jumped down frantically, giving the reins to Bart. He found Annabelle lying on the road. He was sure her arm was broken, hit by the wagon wheel. The worst was the puddle of blood under her limp head. She did not respond in any way, and Thaddeas was too distraught to think clearly.

By the time Ben and Kate got there, Thaddeas was holding her saying, "Annabelle, oh, Annabelle, what have I done?"

Ben quickly took charge. "She's breathing," he said. Kate felt her chest cave in, so awesome was the weight of the horror in it. Annabelle, so full of life one moment, now lay lifeless and pale. Kate knelt down beside Annabelle as Claire sobbed uncontrollably.

"I need a clean cloth to stop the bleeding," Ben said to Kate. "She has a cut. How about your petticoat?"

She pulled up her skirt and tried to rip a piece, but it would not tear. Ben reached over and with one swift motion managed to tear the delicate cotton petticoat. Then he tore it into two long strips. He folded one to make a pad and pressed it against her wound. "Hold this tight," he ordered, and Kate did as she was told. Then he took another strip and wrapped it around Annabelle's head to hold the pad in place.

"Thaddeas?"

Thaddeas nodded where he stood, wringing his hands.

"Get all the young folks into one wagon. Finish dropping them off, and try and get them calmed down. We'll put Kate, Claire, and Annabelle in the other wagon, and head for Doc Malone's. Stop in at Tucker House on the way back to get Mattie if I haven't already been there. See you back at Doc Malone's. Are you all right?"

"No, but I know what needs to be done. Thanks, Ben."

All Kate remembered of the ride to the doctor's was the awful blackness that draped the night's sky and the deafening howl of the wind. She held Claire so tightly that the two seemed as one in the midst of it all.

Chapter 26

The waiting seemed like an eternity, sitting in Doc Malone's small outer room while the doctor and his wife worked fervently over Annabelle, who lay motionless on the big bed in the other room. The small circle of friends comforted each other as best they could while tragedy stalked mercilessly nearby.

Death's presence could be felt, an unseen yet powerful enemy, draping them in a shroud of helplessness. Kate bowed her head in response, seeking her comforter, Jesus, but she quickly jerked it up again as she heard a creaking sound. The door to the adjoining room was opening! She drew a long breath and held it, waiting. . . .

The doctor limped into the room. He ran his hands through his hair, and Kate saw beads of perspiration on his brow.

"It's not good," he said. Huge tears rolled down Mattie's pale cheeks uncontrollably, and Sheriff Larson reached over and lightly gripped her shoulder. "She had a broken arm; we set it. That'll be fine in time. . .some scrapes and bruises, we cleaned them. There was a nasty cut on the back of her head where she must have hit a rock. Whoever stopped the bleeding probably saved her life."

Thaddeas leaned forward, placed his elbows on his knees, and cupped his head in his hands. Then he shook his head as if in disbelief that this could all really be happening.

The doctor continued, "We put twenty-five stitches in mending it, and we had to shave some of her head. But the part that's bad is the bump on her temple. It's responsible for her unconscious state. The good part is that she's stirring, although delirious. There's just no saying if she'll come out of it or not. If she makes it through the night, her chances are better. We'll just have to wait it out and pray. I know the Lord heals folks. I've seen plenty of miracles in my lifetime."

"I believe He will," Kate said. "I just know He will."

"I suggest that Mattie stay and the rest of you go home."

"Maybe I should get Pa," Ben offered.

"No need," Mattie said coldly.

Ben looked confused at the tone of her voice. "We'll be praying just the same, and I'm sure he'll want to come in the morning," he assured her. She did not reply but sat stiffly, staring at the bedroom door.

The sheriff said, "Best do as Doc says. I'll stay here the night and keep an eye on Mattie." Kate nodded in agreement.

"Come on, Thaddeas. We'll drop you off," Ben offered.

First, they dropped Thaddeas off at the sheriff's place. Ben walked him to the door. "Are you all right, Friend?" Ben asked.

Thaddeas's reserve crumbled. "It's all my fault. . .it's my fault that she fell out of the wagon, and then. . .and then, I ran over her." Ben placed his arms around Thaddeas, supporting him until the moment of weakness passed.

"Thaddeas, it's not your fault at all. Annabelle stood up, and it was an accident. That's all. It could have happened to any one of those youngsters on my wagon."

"But Annabelle. . .why Annabelle?" Thaddeas moaned.

"Why don't you come on home with me tonight, Thaddeas. I hate to see you like this."

"No, no. I'll be all right. It's just that there is nothing I can do."

"You can pray, Thaddeas."

He nodded. "I'll do that. Thanks, Ben."

As Ben walked back to the wagon, he noticed Thaddeas was not lighting any lamps, just leaving the house dark. *That would be me, if something happened to Kate.*

He climbed back onto the wagon seat. The night was cold. Claire shivered, tightly squeezed between Kate and Ben on the seat. "It'll be all right, Claire," he patted her cold little hands. They drove on, and Kate cried silently, staring into black nothingness.

Ben went into Tucker House with Kate and Claire, lit the candle just inside the door, and then one of the lamps. "I'll stay if you want," he offered.

Kate managed a weak smile and shook her head. "Your pa will be worried. You'd better go on home."

"Only if you're sure you'll be all right."

"I'm sure," she said. Then, as if remembering something, she suddenly called out, "Ben?" He was immediately at her side. "Thank you so much. What would we have done without you?"

She looked so vulnerable holding Claire's frail hand, her lips quivering. Ben reached out and pulled them both to his breast, holding them in a tight embrace. Then he released them and smiled tenderly.

"I'll be by in the morning to take you back to the doc's."

Kate nodded, and he turned, pulled his hat on tightly, and was out the door.

"Are you hungry or thirsty, Claire?" she asked. Claire shook her head. "Let's go up to bed then." Kate lit the candle again and turned out the lamp.

"Would you like to sleep with me tonight, Claire?" The young girl nodded that she would.

As Kate lay in bed, enveloped in the bleakness of night, she found herself listening to Claire's soft breathing in comparison to the heavy wind blowing outside. She tried to put some perspective into her thinking. *How can the world be so perfect one minute and so dark the next? Life can be good or cruel,* she thought. She remembered again being a little girl in the root cellar, the Indian raid, and holding Annabelle. . . . *Oh, Annabelle.*

Some things are out of man's control; like the way love bubbles up from within for a special person, coloring the world rosy, or the way we are all so fragile and can face death at any moment. Yet one thing remains constant, God's love.

"Oh, Jesus," she prayed. "I don't know if Annabelle is ready to meet you. It's not her fault, Lord. . .with our folks dying when she was so young and Mattie rebelling against you. Please, Jesus, give her another chance and heal her body." Kate prayed whenever she woke as she drifted in and out of a restless slumber.

Mattie could not sleep. She just stared at the bedroom door. Once Mrs. Malone came out to check her, and Mattie asked if she could go sit by Annabelle's side.

"All right, for a little while, but then you must try to get some rest, Mattie. If she comes around tomorrow, she'll need you."

The next morning, bright and early, Ben and his pa headed for Beaver Creek.

"Looks like another windy day, but the sun sure warms a body up," the Reverend said. "It reminds me of God's steadfast love when times are hard." Ben nodded, and then they rode on silently.

Meanwhile, Kate started a fire and tempted Claire with some warm oatmeal. Having Claire to take care of helped keep up her courage. They were anxious for the Wheelers to come and take them to the doctor's, but Kate was still surprised and grateful when they arrived so early. She moved methodically to the door to let them in.

The Reverend reached for her right away, and she fell into his arms. "Well, are you girls ready to go to the doctor's?" he asked. Kate nodded, and they grabbed their wraps off the peg behind the door and headed out. As they drove into Beaver Creek, all sorts of thoughts raced through their minds—thoughts of hope and trusting chased by thoughts of despair and fear.

Soon they pulled up outside of the doctor's house. The Wheelers helped the girls down and led them to the door. Ben paused a moment while everyone searched inside for courage, and then they entered.

The sheriff sat on the settee drinking coffee. He shook his head as if to say nothing had changed. Mrs. Malone popped her head out of the kitchen and rushed to greet them. She shook their hands warmly and took their wraps. "Here, sit down," she said, and motioned toward some chairs.

"May I go in and see them?" the Reverend asked.

"Yes, that would be fine," answered the doctor who had just limped into the room. "There's been no change with Annabelle except her head is more swollen, and Mattie's taking it so hard. She just sits and stares. She won't rest, and she doesn't talk. It's natural and all. . . . Everyone takes grief differently, but I hope you can help, Reverend."

"I'll see what I can do."

"Mattie, I'm sorry," the Reverend said as he entered the dark room. He walked to where she was sitting and took one of her limp hands into his own. She jerked, and her body went rigid. Mattie looked at the Reverend with cold, hard eyes. "I want to help you if I can," he went on.

She pulled her hand away and jumped to her feet. "Then you just tell God ta leave me alone! He's took and took from me. . .until there's nothing left ta give. How can He be so cruel?" she screamed.

"Mattie, I know it seems like that, but He hasn't taken Annabelle. We can't be blaming Him. We need to be seeking Him, asking Him to help us."

"Well. . .He won't help me; I know that! I ain't countin' on His help!"

"May I just kneel here and pray silently for Annabelle?"

"Do what ya want. I'll go get some coffee." She turned abruptly and left the room, walking with shoulders slumped into the sitting room. Kate went to her immediately, noticing the deep dark circles under her swollen eyes.

In the other room, the Reverend knelt beside Annabelle's bed, praying for her healing, and praying for wisdom and insight. Then he nodded and prayed for Mattie, praying that her heart would be softened and she might come to terms with her Maker.

Chapter 27

When the Reverend got up from his knees that morning, he opened his eyes and looked around the room, perhaps expecting to hear directly from God. No dramatic revelation or healing miracle took place within the Malones' bedroom. He only saw the sun's rays, shining in through the windows and splattering warmth across him and the wooden slats on the floor.

He stood and looked once more at the beautiful young girl lying on the big bed and felt his own weakness and need to depend on God. He knew he should pray for Mattie as well as Annabelle. He believed God was listening.

Anyone as old as the Reverend was not sheltered from the frailties of human life. He had seen people suffer and die and had been called upon to bear these burdens with them. His own dear first wife had faded away like the light at the end of day. Yet over the years, his faith in God's goodness and healing power had grown. After all, God also healed people. Many verses in the Bible told about God wanting the best for His people. The Reverend believed that God could use this accident to accomplish good for His children if they would only turn to Him in their time of need.

Most of God's promises had conditions connected to them, and Romans 8:28 was not any different: "And we know that all things work together for good to them that love God, to them who are the called according to his purpose." He knew that if Mattie did not love God, He would not be able to perform His will in this, so the Reverend resolved to pray for Mattie constantly in the days ahead.

When he came out of the bedroom, Mattie agreed to let the sheriff take her home where she could rest while Kate stayed with Annabelle.

Claire asked, "Please, Mattie, before we leave, may I see Annabelle?"

"I'll go in with her," Kate added.

"All right," Mattie said, "I'll wait outside." She turned and walked wearily out the door, followed by her devoted sheriff.

When Kate and Claire entered Annabelle's room, they walked timidly up to the bedside. Kate placed her hand on Annabelle's broken arm.

"Oh, poor Annabelle," Claire said.

"She's sleeping."

"Kate?"

"Yes."

"Do you think God really hears us when we pray?"

"Yes, I really think so, Claire."

"Will he wake Annabelle up if we ask Him?"

"I hope so, Claire. That's what I've been asking Him to do. I trust God to do the best thing for Annabelle. I know He loves her as much as we do."

"How do you know that?"

"It says so in the Bible, Claire," Kate said, bringing Claire's small delicate hand up now, and pressing it to her breast.

"I'd do anything for God if He'd let Annabelle wake up," said Claire.

"Claire, you need to be strong today. . .for Mattie's sake. Do you know what I mean?"

"Yes, Kate."

"Are you ready to go now?"

"Yes, bye, Annabelle. Please wake up. . .we need you, Annabelle."

Kate led Claire out of the room and watched her leave. Then she turned back to the bedside to start her vigil.

Meanwhile, Doc Malone told the Wheelers, "There is no way of knowing for sure, but Annabelle probably will be unconscious until the swelling goes down on her head. She started with a fever early this morning, and I hope that when it breaks, she'll awaken."

The next few days were days of waiting and trying to keep the fever down. Annabelle did not respond to the world around her, other than sporadic movements and words that indicated she was having some dreams in her own world, far away.

Kate and Mattie took turns at her bedside with Mrs. Malone and the doctor always doing their best. Many friends dropped in at Tucker House to comfort those who they would find at home, or at the doctor's house to see if there was anything they could do to help. The Reverend called daily at the Malones', and if he did not find Mattie there, he also would stop in at Tucker House.

Mattie was never so rude to him again as she had been that first morning, but her former smile was replaced by a face set in stone. Thus she continued to withdraw from her family and friends more each day, refusing their comfort and solace.

Ben did his best to encourage and support Kate. He knew it was a hard time for her. She was not aware of what she said or did during those days, but Ben was aware. He watched her in admiration. His heart grew fonder toward her as he valued her inner character, her faith, courage, and compassion. A precious jewel, he desired with all his heart to make this remarkable woman his own.

One afternoon, exactly four days after the accident, kneeling on the cold, hard floor in her room, Claire petitioned God. "I know You are Kate's God. But if You'll help my sister, I'll have You for my God, too. Kate said that You love Annabelle. If You let her wake up and make her well again, I'll promise to serve You. I'll be whatever You want, a preacher. . .a nurse. . .or a missionary. I promise. Amen."

That little prayer hinged on the edge of hope and a turn of events. In the meantime, Mattie returned to Doc Malone's to sit once more with Annabelle. As she entered the room, she was overcome by a sense of helplessness. She felt like a speck of dust in the mighty universe and like her circumstances were of no concern to God. . .if there was a God. She slumped in a chair under the window and waited for Annabelle to regain consciousness.

"Mattie, the swelling is down, and the fever is broken," the Reverend told her.

"She ain't never comin' back, though, is she?"

"Why, I was just thinking she would, any hour now. The doctor said this is the most crucial time. He said that. . ."

Mattie interrupted. "It's all so useless."

"What? What's useless, Mattie?"

"What other people think, what other people say, all the prayin'; none of it changes anythin', does it now?"

"It does for me, Mattie. Maybe you just aren't receiving."

"What do ya mean?"

"I don't mean to be showing disrespect, Mattie, but you're building a wall and not letting anyone through it. You can't be encouraged, supported, or even loved if you don't allow it. You're shutting out your family and friends who love you so much. We want to help, Mattie."

"Love? Whenever I love. . .it hurts. I don't have enough courage to open up ta folks anymore."

"Sometimes love is pain, Mattie. God hurts when His people don't return His love. Jesus died on the cross because He loved us. Isn't that pain?"

With these words Mattie sobbed uncontrollably. "He doesn't love me. How could He?"

"Oh, Mattie, He does love you. I know He does."

"What? What's this?" a raspy weak voice whispered from behind them, so faintly that for a moment they were not really sure it was real.

Then they rushed to the bedside, Mattie trembling as she quickly dropped to her knees at Annabelle's side.

"Annabelle! Annabelle dear, we're here. Everything's all right, Dear. We're right here."

"W—where am I? W—what happened?"

"You had an accident, Dear. But you'll be fine, jest fine."

The doctor was immediately summoned, and he sent them all from the room for a time as he examined Annabelle.

As relief flowed through Mattie, it washed away the stony façade of detachment that had been her way of coping.

"Reverend," she said, "may I speak to ya?"

When Mattie came out of that room, she was transformed. Bitterness and fear fled, and God's Spirit did a wondrous work within her heart. She was filled with new courage and bubbled over with a newfound love and joy.

Hard times continued because even though Annabelle awoke from her state of unconsciousness, she was not herself. The family could see that but did not really know the extent of the problem yet. She acted incoherent, as though she did not know who they were or what they were talking about. The doctor said this was sometimes a normal reaction and she should improve as time went on. Vigils would still be kept at Doc Malone's, because she would not be able to be moved yet for a couple of days.

Much later Kate and Ben rode to Tucker House, quietly recalling all that had transpired that evening. Kate was deep in thought when she realized Ben was chuckling beside her.

"What's so funny?" she asked.

"Oh, I was just thinking of the expression on the sheriff's face tonight at the change in Mattie."

Kate smiled. "Yes, he was rather smitten, wasn't he?"

"Think they'll ever get together?"

"I don't know. They really think so much of each other; maybe there's a better chance now."

"He follows her around like a little puppy."

"And you don't think that's good?" Kate asked.

"It's just amusing to watch, that's all."

"Really?"

Ben reached over and took her hand, but did not share the things in his heart. There had been enough excitement for one evening, and he knew she was not really quite herself yet. He would wait until the time was right. Contentedly, they continued until they reached Tucker House.

After Ben was alone, though, his emotions got the better of him, and he exploded in a burst of song. The amazing thing was he did not even feel foolish as he rode home, singing at the top of his loud baritone voice in the dark of the night, while the stars twinkled God's approval.

Chapter 28

Thaddeas trotted his horse toward Tucker House to call on Annabelle and check her recovery since she had been moved home. *Perhaps familiar surroundings are just the thing she needs,* he thought, *to help her get her senses back. I hope so.* And he nudged his horse on. He had brought along some flowers for Annabelle and soon found himself on the Tucker House doorstep, posies in hand.

"Come in, Thaddeas," Kate said cheerfully. "How nice of you to stop by."

"The flowers are for Annabelle. . . . I should have thought to bring you some, too, Miss Kate," he stuttered.

"Nonsense! Annabelle's the one recuperating, not me. Come along, and I'll take you to her."

Annabelle heard the stair steps creak in protest and cheered that someone was coming up to see her. *Doesn't sound like those who have been attending to me,* she reasoned. *I wonder who it could be? Oh, why am I so confused?* It was frustrating when things were on the very edge of remembering, almost there, and then gone again. It was that way with names, faces, events. Just when she felt it was familiar and she thought she was remembering, she would go totally blank. She could not seem to focus. Everyone was kind enough, but she felt distraught and too weak and tired to do anything about it.

"Hello, Annabelle!" Thaddeas said with forced enthusiasm.

Annabelle looked at the young man standing before her. *What a nice-looking fellow,* she thought. *I wonder who he is?* Then, "Oh dear," she said aloud.

"Well, I am a dear. That's true enough, but I didn't know you were aware of it." He grinned.

"I'm sorry. Just trying to remember." Her eyes fastened fixedly on his handsome face.

He blushed under her steady gaze as Kate said, "Annabelle, this is Thaddeas, Thaddeas Larson. He is the sheriff's nephew." Then to Thaddeas she said, "I'll leave you to visit alone," turned, and was heard stepping lightly down the stairs.

"Well, Annabelle, please don't trouble yourself trying to remember me. I'm not an old friend, but indeed a good one."

She smiled at this and relaxed a bit to watch with fascination as he continued.

"I've only been in Beaver Creek a couple months, and as Kate said,

I'm staying with the sheriff. But perhaps you'll remember I'm your fishing partner. One Sunday afternoon we went fishing at the creek." He paused to watch her reaction.

She shook her head sadly. "No," she said, "I'm sorry, but I don't seem to remember it at all. Do you pick flowers at the creek as well?"

Thaddeas laughed. "Well, your memory may be a little rusty, but your wit is certainly in fine tune. These are for you. Perhaps they will put me in your favor, and the next time I come to visit you, you will count me as a friend. . .a new friend. . .and one that you can count on, Annabelle."

As Thaddeas went to put them in a vase by the side of her bed, she asked, "Will you visit me again?"

"Of course! What are friends for?"

As she mulled this over, another scene developed in the room below. Kate went to the door again, and much to her astonishment, there stood Tanner.

"Hello, Tanner," Kate said, "please, come in."

"Thanks, Kate. Could we just talk outside?"

Kate followed Tanner, and they sat down on the porch step. She waited patiently until Tanner was ready to talk.

"What do you think of Elizabeth?"

"Why, she's very pretty, and she seems nice enough," Kate answered with embarrassment.

"Yeah, that's her. Took your advice, you know. I've got a lot to make up. Hope I can make her happy; I know she'll be good for me."

"I'm sure you'll both be very happy," Kate said, trying to reassure him.

"Aw. . .who am I trying to fool? I came here to tell you. I don't know what love is, but I think I love her," he blurted out.

Kate laughed. "I think you're finding out, Tanner."

"You're not mad, are you?" he asked, regaining his poise and shooting her one of his famous smiles.

"Tanner, I'm just so happy for you. I really am!" she said earnestly. "I'm most happy that you found the Lord!"

"Yeah, me, too. Luke's teaching me. He comes over, and we study the Bible."

"Really? That's great!" Kate exclaimed.

"You know, the Reverend even had a dream about me?"

"Tell me about it."

"Well the Reverend said he was walking through a cornfield when the wind swept him up and set him down on the edge of a green pasture with sheep in it. A voice said, 'Feed My flock.' Then a lamb romped through and destroyed the corn.

"That was me, Kate. . .when I rode through their farm and shot things up. Well, it made him mad in his dream, and he yelled, 'Get out of my corn.' Then the voice said again, 'Feed My flock.' So he let the lamb go. When he did, other lambs followed, and the cornfield sprung up, unharmed.

"The Reverend said when he started the church, he obeyed the voice. I was the sheep. He said other lambs will follow. The Wheelers think that means my friend Jake will get saved. Luke's been praying for him."

Kate covered her mouth with her hand in amazement as she recognized the dream, and shook her head as tears rolled down her cheeks. "Oh, that's beautiful, Tanner!"

"Aw, now don't go crying again," he said affectionately.

"I'm sorry, Tanner. You've just made me so happy."

Just then the door flew open, and Thaddeas walked out. "Hello, Tanner," he said.

Tanner jumped up. "Hello, Thaddeas. Join us?"

"No, I was just on my way out, but thanks and good day to you." Sadness colored his voice, and he hurried off.

"He's been to visit Annabelle," Kate said softly.

"Taking it kinda hard, I see. I'm sorry, Kate. Well, I'd better be off, too. It was good to see you."

As Tanner walked away, Kate called after him, "Tanner!"

He turned and waited.

"I just wanted to tell you; you're a man I can respect." Tanner rode away feeling ten feet tall.

❧❧

Upstairs alone in her room, Annabelle stared out the window, quietly crying as big teardrops fell, wetting her pillow.

Chapter 29

Bare and twisting, the branches reached toward the frosty window that held Claire and Annabelle's gaze as they sat on their bed whispering. "I wish I could go to school with you; perhaps then I could remember again."

"You were always glad to be out of the schoolroom," replied Claire.

"Well, I don't know why," Annabelle said glumly.

"Come on. We'd better hurry and get downstairs for breakfast; it's getting late," said Claire.

As they descended the steps, Claire said, "I'll be so glad when you can braid my hair again. Kate pulls too tight, and my poor head gets so sore. Of course, I don't want to bother Kate with complaining when everyone is so worried about you. I'm glad you're getting better."

"But I'm not, Claire! Everyone just seems to pretend that I am, but I'm not!"

"You'll get your memory back soon enough. Don't worry, Annabelle."

The aroma of hot mush, cooking in a black kettle over the fire, tempted them. It tasted good with fresh bread, butter, and honey.

"Ben said that Luke will be visiting the schoolhouse today. He's going to share with the children about going into ministry and what he expects the university life will be like," Kate said.

Claire's interest piqued. "Ministry?"

"Yes, he's studying to be a preacher like his pa. I thought you knew that, Claire."

"Maybe I did and just forgot. I wasn't interested in that stuff until. . ." She stopped for a moment, catching herself, and then continued, "until now that I'm older."

Mattie nodded, exchanging amused glances with Kate. "Well, I'd better be off then." Claire bolted from the table and grabbed her coat off the peg.

"Whatever brought that about?" Mattie wondered as did the others.

Claire's feet scarcely hit the crunchy, frost-covered ground as she hurried off to school. Little halos, puffs of breath, preceded her as she walked along at a brisk pace, but she did not notice. She thought about Luke's visit. The promise she made to God excited her, and she had many questions. Perhaps today she would find some answers. As she reached the little schoolhouse, which looked warm and inviting, Claire opened the door, and a cheery fire popped and spit its greeting.

"My, you're early this morning, Claire," said Miss Forrester. "Would you like to help?"

"Sure!"

"Very well, then. You may take the slates from the shelf and place one on each of the desks."

"Will we be doing our regular work today, Miss Forrester?"

"Yes, however, I do happen to have a surprise planned for today," she added with a twinkle in her eye.

The classroom filled with wriggling bodies. The children removed their coats and hats and huddled around the welcoming fire. They rubbed and patted their hands to get the color back into them. Eventually they went to their seats, and class began.

The day seemed to drag for Claire. First, they did their sums, then reciting, followed by recess. After recess, Miss Forrester explained the cycle of seasons, pointing out the barren signs of winter. Claire shuddered as they talked about ice formations. Finally, it was lunchtime. Sammy Hawkes chased her above all the others in their game of tag.

Reluctantly, the children returned to the classroom, and Miss Forrester read a story about the bitter cold winter the first settlers experienced when they arrived on the Mayflower. As Claire watched her squint and wrinkle her pointy nose, she wondered if today was going to be any different after all. Miss Forrester suddenly interrupted her pleasant flowing words and announced, "Children, we have a visitor today. May I introduce Mr. Luke Wheeler?"

Claire started in her seat and quickly turned to the door. There he was all right, good old Luke, standing about ten feet tall as it appeared to Claire. He filled the doorway with his head bent and smiled kindly at the children. "Do come in, Mr. Wheeler."

As Luke entered the room and made his way to the front of the class, the children tittered and chattered. "Class, please. May we have your attention?" continued Miss Forrester, and the class obediently responded.

Miss Forrester pulled her chair around to face the classroom and placed another large chair beside hers before Luke knew what was happening. He blushed that he had not helped her. Then she said, "Please, sit down, Mr. Wheeler," and he obligingly sat.

She introduced him and explained, "Mr. Wheeler is going to start an adventure—something that you may wish to do when you are old enough. I will ask Mr. Wheeler some questions, and he will share his plans. Then later, we will let you ask the questions. Now, Mr. Wheeler, what occupation have you selected?"

"I have chosen to be a preacher."

"And why have you decided this?"

"Well, my father is a preacher, as most of you know, and when I was a lad, I wanted with all my heart to do what my father did. I watched him preach, and then I practiced on my brother, Ben. Later, when I was about twelve, I knew I had a real calling from God."

"A calling, can you explain this further to the class?" asked Miss Forrester.

"I'll try, but it's really something you cannot see or hear directly. Rather you sense it within yourself. It's a feeling, and you know what to do. Other people often point out your gifts; that is called confirmation."

"I see. And what exactly do you have to do to become a preacher?"

"I went to school like these children are doing until I graduated from the classroom. Then I went to a secondary school. Now I need to go to a university to continue with more studying."

"And where will you go?"

"Ohio University in Athens, Ohio. If I need further schooling, I will go to the University of Pennsylvania," Luke answered proudly.

"Now, children, you may ask Mr. Wheeler questions."

Sammy raised his hand, and Miss Forrester promptly called upon him.

"W—will y—you p—preach here i—instead o—of your p—pa?"

"That is something I don't know yet. I'll have to wait and see where a preacher is needed when the time comes."

"H—how w—will you k—know where y—you're n—needed?" Sammy asked.

"People will write letters to me, asking me to come and be their preacher. Then I will pray about it."

Mary raised her hand shyly. "Yes, Mary?"

"How did you get so tall? Do all preachers have ta be tall?"

Luke answered quickly with a perfectly serious face, "I got to be so tall from eating all the food my mother put on my plate and from doing my chores without complaining. And God will take anyone, any size."

Claire smiled at that remark, knowing that Luke was teasing, but also happy that God would take her, just as she was.

Soon they exhausted the subject, and Miss Forrester dismissed the children to go home for the day. She thanked Luke warmly. "Whatever can I do to show you my appreciation?" she asked patting her little brown bun to coax her hairdo into place.

"It was my pleasure. You handle the children well. I must compliment you on your efforts."

Claire waited outside the classroom, wondering if they would ever finish talking when she heard the squeaking of the schoolroom floor.

"Luke!" she exclaimed.

"Hello, Claire."

"May I talk with you?"

"Of course. Would you like a ride?"

"Yes. Thank you."

He lifted her into the wagon with his strong arms and set her softly on the seat. "Now, what would you like to talk about?"

"Ministry. Are there women preachers?"

"Very few, but that does not mean women aren't important in ministry. There are many places women can serve."

"There are? Where?" she asked.

"Well, there are missions where women can work. Ladies go overseas as missionaries. Women marry preachers and support their husbands' work in the church. Women join groups or committees to help the needy and sick. . . or they can be nurses." He stopped there and looked over to see her response to this lengthy explanation.

"All that? How would I ever know where to start?"

Luke pulled the team to a stop and smiled tenderly at the girl beside him. "Is this something you want to do, Claire?"

"Oh, yes! I promised God I would. When Annabelle was sick, I told God that if He would heal her, I would go into ministry." She smiled proudly at her little speech.

"Well, God doesn't heal people because of promises they make, you know. He heals them just because He loves them, and He wants to."

"He does?" She looked disappointed. "Well, what would God think of me if I lied and didn't do what I promised?"

"I don't think He would consider that a lie. He can see right into our hearts. He would know that it was your love for Annabelle that was in your heart, and you didn't intend to lie."

"Well, maybe, but I will still go into ministry, just to be sure. So where should I start?"

"By reading your Bible. Read it every day if possible. Start praying. Just do whatever you would normally do, your everyday living. Then when God calls you into ministry, you will hear His voice. It will be a still, quiet voice inside you. Perhaps you will hear it from someone else. Things will fall into place automatically. You have to wait for Him to lead you."

"Can I come to you when I have questions? You're the most intelligent person I know."

"Of course. In fact, I'll give you my address so you can write to me while I'm at the university! How would you like that?"

"I'd rather have you here, but that would be nice. Thank you, Luke."

He gave her hand a loving squeeze, and they rode on.

Chapter 30

Mary Wheeler bustled about her warm, fragrant kitchen, preparing the turkey and stuffing for their Thanksgiving meal. They had invited the Tucker household as well as Buck and Thaddeas. Of course, the ladies at Tucker House would be bringing some of the food. Kate was famous for her pumpkin pies made from the plump ones grown in Mattie's garden patch. Mattie was bringing potatoes and pudding.

There was much to be done, and here she was with a household of men wanting to be of help but only getting in the way. The Reverend finally convinced her that he could wash dishes and clean the pots. Ben swept the sitting room and porch again so he could keep an eye out for the company. Luke took the boys to help with the chores.

The turkey smelled so tempting that the Reverend was hard put to keep his hands out of the roasting kettle in the stone oven. "I hear a wagon. Must be the ladies from Tucker House already," Mary said, wiping her hands on her apron and patting her hair back. "Ben, would you greet them. . . ? Well, look at that, he's already half down the lane before I even get the words out," she exclaimed to her husband.

"Can't say as I blame him, Mary. He doesn't see Kate as often as I saw you before we were married, and that wasn't enough."

Soon the house was invaded by giggling, chattering women along with Thaddeas and the sheriff. "Why, I don't recognize this place, you got it lookin' so homey, Mary. Oh, no harm intended, Reverend," Mattie exclaimed.

"None taken. I agree; Mary is just what we needed around here."

"I think I'll steal Kate for awhile, Mary, unless you need her," Ben said.

"Of course, off with you," she answered.

Meanwhile, Annabelle looked around thinking that it did seem familiar. She went to chat with James and Frank, having remembered meeting them a few weeks earlier at church.

The Reverend announced, "Dinner is ready. We'll pray, and then all file past the food. Just fill your plates and find a seat wherever you can."

After the prayer, Ben and Luke told the story of their hunting escapade—the prize being the day's main course. Luke had tripped and fallen into a mud hole, allowing Ben to shoot the bird. Upon Luke's return to the farm, he had been humiliated when James and Frank had giggled at his muddied trousers. It was not quite the image he wanted to portray.

After dinner, the men retired to the sitting room. The young men challenged each other to checkers and a marble game that the Potter boys' pa had made. Mary, Mattie, and the girls saw to clearing and cleaning the dinner table. "Sounds rowdy in there for checkers," Kate exclaimed, sneaking a peak into the sitting room.

"Aw, you ain't heard nothin' yet," Mary said. The ladies laughed at the joke.

The afternoon flew by as Kate let her thoughts run wild. She imagined herself sitting by the fire with Ben, or pouring his coffee for him in the big chair with his feet propped up on the foot stool.

All too soon the sheriff commented, "Look at those dark clouds. A storm's a-brewing for sure!" A look out the window convinced the others, and they scurried to collect their belongings and put on their coats. Quickly and thoroughly, they thanked their hosts and made their way to the wagon.

Ben helped Kate into the wagon. The sheriff and Mattie climbed into the front while Thaddeas and the girls settled themselves in the back. They covered themselves with blankets to prepare for the cold ride home. Ben gave Kate's hand a squeeze and whispered, "I'm sorry we didn't get much time alone. I'll be over Saturday night, if I may?"

"Of course. I'll count the minutes."

Kate waved gaily as the wagon rolled out the lane.

Annabelle commented, "They are very nice people."

Whenever Annabelle said something to remind the others that she was still at a loss for remembering, it dampened their spirits.

"Annabelle?" Kate said on impulse.

"Yes?"

"See if you can remember anything about that night, the night of your birthday party."

"Kate!" Thaddeas interrupted. "Please!"

"No, it's all right," Annabelle said sadly. "I need to do this. What should I remember, Kate?"

"Well, you were in the back of a wagon like this with your friends. There was hay in the wagon, and you were singing songs. Thaddeas was up front, driving the wagon."

"Thaddeas?" Annabelle interrupted. "Thaddeas?"

"Y–yes. It was I, Annabelle. I'm so sorry; I ran over you and. . ."

"It wasn't your fault at all. Don't go feeling sorry for me. I won't have it. Go on, Kate."

"Sammy Hawkes had just been dropped off."

"Sammy Hawkes?" she asked.

"Yes, you know, Claire's friend who stutters."

"Kate! What a cruel thing to say about my friend!" Claire piped up.

"Sorry, Claire. I didn't mean it that way."

Claire settled back into her corner, pulling her blanket tightly around her, unsure whether to defend him further, when Kate continued.

"He left his hat, and you saw it and stood up to get his attention when the wagon jolted, and you fell out."

Annabelle concentrated very hard on this scenario, willing herself to remember. Finally, she shook her auburn head sadly. "I'm sorry. I just can't remember."

Just then a loud cracking sound turned everyone's attention to the weather overhead. "Oh, no, we're in for it now," Thaddeas warned. "Cover up with your blankets as best you can. I don't think we're gonna make it home before it starts."

"Cuddle together," Claire said innocently.

"Come on, don't be bashful," Thaddeas said, following Claire's suggestion. He was sitting between Claire and Annabelle, and they giggled as they moved in closer.

The rain pelted as if venting out anger for a wrong deed done.

"Ooh, this is fun," squealed Claire in delight.

"It's so cold," Kate screamed back.

"Move in closer," Thaddeas suggested.

"This is just like the day of the barn raising," yelled Annabelle.

"Yes, I remember. We all got soaked," said Claire.

"And you pouted about the Indians, Kate," Annabelle added.

"Annabelle!" They all screamed at once.

"You remembered!" Claire clapped her hands in delight.

"Yes! I remember clearly!" Annabelle exclaimed in joy.

Thus, Annabelle's memory returned in torrents fitting of the situation. The others continued to drill her and pull remnants of memory out of the deep, dark closets of her mind. It was a ride they would never forget. The rain was falling mercilessly, but it did not matter for they were wet with happy tears.

When they reached Tucker House, Thaddeas hugged Annabelle tightly, exclaiming over and over again how happy he was for her. He sorely wished he could go inside and share in the happy event, but he knew they had to hurry off and get their horses out of the storm.

Mattie made a huge fire in the fireplace, and sitting in their nightclothes, the ladies stayed up until the wee hours of the morning listening to Annabelle's remembering.

Chapter 31

Mattie walked into Beaver Creek to inquire about a catalog order from Cooper's General Store. The air outside was biting cold, and she pulled her winter cloak tightly about her, though she was warmed from the inside out, thinking about the surprises she had planned.

"Well, look who the wind blew in!" Mr. Cooper said with a laugh. The old joke was fittingly appropriate.

"Indeed!" Mattie laughed. "And, I've come to inquire about some special things I ordered, if you recall, for Christmas?"

"Ah, yes. But I'm sorry, Mattie, they are not in yet, but any day now, any day!"

"Well, just be sure ya don't say anything if one of the girls comes in for somethin'," she warned.

"Oh, I'll remember for sure, Mattie," he assured her.

"Miss Tucker, hello. How is Annabelle?" Dorie inquired cheerfully.

"Very fine. She's good as ever, and we're all so proud of her. We're thankful she's back to her normal self."

"I'm glad. I wish she could come for a visit. Could she, please?" Dorie pleaded.

"Of course, that's kind of ya to invite her, Dorie," said Mattie.

"How about Thursday then?"

"Thursday would be jest fine, and Annabelle will be excited that ya asked her."

"Thank you, Miss Tucker. I can't wait!"

"Good day to ya then, Mr. Cooper," Mattie said as she left. She was pleasantly surprised when she walked outdoors for snow, huge white flakes, fell, softly wetting her face and sticking to the ground. *Well I'll be!* she thought. *Our first snowfall. I always forget jest how lovely it is!* She felt as young as a schoolgirl as she went about the rest of her errands. Then she heard a call.

"Mattie!" The sheriff stuck his head out of his office. "Come here and visit for a spell!"

"All right, for a minute!" she called.

"Come in out of the snow. Why, you're getting all wet," he said, concerned.

"Isn't it jest beautiful?" she asked, brushing off her cloak and removing her bonnet while he held the door open for her.

"The first snowfall always is," he agreed, nodding his head. "Here, come sit by the fire." He motioned toward his cozy, warm sitting area by the big stone fireplace.

Mattie quickly obeyed. She visited the sheriff often when she came to town. His office was very masculinely trimmed with a set of deer antlers above the fireplace. On the mantel lay an old holster without pistols, fondly placed there when the sheriff received his new one. Also there were a few books for entertainment on long, lonely nights, and an old piece of wood he had been whittling. Directly in front of her on the rough wooden floor sprawled a huge black bearskin, enough to frighten any lady if she was not already used to it being there.

"Are you still cold?" he asked. "I'll get you a cup of coffee."

"I'm startin' ta thaw, but that sounds mighty temptin'."

The sheriff poured the piping hot coffee into two tin mugs and went back to sit beside her. "You sure look cheery enough. Is it 'cause Christmas is a-coming?" he asked.

"Yes, I think that's it. Of course, I have a lot of other reasons to be happy, ya know."

"Tell me, Mattie, what makes you so happy?"

"I'm happy that Annabelle is well again. She's excited about the season, and Dorie Cooper just invited her to come and spend Thursday with her. She'll be in fine tune when she hears that!"

"Yes, I suspect she will at that." He chuckled as he envisioned the two girls together. "And?"

"And I'm happy I'm my old self. I was a bit of a crab there for awhile, and I must apologize right now while I'm thinkin' on it. You were so helpful and supportive through that whole time, and I was jest terrible to ya, Buck."

"Nonsense; don't even mention it, Mattie. You know I care about you dearly. It hurt me to see your pain. I hope we don't ever have to go through something like that again."

"I agree, but if times get hard again, at least next time I'll have the Lord."

"Yep, He sure makes a difference," the sheriff agreed. Then he glanced out the window and said, "You know, Mattie, if it keeps snowing, I may have to take you home myself or just keep you here for a spell." With that remark, he gave her a wink.

"Oh, now, you get that right out of your head, Buck," she teased.

Easily encouraged, he cautiously continued, "You look absolutely radiant today with your rosy cheeks." Mattie blushed profusely. "Have I told you before that I think you're a very beautiful and charming woman?"

"Yes, ya certainly have, and I thank ya again," she said warmly.

"I know we talked about this before, but I feel the need to bring it up again."

"Oh, please don't, Buck!"

"Mattie, I must. You know how I love you."

"I love ya, too, Buck," she said earnestly.

"Then what's holding you back from marrying me? Is it my job? If I quit sheriffing and get a respectable occupation, would you marry me then?"

"Oh, Buck, never!"

"Never?" he echoed sadly.

"Never would I want you ta change like that. Why, sheriffin' is what ya do, and you do it very well, and if I couldn't take ya like you are. . .then I wouldn't be a fittin' wife."

"Mattie, are you saying that you'll marry me?" he asked pleadingly.

"No, that's not what I'm tryin' to say. It's not anything on your part that's hinderin', but somethin' to do with myself."

"What? Why won't you tell me? I love you, Mattie."

She reached over and took his hand, "Buck, I'm sorry. I guess maybe I'm jest afraid of all the changes."

"We'd only make the ones you wanted to make."

"Please give me more time ta think this through. I know we can't go on this way. But, please, let me think about this a spell longer."

He placed her hands between both of his and said, "All right, a little longer, just a little longer."

"Now, I must be goin' if I'm ever to make it home," she said determinedly.

He released her hands and said sadly, "If you must. Are you sure you can make it home?"

She laughed. "Oh, I'm sure, ya old worry wart!" The sheriff helped Mattie into her cloak and watched her leave. Suddenly, he felt very lonely.

What is wrong with me? she thought as she plodded toward home. *How can I lead him on this way? I love him, but I'd have ta tell him about my past. I wonder if he's guessed by now why I always put him off? It would serve me right if he'd up and marry someone else. I'd deserve it.* She kicked the ground soundly, puffing as she walked homeward.

Abruptly she stopped in her tracks, whirled, and headed straight back to the sheriff's office. Moments later, she rapped on his heavy door.

"Mattie! What's wrong? Come in!" the sheriff exclaimed with concern.

"I—I jest came back to say yes, I'll marry ya," she blurted out.

"Mattie, oh, Mattie." The sheriff enveloped her in his arms.

"First, before we make any plans, I've got a story to tell ya. Buck, please sit down and listen."

Chapter 32

Christmas Eve arrived, and a new-fallen snow, fresh and pure, robed the townsfolk in a garment of peace. Was it any wonder that Mattie overflowed with goodwill and charity as she reflected on the miracle of Christmas?

"Oh, Kate, ya look beautiful!" Mattie exclaimed as Kate came down the stairs. Kate had paused for just a moment to gaze in astonishment at a bit of mistletoe that mysteriously appeared at the bottom of the steps before she replied.

"Thank you, Mattie. You look grand yourself. May I inquire as to the origin of this bit of greenery?"

"I confess, I did it. I thought there might be a few handsome gentlemen droppin' in tonight."

"Mattie! I can't believe you're owning up to it. You must be under a spell for sure!"

"I guess I am since I agreed to marry Buck, and I think I'm as eager for Christmas as the girls," Mattie confessed. "Speakin' of the girls, I'd better go hurry them along. Our company could be here any moment."

Left alone, Kate looked about her, and everything looked just right. The smells of the greenery they had used to decorate, fresh coffee, cider, and pumpkin pie mingled sweetly. She felt beautiful tonight with her new soft-flowing green gown and her ebony hair trimmed in green ribbons.

She walked to the window and tried to peer out, but it was too dark to see. As she cupped her face in her hands, the warmth from her breath steamed up the cold window. *It's no use,* she thought, but then she heard bells. *I wonder? That must be Ben and Luke.* She raced to the door.

"A cutter! How wonderful!" she exclaimed as she welcomed them in.

"Yes, would you and the girls like to go for a ride?" Ben asked gaily.

"That will be delightful! Move in here close to the fire and warm up. Mattie and the girls should be down shortly. Here they come now."

Mattie descended just in time to answer the door herself as Buck and Thaddeas arrived. They had walked the short distance and took a moment to shake off the snow and stomp their feet before entering.

"Why, Miss Mattie, you look lovely," Thaddeas said as he walked past.

"A vision of loveliness, my dear," the sheriff added in a low voice and then held out his arm to escort her to the sitting room.

They all stood around the fire chatting for a moment, and then it was agreed that they would all go for a ride except Mattie and the sheriff. As they climbed into the cutter, Claire's blue eyes were on Luke. He felt her gaze and winked. She smiled broadly and continued to watch him, her hero.

This was just the moment he had hoped for. He squirmed and made a funny face.

"What's a-matter, Luke?"

"Come see."

She looked at him suspiciously. "What do you have in there?" She leaned closer.

"It is a Christmas surprise for you, Claire. Something to remember me by when I'm gone." Luke pulled a tiny fur ball from under his coat.

"Mew, mew," it said.

"A kitten! For me? Look, Kate, Annabelle!" She held the little kitten in the air, showing everyone.

Claire thanked Luke with a cold, wet peck on his cheek. "I shall name him Freckles 'cause he has freckles on his nose just like you!"

"I'm honored, Claire."

In the back of the cutter, Thaddeas asked Annabelle how her day with Dorie went.

"It was so fun!" she exclaimed. "It was exciting to watch people come to the store and pick up their Christmas orders, and we helped Mrs. Cooper make tarts and cookies. I think I'd enjoy living in town like you do, Thaddeas."

"Really?"

"Yes, it's so exciting with all the hustle and bustle."

"I'm glad you're back to your cheery self, Annabelle," Thaddeas said earnestly. "Are you warm enough?"

"Yes, I'm fine."

When they reached Tucker House again, Claire was the first to slide off the cutter. "Let's go to the kitchen and get him some milk," she said, toting Freckles.

"Go ahead. Kate and I will unhitch the horses," Ben offered.

Annabelle tagged after Claire, begging to hold the fur ball, and Luke and Thaddeas were amused by all the fuss. "Here, you hold her, Annabelle, while I pour her some milk," ordered Claire.

"Let me get that," Luke said, reaching for the dish that Claire was trying to get in vain.

"I'll bet it comes in handy to be so tall," she said all in one breath. "Now put her down and see if she goes for it, Annabelle."

Out in the sitting room, Mattie and Buck talked in low tones at one end of the room when the small group clamored in upon them. Annabelle and

Claire sat on the floor in front of the fire, playing with Freckles, while Luke and Thaddeas pulled up their chairs close by.

There was a short silence, and Thaddeas took advantage of it. "I have news!" he announced, beaming with pleasure. "I've found a job so I guess I'll be staying in Beaver Creek now for sure."

"Wonderful!" said Luke. "Tell us what it is."

"I'm the new accountant at Green's Mill. It isn't exactly what I want to do with my life, but it's a start in business anyway."

"I'm so glad for you," Mattie said.

"Me, too. I've gotten quite attached to this nephew of mine," the sheriff said fondly.

Meanwhile out in the barn, Ben was just finishing. Kate held the lantern, stomping one foot and then the other, trying to keep warm while he worked. "Are you cold?" he asked, taking the lantern from her and hanging it on a nearby post.

She looked lovingly into his blue eyes. She noticed his freckles—placed in just the right spots on his handsome face. Ben moved closer. Her face was only inches away, breathtakingly close—almost against his—and her soft brown eyes were so close he could see the green specks in them. He saw her black-velvet eyelashes, long and soft. In a moment, he leaned closer and pressed his lips on her sweet, soft ones.

Kate felt the gentleness of his kiss, not forceful like Tanner's. It drew her, and she reveled in the ecstasy of the moment. This was the kiss she had dreamed of; it was everything she had anticipated.

As Ben slowly drew back, he realized how vulnerable Kate was. He saw the flush to her face and the love in her eyes. He felt encouraged and said breathlessly, "My intentions are proper, I assure you, Kate. I love you. Will you marry me?"

"I'd be proud to be your wife, Ben."

"Sweetheart, you don't know how happy you've made me. This is all I could think of since we broke that chair that afternoon you decided to sit on my lap."

She giggled. "Ben! How ungentlemanly of you to bring that up just now."

Ben grinned. "Like I said, it's all I've been thinking about." Then he grew serious again. "There's something else that's been on my mind. I have a confession, and a question to ask you."

"You do? Whatever is it?"

"Well, I'm afraid I was eavesdropping one day, but I didn't mean to and didn't know you were there until I was right upon you. I thought you were crying because you had your head down and wondered what was wrong. Then I heard you praying. So I started to turn away, but I heard what you said. It was the time Annabelle got covered with bees."

"What did I say?"

"You told God about someone you'd met; you said he was handsome and strong and how much you were attracted to him. I guess I don't have the right to ask who it was, do I?"

"Of course you do. If we're to be married, we shouldn't be keeping any secrets from each other, should we?" Ben looked at her wondering if he really wanted to hear and whatever had possessed him to bring it up now. He waited patiently for her to go on. "It was you I was talking about, Silly. Don't you realize that you're the only man I've ever felt this way about?"

"I am? All this time I thought there was someone else."

"I thought you were mighty slow," she teased.

"Hey, now! Well, I guess I was, but not anymore." He placed his hands on her shoulders. "I'll do my best to make you happy, Kate, but I don't have any big plans like Luke. I'm just a simple man."

"You don't have to, Ben. Helping other people comes natural with you, and ministry follows you wherever you go."

"Why, Kate, you're trembling," he said. "Darling?"

She raised a shaking hand and touched his cheek. "With joy. I love you."

Ben pulled her close and held her tight for a moment, then he kissed her properly until her trembling ceased.

Lofty Ambitions

With love to my mother, Annabelle.

Chapter 1

Annabelle's words slapped him as hard as any physical blow might. He leaned against the rough timbers of Sheriff Buck Larson's jailhouse office to steady his trembling nerves. "As far as I'm concerned, this never happened," she snapped.

He had waited too long to give up easily and moved toward her with outstretched arms. "Annabelle, please, hear me out."

"No! I won't listen to any more of this! When I walk out that door, Thaddeas, we shall end this nonsense. I hope you come to your senses!"

Though she strained, the door refused to budge. As Thaddeas watched her, his hopes—four years of patient waiting—dissolved like a puff of smoke before his eyes.

Annabelle pulled and tugged impatiently, but the door simply would not comply. She whirled to face Thaddeas, her green eyes ablaze with frustration. "Well?" Her bottom lip quivered, and she tapped her high-heeled boot impatiently.

He shouldered the door open and searched her face for some explanation. However, she flounced out the door.

Thaddeas collapsed in a heap in his uncle's chair. *Had she misunderstood? Was she appalled by the idea?*

He'd never expected such a refusal. Disappointment flooded over him. His face buried in his hands, he did the only thing he knew. He prayed. "Oh Lord, what am I to do?"

Meanwhile, Annabelle marched toward her home in a huff. *Marry him, indeed!* A small stone lay in her path, and she gave it a sound kick, rousing a wisp of dust. She continued at a brisk clip, muttering under her breath.

At seventeen, Annabelle Larson was a striking woman with an abundance of chestnut-colored hair and emerald eyes, but she was also headstrong and spoiled.

As Annabelle neared her home, a groan escaped her pursed lips when Claire appeared, coming from the direction of the henhouse, a basket of eggs in the crook of her arm.

Claire brightened when she saw her sister. "Annabelle, wait!"

"Oh, Claire, not now. Please, not now." Annabelle brushed her aside and hurried into the house, only to encounter a second member of her family.

"Oh, hello, Annabelle. Is Buck comin' shortly?" Mattie paused from

117

stirring a kettle of beans long enough to wipe her hands on the apron wrapped about her straight, slim figure.

"I–I didn't see him," Annabelle stammered as she rushed by and mounted the steps, two at a time, leading to her room. Alone at last, she slammed the door and heaved herself onto the bed. A gamut of emotions teemed together and surged forth in a torrent of tears. When the storm eventually subsided, she was left feeling drained.

Like a wilted lettuce leaf, she lay draped across her bed.

She could not marry a cousin! This was rationalization at its best, for Thaddeas was not a blood relative. Sheriff Buck Larson adopted Annabelle and Claire when he married Mattie Tucker, giving them his name. Therefore, even though Thaddeas was Buck's nephew, the three young people were not blood related. This fact, however, escaped Annabelle at the moment.

Thaddeas loved the West, but she wanted to go east. With a shudder she thought of her older sister, Kate, toiling on the Potter farm. Annabelle wanted more than that. If she married, he would have to be rich so she could live like Dorie.

Her friend Dorie, whose father owned the general store in Beaver Creek, had moved away to attend school in Cincinnati. Then after graduating, she moved to Charleston to live with relatives, where she now frequented balls, and handsome men attended her every whim and desire. Annabelle waited greedily for her letters to arrive, which read like novels— or fairy tales—and whetted Annabelle's appetite for the flamboyant lifestyle.

Leaning over the side of her bed, Annabelle groped a moment and pulled out a small wooden chest, disturbing a nest of dust bunnies. Opening the lid with trembling fingers, she unfolded the last letter from her lifelong friend and read:

> *I do not believe I shall ever return to Beaver Creek except to visit. After being introduced to society, it would be hard to return to a life of wearing calico and waiting upon customers. My mama gave up a great deal when she allowed Papa to pursue his dreams of the West. I hope you shall not hold it against me or think I am uppity.*

Annabelle sighed and envisioned a magnificent ballroom filled with gallant gentlemen who danced with beautiful ladies. Fantasizing, she saw herself floating in the arms of a handsome cavalier. She fluttered her eyelashes and stole a glance at his face. To her horror, it portrayed her cousin's image.

She shivered as she recalled the hurt look on Thad's face and sat up shakily, dabbing at her eyes. What a predicament! She needed to talk to Kate.

Sheriff Larson stopped in to close up his office and found Thaddeas bent over the desk. "Thaddeas?"

"Oh, Uncle Buck. Is it that late already? I hadn't noticed," Thaddeas mumbled.

"Thaddeas, Son. Is something wrong?" Concern showed in every movement of the sheriff's massive body.

"I'm just feeling low, Uncle Buck."

"You want to tell me about it?" The sheriff prodded his nephew gently.

"I–I offered for Annabelle. I asked her to marry me." In embarrassment, Thaddeas fixed his eyes on his boots.

"Yeah? What did she say?"

"She was angry, didn't want anything to do with me. She said she'd just pretend I never said anything; then she left." Thaddeas moaned. "Uncle Buck, all these years, I've loved her. I've waited so long for her to grow up, and now she refused me. I don't know what I'll do."

"Give her time to think on it, Thad."

"It's hard to figure a woman's mind."

"I know she cares for you." The sheriff patted his nephew's arm, not knowing what else to say, and waited until Thaddeas finally roused.

"Uncle Buck, you better head home, or Mattie will worry about you. I'm going to my room and get some rest now. I've got a big day tomorrow at the mill. David Green purchased a huge order of timber, and all the journals have to be entered right away for he has a buyer coming from Cincinnati."

"All right then, but don't fret, Thad. You know God is big enough for this. He knows what's best for you and how you're hurting."

"I know, Uncle Buck." The sheriff watched Thaddeas shuffle across the room and enter his lodging without a backward look.

Chapter 2

Annabelle looked around the familiar schoolroom. A movement across the room caught her eye, and she watched as Melanie Caldwell, formerly Whitfield, stretched her right hand across her left shoulder to tug at her shawl. Then a long, thin arm reached out, grasped the shawl, and placed it lovingly back onto her shoulders, resting there a moment in an affectionate gesture before moving away. In her left arm Melanie held a newborn, her second, a dumpling of a little girl. A pudgy, red-faced toddler sat on his father's knee.

Annabelle smiled as she recalled how Melanie had chased after her sister Kate's husband, Ben Wheeler, before they were married; but then Charlie Caldwell had moved into Beaver Creek, and Melanie married him soon after.

This reminded her of Thaddeas's proposal. Blushing, she straightened and strained to hear Rev. Wheeler's sermon.

" 'He that keepeth his mouth keepeth his life: but he that openeth wide his lips shall have destruction.' That's found in Proverbs 13:3. Folks, remember this week to treat each other with care." Annabelle shivered. The preacher's words settled and lay in the pit of her stomach like hard pebbles.

On the dirt road that led from the schoolhouse to the old Potter place where Kate and Ben now lived, there was much to attract Annabelle's attention, but she was oblivious to autumn's crisp call. Her attention focused on the backside of Thaddeas Larson. His torso slightly bent, he rode ahead, but far enough behind Kate and Ben to avoid their dust. Thad had not spoken to her today, and she missed his friendly bantering, yet at the same time dreaded his company. She sighed and tried to tear her eyes away from the creaking leather of his saddle and concentrate on her sister's wagon leading the procession.

Up ahead, Ben consoled his wife. "I know it hurts when Melanie says those things, but don't let it get you down, Kate. I'd like a baby, too, but we have each other, don't we?" His blue eyes glistened with emotion.

"You're right, Ben. I suppose the Lord knew it was all I could do just to handle you," she teased. Then growing serious, she said, "Pa's right, though, reckless words do 'pierce like a sword.' " Kate used the name "Pa" fondly, since her own folks died in an Indian raid when she was six. Now Emmett Wheeler was her father-in-law.

Her husband replied, "Melanie's always had trouble with her tongue. Pa also said, 'he that openeth wide his lips shall have destruction.' We must be kind, because she's sure to bring trouble upon herself."

"Her baby is lovely. My arms ache for a child, Ben."

"I know, Kate. I know," he whispered.

Peeking just around the fringe of forest on their left was the "old Potter place." It was not really old. Mary Potter had once lived there with her first husband and two sons, James and Frank. When the Wheelers had moved into Beaver Creek, she was a widow. Later she married Emmett Wheeler, and folks started referring to it as the "old Potter place." Even after Ben and Kate moved in, the name seemed to stick, as there was already a Wheeler farm, and old habits are hard to break.

It spread out before them now, a cabin, barn, corrals, and a large amount of land where field corn had earlier waved brown-tasseled heads. The spread was well cared for, as Ben loved farming. He once told Kate it came as natural to him as breathing.

The wagons pulled into the lane and rolled to a stop. Everyone was hungry, anticipating Sunday dinner, and scattered to help prepare the meal or do the necessary outdoor chores. Time passed quickly, and soon their stomachs were full, yet they lingered around the table.

Sheriff Larson put out the bait. "I got a copy of the *Western Star* in the wagon."

"The *Western Star*?" questioned Ben. "What's that, Buck?"

"It's the newspaper out of Lebanon, brand-new," the sheriff explained.

"How did you get it, Uncle?" Thaddeas asked.

"Well now, remember that fellow by the name of Stone who I locked up yesterday for disturbing the peace?" Thaddeas nodded, and the sheriff continued. "He had it on him, and of course I procured all his belongings before I locked him up. Anyway, when he left, he said to keep it, not that he was overly friendly or anything. Believe me, he wasn't!" The sheriff chuckled, and Ben grinned.

Thaddeas lifted his dark eyebrows in interest. Raised in Boston, Thaddeas had rubbed shoulders with men of the world in his father's leather shop. This influence instilled at an early age a fascination for the country's politics.

Annabelle watched. It was the first thing that had perked Thaddeas up all day. She searched his eyes for their familiar sparkle—they normally brimmed with life—when they suddenly blinked and stared back at her. She blushed and looked away. A glimmer of light shone until they had met hers; then they turned to dark pools.

Later when Kate moved to clear the table, the women rose to help while the men sauntered into the sitting room, and Sheriff Larson went out to the wagon for his *Western Star*. After much discussion, Thaddeas left to stretch his legs.

When he opened the door that led outside, he stopped in his tracks. Annabelle sat on the step, her back to him. He breathed a prayer, swallowed for courage, and moved to join her. As he settled on the step beside her, he sensed her stiffening body, but she turned and acknowledged him. "Thaddeas."

"Annabelle," he said in a soft tone, "I want to apologize for. . ."

Annabelle interrupted him before he could finish his sentence. "Thaddeas, I told you it never happened! Now, I don't want to hear another word about it."

Thaddeas protested, "It did happen, and I am sorry that I offended you. I was wrong. I thought you cared about me."

"I do care about you, Silly; we're cousins. I just don't want to spoil our friendship. You're like a brother to me, Thad."

"Like a brother?"

"That's right. And another thing, you love it here."

"Pardon?"

"The wild West. . .Beaver Creek." She waved her arms to refer to the countryside. "I want to live in the city, see new places, dress in fine gowns, wear jewels, and attend balls like Dorie."

"I see." Her shallow response disappointed Thad. "I've lived in the city, Annabelle. Not everyone goes to balls, only the wealthy. There is also poverty and filth." He studied her reaction.

Without batting an eye she challenged him. "And what is wrong with wealth? Sure isn't any around this place."

Thaddeas brooded over her words. She was still a child. Oh, why did he have to be in love with her? "Thad," she whispered, "there is someone watching us, over there in that clump of trees past the barn." She did not point, but nodded her head in the direction of the barn.

"Stay here!" Thaddeas jumped to his feet in one swift movement and sped toward the spot Annabelle had indicated. "Halt!" he yelled as he ran, but the dark figure also ran and quickly disappeared into the wooded area in the direction of Beaver Creek. Thaddeas raced until he was out of breath, then stopped, panting, and leaned against a tree. The man was nowhere to be found. Thad moved in a wide circle, retracing his steps back to the place where they had seen him lurking in the shadows.

Annabelle soon joined him. "Was it an Indian?"

"No."

"What do you think he wanted?"

"I don't know. But I'm sure it's nothing to worry about. I'd better mention it to Ben, though." His forehead furrowed in concern. He knew that Ben was a peace-loving man who avoided confrontations. "Come on, let's go tell the others."

Later when Thad led the men out to look at the prowler's tracks, Annabelle saw her chance to speak with Kate. "Could we talk?"

"Do you know the trespasser?"

"No, of course not. It has nothing to do with that. I just thought we might have a moment alone." Annabelle realized she did not have much time until the rest would return. "Thad asked me to marry him."

"What? How wonderful, Annabelle!"

"No! It is not wonderful!" she retorted. "I don't want to marry him. His notions are going to spoil a perfectly fine friendship that we have enjoyed for many years."

"You are a beautiful young woman. You cannot expect your relationships with men to stay the same. It is only natural that some will be attracted to you. Don't you care for Thaddeas?"

"Of course I do. But not that way."

Kate considered. "Perhaps then, Thaddeas isn't right for you. However, I've known for a long time that he loved you, Annabelle. You must realize that things probably will never be the same between you again. Either his love will draw you to him or drive you away." Kate patted Annabelle's hand.

"Nothing troubles you, does it, Kate?"

"What do you mean?"

"You work hard and take whatever comes your way without complaining. How can you be content on the farm, working from sunrise to sunset? I want more out of life."

"So do I," Kate whispered. "I want a baby."

"I—I'm so sorry," Annabelle stammered. "I didn't know."

"Well," Kate said, dabbing at her cheek, "now you do. But back to your problem, Annabelle. You said that farm life was not what you wanted, but that is not what Thaddeas wants either, is it?"

"Well, I guess not. . ." She cut her answer short as the others entered, discussing the prowler.

"I wouldn't worry about it, Ben," the sheriff was saying. "Probably just a passerby."

"Strange, though," Ben mumbled.

Chapter 3

The giant wheel, powered from the Little Miami River, turned the great saw that gave life to the mill and the men who worked there. The tool's buzzing intensified to a high-pitched roar and then suddenly returned to the whining hum typical of the usual background drone with which Thaddeas did his work. This meant someone had opened the door to the outer room and closed it again. Thad wondered if it was David Green, coming after the bill of sale that he was figuring. He quickly finished multiplying the numbers before him.

Then he heard the door to his cubbyhole office creak and glanced up to see Sheriff Larson's huge physique in the doorway. "Oh, it's you, Uncle Buck. Come in and have a seat, and I'll be with you in just a minute."

The sheriff nodded and settled into a chair across the desk from Thaddeas and watched with pride. Buck had never had a son of his own, and it pleased him to treat his nephew—who had braved the West to seek him out—as one.

"What can I do for you, Uncle Buck?" Thaddeas pushed aside his bill of sale.

"I just came from Cooper's General Store, and they had this letter from your folks. Thought I'd deliver it."

Thaddeas reached for the letter and leaned back in his chair, tilting it onto two legs as he tore open the envelope. He was always glad to get news from home, and Buck was eager to hear from his brother as well. He smoothed the letter out and began to read.

Dearest Thad,
I am filled with sorrow. Your father, my beloved husband, died this past night. He took ill, developing lung fever.

Thaddeas's chair slammed to the floor, and his eyes filled with tears, which he brushed away with the back of his hand. His fingers trembled, and as he tried to read further, his vision blurred.

"Son? What is it?" The sheriff instantly rose to his feet and went around the desk toward Thaddeas.

"It's Father. He died." Thaddeas looked up at Buck through pain-filled, unbelieving eyes. "Father's dead," he repeated.

"Lewis? Lewis is dead?" the sheriff asked. He pulled a stool to Thaddeas's side and slumped down onto it with his thick legs and gun-belted middle spilling over. His hand gripped his nephew's shoulder. "I'm so sorry, Son." After a moment he asked, "Is there more?"

"Yes, here. I—I can't see the words." The sheriff gently took the piece of paper and read aloud.

> *He has been abed this past week. I should have written earlier to tell you of his illness, but I was holding on to every thread of hope that he would not leave this world behind. He spoke of many things before he parted, expressing his love for you, his youngest son. I know that he envied your adventure, going west and all, wishing it could have been him. Your brother, Leon, is keeping things going at the shop, but he wants you to come home at once so the will can be read. I know that you love the West, Son, but we sorely need you. Please come as speedily as you can. My heart breaks for the loss of your father and the grief that this letter brings to you.*
>
> > *Love,*
> > *Mother*
>
> *Please give my regrets to Buck.*

Thaddeas bent over the desk and placed his head in his hands, his shoulders shaking. Buck embraced him, and they both let the tears run freely as the realization of death sank in.

After a long time passed, the sheriff spoke with compassion in his voice. "Stay put, and I'll find David Green." Minutes later Buck returned for Thaddeas. They moved past towering stacks of clapboards and floorboards. The sweet smell of wood and sawdust went unnoticed as they walked on, heavy-footed, past stockpiles of shingles, staves, and rails. Finally they turned west—with their backs toward the river and the giant wheels that splashed and groaned an appropriate requiem—and walked silently toward the jailhouse.

❧❧

By the following evening, things were in order, and Thaddeas rode to Tucker House to say good-bye. The mill's owner, David Green, did not want to let his employee go, but he paid him what he had coming. He offered his regrets and promised to take Thaddeas back if he should return to Ohio. Mr. Green saw potential in Thaddeas, acknowledging him as an agreeable young man who had done a remarkable job with the mill's accounts. He would miss him.

Mattie convinced the sheriff that she would be fine if he accompanied Thaddeas on the first leg of his journey. She knew rumors of Indian unrest along the Miami and Ohio Rivers worried Buck. At first the sheriff hesitated, but then he quickly made plans. He rode out to Jude Miller's place and persuaded him to watch over the town for a week or so in his absence, deputizing him and giving him a long list of instructions. Then he set about buying the staples they would need for their trip. Finishing up with some last minute details at his office, he picked up Thaddeas there and started toward Tucker House.

Mattie greeted them as they tethered their horses. "Buck! Thaddeas!" Linking her arms in each of theirs, she led them to the house. When they reached the steps, she turned to Thaddeas and said, "It hurts me, Thaddeas, to see ya suffer. I'm so sorry for ya."

"I know, Mattie. Thank you."

During supper, Claire could hardly eat. She swallowed hard and blinked back tears, brokenhearted to see Thaddeas go through such a hard time. Thaddeas cleared his throat, and she gave her full attention. "I've done a lot of thinking today. You're my family, and I love Ohio. I don't want to leave, but Boston is my duty. I don't know if I'll be back. I'll miss you all."

Mattie spoke quietly, "Sometimes life's portions are hard ta take, sure enough, Thaddeas. But you're a man of God, and I know you'll be strong. You'll make it through. We are family, Thad. And we're gonna miss ya somethin' fierce."

"Thank you for letting Uncle Buck see me off. But he doesn't have to come, you know."

"He needs ta go. It's important to him," Mattie replied. The sheriff smiled across the table at the woman he loved.

After dinner Thaddeas approached Annabelle. "I need to talk with you a minute, please, before I leave." It had been a shock when Thaddeas had asked her to marry him, and now it was a greater blow that he was departing from her life altogether. She thought her heart would break to lose him, but upon seeing his sorrow, she answered calmly, "All right, Thad."

He led her to the wooden bench beneath the giant hickory tree beside the house. As Annabelle sat down, she took great pains to arrange her skirt about her. It was something to do. Thaddeas sat close at her side. "Oh, Thaddeas!" she blurted out. "I'm so sorry."

"I—I never thought it would come to this," he said softly. Annabelle looked up, her eyes brimming with unshed tears, and he continued—straight to the point—"I love you, Annabelle."

"I love you, too, Thaddeas."

His eyes brightened at her words, and his eyebrows raised to ask the unspoken question that stuck in his throat. He urged, "Marry me then."

Annabelle remembered Kate's words. *His love will either draw you closer or drive you further apart.* She brushed away a tear that escaped her thick lashes, then reached out to take his hand. He felt the wetness as she answered. "Thaddeas, I can't. My heart is breaking, but I cannot marry you."

He applied pressure to his grip on her hand and asked, "You don't love me then?"

"Not in that way, Thad. But I don't want to lose you. What will I do without you?"

"I don't know if I'll be back."

"You must come back," she pleaded.

"Why? If I cannot have you, Annabelle, I'd be better off to stay in Boston."

"But you love the West. You said the city was too crowded, that. . ."

"Maybe I'll go somewhere else, farther west across the Mississippi. I feel dead inside, Annabelle."

"I do, too," she answered.

"We'd better head back to the house. I need to get home. We'll be leaving early in the morning." Then he turned and said almost desperately, "Annabelle, if you ever change your mind, I'll be there."

Annabelle felt like nothing would ever be right in her world again.

Chapter 4

The flatboat glided smoothly downstream, riding the current of the Little Miami like a leaf catching hold of the skirts of the wind, yet not so free. David Lowry's able hands maneuvered the raft around rocks, trees, and the other obstacles that threatened their voyage.

Thaddeas sat near the edge, hugging his knees and scanning the shoreline. The trees passed like great dark giants, sentinels of a forbidden land. Cynical thoughts nagged at him. *Banished! Snatched from the wilderness that I love.* He reached up to brush away a tear lest his uncle see him cry, then expelled a weary sigh along with a sidelong glance in Buck's direction.

Buck hoped to direct his nephew's attention away from his troubles. "That's all military-occupied land." The sheriff pointed to the east side of the shore where Thad had been staring. "It's the Virginia Military Reserve."

This part of the country was new to him. Thaddeas nodded. Then Buck pointed to round hills that looked like burial sites, and the young man's thoughts returned to the death of his father. "See those mounds, Son? It makes a body wonder what sort of people made them."

Thaddeas choked out the words, "Indians, I suppose."

"Too bad you folks ain't goin' downriver farther," Lowry piped up. "You're gonna miss the great wall."

"Great wall?" Thaddeas looked at the man in wonder.

"That's right," the navigator replied. "Three and a half miles long."

"Have you seen it, Uncle Buck?"

"Yep. It's a sight, made out of earth, stone, and bone."

"Never get tired of seein' it," Lowry remarked, as he deftly steered the boat from the back with a long oar. "Looks like an old snake crawlin' in the grass alongside the Miami."

"Is it a fort?" Thaddeas asked.

"I reckon. No one knows for sure. Folks say it encloses one hundred acres of those mounds." Lowry nodded his woolly head. His words muffled as he leaned over the back of the barge and spit out a mouthful of black juice. Then he continued, "See that knob just ahead? I'm steerin' towards it. When we pass the point, you'll be able to see Waynesville, where you'll be goin' ashore." He grunted and with powerful strokes guided the barge toward the landmark.

True to the man's word, the settlement soon appeared. In minutes

Lowry had docked the boat, helped Buck and Thaddeas get their horses ashore, and pushed off again toward his final destination of New Orleans. The horses were skittish, and the two men spoke soothing words before they mounted. Then they wasted no time leaving the small settlement in their dust, traveling toward Cincinnati by means of Waynesville Road.

Stiff from hours in the saddle, Thaddeas arched his back and stretched his arms. They had ridden hard all afternoon except for stopping twice to rest the horses and drink water, and once when they had lunched alongside the trail. The beautiful spot with a trickling stream had reminded Thaddeas of the many times he had fished behind Tucker House with the girl he left behind. Now there were only dense forests for as far as the eye could see.

"Are you as tuckered out as I am, Son?" asked the sheriff as he rode alongside Thaddeas.

"I feel rusty as an old tin can," Thad replied.

"Well, we'll be hitting Lebanon and the Golden Lamb in a couple hours."

"I think any place would look good tonight," Thaddeas sighed. Fatigue creased his face with heavy strokes, and sorrow shadowed his eyes.

"The first couple days of travel are always the worst," Buck said solemnly. He thought about the long trail ahead for his nephew and the ordeal that awaited him when he reached Boston.

As the first shades of night fell, they pulled up weary but grateful at the hitching post of the Golden Lamb. "A welcome sight and just in time. I think the cold weather is heading in." Buck pointed toward the inn. Thaddeas nodded, taking in the two-story log tavern where a wooden sign, displaying the Golden Lamb emblem, creaked and groaned in the nippy night air.

A lad ran to greet them. "If yar stayin' at the inn, I'll take yar horses for ya."

"That we are. Thank you," Buck said. "We'll check in on them before we turn in. Is supper still being served?"

"Yes, Sir. Veal, cheese, cornbread, and pie, Sir."

"Sounds tempting. Come on, Thad."

Once inside, a full-fleshed woman warmly greeted them. She led them to their room so they could clean up and said, "My name's Martha. Jest seat yarselves at the table in the dinin' room when yar ready, and I'll serve ya yar meal." She bustled away, and the clacking sound of her heels echoed in the narrow hallway. Buck spotted a basin of water, and they quickly washed for supper.

"We best eat so we can turn in," Buck suggested.

"Hope it's as good as it smells." Thaddeas followed his uncle back through the hall and into a large dining area equipped with a huge table where folks sat before the meal the stable boy had described. Buck nodded with approval. He knew the place; it looked good as ever. A cloth graced the table, and a hearth fire warmed the room.

A stern-looking military man passed Buck a platter of ham and veal. He introduced himself politely, "Lt. Wade Brooks."

"Buck Larson, and this is my nephew, Thaddeas."

"I see you're a sheriff. Where you from?"

"Just upriver, Beaver Creek, but Thaddeas is a Bostonian. He's on his way home. And you, Lieutenant?"

"Stationed at Fort Wayne under the command of Capt. William Wells at the moment, originally from Pittsburgh."

"Really? Same as my wife, Mattie."

"I didn't know that, Uncle Buck," Thaddeas interrupted. "I guess I never heard Mattie talk about her family."

Buck turned and directed his conversation toward his nephew. "Yep. She grew up in Pennsylvania. She isn't one to talk much of her past. It's painful for her. She didn't get on with her folks. Her father, the Rev. Tucker, was a strict, mulish man. . . ."

Brooks choked on his drink, and Buck cut his explanation short. "You all right, Lieutenant?"

The tall, rugged man looked quite pale. He nodded. "Yes, please excuse me."

Buck resumed his conversation with Thad. "It wasn't her fault; she's a good woman."

"Of course, Uncle Buck."

Buck stabbed a chunk of meat with his fork and daydreamed about his wife. He pictured her at work, stitching something pretty for one of her customers. Loneliness pricked his already heavy heart.

Thaddeas addressed the officer, "Lieutenant Brooks, what can you tell us about the Indian situation? Does the military expect trouble?"

"It doesn't look good. A settler by the name of Myer was killed, scalped a few miles west of Urbana. A lot of folks are packing off to Kentucky for safety." The hair on Thaddeas's neck bristled at the news, and his eyes widened. "We're keeping a close watch on the Indian chief Tecumseh and his brother, The Prophet, up at Greenville. Have you heard any reports about that pair?"

Thad shook his head. "No, Sir."

Buck joined in the conversation. "But we've noticed lots of Indians milling around lately."

"Actually I'm headed to talk to some Shakers about the Indian village of Greenville," the lieutenant explained. "They paid them a visit not too long ago."

"What does Captain Wells think about it all?" Buck asked.

"Tecumseh and The Prophet vow they want peace. However, at the same time they are uniting tribes from all over the Northwest Territory, even across the Mississippi. Tribes you've never heard of. The captain thinks it looks mighty suspicious. I think the settlers in Ohio need to be on the lookout."

Buck pushed his plate away from him and sank back in his chair. He hated to hear that kind of talk. Things had been peaceful in Ohio for a long time, but the lieutenant was right. His heart sank with the heaviness that had plagued him over the last several days. It was late, and he felt tired.

"Ready to turn in, Thad?"

Meanwhile back at the old Potter place, Ben pulled the barn door closed. *Almost dark*, he thought. *I'm late for supper. Hope Kate's feathers aren't ruffled.* Then he remembered that Annabelle had spent the day with Kate. He pictured them engrossed in woman talk and realized he need not worry. Approaching the house, he picked up his gait, anticipating the meal that would be waiting as well as the companionship of the young women inside. Their silhouettes in the window drew his attention; then he gasped as his eyes caught a figure squatted low, peering into the window where Kate and Annabelle could clearly be seen by the lantern light.

"What in the. . . Hey, you!" Ben bolted toward the crouched man, who jumped when he realized he had been discovered. Instantly, the stranger made for the side of the house and slipped around the back with Ben close behind. "Wait! Hold up, now!" Ben yelled as he gained on the shadow, which enlarged with each step.

A thought skimmed his mind, one of relief that the prowler was not an Indian. Ben was almost within reach and was grabbing for the man's coat when his own foot caught in a tangle of roots and weeds, wrenching his lower leg and jerking him to a stop in midflight. His feet went out from under him, and he sailed forward, hitting the ground with his head. He lay stunned, and several minutes passed before he groggily returned to consciousness. As he recovered, he groped about in the dark.

Ben tried to focus, but his head throbbed, and he was overcome with dizziness. Blood oozed down his brow. He raised himself to a sitting position and remembered the trespasser. Everything was now dark, and he knew the stranger would be long gone, so he eased himself to his feet and limped toward the house. Before he could reach it, he heard his name ring out in the night air.

"Ben!" Kate's voice came from the barn where she had gone to search for him. Seeing the blood streaming down his face, she screamed, "Darling! What happened?" Instantly, she supported her husband and guided him inside, easing him into a chair where she grabbed a clean towel and pressed it to the wound. Then she undid the top button of his shirt.

"Ben! Kate?" Annabelle rushed to their sides.

"I feel better. I'm fine now," Ben whispered.

"Please, stay put. We must be sure the bleeding stops, then I'll take another look," his wife ordered while glancing up at Annabelle.

She saw terror in Kate's eyes and knelt on the floor beside the pair, watching mutely. Annabelle grabbed Ben's sleeve and clung fiercely, while he gently scolded his attentive wife.

"Listen, Kate. You shouldn't have gone to the barn alone after dark. There could be animals, Indians, or prowlers."

"Don't be ridiculous." Kate's voice quivered. "I just went to look for you. I knew you were out there. Now, if you must talk, tell me what happened."

"I–I guess I tripped and hit my head on a rock or something. It must have knocked me out."

"All right. Let's take another look." Kate examined her husband's wound carefully. "It's not deep." She sighed with relief. Then she pressed the towel on the cut again. "Hold this, Darling, and just sit still. I'll get you a drink."

Annabelle quickly jumped up. "No, I'll get it, Kate." Ben watched his sister-in-law dip a cup of water with her back toward him, then he looked into Kate's moist and troubled eyes. The brown swallowed up the green flecks that usually danced there. She was on the verge of tears.

Ben did not like to keep anything from Kate but did not want to frighten her, either. He would ride into town the next day to talk to Buck.

Chapter 5

The wagon jostled Ben and Annabelle as its large-spoked wheels cranked along the road, frigid in the early morning cold. Annabelle clutched her cloak and glanced at her brother-in-law, who unconsciously tugged on his hat to cover the gash on his forehead. He refused to wear the outlandish bandage that Kate had tried to force upon him.

Annabelle shivered. "I cannot believe how cold it is this morning."

"Mm-hm."

"The trees will soon be bare with this sudden drop in temperature."

"Mm-hm."

Annabelle grinned when she realized Ben was not listening to a word she said. "I suppose I mentioned that I was eloping on Saturday?"

"Mm-hm."

His mind rehearsed the previous night's episode, reliving the scene a hundred times. This morning he had awakened, remembering that Sheriff Larson had accompanied Thaddeas to Cincinnati. His head exploded with each toss of the wagon as he tried to recall who the sheriff had deputized and sort out what should be done.

"Ben Wheeler, you are the most preoccupied man I know." Annabelle leaned forward, positioning pink cheeks close to his so he could not escape her miffed expression.

"I'm sorry, Annabelle. I'm not very good company this morning. My head feels like it met the end of a tomahawk, but don't tell your sister."

"Oh, Ben, I didn't realize. I'm the one who should apologize."

Ben smiled warmly and patted her hand. "No need."

They rode the remaining distance to Tucker House in silence. Then Annabelle offered, "I can help myself down, Ben, unless you would like to come in?"

"Yes. I would like to chat with Mattie a bit."

Annabelle hurried into the house, leaving him to secure his rig. "Mattie! I'm home."

"Mornin', Annabelle. Did ya have a good visit?"

"Yes, very good. Ben wants to talk to you."

"Oh?" Mattie laid aside her sewing and found Ben waiting on the porch. "Good morning, Mattie."

"Mornin'. Come on in," she invited.

"Ah, no. I just want to check if there is anything you need, with Buck gone."

"That's kind of ya, but no, I can't think of anythin'. Takin' Annabelle off my hands for a spell was plenty." Mattie winked at Ben, while mentally linking Annabelle's strange behavior of late to Thad's departure.

He chuckled. "I expect Kate got the brunt of that." Then his voice took on a serious but indifferent tone, for he did not want to worry Mattie. "By the way, who did the sheriff put in charge of the town?"

"Jude Miller."

"I see. Well, let me know if you hear from Buck or need a hand with anything."

"All right, thank ya," Mattie called as she watched Ben return to his wagon with a stiff gait. She wondered if he was overdoing it around the farm with heavy lifting. Then she turned her attention to Annabelle and hoped her visit with Kate had lifted her spirits. When she entered the sitting room and picked up her sewing, she found Claire conversing with her sister.

"I'm walking to town this morning to get some things that I need for my box."

"What box?"

"For the box social Sunday night." Claire stole a glance at Annabelle, who slumped in her chair like a giant rag doll at the mere mention of the event.

"It just won't be the same without Thad," Annabelle whimpered.

"It will be fun," Claire coaxed her sister. Though she was the younger by a year and a half, Claire oftentimes acted the more mature. "Come with me. You always have such good ideas."

"Well I don't know," Annabelle mumbled. "Mattie may need me. I was gone all day yesterday."

"Go along." Mattie waved her needle in the air. "But when you get back, I'm puttin' ya both ta work."

Annabelle rose reluctantly to follow Claire out of the room. "Bundle up now; it's cold outside," Mattie warned in a voice garbled from a mouth stuffed with pins.

As they fingered the slick, satin ribbons in Cooper's General Store, Annabelle admonished Claire, "Mattie's got plenty of lace at home, but a few sticks of candy would be nice." Her mind raced, and she imagined the young men she knew contesting over their boxed lunches.

Gradually her attitude changed to excitement, and she hastened toward the candy counter where the mild scents of cinnamon and mint mixed with the heavier aromas of coffee and molasses. A balding head poked around the corner of a row of glass jars filled with tempting confections. Elias Cooper straightened to his full height and beamed when he saw who his customers were.

"Mornin', Annabelle, Claire."

"Hello, Mr. Cooper."

Annabelle inquired about her friend. "How is Dorie? Have you heard from her lately? I wish she'd write more often."

"Oh, yes, we jest received a letter. Would ya like me ta read a few parts?"

"Please do."

Mr. Cooper's long, thinning hair fell forward, hiding his spectacled face as he bent his head to read the letter that he pulled from his apron pocket.

The McClintocks' ball attracted guests from all over Charleston.

He paused to glance at the young ladies, savoring their expressions, and continued.

Miss Delaney made her debut in an ivory-colored gown trimmed in. . .

Elias floundered over the next word.

"May I see?" Annabelle pressed close. Mr. Cooper scratched his bearded chin and reluctantly handed the parchment paper to Annabelle, who scanned over the contents until his stubby finger pointed halfway down the sheet.

"There," he said.

"Rosettes," she sighed.

He snapped the paper back onto the counter.

. . .rosettes. She wore genuine pearls and looked exquisite with her black hair fashioned most gracefully atop her head. Of course all the gentlemen attended her courteously, and I was consumed with jealousy. However, Aunt Adelaide introduced me to an extremely handsome congressman named Brett Powers. The evening turned out to be quite lovely after all.

"Oh, how dreamy." Annabelle clutched her hands to her breast and swooned. "Real pearls, real gentlemen."

She did not realize that a stranger had earlier entered the store and now observed them from where he browsed. He continued to eavesdrop while the women concluded their shopping.

With sticks of licorice wrapped in tissue paper tucked in a shopping basket, Annabelle hooked her free arm through Claire's, in a light-hearted gesture, and guided her sister toward the door.

"Good morning, ladies."

"Sir?" Annabelle was startled to look up into steel-blue eyes set in a face of granite. As she stared, the statue face turned from stone to liquid, with waves of dimples and creases enveloping a gorgeous smile. The eyes twinkled as if the young man knew something humorous about Annabelle. She blushed and turned to move away.

"Ma'am, may I?" He tipped his hat, displaying shortly cropped brown hair, while the same grin spread across the expanse of his face and his eyes dared her to defy him. "May I introduce myself? My name is Charles Harrison."

Mustering up courage, with Dorie's image flashing in and out of her consciousness, Annabelle responded with a slight curtsy. "Annabelle Larson, and my sister, Claire."

"At your service, I am sure. Where are you headed? May I carry your basket for you?"

"That is very kind, but we are on our way home, and I am sure it would be quite out of your way."

"Ladies, please be assured, it would be a pleasure."

"Perhaps another time, Mr. Harrison."

The young man persisted, "May I call on you, Miss Larson?"

Annabelle retorted with a question of her own. "Will we see you at church on Sunday?"

Charles Harrison admired her quickness and the fire that shot from those green eyes. The way in which the gorgeous chestnut hair—framing her upturned face—caught the sun's light enchanted him. "Sunday? Why yes, of course. I'll see you on Sunday then, Miss Larson." Another tip of his hat and he disappeared.

With his retreat, Annabelle could not see the smirk on his stony face, hardened by service in the military. He carried a soldier's stance, straight and perfect, but Annabelle only saw a gentleman. As Charles Harrison formulated a plan, he scowled. He had a long ride ahead of him to make it back by Sunday.

Chapter 6

I t's such a good cause, Reverend," Melanie Caldwell quipped as she bounced the squirmy bundle in her arms.

The preacher reached out to touch the baby's silken cheek. "Luke is excited to present the gift to the orphanage."

"Of course everyone loves the box socials regardless of the cause."

The reverend grinned. "I believe you're right, Melanie. Perhaps I should get the auction started before a few men lose their courage." He chuckled as he straightened his round white collar and moved toward the long wooden benches where the fancy boxes drew the crowd's attention.

Across the room, Claire clutched Annabelle's sleeve. "I hope Sammy gets my box, but I doubt if he has money to spare."

"You're always interested in the most unlikely creatures."

Claire frowned. "Just because Sammy stutters does not make him a misfit. He is the sweetest boy I know."

"Yes, I know you think so. Now you'd better wipe that scowl off your face, or no one will want to purchase your box." Annabelle waved to Rebecca Galloway who had moved up in rank, as friends go, when Dorie moved out of the valley. Rebecca and her young brother, James, crossed the room to greet them.

Married women, outfitted in their best calico prints, chatted in small clusters, secure in the knowledge that their husbands would be obtaining their boxes.

Just as the reverend cleared his throat to call the attention of the folks, Annabelle spotted him. Dressed in a flowing white shirt and dark brown pants, the handsome stranger pushed through the crowd, making a straight track toward her.

"Miss Larson, you look lovely. Quickly, which box is yours, before the bidding starts?"

"Mr. Harrison, what a surprise."

"You did invite me this morning." Annabelle colored slightly as she recalled the conversation. When he had appeared at church and continued his pursuit, she had put him off by talking about the box social.

"So I did," she admitted.

"Please don't say you were just trying to get rid of me." He leaned close, and a delicious musky scent filled the air. "Now, which is yours?"

"I suppose it won't hurt to tell you. After all, there is no guarantee that you can secure it. And it is for a good cause." Annabelle then described her lunch as a disguised cigar box wrapped in soft blue fabric and secured with white lace knotted about a dried chrysanthemum.

As Charles Harrison slipped away, Rebecca gave Annabelle a searching look. "Where did he come from?"

"I don't know," Annabelle answered honestly. "But I intend to find out."

Two strapping country boys, Andy Benson and Bart Barnes, eyed the stranger suspiciously. "Where ya from, Mister?"

"Boston, and you?"

"From here. What's your business in Beaver Creek?"

"I don't believe that's any of your affair." The three eyed each other icily. Then the bidding started.

The reverend waved Annabelle's box high in the air for all to see. Thad's departure had opened the door for suitors, and she was embarrassed that so many young men bid upon it.

Andy seemed most determined. "One dollar." The room grew quiet, then "Two dollars" echoed from the corner where Charles Harrison stood. Annabelle knew instinctively that he would be able to outbid Andy. Her heart beat wildly until the final offer. The reverend handed the coveted container to Mr. Harrison, who flung a sidelong smirk in Andy's direction. The country lad stood with his hands in his pockets.

Annabelle fanned her hot cheeks and looked away from the staring faces. Across the room Claire sat with Sammy, and Mattie had joined Kate and Ben. "Predictable creatures," she whispered to Rebecca. "At least Charles Harrison provides a bit of diversion." Rebecca considered her remark, and Annabelle noticed a mischievous glint in her friend's eyes.

❧❧

"There you are. I thought you had slipped out the back door," the young Harrison accused Annabelle as he led her to a vacant bench situated against a far wall.

"Nonsense."

"Good."

"Mr. Harrison, what brings you to Beaver Creek?" Annabelle quickly diverted her eyes away from the chrysanthemum tucked into his shirt pocket like a prize for all to see.

"Actually, investments."

"In Beaver Creek?" Annabelle questioned as she placed a crisp linen napkin on her lap and handed an identical match to her dinner partner.

"Precisely. There is a road coming through, and I am considering whether to fund it."

"A road?"

Charles reached for a chicken part and nodded. "Ever heard of the National Road?"

"Yes, but. . ." She smiled as she traced the steamy circumference of her mug of apple cider.

Charles wondered what amused her and gently prodded, "But?"

"But surely not, you seem so young. I thought investors were stuffy old men with large stomachs and bulging pockets."

"You have just described my father." They burst into laughter and felt like old friends. Then he unwrapped the tissue paper which held the candy from Cooper's General Store. "Licorice, my favorite." The intensity of his gaze insinuated that she had purchased the candy purposely for him. "I am an adventurer at heart so Father allowed me to come in his stead," he said without taking his eyes off her.

"He must have confidence in you."

This pleased Charles, and he warmed. "Well, the family inheritance passes to me, so, yes, he trusts I'll use good judgment."

"And where is this family?"

"Boston."

Annabelle choked on her food.

"Did I say something wrong?"

"No. I just know someone from there."

"Indeed? Who?"

"His name is Thaddeas Larson."

"Never heard of him. A relative?"

Annabelle sighed. "A cousin."

"I am glad to hear he is not a suitor." Annabelle colored, and he continued, "This pumpkin pie is excellent."

"Thank you."

"Now, tell me about yourself, Miss Larson. Have you always lived in Beaver Creek?"

"Mostly. My parents were killed in an Indian raid at Big Bottom. Mattie Larson brought me and my two sisters here to raise."

His eyebrows arched slightly at the mention of Mattie. "I'm sorry. How old were you?"

"Just one. I cannot remember my real parents. Kate remembers them clearly though."

"Kate?"

"Yes, my older sister, married to Ben Wheeler. Over there." She pointed toward her brother-in-law, who was engaged in a serious conversation with the stand-in sheriff, Jude Miller. Annabelle had the distinct impression that they had been talking about her and Charles. They looked her way as she pointed them out, so she feigned a wave. "Uh-oh, guess we got caught." She frowned. "Here they come. I'll introduce you."

Charles jumped to his feet and stiffened as the large freckled man and another, slightly smaller and older with a star pinned to his vest, approached.

"Ben, I would like you to meet Charles Harrison. Charles, this is Ben Wheeler, my brother-in-law, and Jude Miller."

Charles straightened, resuming his soldiering posture, and stretched forth his hand. Ben carefully eyed the man as he shook his hand. "Have we met before? You remind me of someone."

"Not that I remember, Sir. But it is a pleasure to do so now."

"Welcome to Beaver Creek, Mr. Harrison."

"Thank you. I am enjoying your town very much."

Jude studied the man who stood before him. Annabelle watched Charles Harrison's face turn to a stony countenance, and wondered why he looked as glum as one headed for the gallows. After some small talk, including an invitation from Ben to visit his farm, the men excused themselves and moved away to resume their private conversation, leaving Annabelle and Charles alone again.

Charles turned to Annabelle, "Would you mind if we step outside for some fresh air?"

She glanced at their supper mess, and he bent to lend a hand. When all of the scraps were shoved into the box that Charles had purchased, she reached for her shawl, and they moved toward the door.

"May I keep this for a remembrance of this evening?" Charles asked, plucking the flower from his shirt pocket and twirling it between long, slender fingers. Annabelle blushed close to the shade the flower had once been. He slipped his other hand beneath her elbow. The night was black and cool, and his voice sounded like the distant brook—low and musical. "Annabelle."

"Yes," she said in a tone so low that he was not sure if she had replied.

"You're a special young woman," he said, gazing at the star-studded sky. "This has been a pleasant night." He waited for her to look up and watched her face under the moon's light. "May I call on you?"

This time she consented. "Yes, I would like that."

Charles took her hand, his touch firm and gentle, and Annabelle thought for a moment that he was going to kiss it, but he did not. Then like a vapor, he was gone—and she wondered if he was even real.

Chapter 7

S udden drops in temperature teased the trees, producing spectacular color displays. On this particular day, the sun gilded the leaves to brilliance, but the rider did not pause to admire his surroundings. With a message to deliver, he spurred his horse forward until he rounded the bend that revealed Tucker House. As he focused on his destination, he noticed patches of color like flags waving behind the house. Quickly dismounting, the young man strode toward the spot where he found the women doing the wash.

"Telegram! Telegram!"

Mattie dropped the gown she had just removed from the clothesline and snatched the dispatch from the errand boy. When she realized her discourteous behavior, she quickly added, "Thank ya kindly." Ripping it open, she silently read its contents and then exhaled deeply. "Well, that gave my body a scare. 'Tis the sheriff, and he jest wants us to know that everything is fine. Thad is on his way to Boston, and Buck is stoppin' in Dayton for a short visit with Luke Wheeler."

The message carrier saw that all was well and politely made his departure. "Could I git ya a drink?" Mattie called after him when she realized her manners, but he was too far gone and did not hear the invitation.

"When will Buck be home?" Claire asked. Practiced fingers folded clothes, stiff from the sun.

"He didn't say."

"I'm glad he's visiting Luke." Claire was fond of Ben's brother, Luke, who had been her spiritual mentor. She had corresponded with Luke after he left Beaver Creek for college four years earlier. Now he was involved in the orphanage that was a ministry of the Presbyterian Church of Dayton. "In his last letter, I got the impression that he was a bit homesick."

"Is that all Buck said about Thaddeas?" Annabelle complained.

"Jest that he's safely on his way to Boston," Mattie snapped. "Telegrams are always short, ya know, too costly otherwise." She grew irritable, for she had been looking forward to Buck's return, and now it was to be delayed. Silently, the three women piled the crisp clothing in their arms as they thought about the message. "Run ahead and heat up the iron, Annabelle," Mattie ordered. Annabelle thought Mattie sounded as cross as a general in the army. She resisted the temptation to salute.

Long after the iron had cooled in its spot on the kitchen shelf, and the supper dishes were washed and stacked away in a neighboring niche, the women retired to the sitting room. "Shall I start the fire?" Claire offered with concern for Mattie, who rested with tired feet propped upon a footstool. Freckles, Claire's cat, climbed uninvited onto Mattie's lap.

"Please do," Mattie answered. "My back is achin', and it feels good to sit." She arched like Freckles, working out the kinks.

Claire tossed an armful of logs into the fireplace. She gazed at the fire as it crackled and hissed, then posed a question. "Do you think Thaddeas has to sleep under the stars? Surely there's not always an inn available."

Annabelle envisioned him with his bedroll, camping with strangers in the night. Her eyes burned as she blinked back tears that threatened to flow. *Thaddeas would not be frightened; he is so strong and dependable,* she reasoned. He always talked about God and faith. Just like everyone else around her. She frowned. This frustrated yet comforted her. The frustration stemmed from the knowledge that she did not possess or desire this Christian faith that the rest of the family had. The comfort came in leaning on their strength. Thaddeas had been her pillar, always there to protect her, expect the best in her.

"I'm sure Thaddeas is doing jest fine. I worry more about his grief; he seemed so low. But time heals things like that." Mattie's voice faded away as if she were thinking of another time.

Annabelle felt pangs of guilt, knowing she had caused some of his pain.

"Poor Thad," Claire said.

Annabelle shot out of her seat at Claire's remark, unable to listen to another word, for her conscience pricked her sore spot. Mattie and Claire looked at her questioningly, but just then they were interrupted by a knock at the door. They shifted their gaze toward the large, wooden portal. Annabelle pulled the latch with an unsteady touch to receive the unexpected caller.

"Mr. Harrison!"

"Good evening, Miss Larson."

"Please, come in." The ladies jumped to their feet, toppling the footstool and scaring the cat off Mattie's lap. Annabelle, embarrassed by the confusion, did her best to welcome him.

"Your home is delightful, Miss Larson," he said upon entering. "Why do folks call it Tucker House?"

Annabelle swallowed a lump that stuck like molasses in her throat to explain. "Mattie's name was Tucker before she married the sheriff. Remember, I told you we were adopted? Well, it's been a seamstress shop for many years, and that's the name the townspeople gave it."

Charles digested this information as they seated themselves in the sitting room, and then surprised them by referring back to the beginning of her rejoinder. "Did you know Annabelle's parents, Mrs. Larson?"

Mattie squirmed. "Yes, I did."

"You never told me that before!" Annabelle's voice sounded accusing even in her own ears.

"I—I guess it never came up before. I believe Kate and I have discussed it, though."

"Annabelle's sister?" Charles posed the question, and Mattie nodded. "Was Kate old enough to remember her parents, then?"

"Yes, she remembers clear enough. She used to have nightmares 'bout it."

"I imagine you were a comfort to her—the fact that she had a familiar person to go to."

"I wasn't. . . I knew her parents before. . .she was old enough to remember."

"How did you happen to get together with the girls then?"

Mattie frowned at Mr. Harrison. "Enough talk of the past, Mr. Harrison. I'm sure you young folks have more interesting things ta talk about. I was jest about to make some tea when ya came; may I get ya some?" Annabelle wondered about Mattie's sudden burst of energy and looked at the woman with surprise.

"Yes, thank you," Charles replied.

Claire felt awkward and jumped up to assist Mattie, and as soon as they left the room, Charles turned his attention toward Annabelle.

"I apologize for Mattie. She misses Buck and is on edge tonight."

"I'm sorry, Annabelle, if I've brought back unpleasant memories."

"When I was fourteen, I was in an accident and lost my memory. Sometimes I wonder if there are things I still don't remember." She blushed. "It's embarrassing."

"Don't be embarrassed. Please go on."

"It was a painful time for me. I didn't like the sympathetic looks my family gave me when I questioned them about things, so I just didn't press them. I should have asked Mattie or Kate more about my parents."

Charles seemed lost in thought, and his face turned as dismal as a patch of burned stumps. The room grew uncomfortably quiet. Annabelle tried to concentrate on the gentleman sitting beside her and think of some interesting topic to discuss, as Mattie had suggested, but a heaviness remained. She wondered if it stemmed from thinking of her accident or if her concern for Thad still shadowed her.

"Miss Larson?"

He reached for her hand, but she snatched it away.

"Mr. Harrison, I'm. . ."

"Call me Charles."

"Charles, I'm sorry I'm not very good company tonight. I guess I miss Buck and my cousin about as much as Mattie. We were just talking about them when you came to the door."

"Your cousin?"

"Yes, the one returning to Boston."

"I remember. Well, perhaps tonight is not good. I can call another time."

"Oh, no! I didn't mean that you should leave."

"I think it is for the best."

"Please, Charles, stay."

"Another time, when you are not preoccupied." His voice sounded harsh, and he shot a withering look her way as he rose to his feet.

"Charles, wait. I'm really sorry." She rambled on, apologizing as she pursued him toward the door. He turned abruptly, and she bumped into his chest. They stared at each other momentarily, and then his face took on a look of condescending amusement.

"Give Mrs. Larson my apologies for not taking tea. Good night, Miss Larson."

"Please. . .call me Annabelle."

"Annabelle," he whispered as he brushed her cheek with his finger in the same manner someone might treat a small child.

After she closed the door, she stomped her foot. "Well, I never saw the like! What an impossible man!"

Chapter 8

Buck Larson arrived in Dayton on the October 4, five days trail beaten. From the Golden Lamb, they had traveled on the washboard-rough Old Military Road. In Cincinnati, they tarried a full day until Thaddeas got passage on a vessel via the Ohio River destined for Zane's Trace. After an emotional departure, Buck, struck by impulse, sent a telegram to Mattie that he was stopping in Dayton, another two-day trip on Mad River Road.

Dayton, the city where many rivers came together—the Miami, Stillwater, and Mad Rivers and Wolf Creek—had grown so much since his last visit that Buck hardly recognized it. Iron-tired wagons grated noisily over the paving stones, and children dodged in and out among the merchants gathered on the street.

Buck pulled his red kerchief from his vest pocket and wiped his brow. Then he made his way to Main and Water Streets and dismounted in front of the Newcom Tavern. A clammy kiss of cold air arose from the river and enveloped him outside the two-story log building, which at various times served as courthouse, church, school, and post office. He opened the bulky wooden door and entered, boots creaking on the warped wooden floor. A bushy-haired man with a broom-bottom mustache and white apron greeted Buck, leading him to a tiny table to be served.

After his thirst and hunger were adequately satisfied, he inquired, "Where's the orphanage?"

"Ya mean the asylum?"

Buck's face flinched. The expression sounded callous—too harsh. The man with tumbleweed hair seemed indifferent as he gave directions, and Buck paid him and left.

The orphanage was located on the outskirts of town on a parcel of land sheltered several miles from the riverbank. The thought crossed Buck's mind that it was something to be thankful for; at least the air was not as chilly. He tied his mount at the hitching post outside the stone building that stretched before him. It was long and narrow, and reminded him of a large bunkhouse he had seen on Tanner Matthews's place, a prominent ranch in Beaver Creek.

He banged on the door, and it swung open to reveal a blond young man of six feet, lean and sturdy. Astonishment covered the boyish face. "Sheriff Larson! Buck." Luke pulled the sheriff into an embrace and pumped his hand in a rush of excitement. Released and held at arm's length for inspection, Buck noticed a small crowd gathering about them.

Peeping eyes, huge grins, and thin bodies etched simultaneously into Buck's consciousness. Luke followed his glance and then motioned for the small tykes to come forward. "Come meet my friend Sheriff Larson."

One boy of about seven boldly stepped forward from the huddle. "You a real sheriff?"

"Yes, Lad, but you need not be afraid. I'm here to visit Mr. Wheeler."

"Mr. Luke," the lad corrected him shyly.

Buck chuckled. "What is your name, Son?"

"Barnabus. But you kin call me Barney." That tickled the smaller children, and they giggled and squirmed in turn when Luke led Buck to the group for introductions.

There were fourteen orphans of ages varying from eighteen months to fourteen years. They were dressed in hand-me-down clothes, clean and mended. Luke guided Buck down a long hallway and entered the kitchen— dark and bleak, but warm from the blackened oven-fireplace.

A yellow-haired woman, young and curvaceous, with smooth skin the color of apricots, looked up from her work. She was introduced as Mrs. Catherine. Buck also met her counterpart, Mr. Jesse. Their surname was Murdock, but the children dispensed with such formalities, attaching titles to given names.

The sheriff enjoyed his visit, though the children tugged his heartstrings. He asked Luke about little Barney Forbes, his favorite.

"He is one of five children," Luke explained. "Abigail is fourteen; Brooke, twelve; Hank, ten. Then there is your Barney, who is seven, and his younger brother, Lonnie, five. Their pa plunged to his death in a wagon accident, coming west. The mother also died along the trail from lung fever. The wagon master brought them as far as Dayton, and the orphanage took them in."

"How sad."

"Yes. Actually, Abigail is quite mature and could probably raise them if they had a home. But you see, there was no place for them to go."

The tragedies of the youngsters turned Buck's thoughts homeward to the town he sheriffed. Being Beaver Creek's troubleshooter meant twenty-four-hour duty protecting its citizens, anticipating and avoiding crises. A sense of urgency overwhelmed him. He needed to get back to his charge.

Early the next morning, cutting his visit a day short, he made his farewells and stuffed a letter Luke had written to his father, the reverend, in his vest pocket. Then he headed home.

The afternoon sun toasted Annabelle's cheeks and made her drowsy. Expelling a happy sigh, she threw off the temptation to dismount and take a nap in the piles of leaves strewn along the way. She enjoyed horseback riding and was grateful Sheriff Larson had taught her to ride after he came to Tucker House to live.

Annabelle guided her mount, Dusty, slowly along the dirt road and thought how good it was to get away from home where Buck's absence gnawed at Mattie, making her mopey. It sickened her to watch Claire chirp about like a mother robin, doing extra things to cheer Mattie, and made her wonder why Claire was such a do-gooder, even worse than Kate.

A squirrel darted across the road and scurried to a high limb of an oak tree that canopied the roadway. It scolded her as she rode beneath. Annabelle tried to spot the creature in the maze of twisted gray limbs until the straining action put a crick in her neck. When her gaze returned to the trail, to her surprise, a horse and rider fast approached.

She straightened to full height in the saddle, absentmindedly tidying her riding habit as best she could with one hand. Her hair, which was pulled back in a ribbon, sprung out in various directions where stubborn strands had worked free.

Thus when Charles Harrison caught her vision, Annabelle's natural-looking beauty beckoned. He reined in his horse, for he was going at a brisker clip than she.

"Good afternoon, Annabelle. What a pleasant surprise," he puffed.

"Charles." Annabelle nodded, while holding Dusty in check.

"Riding becomes you. You look beautiful." He could not tell if she blushed from his words or if the sun had burned her cheeks. "Are you headed someplace special?"

"No, just riding. I was about to turn around and head back." As soon as she spoke the words, she was sorry. It sounded like she was fishing for an invitation, and she did not even think she liked this moody person.

"I was thinking about a rest," he said. "It is so lovely here."

"It isn't far to the creek. It is breathtaking there."

"I would love to see the spot. Would you care to dismount and show me?"

"Well, I don't know; I should be getting back." She looked over her shoulder toward Tucker House and recalled how boring it was to watch Claire console Mattie. "On second thought, a small excursion is exactly what I need."

Charles's face registered surprise as he regarded her carefully—a beautiful, copper-haired maiden looking for adventure. He threw back his head and chuckled. Then all in one motion he was off his horse and coming to her side.

Annabelle dismounted with butterfly grace and allowed him to fasten their horses.

"This way; race you." She tossed the challenge into the wind.

"Hey, wait! I don't know where we're going." With longer strides he soon caught up to her. Panting and giggling, they ran side by side until they reached the banks of the Beaver Creek, which meandered in and out through the wooded brush. Annabelle dropped to her knees.

"I've wanted to do this all afternoon," she gasped.

"What?" he asked while settling at her side.

"Sink into these leaves. They smell like autumn."

"Do they? Let me see." He scooped up an armful and buried his face into the scratchy, brittle flakes while inhaling deeply. "Indeed they do." While yet speaking, he tossed them into the air above her head, and they deposited over her like a haystack, tickling her face and clinging to her hair and clothes.

"Oh! You scoundrel!" She shook her head vigorously, and for a moment he thought she might be angry, but she burst into a fit of giggles.

"Here, let me help." Charles rolled over on his side and tenderly picked tree crumbs out of her thick tresses. Her laughter subsided as she gazed into his mirth-filled eyes. The next thing she knew he had lifted her chin upwards and placed a light kiss on her lips.

"Annabelle." He breathed her name.

She gave him a playful push and moved out of his reach, where she scrambled to her feet and brushed off her riding skirt. He lay there looking at her, and she dared to offer him her hand. Pulling him to his feet, she ordered, "Come along, Charles; there is much more to be seen."

"Yes, Madam."

They departed hand in hand.

Chapter 9

Buck swung Mattie round and round until she squealed, breathless. Annabelle and Claire watched from the porch, laughing as the two of them behaved like newlyweds. When the couple finally approached, arm in arm, the girls embraced the sheriff, each in turn.

"Welcome home, Buck," Annabelle said as she released the giant man.

"It is good to be back." Buck's voice was husky.

The women buzzed around him like bees over a honeycomb. Once inside, Mattie set a mug of coffee in front of him and asked, "Hungry?"

"Just a snack, if you have something."

Mattie shined an apple on her skirt and handed it to him. "Now, tell us all about your trip."

"How is Thaddeas?" Annabelle asked.

"Did you see any Indians?" Claire wondered.

"Whoa, one question at a time." The sheriff raised his thick, leathery hand to stop the attack. "Thad held up, a bit haggard from the first leg of travel—but doing good enough. One of the hardest things I ever did was say good-bye to the lad. There was a group headed in his direction, so he won't be traveling alone, which is safer. As for his sorrow, that will take some time."

"Poor Thad." Claire sniffed. "You're sure he's safe then, from the Indians and all?"

"He's in the Lord's care," Mattie pointed out.

"We need to continue to pray for him daily." Buck studied their faces. "The Indians are up to something. We met a Lieutenant Brooks from Fort Wayne under the command of Capt. William Wells. They believe we're on the verge of an Indian uprising. The captain sent him to scout out information on Chief Tecumseh and his brother The Prophet. . . Mattie!"

Buck quickly reached out to steady his wife, who had turned pale and limp. "Are you all right? Please, don't be frightened."

"I–I'm fine," she protested.

"I'm sure we'll be safe here, so close to town." He assured her as he patted her hand.

"Tecumseh!" Annabelle remembered her friend mentioning that name. "Rebecca Galloway told me about him. Surely he is harmless. He's a frequent visitor in their home. Why, she even reads to him."

Buck scowled, considering her comments. Then she added as an afterthought, "It's almost like she's sweet on him."

"Don't be ridiculous." Claire rolled her eyes. "He's an Indian."

"When did you have such a long talk with Rebecca?" Buck asked.

"At the box social Sunday night."

Claire piped up, "Speaking of the social, Annabelle has a new beau."

"Oh, Claire, stop it!"

Claire's face took on a peachy glow as she continued to tease her sister. "Charles Harrison, a gentleman from Boston."

"He's new to the valley. Won't be stayin'," Mattie offered. "He's thinkin' about fundin' the new National Road."

"I thought it was to be government funded," Buck said. "How did you meet this stranger?"

"He's not exactly a stranger. He comes to church. Anyway, we're just friends."

"He bought Annabelle's boxed lunch," Claire giggled.

Mattie took pity on Annabelle and changed the subject. "The reverend is sending the money to Luke's orphanage."

Buck chuckled. "It's not exactly Luke's orphanage, but the children sure look up to him. He's a fine young man."

"Tell us about him and the children," Claire begged.

"There are fourteen children. Such sad stories! There's a set of brothers, little tykes whose folks and siblings died of typhoid; another family of three, deserted by their ma and pa because there were too many mouths to feed." He thought of little Barney and his brothers and sisters. It was too painful; he did not mention them. "The children are loved now. Pity is, it could be too late for some of them. You see, some were alone or abused for years before the Murdocks heard about them.

"Catherine and Jesse Murdock parent them like they were their own, and Luke spends every afternoon with them. He helps with some of the teaching—they have schooling there at the home."

Buck rubbed his chin and nodded thoughtfully. "Yep, Luke is doing good. His faith in God is strong as a buffalo, and along with the Murdocks, he is doing the Lord's work by providing those younguns with love and care."

Claire clung like moss to every word Buck said. "I wish I could help. Do you think I could?"

"Well, I don't know, Claire." The question took Buck by surprise. Annabelle stared in disbelief at her sister.

"Claire! Are you crazy?"

"We were orphans, weren't we? The Lord provided us with a home. There's a Scripture I've been thinking about. Let me read it." Claire brushed past Annabelle in a hurry to find her Bible. In moments she returned. "Here it is. Matthew 10:8: 'Freely ye have received, freely give.' I like that. I think that's the way it's meant to be."

"Are you telling me that God caused our folks to be killed so that we can go help orphans?"

"No, of course not. But when you can feel other folks' pain, you can help them better."

"Well, Claire, you do that enough for the two of us."

"Girls, we can talk about this later," Mattie interrupted. "We'll give it some thought. Right now it's time for supper, and I'll need ya both in the kitchen."

"Oh, Mattie?" Buck called.

"Yes?"

"Do you know anything about a note that was left on my desk at the office, something about another prowler at Ben's?"

"What? Why, no."

"Hm. Wonder what it's about."

❧❧

Annabelle's eighteenth birthday came and went in October. The weeks sped by as she spent many hours with Charles. Riding together had become a regular occurrence since the day they had met accidentally by the creek.

Annabelle battled pendulum emotions. Sometimes she soared in the clouds, romancing with Charles, but most often she sank into depression, unable to get her mind off Thaddeas. Unconsciously, she weighed the differences between the two men.

Unpredictable Charles Harrison swept Annabelle off her feet with suave charm one moment and turned cold as ice the next. Yet he possessed all of the things she coveted—a good family, wealth, charm, and looks. Many nights she lay awake, considering him. He was attracted to her, but lacked any feelings of commitment. She asked herself, *Would he propose marriage? Is that what I want? Would Thaddeas approve?*

Thad had sent two telegrams. The first came from the Spread Eagle Tavern in Philadelphia on October 17, saying he was fine. She worried about his safety until his second telegram arrived on November 4. "Arrived safe, Boston." Her heart remained heavy even with this assurance, and she missed him sorely.

Chapter 10

Thad shook his dark, curly head as he looked about him and hastened his gait alongside his brother. The stench of swine overpowered him. Instinctively, his nose wrinkled its protestation. Boston, referred to as the "swineless city," was not true to its nickname today.

A pig drover, bringing hogs to market, created a general disturbance, maneuvering his herd through the main thoroughfare. Dogs yipped at the strays, which squealed and staggered back into the waddling procession.

When he rounded the corner at Tremont Street, leaving the confusion behind, Thad loosened his necktie in a frustrated effort to resist the phantom that accompanied him wherever he went. Annabelle was ever on his mind. Her words echoed through his memory, *"And what is wrong with wealth?"* He had to admit that it was a great deal more pleasant than the poverty he encountered in parts of Boston.

After living in luxury for the past two weeks, Thad wondered if he had been too hard on Annabelle. After all, he had never been in need himself. But then neither had Annabelle. He grew weary of his thoughts. On an impulse, he turned to his brother. "Leon, where does Mary Beth work?"

"Why, she is a dairy maid."

"I know that, but where?"

"Oh, on Bromfield and Washington."

"Really? Could we swing by there?"

"Of course; she'd like that."

Leon, an older version of Thaddeas, was more suited to city life. He could not understand Thad's infatuation with the western wilderness.

Leon had insisted that Thaddeas return for the reading of the will. Hoping Thad's call to adventure would diminish once he laid eyes on Boston again, Leon planned for his brother to join him in the family business.

Mary Beth Edwards. If that was what it took to interest Thad, well. . .

They turned and walked south, two streets out of their normal trek, and soon approached a large brick building where the dairy women put in their long hours. The huge room they entered smelled musty and looked bleak except for the stone fireplace that graced the very center of the expanse. Here the girls gathered periodically to warm themselves.

Intrigued, Thad and Leon observed the various stages of the process. They noticed an adjoining springhouse that appeared cold and damp, where shallow pans separated the cream. At the opposite wall, some women churned, and others kneaded and pressed cream into a solid consistency, using their hands. There they spotted her.

"Mary Beth!" Thad waved his arm in greeting.

A slender, light-haired girl with turquoise eyes patted a pale lump with delicate hands. As she recognized her visitors, a smile formed. Mary Beth and Thaddeas had renewed their acquaintance when she had accompanied her mother on a recent visit to the Larson home. Mary Beth had changed in the five years Thad had lived in Ohio.

Both attended the Old North Church on Hull Street and held many things in common. Miss Edwards's family occupied the same class as Thad's, that of the wealthy merchant class. The young woman was gentle hearted, yet not bashful. She loved adventure and could always be found out "doing" something. Just so, Mary Beth recently had hired on as a dairy maid to fill in for a sick friend who attended her church, so the girl would not lose her job.

Since his return to Boston, Thad had noticed Mary Beth's attentive manner on the occasions when they had met at church functions, which did much to restore his torn ego. He found her warm and sympathetic.

"Such gallant callers, I am honored." Mary Beth tilted her head in a slight bow, but the words were not meant to mock. Then she smiled brilliantly and motioned with her arm. "See! Is it not amazing?"

"Indeed," Thaddeas agreed. "So many girls in one place."

"Oh, you!" Mary Beth's head bobbed with amusement. "Come. Let me show you how they make cheese." Her enthusiasm was infectious as they toured the dairy. She explained how they used the cow's stomach lining that had enzymes to solidify milk into curds. The women squeezed the milk through cheesecloth, then compressed it in a cheese press. They peered through a long, open window into a room where shelves of cheese aged.

When they completed the tour, she asked, "Now, what really brought you boys around?" Leon nodded toward his brother.

Thaddeas moved close so she alone could hear his voice. "I've been thinking about you, wondering if you would mind if I came calling?"

Her voice, soft and faintly reverberating, was like a caress. "I'd like that."

"Tonight?" Thad asked.

She smiled at him in wonder. "I would be delighted."

"What time would be convenient?"

"Seven o'clock. Oh, no." Her face took on a look of disappointment as she reconsidered. "I promised Mother to take supper to a family who lives on our street. I am sorry."

"Can't I go along?"

"Of course." She brightened. "If you like."

"Good, I'll pick you up in our carriage. Seven o'clock."

"Thank you, Thaddeas."

"Good day, Mary Beth."

"Thanks for dropping by, boys."

"Bye, Mary Beth," Leon called.

"Nice girl." Thad whistled as they walked past the bare trees lining Bromfield Street. Unconsciously, he plucked off a single leaf, nearly the last of its kind, hanging on tenaciously against frost's assault. He released it carelessly, and it floated downward to the ground. "Nice girl," he repeated.

Leon suppressed a grin.

"Look, Leon!" He slapped his brother across the chest. "The potter! Let's surprise Mother with something new!"

❧

Amelia Larson turned the smooth, cool vase, admiring the piece at various angles, then set it aside and patted Thad's hand. "Thank you, Darling."

Thad looked at the plump, soft hand resting on his, cuffed in lace, expressing warmth and caring. Then he considered the sweet, familiar face of his mother, whose eyes now misted. "I want you to be happy, Son."

"I know, Mother. And I am."

"No, I would not call it happiness. Perhaps testing or confusion?"

"You are wise." He squeezed her fingertips.

"But what is so troubling?"

"I love the West. The folks in the Ohio Valley are different from the people in Boston. They work hard and enjoy the small things in life that we take for granted. They need to depend on each other because of destiny itself—weather, Indians, wild animals, cold, hunger—and it makes them a caring lot. They're honest and simple." His mother did not interrupt, yet tried to imagine the Ohio settlers as he painted their description.

"Your cousins, they are lovely girls?"

"Yes, Mother. Kate, of course, is married. She is beautiful, perfection in all ways." Amelia smiled at what must be an exaggeration, but he did not notice. "Claire is pretty on the inside; she is kindness personified. They are Christians. Then, there is Annabelle." How could he describe her?

"Tell me about Annabelle." Instantly, Amelia ascertained that this was the lass who caused Thad's confusion.

"Annabelle. She is quite stunning—no, absolutely gorgeous—full of life. . ." He paused to find proper words to portray the woman he loved. ". . .beautiful as a spring day and deadly as a rattlesnake." He sighed. "She's a redheaded spitfire, irresistible, unreasonable, and, I am afraid, not a believer."

"And you love this girl?"

"Ah, Mother, yes. And she will be the death of me." Amelia waited patiently until he continued. "I've loved her since I laid eyes on her, but she was too young, only fourteen. I waited patiently for her to mature, which she did physically. But she's still a child at heart. Before I got your letter saying Father had died, I asked her to marry me. She turned me down flat. I asked her again before I left, but she said no."

"I am sorry. She must be a foolish girl." So recently experiencing the loss of one she loved deeply, Amelia sympathized with her son.

"She has dreams high as the sky, and they are everything to her. Annabelle covets all that money and city life can provide."

"I do not understand then; what is the problem? Doesn't she know you can provide all of that for her? Surely from the reading of the will, you realize you are a very wealthy young man. Why, with our investments, and. . ."

"Mother," Thad interrupted, "I did not tell her. I wanted her love."

"I see."

Thad scowled. "Of course I did not even realize how affluent we were, until the will was read. It is ironic." A dreamy smile froze Amelia's face. "What is it, Mother?"

"I was thinking of Mary Beth. The two of you are very much alike. You both could have anything money can buy yet stubbornly push to make your own way." She considered their similar convictions. "And you share a strong commitment to serve Jesus."

"You sound like a matchmaker, Mother."

"Do I? I'm sorry."

"Actually, I have been weighing those very thoughts. As a matter of fact, I'm calling on her tonight."

Amelia's face lit, glowing like the oil lamp on the nearby parlor stand, while Thaddeas reddened to several shades lighter than the scarlet velvet draperies hanging across the room.

Thaddeas's mother fingered the lace-edged handkerchief on her lap. "Thad, we want what is best for you. Your brother does not really need you in the shop, but he wants you there. Of course there is plenty of room for you in the business. Leon would go to great lengths to keep you here in Boston, and I hope you decide to stay with us. But it must be your decision."

The servant girl entered the parlor. "Ma'am, dinner is served."

"Thaddeas, shall we join your brother?"

"Yes, I'm starved."

Chapter 11

Mattie Larson's black-booted feet stepped off the distance between Tucker House and Cooper's General Store. She shuffled thoughts as she walked, concentrating on her shopping list: two brown spools for Mrs. Jennings's gown, cinnamon for Thanksgiving pies, and she wanted to look at the woolen stockings.

She lifted her skirts high to step up onto the wooden walkway that edged the shops in Beaver Creek. The timbers had weathered rough, yet she managed to keep her clothing off the splintered edges. A waft of autumn breeze roused a dust devil, and she paused to watch the swirling leaves.

As she shifted her gaze to the folks who occupied the shops and roadways, a tall figure across the street caught her eye. Unnerved, she ducked behind a post and watched. The brown-haired military man made long strides toward The Lone Wolf, the local tavern.

Mattie clutched the breast of her winter cape, digging her fingernails into its deep pile. *Wade! It is you!* Years had molded the boyish face into a stern, sober one; yet she recognized the man. Her heart somersaulted, just like twenty-three years earlier. What should she do? Frantically she rushed into Cooper's General Store.

Elias Cooper noticed the breathless entrance and pale, stricken face. Very little slipped by him, and he wondered why the stranger, a lieutenant, had frightened her.

"Mattie, somethin' wrong?"

"No!" she snapped. "I'm jest needin' some notions." She drew her torso to full height, forced a smile, and marched trembling legs to the back of the store. There hidden from view, she leaned against the rack of many colored threads to steady herself. Her finger twirled the soft spools, and she thumbed a brown one loose from its peg.

"Dear God, what does this mean? What am I to do?" she prayed. Then a picture flashed, and she relived the scene, four years earlier, of a snowy December morning in Buck's office. It was where he had proposed, and she had told him her life's story. She quickly collected the other items on her list. She must talk to Buck.

Moments later she entered the room where she had bared her soul that other day. The furnishings remained the same. She saw the stone fireplace and its wooden-beamed mantel supporting Buck's old holster. The things that

Buck cherished—from his deer antlers to his bearskin rug—and the familiar smells of leather and coffee stirred her, and she flung herself into his arms.

"Darling, what's wrong?" Buck scooped her into his all-encompassing embrace and waited until she could speak.

Her husband's arms felt strong and protective, his chest warm and comforting just like his unreserved love. Mattie succumbed to sobs. "I–I don't deserve you."

"Don't be silly, Mattie. Tell me. What is it?"

"I love ya, Buck. Ya know I do."

Buck smiled. "I'll never tire of those words. I waited so long to hear them." He stroked her back, encouraging her to continue while a knot constricted in his stomach, for it was not like her to respond hysterically. He pulled out a chair for each of them as he mentally prepared himself.

"Remember the day ya proposed, and I told ya about my past?" Buck nodded, and she hung her head in shame, stumbling for words. "I told ya about gettin' pregnant when I was young without bein' married."

"Mattie, there's no need to go over this."

"I never named the father."

"And now you want to tell me?"

Mattie nodded her head. "Lt. Wade Brooks."

Buck sat motionless, taking in the meaning. Putting a name to the fact cut deep. His stomach lurched, yet he remained calm.

"Why are you telling me this now, Mattie?"

"I don't know. It jest seemed the right thing to do. I saw him in town a minute ago. I don't know why he's here. Ya mentioned meetin' him at the Golden Lamb. It was the first I knew he was a lieutenant."

Then Buck remembered Mattie's reaction the day he returned from Dayton, her pale face at the mention of the man's name. How foolish he had been to think she was frightened of the Indians. "Did you talk to him?" he asked.

"No! And I don't want to, but since he turned up, I wanted ya to know, firsthand, from me."

"Thank you, Mattie. It doesn't change anything between us. That's the important thing." He patted her hand. "We'll just take this one step at a time and see it through together."

❧

The wind brushed Annabelle's curved form, billowing her riding skirt and whipping her hair. Even Dusty's mane tossed about like waves of corn silk. The gallop and gale invigorated Annabelle, and she was hard put to rein in at the designated meeting place—the same spot where she had been meeting Charles for weeks.

She smiled, satisfied that she had arrived early enough to arrange her hair before he showed. Just a trace of a musky scent lingered in the air, the same as Charles used. Instantly her curiosity was aroused. Then she noticed a paper flapping in the breeze from a tall beech tree. She dismounted, tied Dusty to a bush, and investigated. It must be from Charles. Snatching the note, she read:

Annabelle,
Another time, another place, and I could have loved you. But that is not to be our destiny. Duty calls me away, just as it brought us to-gether. Please do not hate me. I'll remember you forever, my copper-haired country maiden.

Fondly,
Charles

"Of all the nerve! I cannot believe this! *Country maiden!*" Annabelle crushed the paper and threw it to the ground in disgust. Then she stomped about flailing her arms like a mad hen, muttering loathsome things about Boston gentlemen, ending with, "They think they are so high and mighty, running off to their precious Boston! Everyone I love disappears, back to that horrid place. Thaddeas, I hate you! Why did you leave?"

Hurt and confused, she stooped, picked up the crumpled note, and settled on a nearby log. It was a place where she and Charles had sat together many times. She carefully ironed out the wrinkles with her palm and reread its contents. "Fondly, Charles." Cupping her face in her hands, she succumbed to tears.

Attired in proper military fashion, Charles Harrison dismounted and saluted his lieutenant.

"Sir."

"Cpl. Harrison. What is your report?"

"Confirmed. Her maiden name was Tucker, just like you thought. Their ages, twenty-two, eighteen, and sixteen, Sir."

The lieutenant stared across the brown meadow, perfect jaws clenched under eyes shadowed with heaviness. Then he relaxed and nodded. "As I suspected. The evidence is sufficient. No more prowling around for you. Consider this assignment finished. Let's mount and ride together to the fort. Tell me all you know, Corporal."

Chapter 12

The Larson wagon appeared just as the Thanksgiving bird that turned on Rev. Wheeler's fireplace spit was roasted to perfection. Luke, who was home for the holiday, rushed to greet the guests.

"Luke! It's so good to see you!" Mattie embraced the brawny young man who towered over her, then held him at arm's length. "Jest let me look at ya. Healthy and glowin' with the Lord's blessin'."

"Hello, Luke," Buck greeted the young Wheeler, who returned his iron handshake.

"Your visit meant a lot to me, Buck. Lifted my spirits tremendously."

"It was my pleasure, though it gave me a lot to think about."

Luke gave Annabelle a gentle squeeze. "You've become a charming young woman."

Annabelle blushed under his inspection. "Welcome home, Luke."

Then he spied his favorite, shyly hanging back. Luke held out his arms, and Claire flew into them. Through their correspondence, he knew more about this young woman's thoughts, feelings, and struggles than did her own family. Suddenly aware of this, Claire turned bashful. Luke assessed the situation and released her, taking in the tender age—twelve when he left, fifteen at their last meeting, now a budding sixteen. He tried to ease her jitters.

"I am especially pleased to see you, Claire. I have so much to tell you."

"You do?"

"Yes, and you encouraged me with your faithful letters." Claire soon warmed under his reassuring manner, and her devotion quickened when he asked her about Freckles, the cat he had given her as a gift several years earlier.

Mary Wheeler interrupted the eye-watering homecoming by calling them to dinner. Eleven gathered around the Thanksgiving table. Emmett glowed with satisfaction at having his entire family present.

"Let us pray," he bellowed. "Thank You, gracious Father, for each loved one here today, for the labor of their hands and hearts, for this bounteous food set before us, and mostly for Your precious Son, Jesus. Amen."

Amens chorused the room, and then the place charged with the buzz of chatter and the scraping of utensils against pewter plates. "Tell us about the work you are doin', Luke." Mattie pointed her fork in his direction, giving him the floor.

"Where do I start?" The young man scratched his straw-colored head.

"With the children," Claire nearly burst with enthusiasm. Expectant eyes round and blue, not willing to miss a word he had to say, watched his every move.

"All right. Cody and Gabe Calton are the youngest—eighteen months and three years. Their folks died with typhoid last spring so they've been in the orphanage for about seven months. The home consists mostly of older children, because babies usually get snapped up by relatives or childless families. I'm surprised this pair hasn't."

Luke paused to look around the circle of friends and relatives. Noting their attentiveness, he continued. "Adorable tykes, but it makes things extra tough, caring for a little one with so much to be done at the orphanage—schooling, cooking, clothing, and care. Of course, the older ones pitch in."

Kate placed her hand across her mouth to stifle a sob and kept her eyes glued to her plate. She felt Ben's sympathetic gaze and could not look at her husband for fear of breaking down in front of the family.

"There is one boy who I wish you would keep in your prayers. He is the oldest, fourteen." Luke jabbed at his peas with his fork, scooting them around his plate as he spoke. "Name is Adam Parks. Beaten and left for dead when he was about nine by his ma's new husband, he lived on the streets in Philadelphia until he hired on with a hard man that worked him excessively and also battered the poor boy.

"Adam ran away and ended up in Dayton, where he has been with us for about a year. Last week the blacksmith took him on as an indentured servant. He's a decent man, but Adam doesn't trust people. I pray that he won't run away and end up God knows where, but that he will give it a chance. . . ." Luke choked up and could not continue. "I planned to stop in and visit him, but I made this trip home just when he needed me."

"He's in the Lord's hands, Son. God wants to give us the desires of our hearts. He knows yours, and we're grateful for this visit."

"I want to help, Luke. What can I do?" Claire stood to her feet, and all eyes fastened on her.

Her plea touched Luke's heart. James and Frank had listened attentively, and now Frank nudged Mary. "Ma, Christmas is coming up. Could we do something for the children?"

"Why, that's a wonderful idea! What could we do, Luke?" Mattie joined in the excitement.

"Let's go to Dayton; let's visit them," Claire suggested. She nearly danced, hoping to see the home and get involved.

"Luke?" his father questioned, and silence hovered over the group as they waited for the response.

A huge grin birthed beneath quivering lips to tickle Luke's newly grown mustache. His sea blue eyes lit like candles, and the crinkles in his forehead indicated pleasure. "I—I don't know what to say."

"I say, let's start planning." Buck set his fist on the table like a judge's gavel, and a babbling of ideas erupted.

Frank interrupted, "The kids need gifts."

Mattie ordered, "Luke, have Mrs. Murdock send us a list of things they'll be needin' right away, when you git back."

Annabelle's brow creased in thought. It seemed to her that things were getting out of hand. *Sure the children are sad little ragamuffins, but why do I have to get involved? Where is my life headed?* She answered her own question. *Surely in the wrong direction—visiting the poorhouse itself. Oh, heavens! Every-thing is out of control.* And she twisted the napkin on her lap between two clenched fists.

As usual, Kate and Annabelle sought each other out for a bosom talk. Just now they walked through Emmett Wheeler's apple orchard. Though they were fully cloaked, the air pierced them, stinging their faces a raw pink. Kate's mittened hand patted her sister's arm. "You're going through some hard times, aren't you?"

Annabelle's reply spewed forth like a volcano eruption. "Charles jilted me. You'll never believe it. He left a note hanging on a tree. Said he'd always remember his. . ." She spit out the last two words, ". . .country maiden."

Kate knew the pet name had injured her sister's pride. "Did you love him?"

"No." Annabelle kicked at the ground.

Kate, noting the quick retort and angry response, asked, "Are you sure?"

"I'm sure. I—I love Thaddeas."

Kate clapped her padded hands. "I knew it." Then she hugged Annabelle. "It's no use. He's gone."

"It's not too late. I know! Send him a telegram."

Annabelle giggled. "A telegram?"

"Sure, it would be so romantic."

Green eyes fired, and copper curls bobbed as Annabelle began to scheme. "A love telegram. I'll do it!" The girls stood in one spot, drafting the mes-sage, puffs of vapor shooting upward at each new idea, while rubbing their hands and stomping their feet to keep warm.

Annabelle turned toward Kate. "Thanks so much. I feel better. Ready to go in? I'm about frozen."

"Just one thing, first. I haven't talked to Ben, but I'm going to adopt those babies."

"What babies?"

161

"Cody and Gabe, the little boys Luke described. That is, if Ben is willing."

"Kate, I don't know what to say."

"Pray about it, Annabelle," her sister pressed.

"I can't promise that. You know I'm not big on praying."

"Start. It means so much to me."

"I'm sure Ben will understand. Two babies, already grown—that would sure change things around here."

Kate beamed and they headed back to the house with their spirits soaring in anticipation.

Chapter 13

Taking a reprieve from the blurry numbers dancing before his blood shot eyes, Thaddeas uprighted his taut body, then peered out the foggy window, clearing a circle of vision with his shirt sleeve. The leather shop was grossing large profits, and he would have to speak with Leon about securing new investments.

Surprised, he noticed the late afternoon sky had blackened while he had pored over ledger pages. The heavens rumbled warnings, and the clouds churned, prompting him to prepare for home before the storm's fury hit the city. He set about to put his desk in order when a chill rushed across his back and ruffled the papers he had worked to straighten. Just as suddenly, the door banged directly behind him, causing him to jump.

"Telegram for Thaddeas Larson."

"Here!" Thaddeas waved to the lanky youth who called his name while he took in the bundled body and woolen-scarfed head.

"The wind is stirring up, Sir. Sorry to startle you."

Thad winced as he exchanged the telegram for a coin and wondered what the communication could contain. His last wire had been bad news. He remembered to thank the lad just before he left, and shivered as another mighty gust blitzed through the office.

Easing himself back into the padded chair behind his polished desk, he utilized the armrests and stared at the envelope. "Oh, Lord," he prayed, "prepare my heart." He tore open the seal and pulled out the contents. Greedily he devoured the message all at once, then digested it word for word.

> *Dearest Thaddeas,*
> *Make me yours. I love you. Boston suits fine.*
> *Annabelle*

He ruffled his bushy black hair with thick trembling hands, reading the message until he had it memorized, etched forever as a permanent fixture in his mind. A myriad of emotions surged through his immobilized body—elation, wonder, disbelief, skepticism, then anger. There were few words and many suggestions of interpretation. The part about Boston disturbed him and unseated a wagonload of doubts.

Resentment mounted steadily, and he clenched his fists. This was just

163

like her, making demands: "Make me yours." The next part, "I love you," cut to the heart. He would not be taken in, however; she had said those words before, along with the explanation, "but not that way." And the final blow, "Boston suits fine." Of course it does, suits her high and mighty taste, her lofty ambitions.

Uncle Buck must have told her how the land lays. *She's after my money, my influence. Well, I won't settle for that. I don't have to. What a fool I've been.* He crumpled the paper and hurled it into a wastebasket. Grabbing for his coat, he strapped on his boots and threw open the latch.

A blast of wind snatched at his hat. He pulled it down tightly over his ears, set his shoulders against the tempest, and stomped off for home.

Before he reached his house on Beacon and Spruce, gigantic lacy flakes enveloped him, salting the shoulders of his dark jacket and covering his tracks. The Lord dusted Boston with its first snowfall of the season, but it fell unheralded by Thaddeas, who plodded on single-mindedly.

Stubborn pride settled in like the blanket of fog that so often fell over Boston, obscuring the vision of the city's occupants. It blinded him to the simple truth that Annabelle loved him. Unintelligible thoughts persisted. *She's after my inheritance. She does not want me; I'm like a brother to her—yet she will not release me. How can she be so cruel? I cannot live like this; I can take no more.*

These ideas, like whirring arrows, set him in flight, turning him in the direction of Mary Beth's house. That would clear his head; she was an intelligent woman who cared about him.

Hours later, more to safeguard his affections than anything else, he made a hasty decision and heard himself utter the unrehearsed words, "I love you. Will you marry me?"

Mary Beth drew away, frightened at the intensity of his dark eyes. The coveted words tantalized her willing heart, but her spirit resisted. No trace of romance lit his face, only pain and desperation, unrelentless.

"Mary Beth?" He repeated her name.

"I do love you, Thad, but we must be sure."

"I'm sure. I've never been more determined in my life. Marry me," he urged.

"Yes." The word was soft as velvet, and Thad pulled her almost roughly into his embrace.

Mary Beth's heart whispered encouragement. She genuinely loved this dark-haired beau but sensed his love lacked fullness. Oh, she could not doubt the passion pulsing through his sturdy body, but she wondered if it was enough to last a lifetime.

Thaddeas reflected on his day. What a long one it had been, starting with hours laboring over figures, then the unexpected telegram, and ending with his call on Mary Beth. She was a sweet young thing, innocent, self-sacrificing. He could not ask for a better wife or a prettier bride. After all, how long could one resist such a loving countenance, or those puppy eyes that had revealed infatuation for him from day one?

Then there was their families' joy when they shared their plans. Leon and Mother had been elated to learn he would stay on in Boston—at least for the time being. Who knew? Maybe some day Mary Beth and he would travel west. She'd make a good wife, and she would be willing to live wherever he decided.

Only one thing remained undone, and it would be the hardest, the most final. He swallowed the lump in his throat and scuffed across the room to rummage through the drawer of a small desk that sat beneath his bedroom window.

Settling himself in its accompanying cane chair, with paper and pen poised, he stared at the delicate designs of snow and frost fast forming on the window and penned, "Dear Annabelle."

The words engraved upon his soul played over and over in his mind. "Make me yours. I love you. Boston suits fine."

Thad's thoughts rambled, and he jumped up, threw a couple more logs into his fireplace, and paced the floor. Visions of copper curls glistening in the sun's light haunted him. Eyes green and full of fire, saucy cheeks, upturned nose, and tiny curved body all made up the creature who had commanded his heart for so long.

He collapsed on his bed, burying his dark face and heavy eyes into a comfortable feather-stuffed pillow, and willed Mary Beth's image into his mind. This would not do. He roused himself, returning to the task at hand, and yanked at the cane chair. It toppled over, and parchment paper floated helter-skelter about the floor. This was going to be a long night, but he would not go to bed until this letter was written. Then he could make a new beginning, one with Mary Beth.

Chapter 14

The first week's waiting was the hardest, expecting a telegram at any moment, scanning the horizon for the messenger boy, jumping out of her skin at every knock on the door. Even now, the second week, hope lingered. But if no word came by today, Annabelle resolved that Thad's reply would come via letter, taking four to six weeks—or maybe he would just show up at the door.

Annabelle reined Dusty in at the hitching post just outside Cooper's General Store. She knew, humanly speaking, there could be no letter yet; however, her heart raced as she made her way to the shop. Brushing the wrinkles out of her riding habit, she entered, her skirt swishing to the gentle movement of her hips.

It was enough to stop the heart of Andy Benson. Bart Barnes punched his buddy, "Look, across the street—Annabelle Larson!"

"I saw her." The young man continued to stare even after the massive plank door enveloped her and she vanished from his sight. Without a word, Andy plodded toward the street in the direction of Cooper's General Store. Bart snickered and caught up with his friend.

The country lads paused a moment, then Andy pushed open the portal, and they entered.

"Miss Larson, howdy." Both boys took off their hats and stood still for her inspection.

"Hello, Andy, Bart."

"You here to order some Christmas surprises?"

"In a way. Do you remember Luke Wheeler?"

"Yeah, sure! The preacher's son."

"Right. He works at an orphanage in Dayton, and our family is going there for Christmas."

"To the orphanage? What for?"

Annabelle smiled. "That's the same question I asked. But Claire is so sentimental. She's convinced everyone to get involved, a charity project."

"Oh, I see. Yeah, Claire, she's got a soft spot all right." When Annabelle gave Bart a strange look, he quickly added, "No harm intended, Ma'am."

"None taken." Annabelle looped her arm through Andy's. They had known each other all of their lives, and though she knew he was sweet on her,

166

she did not take him seriously, never considering her effect on him when she offered the slightest encouragement. She chattered as she led him toward the counter. "Mr. Cooper, I'm here to pick up the paper that we ordered."

"Sure, Annabelle, it's in."

She released Andy's arm and expressed delight at the package that Elias unwrapped: a stack of natural-colored parchment paper, cut into half sheets with holes punched in.

"Wow, you aren't going into teaching, are you, Annabelle?" Andy asked.

Laughing, Annabelle denied it. "No. Claire is making diaries for the older girls at the orphanage. She thinks it might ease their pain to write down their feelings. Buck is getting the leather covers made, and Mattie is supplying the ribbon to bind the books together. Wouldn't mind having one myself."

"Maybe Claire will make you one for Christmas. I would if I knew how," Andy said quietly.

"Oh, Andy, you're so sweet," she said in one breath, and then, "Mr. Cooper, do we have any mail?" in the next.

"Jest a letter for the sheriff. Want it?"

"I'll take it." Annabelle placed it in the pocket of her riding skirt and fastened her coat as Elias carefully replaced the wrappings around the parchment paper and then offered her the bundle.

Andy grabbed for it and escorted the young woman outside, where he helped her mount.

"Have a good day," he called as Annabelle rode away. He watched her until she disappeared around a distant bend.

Bart spoke from a few feet away. "Why don't you call on her?"

"My timing is bad, I guess. I was all set to after Thaddeas left. Then that Harrison fellow showed up." Disgusted looks crossed both their faces, remembering the obnoxious intruder.

"I hear he's gone. No one's seen him for weeks."

"I know. Guess now there's no excuse, but I can't find the courage. She's just too elegant." Bart nodded his head in understanding.

❧❧

"Look, Mattie, the paper was in!"

"Land sakes, let me see." They fingered the fragile paper wrappings, then Mattie said, "No! Go get Claire first."

"Where is she?"

"Out in the chicken coop scrounging for feathers. We still need more stuffing for those pillows."

"Even after all those feathers we got from Ben and the reverend?"

"Yes. Now, quickly, go get yer sister."

Annabelle flew out the door, letting it bang. She turned the corner where the giant hickory spread its bare limbs and stopped in her tracks. Snow! The first snowfall of the season in Beaver Creek. She looked skyward, and wet flakes sprinkled her face. The flakes melted upon impact with the earth. She watched the process in fascination, each time expecting a trace of snow to remain upon the ground, disappointed when it vanished leaving only a damp circle.

"Claire! Claire!"

"In here." The call came as she suspected it would from the little shanty where the brown-winged fowl bunked. There was not a bird around, however, for when Claire had approached with gunny sack in hand, they had fled for their lives. Stooped over with hair dangling in her face and spreading down her back, Claire diligently picked at each feather that she spied—a tedious process. She did not look over her shoulder as she spoke. "Yes?"

"Your paper came."

"It did?" She yanked the strings on the mouth of the sack, swung it over her shoulder, and crouched to crawl through the small opening of the coop to greet her sister. "Great!"

"Missed one." Annabelle flicked a feather off Claire's cheek.

The girl scolded, "Hey, don't do that." She bent to pick up the solitary feather that had floated earthward landing on her boot, then noticed with pleasure, "It's snowing."

"Isn't it lovely? Look! It's sticking." The girls paused to take in its beauty, letting childhood memories flood over them. In a matter of minutes, the sky grew dark and the snow fell in heavy flurries.

They started toward the house, amazed that their world could turn white in such a short period of time. Claire glanced over her shoulder and pointed to some fresh markings in the now snow-covered ground behind them. "Tracks! Remember how we used to follow the animal trails after a new-fallen snow?"

"Yes. But these are chicken tracks. And look where they lead. Right up those trees. They're roosting and waiting for us to clear out so they can return to their coop."

This brought Claire's thoughts back to the orphanage. "Hope it doesn't turn out to be a blizzard and ruin our trip to Dayton. Come on!" She hollered and rushed for the house.

"Mattie!" Claire called. "We won't have to cancel our trip for the snow, will we?"

Mattie frowned, fondling the unopened package containing Claire's paper. "I hope not. Depends on how deep or icy it gets. Nothin' we can do to change nature's doin's, so it won't do any good for ya ta worry 'bout it.

Now, let's take a look at that paper."

While Claire opened the parcel for inspection, Mattie planned out loud. "We need to pick up the rest of the new comforters the churchwomen are makin'. There's two more rag dolls ta make. The reverend and Mary's boys are doin' the boats for the smaller boys, Kate and Ben bought knives for the older boys, and the sheriff is gettin' the leather for your diaries."

"And I've enough feathers now for one more pillow." Claire and Mattie beamed with the satisfaction of accomplishment, but Annabelle's mind wandered.

She moved to the kitchen window and pushed the curtains aside to watch the winter storm. A chill tickled her spine, and she shuddered involuntarily. *I hope I hear from Thad before we leave for Dayton. Why doesn't he answer?*

Chapter 15

The weather cleared enough for travel, and a few days before Christmas the entire entourage pulled into Dayton's fogged and frozen thoroughfare without much fuss from bystanders. Such sights, and ones many times more odd, frequently graced the city's cobblestones. Annabelle's and Claire's eyes gaped wide. They hardly ever traveled, and still less frequently to a city.

They took in every aspect of the cluttered streets: the tall, groomed buildings, gloriously attired residents, and tattered beggars. Even as they watched from their wagon, a barefooted woman draped in a gray woolen shawl—partially covering her head as well as her back—stuck out a palm begging for a coin. "Jest need 'nuf for some firewood. My young 'uns are freezin' ta death," she called, exposing a nearly toothless mouth. Claire clapped her hand over her lips in horror as Buck tossed several coins toward the woman.

"Get out of the street!" yelled a small-built man dressed in a suit and overcoat. "Go on. Be off with you." He waved his walking stick, but the woman paid no heed to the insults the man hurled, instead snatching the fallen money off the ground and stuffing it into her bosom. Claire crooked her neck to stare at the woman, who staggered along the street behind their wagon's trek.

Annabelle began to understand how sheltered they had lived. She feared Claire would become fainthearted and reached a gloved hand toward her sister to utter some assurance when a raucous shout caught her attention. A clamor of unruly men gathered, encircling something as they hooted and shouted obscenities. "I believe it's a brawl," Annabelle said, aghast.

Buck yelled back at the girls, "Don't be afraid. It's just a cockfight."

"Oh, how awful." Claire grimaced and covered her eyes.

"Look!" Annabelle nudged her sister. "The theater! Just like Dorie described." Couples milled in front of a shop with a huge sign that announced the show time and performers. Annabelle strained to take it all in—the names on the billboard as well as what the ladies wore beneath their fur-trimmed cloaks.

As the wheels of the Larson wagon rumbled on, slipping into potholes, bouncing over rocks and pebbles, and clacking on the pavements, the jostled passengers soon realized they were leaving the heart of the city. Annabelle breathed deeply.

The smells were less pungent, the fog thinner. They must be going in the opposite direction of the river. But then it was hard to tell as the waters came from all directions and seemed to network everywhere about them.

Claire gripped her sleeve, and Annabelle shifted to look where her sister pointed.

"That must be it!"

Annabelle recoiled, seeing her fears materialize in the form of a drab stone building sprawled out before them, bleak and uninviting. The place looked frightfully neglected and just like Annabelle had imagined the asylum. She was not the least surprised when children appeared, dressed in drab colors and ill-fitted garments.

"Oh, aren't they something?" Claire elbowed her sister, with wheels turning in her head. They were not given time to speculate as Buck instantly appeared to lift them to the ground, where they rubbed out their stiff muscles.

When Luke saw the group, the same ten, all-inclusive, from Thanksgiving Day, he was overcome with gratitude, hugging each in turn, and introducing them to those nearby, which soon included Catherine and Jesse Murdock.

"Land sakes, it's too cold to stand outside. Let's get the ladies indoors," Catherine urged. Mrs. Catherine Murdock took Annabelle by surprise. *Why she's beautiful,* she thought. In one solid look she memorized the woman from her pink oval face to her pointed, high-topped boots. Wearing an expression of rapture and serenity in perfect harmony, she flashed crystal blue eyes encircled in long, dark lashes. An abundance of yellow hair framed the woman's pleasant features supported by a lily-white neck. Her white-collared blouse was neatly tucked into a gray woolen skirt, which swished as she walked away.

"I'll help with the livestock," her equally exuberant husband offered. At his voice, deep and vibrant, Annabelle turned to see what kind of man this woman had married. She drew in a sharp breath, for he easily passed her inspection. *Yes, he would do.* Blushing, she moved to catch up with the other women and the band of children now entering the offensive habitation.

They were led into a long, rectangular-shaped room with many odds and ends of furniture scattered about. Some benches lined one wall, and Annabelle noticed a green settee and several padded chairs situated in a circle in front of a cavernous fireplace. A small table and chairs occupied either end, one with a checkerboard and checkers stacked from recent play.

"This is our parlor, such as it is." Mrs. Murdock waved her arms to include the expanse. "We all meet here in the evening to read or play games and visit. Please, sit there by the fire and warm yourselves, ladies."

"Are we done fer the day, Mrs. Catherine?" a child's voice questioned.

"Yes, Dear." Mrs. Murdock smiled at the towheaded boy who stood before her, shifting from one foot to the other. "This is Barney Forbes." Barney nodded. "Barnabus, why don't you assemble the other children, and when the men return, we will make introductions all around." He agreed and rushed out of the room.

That evening, supper was held in a huge dining hall with three very long tables. Mr. and Mrs. Murdock sat at one table with seven girls, Luke was in charge of six boys at another, and the visitors occupied the third. Mrs. Murdock and two older girls, Amity Jones and Brooke Forbes, both fourteen, served the dinner of stew, dumplings, and apple cobbler.

Afterward when the women visitors moved to help with the cleanup, a bubbly red-haired girl called Lacy spoke up. "No, Ma'am. . .ladies. 'Tis our turn to do the dishes." She motioned to several boys and girls, aged seven to twelve, and they gathered the dishes.

"They take turns with various chores," Luke explained.

"Well, that may be," Mattie said, "but we want ta do our part while we're here."

"Very well." Mrs. Murdock seemed pleased. "But at least relax until tomorrow. I'm sure you're tired from your long journey."

They adjourned to the parlor, and Claire and Annabelle were soon encamped by a group of the older girls. One called Abigail spoke. "Brooke and I are sisters."

Brooke took up where her sister left off. "Hank, Barney, and Lonnie are our brothers." She pointed out two towheaded boys engaged in a game of marbles.

"Five of you?" Claire questioned.

"Yes, Ma'am." Abigail went on, "We don't get many visitors."

"Please, don't call me ma'am," Claire said. "Why I'm not much older than you are, or your sister. Just call me Claire."

Brooke shook her head. "No, that wouldn't be fitting. How about Miss Claire?"

"Good idea!" Claire patted her own sister's knee. "And this is Miss Annabelle, my sister." Suddenly, Annabelle was tongue-tied for the first time in her life.

Across the room Kate rocked, singing lullabies to a shy, sleepy-eyed baby boy. Ben bounced the baby's three-year-old brother, Gabe, upon his knee. Gabe's round, freckled face looked up at him in wonder.

"Give Cody horsy ride, too?"

"I think Cody is falling asleep," Ben answered. Kate listened to Ben's deep, soft voice, soothing the tiny child. She marveled that the boy resembled the large man who held him.

Annabelle, touched with pity, listened to snatches of conversation. The children seemed content with so little. Some excited and others leery about Christmas Day gathered across the room as Luke explained what the special day, honoring the birth of a holy child, would hold, concluding with the promise of lots of surprises.

Long after the stars peeped out, the last of the orphans departed to retire for the evening in their simple rooms, where identical bunks lined the walls. Annabelle wondered if she would survive this ordeal. She felt exhausted.

Chapter 16

Annabelle concentrated on her task of braiding Lacy Gray's unmanageable hair.

"Your hair's the same as mine," Lacy stated.

Annabelle considered the comparison. "I never liked it when folks said my hair was red—it would make me fighting mad."

"I know," the nine year old said softly.

"I'd say, nope, it's auburn, or copper-colored, or my favorite, cinnamon fluff."

"Cinnamon fluff?" The little girl wrinkled her nose, then remarked, "I like that."

"Or cinnamon sticks, since yours is neatly braided."

Lacy giggled.

"Now, quit squirming. We need to hurry. After all, it's Christmas morning."

Annabelle observed those crowded together to hear Luke read the Christmas story. Some reclined in chairs, others sprawled on the threadbare carpet. Excitement danced in the children's eyes. They looked forward to the times Luke read to them from his Bible, for his voice was animated and his large hands expressive. Because it was Christmas, the air was charged with the element of the unexpected.

Between pokes from the tiny fingers of Lacy and her sisters, who competed for her attention, Annabelle watched James and Frank roughhouse playfully with some of the boys who were as noisy as an Indian war party. Barney's head, as always, popped up from the center of the scuffle.

Cody and Gabe cuddled in the laps of Ben and Kate while Claire sat shoulder to shoulder between two older girls. Luke shook hands with a visitor, a burly blacksmith named Luther Woods, but when he came to Woods's indentured servant, Adam Parks, Luke gave the boy an emotional bear hug.

Rev. William Hamer, the Presbyterian preacher under whom Luke served, and his family were present. The dark-haired clergyman wore a look of approval.

At last Luke settled in a chair, opened his worn Bible, and began. Captivated, Annabelle realized Luke recited many portions from memory. " 'And there were in the same country shepherds abiding in the field, keeping watch over their flock by night. And, lo, the angel of the Lord came upon them, and the glory of the Lord shone round about them: and they were sore afraid. And the angel said unto them, "Fear not: for, behold, I bring you good tidings of great joy, which shall be to all people. For unto you is born this day in the city of David a Saviour, which is Christ the Lord. And this shall be a sign unto you; Ye shall find the babe wrapped in swaddling clothes, lying in a manger' (Luke 2:8-12)."

He paused, letting the leather-bound black book rest on his lap. Luke knew there would be questions, like always, and waited patiently for the words to soak into the little sponges camped about him.

"Did he have a ma and pa? The baby?"

Luke studied Barney intently and answered, "Yes. Mary was His ma, and Joseph was His pa. But He was also the Son of God."

"Whew!" Barney exclaimed. "That's somethin'."

Luke continued, "God sent His Son to be the Savior of the world. He let Him come as a baby, so that He might be our Savior."

"Did God leave Him in the manger just like our folks left us outside the livery stable?" Lacy asked with astonishment.

The room grew quiet, and Luke cleared his throat. The Grays had abandoned their daughters when they passed through Dayton six months earlier, entrusting Lacy at age nine to care for her two younger sisters. The girls were found huddled together outside a livery stable. Lacy had explained there were eleven children in all, and her pa always complained that he had too many mouths to feed. Luke figured they needed the older ones to do the work, and the youngest ones had not been deserted solely because they were male.

"I'm sure it was hard for God to send His Son and also hard for your folks to leave you girls. They knew that they didn't have enough food and money to care for you. I know it's difficult to understand. But we love you very much." Luke held out his arms, and the three little girls scooted into them.

"What about Santa Claus?" Lonnie asked. There were snickers around the room from the older children.

Luke tactfully avoided the question and asked, "What about presents? Are we ready to open gifts?" The room buzzed with excitement. "All right. James and Frank, would you like to pass out the packages?" Names had been placed on the gifts, and the two young men carefully matched them to the proper recipients.

～～

Later the girls, tucked in their rooms for the night, cuddled new rag dolls and cherished diaries. The boys were content with their boats and knives, and they all snuggled under new comforters and rested their weary heads on feather pillows.

The exhausting day wound to a close with the adults gathered in front of the parlor fire, discussing the day's events.

"It didn't even snow for Christmas," Annabelle murmured as the heat of the flames licked her cheeks.

"But it was the best Christmas I ever had," Claire remarked. "And snow might have kept us from coming."

"Or stranded us here at Dayton," Annabelle added.

"I wish I could stay and help. Can I, Luke?" Claire's face showed her eagerness.

"We could use the extra help."

"I jest don't know; you're so young." Mattie looked to Buck for support—some reason why their daughter could not remain at the orphanage—but he remained quiet, only responding by placing his arm around his wife and squeezing.

Noting Mattie's strong objection, Luke explained with gentleness, "You cannot stay this time, Claire, without your belongings or Mattie's blessing. Give your folks some time to decide; pray about it. Then if you choose to help, we will be glad to have you."

Claire nodded in resignation, and relief washed over Mattie.

Ben saw his opportunity and jumped in, "Luke, tell us how we can adopt Gabe and Cody."

Luke's eyes sparkled at Ben's request, and he glanced at Jesse Murdock across the room who replied, "If you want to make it legal and give them your name, papers need to be drawn up. We're mighty grateful that you want them. You're fine folks and would make the boys good parents."

"Thank you." Kate addressed the Murdocks anxiously, "How long would it take? We need to leave tomorrow."

"It would be better if we waited, Dear." Ben spoke softly to his wife. "We can return for them."

Jesse agreed. "Probably be best for all of the children to have time to prepare them. It's always a loss to the others when some leave. They take it hard."

As Annabelle listened, her stomach churned with feelings of guilt and grief—a sensation that was now a constant companion. It had first appeared after Thad's proposal and grew more intense when Thaddeas moved to Boston. The same pain tormented her after Charles's note and taunted her on a regular basis since she realized she loved Thad. Its agitation provided a steady reminder of her unanswered telegram.

Now, though, its cause was the sorrow she felt for the children, combined with the knowledge that she was not like Claire. She could never go into ministry. She just wanted to flee, get as far away from here as fast as she could. The miserable feeling boiled her insides.

"Claire, you asleep?" Annabelle whispered to the girl who lay beside her.

"No. What is it?"

"This place upsets me. I feel like I got the jitters."

"Me, too. I can't stand not being able to help. I want to come back more than anything in the world. It means everything to me."

"I can see it's a good thing. They need contributions and support, but it hurts too much to be around them. How could you cope?"

"Well, there's pain all right, but it won't go away just because we walk away from here. And I have peace with God that this is a ministry I'm supposed to do."

"If it is, Mattie and Buck have to let you come. But I'd miss you terribly. The thought of it makes me feel even worse. I keep losing everyone I love."

"Do you mean Charles?"

"No. He hurt my pride, but I never loved him."

"Thaddeas?"

"Yes. I miss him so much sometimes I think I can't bear it."

"Oh, Annabelle, I'm sorry."

"There's nothing that can be done about it. We'd better get some sleep."

"I'll pray for you."

"Thanks."

"Good night."

Chapter 17

At Tucker House a few weeks later, Annabelle listened carefully as her sister Kate explained.

"I'm mixed up. I thought adopting Cody and Gabe would be the best thing on earth, but instead it's set my world spinning."

"What do you mean, Kate?"

"At first it was exciting, planning what needed to be done for their arrival. The loft had to be cleaned. The place had become a storage post. Ben said he'd make two beds and a stand for it. We needed sheets, comforters, pillows, and clothes for the boys." Her voice trailed off at this point, and she lapsed into a state of reflection.

"You look exhausted. Perhaps you're trying to do too much."

"We've barely scratched the surface, and it's driving a wedge between Ben and me."

Annabelle's mouth flew open of its own accord, in an unflattering gesture, at this piece of information. "Why? Doesn't Ben want the children?"

Kate pulled a hanky out of her apron pocket and dabbed at her eyes. "I thought so. Maybe he just wanted them for me." Then she said sarcastically, "The way he's sulking and moping, I can't believe he's trying to please me. I don't know what's wrong with him."

Annabelle did not know what to make of this muddled explanation. Kate and Ben were the perfect couple, and Kate always had everything under control. She patted her sister's hand and listened.

"Ben makes promises that he doesn't keep," she continued between sobs. "He said he'd make those beds, and he hasn't even begun."

"Perhaps he's just been busy."

"Yes, he has. Doing stuff for other people. He spent a couple days helping his father mend fences. He and Jude Miller put up a new outhouse, and he even spent a day fishing with Frank and James. Real important things!"

"It sounds to me like you should be the one who is cross. Why is Ben sulking?" Annabelle became angry at her brother-in-law.

"I don't know. But he's barely speaking to me. I've been doing what I can. Cleaned the loft until it sparkled. Took the wagon to town myself for material and then stayed up all hours of the night knotting those comforters." She sighed. "And sewing little trousers."

Kate remembered the first night she had been up late. Ben had been

178

cheerful enough, even playful. She had to get quite stern with him before he had left her alone to work on them. Finally, he had gone to bed.

She tried to remember when his ill temper had started, but she could not. She was so engrossed in her tasks, the days and nights all ran together. Finally, Ben had understood the importance of the matter and had quit pestering her each night.

Then he started in with his little demands. There had been a few arguments about making their little beds, and now this dreaded silence—each going about their own duties. She shrugged her shoulders; she just could not remember anything she had done to offend him nor could she understand why he was dragging his feet about the children.

"I'm afraid to ask him when he plans to get to the beds. He'll probably bite my head off."

"You poor thing," Annabelle murmured.

"When he finds out I came over today, he might be upset." Kate looked sheepish. "I didn't tell him I was coming."

"I'm sorry Mattie wasn't here. She would know exactly what to tell you. The sheriff and her have their squabbles."

"They do?"

"Yes." Annabelle nodded. "Of course they don't last long."

This information encouraged Kate, who had not known if such arguments were normal or irregular. She only knew they upset her.

A thought suddenly hit her. *Neither Ben nor I had a set of parents to watch as children. There is so much to learn about marriage.* On its heels came another thought. *Quit thinking about yourself. Try to understand Ben.* Next came a great desire to go home and spend some time alone with God. "Well, I'd best be getting home now. I feel much better, really I do."

After the dust from Kate's wagon settled, Annabelle stood on the front steps of Tucker House reflecting over the things Kate had said. *Men!* She thought of her love telegram that continued to go unanswered. *Is that what Thaddeas is doing to me. . .giving me the silent treatment?* She wondered if he was trying to get even with her, to prove something. It was not like him to play games, and he did not leave Ohio angry with her. *Could he have grown bitter in such a short time?*

Two days later Mattie received a caller. This one found her at home and alone. She patted her honey-colored hair, with nimble fingers tucking strands of unruly pieces into place in the twist where they belonged, and called, "Comin'."

The caller heard her voice and stiffened, waiting for the door to open. When it did, Mattie gasped and stared for a long time.

Finally the man spoke. "Hello, Mattie." His voice was familiar, though deeper and edged with tremor.

She flushed. "Hello, Wade."

"May I come in?"

Mattie looked over her shoulder at the vacant house, and many thoughts raced through her mind. *What does he want? It isn't fittin' with Buck not here.* "I–I don't know. . . ."

"I realize I've got no right to ask. But I only want to talk. Please."

Again she hesitated. "I don't think it would be proper. . . ."

Wade pulled an envelope from the inside of his military jacket and held it in full view. "I have a letter from your folks." Mattie's full attention riveted to the document in his fist. The hook sufficiently planted, he returned the envelope to his pocket and waited.

This was unexpected news, and Mattie placed her hand across her fluttering heart. "All right," she said, "come on in."

The six-foot man followed her into the sitting room, taking in the surroundings. The smell of lavender trailed behind the straight, slim back of the woman he had once loved. The realization that she was more beautiful than he had remembered shook him.

While obsessed to know all about her—every detail of the last twenty-three years—he perceived the need to proceed cautiously. The lieutenant noted Mattie's strength, the courageous glint in her eyes, and the firm set of her mouth. Every movement signified stubborn resistance to his presence.

When they were seated, stiff as two starched shirts, Mattie gave him an icy stare. She saw flashes of his youth but mostly a commanding lieutenant, unrecognizable. His eyes, though, were soft pools, and lines of worry grooved his temple.

"Mattie, I know I have acted dishonorably. May I explain?"

"It's not necessary," she snapped.

"But I want to."

"What good can come of it? That's all in the past."

"It needs to be righted."

"How can it be?"

He smiled. "You're a strong woman, Mattie."

"I had to be."

"I was wrong to do what I did. I was young and afraid of the preacher, your father." Mattie's eyes glistened with astonishment. She understood fear of the tyrant. "But that is no excuse," Wade continued. "To leave you to face the bully alone was abominable."

The lieutenant unconsciously crushed the hat on his lap, then ran his fingers through his saddle brown hair. "I joined the cavalry. When my term expired, I returned home, expecting to take up my responsibilities, but you had vanished. I went to visit your father."

Mattie smiled in spite of herself, imagining what that scene had been like. "You must have been courageous," she said, bitterness tainting her voice.

"He disowned you and wouldn't give me any information, so I joined up for another hitch. After the Indian raid, your parents were overcome with grief. That was when I learned you'd gone to Big Bottom to live with your sister, Elizabeth. . .and our baby. But they said you were all killed."

He continued, "I married and had a son." Mattie's brows arched, but still she said nothing. "My son is fourteen, and my wife, Hannah, died a couple years back." Sorrow laced his voice, and Mattie discovered she felt some compassion for the man.

Wade noticed her countenance softening and added with more enthusiasm, "I got stationed at Fort Wayne and made trips along this territory, where I heard of Tucker House and Mattie Tucker. It seemed a miracle, and I just had to know if it was really you!"

Mattie replied, her voice low and reflective, "All these years, I never knew what happened to ya. Then Buck, my husband, ran across you at the Golden Lamb. He mentioned your name 'pon his return."

"Does he know about us?"

"Yes. He knows it all."

"I guess my purpose in coming is twofold." The brown-eyed officer took a gulp of courage. "I come to ask for your forgiveness and to see if our child is alive."

"With the Lord's help, I'll forgive you."

Wade Brooks bestowed Mattie with a generous smile. "Thank you." He hesitated to press her. He had come so far with this woman who sat so straight yet looked so vulnerable, but he ventured, "And our child?"

"I raised three daughters, orphans from the Indian raid; that is all."

"I know. Is one of them our daughter?" Mattie stared at him stubbornly, refusing to reply. "One is the right age," he continued.

Mattie rose. "You have no right to ask. Anyway, what's done is done. What's past is past. Buck wouldn't like ya bein' here." She pointed to the door. "You really must leave now, Lieutenant."

"Very well, Mattie. I see you are distressed. However, it's important for me to know if I have a daughter." He paused to emphasize his point. "My work takes me through these parts frequently. I will let you think about what we have discussed and stop another time."

"Please, don't. I've had a lonely life, but I'm happy now. I don't need you turnin' over old stones, just stirs up trouble."

"I'm sorry you see it that way, Mattie. I just want to make things right."

His next words stuck like tree sap. "If I have a daughter, then I owe it to her."

As Wade Brooks turned to go, he remembered the letter from her folks. "Here, Mattie. And think about it. I know you'll do the right thing and see me again. Good-bye."

After he left, Mattie stared at the envelope that lay on her lap. Finally she tore it open.

Dear Mattie,
We took you for dead, but Wade claims you are alive. I've made many mistakes in my lifetime, but what I did to you was the worst. Please forgive me. Your mother longs to hear from you.

Your Pa,
Rev. Tucker

Mattie wept bitterly until her tears were spent. Then she prayed, "Oh, Lord, I cannot forgive them on my own. Can You help me?"

Chapter 18

Annabelle's breast felt as if it caged a wild bird. She sought to still the fluttering wings beating against her bosom by seeking refuge at a favorite spot. Brushing the snow off the bench with mittened hands, she seated herself where the sun's warming rays could be felt beneath the bare-branched hickory tree, a comfortable haven, alone. Her disappointment and anxiety over the past six weeks since she had sent that telegram had taken a toll on her.

She realized by now that Thaddeas was not overjoyed by her message or he would have sent an immediate reply. The padded letter she now held in her hands contained his answer yet she hesitated to read its contents.

Remembering the night she had sat under this same tree with Thad, she pulled off her mittens and placed them on the bench. It was the night before he had left for Boston, and he had offered marriage. How she wished she could take her answer back, could be in Boston with him today.

Just then a rabbit scampered across the yard—within a few feet of her. Upon the scent of danger, it froze like a statue, except for the tiny, twitching nose. Annabelle murmured to the diversion, "Are you as scared as I am, little fellow?"

When her voice pricked the air, the long ears shot skyward, and in a cotton flurry he hopped away, his giant feet zigzagging a trail in the snow-covered ground. "I guess you are." She sighed. "Well, I can't run away like you."

She carefully opened the letter, smoothing out the sheets of paper on her lap. Picking up the first page, she read:

Dear Annabelle,

I received your telegram today and decided to write a letter. My heart is full, and there is too much to say in a telegram. I have loved you for a very long time, but I believe that our ambitions are far too different for us to make a life together.

Annabelle's hands trembled, and large tears glistened on her cheeks. She instinctively knew her world was falling apart, but she continued to read.

Your ambitions are lofty ones, dreams of gold, pearls, balls, and parties.

Fleeting thoughts of Charles Harrison and the hopes she had harbored at that time flashed before her eyes. She remembered her haughty attitude with Thaddeas and recalled her vain words. She did not know when, but those ambitions had been replaced with hurt, doubts, emptiness, and the all-encompassing loneliness that haunted her since Thad left.

My dreams include hard work and adventure, living my life for Jesus Christ and following His direction. I am looking for a woman who will love me as much as I love her, be willing to live in a shack or a castle—a woman filled with passion and compassion—who would not be afraid to dirty her hands for any task set before her.

A hope quivered in her breast. Yes, she could be that woman. She would show him, let him know that she had changed.

I believe that I have been patient with you, nurturing in our relationship, careful not to force myself or my Lord upon you. You turned my proposals down so emphatically, I can only believe it is not possible that you love me.

"Poor Thad. Oh, I must let him know that I really do love him."

You must, therefore, love my friendship, my money, my influence, or my Boston. But I know you cannot truly love me.

But I do, Annabelle's heart screamed. *I do!* Frantically she read on.

Since coming to Boston, I have met a woman who has all of the qualifications I am looking for in a wife. Her name is Mary Beth Edwards. Her love for me is unselfish and pure. I have asked her to be my wife, and she has accepted.

Annabelle felt the shock of Thad's declaration pulse like a wave through every part of her being, leaving her paralyzed as it inched along. When it reached her feet, it seemed that her life's force drained onto the frozen ground, leaving her a lonely shell of a person. She did not know how long she sat there in denial and grief.

Finally, she realized several sheets of paper remained. *What is this? Endless praises of his betrothed?* Then an urgency possessed her to know more about this woman who had stolen Thaddeas from her. Angry, she gripped the letter and read on.

I am sure that it will not take you long to set your affections upon some other young man. Many will be as spellbound as I was. I will continue to pray for you, that you will come to know the Lord Jesus Christ, and that you will find a life that is fulfilling. I remain affectionately yours,

> *Your cousin,*
> *Thaddeas*

P.S. I have enclosed a letter for Uncle Buck and would appreciate it if you would see that he gets it.

"That's it? That's all? He is dismissing me. He cannot do this! I won't stand for it! The rest of this is a letter—for Buck. This cannot be happening. He said he would always be there for me."

"Annabelle!"

She saw Claire standing on the steps, but the sound of her sister's voice seemed miles away.

"Come in for supper!"

The bewildered young woman waved her letter-stuffed hand in the air, acknowledging Claire's request. How could she face the others? In a whirl of confusion she gathered up her skirts and ran to the house, wherein she flew through the kitchen and clamored up the steps to her room.

"What on earth?" Mattie dropped the dishcloth she held and chased up after her. When she entered Annabelle's room, she rushed to the sobbing girl. "Child, what is wrong?"

Annabelle thrust Thad's letter into Mattie's hand. "Here. Read it for yourself. Thaddeas is engaged." And she burst into another fit of tears. Mattie drew the young woman into her arms and held her tightly. "Oh, Darlin', I'm so sorry. I know how it must hurt ya."

❧

Six weeks had passed since Thaddeas had written Annabelle. Daily, the young man thrust his energy into his work at the leather shop, where his relationship with his brother, Leon, was renewed. His evenings found him with his mother or his fiancée, Mary Beth.

Christmas came and went, a pleasant time when Thaddeas and Mary Beth discussed likes and dislikes and discovered they had numerous things in common. In planning their future, Mary Beth professed undying love and loyalty and a desire to follow Thad wherever he might go. The sensitive creature knew exactly when to tease and flirt, lassoing Thaddeas with love and attention, tightening the knot with pleasant words and passing days.

Just occasionally he questioned his own motives. Once when he had gazed into her eyes, green fiery ones glared back instead of the gentle turquoise ones Mary Beth possessed, and he cursed himself for thinking of another but his beloved.

Another time he snapped back at her when she succumbed without a thought to one of his plans. "Woman," he had said, "don't be afraid to have an opinion of your own. A little pluck is good for the soul." She had cried, making him feel like a beast. Realizing he had compared her unjustly to Annabelle, he determined to make her happy, love her more devotedly.

On this January day, however, his troubles were not romantically inclined but focused on a pressing dilemma.

"Perhaps we should dip into our investments and buy a warehouse to store goods without cost, and later resell the property," Amelia Larson suggested to her two sons.

"I think we should wait it out," Leon urged. "Jefferson cannot let this thing go on for any length of time."

"When I first read the headlines back in December of this Embargo Act, I knew it would be trouble." Thaddeas hit his fist against his thigh in protest of the disturbing bill Congress had passed under Jefferson's persuasion. "Why, England and France are laughing at us—especially England. She's getting richer by the day.

"Last year alone the United States exported eight thousand boots and one hundred twenty thousand shoes. The industry cannot handle this restraint. While the shoes pile up in warehouses, we cannot move our leather."

Amelia questioned her son, "Is there a domestic product that could use our leather, some item we have overlooked? Does it all have to go to shoes, boots, harnesses, and saddles?"

"None that we can think of at the present, Mother." Leon shook his head thoughtfully.

"I was just going to give our workers a raise. They deserve more than fifteen shillings a week," Thaddeas complained. "Now I'm afraid we'll have to lay some off instead. We'll keep on the apprenticeships; they are cheap and will provide good labor when the seas open up again. But I hate to put people out of a job when they have been faithful."

"We could lay off Peterson. He's a troublemaker anyway."

"Yes, I suppose he shall be the first to go," Thaddeas agreed. "I guess our most pressing question is whether we can wait any longer before we take some action."

"I think we should wait," Leon offered.

"I am willing," Amelia agreed.

Thaddeas sighed. "All right." Then he rose to leave. "I'll be in my room until supper, if I'm needed." He climbed the spiral staircase, gliding his hand along the smooth oak banister. Perfectly shined boots stepped off the distance of the long hallway and took him to his large, masculine-looking room. When he opened the door, a crackling fire welcomed him. The scent of rose water filled the air to remind him the maid had prepared a basin to freshen in for supper.

He stared at the large painting above his four-poster bed. The western setting, usually so soothing, depressed him today. Purple mountains loomed, calling his name. The smiling cowboys mocked him as they herded mangy cattle with lassos high overhead and prairie grass underfoot.

He dropped to a kneeling position on the oval rug that warmed the floor at the side of the bed. His forehead pounded as if the cattle in the painting stampeded across his head, and he poured out his troubled heart to God.

Chapter 19

In the days following the announcement of Thad's engagement to Mary Beth, Annabelle went through many stages of coping with her grief. One of her first reactions—anger—she vented upon Andy Benson when he finally mustered up enough courage to call one Sunday afternoon.

"Evenin', Miss Annabelle."

Annabelle watched the young man shuffle from one foot to the other and quickly grew impatient with the tongue-tied intruder.

"Yes?" She tapped her booted foot as if counting off the seconds he was allotted before she shut the door.

" 'Tis a cold day, isn't it?" he ventured.

"Perhaps you'd better state your intentions then?"

"Ma'am?"

"What can I do for you, Andy?"

"Well, I thought I'd. . .that is. . .I'd come callin'."

"What?" Annabelle frowned. "Do you want to see Claire?"

"No, Ma'am. I came to see you, Miss Annabelle."

"That's impossible! Why should you call on me?"

She then dismissed him so coldly that Mattie, who had overheard the end of the conversation, insisted she ride Dusty to his farm to apologize. Reluctantly Annabelle did. She expressed regrets for her rude behavior in all meekness, but Andy—much impressed with her sour temperament—vowed he would never call upon her again, which suited Annabelle fine.

Days on end of melancholy and listless existence led Annabelle toward introspection, followed by extended periods of weeping. This drove Claire wild. She could not stand to hear the wretched sobs penetrating the wall between their dark rooms.

She tried to comfort her older sibling and received tongue lashings in return. Still, she persevered. At just such a time, she approached Annabelle with an idea. "I know just the thing for you," Claire said.

"And what is that?" The tone of Annabelle's voice dripped with acidity.

"Why don't you come with me to work at the orphanage? You can get your mind off Thaddeas by helping the children. A city like Dayton is bound to have many diversions."

"You don't even have permission to go to the orphanage."

"I know. But with your persuasion, Mattie and Buck would give in."

This challenge became a tiny bubble of a catalyst that gradually propelled Annabelle out of her phase of lethargy. She considered. "You think so?"

After lengthy discoursing and debates, Buck and Mattie agreed to allow the girls to move to Dayton. Buck, who never had been against the idea, supported Mattie as best he could, gently assuring his wife that it was the right decision.

He had to go easy with her these days as she was taut as a fiddle. The lieutenant had asked questions around town, then paid her another call, and she was not handling it well. Buck had been present when the lieutenant dropped by, an awkward situation for all of them.

When Brooks left, the Larsons got into a heated debate, for Buck believed Mattie was dead wrong to withhold information from Wade Brooks about his daughter. However, she remained steadfast about it, and there was nothing he could do to bend her thinking. It was her decision to make.

Though Mattie was a good woman who usually channeled her stubbornness in a constructive manner, Buck knew she was hard to come up against head-on. He learned fast that patient nudging and gentle counsel went further in changing her mind than butting heads like a couple of mountain goats.

After informing the girls that they were allowed to help at the orphanage, telegrams ripped like lightning between Beaver Creek and Dayton. The girls sent the first message:

Luke,
> Have permission. Desire to come help at orphanage.
> > *Annabelle and Claire*

Luke replied:

Annabelle and Claire,
> All is set. I will come for you. Arrival February 10.
> > *Luke*

Ben Wheeler held a different telegram in his hand that pricked like a sliver of wood from his corral and needed to be dealt with immediately. He knew if he waited until evening it would fester all day long, so he headed for the house to find his wife. The telegram addressed the issue that had turned his household upside down.

"Kate."

"In here." Kate came out of their bedroom, wondering what Ben wanted.

She had not heard him return from his ride into town. No small talk had been exchanged between the two lately, so she knew something important was afoot if he called her name now.

In the last several weeks life had grown tenser by the minute at the old Potter place, with Ben expelling a great amount of energy on his chores, which he did in silence. Meals had turned into dismal affairs, and most often afterward Ben would go to the barn to check on the animals while Kate burst into a fit of tears. She continued to work on the clothes for Gabe and Cody—the comforters now complete—until Ben fell asleep each night; then she dropped wearily onto the far edge of the bed they shared.

The loft remained empty, and the small beds and table Ben had agreed to make were never discussed. Both Ben and Kate spent time in prayer about the issue. Each, at different times, came to the verge of confession or forgiveness of their spouse, when a swell of pride or new accusations hindered the reconciliation.

Just this morning when Ben rode away with the dust licking at his heels, Kate had fled to her room, dropped to her knees, and begged God to intervene.

Now Ben hung his coat on the peg behind the door and removed his hat. "Please sit down, Kate." She obeyed, fidgeting with her hands in her lap. Finding himself mute, Ben handed her the telegram. "Here."

Kate read the words that her husband had memorized.

Ben and Kate,
 Arriving February 10, to escort Larson girls to Dayton. Could bring adoption papers and boys. Please advise.

Luke

"What does this mean, to escort Larson girls?"

"I stopped in on the way home. Annabelle and Claire are both going to the orphanage for awhile to help out."

"What! Why, I can't believe Annabelle would do this. She usually tells me everything."

"You haven't been the most sociable lately."

Kate's face burned at the insult, and tears stung her eyes. She did not reply. After a loaded silence, Ben continued.

"What answer should I give Luke?"

"No. Tell him no." Kate spat out the words. She got up from her seat and ran across the room to their bedroom, slamming the door behind her and flinging herself across the bed.

Ben instantly wished he had bitten his tongue instead of insulting Kate.

He hated his behavior of the last several weeks, yet continued in the same destructive pattern, powerless to change it. Even with nonresistance a part of his lifestyle, he would rather take blows from any man than suffer the rejection he had been experiencing from his young wife. He found himself wondering if she had only married him to have children. Not able to provide her with them, she now cast him aside like a rusty nail.

Regardless of the truth, he could not go on this way, with life crashing in all around him. He crossed the room to their closed bedroom door and lifted his fist to knock, but he could not. What would he say? He lowered it again. *Lord*, he prayed, *give me the words to say.* Then he gently rapped on the door. "Kate?"

"Go away."

"I'm sorry. May I come in?"

"No."

"Please." This time there was no reply, so he eased the door open and lowered himself onto the bed beside his wife. Her whimpers tore at his heart, and he pulled her into an embrace; they clung to each other. The physical touch began to dissolve the wall of pride and misunderstanding that stood between them. Apologies poured out.

"I'm sorry, Darling."

"What have I done to make you so angry?" Kate moaned.

"I am not angry, just hurt. I feel like you don't want me around anymore."

"Why would you feel that way?"

"You've turned me out, Kate." He did not want to make her angrier and carefully worded his thoughts. "Since we've been married, our evenings were always special. Lately you're preoccupied." She stared at him, trying to comprehend. "That isn't all. I wondered if once we got Cody and Gabe, you'd even share my bed anymore."

Like a shooting star, understanding dawned for Kate. "Oh, Ben, I'm so sorry. I didn't realize what I was doing. I love you more than anything. I've been so lonely without you, and so foolish to let things go on like they have, each of us going our separate ways."

Realizing there was a great deal that they did not understand about each other or about nurturing a marital relationship, Ben pulled his Bible off the nearby nightstand.

"Want to know what the Lord's been saying to me? Of course I was too mule headed to listen."

"All right."

"Here it is. Ephesians 4:26: 'Let not the sun go down upon your wrath.' I vow this will never happen again in our household, if we have to stay up all night talking."

191

"I didn't listen to the Lord either. I'm so sorry."

Recognizing the fragile state of their emotions, they agreed to put off the adoption for awhile, devoting time to each other and their relationship. Thus, Luke was much surprised when he received their telegram which read,

> *Luke,*
> *Not ready to adopt at this time. Will discuss on your visit.*
> *Ben*

Chapter 20

February 10, one month after Annabelle had received Thad's letter of dismissal, she found herself reasonably settled in her new surroundings. Her strenuous days proved to be anything but routine for they centered around thirteen energetic children.

The first week passed, a killer. Every part of her body ached from bending, lifting, toting. With the endless number of chores, Annabelle could not imagine how Luke and the Murdocks had gotten along before she and Claire had come to help. But the ceaseless duties, rather than taxing her, provided a numbing effect, and she could finally get her mind off her problems.

In a short while these new activities became an integral part of her existence, and Beaver Creek seemed like part of a distant dream. This was reality—up at dawn, washing, ironing, mending, baking, and tending the children.

She became especially attached to her young redheaded twin, Lacy Gray. Taking Lacy underfoot meant caring for Lacy's tiny sisters as well. Ever since their parents had deserted them, they tagged along behind Lacy like baby chicks following a mother quail.

Annabelle felt sorry for the little girl because there were no other girls her age to play with, only boys. Not the tomboy type, Lacy oftentimes felt left out.

Sunday was a day they all looked forward to. Sometimes they attended the Rev. Hamer's Presbyterian church in Dayton, but most often Luke preached the Sunday morning meeting in the huge parlor. In the afternoon, following dinner, they relaxed or participated in a special fun activity.

On this particular Sunday they planned to go sledding behind the orphanage on the hills that looked like the rumps of sleepy bears. The children heard the fable told each winter—how all the polar bears from Antarctica came to this particular spot to rest on their tummies and hibernate for the winter. Of course they knew this could not be true for the children often tromped and explored these snow-covered hills, within walking distance.

Today the children, anxious to occupy the slopes again, listened to Luke finish his sermon. "Therefore, children, remember that God loves you in a very special way. Psalm 68:5 says, 'A father of the fatherless, and a judge of the widows, is God in his holy habitation.' This God who created the universe knows everything about each one of you. He is the same God who made the snow."

This caught the children's attention, and Luke set a beautiful picture before them of a magnificent God. "Job 37:5–6 says, 'Great things doeth he, which we cannot comprehend. For he saith to the snow, Be thou on the earth; likewise to the small rain, and to the great rain of his strength.' And this all-powerful God wants to be your Father. He wants you to come to Him with all your cares. Pray to Him every day, bringing to His attention all of the things you are doing, your accomplishments, and your needs. He promises to be there for you.

"Heavenly Father," he prayed, "thank You for creating an ice palace for us, complete with heaps of snow and slick hills that make sleds go fast. Thank You for Your love."

After the "amen," children's bodies scurried this way and that, checking their duties on the blackboard that hung on the wall between the dining room and kitchen. Dishes and utensils appeared. Youngsters carried bowls and glasses, and performed the various errands needed to serve the Sunday meal. Afterwards just as many chipped in for cleanup, eager to be off to explore the snowy hills.

Annabelle walked with Lacy and pulled Neda and Missy on the sled, leaving wiggly grooves that blended in with the tracks made by the other four sleds, thirteen children, and five grown-ups. Annabelle glanced at Claire and thought that life at the orphanage agreed with her. She looked a vision of health. Her cheeks glowed and eyes sparkled as she chattered with those grouped about her.

Puffs of steam encircled them and drifted skyward as they huffed their way uphill to the top of the nearest bluff. The hill was not high but steep, and provided an excellent road course for the outing. When the sleds were lined up on the ridge and loaded with willing bodies, Luke and Jesse pushed them off. Giggles from the spectators nearly drowned out the squeals of the riders. After they reached the bottom, the youngsters headed uphill with sleds pulled behind them to give the next child a turn.

All the children had taken several spins before Luke suggested that Annabelle and Claire take a turn. Side by side they eyed each other, then Luke said, "Ready," and they were off. The wind slapped Annabelle's face soundly, sucking out her breath, spraying snow all the while, and the trees sped by like arrows. Her stomach lurched, then hung in her chest until the sled finally glided to a smooth landing. She sat still a moment while a rush coursed through her veins, settling in her stomach, which returned to its proper place. Then she climbed off as quickly as her bundled body could manage. When she saw her sister's teary eyes and red nose, she called, "Wasn't that great?"

"Wonderful!"

Joyously they made their ascent and turned over their wooden sleds to those next in line.

Annabelle laughed at Lacy's face, screwed up into a frown because she had to double up with ten-year-old Hank Forbes. When Luke called, "Ready," Lacy quickly wrapped her arms around the lad's middle, and as the sled gained momentum, Lacy's cinnamon-stick braids flew straight out behind her and slapped in the air like whips. The ride soon ended, and the boy and girl climbed the hill, breathless and enthusiastic. As the young couple neared the top, Annabelle reached out and pulled the little girl to flat ground.

"What a ride! And Hank's the best. He blocked more wind than Lonnie." Hank, upon hearing the words, wore a grin wide as the prairie.

The day passed by too quickly. Back at the home, happy children turned into grouchy bears that needed to be coaxed into dry clothes. Catherine warmed hot chili, and they gathered for a short period around the hearth, reflecting on the day's events before heading off for bed.

Annabelle and Claire remained long after the others were asleep and gazed into the embers of the fire.

"Are you sorry we came?" Claire asked.

"No, just tired. I was thinking we're lucky that Mattie took us in, that we didn't have to live in an orphanage. No matter how hard we try, there's just not enough time in the day to give each one the attention they need."

"I don't think it was luck, Annabelle. I believe it was the Lord's plan to take care of us."

"If it was Him, then why did He allow our folks to be killed in the first place?"

"I can't answer that." Claire grew weary of Annabelle's resistant attitude toward God and her own inadequate explanations. "I just know that bad things happen. Sometimes they are the result of sin, but God doesn't make them happen. They just do, unless He intervenes—like He did that time you had your accident. He allowed you to live, Annabelle. He has the power and means to get us through hard times and to make good come from them.

"Anyway, because of what we have experienced, we can be of help to these children who are going through similar times. See, there will always be accidents, always sickness, always things that take away parents and leave children orphaned."

"I know what you're trying to say, Claire. I just don't know if I believe it."

"Perhaps you should think heavily on it, Annabelle. You've got saddlebags of disappointments you're toting around. You'd find life a lot easier if you could hand them over to the Lord."

"Maybe. C'mon, time to turn in, little sister. By the way, you don't write Rev. Hamer's sermons for him, do you?"

Claire rolled her eyes, and the girls giggled as they went down the long hallway to their room.

Chapter 21

One day near the end of February, Luke came back from Dayton spilling over with news that deeply troubled him. He paced the kitchen floor as he voiced his concerns to Jesse Murdock. Annabelle and Claire listened as they assisted Catherine with food preparations.

"It's awful." Luke threw his arms about in protestation. "They auctioned off two boys this morning at the public sale."

"Lord, have mercy," Catherine exclaimed.

Claire dropped the potato which she was paring, and it rolled into the basin with the peelings. "There must be something that can be done!" she cried.

"I talked to Harper." Luke's face twisted in disgust as he remembered his conversation with the overstuffed man who ran the sale.

"What did he say?" Jesse asked.

"He said selling orphans makes money, feeding orphans takes money." Luke clenched his jaw and tightened his fist. "I told him he'd be sorry if it happened again."

Jesse squinted his fine-featured face, wondering how Harper had taken the threat. "He laughed," Luke said.

Catherine turned to her young husband with concern. "What can we do, Jesse?"

"I guess I'll go see Rev. Hamer."

"I already tried that. He's out of town until late tonight."

"Well," Jesse said with determination, "Luke and I will visit the parson first thing in the morning. If he can't do something, then we'll pay the governor a call."

Catherine beamed in admiration at her husband, confident that the two men would accomplish much. Before Annabelle could even take it all in, Neda ran into the room, dripping snow and slush on the kitchen floor. "Come quick, Lacy's sick." The little girl's fright quickened Catherine and Annabelle into action. Together they followed the young child, stopping only long enough to grab their cloaks from a peg before they braced the winter's cold. The poor girl lay in a heap outside the outhouse door.

Catherine scooped the child up, crooning reassuring words into her ear as she carried her into the building and to the huge room that Lacy shared with the other girls. Placing her on a bunk and stripping off her coat, Catherine ordered, "Get a basin of hot water and a rag." Annabelle flew to do the woman's bidding and sent Luke back into town after the doctor.

Annabelle stayed by Lacy's side and wiped her hot brow with a wet cloth while the young girl whimpered in pain.

Finally, the doctor arrived. "It's her appendix," he quickly diagnosed, and Lacy was taken away in a carriage. Catherine and Jesse accompanied her to the hospital.

It was eleven A.M. Claire and Luke waited for news and watched Annabelle pace the floor and wonder if she would see her young friend alive again. Annabelle remembered Lacy's last words as they had carried her away. "Jesus loves me. Mr. Luke says Jesus loves me." Now Annabelle turned to look Luke full in the face. He saw her troubled expression.

"Annabelle?"

"Lacy said you told her Jesus loves her."

"He does. Whatever happens to Lacy, you can be assured that Jesus loves her."

"What if. . .if she dies?"

"Then she'll be in His arms. She'll be very happy. Nothing on earth could be as satisfying."

"I know. Living just brings pain."

"Not always, but even the happy times aren't totally fulfilling. Only spiritual things can truly satisfy."

Annabelle hung her head. "Luke, sometimes I just don't think I can go on living."

Luke knelt in front of the struggling woman and took her hands in his. Annabelle felt helpless to the point of nausea. He gave her hands a squeeze, and the Holy Spirit used his tenderness to move her.

Overcome with tears, she fell into his arms. Claire looked at Luke with pleading, misty eyes as he held Annabelle, who wept upon his shoulder. Succumbing to disappointment and loneliness, Annabelle sobbed uncontrollably.

Finally, Luke spoke. "Annabelle, it is time for you to ask Jesus to come into your life. Allow Him to bring you comfort." She nodded, and he began to pray.

She repeated his words in choking little gasps. "Forgive me for my sins. Jesus, come into my life."

As Annabelle spoke the halting words, she felt a peace infiltrating her lightheaded body, and she marveled at it. The burden immediately lifted, and she could not remember why she had not wanted to live. A little spring of joy bubbled in her chest, filling her with hope. "Is this His love?" she asked.

Claire embraced her sister joyfully. "Yes!" she reassured her.

"Now I understand. But I can't explain it."

"It's called faith," Luke said, grinning. "It just wells up within us, and we know that God is real."

"Yes!"

The three of them were still awake when Catherine and Jesse returned from the hospital with the sad news that little Lacy had died on the operating table. Her appendix had burst. Annabelle said bravely, "I have experienced new life, and my little sweetheart is experiencing new life, too, with Jesus. Oh, I wish I could go with her." Her heart burned, and tears streamed down her face anew.

"Jesus needs us here," Luke said.

Annabelle nodded. "I will be faithful. Jesus is all I have now."

Claire knew that, in time, Annabelle would discover many things worth living for. But it hurt her, also, to let Lacy go. She went to Annabelle. "Come, let's get some sleep." Claire led her away.

Over the next few weeks, Annabelle grieved for her little friend. She talked to Jesus about Lacy. It helped. "Don't let anyone call her hair red, Lord. She likes to call it cinnamon." Annabelle devoured the Bible, spending many hours discussing it with Claire at night in their room. Her newfound faith strengthened the ties between them.

One night Claire suggested to her sister, "I think you should write to Mattie and Kate and tell them what has happened to you."

Annabelle quickly agreed. Then she added, "I believe I shall write a letter to Thaddeas as well." As she fell asleep, she transcribed the letter in her mind.

Dear Thaddeas,

A wonderful thing happened to me, and I want to share it with you. I asked Jesus to come into my life, and He did. It is truly amazing, and now I understand so many things that I did not before. I realize how foolish and selfish I was and want to ask you for your forgiveness. Also, I offer congratulations on your upcoming marriage and hope you will be happy.

I am living in Dayton now. Claire and I came in February to help at the orphanage. I have learned that the real "treasures" in life are not those which money can buy. My most precious jewel was a little girl named Lacy who I met here at the orphanage. She lives in heaven now with Jesus. Her short life brought so much beauty to mine. She was the instrument the Lord used to show Himself to me.

I just wanted you to know these things since you were praying for me. I knew it would make you happy. Whether we meet again on this earth, or in heaven, I remain, forever yours,

Annabelle

Chapter 22

Annabelle visited Lacy's grave site. She watched the March wind blow hard across the tiny plot, creating snowdrifts, and remembered the day they had gone sledding and smiled. As she knelt to brush the snow away from the evergreen wreath resting against the small grave marker, she fingered the words carved into the wooden memorial: "Lacy Gray, a precious little jewel, born April 1799, died February 27, 1808."

Remembering Lacy and her courage in mothering her tiny sisters, Neda and Missy, she wondered where the girls' parents were and if they would ever find out that their child was dead. Annabelle thought about her own parents who had died at such a young age. She imagined Lacy looking for them in heaven to tell them all about Claire and herself. Lacy knew about them for they had talked about many things.

Fast-sailing clouds cast a shadow across the grave's marker, and Annabelle looked toward the heavens. The sun peeked out for a split second, and the moisture on the bare limbs that hung overhead glittered. Just as quickly, the brilliance disappeared, displaying branches dull gray and white with snow. "That's what you were, Lacy, a glimpse of heaven's beauty."

Now that Annabelle was a Christian, there was so much to learn. She marveled anew at her peace of mind and thanked God for His love. It was as if everything had purpose now, even the pain. Annabelle put her heart, soul, and body into the work at the orphanage and soaked up the words from the Bible like a sponge. Sometimes she asked Claire or Luke questions about what she read. She came to greatly admire Luke—his intelligence about spiritual things, his enthusiasm around the orphanage.

She started back to the home, and her tracks filled with the drifting snow. Upon returning, she hung up her coat and went to the kitchen to lend a hand. At the open doorway, she overheard Jesse and Luke talking in the adjoining parlor. When she heard what they were saying, she stopped to listen for the subject greatly interested her.

"Rev. Hamer gave me several options. We can make a deal with Harper, assuring him we will buy all children up for sale and requiring him to report them to us immediately. Or we could get up a petition with as many signatures as possible and deliver it personally to the governor in Chillicothe. The problem really isn't just local, you know. Of course moving toward this larger-scale plan means finding willing people to house these children. Perhaps it would be a step toward state funding of orphanages."

"Or even federal funding. You're right, Luke. It's not a local problem. That makes the first option a feeble one. Harper can't be trusted anyway. He would probably up his price and still try to make money off the innocents. But I imagine we'll be forced to start with that option while working toward the other."

"That is exactly what I was thinking, Jesse. It takes time to get things moving in Congress." The two men shook hands in an unspoken pact of the heart.

Annabelle realized she had totally forgotten about the problem. Lacy's sickness and death had all but erased the issue from her mind. She thought if anyone could change things for the better, it would be Jesse and Luke. She turned to go until she heard Jesse ask, "Any other news?"

"I heard that the Indians camped up at Greenville, under Tecumseh and The Prophet, are having it real hard this winter. Women and children are starving. Hundreds of Indians arrived without thought of hunting grounds or survival."

"Why are they gathering? It doesn't make sense."

"The Army thinks they plan to attack. They expect an uprising. The government is soon going to make them dispel, run them out of there."

"They could be innocent, Luke. Maybe they are banding together for religious ceremonies. I hope the Army doesn't break up their camp right in the middle of winter."

"Rev. Hamer said the Lebanon Shakers are getting some food together to take to the camp. He is going to speak to his parishioners to try and get some additional donations. Most folks don't like helping Indians, though, so I don't know how much success he'll have."

"Wish there was something we could do. But we're operating on donations ourselves."

Luke nodded in understanding. "I could write my father a letter. Maybe his church could help some. But again, folks are stubborn as stumps when it comes to Indians. . .except the Galloways." Luke thought a minute. "I'll mention Galloway to Father in my letter. Perhaps he could head a group to round up some food."

Annabelle shuddered. Greenville was not that far away. She was not sure that helping Indians was the right thing to do, but she knew her friend, Rebecca Galloway, was close friends with the Indian chief they were talking about, Tecumseh. Annabelle had seen the Indian in Beaver Creek a few times. He was quite handsome. Rebecca had often sung his praises to Annabelle.

Thinking about her friend reminded her of Dorie Cooper. She had not thought of her in months. Annabelle considered writing her old friend a letter to share what had been happening in her life. *Dorie will never believe it!* she mused. Catherine interrupted Annabelle's daydream, summoning her to the kitchen.

The wind howled like a wild beast, and limbs clawed outside the window of the room Annabelle shared with Claire. Annabelle thought she had never waited so long for spring to appear when the children could play outdoors without the hassle of coats, mittens, and boots. The days seemed so short with never enough hours to get things done. After the children's classroom lessons, it was suppertime, then bedtime. Annabelle pined for the longer, carefree days of summer but did not consider going home to Beaver Creek.

Chapter 23

April sun rays thawed the Dayton area. Trees shook off their wrappings of snow and ice, making streams of the winter's precipitations. Rivulets forged downhill, joining neighboring tributaries. This merging of forces enlarged their beds and bolstered their flow until they were indeed a great force that dumped into the mightier branches of the Miami, Stillwater, and Mad Rivers—even Wolf Creek was of worthy magnitude.

Word spread quickly throughout the city of dangerous water levels. And then the dreaded thing came, April showers. The watercourses continued to swell and gobble up embankments and shorelines.

The children grew restless, unable to play outdoors. Annabelle bounced Cody on her lap while she sought to divert them with a story. A sudden burst of thunder cracked, sounding so close that the children's faces paled and their eyes widened. Before she could reassure them, the door to the main entrance burst open, and Luke and Jesse bolted in. The rain behind them dumped in pailfuls and the water rushed off their coats and boots, making puddles all around them.

Jesse stooped to unbuckle his heavy, mud-laden boots. Annabelle realized the men's hair and clothes were soaked and sternly admonished them, "Better get out of those clothes quick before you catch cold."

"No time. Where is Catherine?" Jesse asked.

Annabelle pointed toward the kitchen and watched the anxious man leave the room. Then she turned to Luke. "What is it?"

"It's bad, real bad. The water is flooding the main streets; people are running for their lives. Buildings are collapsing, belongings going downriver."

Annabelle gasped, "No!"

"Will the water come here?" Barney asked.

"Not yet. We need to pray that it will quit raining. In the meantime Jesse and I are going back to the church. It's on high ground for the time being, and folks are taking refuge there. You women will have to double up the children and make room. I'm sure we'll be bringing some folks to spend the night."

Catherine Murdock followed her husband to the door and forced the men to drink large drafts of coffee before they braved the storm again. Catherine kissed Jesse, and they spoke in low tones. Annabelle turned to Luke.

"Luke."

He looked down at her and smiled. "Yes."

"Be careful. . .and. . .and God be with you."

"Thank you, Annabelle. I'll be fine." Moments later they were gone, two lone men taking arms against the elements. Annabelle looked at Catherine with a fearful expression. Catherine straightened.

"Come, there is much to be done," she said.

That night several families sought shelter at the orphanage. Some Catherine put up in beds, but the rest just found spots on the floor. She, Claire, and Annabelle kept busy serving coffee and drying out clothes by the fire. Annabelle was grateful that Mattie had initiated the comforter project at Rev. Wheeler's church. When the new comforters they brought for the children had arrived, the old ones were stored away. Now these were rummaged out, and the room stank of wet bodies, wool, and firewood.

With all of the excitement, the children were hard to bed down. They made new friends among the stranded and were wound tight as clocks. Long past midnight, Claire and Annabelle tucked the last child in and prayed for the twelfth time—once per child—that the Lord would make the rain cease.

"If the Lord hears the prayers of children, then surely this request will be answered," Claire said as she rubbed a kink out of her neck.

"He listens to the prayers of children. Remember your prayer when I had my wagon accident," Annabelle reminded her.

"Yes. Now what we need is faith that He will do a miracle."

"I believe," Annabelle said. "I have this feeling. When we prayed for Lacy, it was not the same. I think I knew what His answer was going to be. But something within is welling up, this. . .this faith."

"Good." Claire gave her sister a hug. How thankful she was that Annabelle was now a sister in Christ as well.

When they reached the end of the hallway, and just before they reached the parlor, they heard a knock on the door. Annabelle quickly pulled it open, anticipating more stranded townsfolk. What she saw was a drenched blond man, holding a crying child tightly against his chest.

"Luke!"

She pulled him in out of the storm, and he placed the soaked bundle into her arms. "Can you get her dry and rock her?"

Annabelle nodded and carried the small child to her own room, where she clothed the little girl in warm clothes. Singing softly, she rocked her from the edge of her bed, then whispered, "Jesus loves you, little jewel."

When Claire went to bed, she found Annabelle and the youngster curled up together. She covered them with Annabelle's quilt, pulling her own heavy limbs into her bunk for at least an hour's sleep before the morning's dawn.

Annabelle opened heavy eyes and would have cried for joy if she had not remembered the sleeping child lying at her side, for the sun shone, sending beams of comfort into her room.

She eased out of bed and fell to her knees. "Thank You, Lord. Thank You."

Annabelle supervised the children's play and reflected on the happenings of the past week. The first few days had been crazy. There were so many mouths to feed, many extra helping hands, more children underfoot. She was grateful they soon were able to let them run out-of-doors.

Each day the men staying at the orphanage accompanied Jesse and Luke into the city to rescue, restore, and rebuild. First, suitable shelter was found for the homeless. The cleanup seemed endless, and the new construction costly. Every day folks prayed that the sun would keep shining, and it did.

The ground was still mushy soft, which was the reason Annabelle did not hear Luke approach. She jumped when she felt his hand touch her shoulder.

"Sorry, I didn't mean to frighten you."

Annabelle relaxed. "I didn't hear you come." She looked back at the children playing. "They are so happy to be outside again. Look how free they are."

"Thank you."

"For what?"

"For all your help, your work. You pitched in and did the work of two during this disaster."

"I couldn't do enough."

"I know. I felt that way, too. Especially when Clara's parents were killed. If only I had gotten there sooner." He spoke of the little girl he had brought to Annabelle the night of the flood.

"But you saved her life!" Luke warmed under the encouragement of Annabelle, always so vibrant and spunky. He remembered how it used to get her into trouble and was pleased that she had learned to channel all that energy into helping others.

Wanting to express his affirmation, Luke reached out and placed his hands upon her shoulders. "Annabelle, the Lord's done a mighty work in you. You have become quite a woman."

The praise embarrassed Annabelle, and she dropped her eyes momentarily and blushed. His kiss, then, came unexpectedly, and it was so gentle that she wondered if she had imagined it.

Since her conversion, she had come to have great respect and admiration for Luke. She felt a glowing happiness that he paid her such a compliment. He smiled at her now, and his gaze almost unnerved her. Then he spoke softly.

"I got a letter today from Ben. You can read it if you like. It says that he and Kate are ready to adopt Cody and Gabe."

Annabelle's green eyes sparkled with joy. "Oh! I'm so glad."

"Me, too." Luke looked over his shoulder and heaved a great breath. "I better get back to work. There's still so much to do. I'll see you tonight at supper, Annabelle."

The way he said her name made her wonder. Was it her imagination, or was there something special about it?

Chapter 24

"I cannot believe it is coming to this. Everything Father worked for is crumbling." Thaddeas paced the dining room floor, addressing Leon and Amelia.

"It's not that bad, Son. Things are not falling apart yet. It just seems so because the responsibility lies partially on your shoulders."

Leon listened to his brother rant for several minutes. In the short time he had worked with Thad, he had learned it was best to let him vent all his feelings before offering any advice. Now he intervened.

"I think the best thing we can do is close down the shop for awhile, Thad. It does not make sense to be pulling money out of our investments to make goods that will just sit in a warehouse."

Tears glistened in Amelia's eyes. Having been through worse times with her husband, she knew they would survive this, but it touched her to watch her grown-up sons make such decisions. She was proud of them.

Thaddeas nodded. "You're right, of course. Maybe we should pull all the goods out of the School Street warehouse then and keep them at the storefront, since we can't get out of the rent for another six months anyway."

"Good idea. And, Thad, we'll go together when we tell our employees. It's hard, but there just isn't any other way."

"Do you want to go now?"

"Why don't we let them finish the day?"

With business temporarily resolved, Amelia spoke.

"Thaddeas, a letter came for you from Dayton."

"Dayton? The only person I know there is Luke Wheeler. I wonder why he is writing." Amelia handed her son the letter, and he walked away with it, mounting the stairs that led to his room.

Seating himself at his desk, he took a look at the letter in his hand. There was no return address. *That is strange,* he thought. He opened the letter and quickly turned to the last page to see who it was from. *Annabelle!*

His excitement mounted despite himself. With trembling hands he shuffled the pages back to the beginning. Thaddeas cried when he read about Annabelle's conversion, her apology, and her new outlook on life. She mentioned his prayers. Sobs overtook him, and he pushed the letter aside, burying his face in his hands.

Oh, that he could be there to see the change in her. He marveled over the miracle of her conversion and tried to envision what she might be like. In his wildest dreams, he could not imagine her working at an orphanage.

With the need to be alone and think this thing through, he gathered his wraps and started toward the docks. First, he passed through the residential area, a row of brownstone houses occupied by wealthy merchants like his own family. The afternoon sun shone on the manicured wet lawns, creating fields of diamonds.

He wondered how many of these folks dealt with the same problem in their businesses that his family encountered with their leather shop. But his mind did not stay on business long. It returned to the letter from Annabelle. *Helping orphans! I can't believe it!*

Reaching Dorchester Road, he picked up his gait and in no time approached the docks. The familiar sight stretched before him. The fog, which had lifted around noon, allowed the city's shame to manifest itself, the result of the despised Embargo Act.

The docks were jammed, crowded with freighters and cargo ships as well as a hodgepodge of smaller vessels. Sailors slopped the decks for want of something better to do. A group of burly, unkempt men drank and yelled obscenities. When Thaddeas walked past them, one called out, "Cost ya to walk on this here deck. Be off with ya, ya no good 'monger, unless ya got some goods ta ship." This set the others into a gale of laughter. Thaddeas looked away until he passed them. The whole scene disgusted him. *It's best when this place is fogged over,* he thought.

Seagulls swooped down and shrieked out, adding their soprano to the bass of the waves hitting against the crafts and docks. Thaddeas stopped to watch the birds pick through the dirt and sand, then soar across the water, diving to come up with a fish. The smell of salt, fish, fowl, and sea was potent, but it did not call out to him. It was the land across the mountains that whispered his name.

Thaddeas realized how weary he had become of Boston, the sea, the politics. In that moment he vowed to take Mary Beth west. A rush of excitement hit him. They would move up the wedding date! He knew that Leon was capable of handling things here.

Thaddeas made an about-face and ran until he hailed a carriage and, breathless, tried to calm himself as he gave the driver Mary Beth's address on Walnut Street. Within twenty minutes he was standing at her front door.

"Come in, Mr. Larson," the maid invited.

"Could you tell Mary Beth that I am here?"

"Certainly."

He rubbed his arms and shifted feet as he waited.

"Thaddeas!"

"Hello, can we talk?"

"Of course, come into the parlor. You're as nervous as a rabbit. What's wrong, Thaddeas?"

"Nothing is wrong. I just came to an important decision. . .about our future, Mary Beth."

"Sit down, please. What is it?"

"We are going to speed up our wedding date and move to the West. . .as soon as possible."

"I don't understand. Why this sudden decision?" Mary Beth had deliberately set their marriage date far into the future, hoping Thaddeas's love would take on more fullness. He was passionate enough, vibrant energy coursed through his sturdy, well-built body, but Mary Beth knew she did not possess his love and did not know why. Could a man like this only love adventure? Or was there a woman from his past who already owned his heart? He was so commanding, so impulsive. It frightened her.

Hoping his restlessness would settle over the months of their engagement, she had waited expectantly to see the shine of love in his eyes. There was a gleam there today, but from what she did not know.

"Things aren't going well at the leather shop. You know that. There is really no reason for me to stay here anymore. I am itching to go west."

"How soon?"

"As soon as you can arrange things."

Mary Beth acted out of character, for she picked up a nearby cushion and hurled it at him. It caught him square in the head, ruffling his black wavy hair. He gaped at her in amazement. "Mary Beth!"

"You exasperate me!" she screamed.

"Mary Beth, I'm sorry. You said that you would follow me wherever I wanted to go. I. . .I thought you would be happy."

She quickly gained her composure as a new revelation hit her. "Thaddeas! I know what it is. I finally know what it is. You are running away from something. That's it, isn't it?"

"Nonsense."

"I shall not even marry you at all unless you tell me everything."

When Thaddeas realized she was serious, he spoke. "I feel like I'm on a raft fighting against the current—going in the wrong direction—but I can't remember why it's the wrong way."

"Perhaps you are running from love." Mary Beth referred to their own relationship, meaning to encourage him to open up to the love between them.

"No, that's over."

"What?"

"That was over months ago. How did you know?"

She took a deep breath, and courageously forged ahead. They were so close. If they could just talk this out. "Please tell me about her."

"My cousin from Beaver Creek. I thought I loved her, but she had different ideas. She was a gold seeker with lofty ambitions."

"And you wanted her to love you and not your money."

"Yes. She sent me a telegram, pursuing me, and I dismissed her. Since then you came into my life, and now you are all to me."

"I wish I could believe that. Did she free you then?"

"Yes. In fact I continued to pray for her, that she would become a Christian, and now she has. So I am totally free from her and any obligations toward her."

The light dawned in Mary Beth's brain. "When did you find out that she had become a Christian?"

"Just recently. Mary Beth, why does it matter?"

"I believe the reason you feel you are riding the current in the wrong direction is because you need to find out if she has indeed changed." Mary Beth gathered her courage. "Running off to the wilderness probably won't solve your problems. And I am sure of one thing—I won't be accompanying you. I am not so hard up, so needy, that I have to marry someone who loves another. You are not the only available man in Boston, Thaddeas Larson! And you better leave this house before I throw something harder than a pillow!"

"Darling, be reasonable."

"Don't call me darling. The way I see it you have several choices. You may rot in Boston. You can fly to your wilderness. Or you can look up that old flame. It is nothing to me, for we are no longer engaged. Weigh your decision wisely, Thaddeas. Don't make another mistake!" She left him alone in the parlor.

Thaddeas was mortified. Then a grin spread across his face. *Thank you, Mary Beth,* he said to himself as he left the two-story stone home. He knew what this had cost her. Could he allow her to make this sacrifice? He had no other choice. "You're an angel," he called, feeling happier than he had in months.

Chapter 25

I f a farmer had a milk cow, two sheep, ten chickens, and one hound dog, how many animals would he have altogether?" Luke posed the question to the group of young boys seated before him.

Barney dangled his legs, made some scratches on his slate, then raised his hand.

"Yes, Barney?"

"Would that there cow be a Guernsey or a Holstein?"

Annabelle smiled as she watched Luke patiently answer the towheaded boy.

"The cow is Guernsey, there is a white sheep and a black lamb, nine Rhode Island Red hens, one Rhode Island Red rooster, and one short-tailed hound dog used for hunting coon, and oh yes, three baby chicks just hatched."

"Aw, look what ya did, Barney. You made the problem harder," complained nine-year-old Logan.

Slates squeaked as the children added up the sums, and Luke gave Annabelle a knowing smile. She moved methodically behind the boys to see if they placed their number columns straight and stopped to help Barney line up his one hound dog under the one Rhode Island Red rooster.

The dinner bell rang, and the children scrambled to line up at the door. "Think about this over lunch," Luke told his pupils. "See you back here at one o'clock sharp. You may go now."

Annabelle watched Luke with wonder, marveling at the way he commanded the children's respect yet kept the lines of communication open. Any of the orphans could flee to him with a concern, except for the older girls who were beginning to show signs of shy adolescence.

She thought about them now and wondered what would become of them. How would they find husbands, stuck away in a place like this? Amity slipped past Luke just then, taking a quick peek at his face. He smiled at the fourteen-year-old girl, and she dropped her eyes to the floor as she hurried past him. Annabelle realized the girl was enamored, probably had a crush on the teacher.

Annabelle considered this. *I wonder if he knows.* He is good-looking and young. Maybe he grew the mustache to look older. She had always deemed him better-looking than his brother, Ben. Her eyes took in his tall, lean frame, blond hair, and face that was both tanned and freckled. *Those blue eyes would melt any young girl's heart, even though they are never flirty.* The sapphire pools gave his face a kind, attentive expression.

"Thinking hard on something?" Luke asked as he waited for her to join him.

"About you." She reddened. "You're a good teacher, Luke. In fact, you're a good preacher, too."

"Well, that is high praise. And what might you be after?"

Annabelle socked him in the arm, then blushed again as she felt his solid muscles flex beneath her fist. He reached out playfully and snagged her closed hand in the palm of his enormous one, holding it for a moment then releasing it like a hot branding iron.

She thought he acted differently toward her lately and could not figure it out. She shrugged it off. "When will Ben and Kate come for the boys?" she questioned.

"I thought maybe we would deliver them."

"Really?" she squealed in delight.

"Would that please you?" He watched her reaction.

"Oh yes! It would be so good to go home."

His eyebrows arched. This creature was not the same girl who he had once considered shallow and immature. He enjoyed her company now, as well as her helping hands, and hoped she was not homesick.

"I mean, for a visit. And Claire will be glad, too. Or maybe I should ask, who will be going?"

"No plans are set; I've just been rolling ideas around. It's still too muddy to take a wagon; however, it shouldn't be long until we can make the trip. I imagine the Murdocks can do without the three of us for a short while. The volunteers at church like to fill in occasionally. This will give them the opportunity."

"When will you tell the children, Cody and Gabe?"

"Soon."

"Just think, they'll be our nephews."

"I can't wait to see them smothered with Kate and Ben's love."

"Me, too."

Luke's expression changed. "Oh, I wanted to tell you something."

"Yes?"

"Jesse and I talked to Harper. He agreed to cooperate. He gave us his word he won't sell any more stranded children, but we have to pay him to take them in at the orphanage." Luke looked concerned. "I don't trust the man."

"But that is wonderful, Luke. I'm so proud of you and Jesse."

"I guess it's the best we can do. We're starting a petition to work toward changes on a larger scale. Do you want to sign it?"

"Of course."

Luke gave her an intense look. Annabelle met his gaze, sensing that Luke was evaluating her and appraising her with high marks, and it felt good.

Claire hung her dress on the hook beside her bunk and slipped her flannel nightgown over her blond head. She did not climb under the covers but perched on the edge of her mattress with her elbows on her knees, watching her sister brush her hair. She watched the copper tresses elongate and then spring back when Annabelle pulled the brush away.

"You happy here, Annabelle?"

"Yes. Are you?"

"Mm-hm. You've changed so much. I never know what to expect from you."

"I have? I was pretty awful, wasn't I?"

"No, of course not."

"I could never understand how you could be so caring for folks. Take for instance, Sammy Hawkes."

"What about him?"

"See what I mean. You always defended him, always went out of your way to encourage him, just because he stuttered."

"The other children teased him."

Annabelle nodded. "But I didn't care. I only considered my own needs. Since Jesus changed my heart, I regret my past."

"It's all forgiven. Kate will like the changes in you."

"I'd love to have a nice long chat with her."

"Soon enough, you'll be able to when we take a vacation and visit home."

"I can hardly wait."

"Annabelle?"

"Mm-hm." Annabelle laid her brush aside and wiggled under the covers of her bed.

"I think Luke is falling in love with you."

"What?"

"You heard me."

Annabelle sat up straight. "Oh, I hope not! That will ruin everything."

"I don't think it would be such a bad thing to have a man like Luke love you." Claire's voice took on a dreamy quality.

"I am not ready to love anyone, Claire," Annabelle said sternly. "Loving a man hurts like having your insides full of burrs. I'm not ready to go through that pain again."

"Oh, Annabelle." Claire giggled. "I hope it is not like that. Just forget I said anything and go to sleep."

But Annabelle could not sleep.

Chapter 26

I want to thank all of you who helped out with the food for the Indians at Greenville." Rev. Wheeler gazed long and hard at his Beaver Creek congregation. Some squirmed in their seats but remained quiet. No one had nerve enough to disagree with the mission project in this setting. But the reverend knew that as soon as the service was over, many would complain and criticize the project; that is why his gaze bore down relentlessly on several of his parishioners.

James Galloway patted his daughter's hand and exchanged a meaningful glance with his wife. He remained one of the few who had pitched in to help the preacher head up this particular charitable outreach.

Rebecca's thoughts turned to the proud Indian Tecumseh. He was her good friend. It hurt her to see him have to take donations from the white men to feed his people. His braves were proud and able to provide for their own. However, the government had cruelly hemmed them in, continually taking away more rights. Her eyes watered as she listened to the preacher conclude his message and say the benediction over the congregation.

"The Lord bless you. Go in peace."

Outside the schoolhouse, the day burst with the new growth of springtime. Folks gathered in familiar circles to visit. Kate overheard one mother remark, "A body can surely tell that the children have spring fever. Jest look at 'em. I wonder how the teacher can give them any learnin' this time of year."

Nearby, Melanie Whitfield rubbed her swollen stomach—to make a statement, Kate thought. "This baby sure does move a lot. I think being pregnant is just the closest thing to heaven a body can be."

Kate nodded. "When's the little one due?"

"I expect around August."

"You're mighty big for August."

Melanie's face flushed and her eyes glared, hot as two volcanoes. "Might be twins."

Kate nearly giggled. She should not have said that, but sometimes the woman got under her skin. "Wouldn't that be nice," she said sweetly.

Ben had come up behind her and, overhearing Melanie's last statement, interrupted the conversation. "We just might be having twins ourselves."

"What!" Melanie clapped her hand across her mouth in astonishment. "Well, glory be!"

"Ben, you better explain yourself," Kate admonished her husband, but on the inside she was enjoying their little joke.

"We're adopting two boys, Melanie, from Luke's orphanage."

"Oh. Well, I wondered, didn't think you'd be having real children, so long as it's been and everything."

Kate became indignant. "These are real children, Melanie. Two very sweet little boys."

"Why, of course they are, Honey. I didn't mean no harm by it. I just ain't myself when I'm with child, I guess."

Kate thought she seemed very much like herself.

Ben gave his wife a supportive caress and moved away to join a group of men. As he drew closer, he saw forceful arm movements and heard explosions of anger as the men grumbled their opinions. "We're feeding the very hands that are going to shoot arrows in our backs, burn our homes, and scalp our families." Ben turned and walked away. This kind of talk discouraged him.

❧❧

On the ride home, Ben and Kate discussed the sermon and Melanie Whitfield. Eventually the conversation led to Cody and Gabe. Kate's eyes sparkled. "I can hardly wait."

"How old is Cody now?"

"Two years old this month, May 14," she said without the slightest hesitation. "I hope they're here for his birthday."

"They will be, Darling." Ben hugged his wife. "Not to change the subject, but have you noticed how all of Luke's letters sing the praises of your sister Annabelle?"

"It's hard to believe, isn't it?" Ben looked at her questioningly, and she clarified. "That she has changed that much. We so quickly forget God's power, that His love changes lives. I'm real anxious to see her again. She may actually seem like Claire's sister now."

"And yours. Don't sell yourself short, Dear. But what I meant is. . ." Ben scratched his head, and it was Kate's turn to look puzzled. "Sounds like Luke might be falling in love with her."

Kate smiled. "That would be nice, but I always pictured him and Claire together."

"I can't believe you've had such thoughts and kept them to yourself!"

"Only thoughts, Darling. The only romance I'm sure about is ours."

Ben answered his wife with an affectionate pat on the knee.

❧❧

The same day, May 9, Thaddeas arrived in Beaver Creek, dusty and weary. His legs felt numb and weak as he hobbled to the front door of Tucker

House. It looked so good. He raised his fist and pounded. Since it was Sunday, Buck and Mattie were both at home, napping in the sitting room.

"I'll get it." Buck staggered across the room, jumping up from his sleep a bit too fast. "Just a minute, I'm coming," he yelled. Then under his breath he muttered, "Don't need to break down the door."

He pulled it open with a frown, wondering who was disturbing their siesta, and stared full into the unshaven face of his nephew. "Thaddeas! Boy!" He pulled Thad into a bear hug, screaming into the young man's ear, "Mattie, come quick! Thaddeas is home!"

"What!" Mattie scrambled to the door, barely missing Freckles's tail. Her arms flailed with expression. "I can't believe it. Oh, it's so good to see you. Come in."

"We didn't get a letter, so we weren't expecting you," the sheriff stammered.

"Wasn't time to write. I had to get here quick as I could. Started out the first of April and made it in six weeks." Thaddeas seemed proud of himself.

"Why? What was the hurry, Son?"

"I'm home to stay, and I'm going to marry Annabelle."

Buck cleared his throat. "They don't need you in Boston?"

"Nope. We closed down the leather shop because all our goods kept piling up."

"Things got worse?"

Thad nodded. "That Embargo Act is ruining the merchants in the coastal cities." He saw Buck's worried expression and quickly assured him. "Oh, we'll make it all right. We've got plenty to ship as soon as the seas open. In the meantime, Mother and Leon are living off investments. Leon is quite capable of handling affairs at home."

Buck warmed to the idea of having his nephew back and expressed himself, saying, "I'm glad you decided to come home."

"It is home, Uncle Buck. By the way, Mother and Leon send their regards."

Mattie's own motherly instincts toward Thad surfaced. She gave him another hug. "Now, what can I get you? You must be hungry and thirsty."

"I don't suppose you'd have any pie?"

"I sure do. A custard pie."

"And a glass of cold milk?"

Her face crinkled just like he remembered it. "Comin' right up."

Buck studied Thaddeas. "Annabelle and Claire aren't in Beaver Creek anymore. They are helping Luke out at the orphanage. I don't know as any of us will know Annabelle when we see her again. I hear she's made some major changes."

Thaddeas listened attentively. "I'm counting on it."

"And speaking of changes, I thought you were engaged to a girl in Boston."

"That didn't work out, Uncle Buck. It never could because I've always loved Annabelle."

"I see. Well, I wouldn't get your hopes too high."

Thaddeas just laughed. "Uncle Buck, you just wait and see. I'll be needing to get a few supplies before I go on to Dayton," he said, planning out loud.

"You won't need to go to Dayton."

"What do you mean?"

"Luke is bringing Annabelle and Claire home for a visit. Ben and Kate are adopting two little boys from the orphanage, and the girls and Luke are bringing them. They should be here within the week."

Thaddeas brightened and hollered, "This is perfect!"

Buck looked amused. "Annabelle will be surprised, all right."

Chapter 27

Buck's strides mashed down the tall fronds of grass growing on the grounds surrounding Green's Mill. The ground sloped downward toward the bank of the Little Miami River where the mill, a hub of activity, provided many men with work and wages.

David Green had welcomed Thaddeas back to his old job with open arms, which is where Buck found him wearing a frustrated expression on his face.

"Hello, Uncle."

"Morning, Thaddeas. How's it going?"

"Tough as horseshoes." He bent forward so Buck could hear when he lowered his voice to a whisper. "Books are all messed up. It'll take me awhile to get them straightened out."

Buck grinned. "That's why you looked so troubled when I came in. Well, you're just the man to do the job."

"Thanks, Uncle Buck."

"You bet. I thought you might like to know. . .Annabelle is back."

The quill in Thaddeas's hand snapped in two. "What! She is?"

Sunday's confident man suddenly looked like a whipped puppy. Buck compassionately reassured him. "Don't worry, Son. You'll do fine."

"Does she know I'm here?"

"No. Thought we'd let that be a surprise."

Thad nodded as he nervously toyed with the broken quill pieces. "Maybe that is best. Meet her head on before she has time to rationalize. Get her true reaction that way."

"There's a birthday party at Kate and Ben's tonight. Can you come?"

"Whose birthday?"

"Cody. One of the little boys Ben and Kate are adopting."

"Oh! Yes, I'll be there."

"Good." Buck slapped his nephew roughly on the back. "Now you better get back to work."

"If I can concentrate."

❧❧

Annabelle looked out her bedroom window; Tucker House seemed just the same. A robin flew with string in its bill and lit upon the budding limb of the hickory tree, then disappeared within its foliage. "Missed the tulips this year," she muttered to herself.

She examined the few clothes she had brought back from Dayton, trying to decide what to wear to Cody's birthday party. Fingering a soft green gown she had not worn for months, she thought, *I'll wear that, then just leave it here. Not much need for such niceties at the orphanage.* She concluded, *It'll be fun to dress up tonight. I think I'll leave my hair down. It's so bothersome always binding it up.* Catherine encouraged the girls to do so at the orphanage. *Hope Catherine is not overworked without us.* She sighed.

They had arrived late the night before, bunking at Ben's. Luke explained that the boys might be frightened to be left alone with their new parents. Then this morning Luke had brought Claire and Annabelle to Tucker House, where they were greeted warmly with hugs and kisses all around.

Luke agreed to stay on at Tucker House for the extent of their visit, giving Ben and Kate time alone with their new family members. However, he had ridden off about an hour earlier to see his father, Mary, and the boys, saying he would meet them back at Ben's that evening.

Suddenly, Annabelle felt hungry. Deciding to go to the kitchen and find an apple before dressing, she found Mattie bent over the ironing board. "Let me do that," Annabelle offered.

Mattie grinned at Annabelle, then shook her head. "Nope. Not today. Consider it a holiday."

"But it isn't."

"Seems like it, having you girls home. I missed you. Best sit down so we can talk a spell."

Annabelle grabbed an apple out of a shallow wooden bowl that graced the center of the table, eyeing Mattie all the time and wondering what she had to say.

Annabelle crunched a bite out of her apple just as Mattie spoke.

"You happy, Annabelle?"

"Yes."

Annabelle choked and coughed, and Mattie ordered, "Git yerself a drink."

Annabelle's apple rolled to the floor. "Now there's no use wastin' a good apple," Mattie teased.

"Sorry, Mattie." Annabelle picked up the red fruit and washed it off in a basin of water by the kitchen window.

"Sure is lonely here without you girls."

"Consider it a reprieve. It's about time you had a break, Mattie. You've been such a patient mother."

At the word "mother," Mattie's conscience pricked her. "I love you girls," was all she said.

It was quite a reunion at Ben's. Emmett Wheeler's family was there and, of course, the Tucker House group. Kate made everyone feel at home, and Annabelle just knew her sister would make a perfect mother. She noticed, though, that Gabe and Cody acted like lost little boys, excited yet unsure.

"You boys behaving?" Annabelle asked with a serious expression.

"We played today. Ben showed us horsies," Gabe answered as he jumped onto her lap. Cody followed Gabe wherever he went and wiggled his body against hers. Her skirt tugged in his tiny grip, and she gently lifted him and pried the material out of his fists, settling the child in the tiny space remaining that his brother did not occupy.

Kate's eyes followed the boys constantly, and now Annabelle saw a glimpse of sadness in the brown pools and knew her sister longed to have them prefer her in such a way. "Oh, look what your mommy has." Annabelle pointed toward Kate and gave them a little pat and a shove, setting them in her direction.

Nearby, she overheard Luke discussing the Indian situation with his father. "Thanks for helping out. I know what you were up against. Folks around Lebanon practically lynched some of the Shakers who drove the wagon loads of food to the settlement." A mournful cry of Ben's beagle interrupted the conversation.

The dog howled again, then let out some short barks, so Ben went to the door and welcomed the visitor. Annabelle heard the familiar voice of Thaddeas and almost cried at the sound. *It could not be. Thaddeas? No one mentioned that he was home. Calm.* She must remain calm.

Suddenly, she felt ashamed and embarrassed at the telegram and letter she had written him. How forward she had been. She must not appear that way now. Annabelle silently vowed she would not let him see the love in her eyes; she would not ruin his life again. So desperately she longed to make a new start, to have his friendship. But could she stand the pain of it, without his love?

When Thaddeas laid eyes on Annabelle, all of his big talk to his Uncle Buck was just that—talk. He took in the wavy copper tresses. How he had dreamed about their silkiness. Her face glowed as if a halo floated overhead. He grew tongue-tied and ill at ease. Thoughts raced through his mind, *I don't have forever; she plans to go back to Dayton. Don't scare her away again. Maybe she does not feel the same anymore. Oh, why is it so hot in here?*

It seemed like the room faded away as Annabelle watched him move around greeting folks. Then he looked directly at her and came in her direction. Out of the corner of her eye, she noticed Mattie and Buck whispering.

Oh, he looked wonderful. Had his shoulders always been that broad? His hair so dark? His eyes so intense? She rose from her chair and held out her hand to him. He clasped it tightly. The room grew quiet. "Hello, Annabelle."

"Thaddeas."

At that moment Luke slipped out the door to get a breath of fresh air, and Claire followed him. "Wait up." Luke paused and waited for the young woman to catch up to him. She spoke bluntly. "I'm sorry, Luke."

"What?"

She tossed her head toward the house. "About Annabelle."

"You don't miss much, do you, blue eyes?"

"It's been pretty obvious—to everyone except Annabelle."

"I thought Thad was out of the picture," he admitted. "No one told me he was in Ohio. He always loved Annabelle. You think it would be too obvious if I walk a bit?"

"Don't be gone too long." She sadly retreated to the house. Thad had seated himself at Annabelle's side. Claire marveled at how her sister's beauty attracted men. At one time she would have felt a little pity for the man who won Annabelle's heart, but now any man who loved her sister could be proud. She knew Annabelle loved Thaddeas. She wondered what he was doing back. Would he break her heart again? Or would Annabelle break Luke's?

They seemed to be in deep conversation. Annabelle was saying, "Are you here for a visit?"

"No, to stay. I'm working at the mill again."

"I'm glad. Is your fiancée here?"

"No! That didn't work out."

"Oh, I'm sorry." She reached out and touched his hand gently. Luke entered the room just in time to observe the tender scene. Thad lowered his voice so the others couldn't hear their conversation. "I would like to explain it to you. I hope I get the chance very soon."

Annabelle still felt jealous of the Boston lady and resisted the urge to reply sarcastically, for she knew better. "I'll only be here a few days; then I'll be going back to Dayton. . .with Luke." Her eyes glanced across the room at Luke. "This was just intended to be a visit; all of my belongings are at the orphanage."

Thaddeas's heart sank. She would return with Luke? Was there a special connotation in the way she glanced Luke's way? Luke stood where he had entered the room, and Thad's eyes locked with his, each regarding the competition.

Thad turned toward Annabelle, "How about a canoe ride before you leave, like old times?"

"That would be perfect," she replied.

"How would tomorrow evening be?" Thaddeas asked.

"I'll look forward to it."

Gabe rushed into Luke's arms. "Daddy," he called, and the blond-haired giant beamed down at him.

"Uncle Luke is right here." He assured the child while providing him with gentle correction. "There's your new daddy." He pointed toward Ben.

Kate called her sons to come to the table so Cody could blow out his birthday candles. "Come, let's light the candles," she coaxed.

Gabe cried. "We want mommy and daddy to sit beside us."

Cody copied his brother and waved his chubby little hands pointing toward the chairs, "Mommy." Everyone in the room understood that he addressed Annabelle.

"Of course we'll sit by you," Luke offered and he reached out to catch Annabelle's hand, pulling her along. He felt Thad's eyes scald his back and winked at Annabelle anyway, glad to snatch her away. "Aunt Annabelle"—Luke emphasized the "aunt" part—"and Uncle Luke are right here. Now your mother can light those candles."

As the evening proceeded, Luke monopolized Annabelle in a sweet and charming manner, under the guise of making things easier for Cody and Gabe. Thus, Thaddeas was able to observe Annabelle's new unselfish character as she ministered to the small children. The fact that Annabelle and Luke worked familiarly well together did not go unnoted.

Claire determined to stay out of the love triangle and did not offer any assistance with the youngsters. Instead, she helped to serve the food. However, she kept an eye on Luke's smooth performance.

When the time came for the youngsters to be tucked in for the night, Annabelle went with Kate. She found the opportunity to encourage her sister. "It won't take long for them to warm up to you."

"I know. It's all right, really. I've waited too long to give up easily."

"Me, too," Annabelle said softly, thinking of her Boston gentleman.

Chapter 28

Rebecca Galloway knocked on the door of Tucker House, then tapped the side of her riding habit with her fingers in a nervous manner. She sighed with relief when Annabelle answered the door. "Rebecca! Come in."

"Hello, Annabelle. I heard you were back in town and wondered if you would like to go riding with me?"

"Sure, come up while I change." Annabelle motioned toward her room.

"That's all right. I'll just wait outside. It's such a beautiful day."

"Yes, it is. I'll just be a minute."

❧❧

Within the hour, Annabelle mounted her horse with an air of expectancy and shouted to Rebecca, "I really missed riding Dusty." She patted the beast's mane, then acknowledged her friend. "What's been happening in your life, Rebecca?"

"You first. Tell me about the orphanage."

"Working there turned out different than I expected."

"In what ways?"

"I guess I learned to think about other folks' needs as well as my own."

"Was it the children?"

Annabelle nodded. "Especially one little girl named Lacy." She smiled, and her voice took on a soft quality. "We became very close, and then she died."

"Oh no. I'm sorry."

"But she taught me about Jesus."

"Really?"

"Her and Luke."

"Tell me about Luke." Rebecca rolled her eyes, making romantic insinuations.

"Luke is a remarkable Christian man."

"I haven't seen him for years. Is he still as handsome?"

"Very!" The girls giggled. "But as I was saying, when I became a Christian, my life became meaningful with peace and purpose."

"I am happy for you. Now, where are you taking me?"

"To a very special place." The spot, the same one where she had rendezvoused with Charles Harrison so many times, appeared. Today she wanted to see it through forgiving eyes. It was a chapter of her life that needed closure.

They dismounted, and she sighed with satisfaction as they tied up the horses.

"Over here." She led her friend through a tangle of dense trees and knee-high bushy plants. The path, now grown over with the season's lush explosion of grass and weeds, no longer existed. In a short while, they emerged into a paradise of wildflowers.

"Oh! It's beautiful," Rebecca gasped.

Annabelle was surprised by the daisies that waved smiling faces. The last time she had been here, it had been autumn. "Changes," she murmured.

"What?"

"Oh, nothing. Come on!"

They left the meadow to forge through more forest, then stepped into an open area surrounded on three sides by wooded foliage. The fourth supplied a panorama of the Beaver Creek's blue tongue, flowing swiftly onward. The water level was high. "Let's rest on that log." *That looks the same,* she thought.

"It's gorgeous. How did you find this spot?"

"My secret," Annabelle cautioned. "Now, tell me about yourself."

"All right. But brace yourself." Annabelle gripped the log with her gloved hands, eyes enlarged with curiosity. "I've had a marriage proposal," Rebecca said, "and I don't know what to do."

"Really? Who?"

"Promise me you won't tell a soul, not anybody?"

"I promise."

"Tecumseh, the Shawnee Indian chief."

Now, Annabelle's mouth flew open. "What! I don't know what to say. . . he's very magnificent, I've seen him. . .and powerful."

"And brave, and respected by his people," Rebecca added.

"Do you love him?"

"Yes, madly, but how can I love an Indian?"

"Oh, Rebecca, what will you do?"

"I don't know."

"It is so romantic. How did it happen?"

"In a canoe."

"What?" Annabelle recalled her engagement with Thad that evening to do that very thing. However, Rebecca interrupted her thoughts.

"A canoe. I can't tell you why we were out rowing. It's an Indian secret. But he proposed very gallantly and properly. He said he'd only take one wife, and I'd never have to work like the other squaws because he was the chief and could declare it."

"Well, that's good. But aren't the soldiers expecting a war soon? Do you know what he's doing in Greenville? Is that part of the secret?"

"No. He doesn't divulge information like that. But I'm afraid if I turn him down—which is what I plan to do—it could cause a war."

"Poor thing. What a predicament! Rebecca, have you told your father?"

"Yes. We've discussed all the options, and he said he'd support me, whatever I decide."

"But, of course, you can't worry yourself about the outcome. After all, an Indian uprising could just as easily happen if you did marry him. Imagine, fighting against your own family."

"I have," Rebecca said with sadness.

"One never knows what the future holds. If war or peace lies ahead, we can only trust God with it."

"You're right, Annabelle. Talking with you has been helpful." Rebecca patted her friend's hand. "Will you be returning to the orphanage? I know it's selfish of me, but I hope you'll stay. With Dorie gone for so long and then you, it's been lonely."

"I miss Dorie, too."

"Did you hear about her?"

"No, what?"

"She's engaged to be married to a congressman."

Annabelle shook her curly head. "It doesn't surprise me. But know what? I'm not even jealous."

"You didn't answer my question. Is there a chance you'll stay?"

"I really don't know." She thought about Thaddeas; leaving him again would be painful. The two women were silent for a long time. The sun drizzled warm rays, causing sweat trickles on their brow. Annabelle plucked a wild violet and inhaled deeply. Its sweet perfume intoxicated her with spring's aroma.

Rebecca broke the spell. "Annabelle, something else is troubling me, and I thought you should know."

"What is it?"

"Oh, I hate to say this, but a rumor is spreading around Beaver Creek. It's about Mattie."

"Mattie?"

"Yes. Word has it she's been seen with a man other than the sheriff, a military man. I'm sure there is some explanation. And if there is, it would be good for Tucker House to put a bug in some ears. Do you know what I mean?"

"I know there's nothing to it. Gone so long, I've no idea what it could be about. I'll ask her, and we'll get it all straightened out."

"I can imagine the rumors going around about me." Rebecca sighed.

"Oh, don't fret. You've done nothing wrong."

When they left that place, Rebecca felt encouraged, but Annabelle continued to poke at the rumor Rebecca mentioned from every angle, coming up at dead ends.

Chapter 29

Annabelle dismounted and looked toward the house, where she recognized Mattie at a distance, digging in the flower bed. She stabled Dusty and set off toward her. With concern, she slowed her pace when she saw Mattie wrestling with a fistful of ragweed.

When she reached the older woman, she knelt beside her and uprooted some stubborn dandelions. Mattie warned with approval, "You'll git your ridin' clothes soiled."

"Couldn't get any worse. We stopped off by the creek."

"Sure is a nice day."

"Indeed. I think I have spring fever."

"I 'spect you're thinkin' about goin' back to Dayton, the orphanage and all."

"I guess it's always on my mind. I seem to be just living one day at a time."

"That's what we all do, I 'spect."

"There is something that I want to ask you."

"Go ahead, Child."

"I really don't know how to say this, but I hear there's a rumor going around town about Tucker House."

Mattie gave her a quizzical glance, and Annabelle continued. "About you and some Army man?"

Annabelle had never seen Mattie look more stricken. She dropped to the grass, limp like the weeds that lay in a heap between them. Calling up courage, Mattie straightened. "I reckon it's time I told ya. I can't live a lie any longer."

Annabelle held her breath, unable to imagine what kind of deception Mattie could mean. She listened carefully as Mattie told her story in a trembling voice that grew stronger as she spoke.

"A long time ago, when I was about your age, I fell in love with Lt. Wade Brooks, only he wasn't a lieutenant then. We weren't married, but I got pregnant. My pa, a preacher, kicked me out of the house."

"Oh, Mattie, what did you do? What did the lieutenant do?"

"He skedaddled, and I never heard from him again until a few months ago. Now he wants to know about our child. There ain't nothin' betwixt us now; he's jest been houndin' me."

"What happened to your child, Mattie?"

"This is the hard part ta tell. I gave her to my married sister, Elizabeth, to raise."

"That's not so bad. I can understand that."

"She and her husband were murdered at the Big Bottom Indian massacre." Annabelle stiffened, and Mattie's tears flowed unrestrained. Rivers of regret wet her cheeks as she continued. "My child survived. I took her and my sister's own two daughters ta raise as my own."

The truth was hard for Annabelle to accept. "Are you saying. . ."

Mattie nodded. "Kate is my daughter. You and Claire are my nieces. That's why I didn't adopt ya till after Kate married. She was already mine."

"I–I thought it was because you married Buck that you adopted us. Why?" Annabelle screamed. "Why have you lied to us all these years?"

Mattie hung her head as strangling sobs engulfed her. "I already had my seamstress shop in Beaver Creek. Folks knew me, and I liked it here. I didn't want them ta know about my past."

"How could you? This is unforgivable!" Annabelle rose to leave, but Mattie clung to her skirt, preventing her.

"Wait. There's more." Annabelle glared down at Mattie. "Lt. Brooks, Kate's father, hired Charles Harrison ta spy on us. He was the prowler at Ben's place. That's why he left so abruptly."

"He. . .used me?"

"I'm so sorry." Mattie still clutched Annabelle's riding habit.

Annabelle jerked it loose. "I shall not forgive you!" she cried out and ran for the house.

Annabelle isolated herself in her room, where she wrestled with this newfound information. She stomped, ranted, and raved just like the old creature she used to be, then gave in to self-pity and weeping. "Oh, Lord." She moaned. "Kate is not even my sister; she's my cousin. How awful. But Claire. . .yes, she's a sister. Oh, how can this be?"

Eventually there was a knock on her door. "Go away," she shouted.

"It's Buck."

"What do you want?"

"Thaddeas is here to see you."

"Tell him to go away!" Her mind raced. "Wait! I'll be down in a little while."

"Very well." Buck turned away, relieved that she would see Thaddeas. Things were going badly with Mattie broken and sobbing in one room, and Annabelle angry and weeping in another. If only Claire were here—but Luke had driven her into town.

Annabelle found Thad waiting outside. As she approached, Thad's heart quickened with anticipation for he had planned this evening very carefully, hoping to mend their relationship. Then she drew nearer, and he realized something was very wrong.

"Annabelle! What is it?"

"You're never going to believe it."

"Try me," he coaxed.

"Maybe later. I'm not going to let Mattie spoil our canoe ride."

Thad, unwilling to open a new can of worms, quickly agreed. "All right then. Let's go." He offered his hand, and she took it as they walked toward the creek.

"Looks like Buck keeps the path worn down fishing," Annabelle observed. The cool air helped her to gain her composure.

"This looks great." Thad breathed deeply, taking in the woodsy freshness. "I've missed this place."

The footpath declined then turned sharply, and the couple stepped carefully over the jutting roots from the giant cottonwoods that lined the creek bank. "Uncle Buck said the canoe should be beached along here. . . there it is!" Thad pointed with enthusiasm.

The tip of the craft stuck out from behind a mossy rock. Thad hurried to free the small craft and slid it into the water for Annabelle's inspection. "Madam," he offered. As she entered the canoe, he cautioned, "Carefully now." She positioned herself on the far end and grabbed fast onto the sides. "Ready?" Thad asked.

"All set."

Thad climbed in and pushed off the grassy shore. Within seconds they glided swanlike through the water. Annabelle closed her eyes and relaxed. "This seems like old times, Thad," she murmured.

"We've many memories along this creek, don't we?"

"I do recall outfishing you on numerous occasions," she quipped.

"You would!" Thaddeas exclaimed. Then he ventured, "Annabelle, could we start over, you and I?"

Her heart flopped like the fish beneath them. "I'd like that very much," she answered softly, "but I'll soon be returning to Dayton."

"Do you have to go?" Thad pleaded. He reached for her hand, and the canoe wobbled.

Annabelle pulled away and clung to the canoe, but quickly recovered when she realized there was no threat of capsizing. The mood ruined, she complained, "Things aren't that easy, Thad. Right now I'm angry at Mattie."

"What's wrong? What did she do?"

Annabelle slowly spilled out the tragic tale—from her one-sided version, including a few details about Charles Harrison—and finished with a bitter declaration, "I shall not forgive her!"

Thaddeas responded sympathetically, "What a shock. I can imagine how this upsets you."

"Oh, I knew you would understand, Thad."

As he paddled, he spoke. "It reminds me of another story I heard." Annabelle gazed at him skeptically.

"Yes, it's much like your situation. No," he argued with himself, "it's similar but different."

He succeeded in arousing her curiosity. "Really? How?"

"You want to hear it?" She nodded. "There were two women. Each bore a child out of wedlock, but one child died." Annabelle frowned, and he asked, "Follow me?"

She nodded, and he continued, "The women fought over the living child."

"That's absurd."

"I agree, but at any rate, their dispute went before the king."

"This isn't a true story," Annabelle accused.

"Oh, but it is. Do you know what the king said?"

"No."

"Bring me a sword, and I'll divide the living child in half and give one half to each woman."

"How awful. That can't be true," Annabelle insisted.

"Yes, it is. Then the real mother denied the child and said, 'Give it to the other woman.' "

Annabelle puzzled over the story until Thad spoke again. "The story is found in the Bible. You can look it up in I Kings chapter three. Do you understand?"

"I think so. The real mother loved the child enough to give it away." Silence hung for a full count. "Like Lacy's parents."

Thad had beached the canoe alongside a fallen tree where they had a good view of a beaver community. As they watched the creatures, he waited for Annabelle to digest his story. "Like Mattie," she mumbled. "I have to forgive her, don't I?"

"If you want to please Jesus, you have no other choice."

"Do you think He can give me peace about this?"

Thaddeas placed his hand alongside her troubled face and prayed in a soft tone, "Lord Jesus, please give Annabelle Your peace. Help her to forgive Mattie, and heal their relationship. Amen."

Annabelle dabbed at puffy eyes. "Thaddeas, thank you so much. I must get this settled right away. Would you mind terribly if. . ."

"If we left?" He finished her statement. "No."

"Oh, Thad, you're wonderful."

"You think so?"

She nodded while he headed the canoe in the direction of Tucker House.

Annabelle approached the closed bedroom door and stopped to listen. Hearing the heart-wrenching sobs of her aunt penetrate the walls, she pushed, and the door creaked open. Annabelle tried to focus in the darkness that engulfed the room.

"Mattie," she whispered.

The sobs ceased, then sounded intermittently, but she was summoned. "Come here, Child."

She rushed to the spot where the voice had pierced the blackness and saw Mattie's shadow upon the mattress. "I'm sorry, Mattie. I forgive you. Of course I do."

"Thank You, Jesus," Mattie exclaimed. "I don't deserve it. I've done sech a great wrong."

"I understand now. You love us; that's all that matters."

"I love you so much; you'll never know."

"But I think I do."

"I've carried this burden for so long." Mattie sighed.

"Does Buck know?"

"Yes."

Annabelle reached across the inky thickness and found Mattie's hand. "We need to tell Kate and Claire."

"Yes. Tomorrow." The sad tone of Mattie's voice softened Annabelle's heart.

"We'll do it together. Mattie?"

"Yes?"

"Maybe sometime you can tell me what my mother was like."

"I'd be proud to."

Chapter 30

Kate lifted the calico curtain to peek out the window. She wondered, *Who could be riding up at this early hour?* A circle of dust accompanied the wagon containing Buck, Mattie, Annabelle, and Claire. "Looks like we got company, boys." Little Gabe's eyes lit up.

"Who, Mama?" Wetness appeared in the corners of her eyes, for it was the first time Gabe had called her "Mama."

"Why, it's the Larsons, Honey."

"Miss Annabelle and Miss Claire?" Little Gabe clapped chubby hands and ran toward the door, with his little brother close at heel.

"What a pretty picture this makes," Annabelle exclaimed, gathering Gabe into her arms as Claire scooped up Cody.

"Come on in." The tension in the air struck Kate at once.

Buck spoke up. "We come as a family to share some important news." The look on his face and the others' was so sober that Kate almost shuddered.

Ben entered the house at that moment, and Kate motioned him to her side, bringing him up-to-date. "Well, let's go into the sitting room. There are some toys there for the boys, and we can talk."

As the others seated themselves, Kate diverted Cody's and Gabe's attention with the wooden horses and toy wagons that Ben had carved, and they soon were in their own little world of make-believe. "There now, what is it?"

Buck started. "Mattie and I have harbored some secrets that we should have shared with you girls years ago. Last night Annabelle learned the truth, and now Mattie wants to tell you her story, some facts about her past."

Mattie looked at Kate first. "We talked about some of this once, Kate. But, Claire, you were too young at the time, so I'll start from the beginning.

"I made some mistakes when I was about your age. I met a man named Lt. Wade Brooks and had his child outa wedlock."

She paused, and Kate interrupted. "But it wasn't your fault, Mattie." Claire's eyes grew big as pumpkins, amazed with this information and the fact that Kate and Annabelle both knew.

"I made wrong choices. It's always wrong not ta wait till you're married to be intimate with a man. My pa, a preacher, called me a harlot, threw me outa the house. The young man disappeared out of my life."

Mattie was amazed how much easier it was to tell the story this time.

A calm possessed her. " 'Twasn't his fault. We were both young and foolish. We lost track of each other. I went to my married sister, Elizabeth, and she took my baby to raise. That baby was you, Kate."

Mattie stopped, letting the words soak in. Kate cried, "Oh, Lord." Claire's shoulders shook as emotion overtook her.

"I made a new life for myself. Elizabeth bore two daughters, Annabelle and Claire. After the Indian raid that killed your folks, Claire, I came to get ya all. I should have told you girls who I was." She looked at Claire and said, "Your aunt," then glanced at Kate and stated, "and your ma."

The room hung silent except for the low noises the boys made in their play, until she went on. "I fell in love with Buck but put him off for too many years because I didn't feel worthy of him."

He reached out to take her hand. "I shared my story with him, but I carried this burden too long. I release it to ya now. I pray ya will forgive me but won't hold it against ya if ya don't."

Kate and Claire immediately went to the broken woman. Claire spoke first. "Of course we forgive you, Mattie."

She looked at Kate. "Yes, I forgive you." Kate paused and then used the precious word, "Mother."

"I've given this a lot of thought," Annabelle interrupted, "and this does not really change a thing. You're still my sisters, as I see it." Everyone hugged and talked at once.

The boys giggled and jumped onto laps. "Me, too, me, too," said Cody, wanting to get in on the hugs and kisses. Wet smacks were planted on their cherubic cheeks.

The rest of the facts were pieced together as they discussed this new disclosure. Annabelle explained to Ben that the prowler was Charles Harrison, whom the lieutenant had sent to spy out the truth.

Mattie assured Kate that the lieutenant had turned into an honorable man whom she could respect. "He wants ta meet ya, Kate, more than anythin' else in the world. You look like him; you have his eyes and dark hair. He said he has a son, fourteen years old. He'd be a half-brother to ya. Here, I wrote down Lt. Brooks's address at Fort Wayne where he is stationed. I 'spect if he'd get a letter from you, he'd be down here in a flash." Kate nodded. Adrenalin pumped through her veins.

"Thank you, Mattie. This means so much to me. You have given me a f–father." She choked on the words, and Ben placed his arm around her protectively.

Mattie stood and spoke to Kate. "You told me once that love is pain. I know that ta be a fact. I thank everyone of ya in this room for forgivin' me. I'm so glad we all know the Lord, for I know 'tis Him who makes it possible."

Ben then gathered them together in a family circle, placing the boys and their toys in the middle by their feet. They joined hands and prayed.

That evening back at Tucker House in the last hour of light, Luke took Annabelle and Claire for a walk. The evening air invigorated them. "I think I'm getting soft and lazy," Luke admitted.

"Perhaps we need a run," Claire suggested.

"Race you to the creek," Annabelle shouted.

Luke never liked to lose, especially to women. He easily caught up to them and passed them like a storm on wheels.

He flung himself on the grassy embankment and crossed his legs, trying to control his panting. The girls arrived neck and neck and collapsed at his feet. "What took you so long?" he asked.

They both socked him playfully as they sought to catch their breath.

"Look, the water was high here, too." Claire pointed to the waterline mark on the bank and referred to Dayton's floods. The thought sobered them, and they watched the mosquitoes hover over the water as they reflected.

Annabelle swatted at one that dined on her neck. "Ouch!"

"Better head back," Luke suggested. He helped them to their feet and commented, "This has been quite a visit. I'm real proud of both my girls." He now had one on each arm. He referred to Mattie's confession when he said, "You could have been bitter, but you've chosen forgiveness."

Claire answered, "All things are possible with Christ."

"Love is a miracle," Luke answered while looking intently at Annabelle. Then he seemed embarrassed and changed the subject. "We should be heading back for Dayton soon. How does the day after tomorrow sound?"

"Great!" Claire answered, who looked forward to returning to the orphanage.

"I won't be going back," Annabelle announced with resignation in her voice.

Claire understood, her heart aching for Luke. She tactfully excused herself. "I–I'll leave you two alone to talk about this."

They stood in silence until she was out of sight, pausing under the hickory tree. Luke turned toward her then to hear her explanation.

"I have to stay. I'm in love with Thaddeas." She saw the hurt expression on his face. "I'm sorry, Luke. I admire you, nearly worship you, but I cannot let myself grow to love you when I already love Thad. If I go back, I'll become even more fond of you, and it will hurt us."

He took her hands in both of his and looked at her with a steady gaze. As he did so, they were unaware of another presence nearby. Thaddeas, coming in search of them, rounded the corner of the house to catch this intimate moment. He stopped to watch from a distance, which made it impossible to hear what they were saying.

"I understand, Annabelle. I am growing very fond of you." He touched her chin with his finger. "May the Lord continue to bless you. Good-bye, Annabelle." He pulled her into his arms and gave her a brotherly hug.

Thad took a few steps toward them and shouted angrily, "I see how it is then!" They jumped apart in shock and watched him stomp off.

"Thaddeas, wait!" Annabelle ran after him while Luke ran his fingers through his sandy hair.

Thaddeas mounted his horse and kicked. The animal bolted, unused to this kind of touch from his master. The rider did not look back as his name was called. "Thaddeas!"

Chapter 31

Annabelle embraced Claire. "I love you."

"I'll miss you," Claire said with much emotion.

"We've become so close." Annabelle held her sister at arm's length. "You've taught me so much. Thank you for convincing me to try Dayton last winter. I hope you understand why I have to stay."

Claire nodded. "I do. And don't worry." She squeezed Annabelle's arms. "It'll all work out fine. Just remember to keep praying."

"I will."

"Good-bye."

Annabelle nodded and released her sister. Then she turned to Luke while Mattie and Buck lavished Claire with farewells.

Stiffly they faced each other. Luke spoke first. "I'm sorry Thaddeas misunderstood. Are you sure you don't want to come along and provoke him further?" he teased.

"I'm sure." Annabelle smiled.

"All right." Luke grinned. "Keep an eye on Cody and Gabe."

"I will." Annabelle almost wished she could return to the orphanage. It was hard to let Luke and Claire go. "You'll send my chest of belongings then?"

"I'll take care of it personally. Good-bye, Annabelle." Luke pulled her into a final embrace and then let her go.

⌦

That afternoon the heat bore down on Annabelle's back as she rode into Beaver Creek, rehearsing her speech. She reined Dusty in at the sheriff's office, and her boots clacked on the wooden planks of the porch announcing her arrival—if someone had been in the office to hear it—but the sheriff was at Tucker House. It was Saturday, so Thad had the day off from the mill and was inside, sulking in his room.

Annabelle entered the empty office, and her voice echoed as she called out. "Anybody here?"

When there was no answer, she turned to face the door that stood between her and her future, for she figured Thaddeas was on the other side. Swallowing for courage, Annabelle tapped lightly. A few seconds passed; then it opened slowly.

"Annabelle! You shouldn't be here." The words were spoken hotly.

"I probably shouldn't." She returned his glare. "A woman alone in a man's room. . .but I have to make you listen."

"Why don't you send me a telegram?"

Annabelle's cheeks burned at the insinuation, but she had to make him understand. "It wasn't what you thought last night with Luke."

"It's none of my business."

Annabelle sighed. "Thaddeas, please. There's nothing between Luke and me."

Thaddeas scowled.

"I was just telling him good-bye. I won't be going back to Dayton."

He stared at her, longing to believe. She returned his stare, then threw her arms in the air, surrendering. "Fine!" She turned to leave.

"Wait. Please, come in."

Annabelle settled down, picked up her skirt, and stepped over the threshold. The room, bare and masculine, was sparsely furnished. Her eyes fell upon the cot where he slept, covers in disarray.

Thaddeas took control of the situation. "Over here. Let's sit down." He directed her toward a small table with two chairs in the opposite corner of the room. Clumsily, he pulled one out for her, and she seated herself directly across from him.

"Now, what were you saying?" He wanted to get this straight, plain and simple.

She cleared her throat. "What you saw was not as it appeared. Of course, Luke and I are close friends, working together as we have. I hated to tell him that I would not be returning. He was just telling me in his own way that it was all right and was saying good-bye."

"I'm sorry, Annabelle. I'm glad you came." There was a pause, and their expressions softened.

"But you're right, I shouldn't be here," Annabelle said as she squirmed in her seat.

"Never mind that. Please stay. Tell me how things are going with you and Mattie."

"We got things worked out."

"I'm so glad. I knew you would."

Annabelle fumbled with her gloves. "We told Kate and Claire."

"How did they take it?"

"Better than I did. Everything is going to be all right." Thaddeas waited for her to finish. "Actually, nothing has really changed, except Kate has a new father and a brother."

Thaddeas listened as Annabelle continued. "Mattie said she's sending a letter to her own pa. He's been trying to get in touch with her, and she's finally forgiven him. Said when I forgave her, then she realized she had to forgive her folks for what they did to her."

"Annabelle, that's wonderful." Thaddeas reached across the table to take her hand. "You allowed the Lord to work through you, and it changed her heart. I'm so happy."

"Are you?"

"With you here, yes."

"When are you going to tell me what happened to Mary Beth?"

Thaddeas grinned. "She grew frustrated with me."

"Why is that?"

"I was pining away for you."

Annabelle reddened. "Then you were jealous the other night?"

"Terribly."

"I was miserable when you left that way," Annabelle confessed.

"I was, too."

"I have just one more thing to say then."

"What is that?"

"Thaddeas Larson, if you don't marry me, I shall die!"

Thaddeas laughed. "I'm glad to see you didn't lose your spunk. Come here, Darling; of course, I'll marry you."

He held out his arms, and she flew into them, and he pulled her onto his lap, enveloping her. "I love you, Annabelle," he whispered against her ear.

"I love you, Thad."

He kissed her. "Will you be my wife?"

"Of course."

"What about your ambitions?"

Annabelle's face glowed. "Once I had lofty ambitions; now they are even loftier."

"So tell me, what are they?"

"To marry you and serve the Lord Jesus. What else would they be?"

"I cannot imagine any other thing."

Ample
Portions

With love to my children, Mike and Rachel.
May God richly bless your lives with His ample portions.

Chapter 1

A single provocative curl—long, brunette, and tousled—dangled from Miriam Wheeler's otherwise ribbon-tied tresses and captivated her husband. As she spoke, the curl partially concealed her worry-wrinkled brow, but Luke easily detected frustration in the tone of her voice. "The man's behavior was insufferable! He was probably drunk. . . ." Miriam paused to tug at the ends of her apron strings, which would not stretch nowadays to meet across her veritably pregnant middle. Luke's mirthful eyes and the crooked grin spreading across his face did not deter her. Letting the ties drop and setting swollen hands upon the proximity of her hips, she sighed. "Be serious, Luke."

Smiling mischievously, he reached a ready hand to tuck the distracting ringlet back into place and maintained. "I'm trying, Miriam."

Resisting his playful mood, she continued. "Think of his poor wife. For Aaron to insult you, a parson, in such a manner must be humiliating for Ruth. Luke, won't you call on the Gateses tomorrow and resolve this misunderstanding? For her sake?"

The preacher succumbed easily to his wife's beseeching brown eyes which, as always, melted his reserve until no request was too big. He pulled her close. "Of course, Darling," he whispered, "if it means so much to you."

❧

It was the last promise Luke Wheeler made to his wife Miriam before her death. For several weeks he completely forgot about it—but today he had suddenly remembered.

As the young widower stuffed clothes into a black valise, he spoke softly to his two-month-old son, Davy. "I made a promise to your mama, and I need to keep it." Exhaling a weary sigh, he continued. "Just this one last thing, then tomorrow we head for Beaver Creek. It's time you met your relatives."

Davy's newborn arms flailed through the air, and he wailed, his face beet red. Luke picked up the infant that mirrored his own characteristics, stroking the cornsilk hair. "Please don't object. Don't you see? My heart's not in the ministry since. . ." His voice faded.

He remembered accepting his first pastorate job with such enthusiasm two years earlier. That was the year the missionary's daughter swept him off his feet. Accompanying her father on a visit to the States, Miriam had been

239

equally captivated by the new Presbyterian preacher—so much so that before her father returned to the mission field the following spring, she and Luke were married.

The two years that followed were no less than glorious. Luke gave his all to the ministry, supported lovingly by his young wife. Their days were filled with hard work, lightened with laughter, and seasoned with love. But now. . .

Grief marked Luke's worn face with an inconsolable expression. Large grooves cut downward through his cheeks, hidden in part by a yellow mustache. The days when dimples danced there, dodging laughter and smiles, were gone. Today dark circles framed his blue eyes, making him look older than his twenty-five years.

"My brain's fuzzy as a cobweb." He continued. "I feel empty, so far away from God." The baby settled down at the subdued tones of his father's voice, sticking a fist into his mouth to suck. Luke caressed the small face with his thumb, outlining Davy's velvety cheek, pink and perfect. "Hungry again?"

That same afternoon the rhythmic canter of Queenie, Luke's quarter horse, soothed father and child alike. Those living in Dayton, Ohio, in the summer of 1810, took this unusual sight for granted—the giant good-looking widower toting his pint-sized son. Teary-eyed females often paused to sigh at the poignant reminder of Luke's loss.

When they reached the lodgings of Claire Larson, Luke dismounted, confident that he could go to her today with his need. As he walked toward the house with Davy, he thought back over the years that he had known her.

Claire, whose parents had been killed in the Big Bottom Indian massacre of 1791, grew up in Beaver Creek, Ohio, under the care of her Aunt Mattie. When Claire was twelve, Luke's brother Ben married Mattie's daughter, making Claire and Luke cousins.

Claire became a Christian about the time Luke left Beaver Creek to attend seminary in Dayton. They corresponded, and Luke became Claire's spiritual mentor. During this time, the young woman bombarded Luke with many questions about her newfound faith.

After seminary, Luke went to work at Dayton's orphanage. On Claire's sixteenth Christmas, she and her family visited Luke there. An orphan herself, Claire was touched in a profound way by the children. Thus she set out to convince her family of her desire to work at the orphanage. For three years she served there, even after Luke went into the pastorate and married Miriam.

As Luke knocked on Claire's door, he reflected that his cousin was no ordinary girl. Her exuberance and warmhearted nature, constant as the sun's warmth on a summer day, provided the stability he so needed during these days when his world seemed to be crumbling down around him.

The moment Claire opened the door, she swept Davy away from Luke, crooning over the child. In response, Luke's blond mustache twitched just as it always did before it curled upward with a smile.

Claire first examined Davy at arm's length before bringing him to her breast for a long cuddle. "Oh, what a little doll you are! And you're getting so big." Only then did she turn her attention to the grinning parent. "Forgive my manners, Luke. Do come in." He followed her swishing skirts into the parlor, where she asked, "What brings you around?"

Luke eased into a stiff chair, tight and squatty beneath his tall, slim form, which had become even thinner since Miriam's death. He leaned forward to prop his elbows on knees elevated high off the ground. "I wasn't sure if I'd catch you at home, but I was coming this way and wondered if you could take care of Davy for a few hours."

"I'd love to!" Her blue eyes reflected genuine delight that Luke had remembered it was her day off from her orphanage job.

Relieved, Luke returned to his feet. "Great!" He lost no time unbuckling a small leather pouch he wore strapped across his chest. "Here's his bottle and some diapers." He held it out before him.

Claire's infant-filled arms remained clasped in their cradled position as she responded with a tilt of her head and a soft chuckle. "Put it there, Luke, on the table."

He missed the humor in his actions, his thoughts focusing mainly on his nagging mission. "I'm on my way to call on the Gateses—not a visit I'm relishing. Tell you all about it later."

"Oh, there's something else, too." Claire's eyes widened expectantly. Fidgety, Luke recovered his hat from the arm of his chair and mechanically dusted it. "Looks like I'll be leaving Dayton sooner than I thought." A quick glance her way revealed Claire's brows arched in consternation, just as he had expected. "We'll talk later. I'll be back before dark."

With hasty strides Luke made for the doorway. He had dreaded telling her of his plans. She had taken it hard when he first shared his decision to leave the ministry, even trying to dissuade him.

Not to be left hanging like that, however, Claire quickly followed, babe in arms, and touched a hand to his sleeve. In a tone revealing deep emotion and concern for his well-being, she said, "I'll look forward to that talk, Luke. God go with you." His departure left her staring after him with many unanswered questions.

As Luke traveled toward his destination, he thought about his promise to Miriam regarding the man called Aaron Gates. An involuntary shudder of disgust swept over him when he recalled his last encounter with the man the day it all began, at the general store. Luke had unexpectedly bumped into Ruth Gates and recognized her as a woman who attended his church sporadically, always slipping into the back pew after the service started and leaving before it was over. Naturally, he was excited to make her acquaintance and greeted her with the irrepressible enthusiasm of a young pastor. No wonder then, his mouth fell agape when Ruth's husband appeared a few steps behind her with a malicious sneer planted on his tanned jowls. Muttering vile accusations, he seemed determined to pick a fight.

Luke's disbelief had turned to anger when the man thrust his wife aside, causing her to stumble backwards. Beneath the plaid shirt untucked from the man's exertion, bulging arms rippled from muscles toned at sea. Although Luke's nerves bristled and small beads of sweat broke out upon his brow, he did not cower under Aaron Gates's stormy stare. The reddened, glazed-over eyes told the tale. He was drunk.

His loud, slurry voice had caused a scene before the store's other customers. "Keep your sweet talk to yourself, Preacher, and leave my wife alone!" The accusation embarrassed Luke, and he had stammered a futile apology while the intoxicated man pushed past him, knocking several items off the shelf as he stomped out of the shop.

"I'm so sorry, Reverend," Ruth Gates mumbled before she also fled.

When Luke had told Miriam about the man's accusations, she had asked him to call upon the Gateses and rectify the situation. However, circumstances had prevented him from fulfilling this promise as the next day his wife took to her bed, and shortly afterward she died in childbirth.

Beset with an excruciating grief which vanquished all else, Luke forgot about the promise. It was a miracle, all things considered, that he could even perform the most mundane duties required of him over the next two months.

But for Davy's sake, Luke had persevered. His son's initial fight for survival was of paramount importance to him, and toward this effort he poured all his remaining energies. Remarkably, Davy flourished under Luke's tender care. During this time, the idea seeded and grew in Luke's heart that he should move back home to Beaver Creek, Ohio. Subsequently he turned in his resignation at the Presbyterian Church where he pastored.

The day finally arrived when he began to pack. In his haste, he snatched his coat from a peg beside the stove when something floated to the floor, catching his eye. *Miriam's apron!* A sudden pang of anguish surfaced when he knelt to pick it up. He tenderly fingered the cloth, remembering how she had outgrown it in those last days.

This cherished memory stirred yet another, troubling Luke and calling up his last promise to Miriam. And though he tried to cast it off, he could not. Finally, he yielded to his conscience, determined to deal with the matter, which eventually brought him to this place—a mile down the road from the Gates farm.

Chapter 2

With the June sun scorching his bare neck, Luke approached the shaded dwelling that poked shyly through a curtain of beech trees, and it crossed his mind that in his grief April and May had come and gone without his knowledge. A calico dress billowing on the wash line caught his attention, bringing thoughts of Miriam. Townspeople insisted his late wife resembled Ruth Gates. He considered it now for a fleeting moment, then cast the thought aside. No, the Gates woman was much older, mid-thirties at least.

Drawing nearer, within yards of the Gateses' cabin, Luke was startled by angry shouts; instinctively, he pulled his mount to a halt. Listening closely, he picked up fragments of what sounded like men arguing. *What a time I picked to call!* he thought. *But I have to fulfill my promise to Miriam.*

Thus Luke steeled himself to face his obligation as he dismounted and tethered his horse to the closest sapling. Proceeding with caution, he headed toward the house, fully expecting to receive the brunt end of Aaron Gates's bulging biceps.

When he was a few steps onto the porch, however, the shouting ceased, creating a sudden eerie quiet that magnified the creaking of the boards beneath his boots. Luke raised his fist to knock, but upon hearing the pitiful cry of a woman, he instinctively thrust open the door with both hands and let it slam against the wall. It took his eyes a moment to adjust to the dim interior. When they did, his mind rebelled against the horror of the scene even as his body played into action.

Within five feet to the left of a long plank table, Aaron Gates lay in a bloody pool on the cabin floor. Without a second thought, Luke crossed the short distance to kneel beside the ashen-faced man. Ruth Gates, who was already bent over her husband, reached up to clutch Luke's sleeve as she begged, "Please, help us!"

Though Aaron appeared lifeless, Luke immediately snatched his hanky from his back pocket and positioned it over the wound on the back of the man's head. "Can you hold this in place?" he asked Ruth. At her nod, he worked quickly to bring the loose ends around Aaron Gates's head, pulling it tight to stop the profuse bleeding.

Rousing slightly now, Aaron began to thrash about, but Luke restrained the injured man by cradling his head against his own chest. The preacher's mind raced wildly, his temples pounding. Nevertheless, outwardly he appeared calm and rational. *Keep him still and stop the bleeding,* he thought. *Must get a doctor. Ruth can't. . . What? Hoofbeats?* Luke cocked his head to listen. But before he could investigate the source of that sound, Aaron Gates required his attention once again. He gasped, struggling—then finally collapsed, limp within Luke's strong grip.

With that Ruth shrieked, "Do something!"

Frantically probing the man's neck, Luke searched for a pulse, knowing even as he did so, it was too late. Seeing the look on her benefactor's face, Ruth grew strangely quiet, her eyes darting from him to her husband and back, her breath held.

Luke, too, was silent as he gently laid the man onto the wooden floor before he turned his attention back to Ruth. "I'm sorry, Ma'am, he's gone," he said, flinching at her scream.

"No! No! He can't be."

Luke reached out to comfort her, but she recoiled in fear. Puzzled, for the first time he really looked at her. It was then he noticed the woman's swollen face, blackening near the cheekbone. With increasing realization, he identified, too, the smell of alcohol permeating the corpse. In that same instant, he knew she had been the victim of abuse.

Thinking that he understood better now, the young preacher spoke in soothing tones, using her given name. "Ruth, I'm sorry. I'll help you with this. It's going to be all right."

Ruth lifted her eyes and held Luke's compassionate gaze before she swiped at her tears with her apron and moved into his arms. He consoled her as she wept, whispering a prayer for the situation.

Eventually she calmed a bit, and Luke gently placed her at arm's length, gripping her shoulders in support. "I want to help, Ruth," he said, his eyes warm and caring. "Can you tell me what happened here?" Upon hearing that question, the look in the woman's eyes grew wild.

"Ruth, you can trust me," Luke urged. But before she could answer, a shadow fell across the floor from behind them, and Luke jerked his head around to see who had entered the room. The Gateses' neighbor, Uriah Cook, stood in the open doorway, taking in the scene. Instantly Ruth tore free from Luke's restraint and flung herself upon the newcomer, screaming, "Help me! Oh, help me! The preacher's killed Aaron!"

Luke gasped his surprise, "What? Why the woman must be in shock!" Then a gut-wrenching foreboding gripped him as he watched Ruth's convincing performance.

She thrust a finger at Luke, spewing out accusations. "It was awful, Uriah! He came here, said he was looking for his wife, Miriam. . .that he was so glad he found me, and then he. . . Oh, it was terrible." Ruth sobbed into her hands, leaving Uriah to eye Luke warily, noting the other's bloodied shirt and hands. "Go on," he urged. "I won't let him harm you."

"He came after me, but I fought him off, and then he hit me." She gingerly placed her hand to the swollen spot on her cheek.

"That is ridiculous!" Luke exploded, finally having the sense to intervene on his own behalf.

Uriah's face grew flinty, and he pulled his gun from his holster pointing it at the towering preacher. "Shut up and stay put, or I'll put a bullet in your head! You'll get your say." He turned back to his neighbor. "Go on, Mrs. Gates."

She paused a moment, then replied, "He hit me, and then Aaron came in. They struggled, and the next thing I knew my poor husband lay on the floor bleeding. The preacher grabbed me again; then there you were, standing in the doorway."

Ruth turned toward Luke and hissed, "Though you're a man of the cloth, I despise ya!" She spat at the floor and lunged forward while Uriah reached out to restrain her from railing at Luke.

"Let me handle this, Ruth," Uriah said, taking charge. "You sit down now and try to calm yourself." After the woman obediently sank onto a chair, Uriah Cook waved his pistol at Luke and bent slowly over the body to verify that his friend was indeed dead. With this confirmed, he looked at Luke. "All right, easy now, Preacher. I'll be taking you into town to see the sheriff. Now, move!"

"But that's my hanky around his head. I only tried to help. You've got to believe me; I had nothing to do with this," Luke argued.

"Look, I don't know how that got there. All I know is there'll be plenty of time to sort it out 'cause you're gonna be telling your story to Sheriff Watson." Then Uriah turned toward Mrs. Gates and added, "You'd better come along, too."

Ruth's face turned chalky. "I—I can't. Why, my children will be home shortly. They're at the neighbor's seeing a new litter of puppies. I can't let them find their pa this way!"

Uriah had to agree, "You're right. They shouldn't have to see such a spectacle. I'll stop at my place on the way and send the wife over to help you."

Ruth's color returned with her sigh of relief. "Thank you. You're a good neighbor, Uriah."

Having no choice, Luke did not resist Uriah when the man poked his gun into his ribs, motioning him outside. Still incredulous, however, the preacher glanced over his shoulder at the woman who had lied so persuasively, but in return, she met his eyes with a hard look, and all he could do was hang his head. *Lord, what is going on? Why is my whole world crumbling around me. Have You forsaken me?*

❧❧

Luke stepped into the empty cell and flinched when the steel door slammed shut behind him. He wheeled about just in time to see the red-haired lawman twist the key into the padlock and drop it into a deep vest pocket before he cast Luke a final look and turned away.

Like liquid fear, panic coursed through Luke's bloodstream. *Trapped!* He gripped the iron bars and pulled, but the barricade remained immovable. He jerked until his hands felt bruised and the dangling lock rattled.

Surprised at his prisoner's unruly behavior, Sheriff Watson reappeared. "Hey now, Rev. Wheeler, that won't do. You'll wear yourself out. Better just rest up for tomorrow," he cautioned.

Luke's hands slipped downward until they relaxed and fell limp at his sides. He felt the lawman's watchful gaze as a thought struck him. *The sheriff probably thinks I am insane, just like Ruth Gates described me. I must control myself.* Thoroughly dejected, Luke nodded to the lawman, then let his eyes peruse the ten-by-ten-foot cell interior.

To his left, a small bare cot—too short for Luke's tall body—lined the wall. Straight ahead, Luke saw a barred window at chest level. With disdain, he eyed the pewter pot placed against the adjoining dirty wall.

After the quick inspection, he crossed the tiny cell and bent to look out. Facing east, he discerned the sketchy outline of a river embankment, a small portion of the Miami River. The view was a hazy gray, however, as the sun already hung low, and beyond, a fog hovered.

Nevertheless, Luke's heart gladdened with this tiny measure of freedom. *At least I can watch the river traffic!* With the thought came a gentle assurance, and he expelled a sigh. *The very river where I baptize converts. Thank You, Lord.* He crooked his neck and stared out the iron-barred square-foot opening until the stars appeared. Then, breathing in the fresh air as if it were a rationed commodity, Luke poured out his heart to God.

❧❧

The next morning Luke collected his thoughts. *Need to get a lawyer, find someone to take care of Davy until I can get out of here. . . .* His mental list dispelled as obscure voices drifted into his cell from the outer room. He moved to the bars, straining to hear. Thus, the pitiful scene which greeted his visitor when the outer door swung open was Luke's unshaven face pressed against the bars with his hands gripping the cold iron like a criminal.

Claire gasped, and her hands flew to cover her mouth as she stifled a sob.

"Claire!" Luke exclaimed, overwhelmed with emotion.

Sheriff Watson briefly touched the small woman's elbow. "Are you all right, Miss?"

It took Claire a moment to recover. "Yes. I–I'm fine."

"You sure?"

Claire nodded. "May I have some time alone with Rev. Wheeler?"

"Wait here, Ma'am." The lawman left the area and returned momentarily with a chair that he placed just outside Luke's cell. "Call me when you're ready to leave," he said before leaving them unattended.

Claire seated herself carefully while she examined Luke's condition. His tear-smudged face was puffy around the eyes, and his shirt, wrinkled and dirty, hung outside his trousers. While Claire searched in vain for the right words, an awkward silence prevailed.

"I'm sorry, Claire. This is no place for a lady." He indicated the cell, feebly waving his hand.

With this gesture, Claire noticed that what she had thought to be soil on his shirt was actually bloodstains. Tears trickled down her cheeks as she reached for him. "Oh, Luke," she cried. "Is it true they've charged you with murder?"

He grasped both her hands through the bars and held onto them as tightly as one clinging to a life preserver in the midst of a stormy sea. "I've been wrongly accused, Claire."

"I worried all night after the deputy brought me word."

"I haven't slept much either," Luke admitted. "I'm glad you came."

She nodded, her smile tremulous. "Tell me what happened, Luke."

"All right." He released Claire's hands to position himself cross-legged before her on the floor. Expelling a great sigh, he began his story.

Claire listened intently as Luke recounted the details leading up to his arrest. Then she tilted her head, looking thoroughly perplexed. "I don't understand. If this occurred as you say, of which I have no doubt, then why are you here?"

Luke shrugged, holding his hands up in helplessness. "The woman lied. And what an actress she was! Framed me good."

Claire shook her bonneted head. Shafts of sunlight from the barred window warmed her face. "How could anyone believe you would do such a thing?" she asked in disbelief.

Luke sobered. "Claire, I don't know, but they do. Will you help me?"

"Of course. What can I do?" She leaned close to the bars, eager to assist in any way.

"Simon Appleby—I want him to be my lawyer. Can you ask him to drop by?"

"Yes. I'll go right away." She started to rise but was stayed by a gentle hand reaching through the bars.

"Wait, Claire. How's Davy?"

A sweetness lit the young woman's face. "He's just fine, Luke. Don't you worry. I'll take good care of your baby boy."

"I know it's a lot to ask of you, but he's all I have left. He means so much to me and—"

Claire covered his hand where it rested on the bars. "Hush now, Luke. Caring for Davy is no bother. You know I love him."

Luke's countenance softened for a moment, then turned troubled again. "If I don't get out of this, will you take Davy to my brother, Ben?"

Claire stiffened. "Of course, but don't even say such a thing, Luke. You'll soon be free. I'll get Mr. Appleby over here first thing. He'll know what to do."

Luke said, "You know, I was angry with God when Miriam died. I truly didn't believe things could get any worse. But now I find myself on my knees again. I can't say I have a peace about this, but I know He's here with me."

"Then God will keep you strong. Believe it!"

His smile was weak. "Claire, thank you for coming."

The young woman dabbed at her eyes with her lace handkerchief as Luke called out, "Sheriff Watson!"

The lawman's bulky physique appeared so quickly that Luke realized he had been waiting just beyond the door. Afterward Luke sank thoughtfully onto his cot. Having shared with Claire, a true sister in faith, his burden felt lighter. He was finally able to close his eyes to rest.

Chapter 3

Claire twisted long golden strands of hair into a pleasing arrangement, tightly bound at the nape of her slender neck. As she took careful inventory of herself, the looking glass reflected serious blue eyes set in a pale oval face with strong cheekbones sloping downward toward a button chin. Today she did not pinch her cheeks to force a flow of color, but rather with her fingertips traced the collar of the black dress. It fit her mood—dark and bleak. The dress gave her an air of sophistication that surpassed her nineteen years. This day she needed to be treated with serious regard. Luke was depending on her.

Turning from her reflection, she lifted Davy from her bed and smiled down at his beaming face. His cuddly presence warmed her as she started down the stairs and toward the dining room where the aroma of bacon and eggs wafted through the air. Claire's landlady was bent over a plate of hot biscuits, but upon hearing Claire, she raised her head, revealing round cheeks flushed from the stove's heat. "Morning, Child. How did Davy sleep last night?"

"Better. But I think he misses his papa." Claire gave the baby an affectionate squeeze.

"Yes, I'm sure he does." Mary Anders's expression brightened upon seeing her bald-headed Swedish husband, Gustaf, standing at the door dressed in his town clothes.

"Sorry if I'm holding you up," he said to Claire. "I went ahead and got the rig ready to go."

"Not at all," Claire answered politely. She and the older couple, members of the same Presbyterian congregation where Luke served as pastor, shared a common concern.

Gustaf pulled up a chair, while with his free hand he reached out to tickle Davy. "Morning, little one."

At the same time, Mary dished a question out to Claire along with the morning fare. "Sure you don't want me to take care of Davy today while you and Gustaf are busy with errands?"

"That's sweet of you, Mary, but no thanks. I especially want to take him along. I expect it will cheer Luke."

Mary sobered at the mention of Luke's separation from his child, who had been his primary joy in life since Miriam's death.

"Have you heard when the judge will return to Dayton?" Mary asked.

Gustaf's head jerked up in response to his wife's question, and he focused intently on Claire's reply.

"No. They haven't set a date for the trial yet. Everything is so uncertain. I plan to ask Simon Appleby this morning."

Gustaf nodded. "I'll be meeting this morning with some of the townsmen to discuss ways to help out the reverend. The town's all in an uproar since there's never been a murder trial before. And to think our reverend is a suspect in such a thing!" He shook his head with disbelief.

"Oh, my." Mary's ample bosom heaved as she pulled a handkerchief from her apron pocket to dab at her eyes. "Such a sad thing. What a shame." Turning aside, she sniffled. "Gustaf, be sure to ask Micah Brewer about his wife's list." At her husband's puzzled expression, she added, "The schedule, so folks can take turns cooking the reverend a hot meal. My, my." Once more she shook her head. "I don't know what this world is coming to with folks believing that gentle man could have committed a murder."

The room, which usually brimmed with life, now fell silent except for the scraping of utensils. Ruffled curtains, oval braided rug, and calico tablecloth—all products of Mary Anders's handiwork—depicted a cheery setting. But today everyone's hearts were heavy with preoccupied thoughts. The squeaking of Gustaf's chair broke the stillness as he rose from the table.

"I'll be waiting outside, Miss Claire."

"Thank you. Davy and I'll just be a moment."

Claire started across the busy street in the direction of the building marked in bold black letters, BARRISTER SIMON APPLEBY. To her relief, the door opened easily when she gave it a push with her shoulder. A middle-aged, dark-haired gentleman rose instantly from his chair.

"Miss Larson!" he greeted. "Please, come in. Sit down. It's a pleasure to see you again."

Once she was settled, Simon Appleby assessed the woman seated across the desk, cradling the tiny son of his friend and client. His manner put Claire at ease.

"Thank you, Mr. Appleby," she said.

"Rev. Wheeler expressed his great appreciation of you." He watched her eyes widen in surprise. "That is, in taking care of Davy. In fact, he appointed me to look after you both, especially where the child is concerned."

"It's so like him to care about others when he has problems of his own," Claire answered.

"From my experience, folks in jail have plenty of time to think, sort things through."

The crass remark caused Claire to tense, and the baby stirred uncomfortably. "Mr. Appleby, will you be able to help Luke?" she asked, shifting Davy to a better position.

"If it's any consolation, Luke is my friend, too. We go back a ways. I've always admired the young man for his ability in the pulpit, as well as his efforts to provide better conditions at the orphanage. Just as I admire you for your work there, Miss Larson."

He could see Claire relax as he continued. "I intend to devote all my attention to Luke's case in order to prove his innocence." Claire listened as she unconsciously rocked Davy, a gesture not unnoticed by the attentive lawyer. This prompted him to ask, "How have the arrangements been working out with Davy? Are they agreeable?"

"Oh yes! My work at the orphanage remains unhampered, and I'm growing quite attached to Davy. In fact, I plan to set Luke's mind at ease with a visit just as soon as we're finished here."

Simon's gray-streaked eyebrows arched with concern. "You realize, of course, your caring for the child is only temporary?" he asked.

"Yes. Luke told me he wishes for his brother, Ben, to be Davy's true guardian. But surely it won't come to that? Do you have any idea when the trial will be?" Claire drew his thoughts back to the matter at hand.

Simon shook his head. "No. The date's not set as yet. That's to our advantage, however. It'll give me time to build my case."

"I want to thank you so much for all you are doing for Luke. If anything happens to him, I. . ."

Simon leaned across the desk, professionally covering Claire's hand with his own. "I understand, Miss Larson."

◀◆▶

"I don't know, Ma'am." Sheriff Watson's stern voice along with his disapproving scowl sent Claire's heart racing. "This isn't a place for a child."

"Please, Sheriff, just give Luke a few minutes to see his son."

"With the way folks are flitting in and out, you'd think this was a social event," he growled, referring to Luke's parishioners. "It just ain't proper."

Claire's lip trembled as she breathed a prayer and simply asked again, "Please?"

"Oh, all right. But if he cries, you'll have to go." He quickly turned his back to the young woman lest she see the emotion in his eyes. "Come on." He tossed over his shoulder.

Claire followed, now accustomed to the procedure of the outer door swinging open to reveal a vulnerable and unsuspecting prisoner. Today her first glimpse of the preacher bent over his open Bible filled her with relief. Luke jumped to his feet upon seeing her. "Davy!"

Sheriff Watson shook his bushy carrot-topped head but retreated to his usual post just outside the door without further comment.

To Luke's delight, Davy responded with enthusiasm to his father's familiar voice and face. "He hasn't forgotten his pa." Luke's words broke, filled with emotion.

"Of course not!" Claire bounced the excited baby, while holding him close to Luke. She placed a tiny fist between the bars.

Luke rolled Davy's fragile fingers with the tips of his own. The gesture caused Claire's heart to ache. She waited patiently, allowing Luke to savor these moments with his son.

After a few minutes, she spoke softly. "He's adjusted nicely, sleeping through the night now."

"Did you get his cradle from the house?"

"Yes. It's right beside my bed." Claire's cheeks flamed as Luke considered this.

He gently reprimanded her. "Sounds like you're spoiling him."

"Not any more than you," she contended.

Luke shrugged. "I guess I have lavished him with love, all that I had to give." His expression turned melancholy.

The tiny cell area grew quiet until Claire spoke reassuringly. "Luke, I just know that the truth will come out, and you'll be acquitted. Mr. Appleby assured me he is devoting all his time to your case. And God is faithful. He will hear our prayers."

But Luke's dismal mood remained fixed. "I've been so lonely since Miriam died, I'd just as soon join her." His tone, so dejected, frightened Claire.

"No, Luke. Please don't say that."

He avoided her pleading eyes as he voiced his haunting fear. "You realize I might hang."

"Dayton's never had a hanging. Anyway, they wouldn't hang an innocent man!" At Claire's raised pitch, Davy reached out to grab at her cheek, and she unconsciously removed his hand with a gentle gesture while intently searching Luke's face.

He met her gaze unwaveringly, his pain obvious. "Listen, Claire. I haven't lost my faith in God, but you just don't understand what it's like to feel so empty, so alone—"

Claire interrupted. "Perhaps not, but you cannot give up. You will get out of here, Luke Wheeler!"

"Ahem." The sheriff cleared his throat loud enough to warn them of his approach. "Got your lunch here, Preacher. Looks like another fancy spread, too." Sheriff Watson turned to Claire. "I'm sorry, Ma'am, your time is up."

"Please, I'm not quite ready."

The lawman frowned, considering while he balanced Luke's plate precariously on one age-roughened hand. "One more minute," he growled, then disappeared again.

"I can't leave you this way," Claire protested. She fought back tears of anguish and clung fiercely to Davy, whose small downy head snuggled against her neck.

Knowing that their time together was short now, Luke obliged Claire. "Hey, now." He reached through the bars to lightly tap her chin. "Who's to say? Perhaps you're right. It's in God's hands after all."

Claire sniffed. "That's better. I know God will make a way." Then she shifted the baby so Luke could get a last look at his son's face.

"Thank you, Claire, for bringing Davy." He struggled with a lump in his throat as the infant's hand trustingly wrapped about his extended finger. "Bye, Davy. I love you, Son."

Claire made a brave attempt at a smile. "God be with you, Luke. Don't give up."

Chapter 4

God be with you. Don't give up. Claire's parting words echoed in Luke's head, tormenting him for the remainder of the day. Just when he thought he had settled the matter in his heart, accepted the possibility of the gallows, she flung those scraps of hope at his feet. He had gone so far as to welcome thoughts of joining his beloved Miriam in heaven until Claire brought Davy by and left him with those strong words of encouragement.

Later, much sobered by his thoughts, Luke welcomed Sheriff Watson's announcement. "Got a visitor to see you, Preacher," he said, opening the cell door to admit Luke's lawyer.

"Hello, Simon." Luke rushed forward to shake the man's already extended hand.

"Afternoon, Luke." Simon Appleby waited until the sheriff had procured him a stool and was gone before he spoke again. With the chamber door secured and Sheriff Watson out of sight, he began, "Well, Luke, we have a lot to cover today. Might as well make yourself comfortable."

Luke perched on the edge of his lumpy cot as Simon continued. "I'm going to ask you some pretty hard questions. Got to hear your answers to get the whole picture. The prosecuting attorney will be even rougher than I am today, and you need to be prepared. Understand?"

Luke squared his shoulders, nodding grimly.

"Good. Now, what exactly were your feelings toward Ruth Gates?"

At first the question offended Luke, but then sensing Simon's line of reasoning, he settled himself for the staged interrogation. "I thought of her as a sister in my congregation, with concern for her well-being."

"Isn't it true that she markedly resembles your late wife, Miriam?"

"Some think so," Luke muttered.

"You loved your wife?"

"Very much."

"You miss your wife?"

"Of course I do! More than anything." Luke's face flushed as his raw emotions were set on edge.

Simon was ruthless. "Would you say folks thought Ruth Gates looked enough like your wife to be her sister?"

Luke glared at Simon, knowing where this was leading.

"I'm sorry, Luke. See what I mean? This will all come out in the trial. It's better to get your initial reactions behind us so you can respond in a controlled manner in the courtroom."

Luke sighed his resignation. "I understand. Let's keep going."

"Would you say Ruth Gates looked enough like your wife to be her sister?"

"Some might think so."

"Did you think so?"

"I never gave it much thought. Like I said, she was just a sister in the congregation."

"Good. Very good, Luke."

"It's just the truth."

"I know, but without the emotional baggage. Now let's start again with the scene itself. What time did you arrive at the Gates farm?"

"I left home about one o'clock in the afternoon and took Davy to Claire Larson's to stay. It must have been about three."

Simon could not resist. "What is your relationship with Miss Larson?"

Luke appeared puzzled but replied quickly, "She's a distant relative."

"Um-hmm." Simon scratched his chin. "How distant?"

"My brother, Ben, married her first cousin, Kate."

"She's not a blood relative then?"

"No, why?"

"She seems very attached to you and Davy."

"Claire won't be brought into this thing, will she?"

"No, no. Don't worry." Simon shook his head and changed the subject. "Let's proceed. Now this is very important, Luke. What exactly did you hear when you arrived at the Gateses'? Try to remember carefully."

Luke hesitated. "Men quarreling."

"Male shouts? Who? Aaron?"

"Yes, I heard his voice."

"What else?"

"There was a woman screaming."

"Ruth Gates?"

"I assume it was her."

"Can you place the other male by his speech?"

Luke hesitated again. "No, I can't identify him."

Simon paused thoughtfully. "You know, Luke, it was probably the killer. Any hunches? Sometimes clues are tucked away in the subconscious but leave impressions that lead directly to the murderer."

Luke shook his head.

"Any signs of a third person, anything that doesn't fit, a glimpse or sound of one fleeing?" Luke thought hard, reliving the scene in his mind. "Think about the way the room looked. What was out of order? What was lying around?"

"A chair was tipped. I had the impression the kitchen was messy, but it wasn't mealtime."

"Did the room smell like anything?"

"Liquor."

"Was there a liquor bottle?"

"I don't recall."

"Think about the way Ruth behaved. Do you believe she could have killed her husband? Perhaps ushered a lover out the back door?"

Luke shook his head. "There's no back door, but the curtain in the kitchen window caught my eye. It was blowing freely."

Simon chewed on the tip of his pen. "Back to Ruth, what was her reaction when you entered the room?"

"She clung to me, pleaded for my help."

"How did you respond?"

"I placed my hanky about the bleeding wound on Aaron's head. Wait a minute!"

"What?"

Luke jumped up from his cot and ran his fingers through his hair, dislodging a tousled lock that fell damp across his brow. "That's when I heard hoofbeats!" Luke shook his head and raised his arms in a gesture of disbelief. "It entirely slipped my mind." Simon gave him a look of encouragement. Luke paced the floor as he continued excitedly, "Someone must have been riding away! And they rode hard and fast!"

Simon punched a fist into his open palm. "Just as I suspected! I don't believe Ruth killed her husband, though it's still a possibility we must not rule out. If someone else was involved in the argument and fled the scene, odds are that person is the killer."

"And Ruth is covering for him," Luke added, slumping back onto the sagging cot. "It must be someone she loves, considering the show she put on. What an actress. She framed me good."

"Don't get discouraged, Luke. This has been a big help. Now it's my job to figure out who she's protecting. I think I'll just pay Ruth Gates a visit."

"Not much to go on, is it?"

Simon rose and patted his friend's shoulder. "It's a start, Luke."

❦

As promised, the following afternoon Simon Appleby called on Ruth Gates. Upon meeting her, Simon was disturbed that the thirty-five-year-old widow was such an attractive and seemingly intelligent woman. This would make her story more believable and weaken Luke's defense.

Ruth's children were home. They ranged in ages from eighteen to seven. The oldest daughter had been working the day her father was killed. The younger ones were at a neighbor's house. The eldest son, Ruben, did not live at home anymore.

As Simon expected, Ruth's response was cold as a December gale and uncooperative as well. He determined, nevertheless, to uncover some shred of evidence, unearth some emotion that might provide a lead. The children, timid yet curious, watched his every move. Simon turned to the youngest standing nearby. "You must miss your pa." The child remained silent, though her eyes grew large and frightened. Then Simon turned to the eleven year old. "It's not your fault that your pa hit your mama."

"I couldn't stop him," Tom defended.

Ruth's eyes narrowed. "That's quite enough, Mr. Appleby! It isn't proper for you to question the children like this!"

"Sorry, Ma'am. I just don't want them to feel at fault, nor you either. If you tell me what really happened, I'll do my best to help."

"I don't know what you mean!"

"We both know Luke Wheeler did not kill your husband. Let me help you."

"Get out!"

He tipped his hat. "Very well. I'll be on my way then. Thank you for your time."

Simon did not leave the premises. Instead he circled the cabin, searching the ground beneath the kitchen window and the area between the house and the barn. Seeing him, Ruth rushed outside to angrily issue a threat. "I'd much appreciate it if you'd remove yourself from my property. It isn't proper, me being a widow and all. I'll get the sheriff to keep you away if need be!"

"That won't be necessary. I'm on my way. I've found what I was looking for." He gestured toward the area recently swept clean by brush. "Good day, Ma'am."

Ruth stood as still and emotionless as a statue, but as soon as the snoop was gone, she sent Tom scooting out the back with a message to be delivered.

Young Tom Gates panted from his long run to the docks by the Miami River where his pa's fishing vessel, the *Hilde*, was anchored. Just before the breathless boy reached the old craft, he caught a glimpse of a long shadow and ducked behind a barrel reeking of fish guts—a familiar stench to the boy who felt at home on the riverfront pier. The lawyer! This would never do. Tom waited, concentrating on long, controlled breaths until his breathing returned to normal.

A quick peek revealed that the dreaded man's back was turned toward him, and the boy sighed with relief when he saw the lawyer engaged in conversation with a small group of fishermen. Making the most of this opportunity, Tom made a mad dash for the deck of the *Hilde*, where he slipped out of sight without making a sound.

Upon finishing his discussion with three old-timers, Simon pivoted to stroll along the docks, visually inspecting the harbor while memorizing every detail. Early evening activity intensified now. He at least had the name of Aaron's fishing sloop. Checking the vessels moored along the shoreline, he scanned each one until he saw the one painted blue with a white stripe beneath the large cursive inscription, *Hilde*. With quick steps he hastened toward her.

"Watch out! Better look where you're goin', mister fancy pants!"

Simon wheeled about. Before him stood a roughneck, dressed in baggy blue trousers and dingy shirt with a soiled blue handkerchief tied about his forehead.

"You talking to me?" Simon inquired.

The other guffawed aloud at the question, revealing a scraggly beard that all but buried his mouth—a dark gap where teeth used to be. Swishing the black juice in his mouth before sending it in a powerful stream within inches of Simon's leather boots, he replied, "Yeah. You got a problem with that?"

"Umm no–o," Simon purposely drawled, replying with a calm that he could see surprised the roughneck. "Do you?"

Matted woolly eyebrows slanted over dark eyes. "May be purty, but I see ya got spunk. I like that."

"Yes, and questions, too. Did you know Aaron Gates by any chance?"

"Whot if I did?"

"He was murdered last week, and my client is wasting in the town jail, an innocent man. I happen to believe that Aaron Gates was a drunk and woman beater. Know anything about that?"

"Probably was. Don't know for a fact. No law against wife beatin', is there? He was gettin' to be a mean old lout, though."

"Why do you say that?"

"Common fact, that's all."

"Would you be willing to testify to that?"

"Nothing to tell. But I know somebody who might."

"And who would that be?"

The larger man scratched his hirsute chin. "Just wonderin' if it'd be worth my while. . ."

"I can't offer money. The law considers such testimony unacceptable."

He shrugged. "Then you're barkin' up the wrong tree with me, Mister! I ain't no telltale."

"My office is on First Street, if you change your mind. Nice to meet you, Mr. . . ."

"Didn't say whot my name was, did I now?"

"Well, the sign on my office reads Simon Appleby."

"Won't do me no good, can't read."

Simon cringed at the departing man's coarse laughter.

He then turned his attention back toward the *Hilde*, startled, though not disappointed, at his fortunate timing. Tom Gates was just coming out of the boat's cabin, fingering something shiny. Simon ducked behind some crates, watching as the lad looked up and about to see if the coast was clear before he descended from the vessel and dashed off in a dead run.

The lawyer brushed off a section of the pier closest to the *Hilde* and seated himself. It wouldn't hurt to keep an eye on the vessel to see what else might turn up, just stick around for awhile to chat with the fishermen as they brought in their day's catch.

Chapter 5

The tiny cot squeaked and groaned beneath Luke's one-hundred-seventy-pound frame as he thrashed wildly in his sleep. Moaning, tossing, turning as the nightmare seized him, he awoke with a start, bolting upright. Heaving his legs over the side of the bed, he winced as his bare feet hit the damp, night-cold floor. In contrast, his body felt feverish, covered in sweat.

Still caught in the throes of the nightmare, Luke inhaled and exhaled deeply. Terror raced through his heart while with trembling hands he rubbed his neck, where just moments before the rope had constricted painfully, snuffing out his life.

"Oh, God." He wept. "Is this my destiny? Father, please! I don't want to die this way. Davy needs me." Scenes from his dream replayed over and over, haunting him—the suffocating crowd, condemning eyes. He recalled a set of deep blue ones, sorrowful and desperate; then they became faceless and conspicuous from the others. But the following darkness blotted them out, and hopelessness replaced the light as the black hood fell over his face and the rope slipped about his neck.

Luke squeezed his eyes shut to dispel the reality of the images evoked until gently, ever so tenderly, familiar words harkened unto his soul. *"I can do all things through Christ which strengtheneth me."* Lifting his gaze heavenward where dawn's first muted rays filtered through the tiny slatted window, he finally relaxed and retrieved his worn black Bible from beneath his cot. During the past weeks, just to clutch its familiar soft leather binding brought comfort to his fainting soul. Today, as soon as the room lightened enough to read, he would read the rest of that passage.

Meanwhile he breathed another prayer. "Lord, if it's not Your will that I get out of this, I leave Davy in Your charge. Please make a way for him, provide him with Your special care." This brought his thoughts around to Claire, and he wondered why she had not been to visit for several days. *Probably busy at the orphanage,* he thought. *With Davy to take care of now, her responsibilities are even greater. But doesn't she realize how much I miss the child?*

❧❧

Simon walked at a brisk clip, taking long strides in spite of his short legs. The heavy fog allowed the small, dark-suited attorney to pass along the riverfront inconspicuously. Upon reaching the *Hilde*, Simon squinted his eyes. Stroking his groomed mustache with his ringed finger, he scrutinized the vessel.

Well-tuned ears discerned scraps of heated discussion emanating from below the *Hilde*'s deck, and he strained to listen.

"I hope you are satisfied, Clancy!"

"Don't be shoutin' on my lady!"

"What?"

"That's right. She's my ship now! Haw, haw." The sickening guffaw grew louder as two men emerged from the tiny cabin. Through the thick mist surrounding the prow, Simon could only surmise the silhouette of a young man to be Ruben, Aaron and Ruth Gates's oldest son. The other man, his outline not so clearly visible, bobbed with hilarity.

The obscure figure moved closer, bellowing a final remark. "I'll be back for whot's mine tomorrow!" Simon's eyes lit with recognition—the vulgar sea dog from the other day!

Simon planted his polished boots and straightened his broad form to its full five-foot, seven-inch zenith, expecting to be noticed at any time. His skin crawled as the repulsive character swung about and climbed off the boat backwards, pausing to cast a menacing glance about the docks.

The lawyer's gaze never wavered as it fastened onto that one's leering stare, which soon narrowed with recognition. "Well, now if it ain't the fancy snoop again!"

Simon lifted his brows but ignored the slur as he pursued his inquiry. "Did I hear you say that this vessel is yours, Sir?"

"Sir, is it now? Well, I like that. I really do." The man's bearded face twisted into a contortion of glee. "That's right, the rig is mine."

Simon then turned his attention to the younger man stationed at the bow of the *Hilde*. "I was under the impression that this vessel belonged to Aaron Gates," he called out.

"I'm his son. The *Hilde* came to me after his passing." He gestured with his hand. "Just sold it to that one."

"I see. You must be Ruben Gates then." At the confirming nod, the lawyer continued, "I'd like to board the *Hilde* and have a look around. Which one of you gentlemen wants to accompany me?"

Ruben Gates scowled. "Why? What's the problem?"

"Pardon me." Simon moved closer toward the edge of the dock where the *Hilde* bobbed. "My name is Simon Appleby, Luke Wheeler's attorney."

Fleetingly an unrecognizable emotion swept over Ruben's face, but the young man recovered quickly. "I've nothing to hide. Come aboard, though I don't know what good it can do." Then with displeasure he called to the other seaman, "It'll be ready tomorrow, Clancy. Don't bring your grimy face around 'til noon."

Clancy grumbled and shuffled away, wanting no part of the interrogation about to take place.

Once aboard, Simon questioned young Gates. "I didn't see you at the funeral, didn't think you were in town."

Ruben shrugged noncommittally. "Just got into Dayton. I couldn't get here in time for Father's funeral."

"I see. I'm sorry about your father."

The boy's face flushed, then turned angry. "Then why are you defending his murderer?"

"That's why I'm here. You see, I don't believe Luke Wheeler killed your father, Ruben."

Ruben's wind-chapped face reddened further. "How can that be? You forget my mother saw the preacher do it?"

"So she says."

"Why should she lie?" Ruben yelled doubling his hand into a hard fist.

"That's what I'm here to find out. Now, may I have a look around?"

Ruben slowly unclenched his fist and extended his arm to gesture permission. "Go ahead," he growled, his steely eyes boring daggers through Simon.

Unwilling to assist in any way, Ruben perched on a railing, watching the lawyer search the vessel, prodding here—examining there.

A long half hour later, Simon was escorted off the *Hilde* empty-handed.

"I'll see you at the hearing?" Simon inquired, dusting himself off.

"Of course. I plan to stick around to see the preacher hanged."

Simon bit back a retort. "Thanks for the tour." In afterthought he added, "By the way, I don't know what you got for the *Hilde*, but I believe Clancy got a bargain. He sure left with a mighty big smile on his face."

Without a reply, Ruben whirled about and stalked away, disappearing down the small ship's cave-like cubicle.

Simon grinned mischievously, rubbed his smooth-shaven chin, and headed toward Main Street to the jailhouse.

As Simon entered the jail's office, Sheriff Watson looked up from his desk. "Howdy, Simon."

"Rusty, can I see my client?"

"Sorry, but he's got another visitor just now. And she's much prettier than you." Sheriff Watson scowled. "This jail's never seen so many visitors before the preacher came."

Simon arched his round dark brows with interest.

"I suppose you want to wait?"

"No." Simon began to leave, then paused as he cast an inquiring look at the sheriff. "Don't suppose you plan to reveal who this pretty lady is?"

"Claire Larson." The sheriff grunted.

"Just tell Luke I stopped by. I'll be back later on my way home." When the broad of Simon's back was fully toward the lawman, a smile softened his face.

Meanwhile, within the jail Claire's presence dispelled the gloom of incarceration. Her lilting voice and tinkling laughter saturated Luke's cell.

"I wish I could have seen that," Luke remarked, his eyes crinkled at the corners, warm with the light of shared humor.

"He certainly has captured the hearts of all the children. Why, when you're. . . ," Claire hesitated to find the correct words, ". . .free, you'll have to bring Davy to visit the children again, and see for yourself."

"I'd like that. Seems like a long time since I've been to the orphanage." His voice turned husky. "The last few months seem like years."

Claire nodded. She rose from her seat.

"I must return now, but it's been good to see you in such high spirits, Luke. I'll stop in as often as I can. I've been busy at work. We have a new addition, a ten-year-old boy who has attached himself to me like moss. After a difficult start, I believe he's finally adjusting. . . ."

Claire continued talking, but all of a sudden Luke could not hear her—all he could do was see. *Her eyes. They're the ones in my dream! Lord! What are you trying to tell me?*

"Luke?" Claire whispered. "What is it? You wanted to ask me something?"

Luke blinked. "No, no—I was just thinking about a dream I had. Actually, it was a nightmare. But never mind that. You were saying that you've been busy at the orphanage."

"Yes."

"Claire, thank you for coming. I get so lonely here. Having you is like visiting with family. Speaking of which, I have a letter here for my brother, Ben. And one for Miriam's father. Will you post them for me?"

"Of course. Isn't Miriam's father overseas?"

"Yes, he's serving at the same missionary post." Luke reached under his cot, where he kept the few items the sheriff allowed him within the cell, and pulled out the two letters.

As she reached for them through the bars, he clasped her hand. "Claire. . ."

When he did not finish but only murmured her name, she quickly covered his hand with her free one. For one fleeting instant, she felt the depth of his pain, his hopelessness. "I know," was all she could offer. "I know, Luke."

He nodded, then withdrew his hand and thanked her again for coming.

As she rose to leave, she waved the letters. "I'll post these, and, Luke, you have many people praying for you. Keep trusting."

"I will."

"Good-bye then."

"Bye, Claire. Give Davy a kiss for me."

At the word "kiss," Claire lowered her eyes. "Yes, I will."

Pulled by an exquisite chestnut bay, Simon Appleby held the reins taut, maneuvering his small carriage beneath the cool umbrella of a spreading cottonwood tree. Wet in his gentleman's suit, he took just a moment to savor the shade and slight breeze that evaporated the moisture beads gathered over his brow. But his investigative curiosity soon overpowered his need for comfort. He was anxious to examine his newest lead—Claire Larson's urgent summons regarding some important evidence.

Simon hastened toward the sprawling but dismal stone building where he noted clusters of children playing in the fringes of a sun-parched lawn. Claire happened to answer his knock, and upon laying eyes on Simon, relief washed over her face.

"Mr. Appleby! Come in!"

Her excitement contagious, Simon answered, "I got your message. I came as fast as I could."

"Thank you." Claire led Simon down a hallway and into a large parlor as she said, "I think I've stumbled onto something important that may help Luke."

Simon's eyes remained riveted to his hostess's face, rosy-cheeked with expectation, as he seated himself upon the badly worn Windsor chair she offered him.

Without hesitation, Claire poured forth her information. "We've taken in a most precious boy whose name is Clay. Anyway, as we played with Davy one day, we got on the subject of the Gates murder, and the boy revealed some astounding information."

Simon's forehead creased all the way to the center part of his neatly combed hair. "Go on," he urged.

"You see, the boy was a stowaway from Cincinnati. He spent some time on the docks around the *Hilde*."

Simon's eyes sparked. "This is most interesting. May I speak with him?"

"Yes, of course. But you won't frighten him, will you? I want to help Luke, but Clay's only a child."

Simon rose from his chair, closing the short distance between them. His clean, toilet water scent wafted about her as he stooped and took her hand. "Miss Larson," he assured, "I don't wish to harm the boy. I will be as sympathetic as I can, but I must pursue every lead that might help Luke."

"Very well." Claire rose.

"Oh, Miss Larson?"

"Yes."

"Where is Davy?"

"He's taking his nap," she replied. "I'll be just a minute."

Claire left the room and returned with a ten year old who studied Simon with suspicious blue eyes from atop a freckled nose. She introduced the two and Clay relaxed after Simon's friendly handshake. Claire issued a small sigh of relief, then snuggled in close to the child on a frayed settee.

Simon cleared his throat. "Clay, I understand that you have had some hard times. I know the people here, the Murdocks and Miss Larson. They'll take good care of you from now on. They're kind folks. I'm Miss Larson's friend, and I want to help another one of her friends, Davy's father."

The boy smiled. "Davy's a good baby," he said.

Simon chuckled. "Yes, he is. Now, Clay, I want you to know that you can trust me. Do you understand?"

"I think so. You want me to help Davy's pa?"

Simon's nod was slow and nonthreatening. "That's right. Just tell me what you saw on the docks."

Clay cast anxious eyes at Claire, who nodded her assent, and the young-ster began to talk. "I was on the docks long enough to get to know most of the rigs. I stowed away on the *Barnacle*." He glanced at Simon to see his reaction. Simon smiled and waited.

"You sure I won't get in trouble?"

"I promise."

Then the child surprised Simon with his cliff-edged abruptness. "I saw Mr. Gates kill a man and throw him overboard."

Simon scooted to the very edge of his seat, every nerve quickened. "How did he kill him?"

"Hit him."

"Do you know who the man was?"

"Farthington," said Clay.

"Silas Farthington?"

"Yes, Sir." Clay's eyes lit.

From his investigative research, the name rang familiar. "He had worked for Aaron Gates. Do you know why this happened?"

"No, Sir. They were arguing. Mr. Gates was angry. . .and drunk."

"Where were you when you saw this?"

"Down on the docks, loading fish."

"Was there anyone else with Mr. Gates and Silas?"

Clay nodded furiously, and Simon knew in that instant that the boy spoke truthfully. "Gates's son, Ruben, was with him."

"Ruben! Well, I'll be. Anyone else?"

"Yup, but I don't know that one's name."

"Would you recognize him if you saw him again?"

Claire's upward glance was protective and questioning, causing Simon to quickly dispel any thoughts he might have of dragging this child back onto the docks. Nevertheless, Clay answered his question. "I only saw the old man around the docks a couple times. I don't know his name. He looked like an old grizzly bear."

"Thank you, Clay." Simon mentally noted the description. "I'm sure this information will benefit Davy's pa." He reached toward the lad and shook his hand. "You're a brave boy."

"Thank ya, Mr. Appleby."

"You may go now, Clay," Claire said, sending the boy off with a hug.

"Whew." Simon exhaled a long, wheezy breath after the boy was gone. "This is exactly the kind of breakthrough I've been looking for. Maybe now I can get to the bottom of this case. Thank you, Miss Larson."

Simon jumped to his feet with great enthusiasm, and Claire escorted him to the door. She stood there long after the chestnut bay led Simon's carriage out of sight, wondering, hoping, when a tiny hand slipped into her own. "Miss Claire," a small voice pleaded. She smiled down at the child, turning back to the task at hand.

⋙⋘

The door creaked, moaned, and slammed, making its now familiar reverberations; then footsteps clacked, abating until Sheriff Watson disappeared.

"Hello, Luke!" Simon greeted.

"Hello yourself." Luke cocked his head. "You sound extra cheerful today."

"I am." Simon squatted onto the small stool provided. "We've hit upon some new information."

Luke listened intently as Simon retold the orphan's eyewitness account of Silas Farthington's murder. Afterward he rubbed his chin. "Hmm? What do you make of it, Simon?"

"The child was obviously telling the truth, so I paid the Gateses another visit. Ruben denied everything, which comes as no surprise. He said it was just a case of drowning, that I could check the newspaper. I'm certain he's lying." Simon's face reflected distaste as he added, "I also looked up a seedy character I came across at the docks. I think he is somehow involved. Name is Clancy. He could very well be Clay's 'old man'. Supposedly, Clancy bought the *Hilde* from Ruben, but I believe there's more to it than that."

"What did he say?"

Simon snorted. "Clancy? He just laughed uproariously and spit tobacco juice at my boots."

A sigh of disappointment escaped Luke's lips, followed by another question. "I wonder what Aaron Gates was involved in?"

"So do I. And how is Ruben connected? He split from his pa about the time Farthington was found dead. Moved away."

Luke tugged at his mustache thoughtfully. "But he showed up again when Aaron died?"

Simon nodded. "Whatever it is, Ruth must be in on it, to fix the blame on you so hastily. I thought it might be a lover, but now I seriously doubt it, especially if Clancy is involved." Simon chuckled, then stood, rubbed his palms together, and paced in a semicircle. "I need to turn over some rocks."

Luke remained seated while Simon deliberated. "I just wish we had more time," the lawyer issued with vehemence. "These loose ends won't do us any good as they are."

"Can't the boy testify?"

"He could, but Claire wants to protect him. Truth is the jury probably wouldn't believe him anyway. The defense would cut him to shreds with his background, and he's too vulnerable for that right now."

"I understand."

Simon adjusted his necktie and recovered his hat. "I'd better be off now, to do some more digging. I think I'll look up Mrs. Farthington today."

"Simon, before you go. . ." The lawyer turned his attention back to Luke, eyes questioning. "My father arrived. He's got time on his hands. Is there anything he can do to help you?"

"Is he up to it?"

Luke laughed. "And then some."

"Where's he staying?"

"At the Trader's Inn."

"Good. I'll look him up."

"Simon, by the way, he's a preacher."

"Another preacher!" Simon rolled his eyes in a teasing manner, and Luke laughed.

Chapter 6

During the two weeks that had passed since Luke's arrest, his emotions wavered between the confidence that truth would prevail and the full-blown hopelessness that he would never be free again. Though his emotions fluctuated, his deep-seated faith did not. He discovered that his heavenly Father provided him with ample portions of faith—enough to endure each day's trials.

This particular morning Luke agonized upon bent knee. "Jesus, they took You like a lamb to the slaughter, and You went willingly though You knew what awaited." Sorrow filled Luke's spirit, and he sobbed, his chest heaving from brokenness. "Yet You were innocent. Oh, Lord, please restore my faith. Prepare me for my destiny."

From where Luke knelt by his cot, he buried his head in his arms, weeping as he waited upon God. He felt so weak, and today was his trial.

At eight o'clock that morning, Sheriff Watson ushered Luke down the center aisle of the two-story brick courthouse to occupy his place at the front. A swelling peace within Luke's breast assured him of God's presence.

As he passed, a murmur sifted throughout the crowded courtroom. The faces of parishioners and friends conveyed grief-stricken expressions. Many curious stares dotted the throng of spectators. Some even cast sympathetic glances across the room to the widow Gates and her children.

Directly behind the Gates family, Uriah Cook sat with his wife, Emma. The widow's key witness—arms folded across his chest—wore an expression much like a cat with a plump mouse. Emma, however, sat rigid with lips pressed tight together and clasped hands turning her fingers unnaturally white.

Across the courtroom behind Luke, Rev. Emmett Wheeler observed Simon as he leaned sideways to whisper something in his son's ear. Emmett silently prayed for a miracle. As Simon's errand boy over the last several days, he knew the lawyer's case was weak, revolving around assumptions that contained numerous loose ends. He did not fault the man, however, for Emmett had experienced firsthand the lawyer's fervent efforts to solve Luke's case.

Now he watched as Luke gave his lawyer a weak grin. "I trust you, Simon. You and God."

"I wish you wouldn't put me on the same level as God," Simon protested from the corner of his mouth.

"I'm not. I just believe you are His hands in this."

A slamming of the gavel silenced the whispers, and Judge Francis Dunlevy cleared his throat. Emmett Wheeler leaned forward to press his son's shoulder as the judge opened the trial. "The Common Pleas Court of Dayton will now convene to hear the case of *Gates v. Wheeler*. On my left is the plaintiff, Ruth Gates, represented by Edmund Fulton, and on my right is the defendant, Rev. Luke Wheeler, represented by Simon Appleby. Prosecutor Fulton, you may begin."

"My first witness, Your Honor, is Ruth Gates, widow of the murder victim."

The woman at the witness stand fingered the white handkerchief, sheer and lacy, which lay in contrast against the skirt of her dark mourning gown. Equally so, her delicate flawless face made a striking statement framed in the widow's black. The dark beauty's deep brown eyes moved those in the courtroom like the strains of a sad melody, evoking heartfelt sympathy. Ruth Gates raised her dusky gaze full into the face of Edmund Fulton, who now questioned her.

Pacing back and forth, he tread an invisible path seven feet in length. "How exactly did Luke Wheeler respond when you expressed your condolences over his wife's death?"

She answered as rehearsed, "His eyes went glassy, like his soul left his body. Then they fixed on me, and he came at me like a sleepwalker. I was so frightened that I backed up against the stove. I remember knocking some pots off." She twisted the handkerchief. "I was trapped, and he kept coming."

"Did he say anything to you during this time?"

"Yes, he kept calling me Miriam."

"Are you saying Luke Wheeler thought you were his wife?"

Ruth nodded her black-bonneted head emphatically. Leaning forward, Judge Dunlevy gently admonished her, "Please answer Mr. Fulton audibly, Mrs. Gates, so the jury can hear."

"Oh, sorry, Your Honor. Yes. The preacher was acting crazy."

A murmur spread throughout the courtroom.

"What happened after he pinned you to the stove?"

"He tried to kiss me. I screamed, and he hit me." Ruth gingerly touched her handkerchief to her face as if it still ached. "Aaron heard me and ran to the house, where he tore the preacher off me. They struggled, and the preacher knocked Aaron down. He hit his head. The preacher killed him."

"What happened after Aaron fell to the floor?"

Ruth dabbed her eyes before she answered. "He wasn't breathing."

Edmund Fulton's spindly legs whisked to her side.

"I know this is hard, Mrs. Gates. Please, take your time." He raked steely, accusing eyes across Luke.

Luke's red face blanched, and he whispered a silent prayer.

"The preacher begged me to forgive him," Ruth Gates continued. "He gripped my arms so tight they bruised."

Fulton leaned close. "Go on."

"Why, then Uriah came and saved me. Didn't you, Uriah?"

"Shore did!" the man piped up from his seat.

The silver-haired judge glared at Uriah Cook for a moment, then pointed his finger at him. "You, Sir, are not the one on the stand and will remain quiet," he scolded. He transposed his stare onto Fulton, as if faulting him for the disruption.

"That is all, Your Honor," Fulton said with a contrite bow of his head.

Next Luke was summoned to the stand. Edmund Fulton paced, swinging equally elongated legs and arms, then stopped suddenly—a ploy he used to gain the full attention of the courtroom. Expectantly, the crowd hushed immediately in breath-holding suspense. Several people leaned forward in their seats.

"Mr. Wheeler, how long has it been since your wife's death?"

Luke's eyes, windows of pain and sorrow, met Fulton's accusing ones. "Almost three months, Sir."

"Is it true that you loved your wife and deeply grieved her death?"

Luke set his jaw and concentrated on his answer. "Yes, of course."

"Were you acquainted with Ruth Gates before the day of the crime?"

Luke glanced over the crowd, his gaze resting upon the front bench where Ruth Gates sat. In vain he searched her face for some sign of penitence. But her expression remained stony. "Yes," he answered.

"How?"

"She attended my church on occasion."

"Isn't it true that most folks see a resemblance between Ruth Gates and your late wife?"

Calmly Luke answered, "I've heard some do, but personally I don't see it. Mrs. Gates is much older, and her countenance much harder."

Simon stifled a grin at Ruth's gasp of insult, and her lawyer's consequent frown. But Fulton recovered with practiced speed. "So," he said, "you acknowledge that there is a resemblance."

"Yes."

"Were you acquainted with Aaron Gates as well?"

Luke answered, "Yes."

"What were you doing at their home the afternoon of the crime?"

"I went to fulfill a promise to my wife, Miriam."

Luke's answer was an unexpected twist, one which pleased Fulton. The prosecutor's face lit with apperception as he shrewdly abandoned his previously intended line of questioning. Carefully, he stalked his prey. "So your thoughts were preoccupied with Miriam that day?"

Luke conceded. "In a way."

Then Fulton pounced on Luke like a tiger. "Considering your blinding grief and Miriam's resemblance to Ruth Gates, is it possible you mistook Ruth for Miriam?"

Refusal played across Luke's face. "No!"

"Did you strike Ruth when she would not allow you to kiss her?"

"No!" Luke looked to Simon with a silent plea for help.

His lawyer did not respond, though his face indicated grave displeasure at the way Edmund Fulton was attempting to use this—Dayton's first murder trial—to make a name for himself.

Fulton asked, "Isn't it true that Aaron Gates repeatedly warned you to stay away from his wife?"

"What?"

"I understand, Mr. Wheeler, it is hard for you to concentrate in your unstable condition. . . ."

"Objection, Your Honor." Simon leapt to his feet.

"Sustained. Restate your question, Prosecutor."

"Had Aaron Gates warned you to stay away from his wife?"

"Well, yes, but he was drunk at the time. He had no grounds to—"

Fulton interrupted. "What exactly did he say to you?"

Luke grappled for an answer that was not self-incriminating. When he hesitated, Fulton pressed. "I understand there was a public disturbance with witnesses. Shall I call Mrs. Gates back to the stand?"

Luke's shoulders slumped as he mumbled, "He said to stay away from Ruth."

"I'm sorry, could you speak up?"

Luke repeated, "He said to stay away from Ruth."

"That is all. I have no further questions."

Simon Appleby's sweeping gaze stole across the stuffy, overcrowded courtroom, cognizant of those who relied on him—Luke, Emmett Wheeler, Claire, Luke's parishioners and friends. If only he had a stronger case. Nevertheless, after giving his client an encouraging smile, he began to question him.

"Reverend, what did you hear as you approached the Gates home?"

Luke answered with conviction, "I heard two men and Mrs. Gates arguing inside the house."

"Did you enter the house?"

"Yes, because Ruth Gates screamed, a hideous scream. I rushed inside to help."

"What did you find?"

"Aaron Gates lay on the floor bleeding, Ruth Gates bent over him."

Simon paused to allow the jury to visualize this scene before continuing his interrogation. "Where was the third person?"

"Gone out the kitchen window," Luke answered. "It was open, and the curtain was half ripped off the wall. Other nearby items were knocked about. And I heard his horse ride off."

The crowd gasped. Pleased with this response, Simon asked, "What happened after that?"

"I placed my hanky around Aaron Gates's head to stop the bleeding, but he died in my arms. Ruth begged me to help. That was when I noticed her swollen face." Luke's own face dripped of perspiration, which he wiped away with his hand as he continued. "The smell of liquor oozed from Aaron Gates's body, and I assumed he'd hit his wife. Naturally, I tried to console her as I would any sister in my congregation."

Simon urged, "Go on."

"Ruth grew calmer until Uriah came. That's when she turned on me. She made up things to frame me and protect whoever went out that window."

"Thank you. That will be all for now."

As Luke returned to his seat in the front of the packed courtroom, the spectators used the opportunity to stir from their uncomfortable positions. Men wiped their brows and swatted at flies while women tugged at sticky skirts, many fanning their faces.

Simon rearranged his tight necktie and proceeded to call Ruth Gates to the stand. He recaptured the crowd's attention with his sharp questions, like zipping, burning arrows.

"Mrs. Gates, why did you threaten me when I examined the ground outside your house?"

Ruth stammered, "Y–you scared the children. They'd been through enough. I–I just wanted you to leave."

Simon flinched at the mention of her children. This could sway the jury. Against his better judgment, however, he continued with this barbed method of interrogation to pursue the issue.

"Upon examination, I noticed the ground was freshly raked around the outside of the kitchen window, the window which Rev. Wheeler testified was used as an escape route. Mrs. Gates, were you trying to cover someone's tracks?"

"Objection! The witness is not on trial here," Fulton reminded the judge.

"Overruled. Answer the question, please, Mrs. Gates."

Fulton dropped back into his seat.

She thrust her chin upward. "I don't know what you're talking about.

272

I never did such a thing."

Simon played on a hunch. "Were you, in fact, trying to protect your own son, Ruben?"

"No! I was not!" Ruth jumped to her feet. "That man!" She pointed to Luke. "He killed my husband. I saw it with my own eyes, and you're just trying to get him off the hook!"

In response, someone from within the group of spectators yelled, "What weapon did the preacher use? His Bible?"

An outburst of laughter instantly filled the room while the judge's cheeks turned red as July's tomatoes. With white eyebrows poised in consternation, he banged his gavel repeatedly until order was restored.

Simon changed tactics. "Mrs. Gates, if Rev. Wheeler's story is not true, how did his hanky get on your husband's head?"

She shook her head adamantly. "There was no hanky. The preacher's a liar. He made that up, too."

Aware that Ruth's testimony was harming their case and generating undue sympathy, Simon dismissed her to call Uriah Cook as his next witness.

Once Uriah was settled, Simon addressed him. "Mr. Cook, was there a hanky on Aaron Gates's head?"

"No, Sir. I never saw one."

Eyes widened through the courtroom. Luke lunged forward, restrained only by his father's firm grip upon his shoulder.

Simon stared at the witness in disbelief, now wondering what part Uriah played in this deception. Was he the accomplice? Uriah began to squirm under Simon's intense scrutiny.

"Do you know the penalty for perjury?"

"Yes, Sir," Uriah said. "Like I said, there was no hanky. The preacher lied." He gestured toward Ruth. "Everything Ruth Gates says is true. Why, I saw the way the preacher was mishandling her!"

Simon approached the judge. "Your Honor, this deception is much more widespread than I had anticipated. I ask for a recess. I believe I can prove—"

His appeal upset Judge Dunlevy, whose duties included riding circuit, and his departure had already been postponed for this case. Those responsibilities weighed heavily upon him now. "No recess, Barrister Appleby. You should have done your homework."

As Simon wheeled away from the bench, he noticed a pair of leering eyes from the back of the courtroom—Clancy from the docks. The unscrupulous fisherman laughed out loud, as if taking pleasure in the fact that his presence further rankled the fancy lawyer.

❧❧

The sweltering days that followed wore grim and long as piece by piece

Luke's case was decimated. In the end, one of the testimonies that swayed the jury was that of Sheriff Watson.

"No, Sir," he had replied, "there was no hanky when I got there." Furthermore, he destroyed Luke with his closing remark. "After being around the reverend these past weeks, I find it hard to believe he could have killed anybody. Of course he was like a crazy man when I first locked him up."

On the fifth day of the trial, July 8, the afternoon hours waned as the attorneys delivered their concluding statements. Subsequently, the jury deliberated in the upper story of the small brick courthouse for about an hour. Upon their return Judge Dunlevy heard the verdict and swiftly announced his sentence.

"This court finds Luke Wheeler guilty of murder. I hereby sentence him to hang by the neck until dead, the day after tomorrow at noon."

Claire flew to her feet and screamed, "No! No!"

Equally stunned, Mary Anders clasped hold of the anguished woman's shoulders, easing her back onto the bench where she and Gustaf attended to her.

At the decree, the room buzzed with heated discussion and Luke's world spun madly. He collapsed in his seat, oblivious of those about him just before the blackness came. The stinging, he realized, was Simon patting his cheeks to revive him. Sheriff Watson allowed Simon and Emmett to support Luke as he propelled them through the crowd—which hushed as they passed—back to his cell.

Chapter 7

The hoofs of Simon's chestnut bay beat against summer's parched road to the Gates home. *That woman bewitched the jury. She has to have an Achilles' heel. If only I could prove—* Simon ducked his hat-clad head just in time to avoid the sharp claws of an overhanging limb. "Easy, Boy," he soothed and slowed their pace.

A mile and a half later, he dismounted and approached the Gateses' dwelling with apprehension. The place reeked of foul play. The air felt suffocating, the shadows menacing. He removed his hat, drew in a deep breath of the virulent atmosphere, and knocked. After days of courtroom interrogations, the widow Gates's beauty still shocked him. He tapped his hat against his leg. "Mrs. Gates."

"What do you want? The trial's over." Simon thrust his right leg inside. The weight of the door's heavy impact crushed upon him, causing him to stagger backwards. However, he recovered enough to shoulder the gaping door open and push his way inside.

She backed up. Her hateful glare met his smoldering one.

She was the first to relent. "What do you want?"

"An innocent man is going to hang. His blood, as well as Aaron's, will be on your hands for eternity."

Ruth's face flinched, her voice hard. "Is that all?"

"When the truth eventually comes out, you may hang. Are you willing to die for the one you protect?"

Before she could reply, a cry rang out. "Mama!" Young Tom Gates burst through the open doorway, then stopped when he recognized Simon.

Ruth jerked her head. "In a minute, Tommy. We have a visitor who will soon be leaving. Run along now." She motioned for him to leave.

"Yes, Ma'am," the boy mumbled, but he hesitated, allowing Simon just enough time to notice the shiny object that the boy fingered nervously.

"Tom! Wait!" he called out before Tom fled from the room. "What a fine knife you have there! Can I see it?" Pride swallowed up the boy's better judgment, and he thrust it out for Simon's inspection.

Ruth's eyes narrowed in distrust. As the lawyer palmed the metal object, he complimented the boy again. "Yes, mighty fine. Don't recall when I've seen such a nice piece. Where'd you get it?"

"My brother Ruben gave it to me the day—" Tom broke midsentence, catching his mistake upon remembering Simon's appearance at the docks.

The lad's desire to hide the fact that Ruben was in Dayton corroborated Simon's hunch from the first day of the trial: Ruben must be involved. Perhaps he was the one who had fled through the open window.

"Oh, yes," Simon said, "I remember seeing you on the docks that day, coming off the *Hilde*. Here, Son." He returned the knife, and Tom dashed for the door.

Slowly, Simon turned to Ruth with a fortitude that unsettled her. "You realize, of course, it will only be a matter of time until I can prove that Ruben was in Dayton all along, that Aaron killed Silas Farthington, and you are an accomplice to your husband's murder. It would be much better for you if you came forward with the truth now."

Ruth's eyes widened, but her lips remained clenched in a straight, fine line, determined to seal off the truth. Simon tried one last tactic, an appeal to a mother's heart. "Remember, not only is Luke Wheeler a man of God, but he is also a widower and father of a small baby. That little boy needs him. Surely, you cannot allow his father to die."

"Leave now, Mr. Appleby!"

Simon looked at her unflinching face. "You'll regret this until your dying day," he said with loathing.

"Is that a threat?"

"Of course not! Just the hard truth." Deeply frustrated, he wheeled and left.

Luke stared out the small barred window, watching the carpenters. The sound of hammers broke the otherwise eerie quiet. The sweet smell of sawdust mixed with the more repugnant odors of dust and sweat, permeating through the open window. *Where is justice?* he wondered as he listened to the scraping of lumber, creaking of boards, and thunder of hammers driving nails into the gallows.

Thus Simon caught him unawares, gazing into the distant space, when he came to visit. Startled out of his vacant stare, Luke asked him forthrightly, "What does a man do when he knows he has but hours to live?"

Simon straddled the wooden stool in Luke's cell and considered the legitimate question. "Tie up loose ends, I guess, make things right, say his good-byes."

"My relationships are all in order—I'm ready to meet my Lord. I've even forgiven Ruth. I know she wouldn't do this if she wasn't hurting in some way."

Simon nodded, not intending to tell Luke of his visit that morning since nothing good came of it.

Luke continued, "Mostly I concentrate on meeting Jesus and seeing Miriam again. That gives me strength. But it just doesn't seem possible that one minute I can be in this miserable cell, and the next walking on golden streets in eternity, does it?"

Simon shook his head. He certainly could not comprehend it. He could not visualize this man's life snuffed. He shuddered.

"What about the good-byes? Is there anyone you want to see yet?"

"Father's gone to bring Claire and Davy over for awhile. Then he's going to stay with me 'til the end."

"Well, I'll stay here if you like until he returns."

"That would be kind of you. And, Simon, thank you for trying. I know this is not easy for you. You did your best. Don't blame yourself. It must be God's plan for me, to bring me home."

"I wish I could have done more." Simon hung his head.

When Emmett Wheeler returned alone, Simon and Luke looked at him questioningly. He answered their unspoken inquiry. "Claire will be over later; Davy was asleep."

Rising to take his leave, Simon grasped the prisoner by the shoulders, pulling him into a wordless embrace. "I'll be here in the morning. Be strong, Luke," he said in a low tone.

"Thank you, Simon."

Luke watched his friend disappear, then gave a start when his father grabbed his shoulder, turning him about.

"What is it, Father?"

Emmett leaned close to whisper, his face aglow. "There's a plan, Luke!"

"What do you mean?"

"Ssh! Come listen." Again Emmett whispered excitedly, "A plan for your escape!"

"But, Father," Luke argued, "I'm not a coward! This can't be the Christian way."

Emmett placed a weary hand upon his son's shoulder and tried once more to convince him. "Christ eluded the angry mobs."

Dubious, yet wanting desperately to believe his father, Luke grappled with the issue. Was it an acceptable option? Could there be any honor, any scruples in such a thing?

His father reasoned, "Oh, all right. It's not quite the same." His voice raised. "But you're innocent, and to hang isn't justifiable either."

Luke's will to survive, along with his father's pleading, finally persuaded him. With a nod, he conceded, "You're right, Father. If this is the Lord's plan for my life—to escape—I must try it."

"That's my boy," Emmett whispered with relief. "Quickly now, we must go over the details. There's much to be done."

The plan began when Gustaf arrived at the jail shortly before dark. As usual, Sheriff Watson accompanied him to Luke's cell, but when he turned to leave, Luke detained him with a question. "Sheriff?"

Curious, Sheriff Watson turned back toward the condemned one. "Yeah?"

Luke's hands gripped the iron bars, and from where his face was pressed between them, he glanced at the metal lock. "Could you bend the rules a bit? I could really use the support right now."

Sheriff Watson sympathized with Luke. "Guess that won't harm anybody." The sheriff despised this part of his job—attending a prisoner facing death. He twisted the key and waited for Gustaf to enter the cell with Emmett and Luke. With the special privileges allotted a clergyman, Emmett was already inside the cell.

Upon returning to his outer office, Sheriff Watson heard a disturbance out front and hurried to the window to investigate. "Aw, no!" he muttered and fumbled for his hat and rifle, then swung the door open and stood in its wake, his weapon ready. The group gathered outside were many of Luke's parishioners. "You folks need to disassemble!" the sheriff warned them.

"We won't let you hang the preacher," one man shouted heatedly.

"Now listen, you men know the law is the law!"

Meanwhile the three inside Luke's cell scrambled to receive items that were being passed to them through the barred window. Outside, Jesse Murdock, one of Luke's parishioners, poked two small cloth pouches filled with hearth ashes along with a tiny container of tree sap through the tight bars. Then Gustaf drew two bedsheets into the room and swiftly shoved them beneath Luke's cot.

Emmett grabbed the razor that appeared next. "God bless you, Jesse."

"May God be with you, Luke," Jesse whispered back hoarsely. Then after careful surveillance in all directions, he disappeared.

Gustaf motioned at Luke. "You do it, my hand's too shaky."

Luke grinned. "All right. Father, let's see what you look like beneath that beard." Knowing every second accounted for precious time, Luke made quick even strokes across his father's face, and the man's beard vanished, revealing a squarish, shocking-white chin. Gustaf brushed the small, white curls onto a neat pile for reuse, to be pasted upon Luke's own chin later.

Fastidiously, the men worked over Luke to concoct a clever disguise. First, the Wheelers exchanged clothing. Next, Emmett powdered his son's yellow hair with the hearth ashes until it appeared as gray as his own. Gustaf applied a generous amount of tree sap to Luke's chin, then neatly attached

Emmett's shavings, patting and designing a nice beard for him. With satisfaction, all remaining traces of the caper were concealed beneath Luke's cot.

When the time was right and the crowd outside had dispersed, Gustaf called out to Sheriff Watson. "Ready to leave now, Sheriff!"

The lawman arrived, looking haggard from his riotous encounter. On cue, Gustaf began the charade.

"I'm gonna take Emmett to get a bite to eat and give Luke a moment alone." Sheriff Watson cast a glance at the man on the cot with a Bible stuck in his face, presuming that one was his prisoner, and nodded. As they left the cell, Luke used Gustaf as a shield as the older man diverted the sheriff's attention with small talk.

Once outside on Main Street, both men heard the heavy door slam and the latch being locked on the inside. Gustaf whispered, "I see the sheriff isn't going to take any chances of losing his prisoner to a mob." Luke emitted a nervous chuckle at the irony of the situation as they hurried to the place where his horse awaited, saddled.

"Claire'll meet you at King's Ferry with Davy."

"What?" Luke clearly did not want to involve them in any danger.

Gustaf shrugged. "You know Claire. She thought you would want to say good-bye to the child." At Luke's displeasure, he continued, "She would not take 'no' for an answer." He gave Luke a small push. "Now go. And God be with you."

The two men embraced before Luke scaled his spirited brown mount and headed for the river, propelled forward by a steady supply of adrenaline pumping through his veins.

❧❧

Darkness fell across the Miami River in deepening shades of gray. Luke expelled a trembling sigh of relief; he had reached the ferry in the nick of time before its final daily excursion. He paused to consider the many minute details his friends had coordinated to accomplish this escape. But there was no time for sentimentality. Casting the thought aside, he dismounted and scanned the area, but he did not see Claire. Just as well.

Quickly, he approached the two dark, sizable figures that seemed to be in charge of the ferry. "Room for me and my horse?" Luke inquired.

"Twelve and one-half cents!" one man said, then spit tobacco juice into the water.

With trepidation, Luke rummaged through his father's trousers pocket. He was relieved to feel a lump of money most certainly put there intentionally. Withdrawing a small portion, he counted out the fee to the spitter with the red bandanna and dark beard.

The planks of the sloping ramp creaked like an old barn door as Luke coaxed his skittish horse to board the river ferry, which was secured with cables between the east and west shores. Once this was accomplished, he murmured gently to his frightened beast, tethering her to a hitching post near the center of the floating barge.

Luke's eyes searched the dimly lit ferry. He faintly discerned the silhouette of a skirt. It appeared to be the only female passenger among the group. Surely Claire wouldn't have boarded the ferry. He started toward her. "Claire?"

"Luke? Is that you?" Claire giggled tearfully when she was able to make out his features. "You look so funny."

"Come over here by the railing," he whispered. After putting distance between themselves and the other passengers, Luke drew both her and Davy into his arms. "I can't believe this is happening," he whispered against her hair.

"I was so frightened."

"You poor thing. Why did you come aboard? You should not have come at all."

"Not for me, for you. I was afraid you might be killed or wounded, lying somewhere bleeding—"

"Ssh. I'm fine, as you can see." He released her, holding up his arms for her to inspect his person.

Claire wiped her tears away with a free hand and giggled again at the sight of him and his haphazard beard. Knowing their time for good-byes was short, she offered Davy. With the baby in his arms, Luke turned his back to the others aboard and gazed out over the dark water, its choppy surface now barely visible since the stars were not yet shining.

Luke managed to calm his still-thundering heart enough to speak soft endearments to Davy who, in turn, struggled against his father's chest with screaming protest. "Davy, my son. Have you missed your pa?" The baby calmed and eventually quit squirming at the familiar voice. Unexpectedly, Davy swiped chubby fingers across his beard, whacking off a portion of whiskers. "Hey! I'll need those just awhile longer." Luke laughed. He pried the boy's fist open and brushed away the loose stubbles as he turned to Claire.

Before he could speak, however, the barge lurched violently, knocking them both off balance. Claire grabbed for the railing and held tight. Then they were adrift with two men poling the ferry and a strong breeze brushing across their faces. "You all right?" he asked her.

"Yes." She nodded.

"You were supposed to get off before we launched! Maybe I can stop them!"

Claire grabbed Luke's sleeve. "No! Don't cause a scene. That wouldn't be good for your situation."

Panicking, Luke's voice raised. "But what will you do now?"

Blurting the first thing that came to her mind, Claire said, "Just ride the ferry back across. Don't worry."

"But I am worried!"

"Sh! Not so loud," Claire cautioned.

"But you're the only woman aboard." Luke leaned close to confide, "I've never seen the pair handling this ferry before. King must have hired some new men. I don't feel good about this, Claire."

"Maybe more folks will join us on the other shore."

"We'll see," Luke replied skeptically. Not wanting to spend these final moments arguing, he dropped the issue. "Claire?"

"Yes."

Touching her shoulder, he said, "Thanks for coming and for everything you've done for me these past weeks. Father's agreed to take Davy back to Ben in Beaver Creek. When I'm free again, I'll go to him there."

Claire smiled, looking up into his eyes. "I thought as much. And I'm confident you will be free soon."

Luke shifted his touch to her elbow, guiding her to a nearby bench, and they settled in for the remainder of the passage. Half an hour passed in which Luke played with Davy. When they approached the docks of the opposite shore, he reluctantly gave up the child, and at Claire's insistence. . . he finally left them.

However, once aground, he tethered his horse close to the ferry and positioned himself in the shadows. His intention was to watch those boarding, keeping an eye out for Claire and Davy's safety until they were adrift again.

To watch them huddled together in the spot where he had left them was excruciating. An icy loneliness gripped him. What choice had he? Being on the run, he did not know what dangers to expect. He shivered uncontrollably, wishing some women or children would board. But they did not, and worse still, the bearded man with the red bandanna was even now approaching Claire.

"No place to go, Ma'am?" the man asked. Luke strained but could not hear her reply. But he heard the man's coarse laughter and vulgar response. "I won't mind keeping you company on the long ride home."

Luke muttered under his breath as he bolted back toward the ferry. His boots clacking on the wood-bottomed barge caused such a commotion as to startle Claire and her antagonist. When they turned toward him, Luke blurted out the first thing that came to his mind, "Come on, Claire! We must hurry!" He grabbed Claire's arm to lead her and Davy away, but the bearded one was not to be easily discouraged. He followed and spun Luke around.

"What's the hurry? The lady and me was having a talk, weren't we, Honey?"

"No! We were not!" Claire snapped.

The man then took a swing at Luke, barely grazing his chin, swiping off a fistful of fuzz. "Well, what've we got here? An impostor?" He let out a whoop. "Pretty frisky for an old feller."

Luke hollered, "Run, Claire! Get the horse!" Claire flew with Davy, and Luke found himself facing the offender. The man narrowed his eyes. "What're you up to? You got a reward on your head?"

Unexpectedly, the man lunged at Luke, but Luke dodged him with cat-like swiftness, at the same time releasing a sidelong swing that connected soundly with the man's neck. The strike was powerful—pumping adrenaline had maximized Luke's strength far beyond his usual ability—and the man reeled just long enough for Luke to make his escape.

Claire never knew exactly what happened, but by the time she had fetched Luke's horse, Luke was beside her, breathless. Then he was mounted and pulling her up behind him. "Hold on," he hollered, and they galloped off with Davy sandwiched between them, fast leaving the ferry behind.

Meanwhile back at the jail, Deputy Galloway had come to relieve Sheriff Watson for the nighttime shift, just as usual. This was what Emmett had been waiting for. Now it was time to finish this ploy. "Deputy!"

The lawman soon appeared, and Emmett whispered, "My son fell asleep." He rubbed his chin with his huge hand, trying to cover the smooth white area where his beard had once been. At the same time, he pointed to the cot where a lump resembling a man's form—the sheets that had been pulled through the bars—was visible beneath the wool blanket. "Do you mind if I leave for awhile and get a bite to eat?"

"Sure, Reverend," the deputy whispered back. "I'm surprised he can sleep." As Galloway eyed the lump, Emmett walked past him and out of the jailhouse. Exhaling a sigh of relief, he looked heavenward. "Thank You, Lord."

Remembering something, he changed directions and passed beneath the small barred window. He stooped to pick up the items that had been previously flung out the window. Grimly, Emmett stared at the looming gallows before him.

He bowed his head. "Lord, forgive me for this falsehood," he breathed. Lifting his head, he tucked the bundle beneath his arm, turned his back to the ugly structure with its poignant smell of death, and rushed toward his hotel.

Chapter 8

A remote Indian trail sliced across the Mad River Road, penetrating a heavily wooded area. Here Luke veered east, considerably slowing their previously furious gait to forge untamed forest. Not far within this timberland's tangle of decaying tree stumps, strewn logs, and hock-crippling gorges lay a tiny cove where the near-full moon now cast a welcomed glow.

Upon discovering this secluded haven, he slid from the saddle and helped Claire and Davy dismount. Still winded from their narrow escape at King's Ferry, Luke shook his head. "That was a close call! I'm sorry, Claire. I sure didn't intend to drag you and Davy into this."

He slapped off his hat with one hand and ran his other through his ash-powdered hair, raising a smoky cloud that made him cough. "What a mess I've gotten us into!" He yanked his hat back onto his head and began to pace.

Claire's hairpins had fallen out by now, and her hair hung long and wild. She brushed it off her face as best she could, but Davy's pink fist flew up and latched onto a strand. Claire planted a wet kiss on the baby's cheek and ventured, "Luke?"

He stopped his pacing and faced her wordlessly, several feet away.

"It's not your fault"—she motioned wide with her arm—"any of this. The important thing is that you are free and alive. You must not abort your plans because of us. I can ride. See? I even wore my riding skirt."

Luke went to her where she stood clutching her skirt and lightly touched her arm. "Claire, I need to think. Why don't you have a seat over there on that stump and take a rest?"

Claire nodded and settled herself, rocking Davy gently while she rummaged through the baby's pouch. She diapered him, then withdrew a small bottle of milk. Luke watched as the baby sucked hungrily at first, then more rhythmically, and finally started to nod off.

"Do you have much food along for Davy?"

Claire whispered, "Enough to last through the night."

"When you're rested, we'll start toward Beaver Creek. I'm to make a rendezvous with some men coming our way. Arrangements have been made to exchange mounts to confuse the law, put them onto a false trail."

"I know."

Luke's startled look caused Claire to explain. "According to Gustaf, this

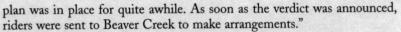

plan was in place for quite awhile. As soon as the verdict was announced, riders were sent to Beaver Creek to make arrangements."

Shaking his head, Luke said, "You don't know how humbled I am, how touched I feel. . . ." His voice faded.

After several moments, he continued, "When we meet up with the riders from Beaver Creek, you and Davy can go with them."

"No!" Claire cringed at the thought of consorting with perfect strangers. Luke swung around and looked at her in astonishment. Her tone had disturbed Davy's slumber. "Please," she begged while rocking the child, "let me stay with you."

"We'll see," he said gently. "But for now, the more miles we put behind us, the better."

Luke recalled that Gustaf mentioned supplies being packed and hoped no one had removed his personal articles normally stashed there. With relief, he withdrew an object made of cloth and leather. Holding the contraption out for Claire's inspection, he said, "A sling for Davy. Would you like me to carry him?"

Claire scrambled to her feet. "I believe I can manage with the help of that sling. Why don't you let me try?"

Luke smiled. "All right. Come here and let me show you how this works." Carefully he reached one arm around Claire while placing the sling beneath the sleeping baby's rump and back. Then gingerly he turned Claire around so he could secure the buckle at her waist and across her back. "Comfortable?" he asked with a mischievous grin.

Claire returned his smile. "Actually, it helps tremendously."

Sobering, Luke apologized. "I'm sorry, but we'll need to ride hard until we get to the rendezvous point. But you can rest there. It's only another hour or two."

"I understand," Claire assured him.

"Ready then?"

Claire nodded, and Luke easily hoisted her up onto the saddle, then slipped in front of her. He cast over his shoulder, "Feel free to hold on or lean against me. If you get sleepy, tuck your hands beneath my gunbelt so you don't slip off."

As they rode, Claire commented, "I noticed the gun. You never carried one before. Can you shoot?"

Luke laughed. "Yes. But this was Gustaf's idea. I hope I don't have to use it." Silence prevailed until Luke remarked, "The Anderses are going to be worried about you."

"I imagine they'll figure out what happened."

"Somehow we'll have to let the others know you're all right." With this thought Luke grew pensive. The night also grew still, except for wild animal calls and Queenie's hooves and creaking saddle gear. The solitary Indian trail led deeper into the woods. As they clipped along, Luke was thankful for the moonlight so he could distinguish the ordinary shadows from any potential lurking captors. He dodged the branches that reached out to apprehend.

After considerable time had passed, Luke became more comfortable with the wooded surroundings. He mulled ideas over in his mind. With a pat, he checked his shirt pocket to see if Gustaf's letter of introduction was safe.

It would present him to the Sweeneys of Cincinnati, Gustaf's sister and brother-in-law. Gustaf had vouched that they would accommodate him. He could make the trip in two days if he rode hard and kept to the main roads. But with Claire and Davy, he might be recognized. They would need to travel cross-country as much as possible. It would be tedious.

Claire's sudden grip at his waist alerted him. Then he heard it, too, the approaching hoofbeats of several galloping horses. Instantly, Luke veered off the trail, and a branch knocked off his hat, which landed alongside the road.

But he spurred Queenie on through a tangle of tiny oak saplings and poplars while the sound of men on horses grew louder. After maneuvering Queenie behind a huge maple tree that hid them from view, they waited for the riders to pass. He patted his snorting beast's quivering neck, hoping to quiet her.

The sudden change in gait woke Davy, and he let out a shrill cry. Luke felt Claire shift, seeking to quiet the child. He scanned the area frantically, mentally planning their escape route should it be necessary.

"Whoa! Hold up!" Luke froze at the words, hoping Queenie and Davy would remain still. Scarcely breathing, Claire listened, also stiff and motionless.

"Let's make camp here." The menacing voice seeped of power and evil. "Billy, search around for a good spot. We'll let Sid and Red catch up with the loot."

Luke whispered, "They're stopping. We've got to get out of here."

Gently, he coaxed Queenie backwards, then reined east toward the wood's heart. Luke hoped the ground was grass covered, and he twinged at each snapping twig. Bushes swished as they inched away. They were about out of danger when Luke heard it, the dreaded discovery. "Look here! A good hat!"

"Let me see."

The hair on Luke's neck bristled, and his every impulse screamed to make a run for it, but listening to intellect, he continued at a cautious gait. The men were still too close and might hear them. And the woods were thick and dangerous. When a safe distance finally separated them from the band of robbers, he muttered aloud, "Thank You, Lord."

Soon they came onto the Indian trail again. "The road must curve," he whispered to Claire. "We're probably only a couple miles away from their campsite." Luke looked both directions, then warily moved onto the trail. He whispered, "Hold tight!" and spurred Queenie into a gallop.

After several miles, when it seemed that they were not being followed, he eased the pace. "You all right, Claire?" he asked over his shoulder.

"Yes. Who were they?"

"Outlaws."

Claire was quiet, and Luke informed her, "We've lost some time. If you and Davy are up to it, we'll keep riding hard now. It can't be much further."

"Yes. Let's get out of here."

A myriad of brilliant stars canopied the moonlight riders. Luke gazed heavenward at God's handiwork and hoped he was in the Father's perfect will for his life. He frowned. What could he do about it now except concentrate on the task at hand? He scanned the trail ahead where the moonlight afforded vision, and he pricked his ears to listen for the approach of riders.

Even so, without warning, a haunting cry pierced the air, and terror shot through Luke's heart. Claire's small hands grasped his waist and clung. He whispered in a tremorous voice, "Just wolves, nothing to worry about." But his hand slipped downward to rest against the gun strapped to his hip. Eventually, her grip relaxed a bit until an owl's shrill hoot directly overhead startled them again.

Nearing one o'clock of the wee hours, they reached Sugar Creek. Luke reined Queenie to the water's edge and turned to Claire. "This is it."

"Where are we?" she asked.

"Sugar Creek, where we're to make our switch."

"But no one's here."

"Not yet," Luke said. "Let's look around." He pointed. "Over there's good cover."

On foot, they investigated the rocky shoreline area Luke had indicated. Deciding that it would serve as an adequate blind, they rested on a large boulder as Davy slept through the sounds of the shallow creek's rushing waters and night chorus of croaking frogs.

"You won't actually let them take Queenie, will you?" Claire's unexpected question startled Luke.

He squirmed uncomfortably. "No, it's not that kind of switch. Ssh! Listen! I hear riders! Stay put 'til we know who it is."

Two horsemen appeared in plain view on the other side of the stream, pausing at the road's end. They gazed across the water, talking between themselves.

"It must be them," Luke whispered.

Hardly a moment later, one called across, "Wheeler! You over there?"

"It's them, all right. But I don't recognize 'em. Wait here." Luke mounted Queenie, urging her slowly into the stream. When the two men saw him emerge from the brush, they, too, entered the shallow creek. Claire watched the riders meet halfway, where the moon cast an eerie silver glow across their partly discernible forms. She heard talking and even laughter as they all came towards her.

Luke motioned her to the craggy edge along the western bank. One of the strangers dismounted, then joined his partner to ride double. At the same time, Luke slid off Queenie. In a low voice meant for Claire's ears only, he said, "I think it's best if you go on with me for now. I'm sure these men are harmless, but I've never laid eyes on them before. Are you willing?"

She clung to his arm. "Oh, yes, Luke! I'd much rather go with you."

"That-a girl. Since you'll have your own mount to handle, why don't I take Davy with me?" Claire allowed Luke to disassemble the baby carrier and helped him into it.

Davy woke, overjoyed to be in the arms of his father. "There little one, how's that?" His son's reaction warmed Luke, and he gave Claire a cheery smile. "Now, let's get you mounted."

"What's his name?" Claire asked, sitting atop a black mare.

One of the strangers laughed. "Just like a woman. Wants to know the horse's name."

His partner grinned. "Sorry, we don't know, Ma'am."

"Well." Claire thought a moment. "I think I'll call him Moonlight."

"Her, Ma'am," the older man corrected.

Claire giggled. "Oh! *She'll* be Moonlight then."

"Why is that, Ma'am?" he asked.

"If it weren't for the moonlight, she'd be too black to see." All three men laughed at her reasoning.

Growing serious again, Luke thanked them. "I'm beholden to you for your kindness, the risk you're taking in helping an escaped convict."

"Ah, no," the younger one answered, "glad we could be of help." Luke eased Queenie next to their horse to stretch out his hand. Both men shook it.

The older one said, "A fine-looking boy you got there, Rev. Wheeler. Good luck to ya."

"Thanks. God go with you."

Luke's benefactors left them to head back across Sugar Creek, and he nudged Queenie into step beside Moonlight. As they also returned to the trail, he explained, "With them riding double like we were and then doubling back to Beaver Creek, anyone tracking us will follow their trail. When they discover we're not in Beaver Creek, we'll be almost to Cincinnati. Hopefully by the time the posse sees they've been duped, our trail will be too old to follow."

"I think it's a good plan."

"In a few minutes we'll come to Beaver Creek Road; only we'll head away from Beaver Creek, south toward Cincy."

Claire nodded.

"Now, we can take it easier. Let's ride for a couple hours, then find a place to camp and get some rest. Can you make it a few more hours?"

"Yes. I'm all fired up!"

Luke laughed. "So is Davy!" Then beneath his breath he murmured, "Poor child."

As promised, a few hours before daybreak Luke found a spot to camp. Set back from the trail, even at this dark hour he could tell it was a perfect spot. The tall grass was enough to hide them, and a brook rippled close by. The sound of water was what led Luke to discover it. There was evidence of previous campsites.

Tired as they were, Luke cared for the horses while Claire tended Davy. Soon camp was made, and two bedrolls were laid out just a few feet apart. An awkward moment occurred when both Luke and Claire realized the indiscreetness of the situation.

Luke cleared his throat. "Sure am glad for the extra bedroll those fellows had on Moonlight."

Claire turned slightly so the darkness would hide her burning cheeks. She chided herself for being so self-conscious after everything else that night.

However, Luke was having similar thoughts, and not for the first time. Every time her grip had tightened about his waist, he'd winced—knowing the impropriety of their wild ride. Would authorities think he had abducted her? Wasn't he responsible for her reputation now, as well as her and Davy's safety?

Suddenly weary, he said, "I'll sleep facing the road. Davy can bed with me. My son and I need to get reacquainted, and you need your rest." He politely turned his back on Claire then and allowed her to climb into her bedroll.

Snuggled up with Davy, his back still toward her, Luke murmured, "Claire?"

"Yes."

"Don't be afraid. We're perfectly safe here."

"I'm not." She sighed. "Too tired."

"Me, too. Come daybreak, we'll move on. This is a good place for the horses to graze and water." In the quiet Luke heard Claire's slumbering breathing. He smiled and kissed Davy's cheek.

Chapter 9

The sound of a woodpecker in a cottonwood tree roused Luke to his first morning thoughts. Today he would hang! But he quickly shook it off as a blurry meadow setting focused. The wild ride through the woods wasn't just a dream then. As his head began to clear, he turned to corroborate his still foggy recollections. The gray bundle would be Claire. However, his movement was impeded by a small lump in his side. Whereupon he felt a little kick and rolled over to look full into his son's upturned face.

"Good morning, Davy," he whispered, cupping the baby's silken head within his palm. "Wide awake and not complaining. You're such a good boy; you deserve better. If your ma could only see you."

Davy cooed, blowing little bubbles from his parted lips. Luke lifted the baby to his shoulder as he raised himself into a sitting position. Eager now to examine their surroundings, he kicked off the scratchy woolen blanket.

Two revelations occurred simultaneously. First, this was a beautiful place; and second, it remained quite a contrast from the gallows prepared for his use this day, were it not for his escape.

All about him, two-foot-high cordgrass glistened wet with dew. Several yards beyond Claire, a brook gurgled. Birds dove from cottonwoods that lined its shore. Patches of bright golden asters dotted the meadow with yellow petals, welcoming in the new day. This magnificent display of nature cheered Luke after his weeks of dreary confinement.

Playfully he tickled Davy under the chin with his forefinger. "Let's clean up a bit." They stole past Claire and squatted by the creek's edge where Luke splashed his face. With a groan, he remembered his disheveled disguise. He took off his shirt and lay Davy on it, then scrubbed furiously, going so far as to dunk his head under the icy water. The vigorous head shaking that followed made Davy giggle and thrash his arms and legs wildly in the air. Shivering, Luke buttoned up his shirt again. Stubborn tree sap still adhered to his chin. Unconsciously, he scratched at it as he contemplated whether to build a fire.

"Luke!" A frightened cry broke the silence.

"Over here, Claire."

"Oh."

Instinctively, Luke turned toward the meadow bedroom. Claire sat with her golden-spun hair spilling all about her face, down her arms, shoulders, and back, her eyes still sleepy.

Only on Miriam had he ever beheld such a glorious sight as a woman's morning hair. Never before had he even considered Claire as a woman to be desired. The idea struck now that the two women were perfect contrasts, yet Claire was every bit as lovely as Miriam. He wondered when that had happened, having known Claire since she was a child. Her hair was as flaxen gold as Miriam's had been dark and shiny. Naturally, he compared the two. Claire was soft and tenderhearted; Miriam, vibrant and joyful. Miriam. . .was gone.

This abrupt realization brought Luke back to the present, where he was mortified at the realization that he was gaping shamefully. And upon seeing Claire's blush, he tore his eyes away, turning back to face the brook. Eventually he managed to put his straying thoughts in order.

A rustling sound alerted him that she was moving about. It sounded like she might be rummaging through the saddlebags. Why hadn't he thought of that? Suddenly curious, he wondered what supplies they did have.

From directly behind him Claire's voice, though soft and musical, startled him. "Things look different in the morning's light." His jump prompted her to giggle. "I'm sorry. I didn't mean to frighten you."

"Silly, isn't it?" he said shakily. "Just edgy, I guess." He glanced up and met her gaze as she settled beside him on a flat gray rock. With much relief, he noted her hair was once again braided and tucked away.

"Davy's last bottle," she offered. "Can I change and feed him for you?"

"Sure." Luke jumped to his feet and scooped the baby up, depositing him into Claire's lap. The child let out a cry when he saw his breakfast.

"Gotta check out supplies," he said and turned away, suddenly unnerved by the responsibilities that bore down upon him. Traveling with Claire unchaperoned could taint her reputation, and Davy was on his last meal. Then there was the danger of getting caught. "God help me," he whispered under his breath as he jerked open the flap on a leather saddlebag.

A glance skyward told Luke it was about six-thirty. Because of the remoteness of their campsite, they had not seen or heard any other riders. With that in mind, he decided to start a small fire and gathered the items needed for coffee and bacon.

By the time Luke had their scanty breakfast prepared, Davy was already fed and changed, and Claire groomed. When their meal was finished, Claire remarked, "You should try some bacon grease."

"Pardon?"

"For the tree sap."

"Oh." Luke rubbed his chin. "Think that would work?"

Wordlessly Claire plopped Davy on his lap and plucked a nearby trillium leaf, which she dipped into the fat. She tapped it with her finger to test its temperature, then smiled in satisfaction. "May I?" she asked.

"Be my guest," Luke stated.

She knelt down before him, her face within inches of his, and he closed his eyes. Carefully, she patted on the fat, then rubbed, scratched, and peeled at the sap.

"Ow!"

"Sorry."

After several minutes, she said, "There, go wash that off."

With a scowl he opened his eyes. The smirk on Claire's face irritated him. "I think you enjoy torturing me," he snapped. Maintaining an injured expression, he headed back to the creek, and when he returned, she had cleaned up the traces of their meager meal. "How's that?" he asked.

"Aside from the red raw blotches, it's a major improvement."

"Really?"

Claire giggled. "I'm sorry, Luke, but you looked so funny with your powdered hair and silly gray beard."

Luke grinned. "It did the trick, didn't it?" He strapped on his gunbelt. "Now we have to make plans. As long as there's no travelers, let's stick to the road. Odds are we'll come across a farm or cabin where we can get milk for Davy. I guess that's our next objective." He frowned. "Aside from dodging the law."

🙟🙝

Back in Dayton, Sheriff Watson carried Luke's breakfast to his cell. As he twisted the key in the padlock, he frowned at the lump under the covers. "Rev. Wheeler, I got your breakfast here." No movement occurred. Sheriff Watson removed the key and pulled open the barred door. Inside, he started toward Luke's cot, suddenly suspicious. Standing over the lump momentarily, he jerked back the covers. With a curse he burst from the cell, slammed the plate he carried down on his desk, and stuck his head out the jailhouse door.

"Deputy!" he hollered at the top of his lungs. Grabbing his hat, he sprinted across the street. Within minutes he reached the small café where Deputy Galloway customarily dined each morning after his evening shift.

Heads turned toward the door when Sheriff Watson entered the cafe, breathless. Instantly, Galloway was on his feet. "What's wrong?"

Watson motioned his younger aide outside, then he wheeled and demanded, "What happened to Wheeler?"

"Wheeler? I don't know. What do you mean?"

"He's gone. His cot was stuffed with sheets, but the cell was empty."

Deputy Galloway squirmed. "I don't know. I'm sure he was there last night."

With another curse Sheriff Watson mumbled, "C'mon." They started back toward the jail. "We've got to get to the bottom of this. So start remembering!" Pale faced, Galloway struggled to keep up with the other lawman. A few strides later the sheriff added, "There'll be a posse to form."

A few hours placed many miles behind Claire and Luke. They topped the peak of a small knoll, and Luke halted Queenie. "Look!" He pointed down at a valley where the road meandered like a river through an open area spotted with clumps of trees and several cabins, corrals, and a barn. "Looks like Davy's lunch might be just ahead."

Claire nodded, her expression a mixture of relief and dread.

"We'll have to come up with a story." Luke had mulled this around in his head all morning, but he felt uncomfortable voicing it. He suggested, "We're a family on our way to Cincinnati. We're going to—"

"Luke," Claire interrupted, "I don't think they'll believe I'm Davy's ma."

He stared at her a moment, frowning, then the implications of Claire's remark struck him, and he despised himself for his obtuseness. "Oh. Of course I wasn't thinking."

Both were thoughtful a moment, then Luke began again. "How about. . . my wife died, you're her sister, and we're taking the baby to your family." He shook his head. "It's still not proper for us to be traveling together, but I guess there's no way around it."

"I think it'll work. It's closer to the truth, which will be better if questions are asked."

Without warning, Luke exploded. "I hate to lie, Claire."

"Maybe we won't have to."

Clenching his jaw in determination, he said, "Let's go."

They stopped at the first dwelling. "Wait here," Luke told Claire as he dismounted.

With Davy still harnessed to his chest, he started toward the small plain cabin. He knocked. After several minutes, an unkempt man with a surly expression opened the door. Rifle in arm, he scowled at Luke and the baby. "Yeah?"

"We're traveling and wondered if you could spare some milk for the baby?"

The man looked beyond Luke at Claire, his expression skeptical. "I'm feeling poorly and would rather you just moved on." He motioned toward the road with his blue linsey-sleeved arm. As he did, a suspender fell off his shoulder and hung in disarray against his untucked shirttail.

Luke hesitated, surmising that the man was nursing a hangover. When he was about to leave, the man stopped him.

"Wait. There's a cow out back. If you want to milk her, go ahead."

"Thank you." Luke reached out to shake the man's hand, but he held it palm up.

"Ten cents."

Luke's eyes bulged. He had not expected the man to charge him, much less so extravagantly. His face grew hot with anger. Such options. Either he could take the man's offer or give him the verbal setting down he deserved, only to have to repeat this humiliating process all over again at the next cabin.

There was no choice. Reaching into his pants, he withdrew the coins and dropped them in the man's grimy paw. Then as he stepped down from the landing, the man called after him, "Stranger! I'll be a-watchin' you. Don't take anything that don't belong to ya, or ya'll be answerin' to this." He waved his rifle in the air.

"Don't worry, the milk's all I want," Luke snapped.

"Hmph!" The man closed the door and stationed himself by the window as Luke left.

After three of Davy's bottles were filled, Luke lost no time in removing himself and his charges from the man's property.

Meanwhile, Sheriff Watson, Deputy Galloway, and the rest of their posse slowed their mounts at Sugar Creek's edge.

"Hold up!" the sheriff hollered, removing his hat and mopping his forehead with his sleeve. "Dismount! Let's check these tracks out before we cross."

Deputy Galloway knelt by the roadside. "Looks like Wheeler went on across. The other tracks belong to more than one horse."

Watson nodded. "He must be heading to Beaver Creek like we suspected then. Let's go get 'em, men."

The rest of the day passed uneventfully for Luke and Claire until late afternoon when huge black clouds rolled in overhead. Casting an upward glance, Luke grew worried, knowing they would need to seek shelter before dark. This was yet another crimp in his plans, for they could not camp out in a storm. If it were just him. . .but it wasn't. With Claire and especially the baby, it was too risky.

Therefore it was with great relief that Luke noticed a column of smoke a few hours later. Paused at a crossroads, he watched it rise above a stand of trees at least a half mile away.

"Look, Claire! Let's check it out."

It turned out to be a secluded, homey-looking farm. Upon nearing, Luke saw a woman and child drawing water from a well and heartened at the sight of them.

"Looks better than the last place we stopped," he said to Claire. "Shall we see if we can stay in their barn tonight?"

The wind whipped, and Claire glanced skyward. The storm promised to be a sure thing now. In addition to its threat, her legs and back ached from riding. Gladly she consented.

As they started forward, Luke cast an unnecessary warning over his shoulder. "Be careful what you say.

"Hello!" Luke called.

The woman looked toward them, setting down her wooden bucket. A few drops of water sloshed over the top, and she swiped at her forehead where perspiration gathered and unruly strands of hair lashed across her face. A gust of wind billowed her skirt, making her appear stouter than she was. She bent forward to send the boy scooting. "Quick! Go get your pa, Matthew."

Luke dismounted and took a few steps toward her. Her expression was wary so he introduced his family. "I'm L—" He paused, wondering if he should use his real name. "I'm Lyle Smith, Ma'am. This is my sister-in-law Chloe and my son, Davy." He cast Claire a guarded look.

The lady nodded. "I'm Elizabeth Jenkins. My husband, John, is in the barn doin' chores."

Claire gave Luke an encouraging nod, and he continued, "We are traveling to Cincinnati. It's a long story, but we'd be obliged if you'd let us bed down in your barn tonight, with the storm coming in."

Before she could respond, the boy returned. "Pa's comin'," he panted.

She motioned for her approaching husband to hurry. "John!"

"Howdy," the farmer greeted Luke warmly.

"Lyle Smith." Luke held out his hand, then nodded at Claire. "Chloe and Davy."

"They're traveling and want to take shelter in the barn, John," the woman explained.

"Nonsense!" he said. "You'll stay at the house. Right, Elizabeth?"

"Sure." Elizabeth smiled. "You can have Matthew's bed."

"That's hospitable, Ma'am," Luke said. "Perhaps Chloe and Davy can accept your offer, but I best stay in the barn." At their perplexed expressions, he explained, "I don't think you understood. Chloe is my sister-in-law."

Elizabeth nodded. "Oh, yes, you did say that. You can stay in the barn then. Yes, that would be fine."

Luke pumped her hand up and down. "Much obliged, Mrs. Jenkins. I was worried for the baby."

"Why, of course you were." She turned to Claire. "Why don't you and Davy come with me while John shows Lyle where to stable the horses?"

"Matthew," the woman called over her shoulder, "can you fetch the water bucket? Then fill up another one for our guests?"

"Sure, Ma," the young boy answered.

"We best get those horses taken care of," John said, "before the storm hits."

Stretched out on sweet smelling hay, Luke lay warm. The barn he shared with the horses and other animals was dry and nearly draft free while outside the wind howled and rain pelted down upon the barn roof. Before he drifted off, he thanked God for providing for their needs. The Jenkinses were surely an answer to prayer. They had graciously offered shelter for as long as the storm prevailed with no questions. With Claire and Davy safe inside their house, Luke was able to get a good night's rest.

The storm turned into a full-fledged fury that blew throughout the night and the next day, finally moving on that following evening. To pass the rainy hours, Luke helped John with his chores and some repairs the man had saved for such a time. Inside, Claire washed out Davy's diapers, hanging them on a makeshift line that stretched across the entire kitchen. She stewed over their slow drying while at her feet, Matthew played with Davy—until he left to plead with his mother for a baby brother.

As Luke worked over a broken harness, his spirits plummeted. He hated the delay the storm had caused even though he was thankful that, unquestionably now, their tracks were washed away. Out the open barn door, he could barely see the house through the downpour.

Wondering about Claire's activities, the idea struck that maybe he should leave Claire and Davy here and go on alone—but her face came to his mind, and with it he envisioned her uneasiness and reluctance to accept such a plan. No, that would never work.

When Luke entered the house at suppertime, the clothesline and its attachments had been cleared away. The meal was hot and filling and did not provide a time for private discussion with Claire. After the meal he pulled out Claire's chair and whispered, "We need to talk."

She nodded. "I'll help with the dishes first."

Luke followed John out to the porch with a cup of coffee. "Much obliged for all your help," John said after a few minutes.

"The least I could do. We appreciate your hospitality."

"The air smells good after a rain. But it looks like it'll be clear tomorrow."

Luke agreed. "We should move on. In fact, I need to talk with Chloe before I turn in. Thanks again." Luke left him to return to the house and find Claire. He wanted to tell her they would be leaving early the next morning.

In the sitting room, Elizabeth rocked with mending upon her lap and

Matthew perched on the hearth, chipping away at a block of wood with a pocketknife, but Claire was nowhere to be seen. "Is Chloe around?" Luke inquired.

"She's in the bedroom feeding Davy." Elizabeth waved a threaded needle in the air, consent that he should enter.

The door to the adjoining bedroom was ajar, so Luke eased through the opening, careful to leave the door open. However, he stopped at the sound of Claire's voice.

She was poised on the edge of the bed with her back toward him, humming and talking intermittently while feeding Davy. The sweetness of the scene touched him, and he paused to watch, thinking about Miriam and wishing she had been able to hold their child, that he had been able to see her like that. When he came out of his reverie, he heard Claire speaking in liquidy-velvet tones to Davy.

"I love your father, you know. I always have, since I was twelve years old." Luke was shocked at her confession. But there was more. "Now I'm a grown woman and love him with a woman's heart. I'll never marry another." She stroked the baby's soft hair, and Luke, aghast, scarcely breathed. "Your pa's a decent man, strong of body and soul. He's the—"

Luke could not stand there any longer, letting her go on like that. He had to make her understand. "Claire!" At the sound of her name, Claire's face instantly paled, and her body stiffened. He slowly walked to face her, placing his hand upon her shoulder. "I'm so sorry, Claire." His eyes appealed. "But don't you see? You can't waste your life on me. I'm just an empty shell of a man."

"No!" She denied it.

"You don't understand." He persisted. "My love went with Miriam to her grave. I've nothing left to give a woman." Her face began to color again, and his voice sounded quivery even in his own ears. "Even one as fine as you."

Unshed tears glistened upon her blue eyes, and his heart lurched denial. Ironically, for one who had just depicted himself as an empty shell of a man, terrible conflicting emotions surged through him.

"You're such a special girl," he began, then corrected himself, ". . .woman. On the other hand, I am a criminal, a wanted man, one without a future."

"But you're innocent," she blurted out with a great sob.

Luke slowly backed away, his voice filled with regret. "The law says I'm guilty. I should have stayed and hanged. You and Davy don't belong here like this. To make matters worse, it's dishonoring to your reputation."

A now trembling Claire jumped to her feet and pushed Luke hard, her blue eyes sparking. "Stop it, Luke! I'll not beg for your love," she snapped. "You! You intruded. Those words were never meant for your ears!"

He could only stare at her. In all the years he had known her, he had never seen such fury. He hardly knew how to respond.

"I—I'm sorry," he stammered. "I had no right. But please understand, Claire. I'll never love again."

"So I've already been told! And I shan't ask you to." Claire pointed toward the door. "Now, get out!" Davy let out a scream, and as she turned to the child where he lay on the bed, she shrieked, "See what you've done!"

Frustrated to the point of anger, Luke strode toward the door. Without turning he said, "We'll be leaving in the morning at sunup."

She glared at his back. "We'll be ready."

As Luke entered the sitting room, Elizabeth dipped her head low over her sewing, which gave Luke another setback, realizing she had overheard their argument. "Good night," he said, his voice cracking.

"Good night, Luke," she answered.

He flinched at the sound of his real name. "Your secret's safe with me," she added softly. "I hope you are innocent. I've grown to like you all."

Luke walked out without a word, stomping toward the barn.

Chapter 10

Luke felt more miserable by the mile. The image of Claire's red, swollen eyes—exceedingly angry as well as sleepless—were branded into his memory. She lagged several yards behind on Moonlight. The only words spoken that morning were those directed to the Jenkinses, expressing gratitude for their hospitality. Mrs. Jenkins's words also seared his conscience. "I hope you get your problems worked out. You seem to be such a nice couple. God go with ya."

Luke grimaced at the testimony he had left with her. The woman had no way of knowing that he was a Christian. But before he could commiserate long on it, another problem presented itself. A dusty cloud appeared on the horizon.

He pulled on the reins and turned to wait for Claire. In moments she caught up with him, chin tilted upwards, her face flushed and blue eyes snappish.

With one hand, Luke supported Davy's harnessed bottom where it rested close to his heart. With the other, he pointed ahead. "Looks like we got company. Better head for the trees." He tossed his blond head to signify which direction. In the quick glance he took at her, he noticed this new development had cooled the fire in her sapphires. Now they shone round and frightened. "Come on," he urged.

When Moonlight's rump disappeared into the stand of thick trees, Luke expelled a sigh. Things weren't going well. He paused to look over the area. With relief he spotted a worn down pathway straight ahead that veered off in the direction they were headed. Taking the lead, he cast over his shoulder. "Looks like we're in luck. We'll follow this trail for awhile."

Though the riding was easy, he wondered where this trail would lead. More outlaws? But the narrow path ran in the direction they were headed, so they continued on it in silence except for the sounds of forest animals and the crunching of twigs beneath hooves.

The slow gait allowed Luke to feed Davy without having to stop. Guiltily he wondered if Claire needed a rest. She was a grown woman. She could certainly ask if she had a need. But when the noonday sun radiated almost overhead, Luke knew a rest was long overdue and dreaded it. As his eyes searched for a suitable spot, his mind searched for fitting words of apology.

"This looks like a good place to lunch," Luke called back to Claire. Her weary expression distressed him, making him wish he had not been so stubborn. Quickly he dismounted, tethered Queenie, and went to Claire's assistance. "Let me get that."

Wordlessly she handed over the reins and stretched the kinks out of her booted legs. As she patted the wrinkles out of her skirt, her eyes downcast, she struggled between the desire to apologize and the urge to lash out in anger. Luke startled her with his touch. "Sorry," he apologized. Carefully, he spun her around. Words escaped him as he stood foolishly before her with his hand still upon her shoulder. He repeated, "I'm sorry, Claire."

His soft tone toppled her emotional teeter-totter. Her hands flew to her eyes, and her shoulders shook unmercifully. Naturally, he enfolded her in his arms like the many times he had comforted Miriam.

Claire cried all the more so Luke patted her back gently. He realized he did not know this woman. He had always thought she was so calm and controlled. Now the sobs kept coming until he hardly knew what to do next. Finally, she began to quiet. Should he speak again? Or would it make her cry all the more?

Luke cautiously released her. Tilting her chin upwards, he looked at her pathetic face. "I'm so sorry, Claire."

"No." She placed a hand upon his sleeve. "I'm the one who is sorry." She hiccuped while attempting a crooked smile.

"Why don't we sit down?" Luke pointed toward a grassy area, and she moved toward it while he removed Davy from the harness where he had been wedged between their embrace.

When the three had settled, Luke picked a few strands of grass, tossing them down again. He opened his mouth, but she spoke first.

"Please, can we just forget this?" She was staring down at her hands; Luke could feel her embarrassment.

"We've been friends a long time," Luke reflected aloud. "In fact, you're probably the best friend I have right now."

Her face jerked up, her gaze fastened on him.

"Of course we can," Luke said.

She hiccuped again and nodded.

The afternoon dragged long and hot even in the shade provided by the thick overgrowth of trees and brush along the unmarked trail they followed. Yet Luke found circumstances greatly improved over that morning's. Their backwoods route put them on the correct course toward Cincinnati. He had made peace with Claire, and Davy napped in his arms.

In Luke's complacent state of mind, he nearly nodded off. It was his sluggish reflexes that permitted trouble to befall them so easily. Claire's piercing scream was his first clue. He jerked awake. *Indians!* They blocked the trail. Panic engulfed him. . . How? . . . When?

A hideous scream rang out, and the braves moved simultaneously to encircle them. Instinctively, Luke reined close to Claire as the savages' painted horses closed in the ring. Luke's eyes darted, keeping all the braves under surveillance. Claire had gone mute; her eyes swallowed her pale face. Her hands clenched a white-knuckled grip upon Moonlight's reins.

Luke willed himself to be calm. He must appear brave. An Indian dressed in tan buckskins jumped off his mount. Instantly, two others followed suit. The redskin poked a long spear at Luke's face, and the other two waved knives and shouted taunts.

The spear was now tight against Luke's throat, pricking it. As he sat rigid, a few drops of blood trickled down his neck, and sweat ran freely down his stoic face. Davy let out a bawl, and Luke agonized. The Indian lowered his spear then and gently poked the child's stomach with it.

"No!" Luke yelled, turning the child aside.

The Indian muttered angry nonsense, but the ones encircling laughed uproariously. At the same time, a brave grabbed Claire's arm and tried to pull her to the ground. She screamed.

"Jesus!" Luke cried out loudly. "Lord God, deliver us!" The Indian's grip upon Claire disengaged as if she burned his hands. She trembled violently while Luke continued to pray with fury. "God have mercy! Protect us from our enemies!" Luke's voice boomed louder than any sermon he had ever preached. The leader grunted, and the Indians slowly retreated. "Thank You, Jesus! Lord, deliver us from the hands of evil!" The Indians continued to taunt the white couple though they mounted, widening the circle.

Luke eyed them warily. "Thank You, Jesus! Claire! Ride!" Luke whooped. They rode hard, side by side, through the gap, without a backward look.

"Thank You, Jesus." Claire joined Luke in prayer. Over and over, they murmured the words. When Luke saw an open meadow to the east, he hollered, "Come on, let's get back to the main road." Crossing it, they continued to veer east. Still they galloped until at last they spotted the more traveled Beaver Creek Road.

It was then Luke cast his first apprehensive look behind them. No Indians were in sight. "Easy, easy." He pulled back on the reins, and Claire followed suit. Still riding abreast, he panted, "Are you all right?"

"Yes!" The wind whipped Claire's fallen hair. Her eyes remained fearful. "But let's not stop!"

"I agree," Luke yelled.

They camped under the stars that night, about two miles from the lights of Beedles Station. So close to civilization, they felt safe. As they sat around the campfire, they talked in tones soft as the dandelion puffs in bloom.

Claire hugged her knees beneath her and posed a question, though she knew its answer. "I wonder what made the Indians turn away?"

Luke stretched his legs out long, his boots nearly touching the fire and remarked soberly, "They looked like they saw a ghost."

"God delivered us. It had to be!" Claire exclaimed. "I don't know how, but He did."

"Yes, it was God," Luke agreed. "Lately I can't seem to get any answers from Him. But today I have no doubt. He intervened miraculously."

"You must believe He still cares about you, has a plan for you."

Claire warmed at the way the firelight revealed, even enhanced, the dimples in Luke's thoughtful smile. "Yes. I feel very much in His hands tonight. Even though the future is unknown."

"Full of surprises," she said wistfully.

"Nothing will surprise me like you have."

"What do you mean?" Claire asked.

"It's your faith that spurred me on. But just when I come to depend on you, you get emotional and act like a woman."

"I am a woman."

"I know that now."

"Now?"

Luke rubbed his still raw chin, now stubbly as well. "Until a few days ago, I only saw you as a girl, Claire, a cousin." Gazing into her eyes, Luke remembered her words to Davy, *I always loved him.* If that were true, unknowingly he had hurt this girl. . .woman many times. He would have to be careful in the future. It still remained, he would never love again. Perhaps now was a good time to emphasize his feelings regarding their relationship. They were talking so freely.

"The truth, Claire, is through all this ordeal, you've held up better than most women, being the emotional creatures they are."

She lifted her eyebrows in teasing protest.

"I'm glad we're friends," he added.

She yawned and said sleepily, "Me, too, Luke."

"Time to join Davy?" Luke tilted his head towards the slumbering child.

"Yes," she murmured as she settled into her bedroll, which was warmed by the fire.

❧❧

Bone tired, the travelers arrived at the outskirts of Cincinnati the afternoon of July 13. Heeding the instructions on the unfolded wad of paper extracted from Luke's pocket, they rode toward the heart of town. Main Street pointed them south toward the Ohio River, where they passed directly in front of the courthouse. Luke gave Claire a wary glance, then nodded at the deputy who lounged against its railing.

A market area lay just ahead. The aroma of tea, coffee, and leather mixed with a variety of vegetables, fruit, and cheeses beckoned. "Shall we stop to buy some milk for Davy?" Luke asked.

"Yes. I need to get the kinks out of my legs before we get to the Sweeneys."

Soon they were browsing through the port city's wares. Claire was intrigued with the women who passed, noting the styles in Cincinnati reflected the eastern cities. She welcomed the bustle of the streets after the lonely days on the trail. Luke, however, scanned the face of every person who passed. Worry rippled his forehead like a washboard.

Claire glanced sideways at him and admonished, "Relax. We made it!"

He gave a weak smile. "You're right." Then he pointed just ahead. "Hats, that's what I need." After trying on several, Luke purchased a tan beaver hat with a wide brim to replace the one he had lost on the trail. As he tugged at the brim, he asked Claire, "How do I look?"

Claire studied him wistfully from the hat down—blond bangs, clear blue eyes, crooked smile, and dimples. "Fine enough," she said, the color rising from her neck upward.

Luke threw back his head and laughed. "I feel like a whole man again." He pointed across the street. "How about a peach?" The fresh fruit, so much tastier than their dried rations, put them both in high spirits. Upon purchasing milk for Davy, they returned to their mounts, ready to complete the final leg of their journey.

They left the market area and rode past homes of various sizes, dodging children playing in the street. Luke kinked his neck to get a long look at a church they passed, wondering what denomination it was. Another market area, much larger than the first, appeared, and Luke told Claire, "We're getting close, according to Gustaf's map."

In minutes they approached Second Street, where they turned to Sycamore. On Sycamore, they headed toward the river again. Claire gasped. "Look!"

She pointed toward the Ohio River. Ships were bobbing in the waves like multicolored corks, sails topped the establishments, and as far as she could see there was blue water. "It's fantastic! I've never seen so much water. Are you sure it's not the ocean?"

Luke let out a whistle. "I'm impressed, too, but I know it's not the ocean. The moist air feels good, doesn't it?"

Claire nodded. "Mm-hm. Can we just stay here a minute and take it in?"

"I feel that way, too. It's overwhelming."

After their eyes had scanned the horizon for several leisurely minutes, Luke asked, "Ready now?" Proceeding then, Luke overheard Claire's groan. He teased, "Better put on your brave face. We're nearly there." Then he nudged his mount forward.

They arrived at a tiny house, similar in many ways to the others that lined Sycamore Street, except this one was strikingly immaculate. Flowers nodded in the breeze, and a stone walkway snaked toward the porch. "This must be it, third house on the left. Let's go meet the Sweeneys."

At Luke's fervent knock, the door swung open, revealing a large-boned woman. She wore her blond hair, streaked with gray, pulled back tight then plaited and coiled about her head. Above rosy cheeks, inquisitive blue eyes thoroughly examined the threesome at her doorstep.

She saw a tall young man, fair and sporting a full mustache and stubbly beard. His face, though now contorted as if to form an opening remark, featured huge, fine dimples. Their points poked far above the unshaven portion of his lower face. His arms curved, cradling a baby.

The small woman with him was also fair, with brilliant blue eyes and a slender nose protruding from a perfect oval face. Her once-white blouse and brown riding skirt were dusty and wrinkled, and the young lady looked capable of collapsing.

With concern Mrs. Sweeney asked, "Yes? May I help you?"

The towering one thrust a letter before her as he sought to explain. "My name is Luke Wheeler. This is Davy and Claire Larson. Claire boards with your brother, Gustaf Anders."

Helga Sweeney glanced at the letter of introduction, recognizing the familiar scrawl of her brother. "Won't you come in?" she offered in a friendly yet mildly cautious tone. "Please be seated." She mistook Claire's nervousness for fatigue and said, "You look about to faint. Allow me to offer some refreshment." Without waiting for their reply, she scurried off and returned with glasses of fresh water. Once their thirsts were quenched, Luke set about to tell Helga his story.

A full hour passed as he recounted his arrest and guilty verdict in spite of his innocence. During this time, Helga Sweeney's face revealed many different emotions. But when Luke told of the spectacular way her brother, Gustaf, had planned his escape, her eyes brightened with wonder. At times throughout the hour, Luke thought she was close to sending them on their way. But now the woman's countenance looked truly compassionate. When he had ended his account, she exclaimed with great emotion, "You poor creatures. Indeed! We shall be glad to help you out."

But even with the woman's assurance, Luke worried that her husband would appear at any moment and fling them out by their ears. He cast the thought off now as Helga patted Claire's hand and asked, "Do you mind if I read this letter from Gustaf now?"

"Forgive me for my rudeness," Luke replied, "by all means." He cast Claire a reassuring glance as they waited for Helga Sweeney to read her brother's letter of introduction.

"Why, you're a preacher yet!" she exclaimed. "Such repayment you have received for your kind deeds!"

By the time Ivan Sweeney arrived home from his day's work at his textile mill, Luke and Claire were feeling much better about the world. A bath and fresh set of clothes had been just the thing for Claire, and the promise of a safe haven made Luke a new man. Davy had been bathed and fed, and Helga Sweeney—whose own children were grown—fussed over the child.

Thus her husband found them. "What's this, Helga," he boomed cheerfully. "We have company? And a wee one, too?"

"Yes, Ivan," Helga said excitedly. "These poor folks were sent here by my brother, Gustaf. They've had such a row of it." She began to describe the injustices as Luke stood and shook Ivan's hand, then politely interrupted to introduce themselves.

Ivan was also big-boned and tall. The Swede had friendly yet strong features despite his ruddy face and many freckles. Luke ascertained that the slightly graying, tow-haired gentleman was competent and well-respected among his peers. It was not long until he also discovered that both the Sweeneys were Christians. It was with gratitude that Luke accepted their pledge of assistance as well as their hospitality and friendship.

Over the evening meal, they discussed Luke's plight. Ivan, who proved to be a well of information, considered their options. "I can give you a job at my textile mill until something else comes up. My business takes me to all parts of the city, and I have connections in many areas. I assure you that your secret will be safe with us. Claire and Davy can board here in our extra room. Luke, you can move into my small room at the mill on East Front Street."

Helga added to this. "It's on the docks but very close. Ivan walks it every day."

Luke replied, "I don't know how to thank you."

"Well, the night's still young, but I know you're tired. If you're agreeable, let's stable your horses and get you settled in at the warehouse."

Later, Luke stretched out on a long, soft bed. He smiled. It felt good to have a bed that fit. Of course, it had been made for the tall Swede. The room was used for times when business kept Ivan overnight. Ivan said it also provided a place for out-of-town guests.

In the lantern's light, Luke looked about him. This room was his for an indefinite amount of time. He smiled contentedly. How plush after his dreary, barren cell! There was a small fireplace with a stack of firewood to its left. By the glass window stood a stand with a flowered washbasin and glass lantern. A chair and small round table draped in a crisp cloth were in the corner by the door. Across the room was a desk equipped with stationery.

At this observation, Luke climbed out of the bed. He rummaged through the items in the desk. Now was as good a time as any to take care of something that had been plaguing him, to set Gustaf's mind at ease about Claire and Davy. He struggled with the wording. This missive must not be connected with him lest he give away his location. Finally, he wrote,

> *Gustaf, we received your three packages, two large and one small, in good condition. We will handle these gifts with care, in the same manner in which they were sent.*
>
> > *Your sister,*
> > *Helga*

He would have Ivan post it in the morning.

With that accomplished, he snuffed the lantern and double-checked the door. It felt good to be on the other side of the lock. Content, he flung himself back into bed, yawned, and soon fell fast asleep.

❧❧

The water slapped lazily against the craggy shore of the Ohio River where Ivan Sweeney's textile mill clung to the bank. Inside, Luke watched with fascination as the water-powered looms wove intricate designs of cotton and wool.

As Ivan showed Luke through his factory, they paused to watch a man carry a wooden block. Holding it by the rails, he dipped it in a tub of steaming red dye, then pressed it firmly onto stretched cloth. A Spanish woman gave it a firm tap with a wooden-handled mallet. When the block was lifted, the cloth was arrayed with tiny red flowers.

Ivan waved his arm, indicating the general area where they stood. "This is where I shall start you, Luke." As the woman prepared the cloth, Ivan explained, "This action is repeated until the design is on a whole length of fabric. Each color requires a separate block. The first color must dry before the second is applied." Ivan's face shone with pride. "It's time-consuming and labor intensive. A good place for you to develop some muscles." The Swede laughed good-naturedly at his own joke.

Luke looked down at his arms, still strong from years of farmwork when living at home. Though they had softened somewhat from his years of ministry, he knew his new friend was only teasing. "Is this the most physical work you have then?" Luke asked.

Ivan laughed. "No, not at all. But you must work your way up. Now, let's introduce you to your coworkers."

Luke soon discovered that the couple they had observed was married. He took an instant liking to the husband. Tony Diago, with his dark hair that curled from the steam of the dye vats, was dark-skinned as was his wife, Maria. Though not as tall as Luke, the young man looked strong as an ox.

Tony was a good instructor, and Luke quickly caught on to the routine. After several hours of laboring over muggy vats, Luke felt capable and began to converse while he worked. He was curious about the other couple.

"Were you born in America?" Luke asked Tony, while hoisting a wooden block and heading for the dye vat.

"Sí." When Tony looked up to answer, his face turned grave. "*¡Tiñe cuidado,* señor! The vat is hot!"

With his attention focused on Tony, Luke had gotten carelessly close to the red tub of dye. As Tony feared—even with the warning—Luke's arm brushed against the great tub. With a howl, he dropped the block, which teetered precariously then started to slide into the vat. Instinctively, Luke reached for it then let out a yell, burning his hands as well.

Tony grabbed the red block from Luke, setting it on a nearby stand, while Maria attended the injured man. "Oh, poor Luke. It looks bad. I'll go after medicine." Maria ran from the room, her bright ruffled skirt swishing.

Meanwhile, Tony grabbed a chair. "Here, sit down, Señor. You look pale." Luke obliged Tony, who rolled up Luke's sleeve on the burned arm. At his touch, Luke gasped. "Oh, your arm's much better than your hands," Tony reassured him.

Maria returned with ointment for Luke's red, blistered hands and arm. "Better go see a *médico,* Luke," she advised. "It's near quitting time anyway. We'll tell the *jefe.*"

Luke prepared to leave then stopped. "Where is a doctor anyway?"

Tony grinned. "Come, Amigo, I'll show you."

❦❦

"Does that hurt terribly?" Claire asked. Wrinkles lined her brow as she concentrated on the job of applying the doctor's ointment to Luke's severe burns.

"No, actually it's soothing." They sat alone at the Sweeneys' kitchen table. The others had retired for the evening.

"Seems I can't do anything right lately," Luke said.

"Nonsense, accidents can happen to anybody."

Luke looked relieved when the last dressing was finished.

"There," Claire said. "I'll be glad to attend to these until they are healed, Luke."

He nodded. "Thanks. The doctor said they should be good as new in a week." This reminded him. "The Sweeneys are so nice. Ivan is going to let me just tag after him for the next couple of days until my hands heal."

Claire's brows arched. "Going to learn the textile trade?"

"Never in my wildest dreams did I consider it. . .before yesterday. A person thinks he knows what he's going to do with his life then wakes up one day, and everything has changed."

"This is all temporary, you know," Claire reminded him.

"Maybe. We really don't know what the future holds, do we?"

"Well, I know what I'll be doing tomorrow," Claire said.

"You do? What is it then?"

"Helga is taking me to visit the orphanage."

"Really?" Luke exclaimed. "That's great!"

"Yes. Maybe I can get some ideas to take back to Dayton."

Luke considered this then replied, "We need to make a plan, you know, to return you."

Claire grimaced. "Not yet, Luke. They'll be able to trace you."

"That's the problem. They'd question you for sure. I'll have to think some more about this. There has to be a way."

Claire grinned. "Anyway, you need me to dress your wounds."

Luke ignored her comment, pressing on with the issue. "Maybe we should send you to Beaver Creek for awhile to visit family. We'd have to find you a chaperone, of course. Then—"

"What about Davy?"

"I could hire a girl to take care of him while I work."

When Claire did not readily reply, Luke yawned. "It's getting late. I'd better go."

"Is your lodging nice?"

"Yes, very. Comfortable, too. And I'm tired."

Claire walked him to the door. "You've had a hard day. I hope you can sleep."

"I don't think I'll have a problem. Good night."

"Good night, Luke."

Chapter 11

A few days passed. One evening after supper, visitors called at the Sweeneys. Helga, who answered the door, recognized the callers. "Tony and Maria! How nice! Do come in," she invited.

As they entered, Maria took in the domestic scene. Luke and a blond woman occupied the settee. The pretty lady cradled a baby. With delight Maria squealed, "Luke! *!Trabieso chico!* You never mentioned you were married!"

Helga rushed forward. "Maria, this is Claire, and Luke's son, Davy."

Claire was afraid to glance Luke's way, knowing how he disliked deceit. She waited for him to correct Maria, but he did not.

"I'm pleased to meet you, Maria," Claire said. "Luke has told me all about you."

Maria giggled. "And this is *mi marido,* Tony."

Tony greeted Claire then said to Luke, "We've missed you at work, Amigo. Well, we did get a glimpse of you with Mr. Sweeney."

Ivan interjected, "Luke is a friend of the family. Now that he's hurt, I can't allow him to stay with the women all day. I would get jealous. So I make him tag along with me."

Tony smiled. "Maria was worried when she saw your big bandage. She begged to come see how you fared." He motioned toward Claire and Davy. "Now that she learned you have *una familia,* perhaps she will not worry so."

Maria interrupted, "Si, *marido,* and now I have made a new amiga."

Claire dressed Luke's burns again after the Diagos left. Usually these moments alone, within the intimate confines of the Sweeneys' kitchen, provided a relaxing end to the day. But tonight Luke seemed troubled. As soon as Claire finished, Luke withdrew his hands, folding them upon his lap.

"You look upset, Luke," Claire ventured.

"Just frustrated."

"What seems to be the problem?"

"I hated lying to the Diagos."

"It took me by surprise," Claire said. "However, if Maria learned that I was just your friend, they would ask questions. This way. . ." She shrugged with her hands.

"This way we weave a story of deceit. Now what will they think when you leave? That you deserted me? Or what if they discover I sleep at the mill?"

"Mm, I didn't think of that. If you're so upset, why didn't you tell them the truth?"

"I don't know. That's why I'm so frustrated. But it's not your fault." Luke digressed to mumbling, but Claire caught the remark: "Seems my whole life is turning into one deception after another."

Starting toward the door, he said, "Thanks, Claire, for dressing these." He held his hands in the air. His gloom saturated the room even after he left.

In the morning Luke walked out to the river as he did each day and gazed across the water glistening like a field of diamonds. Seagulls flapped and dove beneath the water's surface for their breakfast. Down the row of docks where vessels of all kinds were moored, fishermen readied their rigs for the day's catch. The shoreline was abuzz with early morning activity.

Luke wondered as he watched the men work. *How many are running from something, as I am? How many are caught up in deception, victims of foul injustices? How many—* A voice from behind startled him.

"Whot we got here? A runaway!"

Luke spun around, his body ready to spring into action. The face that leered into his belonged to Clancy. Luke gasped. He had never met the man but knew enough about him through Simon. "Sceered ya, did I? The last I heard there was a reward being offered for you."

The man eyed Luke from head to toe then chuckled. "It appears to be my lucky day." Then he sobered. "Are you dumb, Preacher?"

"What do you plan to do?" Luke's eyes narrowed.

"Well, I could turn you in and collect the reward, or you could save me the time with a gift to hold my tongue. My purse is gettin' pretty empty."

"Blackmail!"

"That's right. What do you think your life is worth? Three hundred?"

"I don't have that kind of money."

"Maybe not, but I s'pose with your neck on the block, you can come up with it." The man scratched his long beard. "Tell you whot. I'll give you two days. We'll meet here at the same place, same time as today. If you don't show, I'll turn you in." When Luke did not reply, the man turned to go. He stopped and threw a departing warning over his shoulder. "Don't forget now!"

As soon as the man was out of sight, Luke wheeled and ran inside to see if Ivan was at the mill yet. He knocked on his office door, which was closed.

"Come in."

Relieved, Luke pushed the door open.

One look at Luke's face brought Ivan out of his chair. "What's wrong, Luke?"

"Blackmail. . .Clancy."

"Whoa. Slow down. Who's Clancy?"

"Someone who recognized me from Dayton. He hangs around the docks."

"You sure?"

Luke nodded. "He threatened me with blackmail, three hundred dollars."

"What terms?"

"He said two days."

"Hm." Ivan looked troubled. "Better sit down, Luke."

Luke collapsed in a chair and pounded his fist against the armrest. "I'm done for."

"No. You have two days to find someplace else to go. We'll hide you someplace where he can't find you. Why don't you leave Davy and Claire with us until things cool down."

"I guess I have no other choice unless I want to give myself up. But where could I go?"

"You could disappear on the East Coast in a big city like Boston." Ivan frowned. "Or maybe you should go to the western wilderness. I doubt he'd follow you there. Wait a minute!" Ivan exclaimed. "I have just the thing! You said you wanted to work a job that took muscle?"

Luke grinned. "I have a feeling I'll regret asking, but what do you have in mind?"

"I'm putting some of my goods on a keelboat heading to New Orleans. You could go with it, become a keeler."

Luke leaned back in his chair, closing his eyes. Then he stared at the ceiling as if expecting his answer to appear there in bold letters. He let out a long, slow sigh. "I don't know, Ivan. It's dangerous, and it's harsh work." He held up his blistered hands. "Think my burned lily whites are up to it?"

"I think you're a strong man in body and spirit. You can do whatever you put your mind to. Think about it. It's only a suggestion. I'm sure there are many other options if you don't think it would suit."

"My strength is in the Lord, Ivan."

"All the better. The trip would take about three months. You'd be on the move. Surely folk would give up looking for you by then."

"Davy would be six months old," Luke murmured. "When will it be leaving?"

"Tomorrow morning," Ivan said apologetically.

"The timing couldn't be more perfect. Perhaps God is opening this door for me." Luke reflected, comparing his life of late to a river's current, swirling along with him trapped in it, unable to break free. What choice was there? "I'll do it," he said weakly. "I need to talk to Claire, make sure she'll take care of Davy. Then I'll be back and make plans."

"Good thinking. I'll start to make arrangements."

At his words, Luke strode away.

"Claire, will you get the door, please?" Helga called from the kitchen.

"Yes." Claire propped the straw broom she was using against the Sweeneys' stone fireplace. As she hastened toward the door, she wiped her hands on her apron. Who would be calling at this hour? "Luke!" she gasped at the one standing on her stoop. "What are you doing here in the middle of the morning?"

He smiled. "May I come in?"

"Of course." Claire stepped back to allow him to enter.

Luke decided that he would not let his own apprehensions show concerning his decision. The thought nagged at him that he was getting good at this deceitful stuff, but he quickly cast it aside.

"Something's come up. We need to talk."

Claire tensed. At once she assumed he had found a chaperone to escort her to Beaver Creek. With a frown she followed him to the settee.

"Are you terribly anxious to get home?" His blunt question, presented in such a pleading tone, puzzled Claire.

"No." Claire shook her braided head, "I'm not the anxious one. I never said I wanted to leave."

To her amazement, Luke did not argue. Rather, he seemed relieved. "Would you consider taking care of Davy for about three months? Here at the Sweeneys'?"

Her blue eyes lit, and Luke saw the excitement in her face. "I'd love to! Why, if I stayed. . .I might even be able to help some at the orphanage." Luke nodded, and she continued foolishly, "Perhaps you could get a job there, too." Seeing his troubled expression, she quickly added, "That is, if the textile business doesn't suit."

Luke swallowed for courage. "Claire, I'll be leaving."

"What?" Her eyes snapped. "But why?"

"Do you remember Clancy from Dayton?" Claire nodded. "He's here, and he's found me."

"Oh, no!" she cried. "But that can't be!"

"It's true," Luke insisted. "He tried to blackmail me. Of course I don't want to go that route. So I have to leave right away."

"But where will you go?"

Luke grinned. "Keeling."

"I don't understand."

"Taking a flatboat downriver."

"I know what it is, but how. . . ?"

"Ivan has a load going to New Orleans. It's leaving tomorrow morning, and I'm going with it."

Claire frowned, her bottom lip stuck out, and the thought struck Luke that she looked cute that way. He flicked her chin with his finger. "It won't be so bad. It'll be an adventure."

"As if you haven't had enough excitement lately," she spouted. "And what about your hands? They aren't even healed."

"I'll be fine. Anyway, I don't have a choice."

"How long will you be gone?"

"Only three months. I'd be back sometime in October."

"Three months!" Claire gasped. "That's an eternity."

"That's why I need you to take care of Davy." Luke rubbed his forehead with a bandaged hand. "I really hate to ask you, but I don't know what else to do."

Claire's eyes instantly filled with pity. "Of course I'll help you. It's just. . ." Unshed tears stung. "I'll miss you."

Luke, so vulnerable himself, pulled her into his arms. He whispered, "We have been through a lot together these past few weeks, haven't we?" Claire released a tiny sob as she nodded. He continued to hold her tight for several moments. His heart melted. It was just as well that they put a little distance between them. He slowly released her. "I'll miss you, too."

The *Snappin' Turtle*'s patron, Henry Shreve, knew better than to argue with Ivan Sweeney. Ivan's strange request—that Luke be allowed to stow away on the *Snappin' Turtle* and learn the ropes of keeling—did rouse the seaman's curiosity, but things like that sometimes remained best unexplained. After all, Sweeney's textile business was vital to his own means of income, providing goods to transport on a regular basis. Then there was the fact that extra hands were always needed with casualties on the river being as high as they were. He just hoped this one could survive.

He lifted up the heavy canvas flap and peered down into the deckhouse. "You can come out now."

Luke blinked at the daylight, then crawled out from his hiding place and got his first good look at his twenty-odd crewmates. At first glance they appeared much like himself, being similarly clad. Ivan had provided Luke with the essentials—red flannel shirt, loose blue coat, brown linsey trousers, heavy boots, and beaver cap.

Strapped to Luke's waist was a wide leather belt that held a bowie knife. Unaccustomed as he was to carrying a weapon until the last few weeks, he also carried a pistol. He unconsciously rubbed his one-inch beard.

There was a major difference between him and the others. Their hands were calloused, and their muscles bulged like knots and knurls on a hickory log. Having spent several hours hidden in the cargo box, Luke heard the keelers before he saw them. They sang loudly as they ran the boards. Luke watched with fascination as the oarsmen worked, singing rhythmically. With a single sweeping glance he took in the entire crew of the *Snappin' Turtle*. His gaze paused at the stern, where the helmsman steered from atop a platform with a long oar pivoted to the boat.

Patron Shreve interrupted Luke's observations. "Sweeney said to take it easy on you until you were broke in. Says your hands are hurt." Luke nodded, relieved. "Well that is a shame, but we got work to do, and you'll have to do your share." Luke gulped. So that's how it was. "Understand?" The patron wore an expression that forbade Luke to question him, the owner and captain of the craft.

Luke nodded stiffly, thinking he understood perfectly—that he was in for a lot of trouble. Luke jumped when the patron bellowed, "Snake-eye!" A tall, tough-as-hardtack man of about thirty with long hair and one bad eye whirled and came to stand before his boss. "Over there." The patron motioned. Snake-eye stopped short of Luke, looking him over with his good eye. "This is Wheeler," Shreve said. "Show him the ropes on the broadhorn."

Snake-eye glanced at Luke's bandaged hands and snorted. "He looks soft."

"He is. And it's your duty to toughen him up, keep him alive. I'm putting you in charge of him." The order was just that, and Snake-eye compliantly though unwillingly motioned for Luke to follow. He set him to work at the broadhorn. As Luke pulled the heavy oar, black spittle flew past within inches of his arm, a reminder that his instructor was near, though silent and indifferent.

"Sawyer!" The warning rang out from the captain.

Snake-eye placed his thick, grimy hand on Luke's shoulder to wrench him from his post. Snake-eye then manned the broadhorn himself until the obstacle was clear. A loose tree had caught and now bobbed up and down as the current surged through it.

When the danger was past, he hollered, "All yours again, Whale," motioning with a muscle-laden arm.

"Wheeler," Luke corrected as he slipped into position. He wondered at his own courage.

The grimy hand touched his shoulder again while the one good eye challenged. "Like I said. . .Whale." He purposely accentuated the mispronunciation. "Sounds big, strong. You're under my care now, and I don't want a sissy following me around. Understand?"

Luke nodded, somehow heartened by the idea that the one-eyed keeler was taking him under wing. He only wished his hands didn't ache and thump so. And the rest of his body. . .sissy, Snake-eye had called him. The rest of his body would just have to get used to it.

A westerly wind clipped the *Snappin' Turtle* along about five miles an hour downstream. By afternoon Luke was parched and bone bruised. His bloody hands still manned the oar; however, the wind now did most of the work. The blinding sun caused his head to throb along with his other body parts. Closing his eyes, he wet his lips with his tongue. He would have to grow his mustache longer to protect them.

"Take a break, Whale," Snake-eye ordered. Luke snapped open his eyes and nodded. As Snake-eye slid into position, Luke stood on the cleated footway that ran around the boat between the gunwales and the cabin. He stretched, then rubbed the welts on the back of his neck and wondered how the nasty insects had bitten him through his shirt.

"Hey, First-tripper!" Luke spun around and found himself facing a beefy, bald keeler with a bare, hairy chest and shoulders. A scar curved downward from his left eye to the corner of his brown, curly beard. He stood with arms folded above a firm stomach and his slanted eyes boring on Luke. "You hot, First-tripper? The flies biting you?"

"I'm fine," Luke retorted.

"I don't think so. Do you think so, Skinner?" Luke felt the presence of another keeler move in behind him. He cast Snake-eye a silent plea for help. But his bare-backed guardian shrugged his massive, sun-tanned shoulders noncommittally.

"I know what'll cool him off," Skinner said in a wheezy voice. He grabbed Luke by the back of his trousers and shirt, then tossed him to the floor like a sack of potatoes. Instantly, several pairs of hands flailed over him. Luke struggled, but to no avail as the keelers bound his hands and feet with a rope.

Luke's mind reeled. *They're going to throw me overboard. I'll drown.* He looked around frantically. *And no one is going to stop them!* But instead he was yanked by his hair into a sitting position. He wanted to lash out in anger, demanding they stop whatever hideous scheme they possessed, but he knew if he did, it would go worse with him. With this rough lot, he must act tough. He narrowed his eyes and clenched his jaw. His face shone red with anger. But what he saw next shot fear into his expression. The keelers roared with laughter.

Skinner was waving a sharp razor in front of Luke's face. "Want to know why they call me Skinner?" he wheezed. Again hilarity beset his mates.

Bluffing. He's got to be bluffing. "Not necessarily," Luke retorted with as much calm as he could muster. But the scarred one called Bones grabbed him by the hair again and stretched his neck until Luke thought he would lift off the ground.

Skinner warned, "Now don't move if the sight of blood makes you queasy, First-tripper." With that he began to shave Luke's head. Blond, damp curls fell upon his red shirt, onto his lap, and all about him. When his head was peeled slick and white as an apple, Skinner made to remove his mustache.

"No! Leave it!" Luke ordered.

"Oh?" Skinner liked the first-tripper's spunk and admired his courage. "Do you feel cool enough then?"

Streams of sweat coursed down Luke's bald head. He countered, "Like a snowy day."

Skinner wheezed, "You can keep the rest then, but your poor head's a-sweatin'. We got just the trick for that." Two men hoisted Luke off the floor, where he hung helplessly still bound, head down. Suspended by his legs, Luke thought he was going to throw up. His stomach lurched as the two slung him overboard, dunking and holding him underwater.

Luke gagged and came up gasping and choking each of the three times he was submerged. When he gave himself up for dead, he was suddenly hoisted back aboard and slapped down on the deck. His head hit the floorboards and again hands flailed over him until he was righted in a sitting position. Skinner blasted him several times across the back with his open hand until water spewed forth out of his mouth.

Snake-eye, who had been a bystander until now, commented, "Whale, that's what his name is." The others roared and remarked that his spitting did resemble a whale's waterspout and agreed that from then on "Whale" he would be.

"Whale, you're a good sport," Skinner said as he untied Luke's bindings. Then he gave him a final smack on the back, and Luke's bald head jerked. As his snickering tormenters returned to their posts, he sat there several minutes gasping for breath, glaring at Patron Shreve's back. The man had intentionally ignored the whole episode.

After Luke pulled himself to his feet, he half-stumbled his way over to Snake-eye, collapsing beside the man. "Thanks for your help," he sputtered. "I thought you were supposed to keep me alive."

"You ain't dead," Snake-eye snapped. "Couldn't be helped. Happens to all first-trippers sooner or later."

Luke glared at the man's one good eye. "Any more surprises I should be knowing about?"

Snake-eye smiled, the first human emotion Luke had seen on the man. "Perhaps. But I wouldn't want to spoil your fun, now would I?"

Luke sought to remain furious at the man, but for an unexplainable odd reason he could not. Instead, he found himself grinning back at his instructor.

"Keep your eye out for bears now," Snake-eye teased.

"Pardon?"

"Bear fat! It makes hair grow."

Luke groaned. Then Snake-eye surprised him even further. "Let's go to the cargo box and get some ointment for your hands." He pulled Luke to his feet and started toward the cargo box, pausing to call over his shoulder, "Better get your hat, or you'll get a sunburn." As Luke followed him to the cargo box, his spirits heartened. Somehow he felt like he'd risen a few notches in his crewmates' estimation.

The remainder of the day, Luke became Snake-eye's shadow, willing to learn every task set before him. That evening the *Snappin' Turtle* moored at a wooded bank with a small grassy beach. "Get some rest, or you won't be any good tomorrow," Snake-eye warned Luke. "I'll bring you some grub later."

"Much obliged," Luke answered. As he lowered his body to a reclining position, supported by an elbow, he moaned. He leaned up against a syca-more tree and took inventory of his bodily parts. His hands had quit throbbing with Snake-eye's smelly ointment. He wondered what it was. His arms ached and burned, and his empty stomach growled. Removing his hat, he carefully felt his head with his blistered hands. He grinned. It felt soft as Davy's bottom. He closed his eyes and pictured his son, and Claire's face plainly popped into his mind's eye. His thoughts drifted then, and he fought sleep. He needed to get his bedroll out, to eat something, but he was just too weary.

Chapter 12

A week's ride downriver brought about many changes in Luke's physical appearance. His hands were rough and scabbed, his body was tanned and peeling, and his brown head a mass of peach fuzz. His body still protested, screamed at the long hours of punishment. But he had become accustomed to the routine, though never the men's vulgar language and crass jokes.

Many times he wondered if he would indeed survive this ordeal. At such times, indulging in self-pity, he imagined Davy going on in life without a father, envisioned Claire's tearful expression when she received the news that he had been killed. He shook off the thought. God was able.

Often if the others sang songs too coarse for Luke's liking, he would block out the lyrics by reciting Bible verses in his mind. Those in Philippians were precious to him, especially, "I can do all things through Christ which strengtheneth me," and "But my God shall supply all your need according to his riches in glory by Christ Jesus." A favorite pastime with Skinner and Bones was tormenting Luke with horror stories of what lay ahead downriver. They warned him of the great falls of the Ohio that buried men and boats, sucking them alive into Hades, and spun tales about the killer pirates at Cave-in-Rock. Sea monsters, alligators, and any other leviathan real or imagined in the "Mrs. Sippi" were depicted in gory detail to the first-tripper.

A comforting factor was the alliance formed between Luke and Snake-eye. The man had taken him under wing, taking to heart Patron Shreve's order. On one particular evening, imbibed with liquor Snake-eye grew more talkative than usual. He seemed determined to know what Luke was about. "Why were you holed up in the cargo box when we left Cincinnati?" When Luke did not immediately reply, Snake-eye posed answers. "You burn somebody's house down?"

Luke laughed. He gave his hands a wave. "No, I burned these in a dye vat at a textile mill."

Snake-eye wrinkled his nose. "Sweeney's mill?" Luke nodded. "You running from a lovesick woman?" Luke stifled another chuckle, knowing Snake-eye would not be laughed at a second time and wondered what the man would come up with next. Snake-eye ventured again, "You're too soft for murder. How about blackmail?"

Luke choked. "How'd you guess?"

"Naw. What'd you do anyway?"

Without knowing why, Luke trusted the man. He found himself quietly pouring out his story, and Snake-eye did not once interrupt throughout the whole.

"Unbelievable," he exclaimed when Luke was finally silent. Luke thought he referred to his story; however, the man's exclamation surprised him. "I'm hooked up with a preacher."

Luke grinned. He had a hunch Snake-eye's own past was on the notorious side. "I'd be glad to hear your story sometime. Preachers are good at listening."

"Ssh! Get yourself in more trouble than I could handle if the others catch wind of this—that you're a preacher. Understand?" Luke nodded. Snake-eye continued, "That Clancy you talked about. I know of him."

"You do?" Luke leaned forward with anticipation.

"Yep. I also know something you'd find interesting. Clancy must consider blackmailing his livelihood. He blackmailed Aaron Gates and his son. He saw Aaron murder somebody."

"You know this?"

"Heard it in a pub in Cincinnati, before we headed out. He was bragging about it. That's how he got his fishing sloop, blackmail."

"You don't say? Why, that's helpful, Snake-eye. Say, do you know where I could send a telegram?"

"New Orleans."

Snake-eye's drunken smile made Luke leery, wondering what hideous thoughts were rolling around in the man's mind, but he answered, "Thanks for the information. I owe you."

Shawneetown, a mingling of Indians and whites, river rats of all sorts, was a last link to civilization. Following it came Cave-in-Rock's killer pirates and the Mississippi itself. Remorsefully, Luke watched the town disappear until it remained a mere speck which then vanished behind a curve in the river. Four more hours and they'd pass the dreaded pirate rock near Hurricane Island.

The wind whipped up, and all hands were called upon to keep the craft in the deeper water away from the rocky shoreline. Fighting against weather and current, they had to pick and shovel their way along. The four hours turned into six, making Luke's anticipation soar even higher until the feared warning rang out.

"There 'tis!" Bones exclaimed. "Hurricane Island!"

Patron Shreve shouted, "Gunmen, at your posts! Oarsmen, pull! Under no circumstances go near the shore nor stop 'til I give the order." The patron was pleased that things had gone as planned and they would not be passing the Rock at dark. Daylight hours provided ample time to sail well beyond the pirates' den before they camped for the night.

"Whale! Can you shoot?" Luke acknowledged that he could, and Snake-eye ordered, "Then get your pistol out and cover me while I man the oar."

Luke drew his pistol and checked to see that it was loaded. He had hoped that Cave-in-Rock was just a story Bones and Skinner fabricated to frighten him, but at the patron's reaction, he knew it was real enough. A sick feeling rose from the pit of his stomach.

"That's the Cash River," Snake-eye explained with a nod of his head. "Won't be long now."

The island was in sight. Smoke rose from the shore. As they sailed closer, Luke made out figures around the fire. Why, they did not look like pirates at all! They motioned toward the *Snappin' Turtle*, waving them ashore. "Stranded. . . ," he heard them yell. Luke looked at Snake-eye.

He shook his head. "A trick."

When the men on shore saw that the boat was not going to stop and that the *Snappin' Turtle*'s cannon was pointed in their direction, they ran for cover. However, before they were even out of sight, gunfire sounded, and the water splashed mightily beside Snake-eye. Luke wheeled, searching for the source. "On top!" Snake-eye cried out.

Luke looked up at the high cliff. Could gunfire be coming from there? He saw no one. Then another roar exploded, followed by a scream. Skinner fell to the deck. What Luke saw was ghastly. He stood stupefied, staring. Another blast jerked the boat, throwing Luke off balance. He fell to the deck, his gun misfiring into the air.

"Put down the pistol," Snake-eye ordered. "They're too far away now. Let the gunners take care of it."

"That was our gun?"

Snake-eye nodded as another blast from the *Snappin' Turtle*'s cannon hurled a ball of iron through the air. Luke watched Hurricane Island. Several blazes ignited, but all else was still. "Where'd they go?"

"Crawled back under the rocks they came out of," Snake-eye snarled. "That'll be the end of it for now." He looked sadly toward the bloody pool where Skinner lay sprawled. " 'Til we're going against the stream. We can't sail past then, we crawl by. We'll be lucky if we don't all end up like poor Skinner there." Snake-eye's words sobered Luke since the man had never stretched the truth.

Bones placed a canvas over his friend's body and then returned to his post, shoulders slumped. Another hour passed before the patron addressed his crew. At that time he congratulated them on their performance, pleased that the *Snappin' Turtle* had not been damaged, and expressed his condolences for losing a good keeler. Skinner was buried that night at camp. Luke felt sorrow for their loss, even if it was the one who had made him the brunt of his cruel joke. This crew was a tough lot, but they stuck together.

The *Snappin' Turtle* reached the port city of New Orleans in record time, four weeks. Patron Shreve gave the keelers shore leave while he bargained for their return cargo. Luke shouldered his way through the busy streets of New Orleans, crowded with French Canadians, rivermen, traders, Indians, merchants, and buyers. The shop signs were printed in French, so he window-shopped. He needed to find a place to send a telegram.

"*Bonjour, monsieur,*" a young boy greeted Luke.

"Hello." He smiled in passing.

Turning his attention back to the row of narrow French shops, Luke noticed a window display of maps. He drew close to peer inside. He was in luck! The shop seemed to be a hub for activities such as posting and receiving mail and assessing metals. There was a telegraph machine! Heartened, Luke entered and approached the counter where an elderly bald man stood stooped. Luke cleared his throat. "I'd like to send a telegram, please."

The man shook his head in perplexity, his wire-rimmed glasses slipping down his nose.

Luke repeated himself slowly.

"*Oui, monsieur. . .*telegram." The man understood and handed Luke a paper and pen. Luke wrote his message.

Dayton, Ohio. Simon Appleby. Clancy witnessed murder.
Blackmailed Aaron Gates and Ruben Gates.

"*Non, monsieur. L'anglais est très difficile.*" The old timer waved his arms in the air to portray a problem.

Why don't they hire someone who speaks English? Luke wondered. He rubbed his chin, watching the tiny man who had now turned his back on him. At the sound of Luke's coins spilling out on the counter, however, the man turned and nodded. "Merci."

From beneath the counter, he extracted a chart with the letters printed. Then the man began the tedious job of picking out the foreign words. Luke waited impatiently until the entire message was sent.

At the last tap, Luke announced loudly, "Thank you very much."

"*Vous êtes bien aimable,*" the clerk replied.

With this task behind him, Luke departed to search for Snake-eye. As he made his way through the bazaar of festive carts and stands, a dark-skinned woman with a dazzling smile called out to him. "*Marin! Venez ici!*"

Luke shrugged his shoulders. "Sorry."

Quickly catching on, she tried again. "Sailor! Come here!"

Her fluency of English surprised Luke, and he hesitated a moment too long, allowing her to lean from her stall to bait him. "Come see my wares." She fingered beautiful materials and silken scarves.

Luke blushed.

"A beautiful gift for a lady," she coaxed with painted red lips that were much too full. Her eyes were round and flirting. *"Oui?"*

"Go on," a voice beckoned from behind, and Luke turned to see Snake-eye grinning at him. "Good price," he urged.

The two men moved closer. Snake-eye leaned on the stall as Luke self-consciously fingered the scarves the woman held out.

"What color your lady's hair?" she asked.

"Blond," he answered weakly.

"Red one, perhaps?" she offered.

Luke smiled back. "But what will she do with it? I've never seen her wear a scarf before."

"I will teach you. Come." She winked at Luke; then before Snake-eye could raise an objection, she slipped the scarf around his waist. To Luke she invited, "Now we practice."

Luke laughed loudly, enjoying Snake-eye's discomfort. "It may take much practice," he said.

She shrugged. "No problem."

❦

Everything was more terrifying, more strenuous, or more beautiful going fornenst stream—upstream—since they traveled at a mere snail's pace. Other river traffic consisted of Creoles, French Canadians, Kentuckians, tough, hard men from all parts of the world looking for adventure.

Luke's bare back, now toned with sleek muscles and tanned from August's toasty sun, rippled under his exertion. He easily thrust a twenty-foot pole with an iron point at one end and a knob at the other. The pole was like a third arm to Luke after six weeks on the river.

He worked together with the crew to the rhythm of the patron's chants, "Toss poles!" Spiked ends flew into the water. "Set poles!" Luke grunted as he set his pole into the riverbed. "Down on her!" Luke placed the knob against his shoulder and pushed with all his might.

With the keelers' combined efforts, they overcame the current and slowly moved upstream. "Lift poles!" With a grunt, Luke yanked his pole from the water and dragged it back to his position on the runway. Each time this process was completed, they managed to push the craft farther upstream.

Sweat poured off Luke's now fully bearded face and streamed down his strong back and muscular legs. His scarred, calloused hands were able to give the patron a good day's work. And a good day's work was keeping the craft moving at about a mile an hour.

"Gators!" Snake-eye drew Luke's attention across the river. Luke scanned the shoreline, locating the long, scaly reptiles that intrigued him so. Several lounged on the beach, some on rocks, lifeless. Others slithered into the river. Swimming eyes bulged above the surface of the water, distinguishing the alligators from floating logs.

Occasionally, a leathery tail slapped a rock, propelling a hungry alligator into the river. Nearby, churning water gave evidence of an underwater fight, wherein some unknown creature was becoming the reptile's meal. Luke watched in awe as the giant jaws gaped open and snapped shut, revealing for an instant the huge reptilian teeth.

This was just one of Luke's many unforgettable experiences. The crew, though unruly and crass, would also be forever etched in his memory and some in his heart. Daily he sought opportunities to witness to Snake-eye. However, the keeler would not allow such talk, making Luke wonder what sordid things lurked in the man's past.

One evening in early September, a storm arose. Some men always bunked aboard the craft while others camped ashore. This particular night Luke was in the cargo house on an undersized bunk being tossed from starboard to port side, it seemed. The wind howled, and waves splashed against the keelboat. Lightning ripped through the night, and the thunderclaps kept Luke wide-eyed. He prayed and thanked God that his journey was more than half over, for he had been pushing a keel now for eight weeks.

Luke thought of Davy as he did whenever he prayed, and he brought his son before the throne, as well as Claire. With each passing day, his desire to see her again increased. Her words splashed into his memory like a well-loved poem tucked away in the heart, "I love your father, you know. I always have. I'll never marry another."

A picture that replayed itself often was Claire in that meadow bedroom, her golden hair spilling all about her face, down her arms, shoulders, and back, her eyes still sleepy. He envisioned her cradling Davy, singing lullabies, smiling and looking up at him with her bright blue eyes. He remembered her touch when she had dressed his wounds, soft and tender; her embrace the day he left her, warm and alive.

Luke prayed for these memories to go away, but instead they became vivid and more enticing. His heart ached with loneliness for this woman. At the same time, calling up Miriam's likeness grew more difficult. Even his dreams of her were fading. With guilty pangs he grieved anew. How could he do this to Miriam? Why was God allowing this?

What would happen when he returned to Cincinnati? He was a fugitive. So maybe he did have emotions for Claire, deep-seated ones of love, loneliness, and fear, but the rest remained the same. He was a man without a future. If he sent Claire home, it would hurt her. Would it hurt her more if he loved her, married her?

The cargo room lit as lightning streaked across the Mississippi River's night sky, then fell dark again. Thunder cracked. Luke pulled his woolen blanket over his head.

<hr />

At times when the river swelled too deep to touch bottom, the *Snappin' Turtle's* crew cordelled their way upstream. This meant that some of the men swam ashore and towed the boat by means of long cordelles, or ropes. Put ashore this particular day, Luke and Snake-eye worked to forge a path along the water's edge for those pulling the cordelles. Blood trickled down Luke's face where branches scratched him. Stickers and burrs clung to his beard from the heavy thickets. Wading through a quagmire, Luke poked at the swampy muck with his forked stick, slinging snakes into the river. Just ahead rose a rocky cliff, and they paused to look for the best place to climb.

The other crew members were a quarter of a mile behind them, so they leaned against the stone outcropping to rest. This gave Snake-eye a chance to question Luke about a concern he had been mulling over for the last mile. "It's a miracle we got by without any killings at Cave-in-Rock," he said, referring to their second encounter with the pirates on their return trip. Luke agreed, and Snake-eye asked, "You think your prayers really worked?"

"It's not a matter of my prayers working or not. God hears all prayers. He is in control of the universe."

"If that's true, then why did He let so many bad things happen to you—being a preacher and all?"

"I don't know. But I still trust Him because I know He loves me. Sometimes things happen just because of natural causes, or somebody else's sin. A man murders someone, it's his sin that causes the pain, not God."

"But why doesn't God stop it?"

"Because everyone makes their own choice about God and sin. If He stopped folks, then we'd all be just puppets."

"Humph!" Snake-eye grunted.

"But I believe if we trust Him, He will work things out for our good."

"You think that will happen to you? You sure you won't hang someday?"

Snake-eye's question was one Luke had considered many times over the last several months. "If I do, it will be all right. You see, then I'd be with the Lord in heaven."

Snake-eye remained silent. Luke spoke quietly, "You ready to meet the Lord, Snake-eye?"

"You know I ain't!" he snapped.

"Doesn't matter what you've done with your past, it's all forgivable. If you believe that Jesus is the son of God and died for your sins, repent and trust Him with your life. He'll forgive you, wipe your slate clean, and prepare a place in heaven for you."

"What's repent?"

"It means to change your sinful ways."

"Well, Whale, I'll tell you what. I'll chew on that awhile."

"Fair enough," Luke said.

They rose to begin their ascent when simultaneously they heard a deafening roar and a hideous human scream from somewhere behind them. Immediately they turned back to help their crewmates. As they scrambled toward the sounds of danger, their feet kicked up the swampy water, soaking them to their chests. Luke drew out his pistol, and Snake-eye had his knife ready. The horrendous sounds of a crazed beast's growls and a man's cries crescendoed, and horror flowed through their veins. Then a loud shot rang out, followed by two more, and the hideous growls ceased.

When they reached the rest of the crew, Luke was sickened at the sight. A bear and man lay dead in a heap, the man mangled almost beyond recognition. The crew stood stunned by the ferociousness and velocity of the killer. Snake-eye's gaze met Luke's. Without a word, each knew the other's thoughts; death is unpredictable. And now there was a grave to dig.

Chapter 13

On an unseasonably cold night in early October, the *Snappin' Turtle* docked in Cincinnati's port at dusk. Luke fell into line with all his mates to file past Patron Shreve and receive his pay of forty-five dollars for three months' back-breaking work. He pulled his beaver cap down tight against his ears to keep out the wet chilly wind as he shifted from foot to foot. Reluctant to say good-bye to the crew and apprehensive about seeing Claire again, Luke mulled things over silently.

Snake-eye cut into line ahead of him, and Luke squeezed the man's shoulder. "I'm going to miss you. You were a good instructor, a good mate."

"I'll miss you, too, Whale."

He held out his hand, but Luke unashamedly embraced the man. His voice was thick with emotion. "I couldn't have made it without you."

"Nor I you. After all, you showed me your God."

Luke fumbled with his bandanna, which encased his few belongings, and withdrew something dark. "This is for you, Snake-eye. Something I picked up at Louisville."

"For me?" Snake-eye's one good eye lit with pleasure. "Well I'll be, Whale. This is just perfect. I'll be the meanest-looking—" He saw Luke's frown and changed his thought midsentence. ". . .God-fearing keeler around." He slipped on the black eye patch.

"But I don't have anything for you. Maybe I can buy you an ale at the local pub?"

"Sorry, but I have a family waiting. Anyway, I don't drink."

Snake-eye grinned. "I remember. Old habits are hard to break."

"I have confidence that you will do so," Luke said.

After Snake-eye and Luke received their pay, they parted ways just outside of Sweeney's textile mill. It was closed up for the evening, but Luke knew where an extra key was hidden.

❧❧

Claire answered the door and waited for the stranger to speak. The face beneath the beard seemed familiar. "Luke! I can't believe it's really you. Thank God you're back safe."

"Don't cry now. It's so good to see you, Claire. I've missed you."

"Oh, I've missed you terribly," she blubbered. "This is so wonderful. Come in!"

A six-month-old child rolling on the floor paused to see who had entered the room, his blond curly head tilted toward Luke. Luke rushed toward him, astonished at his son's growth, even though he had known it would be that way. The baby crawled as fast as his four limbs would carry him in the opposite direction; however, Luke scooped him up into his arms. Much alarmed, Davy screamed hysterically, flailing his dimpled arms and kicking his chubby legs.

Luke bounced, cajoled, and murmured to the child, but to no avail. "Davy, Davy. Come now, it's just your pa." Seeing that the child was not going to settle down, he finally relinquished him into Claire's outstretched arms. He clung tight to her neck and gradually diminished his crying while stealing glances at the stranger.

"Da-da-da!" Davy blurted out angrily.

Luke's face shone with surprise. "He talks!"

"I don't think he knows what he's saying." Disappointment laced her words. "Luke, I'm sorry he doesn't remember."

Luke threw up his hands to stop her apology. "No, it's all right. Three months is a long time—half his lifetime, in fact."

"I'm sure he'll make up to you fast, probably by the end of the evening."

"Where is everybody?"

"They are visiting their daughter in the country. Ivan took the afternoon off. They should be home by tomorrow noon."

"That explains why I didn't see him at the mill. He'll be surprised when he hears we're back. The trip went better than usual, and we made good time."

"Why don't we go to the kitchen," Claire suggested, "and I'll heat up some supper for you while you tell me all about it." She set out coffee, cheese, and bread for Luke to nibble on while she heated up leftover stew, stirring as she listened.

"Oh, this is good," Luke said. "Half the time I honestly didn't think I'd make it back. Mm. Such comfort."

Claire smiled. "Was it really that bad?"

"Worse. You can't imagine. The first day aboard they hog-tied me, shaved my head, and dunked me overboard."

"They what?" Claire stared at his long, full beard in wonder.

"It's true. Of course it's grown back by now." He felt her eyes on his face. "And, well this"—Luke rubbed his beard—"makes a good disguise." Claire laughed, and Luke liked the way it sounded—like bells.

She tested the temperature of the stew with the tip of her finger and licked it clean. "What else?"

"Well, there were alligators. Scaly, about seven feet long, heads about half as long as their bodies. Their teeth are enormous and their strong tails deadly. They crawl and swim along the banks of the southern Mississippi."

"Ugh! Are they dangerous?"

"If you get too close. Then there were snakes, yellow jackets, and chiggers."

"Chiggers?"

Luke nodded as Claire handed him a bowl of steaming stew. "Mm. Thank you." He took a huge bite, then talked between bites. "Part of the crew camped out on the shore, and part stayed on the *Snappin' Turtle*. These little mites are so tiny you can't see them, but you could sure feel them crawling under your skin."

"What did you do?"

"Rubbed them with ale."

"That relieved it?"

"Yep. Killed them."

"What about the crew? They sound mean."

"Rough characters. But after I got used to them, I could abide them. Even got to like a few. And made one real good friend, Snake-eye." Claire saw the admiration in his eyes. "Three men died on the journey. One drowned during a storm, one was killed by a bear, and one killed by river pirates."

"How awful!" Claire clapped her hand across her mouth. "I knew it must be dangerous. I'm just so glad you're here safe."

Luke knew someday he would share more of his adventures with Claire, but tonight he did not want to upset her further. "Sit here beside me, Claire." Slowly she pulled up a chair. "I thought about you a lot. I really missed you and Davy. You both mean a lot to me."

Claire wanted this moment to last forever, and she longed to reach across the table and touch his hand as she had the many times she had dressed his burns. However, his comment reminded her that Davy was out of her sight.

She rose from her chair. "Davy's too quiet." Luke pushed his plate away and followed her back into the sitting room to look for his son.

Davy had wadded a torn piece of Ivan's newspaper and was chewing on it. As Claire pried it from his chubby little fingers, he protested loudly. Luke suggested, "Maybe this will cheer him." He pulled a leather string of brightly colored beads from inside his vest pocket. The child's eyes lit with pleasure. "Come to Papa." Luke dangled the beads, enticing the child to venture closer. Soon he had Davy on his lap. He turned to Claire. "He's gotten heavy."

"Sixteen pounds now," she said with pride.

"Da-da-da," Davy babbled, clapping his hands. Even though the words were indiscriminate, Claire's eyes teared with joy.

They sat together on the settee, and after awhile Luke remembered. "Oh. I have something for you, too." He pulled out a tiny parcel and handed it to Claire.

With delicate fingering, she removed the wrappings. "Oh, it's beautiful." She examined the long red silk, letting it flow through her hands.

"May I show you how the women in New Orleans wear them?"

"You bought it in New Orleans? How exciting."

Luke grinned wide, then set Davy on the floor with his beads. He felt like a child with two new toys, not knowing which to play with, wanting to hold Davy, yet wanting to be close to Claire. He stood and motioned for her to join him. "May I?"

She handed him the scarlet scarf and carefully he encircled her waist with it. His grip on both ends of the scarf, he tugged until she stepped toward him. His tanned face was within inches of hers. Claire's blue eyes transfixed him. Slowly Luke leaned forward and placed a soft kiss on her unsuspecting lips.

When he pulled away, he said breathlessly, "I didn't plan that."

Claire blushed, still in the confines of his grasp upon both ends of the scarf. His tender gaze almost did her in. He fumbled then at her waist to tie the scarf. "Hold still now," he teased. Though his hands trembled, he felt such contentment, such joy at her closeness.

When he released her, she was much surprised to see a knot that resembled a rosebud. "It's lovely. How did you learn to do that?" Her eyes and tone were mildly accusing.

He rolled his eyes. "Don't ask. Perhaps I'll tell you someday."

"Another one of your adventures?" she teased.

"Exactly."

Wanting to change the subject, he knelt beside Davy, tickling him under the chin. The child giggled. "It's about your bedtime I imagine. I'm looking forward to a good night's rest myself, one without worry. Good night, Son." He took Davy into his arms and kissed him. Davy pulled away from his face and reached out to grab a handful of the straw-like whiskers.

"Ouch!"

Davy giggled at his father's exclamation, and Luke tossed him about playfully for several minutes, finally returning him to the floor.

"Listen. Since Ivan isn't home and I can't go to work in the morning, how about if I take you and Davy shopping."

"I'd love to," Claire responded.

"Good. I got paid a handsome sum for keeling, and we all left Dayton with so little. Make a list of items you and Davy need, and I'll stop by about. . . When can you be ready?"

"Nine o'clock?"

"Good."

With that settled, Luke moved toward the door, and Claire followed. When he turned to say good night, he saw the love in her eyes and felt like a drowning man. Once more the plaguing thought came, *You're going to hurt her.* "We need to talk. Sometime soon. About the future. . ."

Claire nodded although she did not understand.

As Luke walked back to the docks, he wondered if Claire thought he would be sending her away. Perhaps he should. But that was not what he wanted to do.

Luke, Claire, and Davy walked through the marketplace and toward the shops of Cincinnati. Claire smiled up at Luke under her blue bonnet that matched her eyes, deep as the Mississippi. He had trimmed his beard and looked quite presentable in a crisp shirt that had been laundered and hung in his room awaiting his return. Proudly jostling his son, he returned her smile.

"Sixteen pounds, huh?" Luke asked.

"At least." She grinned up at him.

At times he took her elbow to guide her around holes in the plank walkway or around passersby.

He wondered why he felt so giddy. Was he that much of a landlubber? Was it just the crisp early autumn morning? Or could it be the woman and child accompanying him? This woman evoked a warm feeling from him, as if she touched his very soul. Thinking of his river mates, he smiled. A soulmate. That was a good description for Claire. They had worked together years earlier in the Dayton orphanage, and she had often helped in his ministry. When Miriam died, she was there. . .soulmates. He beamed at her.

Claire stole a glance at him. Her own face reflected the radiance that shone on his.

As their packages began to mount, Luke chuckled. "Perhaps we should have brought a rig."

"Maybe we should call it a day," Claire suggested cheerfully.

"No, not yet. I want to stop at the dressmaker's and buy you a few gowns."

"Oh, no. That's not necessary."

"I insist. Helga Sweeney will probably be glad to get her gowns back."

"I doubt it," Claire answered. Luke looked to her for understanding. "They've all been altered." Then Claire teased, "Surely you don't think we are the same size."

Luke reddened. "No, not at all." His eyes passed slowly over her figure, and Claire was sorry she had spoken so bluntly. "Yours is perfection."

"Luke!" He always had been a tease, before Miriam died.

He laughed. "A compromise then. One pretty gown for the lady who has taken care of my son for three long months in my absence."

Inwardly he rebuked himself, for at his words her expression fell. But there was plenty of time to prove his heart was filled with more than gratitude.

"Very well," she answered.

Inside the shop, a matron hustled to their side to welcome them. "May I help you?" the dark-haired woman asked. She was dressed exquisitely herself, which made Claire blush.

Luke removed his hat. "Please. We are looking for a pretty gown for Miss Larson. Do you think you could help her?"

"Why, indeed! Come right this way, my dear." Claire cast a look of despair over her shoulder, and Luke watched her disappear into a fitting room. The dressmaker then brought several gowns for Luke's inspection. After he selected two, she settled him on a chair with Davy on his lap. She assured him Claire would model the gowns in just a moment.

True to her word, Claire soon reappeared in a blue gown of silk and lace. He watched her finger the skirt with admiration. "That is the one," he said with a wave of his arm. "Don't even try the other one. You look lovely in it, Claire." Then he motioned to the dressmaker. She came closer, and he whispered. With a wink, she hustled Claire back into the dressing room and disappeared. Shortly she returned to Luke with an ivory satin. "How is this?"

"What are you two up to?" Claire called from the fitting room.

"She's finding you something to go with the red scarf," Luke answered. Claire admonished him. "Luke. You said only one."

"Please, I want to."

Finally leaving the matron and her store behind, they turned a corner where no one was within sight. Unexpectedly for Luke, Claire reached up on tiptoes and set a kiss, light as a feather, upon his cheek.

"Thank you," she murmured.

The innocent act sobered him. "I wish I could do more for you," he mumbled, then wheeled her around and gently took her elbow, directing her swiftly down the walkway. "We'd better call it a day. With Davy, I don't think I could carry another package."

They walked in silence for awhile until Claire asked, "What is it you wished to talk about, Luke?"

He looked at her questioningly, as if she spoke a foreign language.

She continued, "The other night when you said. . ."

"Oh." Luke slowed his pace.

They were entering a quiet and peaceful residential area. Autumn's first fallen leaves crackled beneath their boots like a campfire and shone just as colorful with tongues of red, orange, and yellow.

"I wanted to talk about us," Luke finally said. Claire's skirt rustled against the parcels she carried, and her cheeks were rosy from the exertion of the long walk. She waited for his explanation. "We need to talk about the future."

"You want to send me away?" she asked.

"No, but I should."

"No? You want me stay and help with Davy?"

Luke glanced sideways at her. Her hair hung long with golden wisps encircling her face beneath her bonnet. She nearly took his breath away. When had he fallen in love with her? Somewhere on the Mississippi, he realized.

Luke set Davy down in a grassy, manicured lawn along with their packages. The child began to play with the brown paper wrappings. Slowly Luke turned to face her. Claire's eyes were so deep, Luke again felt that drowning sensation. "I don't want to hurt you," he blurted out. "If I send you away, which I should, that would hurt you. If I asked you to marry me, that would hurt you, too."

"Marry you?"

"It would be the proper thing to do. After all, we have been traveling companions. But don't you see? We'd be on the run. I could still get hanged. It just isn't fair to ask you."

She reached up and touched his cheek. "You've changed so much. When you went away, you were an empty shell of a man. But you have come back brimming over with life itself."

"I had ample time to think. I guess when one struggles so hard just to stay alive, one begins to appreciate life. Those months keeling, all I could think of was you, Claire. I don't know when it happened."

"Are you saying. . ."

"I love you." They stood just a foot apart, an irresistible force pulling them together. Claire closed her eyes, expecting his kiss, and that was why she did not see the man approach.

"Well, look who's back!"

The despicable voice set the hair on Luke's neck on end. He spun around. "Clancy!" As he faced the repulsive face contorted with glee, Luke's eyes narrowed. "You miserable blackmailer!"

Claire gasped, then rushed to sweep Davy into her arms.

Clancy scoffed, "I ain't gonna hurt the boy. It's his pa I'm after." Then in a malicious tone he taunted Luke. "Thought you could get away, did you? Well, I believe you owe me somethin', and I mean to have it."

Chapter 14

Claire descended the Sweeneys' staircase, her chin set in defiance, while Luke paced at the bottom of the landing. For the past hour while Claire put Davy down for a nap, he had gone over every available option. Now his mind was set. When he heard her footsteps, he looked up.

"I've decided. You must go home," he said abruptly. "There's no life for us together. This man means to hound me wherever I go." Luke seethed with anger.

Claire touched his arm. "We could go to the East Coast. Surely the cities are so populated that he'll never find us there."

"You don't understand, Claire." He shook his head. "I've involved you in this too long already."

She ignored his admonitions. "We could change our names." Luke sighed and looked long and hard into her face. It was inviting. Could anyone find them in Boston?

As if reading his mind, Claire suggested, "Or we could go to England."

Luke grinned. Then he pulled her into his arms. "You would be willing to flee the country with me?"

"Oh, yes. I would go anywhere that you could make a new start. I've waited so long for you, I'm not about to give you up now."

"And I've just found you. Perhaps that is what we should do. Go somewhere far away, where no one will follow." He stroked the back of her hair and murmured, "I love you, Claire." He kissed her then, and though his passion ran deep, he was gentle with her for she was an innocent. So sweet and pure.

❧❧

Ivan, who had been Luke's sounding board for the last hour, peered across his desk. Luke's astounding keeling stories had kept him riveted. Now he listened in disbelief as the younger man detailed his recent encounter with Clancy.

Ivan shook his head. "I just cannot believe that the minute you get back, you are discovered. After all this time. That Clancy is a bad one."

"I agree, but I have a plan."

"Oh?"

Luke felt as excited as a schoolboy. "Claire and I would like to be married as soon as possible."

"You don't say! I think that is a great idea, Luke. Congratulations! So Claire gets in on your next escapade?" At Luke's frown, Ivan quickly added, "I didn't mean any harm in that. Guess maybe I'm just a little jealous of your adventures."

Luke shook his head. "Well, this time I plan to flee the country."

"And go where?"

"I don't know yet. I thought perhaps you could give me some advice."

"Hmm. I may have to think on that awhile."

"We haven't much time. If Clancy turns me in—"

"Yes. I see your position. Did you ever consider missionary work?"

"Why, yes, of course. But what are you thinking?"

"China, India. . ."

Luke leaned back in his chair and rubbed his head. He had not considered anything as drastic as that. "I don't know. I would have to talk with Claire."

"I have contacts. If you could get to Boston, spend the winter there, next spring I could get you on board a merchant ship sailing to the Far East. From there you would be on your own."

Luke moved to the edge of his chair. "Perhaps it's not such a bad idea. It would mean breaking ties with all family, but under the circumstances. . ."

"If you are serious about marrying Claire, I suggest you do it tomorrow. The sooner you are off, the better."

Luke smiled. "I am serious. She said she's loved me all her life. I think perhaps I have loved her for as long as well. I was just too blind to see it."

Ivan was someone he could fully trust. He turned to him now with a question that had been plaguing him for many weeks. "Ivan, is it wrong for me to love again after losing my wife? Sometimes I feel so guilty."

"No, Luke. I believe God has brought the two of you together."

Luke nodded.

The following day a wedding ceremony took place at the Sweeneys' with just a small circle of Luke's friends. The Diagos from the textile mill attended. Maria had deepened her friendship with Claire over the months of Luke's absence, learning the truth of their relationship. Snake-eye stood up for the groom, grinning. Ivan Sweeney waited at the bottom of the staircase to accompany Claire down the aisle.

As she descended, wearing the ivory satin with the scarlet silk scarf fashioned into a rosebud at her waist, Maria Diago cried tears of joy. Helga held Davy, who babbled, to Luke's delight, "Da-da." The Swedish woman dabbed at her eyes with her handkerchief.

Ivan escorted Claire to the far end of the sitting room, which was arrayed with bouquets of multicolored chrysanthemums, and presented her to the groom. Luke placed her tiny hand in the crook of his arm and gazed lovingly into her Mississippi eyes. Despite all hardships they had encountered, re-gardless of the dangers they still faced, he thought he would never be hap-pier—his heart never fuller—than at that moment. He believed God in His mercy had lavished upon him more than ample portions of love and blessings.

The ceremony was short, and Luke soon found himself repeating his vow. "I do," he said with emotion.

"Claire Larson," the parson asked, "do you take this man to be your lawfully wedded husband, to honor, love, and obey all the years of your life until death do you part?"

"I do," Claire said, her face a vision of joy.

But just as the preacher announced, "I now pronounce you man and wife," unexpectedly, the front door exploded. A badged man with a drawn gun shouted, "Everybody freeze!" Pointing his weapon at Luke, he turned to-ward Claire with regret. "I'm sorry, Ma'am, but that part about death may come sooner than you expected. I'm here to take your husband back to hang."

Claire's legs gave way, the room darkened, and she fainted dead away. As Luke moved to catch her, Snake-eye made a dive toward the lawman, who released a shot into the room above Snake-eye's head then pointed it at the keeler's chest. "I said, don't anybody move!"

Maria screamed uncontrollably, and Davy began to cry. Deputy Galloway, backed by a posse of three, barked orders. First to the Spaniard, he said, "You can go, and take that woman with you." He nodded toward the screaming Maria. Then to Helga, "You can leave, too."

"This is my house!"

The deputy frowned. "Can you quiet that baby then?"

Cradling his unconscious, limp wife, Luke glared at the deputy. He nod-ded at Tony. "Better take Maria and go, Tony. There's nothing you can do."

"Sí, señor. I'm sorry."

With the Diagos gone, the four apprehenders closed the door and gave instructions. "Get something to bring Mrs. Wheeler around," the lawman told Helga. "We'll be taking him to the Cincinnati jail."

Mrs. Sweeney gasped. "Oh, no." Ivan slowly moved to his wife's side.

"Sit down, Dear. I'll get a wet rag." In moments he returned, and Luke dabbed Claire's face with the cloth until she regained consciousness.

"I'm so sorry, Darling," he murmured over and over.

❧❧

Luke's wedding night was spent under the constant, watchful eyes of Deputy Galloway in the Cincinnati jail.

"You're beautiful," Luke whispered through the bars to his new wife.

"There must be something we can do."

He squeezed her hand. "I'm through running, Claire. It's up to God now."

Her chin rose defiantly. "We must not give up."

"You must go and get some sleep, my love. The days ahead may be demanding."

"But I must keep praying," she protested.

"God knows our hearts. He is able. Let it go, Claire. Go home to the Sweeneys. It is my first husbandly order."

Claire smiled weakly at his attempt at a joke, and he kissed her good night before sending her off.

Ivan and Helga came to visit the next morning at daybreak, and plans were made to leave Davy in their care so Claire could accompany Luke to Dayton. Ivan offered to send a telegram to Luke's family. The Wheelers thanked the Sweeneys repeatedly for all they had done and expressed regret for the trouble and sorrow they had caused. The deputy then dismissed the Sweeneys with a word of warning about harboring fugitives.

Claire wore her camel-colored riding skirt and white blouse that had been previously packed for their honeymoon. After breakfast, a posse of four set off with their prisoner. Luke's scarred hands were bound, and two armed men rode ahead, one holding Queenie's reins. Luke and Claire, at their dust, were mercifully allowed to ride abreast. The deputy and fourth man brought up the rear.

"I'm sorry they've tied you. It must be painful." Claire spoke softly to her husband of less than twenty-four hours.

"At least I have the joy of you here by my side."

Claire longed to comfort him, to caress that troubled face that portrayed such a brave front. She would be strong, at least until this ordeal was through. "I love you," she said with a valiant smile.

He winked at her. "Hold your head high, Mrs. Wheeler. Don't let them rob you of your spirit or your joy."

"Never!" she exclaimed.

But as the day wore on, Claire and Luke both wilted in their saddles. The posse drove them hard with little consideration given to Claire being a woman. Deputy Galloway would have preferred she stayed behind.

That evening Claire was allowed some moments of privacy. When she returned, she spread out their bedrolls, placing them side by side close to the fire as Luke watched with his bound hands. The night was cold for October, and Claire shivered as they lay their bundled bodies close together.

Deputy Galloway cleared his throat, then apologized. "Sorry, Wheeler, gotta bind your feet at night." Claire's eyes narrowed in the dark as the man tied her husband. "And you," he said, pointing at her, "don't be getting any ideas about setting your husband free, or you'll get tied, too. Understand?"

Claire nodded. When the man left, Luke whispered, "It's all right,

Claire. Don't cry now. Be strong. He can't take away our love for each other, can he?"

"No," she sobbed.

"He can't take away our love for the Lord, either. In fact, he is no match whatsoever for Christ Jesus. Whatever happens from now on, remember it must be in the Lord's will for our lives."

"We are in this predicament," she whispered vehemently, "not because it is God's will for us but because of someone else's sin." Claire referred to Ruth Gates.

"Nevertheless, God is in control."

Claire continued to shiver uncontrollably. Luke lay as close as he could and prayed for her, that she would not have to suffer any more than necessary. Davy was young; he would survive. But somehow he must convince Claire to go on without him after. . .

One man stood guard, sitting on a hickory stump, his rifle propped across his legs. His gaze traversed from the fire to the sleeping prisoners, to the deputy and his comrades, to the woods behind them, the road beyond, and back to the fire. But he was no match for the craftiness of the deer-footed keelers who even now crept up behind him.

Snake-eye gave the signal, and his men sprang into action. The one-eyed leader conked the night guard over the head, knocking him senseless. Three others descended upon the camp in a howling invasion. Sure that Indians were attacking, Claire and Luke bolted upright, and the lawmen leapt to their feet. Before they could raise their weapons, the keelers were upon them—some flashing knives, others pointing pistols at their heads.

Snake-eye warned, "Put down your weapons, and nobody gets hurt." Slowly, Deputy Galloway threw down his gun. It was the maniac pirate from the wedding who probably still carried a grudge! The others of the posse followed suit.

"Tie 'em up!" Snake-eye ordered, then he rushed to Luke and cut loose his bindings. "Howdy, Whale." He grinned. "And Mrs. Whale." Claire threw back her head and laughed out loud. With his free hands, Luke pulled her close, tugging her blanket up tighter around her shivering body. "Let's get out of here," Snake-eye hollered.

"I can't," Luke answered.

"What?" Snake-eye and Claire cried out in unison.

Luke turned to Claire then back to Snake-eye. "I won't run anymore. I can't live that way. I've made up my mind to face whatever is in Dayton."

"But, Luke!" Claire shrieked.

"I have to, Darling. If I don't do this thing, my faith means nothing anymore. I can't explain it. I just know it's right."

"Well, I'll be," Snake-eye exclaimed.

Luke grinned at him. "You were magnificent, like always. But now you need to get your men out of here. I'll give you time to get away, then cut them loose."

"Well, I never. You're sure about this?"

"Positive."

Snake-eye embraced Luke. "God bless you then, Brother."

"And you, my friend."

Snake-eye tipped his hat at Claire, whose face was stained with tears. "Trust him, Mrs. Whale. He's a good man." She nodded, and Luke protectively placed his arm around her. Before Snake-eye left, he gifted Claire with two wool blankets from his own pack.

❧❧

"It's all right, Claire," Luke said when they had gone. "I know it's the right thing. Come here." They moved closer to the fire and wrapped themselves in the extra blankets where Luke could keep an eye on the tied, gagged lawmen. He gave his mates plenty of time to disappear by ignoring the squirming, mumbling deputy. A tiny Bible provided assurance. By the firelight, Luke read to Claire from the Psalms. When her eyes grew heavy, Luke helped his wife into her bedroll, covering her with the extra blankets.

❧❧

A few hours before daylight, Luke cut loose the ropes that bound the lawmen. Deputy Galloway jumped to his feet and sputtered angrily, "You could at least have taken the gag off!"

"And listen to you beg me to untie you? The last few hours were most peaceful. Anyway, how could you deny a condemned man a few hours' prayer with his Maker and time alone with his bride?"

"Why did you do it? You could have escaped."

"I'm an innocent man. But I'll not run anymore. God is big enough to see me through this."

"What about her?" the lawman asked, nodding his head at the sleeping woman.

"He is able."

"I see." Deputy Galloway considered his prisoner. Sometime during the night, the deputy's opinion of him had changed. "I don't suppose we'll need to tie you up anymore until we see the skirts of Dayton." He motioned toward Claire. "Better get some rest yourself." Before he turned away, he added, "Wheeler, sorry your wife was cold. You're not the kind of people I thought you were. Guess I was just holding a grudge. Sheriff Watson sure was mad when you escaped under my watch. But I'll see to it that you're both treated with more consideration."

Chapter 15

Two days later, just before sundown, the appearance of the six dusty travelers caused quite a stir in Dayton. Folks stopped to ogle. Children ran alongside shouting vicious taunts at the prisoners. One small boy picked up a stone and hurled it at Luke, hitting him in the neck.

"Hey now, stop that. Go on home," Deputy Galloway shouted. But the boys still trailed. Tears streaked Claire's dirty face. Her husband was innocent. Why must he go through such humiliation?

Word spread like wildfire throughout the town. By the time they rode up to the jailhouse, a small group of Luke's friends and parishioners had gathered, including Mary and Gustaf Anders. Luke's face lit when he saw them. The men removed their hats and stretched forth their hands.

Deputy Galloway smiled and nodded at Luke, then cut his hands free. Wearily the Wheelers moved through the crowd, shaking hands with their friends, embracing and receiving blessings. Claire fell against Mary Anders's stout bosom, and the older woman murmured, "Oh, you poor dear, you poor dear. They going to let you come home?"

"I don't know, Mary."

Sheriff Rusty Watson watched from the threshold of his open doorway. His brows furrowed in disapproval when Deputy Galloway cut Luke's bindings. He hoped that this reception would not get out of hand. "Let 'em pass through now!" he called loudly. No one seemed to hear, but after several tense minutes he closed the door behind his prisoners. Sliding the bar across it securely, he breathed easier.

"Pleasure to see you again, Reverend," he greeted as he led them to the barren cell that Luke had previously occupied. With the Wheelers behind bars and the key twisted and removed from the lock, Sheriff Watson leaned against the wall.

"There's no reason to lock up Claire!" Luke said in exasperation.

"I need a few minutes with my deputy," Sheriff Watson replied. "Then I'll be back."

Luke left Claire standing alone in the middle of the cell and went to the barred window to look out. In a few minutes he would know his fate. Was there any hope?

Sheriff Watson turned to his deputy. "What's the story, Galloway?"

"If I'd have believed the man was innocent, I might not have worked so

338

hard to capture him. I guess I was set on revenge because he made a fool of me the night of the jailbreak."

"You think he's innocent?" the sheriff asked, surprised.

"I do. Wait 'til you hear what happened."

Upon hearing Deputy Galloway's full explanation, starting with his prisoner's wedding day and including Luke's honorable behavior when the keelers tried to break him free, Sheriff Watson returned to Luke's cell.

"You're free to go, Mrs. Wheeler." Relief washed across Luke's face. "You can stay with the Anderses. There'll be a private hearing where you'll be required to answer some questions. But I'm afraid short of a miracle, your husband will hang day after tomorrow at noon."

"No!" Claire screamed. "He can't! He's innocent!"

"That may well be, Ma'am, but the law is final."

Luke drew Claire into his arms, and she wept on his shoulder. The sheriff said with compassion, "I'll give you a few minutes alone, then Mrs. Wheeler will have to leave. Let me know, Reverend, when she's ready." He left them alone.

"Claire," Luke murmured against her hair, "I need you to be brave."

"No! We can't let this happen. Our life together is just beginning," she sobbed.

"Perhaps the Lord did not intend for us to be together this way. If I hadn't escaped the first time, you wouldn't have been pulled into all of this. I wouldn't have brought such shame upon you."

"Don't talk this way, Luke," she begged, pulling on his arm. "I won't let them take me away."

Luke's eyes narrowed, and his voice came out much louder and sterner than he had intended. "You must!"

His command sobered her. "I–I'm sorry," she whimpered, struggling to gain her composure.

"That's much better." Luke lifted her face, and she looked at him through blurry eyes. "Perhaps you can contact Simon Appleby for me."

She nodded. "I–I'll do that right away."

"Thank you." He gave her a quick embrace, then released her as he moved toward the barred door.

"Sheriff!"

Sheriff Watson appeared, then led Claire out of the jailhouse. As she departed, the sheriff called after her. "Of course you know you're not to leave Dayton."

"Of course," she replied calmly. As she looked around, she saw no one she recognized. She headed toward Simon Appleby's office. It was a good distance, but she needed the time to think.

"Simon!" Luke exclaimed. "You're a welcome sight."

The two men embraced, then Simon spoke right at the heart of the matter. "I think I have good news. I got your telegram about Clancy. He's the one who tipped the law on your whereabouts. When I got your telegram, I'd hoped you wouldn't return to Cincinnati."

"I was there only a few days. In fact, I would have been gone by the next day. I had to see Claire and Davy."

"That's what they expected you to do."

"What's the good news?"

"At my insistence, Clancy has been apprehended. He's being brought to Dayton and should arrive tomorrow." Luke's eyes lit with understanding. "As soon as he arrives, I'll ride out to the Gates place. His testimony, the fact that we'll have proof Aaron Gates murdered Silas Farthington, may persuade them to tell the truth."

Simon stroked his mustache. "With Ruben as an accomplice to that murder, he may not want to add your death to the list of offenses he'll be tried for. Since our time is limited, if Clancy doesn't arrive by noon tomorrow, I'll go ahead and do what I can to force a confession."

Meanwhile, Luke's father and brother, Ben, rode into Dayton. Before they approached the crossing of Main and Third Streets, Emmett heard the familiar, horrible sound of scraping boards and pounding nails.

"Come on!" He urged his horse forward. Just as he thought, three men were working to reconstruct the gallows for Luke's hanging. Ben's usually ruddy face paled. "Father?"

"Let's hurry."

Only minutes later as Simon was leaving the jailhouse, they jumped from their mounts and hastily tied them to the hitching post. Emmett ran toward the familiar attorney. "Simon? Is that for Luke?"

"I'm afraid so," Simon answered. "I've just been with him. I'm going to do my best to get him freed. Luke can tell you. I must go now."

"I understand. God go with you." At the barrister's departure, Emmett and Ben hurried inside. When they were ushered into the inner room where Luke's cell was, they found him standing with his back to them, stooping to gaze out the barred window.

"Luke?"

He whirled at the familiar and beloved voice. "Father! Ben!"

Sheriff Watson did not smile when he told the elder man, "Hope you don't mind if I don't trust you inside the cell this time, Reverend." Although it hadn't been proven, he knew that Emmett Wheeler had helped his son escape.

Emmett smiled sheepishly while the sheriff pulled up chairs for Luke's family. Hands gripped hands through the bars. Tears trickled down all three faces, but Luke quickly brushed his aside. He was astonished at his own strength; however, he knew the Lord was giving him an ample portion of faith for this hour to face death.

"Father, Ben, did you know that Claire is now my wife?"

"Yes, we heard. That is wonderful news, Son."

"Because of me her life is ruined."

"You only returned her love, and love surpasses all. Be assured, Son, we'll take care of her and Davy."

"Thank you. How is everyone?"

Ben answered, "Heartsick with what's been happening to you, Brother. But otherwise well."

❧❧

Later that evening, Emma Cook climbed out of bed to see where Uriah had gone. When she heard the familiar voice of their neighbor, Ruben Gates, she ducked behind her bedroom door, eavesdropping.

Her husband boasted loudly, "You ain't got nothing to worry about, Ruben. They'll hang him high this time. Then it'll be finished." She shuddered at the look of vengeance upon his face.

"He'll get his just deserves."

"I hope you're right."

The door slammed then, and the voices grew fainter. Emma Cook took a deep breath. She thought back to the day when Aaron Gates had been killed, when she had stayed with Ruth and the conversation she had overheard. She began to tremble. Sitting back on the edge of her bed, she rocked herself, murmuring unintelligible phrases.

The door slammed again, and she slipped beneath her covers, feigning sleep as her whistling husband entered the room and pulled off his boots.

❧❧

Puffy-eyed, Emma Cook prepared breakfast for her cheerful husband. The eggs sizzled in the skillet, and the coffee brewed on the top of the stove. Uriah stepped close behind his wife and grabbed her by the waist. "Morning!"

"Good morning, Uriah. You're happy today."

"Yep. Got good cause, too."

Provoked at knowing what that good cause was, she smacked the eggs rather hard onto his plate, and the yolk of one broke, but her voice remained calm. "What's that, Uriah?"

"The law brought back the runaway preacher. He's to hang tomorrow noon." He then looked at the plate set before him. "You broke my egg."

"Sorry, Uriah."

Silence lingered except for Uriah's scraping fork, and after Emma had poured coffee into brown mugs, she seated herself across from him.

"It's not like you to be on the wrong side of justice. You've always been a fair, honest man. A good man." Uriah glared up at his wife as she said, "But you're wrong in this. You know that preacher is innocent."

He slammed down his fork. "You're just like my mother, falling under the preacher's spell." He stood up and pointed a thick finger at her. "You stay away from that devil! You hear? I lost my appetite!" He pushed back his chair and walked to the door. Before he went out, he turned back to his wife and said in a much lower tone, "I thought better of you, Emma. Truly I did."

❦

Claire lingered over her morning tea with Mary Anders. The older woman wanted to know everything about their trip. She was an extremely emotional listener, but Claire trusted the woman's good counsel.

"I wonder how Davy's doing," Claire murmured.

"I'm sure he's fine." Mary stirred the sugar into her second cup of tea as she stole a glance at Claire's distant stare. Curiosity provoked Mary to change the subject. "I sure was surprised to hear that you and Luke got married." She motioned with a dimpled hand. "I'm glad you could find a bit of happiness in the midst of all this."

"Oh, Mary," Claire confided, "it's not like that. I think Luke just married me because it was the proper thing to do. We'd spent so much time together alone. When I ended up going with him, he was worried about what people would think."

Mary showed surprise at Claire's confession. "But, Dear, I know a look of love when I see it. And I saw it in Luke's eyes. He's not the same man who left here. Why, he adores you."

"There was a time I thought perhaps. . ." Claire turned her face away from Mary.

"Yes?"

She sighed. The woman would not let it lie. "He told me several months ago that he would never love again, that he was an empty shell of a man. But when he returned from keeling, I thought he'd changed. He even told me he loved me."

Mary Anders looked puzzled, and Claire tried to explain, "But looking back, now I understand. He knew I'd get hurt no matter what, so he did what he thought was best by me. I think he married me to protect my reputation."

Mary tried to reason with Claire. "Of course you have doubts when you didn't even get a honeymoon. All new brides do. If you'd been allowed any time alone with him, you'd know he loves you."

Claire shook her head with its neatly coiled braid. "No! He had the chance to escape. We could have left the country and had a life together. But he chose to hang. Don't you see? He chose death. . .over me." Her voice broke with emotion, but she blurted out the rest, "He still wants to be with Miriam. He knew all along I'd be released from this marriage by his death."

Mary rose and moved to Claire, patting her back. "Now, now. You can't go on thinking such things, Claire. I believe your imagination is working overtime. I know for a fact that Luke is a very honorable man. If he told you he loved you, then he does."

"He always treated me like a sister," Claire cried.

"Because he's a proper gentleman."

"No. He's been cool toward me."

"He's under a lot of stress right now. I'm sure he's just trying to prepare you for the worst."

Claire stood to face Mary. "If I lose Davy, too, I don't know what I'll do."

"Lose the child? Why would you?"

"Ben is here. Luke always talked about Davy going to live with him. Ben and Kate, my cousin, can't have children of their own. They have already adopted two boys. I imagine they think Davy would complete their family just fine. But they can't have him! He's mine now!"

Mary gripped Claire's shoulders. "Claire, stop this! I know the stress is awful for you, too. But you're just talking nonsense! Now get yourself ready, and go visit your husband. You tell him your doubts. For your own peace of mind, you must get this settled."

Claire shook her head. "No. He already has so much on his mind, how can I cause him more grief? Oh, Mary, I'm so confused." Claire moved into Mary's arms and accepted the comfort they afforded.

❧❧

The loose, dry earth billowed upward from the pounding horse hoofs, covering Emma Cook with a cloud of gagging dust. Nevertheless, she continued at a fast clip, often looking over her shoulder to see if Uriah pursued, until she entered the outskirts of Dayton. She straightened herself in the saddle and guided her mount through the traffic until she came directly in front of the building marked BARRISTER SIMON APPLEBY.

Carefully she tethered her mount and approached. Her heart pounded, and her husband's angry voice echoed in her mind. *You're just like my mother, falling under the preacher's spell. You stay away from that devil! You hear?*

Nevertheless she proceeded. Before entering she brushed off her clothes and straightened her bonnet. The door was unlocked and swung open freely, groaning eerily. The room inside was dark and empty, except for a mammoth desk, masculine furniture, and rows of books.

With a sigh, she whirled to leave and nearly collided with Simon

Appleby, who stood in the open doorway. She gasped.

"Mrs. Cook, I'm sorry if I frightened you. May I be of help?"

The woman's voice trembled. "Are you still the preacher's attorney?"

Simon's heart leapt. "Yes, I am." He took a few steps into his office, closed the door behind them, and drew open the window coverings. "Come. Sit down and we'll talk."

"Thank you." The thin woman took the seat offered and waited, her face expressing pain.

"Now. What can I do for you?" he asked kindly.

"The preacher didn't kill Aaron Gates."

Simon slid to the edge of his seat. "Why do you say that?"

"If I tell you, can you help me?"

"Yes. You have my word."

"My husband will be furious when he finds out I came. He's really a very good man. But this whole thing—it's like he's not himself. I–I don't know what to expect from him."

"I understand. Sheriff Watson and his wife often provide housing for witnesses. I'm sure you'd be welcome to stay with them for awhile, if it comes to that. Or I can go with you to talk to Uriah."

Emma wrung her hands. "Thank you."

Simon smiled encouragement. "What do you know?"

"That day when Uriah hauled the preacher in to the sheriff?" Simon nodded. "Well, he stopped by home and told me to stay with Ruth. When I got there, I overheard her and Ruben talking. You see, Ruben and Aaron had been arguing. When Ruth tried to intervene, Aaron hit her. Ruben tried to help her and pushed Aaron hard. He accidentally killed his father. Then when the preacher came, Ruben went out the window."

Emma looked down at her hands. "I should have told the truth at the beginning, but I didn't want to go against my husband. When I told Uriah, he told me to keep quiet. Then when the reverend escaped, I thought it would be all right."

"Why did Uriah testify against Rev. Wheeler?"

Emma's face saddened. "When he was a small boy, a preacher ran away with his ma. All the time he was growing up, he heard his pa talk about slick-talking preachers. He was good friends with Aaron. Aaron didn't want Ruth going to church. Before his death, he'd been filling Uriah's head with nonsense about Rev. Wheeler."

Simon nodded. "I understand."

"He warned me this morning not to side with the preacher. He won't understand. He's just not himself right now."

"Don't worry, he'll come around."

"But that isn't all. Ruben came to the house last night. I don't know what they're up to."

Simon reached across his desk and took Emma's hand. "You are a very brave woman. You have saved an innocent man's life." Emma hung her head shamefully as he spoke to her. "If I go with you, do you think you could tell your story to the sheriff?"

Emma's face took on a new look of determination. "I've come this far. There's no turning back now."

"Good. Someday there will be another trial, and you will be called on to testify. I will stand by you all the way and see personally to your safety."

"I understand."

Simon released her hand then and rose, going to her side. "Mrs. Cook?"

She also rose and followed him out. He turned toward her again with a reassuring smile. "It's just a short walk."

Chapter 16

Sheriff Watson knocked on the door and waited, exchanging glances with Simon, who removed his hat.

The door swung open, and Ruth Gates placed her hands on her hips. "What do you want?" Her rude question left a scowl upon her face.

"May we come in?" Sheriff Watson asked.

"I'll come out. I don't like to upset the children, although Mr. Appleby seems to delight in it." Her sharp look stabbed Simon, but he did not offer a rebuttal.

Sheriff Watson asked, "Is Ruben here?" Ruth reddened slightly and nodded toward the barn. "Out there."

"I'd like for him to be in on our conversation. Shall we walk that way?"

Ruth shrugged her shoulders and led them toward the barn, calling out to warn her son when they were within hearing, "Ruben, Sheriff Watson's here!"

She stopped several yards from the barn, and Ruben appeared in the open doorway, rifle in hand. He leaned against the wooden frame. "You here to tell me that you're finally going to hang my father's murderer?"

"I don't think you'd like it very much if we did that, Ruben."

Ruben straightened. "You're wrong. It's exactly what I want. Justice."

"But then it would have to be you standing on the gallows tomorrow."

Ruth's eyes darted from her son to the two intruders. Simon was watching her, ready if she made a move; however, she stood rigid and motionless.

"That's very funny," Ruben sneered.

"No, it's not. We have evidence that you struck the blow that inevitably killed your father."

"That's not true!" Ruth denied. "It was the preacher!"

"Evidence, pooh!" Ruben spat on the ground at his side.

"Emma and Uriah Cook know the truth," Sheriff Watson said.

"No!" Ruth screamed.

Sheriff Watson turned to answer her, and Ruben used the opportunity to hoist up his rifle and point it at the sheriff while he edged away from the barn, moving toward his horse.

"You'll not get far," Simon shouted.

"We'll see."

Before he could mount, Ruben heard the cock of several guns behind him and whirled toward the sounds. Deputy Galloway and two others stood, ready to shoot. "Drop it, Ruben."

Simon grabbed Ruth by the arms, restraining her, while Sheriff Watson confronted Ruben. "Why don't you tell us the truth for once? I'm not itchin' to hang anyone. You can trust us, Ruben. We want to help you."

Ruben didn't reply. Sheriff Watson continued, "We've got Clancy's story and Emma Cook's. Now let's hear your side of the story."

Ruben closed his eyes and nodded.

Ruth began to sob.

❧❧

That evening a group gathered at the Anderses' home. Mary had cooked a celebration supper as soon as she heard of Luke's release. Now they conversed in the sitting room, going over the day's astonishing events.

"Aaron Gates was not a bad man," Simon explained. "He began to have terrible headaches and eventually took to the bottle to relieve the pain. Ruth said that was when his character changed. He couldn't handle his liquor."

Luke turned to his wife. "I found out the whole story about Clancy." Claire tilted her head, listening attentively. "One night on board the *Hilde*, Aaron was in a stupor and beat up an employee, Silas Farthington. He threw his unconscious body overboard. Ruben was there at the time and tried to save the man, but he never surfaced—he drowned."

"And Clancy saw it?" Claire asked.

Luke nodded. "Yes. He began to blackmail Aaron."

Simon interrupted. "But first Ruben left Dayton. He was tired of watching his dad go downhill."

Luke continued, "Clancy found Ruben in Cincinnati and tried to blackmail him as well."

"But that didn't work," Simon interjected. "Ruben returned to talk the situation over with his father."

Gustaf Anders rubbed his balding head. "That was what they were arguing about the day you visited the Gateses, Luke?"

"Yes," Luke agreed.

"Mercy me. Such a sad thing," Mary murmured in her usual way.

Simon further explained, "Ruth Gates tried to intervene, and Aaron struck her. That frightened Ruben, and he pushed his father away. There was a bit of a struggle. Aaron fell, hitting his head on the edge of a chair. I don't believe any of it was intentional."

"I just happened to arrive at that time." Luke gestured with a wave of his hand. "And Ruth sent Ruben out the window. Later when Uriah appeared, Ruth conveniently put the blame on me."

"Why would Uriah lie about the hanky like he did in the courtroom?" Emmett asked.

"Because he hates preachers." His bearded chin in his hand, Luke pondered his own statement.

Simon explained, "Uriah's mother ran away with a preacher when he was a small boy. His own father drilled it into him that preachers were liars, womanizers, and bad. At first he simply believed the worst of Luke. Later he just wanted revenge for that one in his past."

"Oh, how sad," Claire said. "I'm so glad Emma had the courage to come forth with the truth." She looked across the room at the attorney she had grown to respect. "Do you think Uriah will forgive her?"

Simon nodded. "Yes, I think he'll come around. But the trial could be a painful one."

"For all of us," Luke said. Slowly he continued, "And then there is the pain of forgiving."

Claire added, "The Lord's portions are ample. He has seen us through so much already. Surely He will help us forgive."

After Simon had gone home, Luke said to the others, "I'm really tired. I think I'll go out to my place tonight. It's been empty for months. I just need some time alone to sort through things."

Claire felt a lump constricting her throat. Everything had happened so fast. She had not thought about their life together. Had she expected him to stay with her tonight? She felt Mary's gaze upon her and blushed.

Luke walked to her then, gently removing her hands from her lap. Caressing them, he said, "It's been a long day for all of us. Get some rest tonight. I'll be by in the morning, and we'll make plans." He kissed her lightly on the cheek. Claire remained sitting, her back stiff.

Gustaf saw him to the door. "I'm so pleased this is over. God bless you, Reverend."

When he had gone, Claire gave Mary an I-told-you-so look and fled up the stairs to her room.

Chapter 17

Luke lit a candle in the dark house and looked around at the familiar rooms, furnishings that he and Miriam had picked out. He moved into the kitchen and fingered once again her apron hanging on the peg. He'd never had the heart to pack away her things. Now he wished he had.

Slowly he made his way through the cobwebs into the bedroom. He took a deep breath. There on the bed lay a dusty black valise, packed and ready for the trip he and Davy never took. Davy's cradle was missing. He remembered. Claire had taken it to the Anderses' home.

Claire. He knew he could not bring her to this house for their first night together, not with Miriam's things still here. Anyway, the place was filthy, like he knew it would be. He had seen the hurt in her eyes, but he was just too weary to deal with it tonight.

She knew he loved her, and that was all that mattered. Tomorrow they would make plans to go on a honeymoon. He would ask Mary to pack up Miriam's things. It would be better that way.

He set the valise on the floor, undressed, and climbed into bed. Weary as he was, he thanked the Lord for bringing him through this terrible time. He prayed for Davy and thanked God for Claire. Then he drifted off, dreaming of his new wife.

The following afternoon was hot for late October. The sun shone brightly through the lofty but nearly bare oak and elms, providing a blanket of warmth over the sparkling autumn meadow. Luke and Claire lounged on a woolen striped blanket, strewn with multicolored leaves and picnic remains.

"Come here, Darling, closer," Luke coaxed.

Cautiously Claire moved closer, their shoulders touching. Luke stretched his arms out toward the sky. "It feels so good to be a free man."

"You're not exactly free," she corrected.

His brows furrowed. "Why not? Are you thinking of the trial? Sheriff Watson said I could come and go as I pleased as long as I was here for the trial."

"I imagine that will be a few weeks away." Claire sighed.

"Does it trouble you?"

"No. That wasn't what I meant. You're not exactly free because of our marriage," she murmured so softly he strained to hear.

He cupped her chin in his hand. "But that's the best part."

Claire burst out, "Luke, I wish you would not pretend so. I know why you married me." She gulped. "I know you don't love me."

"What?" Luke was so astonished he dropped his hand and stared at her, unable to find his tongue.

She rattled on. "I'll never be a burden to you. I'll not ask you to love me. And I'll do my best to be a good mother to Davy."

"Why I know you will, Darling." As he looked at her jutting chin, so determined, and her quivering pale cheeks, he suddenly understood.

He took her hands in his again. "Listen, Claire, to what I tell you. I loved Miriam and grieved at her loss. You know I did. What I said that night about never loving again. . . I guess I was just plain blind."

Two tears trickled down Claire's velvety pink cheeks. He longed to reach out and brush them away, but could not bring himself to release her tight grip upon his hands.

"I guess God in his wondrous mercy had other plans. He unlocked my heart again and allowed me to love you. I dreamed of you every night when I was keeling. I missed you terribly. I discovered I was in love with you all along. Now I know I even loved you as a little girl with pigtails. I love you as I've never loved anyone before. Can you believe me?"

"I–I don't know. It's so sudden."

"Sudden? After all these months together?"

"The realization of it is."

Luke pulled her close. He kissed his wife with all the fervor he felt. She gasped and stroked his cheek. With delight she said, "Why, I believe it's true! You do!"

He laughed, throwing back his head. Then he captured her hand, "What about you, Claire? Do you feel burdened to be shackled to me?"

"Why no. I'm happy, I'm. . ."

He waited for her to say the words. The truth of those words several months ago had given life to his own dormant feelings. She could not refuse his pleading eyes.

"I love you, Luke. I always have."

"I'm a fortunate man. Can you forgive the many times I spoke to you so heartlessly, threatening to send you home?"

"You tried to do what was best."

He looked out across the meadow. The slight breeze occasionally sent brittle leaves swirling downward to the earth.

"Luke?"

"Hm?"

"Can you forgive the Gateses, the Cooks?"

Luke smiled. "I already have." Claire looked surprised. "Last night when

I lay in bed, I counted my blessings. Well, of course, God brought that to mind. I struggled with it for awhile. But I so want for you and me to have a perfect start. I couldn't let anything hinder our chances. Do you understand?"

"Yes."

Luke recalled as did Claire some of those times they shared over the past few months. In doing so, he remembered his disguises. With a sudden cheerfulness, he turned to her. "So tell me, Mrs. Wheeler, what do you think of my new look?" He turned his face from side to side, a broad grin enveloping his face.

Claire touched his smooth chin. "I like it. Now I can see all your dimples."

He gave her a thank-you kiss, then coaxed, "Why don't you lay your head in my lap while we discuss our honeymoon plans."

Claire blushed but acquiesced. "What do you have in mind?"

"Do you think you'd mind terribly if we camped out, like we did so many times together?"

She sat upright. "I'd love it. The weather has warmed."

"It could turn cold again."

"We'll have each other to keep warm," she ventured.

"We could honeymoon our way to Cincinnati, visit our friends there, pick up Davy, maybe stop in Beaver Creek and visit family."

"Oh, yes." She nodded with enthusiasm. "I'd really like that."

"Then we could come back and settle in here," he suggested. "There would be the trial, of course."

"You know your congregation will want you back. What will you do?"

"I'll talk it over with my beautiful new wife, and together we shall decide."

Claire snuggled her head back onto his lap. "She'll probably say she wants you to return to your pastorate."

"I thought she might." He looked down at her, his heart aflame with ample portions of love and desire.

Castor Oil and Lavender

As always, I appreciate my family's encouragement and would also like to thank Rebecca Germany for the opportunities she's given me, and for her expertise as a writer and editor.

Chapter 1

Randolph Cline peered at him from across the massive polished desk. No matter how intimidating it was to be the recipient of that condescending gaze, the doctor was determined not to show it. Dr. David Wheeler gripped the chair's smooth walnut armrests and leaned forward. "With every hour that passes, the condition of our city only worsens."

"Let me get this straight. You're suggesting that I hire immigrants to sweep Cincinnati's streets?" Cline's balding forehead wrinkled. "And would you also like me to finance the counting of stars? Perhaps for the sake of science?" Apparently he didn't expect an answer to his question, for after shifting in his chair—which seemed to be a habitual gesture—he continued with his argument. "I'll agree that our city is swarming with the ragged and pitiful, but until you can show me how I will profit in this venture, I cannot help you."

David realized that 1837 was a year of hard times for the nation as a whole, but he also knew that men like Cline continued to prosper. All in all, Cincinnati still boomed. The doctor pressed his boots against the other man's imported rug and pasted on a smile. "Oh, but you will greatly profit. You might spare your own life or the lives of your family." Cline's eyes looked heavenward indicating disbelief, but David continued. "It is only a matter of time until another bout of cholera hits Cincinnati. With your donation, other respectable citizens will follow suit and also contribute. What seems to you an impossible task can be accomplished, and everyone benefits."

Randolph Cline pushed back his chair and eased himself onto his feet. David saw a flicker of pain wash across the man's face and mentally clicked off a list of maladies that might be tormenting him: *Back pain? Too early in the day for indigestion. Possibly hemorrhoids?*

"Beautify the city. Sounds nice. But not practical," Cline said. David stiffened when Cline touched his shoulder. "Now, I need to prepare for my day and upcoming appointments."

He followed Cline to the door, voicing a final plea. "The city's board of health supports this project. Dr. Drake says—"

Cline's hands flew up as if to ward off some odious pest. "Do not bring up that man's name. Had I known he was behind this, I wouldn't have given you the hour." He pointed a finger at David. "You are young and impressionable so let me give you a word of counsel. Treat the sick, and let the lawyers take care of the city's problems."

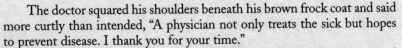

The doctor squared his shoulders beneath his brown frock coat and said more curtly than intended, "A physician not only treats the sick but hopes to prevent disease. I thank you for your time."

He left the land developer-textile manufacturer's office more determined than ever to promote his project of cleaning up Cincinnati's filthy streets. Lives depended upon it. But one thing was certain. He could cross Randolph Cline off his list of prospective donors. David smiled grimly. He would not mention Dr. Drake's name to his next candidate. Which was. . . He pulled a list from his pocket. Number two, Vernon Thorpe. Number three, Zachary Caulfield.

David set his back to September's early morning sun. It peeked over the buildings of the finer district of Cincinnati. Mentally he rehashed the meeting as he strode toward his one-room dwelling, which was attached to the clinic where he received patients.

Later, entering the building by a side door, a fluffy, brown-streaked cat pressed against his leg. "Hello, Gratuity." The cat waltzed in and out of his steps. "Did you find yourself a meal last night?" David stooped to scratch the purring cat's head, then straightened. He placed his fine, brown frock coat on a hook, jerked off his cravat, and crossed the room to an inadequate bed. A maple wardrobe was wedged between the wall and bed, its doors too warped to close.

He sat, and the cat joined him on the bed. "It didn't go well, Gratuity. Mr. Cline would not be persuaded. Narrow-minded. Cannot see the necessity of prevention. Only interested in his fat purse." David pulled off his tall leather boots and wiggled out of his tight pantaloons, exchanging them for a comfortable pair of loose trousers from the wardrobe—some he had bartered from a beggar at the Ohio River docks. His elbow poked through a hole as he slipped into the sleeve of an old coat. "Drake says it only takes a couple enthusiastic persons and then everything else will fall into place." Gratuity finished a spit bath and curled up into a purring ball of fluff. "Some sympathy I get from you. Have a good nap."

After retrieving his black physician's bag from his clinic, David started north toward the canal. His thoughts shifted to an entirely different problem—the patient he was going to visit. If only people didn't bring all their superstitions with them when they emigrated from the old country. He was positive that Mrs. Schroeder's illness was all in her head, a so-called curse resulting from a dispute with a neighbor.

Raised by missionary parents in West Africa, David knew how destructive such pagan beliefs could be. Mrs. Schroeder's physical decline had become more evident with each of his house calls. Death's door would open wide unless he could think of a cure. Reasoning with this patient was futile.

His path followed the narrow stone canal. The new day burst into wildlife song, inspiring him. He quickened his step, chuckling at the simplicity of the remedy, veered off the cobblestone pathway, and sloshed through the weedy grasses where he toed the soggy leaves and twigs until he spotted his prize. "Aha! There you are." Dropping into a squat, he let go of his black bag and snatched up his unsuspecting prey. It croaked and lunged. Grasping the slimy, long-legged creature more tightly, he held the frog up to his face. Its legs dangled.

All in an instant, memories of long-gone boyhood days by the Niger River of Africa lightened his morning's cares. David stared into the bulging eyes. "You, little fellow, are going to do an errand of mercy for me."

A rumble of male laughter and several feminine giggles brought David's gaze back toward the footpath. He stuffed the amphibian into his pocket, but upon feeling a gaping hole, shifted it instead to the opposite side.

Sure. It was unconventional. But if he could keep the woman's physical body from perishing, there was still hope for her soul. Retrieving his bag, he whistled his way back to the path and, stride quickening again, headed past the tallow factory and pork-packing plant toward the canal crossing at the locks.

On Thirteenth Street, counting buildings to distinguish Mrs. Schroeder's place of dwelling from the similar ones within the rows of three- to five-story brick buildings, he veered to enter a dismal establishment's door, then climbed the steps two at a time until he reached the landing of the third floor. After a quick rap, he stuck his head inside the apartment.

"Mrs. Schroeder? It's me, Dr. Wheeler. I came to see how you were doing today."

A moan sounded from a round lump of covers on a narrow cot in the far corner of the room. David easily interpreted the German mumbling. "That frog in my stomach is eating my insides. Will you find my son and tell him that I love him?"

"I'm sure you can tell him yourself," he replied using the woman's native language.

"No. I'm dying."

"Nonsense. I brought you a cure."

A tousled head shot up from the disheveled lump. The eyes were hopeful, but the head shook in disbelief.

"A strong potion."

She sat up. "A potion? Well, maybe. *Ja,* I have heard of such things."

"Let's not waste any more time then." David began a merry version of a German song as he took a spoon and bottle from his bag and helped the woman swallow a dose of ipecac.

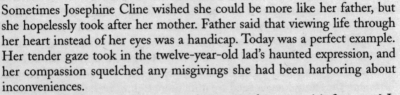

Sometimes Josephine Cline wished she could be more like her father, but she hopelessly took after her mother. Father said that viewing life through her heart instead of her eyes was a handicap. Today was a perfect example. Her tender gaze took in the twelve-year-old lad's haunted expression, and her compassion squelched any misgivings she had been harboring about inconveniences.

"Say, Charles, won't your mama be surprised to get a visit from you? It might be just the thing to nurse her back to health."

"Happy I am to work for your papa. But for Mama, I worry. *Ja*, to see her is *gut*. Maybe for Mama is *gut*, too."

Hugging her velvet cloak against her body to keep out the September morning's chill, Josephine noticed the threadbare condition of Charles's wool coat, mentally making a note to bring it to her mother's attention. Of all the Elm Street orphans her mama clothed, she would be embarrassed to discover that someone under her care was ill clad. "Are you warm enough?"

The lad's hand swiped the air. *"Ja."* His head bent low as if it was his duty to watch his boots navigate the granite footpath.

Josephine's heart tugged. Her father's apprentice might possess a youthful, even angelic face, but most of the time he exhibited manlike courage. Father thought highly of Charles to allow the apprentice time off his job at the textile factory to check up on his sick mother. But Father always possessed insight and practicality. That was why he had added the stipulation that Josephine must accompany the boy. Father wanted to make sure Charles didn't take flight or squander a precious day's time. She was along to chaperone. It would make a good report to the charity society to which she belonged. *Oh, Lord.* She glanced heavenward and sighed. *Forgive my petty thoughts.*

Charles's gait quickened. Josephine swept her hood away from her face and glanced sideways at the boy. His expression was happily animated, and his feet seemed to remember their way home now. They passed the tallow factory and pork-packing plant, fast approaching the canal locks.

On Thirteenth Street, Josephine exhaled visible puffs of air and lifted her full skirt and three petticoats to scurry up the steps, keeping at Charles's heels all the while wondering how he could tell his tenement from all the others. Was it perhaps more run-down? Even so, the lad seemed glad to be home. But the instant they crept into the stale room, she sensed that they were not alone. A quick glance took in the scene. A physician bent over a woman, one who suddenly rose up from her bed and heaved on top of the doctor's boots. Josephine instinctively clutched Charles by the shoulders to keep him from rushing forward as the woman retched.

Gradually Josephine became aware that the man in the room did not have the appearance of a doctor though he carried a black medical bag. His shabby attire resembled that of a beggar's. And he certainly did not behave like a doctor, singing at the woman's bedside.

Josephine watched him thrust his hand into a pocket and withdraw a. . .a *frog!* With a jubilant glint in his blue eyes, he tossed the amphibian into the mess on his boots, then from the tone of his voice—for she could not understand the foreign conversation—he must have ordered the poor woman to rise up off her sickbed. And more to the wonder of it all, she did. Then while Charles watched with his mouth agape, arm in arm his mother and the long-legged man danced a jig as if this was some grand celebration.

Before she could fully fathom the meaning of all that had just transpired, Charles broke loose from her grip and rushed into the mess. Josephine grimaced.

"Mama!" The boy released a stream of German.

The man turned and stared at Josephine as if he had just noticed them. Her face heated.

"Miss Josephine! Mama's healed! The curse is over." Josephine shuddered, wishing for an instant that she had stayed at home in her warm cozy bed and that Charles had not returned to his old home at all but stayed where he was safe and life was normal.

The blond man rolled up his threadbare sleeves and headed for the washbasin. Josephine felt like she ought to be doing something to help restore order. But before she could move, the mother rushed across the room cackling some foreign protest. It appeared that she felt well enough now to see to her own needs.

Josephine blinked twice. The medical imposter accepted payment for the fraudulent cure without hesitation over the fact that the woman might not be able to afford her next meal. He rattled off more German and headed toward the door seeming very pleased with himself.

Josephine's anger surfaced over the injustice. "Charles. Talk to your mama while I see the doctor out."

The man flinched. One of his blond eyebrows slanted upward as he studied her.

If he expects to get away with this atrocity, then he is wrong, she fumed. *I will show him that he cannot take advantage of poor immigrants.* "I would have a word with you," she said, her tone barbed.

He wore a mustache, and his blond sideburns extended into a thin beard, which framed his face. He gave her an odd half smile, bid Mrs. Schroeder and Charles a warm farewell, and strode out the door without the courtesy of a reply.

Josephine's many skirts swept up a cloud of dust from the floorboards, and she fled down the stairs after him, her hot gaze never leaving his back. "Will you wait? I wish to speak with you!"

At the bottom of the landing, he shouldered open the door, stepped outside, and wheeled about abruptly. She stopped just inches from colliding into him. Retreating a few steps, she glared up into his twinkling blue eyes. "You, Sir, are a fraud!"

He cocked one blond eyebrow at her for the second time that morning and looked down his fine Roman nose. Then he had the gall to smile. His voice was soft, his English perfect, and he addressed her as if she were a small child. "Miss. The eye can be deceiving. I assure you that you are working yourself up over nothing. Let me explain—"

"I saw what you did with that frog. You acted like she was under some curse. And you took payment. Only a worm would grovel so low."

His eyes narrowed. He mumbled. Josephine heard the words "insulting mouth." Who was he to reprimand her?

"I plan to turn you in to the proper authorities."

"An unbridled mouth is an unattractive trait in a woman." He bit off his sentence as if he would have said more but thought better of it and turned away.

"You have not heard the end of this!"

This time he did not even flinch.

Josephine placed her hands upon her hips. *Arrogant pauper*. Her face burned with humiliation over the way he had treated her, walking away from her as if she and everything she had said were insignificant. *Doctor. Hah!* She would see that he was tracked down and brought to justice for his misdeed. How could anyone behave in such a manner? Surely her father would know what to do with a man like this.

The tenement door flew open. Charles stuck his head out. "Mama wishes to meet you."

Josephine unclamped her so-called *insulting, unbridled* mouth and exhaled deeply, trying to appear congenial for the lad's sake. "Of course, Charles. I want to meet her, too."

Chapter 2

His good nature prevailing, before David even crossed the canal, he chuckled to himself over the incident he had just incurred. The woman's anger had progressed to a boil much like the steam engine that powered Cincinnati's new steamship, the *Moselle*—the ship that was on everyone's lips and appeared in so many headlines. He could have sworn he saw steam puffing from her ears. Perhaps God should have designed female creatures with safety valves. He chuckled.

The funny thing was, he couldn't blame her for thinking he was a fraud. At first her accusation had galled him because he detested the quacks that had infiltrated Cincinnati, giving people false hope. In fact, his mentor, Dr. Drake, frequently discussed that very thing with him—how to protect citizens from those who practiced medicine without the proper qualifications. Anyway, how was that lovely creature to know that David had a framed medical diploma hanging above the bookcase in his clinic?

It was kind of cute the way she stood up to him, defending Mrs. Schroeder. He should have made her listen to his explanation instead of spouting off at her. What had he said anyway? Something about an unbridled tongue? That had certainly brought color to her cheeks. He chuckled again. No woman liked that kind of talk. Perhaps he was to blame for shoveling coal onto her smoldering fire. But then what did he know about women or what they liked? Not much. Anyway, no doubt he would never see this one again.

"Good morning, Dr. Wheeler."

"Good morning to you." David nodded at the boy vendor and exchanged a coin for a paper, which he thrust beneath his arm. No patients waited on the clinic's stoop. This meant he might squeeze in breakfast before he went to work.

Early mornings were his favorite. He took pleasure in donning old clothes and going on the prowl for patients—the kind that would not feel comfortable or be able to afford coming to the clinic. The needs were great among the people who inhabited areas like the slummy district along the Ohio River docks or along the canal. Very seldom was a morning unproductive.

Though some of his medical comrades thought he was eccentric, David found his method of treatment most practical. It was similar to the way his parents had performed their services in Africa.

Gratuity greeted him with purrs, rubbing against his legs. In keeping with his daily ritual, David read snatches of news to the cat while cracking eggs into an iron skillet. As the eggs sizzled, he hurried to change into a third set of clothing: this time a linen shirt and trousers. He fastened his suspenders and slipped into a wool waistcoat. He hated cravats and never wore them to the clinic.

Scorched egg stench reached his nostrils, and he hurried back to his breakfast, scraping the unappetizing meal onto a plate. As he forked down his fare, he finished flipping through the pages of the *Cincinnati Gazette.*

"Listen to this, Gratuity. Benefit dinner for the women's workhouse to be held at the home of Zachary Caulfield." *Number three on my list,* he told himself as he slid his plate to the floor and mumbled, "Come get your leftovers." The cat's hesitancy made him sorry he had burned their breakfast once again. He stacked the dishes and pulled on his brown leather boots. "Perhaps I need to attend that dinner next week, Gratuity. Might meet some folks with money to spare for our cause." He grabbed his bag. "Let's go see what this day has to offer. Shall we?" The cat slipped out the open door and disappeared. David strode toward the clinic and withdrew a key from his pocket.

Josephine slipped off her cloak and draped it over her arm. "What an exhausting morning."

Her mother looked up from stitching a comforter. "Sit down, Dear. Tell me about it. How is Mrs. Schroeder?"

Sinking into a mahogany and rose upholstered chair, Josie propped up her legs and crossed her feet on a matching stool, reveling in the comfort. "Mrs. Schroeder is fully recovered."

"But I thought she was on her deathbed. Was it just a rumor?"

"I do not know, Mother. She does not speak English, you know. But she is fine now. Some beggar masquerading as a doctor spoke mumbo jumbo over her, and she seemed good as new."

"You look tired. Was it far?"

"No. But I did help her clean up the place. She has so little." Josephine's gaze settled on the silver wall sconces, and she wished there was more she could have done to help the sweet woman.

Mrs. Cline went back to her stitching with renewed fervor.

"But I think what wore me out was that infuriating doctor. I mean to tell Father about him."

"Yes." Her mother nodded sympathetically. "I'm sure your father will know what to do." She glanced up. "Josie, you look like you could use a nap."

"No time. This afternoon I'm helping the cook."

"I'll never know where you get that love for cooking."

"Or you, your love for sewing."

Mrs. Cline's face lit with pleasure. "Perhaps we should make one of these for Mrs. Schroeder, too. What do you think?"

"Oh, Mother. I believe anything would be appreciated. And winter is just around the corner. That reminds me. Charles needs a new coat."

"Charles?"

"Father's German apprentice."

"Oh, yes. Of course. I will take care of it."

Josephine spent the rest of the day helping the cook with dinner. That evening she gave her hair a final inspection and hurried back downstairs. When she entered the dining room, a servant pulled out her chair.

"Hello, Father."

"Josie." He nodded at the servant, who disappeared into the kitchen and returned with steaming dishes of spiced pork and roasted vegetables. Heads bowed, silent prayers were issued. "Your mother tells me that you had quite a morning."

"I lost my temper." Details of her morning spilled out as Josie shared dinner with her parents. She brushed aside their cooking compliments and concluded her narrative with, "I want to turn him in to the authorities. How do I proceed?"

Mrs. Cline interjected, "I told her you would know what to do."

"Did you get the man's name?"

"I had to get the information from Charles. It's Spokes."

"Hmm. Never heard of him."

"The way he was dressed, I'm sure he doesn't have a real practice."

"If he doesn't have a practice, then there's not much we can do to hinder him except run him out of town."

"Don't you have a man who could do an investigation?"

"Yes, but that all costs money. Is this really that important to you?"

Josie felt her cheeks heat, and she nodded. "Yes."

"I'll see what I can do. Say, I know what will get your mind off the scoundrel. We're invited to a formal dinner."

"Something we'll need new gowns for?" Mrs. Cline's eyes sparkled.

Josie grinned. "Do tell us about it, Father."

❧❧

A steady stream of carriages deposited Cincinnati's posh and prosperous at the entrance of Zachary Caulfield's luxurious Victorian estate. David had walked. He waited in the dark shadows of a tall tree to take it all in. A row of gas lamps lined the street where stylish figures paraded by. Cincinnati was a crossroads between the backwoods and the civilized, but its prominent society did not lack in manners or elegance.

He adjusted his despised cravat before stepping out from the shadows. A doorman checked his invitation. He wished Dr. Drake had been able to accompany him, but the doctor was traveling again. It had taken some finagling, but David had been able to obtain an invitation through connections with Clay Buchanan, a friend of Drake's who was on the board of health.

Stepping into the room where about twenty-five people had gathered, David studied his surroundings: elegant tables clad with white cloths, enough appetizers to make his stomach rumble, and people clustered off not only according to occupation and social fabric, but also according to Yankees and Southerners.

With the food as a lodestar, he worked his way through the crowd, happy to stumble so quickly upon Clay Buchanan.

"Come here, Doctor. We were just discussing the East versus the West."

Handshakes admitted him into a small circle of men. Clay Buchanan proceeded to press his point. "The East is static, conservative, old; the West is dynamic, progressive, young."

It went without saying, and David only half listened to the flames of conversation that leapt up about him. He was more interested in the information his eyes could glean. When he spotted two gentlemen whose names were on his list, his heartbeat quickened. *Vernon Thorpe and Quinton Wallace.* His mind warmed to the possibilities of how he might introduce his subject.

As he watched them, the two men turned their gazes to a small cluster of women. Wondering what had captured their attention, David fixed his gaze in that direction. To his great surprise, he recognized one of the women as the boiling steam engine from Mrs. Schroeder's. Only tonight she looked like an angel.

In a swirl of blue silk with a string of pearls at her creamy neck, she glided through the maze of guests. Fascinated, he crooked his neck and leaned sideways to keep her in his view. Her hair was swept up in a most becoming arrangement of brown curls. He could see why she had turned the other gentlemen's heads.

David turned to Clay Buchanan. "Say. Do you know who that young woman is by the fireplace?"

"The pretty one in blue?"

"Yes, she's the one."

"That's Josephine Cline, Randolph's daughter."

No other name could have doused his fire so quickly and thoroughly. He frowned, assessing what he knew about the father and transferring the man's attributes to the daughter.

She looked up. Their gazes locked. He struggled to pull his away but couldn't. She stared back at him in such a brash manner that he cocked his brow at her, shifting the blame of his impropriety upon her.

Instantly, her eyes widened with recognition. The color of her cheeks deepened, and her brown eyes narrowed again. In a queenly manner, she thrust her chin in the air, grabbed a fistful of skirt and lacy petticoat, and marched toward him—a flurry of blue silk.

With each of her steps, it grew more evident she had not forgiven him and meant to continue where they had last left off. David frantically searched the room for a means of escape. *The terrace.* He wheeled about and started toward it.

"Mr. Spokes. Is that you?"

Who was Mr. Spokes? Curiosity proved to be his downfall. He chanced a backward glance.

She rushed forward. "Wait!"

His spirits sagged. It *was* him she was after. And she *was* going to make a scene.

Chapter 3

David took several steps toward the terrace, hoping he and Miss Cline could take their conversation to a private location.

"It is you." Miss Cline brushed past him and blocked his path.

"Excuse me? Are you speaking to me?" *Maybe if I feign ignorance she will go away.*

"You know very well that I am."

David sighed. "What may I do for you, Miss? I do not believe we have been introduced." *That should put her in her place.*

"Oh, but we have. At Mrs. Schroeder's."

"Ah, yes. I remember."

He felt embarrassed under her scrutiny.

"I almost didn't recognize you." A gleam of cunning suddenly appeared in her eyes, one that David did not trust. "I'm Josephine Cline. Come. I'd like to introduce you to my father."

"Ah, Miss Cline. I've already met your father."

She looked quizzically at him. "Well, then you must say hello. I'm sure he would be interested to hear about Mrs. Schroeder's health. Do come along." She tucked her gloved hand beneath his arm and tugged.

David could not believe her forwardness. "Look, Miss Cline. I would like to explain about that day." He grew impatient. "Can we please stop a moment?"

"I didn't take you for a shy man," she argued, while still guiding him across the room. She gave a little wave. He felt her grip tighten upon his arm "There. Father saw us. He's coming. You two can have a lovely chat about Mrs. Schroeder."

David jerked loose from her grip and straightened his frock coat. His voice resembled a low growl. "Your little game has been most amusing. Now if you will excuse me, I was about to get a bit of fresh air out on the terrace."

"Josephine? Did you want me?"

Mr. Cline loomed into David's vision before he could flee. Randolph Cline's gaze bore questioningly into David's, making his skin crawl worse than it had that day in the man's plush office.

"Yes, Father. I wanted you to meet Mr. Spokes. Remember? I mentioned him?"

David shrugged and shook Mr. Cline's hand. "So nice to see you again."

"Dr. Wheeler." Randolph Cline's expression gradually changed to one of amusement. "Spokes. That's a good one, Josie. No wonder I didn't know whom you were talking about."

Miss Cline's cheeks turned bright red. "Our mystery has been solved, Father. You can call off your investigators." David noticed her painstaking enunciation of the word "investigators" and felt uncomfortably warm beneath her gloating defiant gaze.

The two gentlemen David had earlier noticed and wished to speak to regarding the funding of his city cleanup plan broke away from a group of affluent men and began to approach. Josie gestured. "Please join us. Have you met Dr. Spo—Wheeler?" Her cheeks momentarily reddened again.

For one foolish moment, David hoped fate was turning in his favor. He strode forward and thrust out his hand in greeting. But warnings flashed through his mind. Randolph Cline would react negatively if he introduced the subject of his project to clean up the city. Meanwhile, Cline's daughter continued her irritating game.

"Gentlemen, Dr. Wheeler has a new cure. Would you like to hear about it?"

"A new cure? Do tell us."

"Come now, Doctor. Don't be shy," she coaxed. "Tell them about the frog you keep in your pocket."

David managed a smile. "She's teasing you. It's a private joke between us."

"Modesty does not become you, Doctor. Tell the gentlemen how you tricked Mrs. Schroeder, convincing her she was cursed. It was quite disgusting, the way he abused the poor immigrant woman."

All three men frowned at the change of tone in Josephine's voice.

"Miss Cline, I do apologize for not explaining earlier. You see, I grew up in Africa where things like this were common."

Several eyebrows slanted. Randolph Cline's resembled a flock of flying geese. "You're talking about curses?"

"Why, yes." Josephine nodded.

"You put a curse on a woman?" one of the other men asked.

"No! I did not. I assure you that. . ." David felt the noose around his neck tighten. He fiddled with his cravat.

"Yes! He did. I saw it with my own eyes," Josephine argued.

"Look, Miss. You don't know what you're talking about. I told you—"

"Do not raise your voice to me. See, Father? He is a quack. And a rude, arrogant thief."

David's temples throbbed. "I am not a quack or a thief. You do not know anything."

"Well! I know what I saw." Josephine turned to her father. "Are you going to let him talk to me this way? He deserves to be. . .to be run out of town."

"Run me out of town? Hah!" David's voice rose.

"I do not like the tone you are using to speak to my daughter. What kind of doctor are you anyway? I'm beginning to understand why you came to my office begging money. You're a slyboots, aren't you?"

David heard a chorus of gasps. The crowd was beginning to press around them. Otherwise, the room had quieted. But David's ears buzzed and bile choked his throat. "This is absurd. If only you would let me explain—"

"We'll have to ask you to leave, Sir," Mr. Caulfield said.

Where had he come from? Incredible. The host himself asking me to leave. David felt a vise latch onto his arm. A large black man propelled him forward. "Let me go!" David struggled to free himself but saw it was in vain. "All right! I'm going."

"Release him," Zachary Caulfield nodded.

The vise fell away from his arm. David jerked the tails of his frock coat and cast Miss Cline a furious look. She edged closer to her father, and he clutched her protectively.

"Please leave the premises," Zachary Caulfield repeated.

David clenched his jaw and strode toward the door. A path magically appeared through the crowd. The doorman held the entry door wide open. David strode through. Anger surged through him, outranked only by his burning humiliation. The last thing he heard was something muttered about "Drake's prodigy."

❧❧

"Mother!" Josephine crouched over the prone woman, patting her cheek. "I'm sorry, Mother. Do come around."

Mrs. Cline raised her head. When clarity shone in her eyes, she muttered, "Randolph. Take us home."

Easily whisking her up into his arms, he looked at his daughter. "Josie?"

"I'll get our cloaks." Josie hurried to the doorman, who had their wraps already draped across his arm. She picked up bits of conversation.

"Beautiful dinner party ruined. . ."

"Exposed. A quack."

"Bravo, Miss Cline."

She hurried back to her parents, feeling more horrible by each passing minute for the scene she had caused. One more mark against her. Already she did not measure up to the etiquette rule book. Now she had argued publicly. No lady would ever do such a thing. For her own sake, her reputation didn't matter, but she hated to embarrass and disappoint her parents.

"Put me down, Randolph. I can walk." A chorus of female giggles erupted. Josie squelched back the rising humiliation, draped her mother's cloak over her rigid shoulders, and turned to their hovering hosts. "Please accept my apologies. I do not know how to make amends."

"Yes, so sorry," Randolph Cline mumbled.

Mrs. Cline sniffed.

"Accepted. Run along and everything will be just fine. Don't you worry. A little excitement always makes a good party. Anyway, it was Drake's prodigy who caused the ruckus."

Mrs. Cline swiped away a stream of fresh tears.

Right as it had seemed to entrap Dr. Spokes—Wheeler—whatever, Josie wished she could turn back time, do things differently.

Never had such a humiliating scandal befallen David before. He hastened west, away from the Caulfield estate, wanting to put as much distance as possible between himself and the horrible Josephine Cline, the whole belittling scene. A branch scratched at his face.

"Ow!" He swiped at the night air, not breaking his stride.

An owl hooted, "Fool."

He felt the taste of blood on his lips and pressed his palm against his face. It was sticky. His foot struck something solid, and the next thing he knew, he was flailing through the blackness.

A damp cloth against David's face awakened him. The gas lantern on the nightstand hurt his eyes, and he blinked.

"There, there. Careful." Clay Buchanan's round face with its gray, bushy sideburns loomed over him.

"What happened?" David tried to rise. A pain exploded in his head, and he groaned.

"Slowly now. You know better than that."

David fought to remember. His head had hit the cobblestones, and he had looked up into a star-studded sky. But that was all.

Clay pressed the cloth against David's cheek again. "Scratched up your face. Hold still while I clean it. And you have a concussion. A fitting end to your spectacular evening, I would say." He chuckled.

"Ow!" David closed his eyes, and bits and pieces of his memory speared him between the throbs of pain in his head. Eventually he remembered the whole sorry evening. "Take me home, please."

"I don't want to move you until morning. Don't worry. Your troubles are not going anywhere. They'll still be here tomorrow." Clay chuckled again. "When you asked me the lady's name, I saw you were interested. But I sure never thought you would start a whole big row like that. What got into you anyway?"

"Me?" David raised his head again, only to feel the crashing of pain and lay back on the bed. "As you said, this can wait until morning."

The next time David opened his eyes, it was to shards of sun from a lace-curtained window. It appeared to be late morning. Slowly he lifted his head. It felt dull, but nothing like the pain he had endured the night before.

"Dr. Wheeler, I'm glad you are awake. I was worried." He lifted his head to look at the woman who had entered the room. "Are you ready for breakfast?" Clay's servant asked.

"That sounds wonderful." David grimly remembered he had missed his dinner. As he picked through his memory, a sumptuous tray preceded the woman back into the room. He picked up the fork. "I'll be dressing next. I need to get to the clinic."

"Your clothes are there." She pointed. "But there's no need to hurry to the clinic. Mr. Buchanan went over early this morning to see to matters. He said you were to take the day off."

Swallowing a bite of fluffy eggs, David grinned at the woman. "Thank you." He had no intention of wallowing his day away. He would finish this delicious breakfast, dress, and go see what was happening at the clinic. For all he knew, there could be a whole band of respectable citizens surrounding his building, ready to take him at gunpoint down to the docks and stick him on a boat to China. China might not be such a bad idea.

That is as long as there was no one there by the name of Cline. He had all he could take of that family. Randolph Cline was a miser, only cared about his own pocket. And Josephine? Well, she was a tigress who coldly calculated her prey, and once she had them by the throat, she savored the blood. His conscience pricked at the depths of depravity to which his thoughts were sinking. He argued with himself. *Hey, I bled, didn't I? And it was her fault. Everything was all her fault.* "Africa, maybe that's where I should go. My parents would be glad to see me."

"Excuse me? Are you speaking to me?" Clay's servant asked.

"No. I guess I was talking to myself."

She looked at the bump on his head, her expression skeptical. "Are you done with this tray?"

"Yes. Thank you." When had his life become one humiliating episode after another? And more to the point, how was he going to bring closure to this mess of misunderstandings and turn matters around? As soon as the servant was gone, he threw back the covers. He still had a headache, but his clothes went on easy enough. Now if he could just make it to the clinic.

Chapter 4

David dreaded what might be happening at the clinic. But when he arrived, instead of an angry mob outside, there was an eerie quiet. He opened the door. His waiting room was empty, but he heard voices coming from behind a curtain. When he drew back the canvas barrier, his assistant, Tom Langdon, looked up with surprise.

"You all right? Mr. Buchanan said you had a concussion."

"I'll explain later." Tom's patient wore a pale, strained face. His leg was exposed and bound with a tourniquet.

"Snakebite," Tom explained.

"Looks swollen." David loosened the tourniquet. "How have you treated it?"

"Bled him, was getting ready to administer a compress."

David opened his medical bag. "I've got some oak tannin here. Let's use that on the compress. Any vomiting?"

"No," the patient answered. "But my stomach feels upset. And my head is splitting. Am I going to die?"

"How long has it been?" David asked.

"A couple hours now," Tom said.

"I'm sure you'll be just fine, but we'll keep you here today just to be sure." The man nodded. "My leg feels numb."

David finished treating the man and left the room. Tom followed. But the bell on the clinic's door jingled drawing their attention.

Clay Buchanan asked, "How's the head?"

"Better," David replied. "Thanks for taking care of me."

"I followed you last night. Thought you might need an ear. But I nearly fell over you. Found you hugging a dead hog. Surprised you didn't smell the animal."

"I was too angry."

Tom listened attentively to the other two men.

Clay waved the morning paper. "Have you seen this? Headline calls you the mumbo jumbo doctor."

Tom's eyes widened.

David swiped a hand through his hair and stared at the newspaper, dreading to hear what story had been written about last night's incident. Finally he reached out his hand. "Let me see that." *Benefit dinner ruined when mumbo jumbo doctor puts curse on woman.*

He drew his eyes closed, then opened them and frowned. "That's why the place is deserted today. She's ruined my practice."

"Nonsense. You can fight this," Clay said.

"Obviously you have not met Josephine Cline."

"I most certainly have. She's a wonderful young woman: compassionate, hardworking, very intelligent, civic-minded. . . ." His voice diminished. "Well, she is."

David glanced heavenward. "Does she by any chance have a twin sister?"

Clay chuckled. "Say, you're not in love?"

"Are you crazy? She's the kind of woman you want to stay as far away from as possible. I was considering China. Or maybe it's time to return to Africa. What am I going to do about this mess?"

"Get the paper to print a retraction. Make amends with the people you've alienated."

"That's the best you can come up with? Those men I alienated were on my list for funding the city cleanup project." He smiled sheepishly. "You're on my list, too."

"Practice on me then. Don't look so glum. You were going to make appointments with half of these people anyway. Now you have your foot in the door. It'll make for a good laugh."

"Sounds good. But you're not the one who's going to risk getting the boot."

Clay tilted his head. "On the other hand, there is another option."

"What?"

"You could let Josephine Cline get her wish. Pack up. Go abroad."

"I won't do it! But what about Randolph Cline?"

"My advice would be to stay clear of him. He dotes on his daughter."

"Naturally. Two of a kind."

"Well if you've got things under control here, I'll mosey on home."

"Thanks again, Clay. For everything."

"Think nothing of it. Only don't let me down."

David gave a reluctant nod. Clay exited. David released a weary sigh and turned to find Tom watching him. "What?" Tom quickly busied himself, and David started back to check on his only patient.

❧❧

Two days passed. On the third, Randolph Cline brought home some startling news for Josie. "I ran a thorough investigation on your Dr. Spokes."

"Father, please."

"The results indicate that he's a young eccentric, but he's not a quack."

Josie fingered the fabric of her skirt. "But the frog."

He handed her the newspaper retraction. "The woman's illness was in her head. Wheeler tricked her, but he did it for her own good. As I said, he's not ordinary. But he has a certificate to practice medicine. He's apprenticed under Daniel Drake, and he runs a reputable clinic."

Josephine frowned at the article. "What about taking payment for trickery?"

"I don't know why he did that. Doesn't seem ethical."

"And the way he was dressed?"

"Every morning he mingles with the poor. My man followed him. It's some kind of a disguise, to blend in."

Josie felt sick. "A costume." She pressed her hands against her stomach. "What have I done?"

"Don't worry your pretty little head about it. Like I said, he's a colleague of Drake's. I don't care much for his kind. Full of crazy ideas about improving conditions of the city, social injustice. Wouldn't feel bad if we had run him off."

Furrowing her forehead, Josie considered her father's explanation. "Thank you. You've given me much to think about."

She quietly brewed over the matter for several days even though everyone else in her household deemed the incident over. Even her mother brushed the mention of it away, saying, "Trust your father, Dear. He always knows best in these matters."

And Josie tried. She really did. She even prayed about it. But the nausea and worry remained until finally she determined to make amends.

❧❧

The clinic was an ordinary building from the outside. The district was not shabby or run-down exactly, yet there was nothing prestigious about it either. Josephine wondered if Dr. Wheeler had purposely chosen its location. Doctors were judged by the people they treated, affluencewise. Or was there something lacking in the doctor's abilities as she had at first imagined? Something kept him here, ministering to the middle lower-class population.

She pushed the door open, and a young plumpish man looked up from a set of books. "I'm Tom Langdon, Dr. Wheeler's assistant. Have a seat, Miss. There's a wait."

"I would like to speak with Dr. Wheeler. Is he available?"

"Are you a patient?"

"I need to see the doctor." Josephine nodded. "I'll wait my turn. Is he always this busy?"

"Sometimes." The young man leaned forward. His cheeks went pink. "There was a bit of a scandal about the doctor, and the clinic was empty for a couple days. But it was all just a rumor some woman made up. Dr. Wheeler's on the up and up. Anyway, I think everyone who was sick was holding off until they realized that, and now they all showed up at once."

Josephine felt her cheeks warm. "I hope he is as good as you claim." On the wall above a bookcase was a framed medical certificate. Josie inspected it, then seated herself. Tom Langdon left her and disappeared behind one of the curtained sections. Across the room, behind the desk where the doctor's assistant had been sitting, was a row of shelves containing jars of human organs and a skull. Why did doctors have to display such gory specimens? Crossing her arms, she planned what she would say to Dr. Wheeler and wondered how he would respond to her presence.

A male patient soon appeared from one of the curtained areas. He nodded at her and passed before he exited the clinic. After that the assistant poked his head out from behind the curtain. "You may have this room, Miss."

Josie went into the narrow room with only two solid walls. Much was crammed into the tiny area with a table taking up one entire end. On it were a microscope, a stack of papers, an array of splints, medicine, ointments, and a jar of leeches. Another table occupied the center of the room. Once the assistant left, Josie, feeling impish, hoisted herself up onto that table. A series of groans sounded from the other side of the curtain. Next she recognized the doctor's voice.

Mrs. Patterson rubbed the small of her back to show Dr. Wheeler where the pain was located.

"Here?" he asked, prodding the spot.

"Ah, that's it."

David felt the hard stays of a corset and frowned. "How long has this been hurting?"

"About a month."

"Could you walk across the room and back, please?" He watched as Mrs. Patterson's high-topped boots clapped the floorboards. Her hip jutted out more on the left side. "Mm-hmm. I see the problem."

"You do? Can you cure it?"

"No, but you can."

The woman's chin tipped upward. "What do you mean?"

"Sit down and let me explain." Mrs. Patterson eased into a chair. "You have reached a crucial time in your life. The first signs of back pain. You have two choices. You can remedy the situation, and since this has only been hurting about a month, hopefully the pain will gradually leave until you are back to normal. Or you can continue as you are until the pain is unbearable and the problem is irreparable."

"Well!" she huffed. "Of course I wish to remedy the situation. Otherwise

I would not have come to your clinic today."

"It's very simple really. Only most women object."

"Quit with the riddles, Doctor."

"Get rid of the corset."

"Why! I never!" Mrs. Patterson's face reddened.

"You must carefully consider whether you wish to be free of pain or fashionable. The corset is contrary to the way the body is designed to function. I am counting on women like you to spread the truth. We must put an end to this harmful tradition. Do you have the courage to join me in this new healthy manner of living?"

Mrs. Patterson carefully considered his recommendation. After a moment, when her face had returned more to its original hue, she said, "I do believe you are right, Doctor. My corset is going into the hearth."

"Good. And let me tell you a secret." Mrs. Patterson leaned close to him, and David whispered into her ear. "Your husband will love it."

"Oh, Doctor."

"Try this treatment and return in two weeks to report your progress."

David backed out of Mrs. Patterson's compartment and pulled back the curtain to the adjoining room. He turned. The canvas went limp in his hands. Josephine Cline challenged him with her brown gaze. He had to squelch the urge to flee. But as he stood motionless, little nudges of reason worked their way into his consciousness. *Now's your chance to clear up past misunderstandings. She's only flesh and blood, nothing worse.* He jerked the curtain closed behind him and faced his adversary.

"Miss Cline. What can I do for you?"

"I have this pain in my stomach. Sometimes in my head."

David scrutinized her. "Is this another one of your games?"

"Aren't you going to ask me when it started, as you do your other patients?"

"So I can add eavesdropping to your misdeeds?"

She shrugged. "The walls are thin. Go on. Ask me when it started."

David crossed his arms. "When did your symptoms start, Miss Cline?"

"The moment I learned the truth about you. I've felt horrible ever since."

"And this truth is?"

Josie jumped off her perch and gave her skirts a yank where they had caught on the edge of the table. "I am trying to apologize."

David shrugged. "It is something, I suppose. Although the damage caused by your accusations is probably irreparable."

"You could have told me what you were up to."

"Why? I don't even know you."

"I may have been wrong about your medical background. But I wasn't wrong about you. I still believe you are an arrogant, pompous man."

As the heat crept along the top of David's ears and over his brow, he realized that he was losing control of the situation again, heaping coal on the lady's boiler engine. And she had been right about one thing. The walls were thin. If he didn't calm her down, she would run off any patients that he still had. Ignoring the mounting irritation he felt and intentionally softening his tone, he said, "Forgive me for my rudeness. You caught me by surprise. Can we take this discussion elsewhere? Perhaps I can buy you dinner?"

"What?" She stared at him as if he had just eaten a mouse or done something equally outrageous.

"I have patients waiting, but I also want to get this matter straightened out. Now that the shock of seeing you is over, I believe I can behave like a gentleman. How about the Emerald Inn? I can pick you up around seven o'clock."

"No."

"Miss Cline—"

"I will meet you there."

He cocked his brow. "Oh? Tonight then?"

With a nod and flurry of skirts and petticoat, Josephine agreed and disappeared.

Relief washed over David to be rid of her. But quickly following came a dread of what the evening had yet to hold. He stared at the jar of leeches across the room. He certainly was not arrogant or pompous. But he supposed he had behaved badly.

Chapter 5

By six o'clock, David felt as if he had caught Miss Cline's symptoms. His queasy stomach and dull head reminded him of his meetings with Vernon Thorpe and Quinton Wallace. But both of those meetings had turned out fine. Only Zachary Caulfield had not forgiven him yet. Clay Buchanan had correctly predicted that the publicity he had received at the benefit dinner incident would indirectly benefit his cause. Still, tonight was a different matter. He wished he could somehow get out of his dinner date with the explosive Miss Cline.

Still dressed in his clinic clothes, he sat sprawled, his legs stretched out in front of him. One arm dangled down, and he stroked the cat's head. "Gratuity, what if this is another one of her games? What if Randolph Cline shows up instead? Or a policeman?" His tone cheered. "Maybe she will not show up at all." But something told him that he would not be so fortunate.

"Mew."

"Time already?" As if facing the executioner, David rose. He checked his hair against a mirror and put on his top hat. The moment he opened the door, Gratuity whisked out without a backward glance. "Thanks for the moral support," he shouted after her.

Several minutes early, he secured a table inside the green, ornately trimmed restaurant and put on his professional face—the one he used when dealing with incorrigible patients.

He felt her presence the moment she entered the room. Or did he smell her? *Lavender.* Now he remembered how the soft flowery scent always enveloped her. Its fragrance had lingered in his clinic for several minutes after she had left. It wasn't a bad smell, though he preferred the stringent odors at the clinic.

The waiter ushered her toward him. David sprang up, his chair grating across the floorboards, and waited. "Good evening, Miss Cline. Please, have a seat." He turned to the waiter. "Give us a moment, please?"

"Yes, Sir."

Josephine gave David a tremulous smile. She seemed vulnerable. *Impossible.* He smiled back. "Shall we place our orders before we begin a discussion? I would recommend the pork."

"Spoken like a true citizen of Porkopolis," Josephine said.

Once the waiter had taken their orders, David tapped a long forefinger on the table. "You were right. I should have explained my behavior to you that first day. I also detest frauds. You injured my pride. Perhaps, like you say, I am arrogant."

Josie sighed. "If you can entertain the thought, you probably are not. My pride was also wounded." She looked down at her lap. "Every time I think about how you were tossed out of Mr. Caulfield's dinner, I feel sick." She met his gaze again. "I'm sorry."

"Let's put it behind us." She nodded, but David could see she was not ready to do that. "Something more troubles you?"

"Do you really go out looking for patients in the. . ."

"Slums. You can say the word." When a flush crept up her neck to her face and her eyes took on that familiar brown snappish glint, David realized it was true. He was arrogant. "Forgive me. I have this problem. I go out of my way to cater to the poor, the disabled, and the elderly; but to the young, the beautiful, and the rich I am hard, crass, and—"

"Boorish."

"Er, rather."

"So you do put on a shabby costume and go down to the slums?"

"Yes. And I won't apologize for that. I love doing it."

Her gaze softened, reminding him of the brown leather cover on his Bible. Something about it was endearing. Her voice softened as well. "I do, too."

For a moment he had to struggle to comprehend their conversation. "I seem to remember a velvet cloak and a blue silk gown."

Her eyes sparked again. "Not literally. I want to help the poor, put an end to social injustice. I want to do all those things that Father despises you for."

"I shall sleep better tonight knowing your father's low opinion of me."

She chuckled. Her laughter had a musical lilt. Their food came. After awhile, Josephine tilted her head, fascinating him with her spattering of freckles. Usually her face had been too blushed—either from anger or embarrassment—for them to shine through. She asked, "Why did you accept Mrs. Schroeder's payment?"

"Most people do not like to receive charity. It's insulting."

"That's nonsense. Why I'm a member of several charitable societies."

"Is that a fact? And you've met the recipients then?"

"Well, no. But I know from others who have that the things they receive are appreciated."

"Perhaps they are needed. Medical treatment is needed. But it destroys a person's self-respect to have to accept charity. It restores a person's dignity to pay a fair price for services or products. That's why I take whatever kind of payment they offer. I do not require it, but I accept it. There's a difference. I'm not a thief."

The freckles disappeared again. "I understand your reasoning but do not necessarily agree that people always feel that way about getting their needs met."

"When I first went into practice, I offered to donate my time. Dr. Drake warned me that I'd be better received taking a modest payment for my services. I soon learned he was right, although I should have known better just by watching my folks."

"Father says that the needy should be glad for whatever they get."

David felt a prick of anger over Randolph Cline's perception of things. It was a pity that his daughter seemed to be following in his footsteps.

"What did you mean about your folks?" she asked.

"They were missionaries. I have learned to apply some of the same principles that they used in interacting with the natives in my dealings with. . ."

"Folks from the slums? Trouble saying the word, Doctor?"

"Has anyone ever told you that you have an impertinent tongue?"

She smiled. "No, but someone did allude to something about an unbridled insulting mouth."

David pushed away his plate. "A very pretty one also. It's been a pleasure, Miss Cline. May I walk you home?"

"No, thank you. The slate is clean? Between us?"

"Spotless."

"I'll be on my way then. Thank you for the dinner. It was enlightening and very gracious of you to suggest it."

He watched her depart. Such a tiny waist. She must wear one of those ridiculous corsets. Though he doubted its necessity. After she was gone, the fragrance of lavender still lingered. David scrunched his forehead trying to remember what the medicinal value of lavender was. Ah, to relax. To relieve nervous tension. How ironic. He found it titillating.

⌘

The following morning was Saturday, and the Clines always breakfasted together on that particular day of the week before they left to go their separate ways. Normally, Josie and her father used the time to discuss some interesting topic. Today she could not get Dr. Wheeler out of her mind.

"Father, what makes a person eccentric?"

"Stubbornness. They refuse to accept the normal rules of propriety, do not fit in with society, so forth."

"You think it's a negative thing then?"

"Of course. Don't you?"

"I suppose."

"If everyone just did what they felt like doing rather than conforming to the rules laid out by society, whatever that society—a city, a business, a family—then the world would be chaotic. Don't you see, Josie?"

"But what if that eccentricity really helps others? What if a person's actions only seem outrageous because they are uncommon in that the average person does not possess enough courage to perform them? For instance—say soneone has a particular need. The eccentric person, putting his own needs aside, risks ridicule or danger in an effort to help meet that other person's need. Could worry that we might be called upon to duplicate such a selfless life lead us to say the action was abnormal or eccentric when really it was brave?"

Randolph peered at her over his tea. "Are you thinking about that doctor again?"

"Perhaps I am."

"All right. Let's consider him. He makes the perfect example. Here's a man who could spend his time treating the sick. When one has a diploma and a clinic, wouldn't you think that taking care of the sick people would be the thing he should do? But, no. Instead, he wants to hire immigrants to sweep the city clean of refuse. Only he doesn't want to use his money. No. He comes to me and asks me to fund his ridiculous idea. Then he threatens me by saying my family will die of cholera if I don't. Now, that's eccentric. And there's not a good thing about it."

Josie was amazed. "He threatened us with cholera?"

"He certainly did. Made me feel like it was all my fault that the city has problems."

"Do not talk about that disease in this house," Mrs. Cline clipped. "I shall not allow it."

"Sorry, Dear," Mr. Cline said. "I did get carried away, didn't I?"

"Sorry, Mother," Josie dittoed.

"Apology accepted. Now let's talk about something pleasant."

Everyone studied their eggs and bacon, trying to come up with a topic.

"Did you know that the orphanage has doubled since it opened its doors? Now that's a good thing, isn't it?" Mrs. Cline asked.

Josie blinked. She knew her mother meant well.

"All those poor children," Mrs. Cline murmured. "See how fortunate you are, Josie?"

Josie blotted her mouth with her cloth napkin to keep from smiling. "Yes, Mother." The room grew quiet again, and Josie remembered Dr. Wheeler's claim that people didn't like to receive charity. She wished to test his theory. "Mother, what are you doing today? Would you like to go with me to visit Mrs. Schroeder?"

"Why I suppose I could."

"Do you think we could take one of those comforters you made?"

Mrs. Cline's eyes lit. "Oh, yes. Let's."

Randolph Cline pushed away from the table. "You ladies be careful. Take the carriage."

"I'd rather walk, Father. It's not far."

"But your mother—"

"If Josie recommends it, I'm certainly courageous enough."

Mr. Cline covered his smile in his napkin. "Well, I suppose. . ."

Mrs. Cline pecked her husband on the cheek. "Don't you have a land deal or something to attend to?"

"I can take a hint." He picked up his topper. "Good day, ladies."

"Bye, Father."

As soon as he was gone, Josie turned to her mother. "Let's go pick out a comforter. I'm sure Mrs. Schroeder will be most appreciative."

Chapter 6

Josie slowed her pace to match her mother's as they started toward the canal that cut horizontally through their city. Glancing over, Josie asked, "How do you feel?"

"This walking does me good. My back was a bit stiff this morning. I believe it is all the sewing that I do."

Josie leaned close so Charles couldn't hear. "Have you ever considered going without a corset? I hear it helps the back."

"You sound just like your father."

So there *was* something that Dr. Wheeler and Father agreed upon. Josie bit back a smile. They passed rows of rectangular blocks of houses and the occasional conspicuous mansion.

The first of autumn's leaves made the cobblestones crunchy. Squashing the brown and yellow bits of beech, poplar, and hickory beneath her boots, she prayed. *Lord, why does this man intrigue me so?* She lifted her gaze upward. Gilded church spires speckled the horizon. Overhead, fluffy clouds sailed by. God's presence was subtle yet all encompassing.

Man's presence was also evident. Smoke poured from chimneys of the steam foundries. Behind them, steamboats hissed past Cincinnati's busy quay on the Ohio River. And when they reached the canal, the stench of decaying animal flesh overpowered the fresh scent of autumn.

Josie looked over her shoulder before crossing the canal. "How are you doing, Charles?"

The immigrant boy peeked from around the bundle of comforter. "Fine I am, Miss Cline."

They crossed, and soon Josie recognized Mrs. Schroeder's building. Upon their last visit Charles had informed her it was the one by the sausage man. "Here it is, Mother." She rushed forward and opened the side door. They climbed the steps to the third floor, and Josie knocked.

Mrs. Schroeder's face broke into a smile as soon as she recognized Josie and saw her son. She motioned them in and rattled off a string of foreign words.

Charles was crushed in his mother's embrace, unable to reciprocate with the bundle in his arms.

"Tell her that we would like her to have the comforter, Charles," Josie urged.

Josie watched mother and son converse.

Josie watched the woman's expressions change and wondered what was being said. She was able to relax when Mrs. Schroeder chuckled, put her arm around her son's shoulder, and motioned for Charles to place the comforter on the bed. The next thing she knew, they were being led to a small table. Josie and her mother took the only two chairs, and Mrs. Schroeder brought out an apple dish and made them a pot of tea.

"What is this?" Mrs. Cline asked.

"Strudel," Charles replied. "Is *gut.*"

Josie felt very guilty taking the woman's food, but Dr. Wheeler's explanation about accepting payment helped her to enjoy the light meal. It tasted scrumptious, melting in her mouth.

When they rose to leave, Charles translated the farewells and said that he would catch up with them.

"Father will have your hide if you do not," Josie warned, then led her mother down the stairs and back outside. Another pang of guilt accosted her, this time from remembering how she had chased after Dr. Wheeler, hurling her insults. Amends were made, she reminded herself. She must put it behind her.

"That was so rewarding, wasn't it, Dear?" Mrs. Cline asked on the walk home.

"Yes, but the money Mrs. Schroeder received for Charles's apprenticeship will not sustain her forever. She's going to have to get a job."

"Maybe the women's workhouse can find her something. That reminds me; I've got to find someone to replace Dr. Fitch. He was scheduled to hold a clinic for the women but got called away because of family concerns. I could ask Dr. Cook, but he's so crotchety."

"I know the perfect person for your clinic. Dr. Wheeler."

"Now, Josephine, how can you say such a thing? After all the trouble that man caused."

"I caused the trouble. He told me that it's his life's work to care for the poor."

"When did he tell you that?"

Josie did not want to admit that she had met with the doctor. "When we spoke, of course. And Father told me where his clinic is. I'll ask him if you wish."

"I don't know what your father would say about it."

"Let me handle Father, and consider it done. Now, about Mrs. Schroeder getting a job: Do you think we should discuss it with Charles?"

"What to ask me?" panted the young man.

Josie turned. "Charles! What are you doing with that comforter? You were supposed to leave that with your mother."

Mrs. Cline wheeled about. "Oh, no. Didn't you understand that was a gift for your mother?"

His shoulders stiffened. "This kind she does not use. German feather covers she likes."

Josie fingered the puffy cloth. Her voice saddened. "She rejected our gift?"

"To you, we thank."

"Well, Josephine. There are plenty of others who might use this comforter." Mrs. Cline's voice was prickly.

"Are there, Mother?"

The older woman's voice softened. "There is always the orphanage."

Josie felt a rush of tears and pinched the bridge of her nose. "Charles, would you like me to carry it for awhile?"

"No, Miss Cline. Fine I am."

David grimaced, then continued to clean the decaying skin tissue surrounding the snakebite. He reapplied a compress and bandage.

"Looks nasty. Doesn't it, Doc?"

"Did you stay off your leg like I advised?"

"Not entirely."

"This is a serious matter. Some folks die from snakebite. You don't want to lose your foot, do you?"

"You didn't tell me I could lose my foot."

"How did you get here?"

His patient looked at the floor. "Walked."

"I was afraid of that. I'll have my assistant take you home. You are to stay off this leg until I tell you different. I'll come out to your place morning after next."

"I'd appreciate that. And I'll stay in bed. I promise."

"But if it looks any worse, you get word to me, and I'll be out sooner." The patient nodded. "Yes, Doc. Thank you."

David swiped an arm across his brow and opened the curtain to his next patient. His stride broke. "Miss Cline?" He eyed her carefully. "What brings you back to the clinic?"

Josephine slid down off the table, her skirts swishing around her ankles. "Dr. Wheeler, I need your help. Oh, don't raise your eyebrow at me. Did you know you have a habit of doing that?"

"No, I didn't. What kind of help?"

"Mother volunteers at the women's workhouse. It is a society which finds jobs for women and meets various needs."

"I'm aware of the organization. Go on."

"We were wondering if you would be able to hold a clinic. There goes that brow again. It's quite intimidating, you know."

He doubted that anything could intimidate Miss Cline. "When?"

"At your convenience. You did mention that you had a heart for the poor, the—"

"I remember what I said. How about Friday? I could be available from noon on."

"Perfect. Mother will be so happy."

"But I have a condition. Now you're doing it. The eyebrow thing."

"I am not. Am I?"

"Very prettily, too."

Josephine's face reddened. "What is your condition, Doctor?"

"That you serve as my assistant."

"But you have an assistant. Tom Langdon. Can't you bring him?"

"Tom will need to cover here. Sorry, that's my condition."

"But I know nothing about medicine." Her gaze flittered around the room. "Do you think I'm capable?"

"I do."

Josie stepped forward and held out her hand. "Very well. It's a deal."

David shook the small gloved hand and sealed their agreement. "I'm looking forward to it." Her gaze softened, and David suddenly felt uncomfortable in a nice sort of way. He broke away from her gaze and asked in a rather gruff voice. "Have they held clinics before?"

"Yes."

"I guess they'll know what needs to be done to prepare."

"I'll check with Mother and let you know if she has any questions."

"I'm curious, Miss Cline. Does your father know about this?"

"No, Dr. Wheeler. He does not."

"Do you think you should tell him?"

"He says you are eccentric. I'm sure he would not approve."

David wondered if Miss Cline also thought he was eccentric. Of course she must. But there was something else in her gaze that held approval. Why not? Wasn't Miss Cline a bit of a bluestocking? "Ordinary" was probably not even in her vocabulary.

"On Friday then," she was saying.

David strode forward and pulled back the curtain for her. "Miss Cline?" She paused. "Yes?"

"The next time you call, you have merely to tell my assistant you wish to speak with me. You do not need to wait until it's your turn as if you were a patient."

"Are you sure? He has not been very cooperative in the past."

"I'll speak with him."

"No, thank you. I'll take care of it, Doctor. Good day."

David watched her depart. She stopped in front of Tom. "Why does he keep such gory things in his office?" she asked.

"To impress his patients," Tom answered with a blush on his plump cheeks.

David could not hear her reply after that, but whatever she said, it made Tom smile. Did she always cause a stir—dazzling, infuriating, affecting in some way everyone she met? She had certainly turned his world upside down. He had never wanted to see her again, had even contemplated China. Now she seemed to have him at her beck and call.

It was as if she felt his eyes upon her back, because just before she exited the clinic, she turned around and gave him a little wave. David gave her a stiff nod, feeling the heat rush up his neck and face. Tom shook his head as if he understood, then asked their snakebite patient. "You ready to go?"

Jerking his gaze away from the door, David pulled back the adjoining curtain.

Chapter 7

On Friday David easily recognized Mrs. Cline, remembering her from the Caulfields' benefit dinner—the one he wished he could blot from his memory. From her expression, Mrs. Cline seemed to also recall the events of that calamitous evening. Josephine had not mentioned that her mother held ill feelings toward him, but it was only logical that she might, for both women lived under Randolph Cline's influence.

As she approached him, she tilted her head slightly as if she studied an enigma. But her voice was pleasant. "So kind of you to come, Dr. Wheeler."

"I am happy to oblige."

She turned to retrace her steps. "If you will follow me, I will show you where to set up your clinic."

They passed a large open workroom where a group of women unraveled short lengths of rope. David was familiar with the procedure of removing the oakum for use in caulking ship seams. Others were busy with sewing projects. Several cast him curious looks. He and Mrs. Cline rounded a corner. Already a line of women had formed.

"Here we are. Let me know when you've finished attending to the sick. I'll send you some new applicants to determine if they are able-bodied or infirm."

David addressed the women waiting in line as they passed. "I need a minute to prepare." Nods and murmurs followed. Then he thanked Mrs. Cline.

"Josephine should be along shortly."

"Good. Her help will be appreciated. I like to have another female present in situations like this."

Mrs. Cline departed, and David laid out his instruments and medicine. The reason he had given her for asking for Josephine's assistance was not the only reason. His curiosity had not been satiated regarding her. It would be a good test of her character—setting her up in a situation where she would be called upon to respond to the needs of others. He supposed he judged everyone by this standard though he knew it was not fair to do so. Every person had their own niche in life. Even so, he had to know if Josephine would meet his particular expectations.

The door opened. Josephine wore a gray wool dress. It was very becoming. Practical. He liked it.

"Looks like we'll have a busy afternoon."

"Hello, Miss Cline. I hoped you would come."

"I promised, didn't I? What can I do to help?"

"You may admit our first patient."

This was a middle-aged, reed-thin woman with a burdensome cough. First, David put on his stethoscope and listened to the woman's frail chest. Next, he poured some medicine in a spoon, instructing Josephine to administer the dosage. As he prepared a small bottle for the woman to take with her when she left, Josephine spoke soothingly to the woman, even eliciting a smile from the drawn face.

David drew Josephine aside. "She needs nourishment. Can the workhouse provide a hearty soup for her and any of the others whom I designate?"

"I'm sure they can. I'll go make arrangements if you like."

"Yes. Take her along and see that she is cared for. But please hurry back. I need you."

Josephine smiled. "I will."

Turning back to the woman, he said, "You need to eat well and rest until this cough is gone. Miss Cline will see that both are arranged."

The woman left with Josephine. David admitted the next patient who was pregnant but appeared healthy.

He examined her and two others before Josephine returned. "Just write down the names of the women who need food, some other special item, or time off work. Their addresses are on file, and it will be taken care of," she said.

"Good. Thank you. I should have asked about that before we got started."

"Mother apologizes for not giving you the information. She admits that she was distracted. Rather intrigued with you."

"Oh?"

"Your name did come up at our dinner table after the night of our. . . incident."

"She must trust your judgment to allow me to step into this facility."

"I hadn't thought about it that way. I guess I did put her on the spot. But I think she likes you."

David felt intrigued by the way Miss Cline's voice softened when she admitted it, almost as if it mirrored her own feelings. But Miss Cline was not one to hold back her thoughts. If she felt that way, she would just say so. And she hadn't. It occurred to him that while he had subconsciously been subjecting Miss Cline to testing, she was probably doing the same to him. He wondered if he would pass her inspection. Probably no one could ever score high enough to compete with her father.

"I appreciate your mother's open-minded spirit. Now let's admit the next patient."

The line finally dwindled, and the new applicants were also examined. Well after dark, Miss Cline sank into a chair and rested the side of her face in the cup of her hand. "I'm exhausted. How do you do this every day?"

"Not every day is this busy. Can I hail a hackney for you or walk you home?"

"Yes, but let me help you clean up first so that we can both leave."

Not lacking in Miss Cline's demeanor was perseverance. He liked that. In fact, he hadn't found anything negative about their teamwork. It seemed that she was not going to disappoint him after all.

Outside the women's workhouse, David held up a gas lamp. The bleak brick building with its dreary stone wall loomed behind them. No hackney was within sight. He hated to send her back inside again. "I'll have to hunt one down for us."

"Wait." She lightly touched his forearm. "That's too much trouble. I'll just walk home."

David gazed down the dark street, not knowing how long it would take to locate a hackney. "Only if you allow me to escort you, Miss Cline. It's the least I can do. I wouldn't have made it today without your help. I'd still be working, and women would still be lined—"

"Yes. That would be nice. But please, call me Josephine."

He offered the support of his arm, and she took it. At first they walked in silence. The lantern provided light for their path and was especially helpful when they encountered a new construction area and found it necessary to dodge bricks and trash.

"Careful. This litter is so dangerous," he said.

"The city is expanding rapidly. That is a good thing. Father's business is booming."

Besides being in the textile business, Mr. Cline was a land developer. Quite possibly the materials strewn across the way were results of his very own projects. David could barely hold back his contempt for the sloppy conditions.

"Father would have come for me himself tonight, but he was taking a steam bath."

David stiffened.

"Did I say something wrong?"

"You are perceptive. Are you sure you want to hear my opinion?"

Her voice took on an edgy quality. "About my father?"

"About steam baths."

"Oh. What about them?"

"There's nothing harmful about them, but they're not beneficial either. I'd categorize them under leisure and relaxation. And please do not tell me that your father imbibes lobelia."

"But it is highly recommended for many ailments. A friend of Father's introduced him to its beneficial qualities."

"Zero. That's its medicinal value. I suppose he also takes the waters."

Josephine withdrew her hand. "I do not like your tone of voice."

"I'm sorry, but I believe that you should learn the proper use for the word *quack.*"

With that, she released an unfeminine grunt and hastened her pace away from him.

Realizing that she would most likely stumble and injure herself if she did not walk within the lantern's circle of light, David hurried after her, grabbing her arm. "Josephine, wait."

She jerked away and continued to walk. The lantern picked up some new structures, and he grabbed her arm again, "Look out. Stop."

Definitely angry now, Josephine stopped and whirled to face him. Her lips were firmly pressed together; her freckles stood out against her white face.

"I'm sorry," David said. "I didn't realize I was full of all that hostility. I. . . Please, forgive me."

She gave one nod but kept her distance from him as they commenced to walk. Silence invaded the blackness. David cleared his throat. "I worked beneath Dr. Drake. He is a marvelous physician. His genius far exceeds the medical field. He's been opposing the practices and the whole theory of steam and lobelia. It's something we feel so strongly about. I'm sorry I made it personal."

Silence continued to pervade, except for the sounds of boots on cobblestones and the rustling and chirps of night. David remembered the meeting in Mr. Cline's office and that Josephine's father had looked as if he had been experiencing pain. "How is your father's health?"

"He has some problems. But I'd rather not talk about them."

"All right. I don't suppose he would accept my help anyway."

"You are correct on that account. Well, Doctor, my street is just ahead. I can make it fine on my own now."

"I'll see you to your door."

"As you wish."

The silence prevailed, but the houses loomed larger. In Cincinnati, it was commonplace for the mansions and normal-sized houses to be mixed. As they approached the Cline residence, David felt as if a fist squeezed his heart. Any hopes he might have entertained about friendship with Josephine fled when he realized which house she claimed as her own. It was one he had oftentimes admired. It was outlandish and completely out of his class. It only solidified how wide the ravine was between him and the Clines.

"Here we are." Josephine turned toward him. She sounded as if her anger had finally subsided. "Thank you for everything. The clinic. Seeing me home."

"It has been my pleasure. If there is anything I can do to help again, I am at your service."

"Good evening," she said in a dejected tone.

He understood. It matched his feelings. The gulf between them was so vast, yet there was a part of him that wished he could explore the mystery of Josephine Cline.

As he walked home, he went over their past encounters. Every single time he saw her, he had been strongly affected. True, most often it had been adversely; still, she remained a challenge dangled in front of him. The challenge presented was to explore the many facets of this woman's explosive personality. Yet with every encounter he had discovered areas of contention.

She had not passed his test after all. He felt like a teacher who hated to give the low mark. Disappointment and sadness loomed darker than the night. And so he picked his way home. At least Gratuity would be there waiting, glad to see him. His stomach growled. He needed to eat something though he didn't know what to fix. Food and a good night's rest. Then he would feel better.

Oftentimes he felt this way after helping patients with illnesses that were painful or fatal. The only comfort he could find at such times was in his faith in God. The worn, brown leather Bible that waited on his bed appealed to him even more than a meal. His steps quickened.

Chapter 8

All things are full of labour, David read to himself, then said, "Listen to this, Gratuity. The king and writer of Ecclesiastes felt just like I do. 'The eye is not satisfied with seeing'—bodies weakened with sickness and pain—'nor the ear filled with hearing'—rattling coughs, fears of the aged, unfulfilled dreams."

"Meow."

"You, too, eh?" *Weary. That pretty well sums it up. I am weary.* Ever since he had gone to the clinic at Josephine's request two weeks earlier, his spirit was depressed. The melancholy that had struck him outside the Clines' opulent residence had settled in and nested. His outlook was as bleak as the chill that had swept through the city, bringing with it the onset of sickness.

"Tonight there's a lecture on Indian land treaties. Dr. Drake suggested I attend. Maybe he's right. I'm not stretching my mind enough. I need to rise above this, somehow."

"Meow."

❧

"You're not going to another lecture, Josie," her mother scolded. "About next the young men will be calling you a bluestocking."

"They already are, and you very well know it. But I don't care. That just shows how shallow men are these days. All except Father, of course. And he is looking forward to our attending it together."

"I suppose. . . Perhaps I should have a talk with him about dragging you to these functions."

"Nonsense. Ready, Darling?"

"Yes, Father." Josephine placed a juicy kiss on her mother's cheek. "Don't worry, Mother. It will give you wrinkles."

Mrs. Cline smiled. "Oh, run along then. Both of you."

"Sure you don't want to join us?" Mr. Cline asked, giving her a squeeze.

"No. I've got some sewing. Maybe next time I'll go."

Josie and her father chuckled all the way to the carriage over that possibility. They were among the last to arrive and slipped quietly into two vacant seats near the back. The speaker had already taken his place and announced his topic, Indian land treaties.

Since Tecumseh died in the War of 1812 and his brother The Prophet more recently, Ohio has been at peace. But only because of mass Indian removal, and now new treaties are being signed to take away Indian land.

Josie listened attentively until her eyes meandered over the backs of the men and women between her and the speaker and snagged upon a particular set of shoulders. She studied the man, wishing he would turn so she could see if it was David.

A coughing spell from across the room caught his attention. He turned sideways. It was Dr. Wheeler. What a lovely opportunity with such a perfect line of vision to discreetly scrutinize the man who was even more fascinating than the lecture. His face was lean and pleasant. She wondered why she had not noticed before how incredibly handsome he was. His hat was off, revealing a shock of wavy blond hair parted on the side and full above the ears. Sideburns a darker shade of blond lined his jaw and became one with the even darker beard that encircled his fine chiseled chin.

His blue eyes looked concerned. She had to admire the way the physician in him always oozed out. She imagined that he was mentally diagnosing and would not be surprised to see him rise and cross the room to treat the man with the coughing spell.

The sick man rose and hurried outside. Heads turned. The speaker hesitated until the room quieted again, then continued. And not to disappoint her, Dr. Wheeler rose and followed the man outside, black bag in hand. He was the most stubborn and opinionated man she'd ever met, but at least his heart was in the right place.

What a coincidence that he should be in attendance. Ever since she had helped him at the clinic and they had argued, she had tried to put him out of her mind. He was trouble—had been from the start. But she had not been able to dismiss him, and the more she had thought about him and their last discussion, the easier it had been to forgive him for it. Not because she agreed with him, but because she could sympathize with him and understand why he felt so strongly about the steam baths.

And now, just seeing him stirred up that strange longing that she always felt regarding him. It must be her natural curiosity. Father said it was a good thing. Mother thought it was part of the reason she was still single at twenty-two. For Josie it only kept life interesting.

The doctor reappeared and took his seat again. Josie felt her heartbeat quicken. This handsome intriguing man aroused unexplainable desires. She began to imagine what a friendship with him might be like. But how could she get close when he displayed such an indifferent attitude toward her?

Although the plight of the Indians interested her, she could not wait until the lecture was finished, and finally it did come to an end. But before she could reach the doctor, he was headed for the door. She grabbed up her skirts and hurried after him.

"Dr. Wheeler." His back visibly stiffened. He turned, and she gave him her most engaging smile, determined to penetrate his aloof exterior. "It is so good to see you again."

"Josephine, I am surprised. I did not notice you in the crowd."

"You sat in my line of vision. You look tired. Your practice must be busy."

He shrugged. "Just the usual. But I have felt a bit tired."

"Perhaps you need a diversion."

He smiled. "That's why I came tonight."

She plunged ahead, briefly touching his coat sleeve. "There is a new exhibit at the Western museum. I was planning to go see it next week."

"We go about in different circles, Josephine."

"Nonsense. We are both here tonight, aren't we? Will you be my escort?" The doctor studied her. She felt the heat rise up her neck. "And please, do not cock your brow at me."

He smiled. "If I refuse, you will probably do something dreadful. Something my practical brain cannot even conjure up. It's frightening. I have learned from past experience, when the lady speaks, I need to listen."

"It is settled then. You can pick me up at one o'clock on Saturday. Be prepared. I intend to present you to Father. Here he comes now. Be off, and I'll see you next week."

The doctor chuckled and shook his head at her before he ducked out the door, and she felt a little taste of victory.

"Was that your Dr. Spokes?" Randolph asked.

"Why, yes it was. He's a very fascinating man. In fact, he is taking me to the Western museum next Saturday.

"I do not like it, Josie."

"Please, Father. Don't cause a scene."

Randolph frowned. "We'll talk about him later."

❧❧

David almost wished he had his melancholy back. At least it had been consistently reliable and had not interfered with his work. Instead, after seeing Josephine again, for the remainder of the week he had been on an emotional seesaw. The highs were: Josephine was healthy, fresh, revitalizing. Spring in the middle of autumn. His days were not so monotonous, but rather they were filled with anticipation of what their next encounter might bring. No doubt when they attended the museum together, their outing would include another lively discussion.

But when the seesaw dipped, his thoughts scraped the ground. Probably there would be a controversy, and very likely even a scene when Mr. Cline entered the picture. And even if everything went well, in the end he would get hurt. As intriguing as she was, he knew that a friendship with her would never work.

He remembered his boyhood days and how intrigued he had been with African insects. Even though he knew better, many times he had held on until he was either bitten or stung. By the end of the week, he had convinced himself that it would be better to release Josephine before the same thing happened with her. Somehow when they attended the museum together, he would convince her that it was for the best.

❧❧

The hackney pulled up outside the Clines' residence, and David climbed down and went to Josephine's door. A servant admitted him and told him where to wait. It was not long before she appeared—a vision, just as she had been at the benefit dinner. Her beauty sent a foreboding feeling up his spine. He needed to put on his guard.

"You look splendid," she said.

"I believe I was supposed to say that. You are quite lovely."

"And you are fortunate this time. Father is gone."

He escorted her out and helped her into the hackney. It lurched forward.

"I never know what to expect from you," she said. "Sometimes you are dressed in rags. Other times you are the epitome of fashion."

"Let's not exaggerate, shall we?"

"You choose the topic then, Doctor."

"We can talk about fashion. Did you know that wearing a cravat too tight is unhealthy?"

"I did not. Do you suppose that styles will change to accommodate comfort?"

"By all means. One day we will all be wearing sacks again."

Josephine smiled. "After everyone else conforms, then maybe I shall wear a sack. I believe you would do it today if it were to help someone."

It was the way she softened her voice again that squeezed his heart. He felt his guard slipping, and he swallowed. "I believe we have arrived." The coach lurched to a stop. David opened the door and jumped down, offering her the aid of his hand. "Shall we?"

The new exhibit was full of outrageous art: a life-size painting of a maniac, an anaconda devouring a horse and rider, and Col. David Crockett grinning the opossum off a tree. As they toured the museum, Josephine was all that was charming and sweet. He knew that if he was to stick to his plans, he was going to have to speak with Josephine before she endeared herself further, or worse, before he drowned in her sea of loveliness and perfection.

"Josephine, let's leave this crowded room," he whispered. "It's not healthy to breathe in all this stuffy air."

"By all means, I commend my health into your capable hands."

They entered a room of science, and he turned to face her. "I wish you would not do this," he said.

"What? What am I doing?"

"You are being too charming for my own good. This is going nowhere."

"I do not understand."

"Us. It won't work."

"I do not intend to let you analyze our friendship with logical deductions."

"You are too late. I have already done so."

"You have weighed the pros and cons and found me wanting?"

"No. Not you. You are witty, vivacious, and dangerous. It is me. I do not have time to exert energies in such entertainments. I have aspirations, causes, very serious day-to-day issues, boring things that fill my life. I have no time for amusement and games, engaging as you are. If you respect me and care for me at all, you will honor my wishes."

"You're afraid of Father. I know that he can be quite intimidating. He knew I was coming with you tonight. Once he gets used to the idea of—"

"Oh, for pity's sake. Have you not been listening? You are. . .are lavender, and I am castor oil."

"That is the most ridiculous thing I have ever heard. I'll tell you what you are. You are a fool."

"I'm sure you are correct. Come. I will see you home."

He was miserable. Josephine would not look at him the entire ride across town, only stared out the small window. When she finally did, her eyes were red rimmed. But he had to be strong, end it now before he really got hurt. Although he wondered how it could hurt any worse than this. He helped her out of the carriage.

She paused. "At one time I thought you were mysterious. Now I think you are dull, stupid, and insipid."

"Insipid," he murmured, after she was gone. "That's probably true. But stupid?" He climbed back in the hackney, leaned back more weary than ever, and wished he had never laid eyes on her.

Chapter 9

David was on his way to the hospital and had just passed the Cincinnati College when he spotted a group of young men dicing. Usually he broke up such a gang. Not only was the practice illegal, but he hated to see boys get drawn into such an addiction. Today, however, he guiltily looked aside for he was in a hurry. Across the street was Dr. Drake's eye infirmary and marine hospital. He quickly made his way into the building and down a long hall, where he knocked on a closed door.

"Come in." Drake, who greatly resembled an older version of Abraham Lincoln, looked up, his face swallowed up in his smile. "David, I heard you caused a scandal in our fine city."

David gave a grim smile. "Just a bit of a stir. How was your trip?"

"Successful enough. I'm anxious to work on the resource materials that I have collected. But let's talk about you. How's the clinic?"

David leaned forward, his elbows resting on his legs, his face cupped in his hands. "It was a bit slow with the scandal and all, but has pretty much returned to normal. My assistant, Tom Langdon, is such a help."

"You must not get too dependent upon him. Why don't you send him over here to help out at the hospital when you are not so busy. It would be good experience for him."

"I suppose I could. If you think so."

"Good. We can use him. Now, let's take a look at that list of names I gave you before I left." David withdrew it from his pocket and gave it to Dr. Drake, who summarized the results aloud. "Randolph Cline, crossed off the list. Vernon Thorpe, Quinton Wallace, and Clay Buchanan all have contributed generous sums."

David felt embarrassed that he had not done better. "I didn't make a very good showing, did I?"

"It's a start. I've done this myself plenty of times. I know it's not an easy task. That's why I gave it to you. I have confidence in you, David. This negative attitude is uncharacteristic of you."

"You're right. I'll pull up my bootstraps, Sir."

David left the hospital with a determination that wasn't there before. Dr. Drake certainly knew how to motivate. Why, just a short visit with the man made David feel like he actually could make a difference in the world, or at least in Cincinnati. Maybe even Ohio. He felt a surge of excitement that had been missing and wanted to pass it on to Tom. The boy deserved some encouragement, too.

But later that day in speaking with Tom, David discovered the young man wasn't eager about his new assignment at the hospital. David did what he could to raise Tom's spirits and kindle enthusiasm in that part of his assistant's new job assignment even though it meant more work for himself at the clinic.

In the evening, David prayed over the two remaining names on his list: Zachary Caulfield, who still had not forgiven him for ruining his benefit dinner, and Bartholomew Hastings. He prayed that by word of mouth the circle of donors would enlarge.

After that his days were packed and busy. As autumn progressed, daylight hours shortened. That, combined with Tom's time spent at the hospital, caused David to drop into bed each night exhausted.

Josie peered outside her bedroom window at what remained of the cook's pumpkin patch. She felt restless as if she were on the brink of change or discovery but it was just beyond her reach. She could not tell if the feeling had made her pray more or if her frequent prayers made the nudge stronger. Her fingertip followed a stream of liquid down the frosty glass. *Lord, what are You trying to tell me?* A knock at her bedroom door interrupted her prayer. *Sorry, Lord. I guess we'll have to continue our discussion later. There's always something to take up my time. Forgive me for my bad thoughts. Help me to be agreeable.* "Yes?"

"It's Mother. May I come in?"

"Coming." Josephine fastened her wrapper and padded across the floor. "I didn't wake you?"

"No. Come in."

They sat together on the bed. "I was wondering if you wanted to help me out at the workhouse today? One of our volunteers canceled. And I remembered how well you handled things when you assisted Dr. Wheeler's clinic."

"When are you leaving?"

Her mother looked apologetic. "Right after breakfast. It will be a long day."

Josephine gave her mother a quick hug. "Then I'd best get dressed right away."

"Thank you, Darling."

As soon as her foot crossed the threshold of the women's workhouse, vivid memories of her time spent with Dr. Wheeler accosted her—the remembrance of how he had rejected her offer of friendship. He had made it plain that she was a hindrance to his high and lofty plans. And to think she had thought him fascinating. Stubborn and unapproachable were more like it.

Certainly David Wheeler had dual sides to his personality. There was the man who dressed shabbily to better serve the poor. He was compassionate and gallant. But his other half was rude and prejudiced against the rich. Unfortunately, that was the one whose acquaintance she had made.

"Josie?"

"Yes, Mother?"

"Come let me show you the forms that need to be filled out by new applicants. You can sit at this table to help with the interviews."

First was a cane-wobbly woman, kicked out of her home because she could not walk to her job anymore. Her hands were still good, but work was unavailable. Her family was dead, and she was alone in the world. She was a perfect candidate for those who resided full time at the workhouse. Josie's heart warmed when she saw the woman's one possession—her Bible. Once the interview was ended, another workhouse resident in charge of newcomers took the sweet old woman away to get her settled in.

Josie's next candidate was quite a contrast—a young woman with a toddler in tow. She still had a home but had lost her job and needed money to pay her rent. Together they compared a list of available jobs to her qualifications. Josie was glad they could offer her a job at the textile factory. The woman only needed to obtain a letter of recommendation.

The third applicant started toward Josie when a resident burst into the room breathless. "Mrs. Cline, where's the wardress? There's a fight!"

"Oh, I do hate these," Mrs. Cline murmured, stumbling to her feet.

"I'll go find her," Josephine assured her mother and hurried after the messenger. By the time they reached the scuffle, the wardress had already arrived and broken up the fight. But the entire incident greatly affected Josie. When she returned to her mother, she asked, "What will happen to them? One of them was pregnant. And she was so young."

"They are allowed three misdemeanors. After that they must leave. The penalty is extra work or less food."

"That's horrible," Josie said. "I thought this was an institute to help women, not a penitentiary."

"You cannot help a troublemaker. They ruin things for all the others."

For the remainder of the day, Josie thought about the incident. That evening the matter still disturbed her. She prayed about it, thankful that she could go to the Lord with her problems. Where did people turn when they did not know Jesus? She tried to imagine what it might feel like to have to carry a burden all alone. The loneliness and desperation that enveloped the applicants haunted her.

It was no wonder that all that ugliness tumbled out in uncontrollable emotions causing disruptions with other innocent persons. The women at the women's workhouse carried more problems than most. They stored it up until something happened to cause them to explode or act out their frustrations—just as she had witnessed today with those two women brawling over a minor incident. She probably would have done the same thing. They could not help themselves.

Her mind scrabbled for a solution, something that might help them cope. Of course they needed to know the Lord. Then an idea struck. In awe, she thanked the Lord for it. It seemed right, but was it feasible?

David pushed back his breakfast plate of scorched eggs and stretched his legs, his gaze fastened to the morning newspaper. A hand-sketched picture drew his interest, and he straightened, carefully studying the young woman whose familiar face and name set his heart to pounding. *Josephine Cline addresses board of women's workhouse.* What was she up to now? Curious, he pulled the paper close to his face to better read the details. He shook his head in admiration and wonderment. "Listen to this, Gratuity. 'Josephine Cline's idea of assigning a personal patroness to each woman at the workhouse was readily received. Volunteers are now needed. A personal patroness would meet once a week for one hour to discuss the resident's personal problems and give advice. Although the personal patroness plan would aid individuals and head off many workhouse problems, and it cannot be denied that it is a good plan, the question remains: Can enough volunteers be found?' "

A fountain of excitement bubbled up inside him. He had been pretending these past several weeks that he had never heard of Josephine Cline, never looked into her soft, leather-brown eyes, never smelled the scent of lavender. One could do that. Suppress a thing for awhile. But not forever. It was bound to surface time and time again. The question was: What was he going to do with these tangled feelings he felt for Josephine?

The cat meowed. He needed to quit his daydreaming and get to the clinic. But tonight, if she entered his thoughts again, he would pray about the matter. Just to make certain, he left the paper lying open to her picture.

Chapter 10

E ven though Josephine was a closed chapter of David's life, after reading the newspaper article, his fingers itched to reopen the book and explore her captivating pages. Every fiber of his being pricked with an awareness that he had missed the major point before. That he needed to reexamine the text for that missing element. Oftentimes he read a favorite book more than once, savored endings over and over. He shook his head. What was he doing comparing Josephine to a book?

She was flesh and blood and lived in a real and intimidating house. It loomed before him this very instant, tall and ominous, challenging his spontaneous idea of calling upon Josephine to congratulate her on her recent achievement.

It was only a house, after all. He knocked. The door opened, and a servant inquired of his purpose.

"I wish to call upon Miss Cline if she is available."

"And whom shall I tell her is calling?"

"David Wheeler." He stepped inside and waited in the entry while the servant left to find Josephine. The wall tapestry reminded him of the textile factory that Mr. Cline owned shares in. He hoped that he would be spared the embarrassment of meeting either Mrs. or Mr. Cline.

Light footsteps sounded beyond the entry, and David straightened.

"Doctor. What a surprise." Josephine looked shocked but greeted him with a warm smile.

"I hope I did not pick an inconvenient time to call. I. . ." *Babbling, I've turned into a babbling fool.*

"I do have another guest. But I insist that you join us."

"Oh, no. I do not wish to intrude. I'll call another time."

"Nonsense."

"I only intended to congratulate you on your idea for the workhouse."

She colored and stepped close. "Thank you. But please, do join us." She whispered, "I'd really like to talk to you."

It was just the encouragement he needed. He felt her gentle touch on his arm and allowed himself to be drawn into a large parlor. To his surprise a young, dark-haired man rose.

"Dr. Wheeler, this is Otis Washburn, reporter for the *Cincinnati Gazette*." David acknowledged him. "I've read your articles on abolition. Am

I interrupting an interview?"

"No," Josephine said.

"Yes. We were. . ." The reporter who spoke at the same time as Josephine drooped under her sharp glance and sank back onto his chair in silence.

David found humor in the way that Josephine took charge of the situation, and like the reporter, David did not have the courage to cross her so he seated himself. The room grew quiet except for Washburn's muffled cough. David clasped his hands together and gazed about the room. Finally, he ventured, "I found today's article about the women's workhouse quite compelling."

"Did you?" both Josephine and Otis Washburn asked simultaneously.

"Why, yes. The idea of a personal patroness is ingenious."

The reporter leaned forward. "Which is exactly what I told Miss Cline the night we attended the benefit ball together."

A burning sensation surged up the back of David's neck, flushed his face, and settled like a dark cloud across his eyes and temples. There was no way he could conceal his shock and disappointment over Washburn's disclosure that he and Josephine were socially connected.

Josephine frowned and fidgeted with the lace on her bodice. "Now I need to figure a way to attract volunteers. That is why Mr. Washburn is here."

David stood. "I wish you success. But you will not get anything accomplished with me in attendance. I'll call another time."

The reporter stood and offered a handshake. "That is good of you, Doctor."

Josephine stepped forward. "Please, don't go."

"I really have to. I didn't intend to stay."

"At least let me see you to the door."

"No, Miss Cline. That is not necessary."

"Very good of you, Sir. Josephine, I have an idea that might. . ." Washburn's words faded as David made his humiliating departure.

The cold night air slapped his face. What on earth had he been thinking? Josephine did not need his congratulations. She probably had oodles of friends encouraging her, many wishing to be more than friends. In fact, she probably had oodles of suitors with that baby-faced reporter vying to be added to her list.

As he walked, he rehearsed everything he had said and calmed when he realized that he had kept things impersonal. He had done nothing wrong. He only congratulated her on her accomplishments, which were in the area of service that interested him. It had been a socially correct thing to do, nothing more. She would not be able to imagine anything personal. Now he only hoped Josephine would not stir up anything else that involved him. Maybe this would be the end of the story—where he and Josephine were concerned.

❧❧

Josephine could not get the doctor off her mind. She wondered why he had seemingly changed his mind about cutting off their ties and called upon her the previous night. She reviewed the circumstances of their previous encounters. She had always been the pursuer. At first because she wanted to run him out of town. How long ago that seemed now. Then later to make amends. But after that she had to admit she had just been interested in him. Still he had perceived her intentions and had broken it off between them in the plainest of terms. So why had he come calling? His actions were out of character. Congratulations seemed a flimsy excuse.

He must have changed his mind about her. Her heart raced. Could it be? Or was the issue as simple as he had claimed? If he had changed his mind, why had he left her house in such an abrupt manner? Jealousy or uncertainty over Otis Washburn? Over and over Josephine played the questions through her mind.

A trip to his clinic to apologize for the situation of the night before might be in order. If he was willing to renew their friendship, it might be the nudge he needed. Would that be too forward? Maybe that was the whole problem: He didn't like forward women. He'd said that he didn't like ones with *insulting, unbridled* tongues. She smiled. She couldn't change her personality. With the decision made, she slipped into her cloak and tied the ribbons of her bonnet in place. After leaving a note for her mother, she stepped outside.

Josephine followed the granite paving down the tree-lined causeway of shingle-to-shingle and shoulder-to-shoulder shops and businesses. She paused outside the slate-roofed building with the familiar decorative cornice work and drew in a deep breath, preparing herself to enter. But the door before her magically opened without her assistance.

"Whoa, Josephine!" Dr. Wheeler jerked to a halt outside his clinic and smiled down at her.

His cheerful countenance encouraged her. She returned his smile. "I was hoping to speak with you."

"I'm getting ready to take lunch." He paused momentarily. "Have you had yours?"

"No. Is this an invitation?"

Producing evidence of his bagged lunch, he said, "I'll share mine with you. But I haven't much time."

"I'd like that. Where are we going?"

"Come and you'll see."

She fell into step beside him. They passed storefronts and wood-shuttered windows, but neither broke the silence until they arrived at a plot of vacant land with a stand of oak trees in a secluded area. Squirrels rustled the November-brown grass and crisp leaves.

"What a perfect spot. Do you come here every day?"

"As often as I can get away."

A bird trilled overhead. Otherwise it seemed that they were alone rather than just a stone's throw from the city's hustle and bustle. "I feel like I'm intruding upon what must be the last uncivilized spot in our fair city."

The doctor chuckled as he unwrapped his lunch of smelly cheese and hard bread. "An exaggeration. But it serves as a park. The city board would be smart to buy it up and make it into a real park. But they do not want to do anything that will create a tax. How are we going to ever have a decent city if such measures are not taken?"

"Cincinnati's a place where folks can come and become rich. That's what Father says."

The doctor smirked, then ripped his sandwich in two and offered her half. She peeked between the slices of bread and winced, fearing she would offend him if she did not partake. When he looked up at her again, she swallowed a bite and challenged, "Do not hold in your thoughts on my account."

"But I don't want to ruin our picnic."

"Just tell me."

"I thought that sounded like something your father would say or maybe even something I have already heard him say. I wonder, Josephine, has your father taken over that bright mind of yours entirely? Or is there a section that is still uniquely you, the charming lady?"

"Please do not sugarcoat your words."

"I'm a plain man, simple, straightforward."

"On the contrary, you are a duplicate of your hero, Dr. Daniel Drake."

"Do you know him?"

"Father. . . ," Josephine faltered, then jutting her chin in the air, continued, "Father told me about him and his ideas. He says you are one of his prodigies."

"I would imagine your father has pointed out to you the many differences in our views. It would seem it all only goes to prove one thing. You and I are like oil and water."

She turned her gaze heavenward in disgust. "Ah, yes. Castor oil and lavender water. I remember. I will admit you do irritate me at times. But I also get this glimpse of a good side of you. I'm not willing to disregard our friendship yet. Goodness. If people always had to agree, they wouldn't have many friends, now would they?" She slipped the remainder of her half of the sandwich into her pocket without his noticing.

"Is that why you came to the clinic today?"

"I suppose in part. I wondered why you really came to see me last night. And I also wanted to apologize for your reception. I did not mean for Otis Washburn to frighten you away."

"It sounded like your relationship was more than business."

"It was strictly business."

He struggled. "It was an inopportune time. You have nothing to apologize for. And I only wanted to congratulate you for your efforts at the workhouse. I do admire your caring spirit and your desire to help others."

"I believe that is what I admire about you. That is why I'd like to be friends. Perhaps you can teach me about helping others. Oh, I know what you said. You are a busy man. But surely you can spare me a little time?"

He gazed across the lot, taking time to word his reply. "There are many things that fascinate me. You are one of them. But I need to stay focused on my goals. I fear that a friendship with you would be too distracting."

"I do not understand what is wrong with a little distraction."

"Let me restate my real worry. I fear that knowing you is going to hurt. I'll be torn in two directions; we—"

"You worry an awful lot for such a young man."

"This discussion has been delightful, but speaking of worries reminds me that I need to be getting back to the clinic. I will reconsider your friendship proposal, Josephine."

She stood and straightened her skirt. "I'll say good day then. Thank you for sharing your lunch, Doctor. And for your honesty." She turned and started to walk away.

"Josephine." She paused to look back. He smiled broadly. "You dropped something. And the pleasure has been mine."

It was the sandwich. She shrugged and smiled sheepishly. "I suppose the squirrels are hungrier than I am."

Chapter 11

D avid knocked on Dr. Drake's door and waited. When he was welcomed inside, he followed Drake to the kitchen where the older man poured them each a cup of tea.

"Let's move to the parlor and be comfortable," Drake suggested.

It was an unexpected pleasure to be singled out as a guest in such a home where entertaining groups was commonplace. Drake was a wonderful host, and the conversation was always lively. Many times David had sat in this parlor and listened to a debate or lecture. Tonight he felt honored to be counted among the many friends of Drake's influence, for his acquaintances spread across the nation and came from high positions.

"Put your feet up, my friend." Dr. Drake set his cup down and leaned back in his chair, taking his own advice.

"How is my assistant doing?" David asked.

"He has perseverance, but he is not really ambitious."

"He does not like working at the hospital. He seems better suited to his work at the clinic." He felt guilty for not doing a better job of defending Tom.

"I suppose it is best. How about your cleanup project?"

"I was hoping you would ask. I've an idea I wanted to get your opinion on. I met this reporter, Otis Washburn, who has done a story on a friend of mine. It was about her work at the women's workhouse." Dr. Drake leaned closer, and David continued. "What if I invited a few colleagues and some of the men who sit on the board of health to dig drainage ditches and shovel waste—a workday? I would ask Otis Washburn if he would want to do a story on it to encourage others to participate in our plan."

"Or at the least, they would see your earnest commitment and be more inclined to donate money."

"Exactly."

Drake nodded. "The nation is going through a recession, which isn't helping our organizations that need funding. I'm having trouble getting backing for my hospital, barely breaking even. It does get old begging for money."

"I know the country's finances are tight right now. But Cincinnati's pockets are still bulging."

"Give it a try then. Now drink your tea. Then I'm going to quiz you about this woman friend of yours. I thought you'd been acting differently lately. I sure do miss my Harriet."

David took a couple large gulps of his tea, at first wishing that the other man was not poking into his private life, then realizing he really did need someone to talk to about the woman that both mystified and terrified him. "Josephine Cline's her name. Daughter of Randolph Cline."

Drake's expression turned mysterious as if there were some hidden secret connected with his thoughts, possibly dark, but then he relaxed. "Ah. The bluestocking who brought that scandal down upon your head. Friends, eh?"

"Our relationship would probably better be defined as sparring partners or debating opponents. At first we drew the line, but our paths kept crossing so we've worked at being civil."

"Do you find her attractive?"

David grinned. "Extremely. And I believe the feeling is mutual." He coughed. "She pursued me a bit until I told her I was not interested."

"Why did you do that?"

"We're just too different."

"Nonsense. I hear she's very brilliant. You only need to get her away from that father of hers, and you'll probably find out you have much in common."

"She reveres her father."

"Wait. Back up a bit. What happened when you told her you were not interested?"

"She seemed offended, and we went our separate ways."

"So she's not really your woman friend any longer?"

"After reading the newspaper article about her, I had to see her again so I called on her at her house. That's where I met Otis Washburn. Then she came to my clinic last week to see me."

"Did you treat her kindly?"

"I shared my lunch with her."

"Hah! That would frighten anyone away. But as compassionate a man as you are, I knew there must be some romance in your blood. Do not fight it, my son. I was never happier than when my Harriet was alive. I envy you."

David shrugged. "She proposed friendship. It scares me more than anything I've ever faced."

"Spoken as a true male. What scent does she wear?"

"Lavender."

Drake shook his head and chuckled. "Life will never be the same for you. Might as well pursue her."

"Her father hates me."

Drake's eyes hooded as if he understood. "The perfect challenge."

"That's just it. I'm not sure I can handle all the disruption in my life. I liked it just the way it was." Drake tried to cover a yawn, and David gulped down the rest of his tea. "I didn't mean to bore you with my private life. I really must be going."

"Nonsense. I enjoyed our little talk. Drop in at the hospital again soon."

The *Cincinnati Gazette*'s newspaper office reeked of ink and paper. A man with gartered, rolled-up sleeves glanced at David. "Can I help you?"

"Looking for Otis Washburn."

"You're in luck. Usually he's out and about. But I saw him go into the back room. Have a seat." He nodded toward a bench by the door.

David seated himself, taking in the operation of the printing press, the clamor of wood against paper. He drummed his fingers against the armrest, reassuring himself that this was an important step toward a goal.

Very soon the young, dark-haired reporter entered the rear of the room. Washburn didn't seem to recognize or notice him so David stood and cleared his throat. When Washburn looked, David stepped forward.

"Mr. Washburn." The greeting drew a blank expression. "We met at Josephine Cline's." The dark eyes narrowed. "I've come about a story."

The face reddened. He looked over his shoulder. "Let's sit over there." David followed him to a table. "Is this about Josephine?"

"No. Not at all." The reporter visibly relaxed. "I suppose you've heard the debate over the causes of cholera?"

Washburn leaned forward and plucked a pencil and paper from his pocket. "I'm listening."

As the reporter warmed toward him, David discarded the last trace of animosity he held against the reporter for Josephine's sake and got into the explanation of his story, answering the reporter's questions regarding his theories, or rather Dr. Drake's theories, about cholera being caused by invisible little animal creatures that lived in the filth. "You're not going to make sport of this, are you?" David asked.

The reporter's brow wrinkled. "Let me ask you a question first before I answer that. Are you seeing Josephine?"

"No. But neither are you from what she says."

"Perhaps not at the moment. But I want you to know I am pursuing her. I'm not sure if I should help you."

"Josephine and I are merely friends. I did not have to bring my story to you. I only did so because I thought she was our mutual friend. I could have taken my story to anyone else."

"And I can make a living writing about abolition. Let's leave Josephine out of this for now. I'll give you your story, printing the facts as you give them to me. But I might have to do a follow-up story or two with Dr. Drake about his little imaginary foes."

"Better check your notes. The word was 'invisible.' "

The reporter shook out his paper. "Ah. Yes. Right you are." He grinned, and David wished he had taken his story to a stranger.

❦

"Miss Josephine. You have a caller." The servant gave a perfunctory nod.

"Mr. Washburn. How nice to see you again."

"I came to inquire how the last article worked for you. Did you get volunteers to be personal patronesses to the residents of the workhouse?"

"We did. The program has been implemented. We do not have a patroness for each resident yet, but with time perhaps it can happen. Thank you for your help. You have been too kind."

"Selfishly so, I admit. Actually, I am here on two accounts. I was wondering if I could take you to dinner tonight."

She was afraid that his call might be coming to this. One evening attending a benefit ball with the young man had been enough of his company to suit her. It was never pleasant to let down a young man's hopes. Though the older she got, the less frequently she found herself in such straits.

No excuse presented itself so she opted for the truth. "I hope I have not given you the wrong impression. You are a very fine man, but I only meant our meeting to be about business. If I implied anything else, you have my sincerest apologies."

Washburn reddened and cleared his throat. "You have been quite proper, I assure you. Do not trouble yourself about it any further. But I did enjoy that evening we attended the benefit ball."

"It is best left as a good memory then. And I will think kindly of you when I recall all that you have done to help the women at the workhouse."

"I see."

Washburn chewed on his bottom lip, and Josephine hoped he did not come up with some other angle. How much clearer could she make it? She waited patiently. The room grew very quiet. She wondered if it would be too rude to dismiss either him or herself.

He stood. "Thank you for seeing me. I wish you the best, Miss Cline. And if I can ever be of service again, please consider me able and willing."

"I'll see you to the door."

"No need. I remember the way."

Josephine watched him depart. He was handsome in his smart attire, intelligent, and attentive. She sighed. He had told her that he entertained ambitions of owning his own newspaper one day. His inquiring mind made him an interesting person. They had enjoyed several lively conversations. Unlike many men, he was open-minded when it came to women's opinions and appreciated her curiosity in civic affairs. Most likely he would be successful. She thought wryly that he was everything she should be looking for in a man.

Instead, her thoughts were fixed on a particular eccentric doctor. A man who was not attentive but rather held her off as if she had the plague. A man who could be blunt, rude, and irritating. A man whose ambition was helping the down-and-out and who hoarded his time. Why hadn't David called upon her? She had done everything but offer her friendship on a silver platter. Was the man blind? If she had any sense at all, she would forget about him altogether. But she wasn't ready to do that yet.

Maybe it was time that she had a talk with her mother. Perhaps she could give her advice on how to charm the doctor. Wasn't that what any other female would try? After all, Mother had landed her father, and he was a real catch. Her mother had had several other suitors, too. She knew much more than Josephine about wooing men. It could not be denied that Mother was beautiful, and men always seemed to attend to her. The idea of attracting a man's attention had never enticed Josie. Until now.

Chapter 12

Half a dozen shovels hissed into the sludge and splattered muck into vats. David had arranged for the refuse to be loaded onto a flatboat and dumped into the deeper rushing waters of the Ohio River. Next to him an Irishman set the pace. David huffed, finding it hard to keep up with the short man, brawny from hard labor working the canals.

Garbage from the city drained toward the river but collected along Second Street, forming a stinking common sewer. Everyone detested the stench that rose from the area night and day. To eliminate the problem, several men were digging a new drainage ditch so that future rains could wash murky waters all the way into the river.

"Is it true that just breathing in the air might make you sick?" the Irishman asked.

"It's a possibility."

"It's a fear we have. Those who live here."

David hardly knew how to reply. He hoped his efforts would be enough to protect the Irishman and those like him, yet he could not guarantee anything. Only the poorest lived or worked in the area. Although businesses performed their functions along the docks, it was the low-paid laborer who actually performed the work.

Since he had picked up a shovel, he actually felt guilty over the fact that he had been collecting funds to hire the work done—for it was a humiliating and degrading job. Even more amazing, the majority of his volunteers were the poor folks who lived in the area, many of them black. Those he would have hired were doing the work for free.

A splatter of muck struck David in the eyes. He swiped it away with his sleeve. The Irishman laughed.

"Some say that cholera is the result of loose behavior."

"I don't believe that. Cholera originates in places like this. Places where—"

"Us poor folks live."

"Contamination. Stagnant water."

"So you don't think it comes from God?"

"You mean punishment for sins?"

The Irishman nodded.

"I'm no preacher, though my father was, but the Bible gives many examples where Jesus loves the poor and came to save the sinner. No, I don't think so. If that were the case, I'd probably already be dead."

The Irishman seemed relieved. "I know about God, but I don't always act like it."

Before David could reply, the Irishman's gaze lowered. David looked up to see what had caused the man to withdraw from their conversation. It was Otis Washburn approaching in his fine attire, an expression of distaste on his face.

"This place reeks. How can you stand it?" Otis Washburn grimaced.

David loosened the knot on the handkerchief that covered his mouth. It had been stifling his conversation with the Irishman. "Is that a professional question?"

"Sure it is," Washburn said and grinned.

"The way I see it, the citizens of Cincinnati do not have a choice. This is not a pleasant task. But burying people is even a worse prospect. The lesser of two evils."

"Referring to the possibility of cholera?"

David nodded.

"But you're barely making a path through the muck. You're never going to finish. Will you be back tomorrow?"

"Not tomorrow. But next week. I'm hoping that the next time there will be more of us."

"Are these men being paid?"

"No. Everyone is volunteering their time."

"Who are they?"

"Some medical colleagues and students. One is a member of the board of health. Many are residents of the area."

"Residents? How did you get them to help?"

"They do not enjoy living like this. Of course they want to encourage efforts to clean up the place. The next time they'll help recruit volunteers."

"But weren't you seeking funds to pay these people? Looks like they'll do it for free. What will happen to the funds you've collected?"

"I haven't collected any money yet, only pledges. There are people who live in the German part of town, Over the Rhine, who will accept any job."

The whistles from two steamships shrieked, and the reporter's eyes lit. He turned his gaze to the river. "The *Moselle* and the *Goose* are racing again."

David also looked toward the Ohio River. "Someday there's going to be an explosion. They favor speed in lieu of safety when it comes to those big boilers."

"Where is your sense of competitiveness? Being the fastest ship is good business. They get the contracts and the glory, too."

"I'm more concerned with sparing lives."

Washburn frowned. "Back to the subject at hand. If you do get it cleaned up, what then? How will you keep it clean?"

"We're digging drainage ditches. Of course when large spring floods come, it will take another community effort to help clean out cellars and low areas where refuse collects. But the drainage ditches should even help with the melting snow in the spring."

"So you've got it all figured out?"

"You mock me. How can I convince you that the support you can solicit through the *Gazette*'s story will benefit the citizens of Cincinnati? How can I persuade you to jump on board and help with this worthwhile project?"

"You insult my intelligence."

David leaned on his shovel. "Take care what you publish. You have an obligation to the people of Cincinnati. Do not take such a responsibility lightly."

"That sounds a lot like a threat."

"Only the truth."

"Truth is something each person must find for themselves."

"I don't agree. It's always the same whether people find it or not."

Washburn chuckled. "One thing I know for truth: When you finish here, you'll need to take a long bath. I believe I have enough for my story." He tipped his hat. "Doctor."

David watched the reporter leave. He repositioned the handkerchief over his mouth and returned to his shoveling. As he worked, he wondered how he managed of late to defeat his own good purposes. He only hoped that he didn't end up in another scandal of some sort. The earth opened as his tool sliced in. The smart-mouthed reporter was right about one thing: A long hot bath was more than called for.

❦

"Mother. Can you spare some time for me?"

Mrs. Cline turned away from her sewing project. "I'm always happy to chat with you, Dear. I just didn't hear you enter the room."

Josie lounged in one of the plush parlor chairs beside her mother. "I need some advice."

Mrs. Cline's face lit with pleasure. "Oh? I'll be delighted to help if I can."

A sudden rush of heat warmed Josie's neck. "I've never given much thought to attracting men, but now I've met someone, and I'm wondering how to catch his interest."

Her mother could not disguise her surprise though she kept her voice level. "My, my. You wish to charm a gentleman?" She struggled to compose her enthusiasm. "It might help if I knew who he was."

"I guess I was hoping for some sure remedy that would work on all men. But I don't suppose all men are equal." She shrugged and stood. "Never mind. Nothing may even come of this anyway."

"Nonsense! You are most charming." Mrs. Cline studied her daughter. "I do not mean to brag, but I've never had a problem with men. I will help you. Now tell me everything."

Josie sank back into the chair and sighed. "It's Dr. Wheeler." Her mother's eyes widened, resembling the teacups stacked in the cabinet on the wall behind her. "You are disappointed. He is the most interesting man I've ever met. He's quite compassionate. And you have seen for yourself that he is extremely handsome."

"How well I remember his passion and the uproar he caused at the fund-raiser dinner."

"He had every reason to be angry. I falsely accused him."

"Hmm. From what I gleaned watching him at the workhouse, his type is probably sincere, serious. If he's a doctor, he's probably very studious and devoted to his work."

Josie was pleased and amazed at her mother's understanding. "You have accurately described him. I think he is attracted to me, but he's very jealous of his time and thinks a friendship with me will infringe upon his career."

Her mother looked aghast. "All of this has already been discussed?"

"I'm not shy, Mother."

"No. Of course not. If it is the doctor who you want to attract, then I will help you. And if nothing comes from it, at least the practice will be good for you."

"Mother!"

Mrs. Cline was not chagrined and delved into the perplexity with all earnestness. "Let's see. I think we need to appeal to his sense of reasoning, make loving you seem the most logical conclusion in the world."

"Love? I only want to be his friend."

"Really? Whoever heard of such a thing?" She rattled on before Josie could form a sound argument. "We can start there, I suppose. Make a list of the things that your love—"

"Friendship."

"Friendship would offer. Then go down the list one by one until you have made each point evident to him. Think about areas of his life that knowing you would enhance. Then when you have thought about how you will apply yourself, plan a strategy that will demonstrate explicitly."

Josie frowned. "I do not want to trick him or coerce him into anything. I was just looking for some simple ways to attract his attention."

"I didn't mean to make things sound complicated. It's just a matter of applying your charm."

"I suppose. It's all new to me. Thank you, Mother. I think I'll go work on my list."

"What list?"

Josie jumped at the sound of her father's voice.

"Ingredients of a recipe. One that has been handed down among the women of the family," Mrs. Cline said, a glint in her eyes.

"Oh." Randolph Cline sat down with his newspaper. "You'll never guess, Josie, what your scandalous Dr. Spokes is up to."

Josie and Mrs. Cline instantly gave him their attention. Josie tried to sound nonchalant. "I haven't heard any rumors."

"Otis Washburn, your reporter, came to see me today."

"Father, he's not my doctor and definitely not my reporter."

"He told me that Spokes was shoveling manure down at the docks. Remember when he asked for my help in cleaning up the city? Well he must not have gotten much response because he's down there doing the work himself." He chuckled. "If I didn't dislike the man so, I'd credit him for his grit. He apparently hopes to drum up some excitement over the project by giving the story to your reporter."

She ignored her father's teasing. "Why did Mr. Washburn tell you about it?"

"He found out somehow that I'd turned down the doctor. Washburn wanted to interview someone with an opposing opinion on the issue. I don't believe he thinks much of your doctor either."

A lump formed in Josie's stomach. Her father was forming an even bigger wall between her and David. "Is the article in there?"

"No. It will be in tomorrow's paper."

"I'll be sure to read it. I think I'll go to my room now. I've some things to attend to. Good night."

Josie cast her mother a beseeching glance, then hurried to her room and closed the door behind her, throwing herself across her bed to think. This could not turn out well. Whatever her father had said, it was bound to make David angry. And it was all her fault. She should have told her father how much she liked David from the beginning. Perhaps then he would have defended David for her sake. Her father loved her and would do anything for her. But now David's anger over this new incident was sure to spill over to include her. And to think that only minutes ago making a list was her biggest concern.

It occurred to her that maybe Otis Washburn was doing this because he was jealous of David. And if that were the case, David would have even more reason to blame her. There was nothing to be done about any of it until she had read the article. If she thought it would do any good, she would go to the *Gazette*'s office. But of course it wouldn't, for the story was probably already going to print.

Chapter 13

David hurriedly sliced some bread and cheese and poured himself a steaming cup of coffee. He could hardly contain his curiosity over the morning's paper. With a snap of his wrists, it fell open, and he scanned the headlines for the article.

LOCAL DOCTOR PRONOUNCES WAR AGAINST INVISIBLE ARMY. David groaned as he read:

> Grimy from head to toe and reeking, Dr. David Wheeler led a band of doctor colleagues and medical students as well as a few local residents in what he proclaims to be a citywide cleanup campaign. Although his reasoning seems a bit absurd—rounding up the invisible animal creatures that cause cholera and other disease and disposing of them into the muddy waters of the Ohio River—no one is complaining about his efforts.
>
> Sensible citizens realize that the stench from Second Street is a detriment to health. So although the doctor's reasoning may be debatable, the results are favorable.
>
> He hopes to bring the need to the attention of Cincinnati's prominent citizens. You may show your support by donating funds. The money will pay immigrants to perform the required labor. Dr. Wheeler was encouraged when many local residents also pitched in to help, eager to see the sludge and slime removed from their neighborhood.
>
> The question remains: Will his efforts be worthwhile? Will they make a difference? Dr. Wheeler's response to this question was that new drainage ditches to the river are being planned and another workday is scheduled for Saturday of next week. He invites anyone who has some spare time to come with shovels and join in the adventure.
>
> In order to get a feel for the response of the public, I interviewed Mr. Randolph Cline, land developer and textile factory owner.

David's pulse increased. What sort of trick was this? Hadn't Washburn poked enough fun already?

It seems that the good doctor has made his rounds, for Randolph Cline was already familiar with the campaign. The doctor had confronted him about a month earlier to beg funds. From the mouth of Randolph Cline: "The plan is foolhardy because it wastes money on something frivolous. The nation is presently in an economic panic. It is already a tight year financially. There are plenty of real problems for Cincinnati's citizens to consider. Issues pertaining to shipping and land development. Pursuits that enrich our city, not just beautify it."

Randolph Cline also felt personally belittled when the doctor used threatening tactics, indicating that Cline's family could be the next to die of cholera. I also asked Mr. Cline what he thought about the local residents who showed up to volunteer. "That is how it should be. Everyone should sweep their own stoop, clean their own property. Then we wouldn't have this problem. Why should I pay to clean up someone else's dirt or worse? Anyway, it is a well-known fact that Dr. Wheeler is an eccentric."

I would be remiss if I did not present the question to you, the citizen. Is Cincinnati clean enough? If not, will you join forces with Dr. David Wheeler and do something to help? Mr. Clay Buchanan of the Cincinnati Hardware Store says that he will furnish free shovels to anyone wishing to get involved. This should come as no surprise as Buchanan is a member of the board of health.

David shook his head. Washburn treated it all as a big joke. He felt discouraged over the results he would get from such an article as this. One thing for sure, next week he wouldn't ask Washburn to cover the story. And as for Randolph Cline, he was fast becoming an opponent if not an enemy. He supposed that would put an end to any dreams of pursuing a friendship with his beautiful daughter.

❧

Josephine read her father's newspaper and shuddered. It was a far cry from the kind of support and coverage Otis had given her regarding her idea of a personal patroness for each woman at the workhouse. As for her father, she was disappointed with him for the first time in her life. Of course he had no idea of her feelings for the doctor. It was not like he was deliberately hurting her. But just reading the article and imagining how David might be feeling about it caused her to view her father's opinions under a new light. He had sounded cold, money-hungry, uncaring. She had never crossed purposes with Father before and feared the results of such a course, not wanting to hurt him.

Would there be any hope now for her and David? Perhaps it was foolish to wish that David and her father might accept each other. David might even refuse to see her again. Several times he had implied that she blindly followed after her father's viewpoints. If she went to him and told him that she did not agree with her father on this issue, it might open a door toward a relationship. Then if her father would reconsider his stand when he saw how much it meant to her and give David a chance. . .

Spurring herself on with such hopeful thinking, she took out the list she had been compiling, considering the first point: *David and I are both interested in the well-being of others, especially the downtrodden.*

Keeping in line with her mother's suggestions, now she needed to plan an event to demonstrate this point. She chewed on her pencil pensively. Suddenly, the solution was obvious. One that would win his heart if nothing else could. By this one action she would not even have to say a word about the newspaper article—except perhaps to explain to her father afterward. He would be livid when word got to him that his own daughter had showed up at the doctor's next workday, shovel in hand. To be sure, it would cause a scandal. But as long as the doctor appreciated her efforts, she didn't care what the rest of the world thought.

That afternoon David looked up to see Tom Langdon poke his plump head through a gap in the clinic's curtains. "A Mr. Bartholomew Hastings to speak with you." David had approached the man weeks ago about the cleanup campaign, but he had refused to donate any funds. David had attributed it to the benefit dinner scandal. He wondered now if Hastings had changed his mind.

"Mr. Hastings. What can I do to help you?"

Hastings thrust his hand inside his vest and withdrew a pouch. "I'd like to make a contribution to your cause. I'm not sure about your tiny invisible animal theory." He chuckled. "But I like your determination. You've won me over, Doctor."

"Thank you for your generosity. The citizens of Cincinnati thank you. I'll take this to the bank right away. I believe I mentioned before that I have set up a fund which will be supervised by the board of health."

"Yes. I imagine you'll be working with them a lot in these coming days." He grinned as if he were privy to some great secret.

"I hope so. Be sure to pass the word."

He chuckled again. "Oh, word is spreading. I'll run along now. We're both busy men."

"Thank you again."

Once the man had disappeared, David let out a whoop and pumped his arm in the air. After that, his imaginings of crossing another name off his list were interrupted as the bell on the clinic's door jingled again.

"Congratulations, Doctor."

This time it was Clay Buchanan. David smiled. "I guess you've read the paper, too."

"Indeed I have. And I overheard your jubilance after Hastings' departure. But the fact is, the board met this morning. We've decided to bring you aboard, Doctor. Your methods may be unconventional, but we think you're just what we need. What Cincinnati needs. Will you accept the position?"

"I'm honored. How can I refuse?"

"Wonderful!" Clay patted David's shoulder. "We'll call a meeting to indoctrinate you and help organize your next workday."

With the assistance that David received after that from the board of health, everything escalated so fast that by the morning of the next workday fifty people had gathered, many with shiny new shovels donated by Clay Buchanan's store. Many had returned, such as the Irishman, and David recognized several of his former patients.

The board helped to instruct the volunteers. An engineer, whom David had recruited the previous week, supervised the digging of new drainage ditches. David had finished organizing this group when he felt a light tap upon his shoulder. He turned.

"Josephine?" His mouth fell agape. "What are you doing here?"

She lifted her shiny new shovel and pointed toward Clay and some of the other board members. "They insisted that I report directly to you."

He pointed at the shovel in her grip. "Surely you do not intend to use that?" The skirt of her pretty wool dress was already soiled beyond repair. "The job is strenuous and foul."

"I'm strong. I can work for awhile."

David warmed at her enthusiasm. "Really, Josephine, I do appreciate the gesture. But I am sure there is something more suitable that you can do to help. We could use some refreshments. I know it is short notice, but if you could organize some women—"

She surrendered her shovel to him. "I'll do it."

Again he felt astonished. "Great!" Relief and an overwhelming gratitude for her cooperation rushed in.

She flashed him a smile and started to go. He had to squelch the urge to hug her. "Josephine."

She turned.

"Thank you."

"Just doing my civic duty, Doctor." She smiled again and left.

He leaned against the shovel she had abandoned. Joy curled up inside him.

True to her word, an hour later she returned with several other women and continued to be a bright spot in the mire and ooze.

Another incident occurred, however, that was not so favorable. "Doctor! Come quick!" David wheeled about. "We found a black man, half dead!"

Abandoning his shovel, David hurried after the messenger to the circle of men who had gathered around the victim. He barely breathed. "Let's get him to the hospital."

"It's the bad air. We're all going to die," someone said. Several shovels fell discarded. Men fled. Others hesitated, as did David, for he did not know whether to go along to the hospital or stay and reassure the volunteers. The matter was decided when his assistant, Tom, suddenly appeared.

"Want me to take him to the clinic?"

"No. To the hospital so I can stay here and try to keep everyone calm." Thankfully David left the patient in Tom's care and turned to reason with the group of disgruntled men. "That man had nothing to do with what's going on here. He wasn't one of our volunteers."

"What's wrong with him?"

"I don't know."

"Then you don't know for sure he didn't get sick from the rotten air."

One of the board members drew David aside. "Perhaps we should call it a day."

"You're right." He turned back to the agitated group. "Everyone go home. Better to be safe. And thank you for your participation. Cincinnati thanks you!"

The men began to disassemble, murmuring. David felt exhausted, bone weary.

"David?" a female voice asked. "What happened?"

"Oh, Josephine." David backed away from her. "I'm so dirty."

She smiled and shrugged. "I don't care. I'm not afraid."

"You're very brave. Thank you for helping. We're quitting for today."

"I'd better get Mother then and—"

"Your mother came?" David asked, incredulous.

Josephine chuckled. "I didn't want to face Father's wrath alone."

Once again David felt the urge to hug her. But, of course, that was impossible. "Will you go to dinner with me tomorrow night?" He blushed. "I hope the stench will be gone by then."

"I'd love to meet you for dinner."

For the moment, he cast Randolph Cline's likely reaction from his mind. "The Emerald Inn at seven o'clock."

Josephine nodded, picked up her ruined skirts, and tromped off. In David's eyes she was every bit the lady.

He stood there watching her departure. Somewhere behind him he heard evidence that the *Moselle* was racing again. Around him clouds of smoke drifted over the city's steam foundries. Beyond, Cincinnati's green hills looked hazy and indistinct.

Josephine and her mother giggled together as they soaked in tubs of hot water and suds. "That was the most outrageous thing I've ever done in my life," Mrs. Cline admitted.

"And it was only number one on my list," Josephine said as she gave an impish grin.

Mrs. Cline groaned. "What have I done? I'm afraid to ask, but what is number two?"

"He's a terrible cook."

"And you're an excellent one." Mrs. Cline wrinkled her brow. "How do you know he's a bad cook?"

Josephine blushed.

Chapter 14

You are not going out!" Randolph Cline thundered. "I wish to speak with you."

Josephine bristled at the unusually harsh tone and bossy command. "Father, I am not a child. I am twenty-two years old."

His eyes narrowed. "With yesterday's stunt it appears you are about five years old." His words hurt, and he must have sensed it for he added in a softer tone. "What are you up to now? It's late to be going out."

"I'm meeting a friend for dinner at the Emerald Inn."

He calmed even more and appealed to her in earnest. "Come sit beside me, Josephine. This is all so unlike you."

Of course she had known this discussion was due, only the timing was horrid. She perched on the edge of the couch. "All right, Father. But I am in a hurry."

He ran a hand through his neatly combed hair. "I cannot understand why you and your mother joined this cleanup crusade. Surely you understood that I was opposed to it? After that article in the *Gazette,* this looks bad for me, Josie. If I cannot handle my own household, others will think I am weak. It puts my business in jeopardy."

"Handle your household? Do you mean to infer that we are your puppets? I am shocked, Father. I always thought you encouraged me to use my brain. And now for the first time that I have a different opinion, you mean to squelch it."

"You have always thought and acted wisely before."

"Just because I agreed with you?"

His facial muscles tightened. "I am your father. I have authority over you and your mother."

"Isn't that a bit harsh?" Mrs. Cline interjected as she entered the room. "You've always encouraged our charitable pursuits, Randolph."

Josie patted his knee. "And if it is any consolation, I did not do anything to intentionally make you look foolish. I only did this because it is something that I personally believe in."

He narrowed his eyes. "Why have you changed your mind about Dr. Spokes?"

After giving her father a dirty look for ridiculing David's name again, Josie said, "It is simple. I was wrong about him. He's a very nice, sweet man."

"Nice? Sweet?" Randolph's mouth twisted with distaste.

"I believe this can all be settled by inviting the doctor to dinner," Mrs. Cline suggested.

Josie and her father both stared at Mrs. Cline as if she had grown two heads. Josephine recovered first for upon giving it a little thought, it wasn't such a bad idea. In fact, it fit in quite nicely with number two on her list.

"I'm sorry we upset you, Father. But I must hurry before I miss my friend. Can we talk about this later?"

"Who are you meeting?" he asked again.

Josie scooted off the sofa and gave her father a kiss on the cheek. "Just a very lovely friend. Thank you for worrying over us. Why don't you and Mother plan a date for inviting the doctor over?" She eased away and started toward the door. Behind her she heard her father's mutter.

"I didn't agree to any such dinner."

"Nonsense, Darling. . ."

Josie smiled. She knew her mother could charm away her father's objections. Her appreciation of her mother's feminine abilities was increasing. Now if she hurried, she would not be too late for her date.

<hr>

David smelled the lovely lavender scent and looked up in anticipation.

"Forgive me for being late. I hoped you would not give up on me."

"I was worried. I do not like your coming unescorted. We're going to have to do something about our meeting like this. We must be open with your father."

"I agree. When I left the house, Mother and Father were planning a date to invite you to dinner. That's why I'm late."

"What?"

"I don't mean to be forward. You did say we're going to have to do something about meeting like this."

"But your father wants me to come to dinner?" He narrowed his eyes. "Is this some kind of trap?"

She frowned. "You're getting dangerously close to being rude."

Josephine was right. He had responded badly. "Forgive me. Let's order, then we'll start again. I promise to be a gentleman."

"Agreed."

Josephine gave her order to the waiter. Her face was still flushed from the outdoors. The radiance of her face captivated David. Once the waiter had gone, he told her so. "Miss Cline, you look lovely this evening. And I mean that with all sincerity. The only thing that could compare is the loveliness of your heart." He chuckled and shook his head. "I still cannot believe that you showed up with a shovel."

Her eyes lit. "Which reminds me that I hear congratulations are in order. You have been elected to the board of health. Surely this will help to serve your purposes."

"It already has. Do you know that I got the whole idea from watching you?"

"I do not understand."

"The way you helped out at the workhouse—doing something out of the ordinary—made me consider my situation and how I could apply myself."

Josephine giggled, covering her mouth.

"What's so funny?"

"Why, you were my inspiration. The way you go to the slums canvassing patients. Your example provoked my actions at the workhouse."

David leaned close, propping his chin in the cup of his hand, his elbow resting on the table. "Do you suppose we complement each other? Surely we cannot be bringing out the best in each other? I mean, all this time I thought we were like—"

"Two explosive elements." She shook her head. "Surely not. It must be an isolated case. I'm sure we'll be back to bickering before this dinner is over."

"Not if you keep behaving in such a captivating manner."

She shoved her hand toward him across the table. "Could it mean that we are friends at last?"

He clasped it tightly. "Yes, Josephine, I suppose it does. *O dofo ho ye ha.*"

"What does that mean?"

"African. A good friend is hard to come by."

"It's beautiful. Thank you. Does this mean that you will come to dinner then?"

David withdrew his hand and closed his eyes. When he opened them, she was dabbing at her eyes. They were teary. "If they invite me, I will come." He smiled. "But I am curious—who will be cooking this dinner? Servants? Your mother or you?"

She giggled. "Probably a combination of all three of us."

"I shall look forward to it."

❧

Their food came, and for awhile they turned their attention to it. Josie felt a little guilty over his comment about their complementing each other in their efforts of benevolence. It seemed eerily close to her own wording of point number one on her list. And number two was on its way to being implemented. Since things were going so well, perhaps she should move right along to point number three on her list—encouraging each other in their faith in Christ.

"You mentioned that your parents were missionaries in Africa. Tell me about your family." His expression instantly revealed a love for his family.

"My mother died when I was born. But Claire, the woman I call my mother, cared for me from the beginning. My father was a preacher. When I was a baby, he was framed for murder. For awhile he and Claire took me and hid from the law. In the end, he was acquitted. By this time he had fallen in love with Claire. They married and returned to Father's church. But only for a short time. Then they took me to West Africa with them while they served as missionaries. As it turned out, Claire and Father never had any other children."

"That is quite a story. What an intriguing past. No wonder you are an extraordinary man."

He shrugged.

"Are your folks still living?"

"Yes. But they are presently abroad."

"They must miss you. How long have you lived in the United States?"

"They came home while I was a teen. I stayed in Beaver Creek, Ohio, with relatives when they returned."

"Oh? What relatives?"

"I have a whole gang of them. I call them the Tucker House bunch. "

"How is it that you came to Cincinnati?"

"I heard about Dr. Drake." His tone was reprimanding as if she should have known.

"Of course," she said, feeling an aversion toward this Dr. Drake who had such a hold on David. She had only met Drake once or twice.

"When did you come to Cincinnati?" he asked.

"I was born here."

The waiter interrupted with a question about dessert, but they both declined.

"I should be getting home before dark."

"I'll hail a hackney and take you home."

"That isn't necessary."

"But it is. Come."

David found a hackney and assisted her into it. He was so considerate. Her thoughts rambled. "What happened to the man you found half dead?"

"He survived, but he's very weak. It's a shame. He has no home. He's not a slave, but he cannot find work. Always on the move."

"I'm sorry." They both grew reflective. Eventually Josephine asked, "Do you think this will stop the volunteers?"

"I don't know. People have erroneous ideas about cholera. Some still believe it's a moral issue and cholera comes from the poor and immoral." He scowled. "Ridiculous idea."

"I'm proud of you. The work you're doing."

"That means a lot to me."

They rode in silence after that, but it was a comfortable quiet. She realized that although they skirted around the subject, they hadn't actually talked about their faith in God. She would bring it up the next time she saw him. She felt assured that there would be another time. He'd promised to come to dinner, and he'd said those beautiful words about friendship.

The carriage jerked to a stop. David stepped down and then helped her descend. He continued to hold her hand.

"Thank you for a lovely dinner," she said.

"I'll look forward to our next one," he replied.

Josie walked to her front door and turned back. David still stood outside the hackney's open door. He waved. She waved back and went inside, her heart happily skipping.

Chapter 15

I'm going to lunch. Go ahead, Tom, and take care of our next patient." Outside the clinic, David inhaled the crisp November air and felt happy. In the past week there had been another workday. And he hadn't even had to be there. Some of the other board of health members had taken charge. David had been overloaded at the clinic with winter sicknesses. The event had been successful. Even Zachary Caulfield, the last person on his list, had come over to the cause and donated money. This was after Mrs. Caulfield helped Josie and Mrs. Cline with refreshments for the workers.

All in all, his project had been successful. And now with winter's approach he felt confident that the cholera would be suppressed. Of course in the spring the campaign would need to be taken up again.

As he walked, his thoughts turned to Josephine, and he wondered why he had not heard any more about the proposed dinner invitation. Perhaps there had been a disagreement at her household when the intended dinner had been discussed. Maybe he should call on her. But he didn't want to get her into trouble. He chuckled. She wasn't bashful. She would show up at the clinic one of these days. Heaven knew he had enough to keep him busy in the meantime. Of late his clinic overflowed to the point that he sent many of their patients directly to the hospital.

He rounded a corner and noticed some boys dicing. "Shall I call the authorities?" David asked with sternness.

Instantly, they scattered. When he looked up at the pathway again, the object of his thoughts stood before him, bundled in a winter cloak and muff. She waved. Her cheeks were flushed from the cold. Some errant hair framed her smiling face. His steps quickened toward her.

"Hello. I didn't know if you still came here since the weather's gotten so cold."

"Today is the first time I've been able to get away all week. The clinic is so busy right now."

"I've been busy also. With the cold turn, we've admitted more women to the workhouse. I'm sorry I couldn't make your workday. But I did make arrangements for some other women to take my place."

"Don't be sorry. I didn't make it either. All your efforts are appreciated."

"Did it go well?"

"Yes. Each time we get more volunteers and more exposure."

"Speaking of exposure, it probably wasn't the wisest idea to employ Mr. Washburn to cover your story."

"So I discovered. I believe he was jealous over you."

Josephine colored. "Probably. But I certainly haven't encouraged him. Would you like me to have a talk with him?"

"No. Don't worry about it. Let's sit. You want to share my lunch?"

"What do you have?"

"A sandwich."

"I'll just watch you eat."

"So what brings you here?"

"I've come to extend that dinner invitation we discussed earlier."

David smiled. "You actually procured one? Does your father know?"

"Yes. And he's promised me to be open-minded. And you must promise me the same."

"Of course. When?"

"Friday evening. Now I've got to go."

"Thank you, Josephine. I'll be praying about this dinner."

She gave him an enormous smile. "Me, too. Bye, then."

David watched her leave. The scent of lavender in early winter was a strangely wonderful thing.

Friday evening arrived. David's step was lively. His heart already beat madly. He rounded the corner two blocks from the Clines'. Once again, it troubled him to see a group of young lads playing dice. They recognized him and rose to scatter before he said a word. But as the lads made to disperse, he noticed a familiar face. "Master Schroeder! Wait!"

The boy stiffened, turned slowly. He looked instantly remorseful. David hurried to the lad. "Since when have you taken to the dice? Surely you know that is a perfect way to squander your money. And it is illegal."

"Some money I saved. Not enough. To make it grow, I wanted."

"Is your mother ill?"

"She's *gut*, but gone is Papa's money. In the streets she'll be."

"I'm sorry. But if it should come to that, I hear the women's workhouse is not such a bad place. Your employer, Randolph Cline—his wife and daughter work there."

"She'll not go there. To die she would first go. A job she had until another curse the neighbor did. She lost it then."

The superstition again. Remorseful that he had not followed up on presenting the gospel to the woman as he had earlier planned, David grasped at the opportunity to get involved again. "I'll make you a deal. You quit dicing, and I'll go visit your mother and see what I can do to help her."

The lad nodded. *"Danke."*

David hoped Mrs. Cline would have an idea of a job for Mrs. Schroeder. He would speak to her tonight if the opportunity presented itself.

He knocked. The familiar servant invited him in, seated him, and withdrew to find Josephine.

"David." Josephine swept into the room dressed in a pale green silk gown. "I'm so happy to see you." She moved close and whispered, "You look very fine. Let me take you to meet Mother and Father." She drew him down the hallway and just before they entered an adjoining room released his hand and gave an encouraging smile. "Ready?"

He nodded though he dreaded the encounter as much as the plague. They entered the room. Randolph Cline was reading, and Mrs. Cline sat beside him. Both of them looked up. Josephine said, "Our guest has arrived. May we join you?"

"Please do." Mrs. Cline agreed with a smile.

Randolph set his reading material aside. He leaned back, twiddled his thumbs, and quietly studied David.

"Thank you," David said. "It was kind of you to invite me."

The room grew awkwardly quiet, and David remained standing. "Sit down, Doctor. Seems the women cooked up more than dinner this evening. We might as well make the best of a bad situation."

"Father!"

"Randolph!"

"Quite so, Sir," David said, seating himself.

Once again the room grew oppressively quiet. "You've a lovely home."

"I've worked hard for it," Cline growled. "Don't squander my money."

David glanced at Josephine. She was biting her lower lip; her pretty brow was furrowed. Much to David's relief, a servant appeared and announced dinner. David was seated across from Randolph between Mrs. Cline and Josephine. They waited as the servants brought various dishes.

"You set a lovely table, Mrs. Cline."

"The cloth was my mother's."

"An heirloom?"

"Why, yes."

"Lovely," he said again for want of something more intelligent to say. Then he remembered something that might be of interest to his hostesses. "Oh. I brought you ladies something. The name of a woman who would like to be one of your personal patronesses."

He reached into his vest pocket, and when he withdrew his hand, several dice rolled out onto the table. When they tumbled, he quickly made a mad grab for them realizing how bad such a thing must look. As he did, he knocked over Josephine's glass, and dark juice splattered making a giant stain on Mrs. Cline's beautiful heirloom tablecloth.

She gasped. Both hands covered her mouth.

Randolph quickly leaped up to avoid getting a lapful of liquid. From his lofty position he glared down at David.

"I am so sorry. I apologize." David frantically grabbed at things until Josie grabbed his sleeve.

"Stop. It's all right. Please, stop."

David nodded and rose. He stood back so the servants could clean up the mess.

After what seemed like an eternity, Mr. Cline sat back down, mumbling something about *still causing a ruckus.*

The atmosphere at the table grew painfully quiet. Josephine took up the paper with the woman's name and slipped it into her bodice.

"Let me explain about the dice. I broke up a group of lads playing on the street."

Randolph Cline raised a disbelieving brow.

"In fact, you would know one of the lads," David said. "That Schroeder boy. Isn't he your apprentice?"

Randolph scowled. "He was gambling?"

"Yes, but he gave me his dice. In return I am supposed to call upon his mother and see if I can find her a job. I thought maybe you could help, Mrs. Cline. I intended to ask you about it."

"Well, of course, she can come to the workhouse, and we'll see what we can do."

"The boy doesn't seem to think she would come. She doesn't like charity."

"That's sad. I don't know what we can do if she will not accept our help."

The room grew quiet.

"Taste your food, David," Josephine said.

David took a bite and was wondrously pleased. "This is so delicious."

"Josephine made it," Mrs. Cline said.

"I had no idea you could cook like this. That's the bad part about being a bachelor. My cooking is so terrible my cat won't even eat it."

Josephine blushed.

"Maybe you should hire Mrs. Schroeder to do your cooking," Mr. Cline suggested. His eyes held a shrewd glint of satisfaction.

"That's a wonderful idea," Mrs. Cline agreed. "What do you think, David?"

"I could use some help." David thought about how he wanted the opportunity to speak with Mrs. Schroeder about the Lord. "Yes. I believe she just might do it. I'll ask."

The rest of the meal passed uneventfully in comparison to its beginning. But when they rose from the table, Randolph Cline asked David, "May I talk with you privately?" Josephine looked as if she wanted to intervene on David's behalf but wasn't sure how to accomplish it, so he had no choice but to follow Randolph into his study.

"Josie always was one to bring home strays."

David did not want to play games. "It seemed like you and I got on well enough until I mentioned Dr. Drake's name. What is it between you two?"

The point had hit its mark. "A private matter. Nothing that concerns you." He eased down into his chair.

"Did you want to speak about Josephine, or do you wish for me to diagnose your malady? Is it back pain?"

Randolph scowled again and disregarded the latter part of the question. "What are your intentions regarding my daughter?"

"We would like to be friends."

"You're not intent upon courting her?"

David choked and coughed. "Excuse me?"

"You're a doctor. You know about men and women, courting, marriage, babies."

"Please. I would describe our relationship along the lines of sparring partners. We click intellectually."

Cline's face softened. "My Josie is very bright. That's why it puzzles me that she brought you home."

"I'm an honorable man. I can give you credentials if that's what it takes to be allowed to have a friendship with Josephine."

"I've already checked your credentials. A long time ago. The only thing that comes up short is your eccentricity and your connection to Drake. I'm willing to give you a try. But just remember that I'll be watching you. Don't slip up."

"I'll remember. Now let's talk about your hemorrhoids."

Randolph's mouth gaped open. "How did you know? That daughter of mine—"

"Didn't say a word. I can tell by your actions. Let me get my black bag. I've got some turpentine and castor oil in there that will make a new man out of you. And if that doesn't work, we'll try some salt in buffalo tallow."

"Humph!"

Chapter 16

D avid. Come in. Sit down." He did so, wondering why Dr. Drake had called this special meeting. "I'm very pleased with the outcome of your cleanup campaign."

Efforts had been switched from actual cleaning up of debris to digging drainage ditches. The weather would soon turn the ground frigid, and once it snowed, the debris would not be a problem until spring. The drainage ditches would accommodate spring floods and snow runoff. Most of the funds collected had been put into hiring engineers and labor for the digging. Each morning after David made his trek along the docks or the canal, he would swing by various sites and speak encouragement to the workers.

"I'm happy enough with the results. Of course I'll take the matter up again in the spring."

"Your appointment on the board of health will remind you of keeping to your goals, I am sure. But I am so pleased with your work that I've an offer to make you. I want you to become my personal assistant."

Panic struck David. Winter was around the corner. Sickness had already snowballed. He didn't have time for anything new. "What did you have in mind?"

"Frankly I could use some help soliciting funds for the hospital."

David detested soliciting. Above all things, he did not wish to acquire another fund-raising project. "I'm very busy. The clinic is overflowing. I'm afraid I shall have to decline for now."

"You could give the clinic to your assistant to run."

Releasing a large sigh, David shrugged. "Honestly I don't see how."

"Come work with me at the hospital. Travel with me. Help me with my writing. All my projects." Drake chuckled. "I can see that I've overwhelmed you. Take some time. Give it some thought. But remember. I need you."

Give it some thought, David repeated Dr. Drake's words as he stepped out into the street. The sky looked menacing. He pulled his cloak tight around his neck and tried to take in the propensity of Drake's offer. It was the compliment of a lifetime to be asked to be his personal assistant. Quite the achievement. He never would have dreamed that Drake would even consider it. But even more amazing was that he didn't want to do it. He didn't feel like he could find contentment in shifting from one thing to another like Drake did. And now with his budding friendship with Josephine, it didn't seem prudent to take on more work. The obvious deterrent was how this position with Drake would push her father over the edge.

On the other hand, how could he dismiss such an honor to work with the greatest physician he had ever met? He couldn't do it lightly.

He glanced upward again and sniffed the air. Their first snow might arrive this very day. By the time he had reached this point in his thoughts, he had also arrived at Mrs. Schroeder's apartment. He knocked on her door.

"Doctor. Come in."

The living quarters were cold and somehow bleaker. "How is your health?" David asked. It was hard to tell if the woman was thinner with all the layers of clothes she wore.

She spoke in her native language. "Fine, thanks to your potion. But that old hen next door hasn't gotten any easier to live around."

"I'm sorry to hear that."

"What can I do for you?" she asked.

"I was hoping that you could help me out with a problem. You see, I live alone, and I'm a terrible cook. You wouldn't know anyone who I could hire to help me out?"

Her eyes brightened. "Do you like German food?"

"I do. Believe me, I'd be grateful for anything that I didn't have to cook."

"How much would you be willing to pay? I don't mean to sound negative, but by the looks of your suit, you don't have much money to spare."

He mentioned a tidy sum.

Her eyes looked disbelieving. "You sure you can afford that?"

"You have my word."

"I believe I'd like to apply for the job myself."

"Hired! When can you start?"

"Today."

"Excellent. Here's some money for supplies. I live across the canal at Vine and Eighth Streets."

"Really? I would have guessed you lived down at the docks or—"

"I live behind my clinic."

"My, my. You are full of surprises today."

"My kitchen is very small. Make yourself at home there. I never know for sure when I'll be home. But I want you to leave before it gets dark. You can just set aside my supper for me."

"But what about washing the dishes?"

"I can wash dishes. I just can't cook."

"Or you can leave them for me for the next day."

"We can work out the details as we go."

"Thank you. I really need a job. I believe fate has been good to me and that curse has been reversed for good." She cackled. "If only the old hen knew."

"I'd rather believe that God has brought us together."

Mrs. Schroeder gazed at him with worshipful eyes, and David knew she had missed the point. But he hoped that with her coming to his house they would become friends and that he would have an opportunity to explain further what he meant by that statement.

He returned to the clinic, walking via the canal and thinking about his morning. Accepting the position with Dr. Drake would probably mean there would be no more time for walks along the canal or down at the docks. He crossed over the canal and was surprised to see Otis Washburn was also strolling along Court Street. But what was really intriguing was that he had a woman on his arm. A very attractive one. The reporter did not see David. His attention was entirely engrossed by his lady friend. David felt a surge of relief, hoping that this meant that Washburn would not be pursuing Josephine. It wasn't as if he had any claims on her, and Josephine had even said that she was not interested in Washburn, but still, David hoped that this other woman would keep Mr. Washburn occupied.

Things hadn't been perfect the other night at the Clines', but at least Randolph had not kicked him out of the house or demanded that he leave his daughter alone. In fact, David enjoyed standing up to the man and relished the ensuing challenge. But if he accepted Drake's offer, no doubt the door would slam in his face. It was either the opportunity of a lifetime or the very thing that would ruin his life.

Josephine wrapped her muffler about her neck and stepped into the crisp air. She had just come from church services, and now she was on her way to the workhouse to visit with one of her wards. She had first met Rosemary the day that David had held his clinic at the workhouse. She climbed the steps and entered the brick building, placed her cloak and muffler on a hook in the cloakroom, then proceeded down the long hall to the dorm where she was to meet Rosemary. She joined Rosemary on her meager cot to talk.

"How have you been feeling?"

"The baby moves a lot. But *gut* I am."

"I'm praying that your child will be strong like you."

The young German woman dipped her head and raised sad eyes. "Sometimes March seems far away. Other times I do not wish the day of birth to come. This child. How will I raise? I know not anything about being a mother."

"Neither do I. But if you love the child, that will be enough."

"True this is?"

"There is another person who can help you more than anyone. He can be a father to the baby."

Rosemary's eyes widened. She shook her head. "I need no man."

"You need this one. His name is Jesus."

"You speak of God." Rosemary smiled.

"Yes. Do you know Jesus?"

"No. But this I believe. You do. If you pray for me. It helps."

Josie reached out and touched the younger woman. "I will pray. And I will pray that you will know Him as I do."

"Look!" Rosemary pointed out the bleak square window. "It snows!"

"Oh, my! Come!" Josie grabbed Rosemary's hand, and together they went to the window and watched the large flakes descend. As the snow blanketed Cincinnati, it seemed to cover its imperfections.

The large flakes piled up outside the clinic. Tom kept the fire going all afternoon, but once the snow started, the stream of patients lessened. At such a break, the clinic door blew open and David's new cook stepped inside.

"Whew. The snow's coming thick."

"I had hoped you would have headed home by now. I should have checked in on you," he returned in German.

"I'm on my way. I wanted to tell you that there's a stew on your stove."

"Did you make yourself a meal of it? That's part of the pay. You eat a portion of what you fix."

"But that's not right."

"It most certainly is. How are you going to find the time to cook for yourself? By the time you walk home, you'll be tired. It's the only way that this arrangement can work out for us. Now hurry over there and eat and be on your way."

Mrs. Schroeder glanced back outside. "If it wasn't coming down so hard, I'd stay and argue."

"Go."

She chuckled. "I'm going. I'm going."

Tom chuckled. "What was that all about?"

"Food."

"Ah!"

An hour later the snow was only lightly falling. It was so beautiful that it gave David a sudden inspiration.

"Can you close up here? I've an errand to run."

"Certainly."

David hurried out to make his arrangements. By the time he was finished, his mouth was watering for Mrs. Schroeder's stew. It was still warm and delicious. He set out a small bowl to cool for the cat who rubbed against his leg.

"It's as delicious as it smells. You're going to love this."

His clock struck seven. It was time. He put the bowl on the floor and dashed out the door, brimming with excitement. Within the hour he manned a horse-driven sleigh toward the Cline residence. He jumped down, secured the horse, and knocked. The servant invited him in to wait for Josephine.

"David." Josephine's laughter tinkled like the bells on the sleigh. "Look at you. You're all snowed on. Isn't it wonderful?"

"I thought it was cause for a celebration. Winter's first snow. Come look outside."

Josephine peered out and gasped with delight. "You brought a sleigh! What a thoughtful man you are. I'll just be a moment."

"Dress warm!" he called needlessly after her.

When she returned, David helped her into the sleigh and positioned a lap blanket across her legs. "Giddyap!"

The sleigh lurched. "Ooh! I haven't had this much fun since I was a child."

"Neither have I." David laughed. The snow felt cold and wet against his face. "I can't keep you out in this long, so let's enjoy it while we can."

The street was beautiful with its white carpet, gas lanterns, and other horses and sleighs. It was just the sort of thing that was wonderful enough to be impressed upon one's mind as a forever memory. "Oh, look! Everyone has the same idea."

Josephine studied him. "I wouldn't have thought this snow would make you so happy. Didn't you say that it would halt progress on your project?"

"It does, but I was expecting it. Part of the reason that I am so happy is your father's wonderful suggestion and my full stomach."

"Mrs. Schroeder?"

"Yes. She cooked me up a hearty stew and seemed as pleased with our new arrangement as I am. It seems many things could be changing in my life."

"How is that?"

"Dr. Drake asked me if I wanted to become his personal assistant. Give up the clinic." As soon as the words were out, David wondered why he had divulged that bit of information. He had meant to keep it to himself while he considered it. It must have been the mood, the happiness bubbling over inside.

"But you love your work."

"I know. It's a difficult decision." He wished more than ever he hadn't brought it up. He didn't want to spoil things.

"I'll pray about it for you."

"Thank you."

"I had a good day also. Remember the pregnant girl from when you held the clinic at the workhouse?"

"Yes, I do."

"Rosemary is German, and she's teaching me some of the language. We had a nice meeting today. In fact, we were together when we saw the snow through her window." Josephine looked shy. "I was trying to tell her about Jesus."

"How did she respond?"

"She wants me to pray for her."

"That's a good start. I'm hoping to lead Mrs. Schroeder to God's throne. When I first met her and she almost died from that alleged curse, I begged God to save her, hoping that He would have a chance to win her soul. Then I forgot about her until I saw her son the other day dicing. I guess it was God's reminder. I know that when He's behind a thing, it will happen. It's not of my own doing. It's always God, pure and simple."

"But we still have to explain it to them."

"Yes. It all happens so naturally if it is of God."

"I'm happy to know about your faith in God. You mentioned that your parents were missionaries, but I did not know how it was with you and the Lord."

"It is well with me and the Lord. I am glad that we can talk of such things together."

By this time they had circled the city and returned outside the Clines' residence. Josephine's face and hair were wet, her cheeks rosy, and her eyes bright. She looked wonderful. "I wish our ride could go on, but I must get you inside to warm up. Doctor's orders."

Josephine clasped his arm with her mittens. "Thank you so much for this enchanting evening. I don't think I shall ever forget it. Please, do not get down. I'll be fine." She released him and jumped down before he could object. "Bye!" She waved.

A warmth churned inside David's chest. He waved back, then waited until she had disappeared inside the large, austere house. He could not remember when he had enjoyed himself so much. "Giddyap!"

Chapter 17

December days grew cold. Snow piled up. Mrs. Schroeder came whenever the weather permitted, and David made sure that she did not go hungry. Sometimes they dined together. He would read from his brown leather Bible and translate into German. Gradually the immigrant woman received a foundation of biblical truth. He anxiously watched for what the Lord would do with these seeds, confident God would work a miracle in her life.

His work brought satisfaction. His friendship with Josephine was burgeoning. Oftentimes they still disagreed in their discussions, and Randolph was still a touchy subject.

With an inward grin, he remembered how Randolph had reluctantly admitted that his relief from hemorrhoids had made him a new man, that he could even ride horseback again. He had offered to pay David for his medical services, but he had declined. Still, dinner at the Clines' oftentimes left David feeling that he had been weighed and found lacking.

Today David was eagerly anticipating a social engagement with Josephine. They were going Christmas shopping together. Mrs. Schroeder had even volunteered to spend her day making tea and chaperoning so Josephine could meet Gratuity. Women. They had such funny ideas. Being friends with Josephine was complicated. There were always the rules of propriety to keep in mind. Even though they were merely friends, her reputation needed guarding.

The idea of meeting Gratuity had stemmed from Josephine's remark that David was putting on weight since Mrs. Schroeder was cooking for him. When he replied that he was not fat compared to his cat, Josephine had become intrigued with the idea of his having a pet. This fascination increased until she had become adamant about meeting his cat. Jokingly he had told Mrs. Schroeder of his plans to bring Josephine to the clinic and introduce Gratuity. It was then the older woman had insisted that she prepare her apple strudel and tea for the special occasion and that he bring his young lady to his home where she would be their chaperone. Josephine had been delighted with the idea. And David was delighted over any event that would allow him to spend time with Josephine.

He knocked on the Clines' door. Mrs. Cline greeted him warmly and struck up a conversation until Josephine appeared. "Will you dine with us tonight, Doctor?" the older woman asked.

"Thank you for the invitation, but my cook is making me a strudel and insists that it must be eaten hot. In fact, she has offered to chaperone so that Josephine can sample it. Why don't you join us? We'd love to have you."

"Oh no. I wouldn't dream of intruding upon your afternoon."

"You're welcome to come, Mother."

"No. I've other things to attend to. But do come to dinner soon, Doctor."

"He will. I'll see to it."

David shrugged, and Mrs. Cline chuckled. "Have fun, dears."

As soon as they were outside, David joked, "If only Papa were so warmhearted."

Josephine bumped against him playfully. "Give him time. Minds, bodies, and hearts all take time to heal."

David swept off his hat and bowed deeply. "I salute you, Miss Poet Divine."

She smacked his arm. "Do stop and be serious. We need to think of a gift for—"

"Oh, no. I'm not choosing a gift for Papa."

"Rosemary at the workhouse. I thought maybe she'd like something for the baby."

"Ah. Little things, easy to carry. That is *gut.*"

"You are in fine fiddle today. But so am I. And I'm looking forward to seeing your home and meeting your fat cat."

"Mrs. Schroeder has promised to make it presentable and most importantly not to let the cat out."

Josephine said wistfully, "I wish I could speak German so I could relate to her. The language is hard to learn."

"Don't give up. Which reminds me. What should I give Mrs. Schroeder for Christmas? It's the perfect opportunity to give her something without her arguing about accepting charity."

"Oh, yes. I do remember how she refused my comforter."

"What comforter?"

Josie reddened. "Right after you told me that folks didn't like to take charity, Mother and I took her a comforter. Only, she refused it. That was the first time, I believe, that I thought maybe you weren't entirely wrong on every issue."

"And you never told me."

Josephine stopped abruptly. "I've got it! What we can get Mrs. Schroeder." David stumbled to a halt and tilted his head, waiting. "Charles told us his mother liked feather blankets. That's what they use in Germany."

"Perfect!" In his exuberance, David swept up Josephine and spun her around. When they stopped, her face shone and her gaze revealed an emotion that made David's heart squeeze. The discovery that Josephine was more than a friend overwhelmed him. He quickly withdrew. "I beg your pardon. I guess I got carried away." Her expression turned to one of confusion so he mumbled, "Come." Then snatching hold of her hand, he hurried them forward as if they were on their way to a fire.

Hours later the moment had been entirely forgotten. They trudged toward his living quarters, shopping weary. At the sight of home, his stomach growled. Josephine giggled.

David opened the door to the smell of apples, cinnamon, and the wood fire. Gratuity pranced around their feet.

"Oh, you adorable creature!" Josephine knelt.

"Careful, she's not used to strangers."

Scooping the cat up in her arms, Josephine only smiled at him then returned to scratching the cat's head. "What's your name, Beautiful?"

"Gratuity."

A slow look of recognition came over her features. "A patient?"

"Yes. And one of God's small blessings."

"God?" Mrs. Schroeder asked, repeating one of the few English words she recognized.

David spieled off a string of German, then turned back to Josie. "She welcomes us and wants us to sit and eat."

Josephine thanked Mrs. Schroeder and asked David to translate. They talked about how much Josephine's father liked Charles and how well he was doing. They chuckled over how fat David was getting, though he knew they were only kidding him.

When the conversation lagged, David wondered what Josephine was thinking about his meager apartment. His modest furnishings had never bothered him before. But now he wished to please her and regretted his negligence in making it homey or nice. The mixture of nearly broken-down furniture and odd assortments of masculine items had been haphazardly collected over the years. The only cheery things in the room were those with breath in them: Mrs. Schroeder, Josie, and Gratuity.

They invited Mrs. Schroeder to join them in their meal, but she insisted on serving. And then when it was time for Josie to leave, Mrs. Schroeder stayed to clean up.

On their way back to Josephine's house, she asked, "Do you think Mrs. Schroeder will accept a feather blanket?"

"I think she will. But how shall we accomplish it?"

"It can be a project for some of the women at the workhouse. I'll split the cost with you."

"I can pay for it. I know my place doesn't look like much. But I've got a bit of money stashed away. I've just never given any thought to houses or furniture or anything like that."

Josephine touched his sleeve. "Don't do this, David. I thought your little place was a perfect abode for such a person as yourself."

"Meaning?"

"Dedicated to your work, sacrificing your life for others."

"I suppose some people can have a piece of both worlds. You seem to. But I've never had a desire for things. I hope you realize that a man like me has nothing much to offer a woman except friendship."

"I could take offense at that remark, but knowing you as I do, I won't. I value our friendship above any other that I have. Will you just accept that? And will you accept me as I am? Father, mansion, and all?"

"How could I not?"

They had reached her home by this time. "Do come inside, and see Mother's reaction to these tiny baby things."

"I would love to, but I've committed myself to Dr. Drake this evening."

"Oh?"

David detected jealousy or hurt. "I'm sorry. I shouldn't have promised but—"

"No." She pushed his coat front, and her voice softened. "It's fine. You go ahead. There will be other times. I'll let you know about the feather blanket."

He clasped her hand and squeezed. "Thanks, Josie." Her face reddened at the endearing form that he had used of her name. And David's heart warmed another notch toward her.

David slipped into the room filled with his medical colleagues. Dr. Drake had already started to explain the reason for calling them all together.

"As the eye infirmary remains a success, aside from much-needed funds, I'm looking for volunteers to learn the art of this particular surgery. It's taking up so much of my time that I need other physicians to fill in."

David squirmed in his chair, grateful at least that this meeting had nothing to do with the doctor's previous offer to him. Putting that issue aside, he considered Drake's appeal. David didn't wish to spend his valuable time at the hospital. He enjoyed the practice that he had at the clinic. Of course it would be helpful to learn a new technique or two, but not at the expense of turning the clinic over to his assistant.

After the general plea and following lecture, Drake served hot apple cider and mixed with his guests to round up recruits.

"So, David, are you ready to learn eye surgery?"

"I'm ready to *learn*, Sir. But the way things are at the clinic right now, I cannot afford to spend the time at the hospital. Perhaps someone else is more inclined—"

"Nonsense. You should always be willing to learn new things, David. You must not grow stale."

"But I have my mornings doing field work already, and Tom Langdon and I have our hands full at the clinic."

"Think about it. I know I can count on you. Come to the hospital in a day or two, and let me know. And we need to talk about the other. Soon." He walked away toward another young physician.

David sighed, said his farewells, and headed home. It had been a day of revelation, and he had much to think about, pray about. First, there came the realization that Josie was more than a friend. And now this.

Chapter 18

Josie watched David balance the awkward package. His face was flushed from the cold and exertion. His blue eyes shone. They crossed the canal and headed down Thirteenth Street to Mrs. Schroeder's apartment.

"I hope she accepts it," Josie worried out loud.

"Don't worry. I know how to handle her."

"I suppose you do. You can be very charming when you set your mind to it."

"Ah, yes. That's what everyone calls me, the charming doctor."

"Are you sure you don't mean 'the eccentric doctor'?"

"Exactly," he said with a wry smile.

Josie chuckled. She wished Father had agreed to invite David to Christmas dinner and feared he would be offended when he learned he wasn't invited. She knew David had family and wondered if he would be traveling north to visit them. She was thankful they had planned this outing to present Mrs. Schroeder with the feather blanket. The crisp air stung her lungs. She buried her face in her fur muff.

"Cold?"

"Walking keeps me warm, but don't you think the weather's turning colder?"

"And darker. Could snow again."

Josie fondly remembered their sleigh ride. "Have you visited Mrs. Schroeder since you hired her? Do you think she's staying warm enough?"

"I haven't called on her. But she claims she is. Dropping in today unannounced was a good idea."

"As long as she's at home."

David peered over the package at her. "You're kind of cute when your forehead wrinkles like that."

She wrinkled her nose at him, too.

"Here we are. Ready?"

Josie nodded. If not for David, she would have been afraid to approach Mrs. Schroeder with another gift offering even though the woman had acted warmly toward her that day at David's home. When one couldn't communicate in the same language, it was hard.

"Don't forget to translate everything to me."

"Nudge me if I don't."

"Maybe I'll pinch you."

"You do, and you had better run fast."

She giggled. Together they climbed the steps. David knocked on the door, and it slowly cracked open.

"Doctor. Come in," Mrs. Schroeder said in German.

Josephine followed David into the warm apartment. "Merry Christmas." David grinned, placing the wrapped package on the table, and then translating for Josephine.

"What is this?"

"Open it."

Mrs. Schroeder unwrapped the paper. She placed her palms against her pink cheeks in astonishment. "I am so ashamed." Tears pooled in her eyes.

Josephine and David looked at each other in dismay. Mrs. Schroeder spoke again. "What? What is she saying?" Josie asked with concern.

"She says it was cruel and prideful of her to say that she preferred feather quilts. But so thoughtful of you to make this."

"Tell her that the women at the workhouse helped. And be sure she knows that it is from you, too."

David and Mrs. Schroeder exchanged sentences. Finally, the woman approached Josephine. "Thank you, Miss Cline," she said in broken English. "Very lovely you are."

Josephine looked at her in amazement. "You are learning English?"

"My gift to you."

Through the blur of stinging tears Josephine saw David cross his arms and gaze proudly at Mrs. Schroeder. "What does she mean, David?"

"She wanted me to teach her some English. It was her gift to you."

Swiping back her pooling tears, Josie stepped forward and gave the older woman a warm hug. After they separated, both dabbed at their cheeks.

"Tell her that I am also learning some German words."

David did. Mrs. Schroeder replied, and he chuckled. "I believe she is matchmaking. She suggested that I should be your instructor."

Josie squeaked, "Matchmaking?"

"I'll explain to her about our friendship later. I'm sure she'll question me all about you again."

Swiping at some fresh tears over the way he had scoffed at the idea, Josie nodded. Mrs. Schroeder motioned for them to sit and began hustling to prepare them something warm to drink. When the older woman's back was turned, Josie whispered to David. "The place seems snug and warm. I believe she's doing all right."

Later when they left Mrs. Schroeder's building, the snow was falling.

"This makes it seem like Christmas," Josephine said, remembering their November sleigh ride.

"I believe after this I won't be able to watch it snow without thinking of you."

Josie smiled. He could always read her mind. Sometimes he was so sweet. "Are you going home for Christmas?" she asked.

"You mean to visit family?"

Josie nodded.

"No. I cannot get away right now. Dr. Drake's got some newfangled ideas, and I'm so busy I can hardly find the time for anything." He sounded resentful.

"What sort of newfangled ideas?"

"He wants me to learn to do eye surgery."

"That sounds like a good idea."

"He needs surgeons who will give him a break at the hospital. But I'm busy enough with my own work at the clinic. Still, how can I refuse him? It's an opportunity of a lifetime, and I owe him so much already." He shrugged. "All of Drake's ideas are good. It's just that he has his hands in so many different things, and he seems to accomplish everything so well. I feel like I'm letting him down, lazy or something."

"Nonsense!" Josie frowned. "How can you say that? You do not have to be like him to be special. Can't you see how unique your ministry is?"

"Sometimes I wonder. My parents accomplished so much, dedicating their lives to missionary work. Dr. Drake's achievements in medicine and science are astonishing. The whole world benefits, while I accomplish so little. If I did do the eye surgery and work at the hospital, it would fit in better with his plans for me and his other offer."

"Being his personal assistant?"

"Yes. But it also eases me out of my clinic work. It's a tough decision. And I know being Drake's personal assistant would not endear me to your father."

Josie grew angry over David's belittling of himself. He really believed that he was not meeting others' expectations. He was an excellent physician and had made a difference in many lives. "You've been teaching me to think for myself. Now I want you to do the same. You are a special person, talented in the ways that God created you. Your ambitions may be different from any other man's, but they are the ones you were designed for. You must use your talents accordingly and only be concerned that you do your best and not how you measure up with any other person's expectations of you."

David looked down at her with surprise. "Not even your expectations?"

"Be serious."

"I am."

"Then you are overly concerned with pleasing others."

"I will think about that, Josephine. In the meantime, tell me what you are doing for Christmas."

"Nothing special. We will go to church. Mother will cook. Father will read the Christmas story."

"I have an idea, but I'm not sure if it will fit in with your plans." Josephine listened. "If the weather stays this cold and the canal freezes solid, maybe we could find some time on Christmas Day after your family festivities to go ice skating."

"If the weather holds, I will make the time. It sounds delightful."

"Good." They looked up at the Clines' residence. Fresh snow covered the walk and windowsills. "Thank you for everything you did for Mrs. Schroeder."

"I enjoyed it so much. I'll see you on Christmas afternoon then, if the weather holds."

David squeezed her mitten-clad hand and smiled warmly. "Bye, Josie."

She paused outside her door and turned back to watch him walk away. The back of his coat was white from snow. She looked down at their footsteps in the snow. This man was special. She hoped he would come to appreciate that.

⊰❦⊱

Christmas Eve afternoon, Mrs. Schroeder cooked David a turkey dinner.

"You are still here. I am glad. I wanted to wish you a Happy Christmas."

"That is why I waited. I have a gift for you."

David took the rectangular package and examined it. Carefully he unwrapped the paper. It was a small wooden box, intricately carved.

"It is from the homeland. I thought it was something you could use."

"I will cherish it. Before you go, may I read the Christmas story to you?"

"Yes. I was wondering if you would. Some of the things you have told me have my curiosity."

With Gratuity curled up at his feet, David read the story and translated from Luke 2:10–11. "And the angel said unto them, Fear not: for, behold, I bring you good tidings of great joy, which shall be to all people. For unto you is born this day in the city of David a Saviour, which is Christ the Lord."

"You are my savior," Mrs. Schroeder said. "You are an angel."

"No. Just a human. There is only one Savior."

"His power is strong? You used His power to break the neighbor's curse?"

David hardly knew how to form his reply. He did not want to lie. But he knew she was not ready to hear about the frog's help quite yet, even though he realized someday he would need to disclose his secret.

"His power is stronger than any evil. It is enough that the crucified Jesus was brought back to life again. Just as you can be if you only have faith."

"Tell me about faith," she said.

David explained how faith in Christ saves mankind from sin. And when Mrs. Schroeder asked if this Jesus would take her side or her neighbor's, he had to explain that God is not prejudiced.

"That was a good story. Now I must go and prepare Christmas for Charles."

"Thank you for taking the time to listen. And for this gift. Tell Charles Merry Christmas for me." He wished that she had better understood the true meaning of Christmas.

"I will. Now you must eat your meal before it gets cold."

He nodded and breathed a prayer, releasing this special woman over to the Lord's care.

Chapter 19

Dr. Drake's Christmas party caused David to feel lonely. Though it was good to spend time with his colleagues and friends, Dr. Drake's usual inspirational speech only left David feeling frustrated. Until he met Josephine, he had lingered on every word from Drake—every idea inspired him. David wondered if this let-down feeling came because he had been depending upon Drake more than God. Something Josephine had said that day they visited Mrs. Schroeder had been nibbling at his mind. Something about he and God choosing his course and being content with it.

At one point in his life, David had thought he had done that. It was when he made the choice to remain in the States and go into medicine rather than return to the missionary field with his parents. Of course, for a time they had expected him to return to them with his medical experience and join their work. But he hadn't felt led to do that. That was when he had felt confident he was on the right track with his life and following God's leading, even though it had been a sacrifice to be without family. When had he turned the reins over to Dr. Drake?

It was complicated. Drake was his teacher, his mentor—an intelligent, inspiring leader. Was this urge for independence the result of his association with Josephine or was it God's leading? The last time he had experienced such desperation, he had chosen a Bible study in Ecclesiastes. Seeking that special closeness with God, he got out his Bible and turned to the same passage.

He read about the beauty and burden of man's labor and listened carefully for God's Spirit to gently whisper direction. When he came to the middle of chapter four, the words gripped him. "Two are better than one; because they have a good reward for their labour. For if they fall, the one will lift up his fellow: but woe to him that is alone when he falleth; for he hath not another to help him up. Again, if two lie together, then they have heat: but how can one be warm alone?"

Josephine's concerned voice came to him. *Do you think Mrs. Schroeder is staying warm enough?* Other thoughts tumbled through his mind. *Friends help each other. Mates keep each other warm. Two are better than one.* Now he really felt lonely.

"Lord, I feel like I am floundering. What am I missing? Do I need to make a change in my career? Am I not spending enough time with You? Is

Josephine confusing my life? Why am I so drawn to her? What are You try-ing to tell me? I do not want to go down the wrong road. I want to stay in Your will."

Gratuity's mewing interrupted his thoughts. "What is it, Girl?" He opened his eyes. The cat had a Christmas gift for him. It lay at his feet. "Gratuity! You take that mouse outside." But the cat snapped up its unap-preciated offering and ran under the bed.

❦

Josephine watched through the frosty pane for David. She hadn't long to wait until she saw his straight, fit form bounding up the road. She quickly plunged into her cloak, grabbed her skates, and headed outside. "Merry Christmas!"

He smiled broadly. "I could not come empty-handed on Christmas Day. Will you accept this small token of our friendship?"

"Of course. But I have something for you, too. Shall we open them upon our return?"

David nodded, and she hurried back into the house to leave the pack-age. When she returned, he was whistling.

"Let me carry those." He took her skates. "How was your day so far?"

"Lovely. And neither Mother nor Father could fault my eagerness to go skating, though both were concerned about my safety."

"Don't worry. I won't let anything happen to you."

"That's what I assured them. How was your day?"

David shrugged. "Festive enough. Only I could see how lonely Dr. Drake is. He still misses his wife. Somehow the loneliness seeped over onto me."

"Well, I shan't give you time to think about that any more today. Oh, look!"

There were several couples on the ice. The women's long, full skirts made a pretty picture, like winter flowers. Everyone was bundled. Many glided gracefully while some children were learning the art. Josephine clapped. "I'm so excited."

When they reached the ice, David offered, "If you let me help you with those skates, you won't have to sit on the cold ground."

"All right." She slipped her skirt just high enough for David to assist her. Still kneeling in front of her, he suggested, "Take hold of my shoulder so you don't lose your balance."

She used his shoulder to steady herself. The moment she touched him, it felt as if the day had warmed at least fifteen degrees. His touch was gen-tle, capable, that of a doctor tending a patient. Yet it also seemed personal the way he helped her slip into the skates.

He made the final adjustments and helped her to a nearby tree. "Hang on here while I put mine on."

She giggled as he sank to the ground and his manner changed from gentle to awkward motions, much tugging and grunting. "You must not have much confidence in my abilities by the way you've attached me to this tree."

"Just remembering your promise to your father. Until I'm rigged up, I don't want you skating off by yourself. All done." He stood up and offered his hand. "Ready to give it a try?"

"Let's go."

They clomped through the frozen grass, which was easy to walk in, but the drop-off to the ice was a bit trickier. David jumped down first. His legs went out from him, and he landed on his rump. She giggled, and he quickly jumped up and steadied himself. "Your turn." He positioned his heels together so he wouldn't slide away and grabbed her by the waist to ease her down onto the ice. They teetered a bit then found their balance. Taking her hand again, he led her toward the center of the ice. "You are very good."

"Thank you. So are you, Doctor."

Josephine loved the opportunity to hold David's hand—to bump up against his strong, solid body. It made her feel feminine and protected. And the way he kept smiling at her made her feel cherished. She only hoped he cared about her in a special way and that it was not all her imagination.

The afternoon was even more wonderful than she had imagined it might be. She wished it could go on forever. But eventually the crowd thinned and the wind picked up. It would be futile to pretend that she wasn't cold and her legs and feet weren't tired and wobbly.

Maneuvering off the ice was a little easier than getting on. David climbed up the embankment and reached back to easily pull her up onto the snowy grass. They returned to the tree, and this time Josephine backed up against it while David removed her skates. "Are your feet frozen?"

"Yes," she admitted.

"We'll take a hackney. I fear I kept you out too long."

She watched him remove his own skates. "It was so fun. I don't regret it."

"You are a good sport." He held her hand again. "Come. Let's catch that one."

Inside the hackney, Josephine shivered.

"You poor thing. Here, come close." David placed his arm around her shoulders and drew her into his warmth. He whispered into her ear, "Two are better than one. Ecclesiastes."

His breath was warm and sweet against her cheek. She turned toward him. He was gazing intently at her, and she could not look away. Slowly he lowered his face. He was going to kiss her. Her heart raced. There was no time to consider what it all might mean. She felt drawn to him. The kiss was like his touch had been. Gentle. He pulled away and smiled. She blushed. He touched her cheek. "Merry Christmas, Josie. I shall always remember the fun we had together today."

She took a deep breath. "David, I. . .me, too."

"Warm enough?"

"What? Oh." She smiled, embarrassed. "Yes."

He leaned back in the carriage, his arm still around her possessively, and neither of them spoke again until they had reached her house. She wasn't sure what to make of it. And she was afraid to stir, lest he remove his arm and the dream would disappear like vapor. But when the carriage lurched to a stop, he moved away from her and descended, then helped her down. His hands against her waist did not linger, and she wondered if he was regretting their kiss. His gaze did not meet hers.

"You must come in. We need to exchange our gifts."

"Are you sure?"

She looked up at him. "Yes. And you will join me for some warm cider."

"Sounds heavenly." He was looking at her with that strange look again, like he had just before he kissed her. She swallowed and nodded, and they went into the house.

Soon they were seated in a small sitting area with a gigantic fire and two steaming cups of cider. After several warming swallows, they set them aside and turned their attention to opening their gifts.

Josephine caressed the cover of *The Adventures of Captain Bonneville*. "I'm so excited. I shall start to read this tonight."

"I wasn't sure, but I thought you would enjoy something adventuresome since you attended the lecture on Indian treaties. There's an inscription."

She turned the beginning pages until she found it. *I look forward to a discussion when you have finished.*

David fumbled with his gift. It was so fragile and tiny. Finally, the paper fell away. His eyes lit, and he smiled as he held the delicate glass snowflake by its gold thread. "It's perfect."

She was touched by his tone. "When I saw it, it reminded me of you."

"It's a perfect symbol of our. . ." It sounded like he had a lump in his throat. ". . .of our friendship."

She ventured, "Many faceted. It's very special. Like you, David."

"Thank you." He gazed at it in his palm, caressing it with his finger.

Long after he was gone, and she was alone in her room with the book he had given her, the memory of it lingered in her mind.

Chapter 20

After Christmas David decided to receive eye surgery instruction from Dr. Drake. Aside from a flood of patients at the clinic, there were now sketches and notes to pour over. Josephine was pushed to the back of his life for several reasons. First, he knew he had advanced their relationship to another level when he had kissed her, and it frightened him. So he put off seeing her, feeling unfamiliar with this new stage of their relationship.

The matter was so uncomfortable to consider that when Dr. Drake had once again confronted him about learning eye surgery, this time he had jumped at the chance to bury himself in his work.

As the days turned into weeks, he was surprised that Josephine had not taken the initiative to call on him at the clinic. During those times that he thought about her, he hoped that she was well and wondered if she was avoiding him. Maybe she also regretted the kiss and did not feel attracted to him the way he felt attracted to her. If so, this time apart would do them both good.

And so it had gone until one day in mid-January when Mrs. Cline stopped in at his clinic and scolded him soundly. "I would think when one's friend has pneumonia one would visit her. Especially when one is a doctor."

"Josie?"

"She's been very ill. But worst of all, she thinks you've abandoned her."

David grabbed his coat and yelled over his shoulder, "Tom, take over here." Nearly pushing Mrs. Cline out the clinic's front door, he asked, "Has she seen a doctor?"

"Of course. How else would I know that she has pneumonia?"

"But this is a very serious thing." He of all people knew how pneumonia could snuff out a person's life. He panicked at the thought of his Josephine being in the clutches of death. "Why didn't you contact me sooner?" They climbed into Mrs. Cline's carriage.

"Josie wouldn't let me."

He dipped his head in his hands and mumbled, "I've been so busy, too busy."

"She's over the worst of it. Don't fret so."

He relaxed a bit. "Thank you for coming for me."

"She doesn't know I've gone for you," Mrs. Cline said curtly.

When they arrived, she led the way to the sitting room where Josephine reclined on a couch ensconced in blankets. Her head was propped up on a pillow, her hair spilling around her face and shoulders. She looked angelic. He drew in a breath and held it. Mrs. Cline left them, and he rushed forward.

"Josie, I'm so sorry."

"David? You finally came."

"You have every reason to be miffed. I didn't know you were ill. I was just so busy learning eye surgery, and the clinic's been busy."

She waved. "Don't do this." But she did not say anything else. She just gazed at him with a betrayed expression. "I missed you."

So many emotions flooded over David. He was angry with himself for abandoning her. He felt protective and wanted to scoop her up and hold her to his chest. He wanted to examine her and make sure that she was improving. "Why didn't you send for me?"

"I thought you would come. Every day I thought you would come. I thought. . .we were friends."

He clasped her hand. A tear slid down his cheek. "I'm a fool." The clock chimed. "And I'm late." He jumped to his feet. "Surgery. I'm supposed to be at the hospital. When I heard about you, I forgot all about it. It can't be helped. I have to go. But I'll be back."

Her voice saddened. "Go then."

"I'm sorry."

❧

Josephine watched him leave. Then she pulled the blanket over her head and wept. The day they had gone skating, she thought he had shown signs of devotion. But he hadn't called, and then she had gotten so sick. She'd kept waiting for him to come. He didn't. Then she had remembered how he had told her that he was lonely, missing his family. And she wondered if he had only shown such affection that Christmas Day because he had been feeling weak and lonely.

At first she had resolved not to let it bother her, but it did. At times she thought she could wait for him to realize how much he needed her. There was no doubt anymore in her own mind that she needed him. But at other times she grew weary of waiting and sometimes even angry enough that she wished he would stay away. But then he came to call upon her. And now she was even more confused.

Once she'd recuperated, she was going to have to help the doctor discover his feelings for her. She was sure she had seen evidence of the beginning of love in his eyes. Yes, she would think about that.

❧

The rest of January taxed David's patience. First of all, he was still busy at the hospital. Secondly, Tom Langdon had gotten the idea that as soon as he

453

finished his internship, he was going to go to the backwoods to practice medicine. Then David would be left alone again. Thirdly, the only times he could see Josephine was when he called on her at her home, where Randolph Cline always made him feel unwelcome. It was as if he blamed her illness on him.

One particular visit remained vivid in David's memory. Josie had expressed regret over falling behind on her German lessons, and he had offered his services.

"I can give you a lesson or two."

"But what would you teach me?" Her expression had teased.

"How about the word for good health? *Gut Gesundheit.*" She repeated it several times. "Special lady—*speziell Dame.*"

Josie practiced, then surprised him by asking, "How do you say 'handsome doctor'?"

"*Stattlich Doktor.* You may say that as often as you like." It had been the perfect opportunity to lead into the word for love, but he had lost his nerve. Instead he remembered the sadness that had filled her brown eyes when his next word was *friends.*

After that and with the general course of events, he and Josie had regressed in their relationship, back to the more comfortable stages of friendship they had earlier experienced. The door to a deeper relationship had closed. With time, calling on her had become perfunctory. It suited him most days. Though, sometimes, he had to admit there was a longing that he had to stifle. He had become expert at doing that and at covering up his emotions.

With February came sadness. One morning David went to the docks to check on the homeless. He discovered the dead body of the black man who had been found ill during one of their workdays. It deeply moved him, for the man had always been so sweet and thankful each time David called upon him. He trudged through his morning heavy of heart, finally finding himself at Josephine's door.

"David. What's wrong? You look awful." Josephine drew him inside.

"I found a friend at the docks this morning, frozen. My house is nice and warm and cozy, and my friend was frozen."

Tears welled up in Josie's eyes. "Oh, David, I'm so sorry."

"Sometimes the weight of death is heavy."

She nodded, her eyes moist. "I cannot even imagine how you must feel."

They sat in silence for a long while. Eventually, he said, "I must go. I just needed someone."

"Two are better than one," she said, repeating what he had once told her.

"Especially when the other one is you," he replied.

❧❧

Josephine finally convinced her mother she was well enough to resume her visits to the workhouse.

"I almost didn't recognize you," Josie told Rosemary. "You've gotten so—"

"Fat. The word is fat."

Josie giggled at the young woman's expression. "All pregnant women look roundly beautiful. Is there anything I can pray about for you?"

"I worry for the baby's birth. A proper home I need to find."

"I'm sure God has a plan for you." Josie squeezed the woman's hand. "We just need to seek it."

As Josie worked, she was reminded that physically she was weaker, thinner. But she was confident that her strength would return. Many people didn't survive pneumonia. She was fortunate. If she weren't so tired, she would stop by the clinic. Wouldn't David be surprised to see her out and about?

Their time together had become rather dull and routine. Before her illness, they had done many exciting things together. She wondered now what she could do to spice things up, to jolt him out of his complacency, to move their relationship forward again. She intended to look over her list when she got home. She needed a plan that would grab David's attention.

Chapter 21

Josephine reclined and read the perfectly penned list of things her friendship with David could offer him:

We both share the desire to help others
Cooking and domestic abilities
Encourage him in Christian faith
Feminine appeal—attraction toward each other

Then she read the note added at the bottom, her mother's words: Demonstrate in ways that he can understand.

She thought she had worked at each of these points. Was she missing a point, or should she expand one of the points she had already listed? She brewed over it for at least an hour, trying this or that in her mind and considering the consequences.

The point about cooking abilities didn't even apply anymore. By persuading him to hire Mrs. Schroeder, her father had cunningly undermined one of her drawing points. How about intellectual stimulation? She grinned. It was something that any man in her life would need to appreciate. There was *The Adventures of Captain Bonneville* he had gotten her for Christmas. She had finished reading it. She could invite him over to discuss the book.

She glanced over the list again. *Attraction toward each other*. David didn't seem to really notice her anymore. She would change her appearance. With her illness, her skin had paled causing her freckles to stand out on her face. Perhaps she would try egg whites and go for that glazed effect that was so popular. A new hat wouldn't do for an indoor book discussion, but she could get one for another time. She had always been rather plain and conservative. Maybe she needed to try something more frilly, something to shock his sensibilities, make him see her as a woman. A new scent! The one she had always used, lavender, why she couldn't even smell it on herself any longer. She had heard that spiced rose water was all the rage.

With anticipation she put her plan into action, and finally the night of the anticipated book discussion arrived. Judging from the range of emotions displayed on David's face after he had entered the room, Josephine thought her plan might be working. He certainly appeared to be noticing her as a woman. First there had been surprise, then puzzlement, and now his face seemed to glow of pleasure or something likewise agreeable.

"My, you are dressed festively tonight," he said.

"When one's father is in textiles, it doesn't look good to dress shabbily."

"On the contrary, you look up to the occasion." He leaned closer, then frowned.

"What is wrong?"

"Have you changed your fragrance?"

Josephine felt her face heat. "Spiced rose water. It's all the rage."

"It's nice. But I really loved the lavender. I associated it with you. I'm relieved to see you have some color. When I first entered the room, I was concerned for your health. You looked so pale."

"You don't say."

"Now I've offended you. I didn't mean to. It's just that I've grown accustomed to you, or thought I knew you, and tonight I feel as if I'm sitting with a stranger."

"Do you find this new person interesting?"

"Absolutely charming."

She leaned close. *"Danke."*

Shock covered his face again. "What else have you done?" His voice was fatherly, chastising.

She jerked away and straightened her back. "You find something else to criticize?"

"Never. Only I loved your freckles, Josie. And well, your face looks glossy."

"Egg whites. Plautus says a woman without paint is like food without salt." She gave an exasperated look. "You certainly are stuffy."

"I am not. Why do you think you have to change your looks? You were plenty salty before."

"I was dull."

"Hah!" He threw his head back for a good laugh. "You have never been dull, Josie. Goodness, I'd only begun to feel comfortable and safe around you."

"Maybe I don't want you to feel comfortable and safe. Anyway, I invited you over to discuss literature not to discuss my personal appearance."

"Very well, forgive me. Let's see, we've already discussed Plautus. Washington Irving was in store for tonight, was he not?"

"He was."

"I shall let you begin our discussion." He leaned back and continued to watch her with disconcerting awareness, and a tinge of shock and amusement.

She squirmed. "I find his descriptions of the Indians fascinating."

"This does not surprise me. I do, too. He does help us to see their personalities; each tribe was very different."

"I liked the Flatheads because it sounded like they were polite, peaceable, and treated everyone with respect," she said.

"Aren't they the ones who loved to race horses and gamble? As I recall, your folks didn't find it amusing when those dice rolled out of my pocket onto the dining room table."

She smiled. "And you knocked over your drink and stained Mother's cloth."

"She forgave me."

Josie reasoned. "To the Flatheads it was merely recreation. Everyone has to have recreation."

"True. What you said about showing respect, I like that. Everyone deserves that kind of treatment."

"I imagine you learned that from your parents."

"Yes. Did I ever tell you that Claire's parents were killed by the Indians?"

"No. What happened?"

"The Wyandots. It was when they were being pushed off their land. Mother says she forgave them. It was all very tragic. Just like any war."

"I felt sorry about the way things turned out for the Wyandots."

"My aunt's friend knew Tecumseh."

"Really?"

"It's a long story."

"Please, I would love to hear it."

When he had finished, she said, "It's a sad story. I didn't want this to be a sad evening."

"What did you want it to be, Josie? Seems like you went to a great deal of trouble to get my attention. What are you trying to tell me?"

She shrugged. "Only that I'd like to get more reaction out of you."

"I have been predictable, haven't I?"

"The *stattlicher Doktor* has been very predictable lately. He does not seem to be the same man who showed up at my doorstep with a sleigh. I thought perhaps I was at fault, that I was boring you."

"Oh, Josie. Never. It is all my fault. I've intentionally pushed my feelings for you away."

"What feelings, David?"

"Fond ones."

She waited, but he did not expound. She had given him every opportunity to express his affection for her. But if there was to be any kind of romantic relationship between them, he would have to be able to express his heart and be willing to open up to her. It seemed like she had done all the chasing in this relationship. Well, she would not propose to him! His reluctance suddenly made her angry, weary. "Perhaps you can tell me about them another time, *stattlicher Doktor*. Suddenly I'm feeling tired."

David stood. "I understand. I've had an enjoyable evening. Thank you for making it special. I really will try harder to be a better. . ."

It was as if he knew it would anger her to say the *friend* word tonight so he did not finish his sentence. It hung there between them, unfinished. She took pity on him. "I know, David. Another time then."

David did not hail a hackney. He needed to walk and think about Josie's strange behavior. He still couldn't believe how she had arrayed herself in such an extreme manner with the glossy face and the rose water. Didn't she know that he loved her just the way she was?

Loved her? She had nearly caused him to admit his love for her. Why hadn't he? She had transformed from alluring to angry, practically tossing him out the door. He felt like she had not only dismissed him, but dismissed them. What if this time, she let him go for good?

It was what he deserved. He was predictable, boring, standoffish, and a whole lot of other words that she might have flung at him if he had stayed around much longer.

Stattlicher Doktor. She'd called him that twice. But the second time he had felt like the hatchet was going to fall on his neck any moment. She had mocked him, her mouth twisted as if she had a bad taste in it. Was that what he was becoming to her? A bad taste? A disappointment? Heaven forbid. As soon as he got home, he was going to fall on his knees and pray this through. He did not want to lose Josie. He could not bear it. Whatever it took, he would make things right between them again.

Chapter 22

Josie held Rosemary's clammy hand and stroked her forehead. "Everything is going to be fine. Be strong, Dear. The doctor is on his way."

"Pray." Rosemary groaned. "Please."

Josephine gladly slid to her knees beside the woman's bed. This was the first time she had been with a woman who was delivering a baby. Although a midwife was preparing to deliver the baby in case David didn't arrive in time, Josephine had also been called at Rosemary's request. Now Josephine trembled inside at the woman's pain and panicky eyes. Yet she tried to remain calm and reassuring. To do this she focused on her faith.

"Dear Lord. We have come to You before regarding this little one who will soon be born into this world. We pray that You will bring the baby safe and whole and protect this mother and ease her pain."

"Hello, ladies."

"Doctor."

"David." Relief filled Josie's voice. Although she had not seen David for a week, since the night she had made a fool of herself, she welcomed the sight of him now. Fear for Rosemary clutched her heart, making the mixed emotions she had been feeling over David seem trivial in comparison.

"Help me, Doctor. Please."

"Of course. Try not to worry, Rosemary. Who is going to give me a hand here?" He looked at Josephine.

She jerked away her gaze and pointed at the woman who would serve as his assistant. "She is." Then Josephine turned back to Rosemary. "I'll be just beyond the door, praying. The doctor is very capable."

A quick glance up at David revealed his warm expression. She gave a nod and left the room. Outside the closed door, Josie paced for what seemed like hours. Her thoughts ranged from worries over Rosemary's welfare to the state of her relationship with David.

It actually hurt to be in his presence and not be able to express the love she felt for him.

"Josie? Has the baby arrived?"

"Oh, Mother. I'm glad you're here. I don't know. It's been so long."

"Sometimes it takes awhile for babies to find their way into the world." A tear slid down Josie's cheek.

"Don't be troubled. Rosemary is in God's hands."

"No, it's not that. It's just David." She bit her lip to keep it from trembling.

"What has he done?"

"It's what he hasn't done."

"Oh." Mrs. Cline drew her daughter into an embrace. "All I can say is he doesn't know the joy he's missing not making you his own."

Josie hiccuped. A baby's cry filled the air. She covered her mouth and giggled through her tears. Her mother hugged her again, and Josie found herself crying and laughing at the same time. "I hope Rosemary is all right."

David's female assistant stuck her head out of the room, face all smiles. "We have us a little boy. The doctor's finishing up."

"How is Rosemary?"

"Fine."

Josie blotted her tears away and waited for the door to reopen. Finally she and her mother were invited into the room.

Slowly they approached the bed. Cradled in Rosemary's arms lay a red wrinkled infant with fuzzy blond hair. The baby's eyes were closed.

"Oh," Josie whispered. "How tiny and perfect." She lifted moist eyes to Rosemary. "I can see already that you are going to make a good mother."

"If only a decent home I had for him." As if she knew what Josie would say, the new mother added, "I remember. Just do my best."

"Trusting God helps," David added. "You have a fine boy."

Josie jerked at the sound of David's voice so near her ear.

"Doctor is right. Miss Josephine trusts God for me. It helps."

David gave instructions to the woman who had assisted him, then said, "Looks like I'm done here." He whispered to Josie, "May I speak with you in private?"

Josie glanced at him hesitantly. "I'll be right back, Rosemary."

"Sleepy, I am."

Outside the room, David asked, "How are you doing?"

"Exhausted. My first baby."

"Really? From what I could see, you were just what Rosemary needed."

"God is Who she really needs. But I won't give up on her."

He squeezed her hand. "I've got to get to the hospital. But I'd like to see you soon. Tonight? We need to talk."

"Yes."

"Get some rest."

❧❧

David was relieved that the delivery had gone well. As he walked back to the clinic, Josephine's remark about Rosemary needing God kept playing in his mind, strengthening his resolve to have another talk with Mrs. Schroeder. In fact, he would pop his head inside his apartment now in hopes of catching her. He hadn't spoken with her in days. Then he would check in at the clinic. His thoughts briefly turned to his assistant. He wanted to tell Tom how much he needed him and try to encourage him to stay at the clinic.

"Doctor. See I've cooked you a hot stew for such a cold, windy day."

"Smells delicious! And I'm ravenous. Just delivered a baby."

"How wonderful." Her expression full of awe for several long moments slowly changed to teasing. "Shouldn't you be having your own babies soon? Miss Cline is a good candidate for you."

"If I go and marry, you might have to find another job. And I would miss you."

"Perhaps. But God provides."

"What?" David's head jerked around. He was surprised at the woman's confession.

"Your God provides. You always say this."

"Do you believe it?"

"All these days I watch you. Now I know what you say is true."

"The woman who had the baby, she needs a miracle. She needs a home and a job so that she can bring the child up properly."

"Does she not think that God will provide?"

"She trusts in Josephine's prayers but doesn't pray herself. She doesn't know Jesus. Let's put it this way: It's the difference between being a friend of a friend of the king or being a friend of the king himself."

"Oh." She sounded as if she was understanding for the first time.

"Would you like for this Jesus to be your friend and companion, to save you?"

Mrs. Schroeder nodded. "I know I sin. I hate my neighbor. But if what you say is all true, then I must not hate her. I cannot change. I hate her."

"This is true, but you do not need to worry about it. Jesus will help you to forgive her."

"There is much to forgive. Especially her cursing me with the frog. I could have died."

"I have a confession. I should have told you long ago. The curse was not real."

"How can you say that? You saw the frog yourself."

"Yes, I did. We became friends that morning during my walk to your home. He was in my pocket. He helped me trick you so that you would get better."

Her eyes narrowed, and she shook her head. *"Nein.* It was the potion."

"The medicine made you heave. I tricked you. But only because I cared and didn't want you to be sick." David watched a myriad of emotions flicker across the German woman's face, including anger and doubt. He quickly added, "You didn't know about Jesus. I know it was wrong to pretend, but I thought that if I could save your body, God might be able to save your soul."

"You are a good man. I cannot be angry."

"Jesus wants to make you His."

"Pray with me."

David did. Afterward he saw that there had been a transformation in Mrs. Schroeder's countenance. She was now a true child of God. Eventually their conversation returned to the baby who had been born. "Rosemary needs to find Jesus, too. Will you pray for her?"

A light shone on Mrs. Schroeder's face. "She can live with me. I have room for them, and I would love to have a baby in the house. And if she lives with me, I can pray for her and never quit until she knows Jesus, too."

David was so surprised. "Why that's a wonderful idea. Wait until I tell her and Josie!"

"Yes. You do that. I hope it makes the woman happy. Then you tell Miss Josephine that you wish to marry her. Maybe then I will forgive you for the frog."

"You'll forgive me anyway. But I will consider it."

❧❧

That evening, David's manner toward Josie had changed. She attributed it to an emotional day. Josie listened attentively as he freely spoke of Mrs. Schroeder's conversion and about the sappy feelings he always felt after delivering a baby. Her heart melted, and when he told her about Mrs. Schroeder's offer, she shared his excitement. "I can't wait to tell Rosemary. It has also been an eventful, emotional day for me as well."

"How is this?"

"The workhouse received a letter from another workhouse. They want me to come and teach them about our program of personal patronesses."

"That's wonderful. What an opportunity for you."

"I never thought about sharing the idea. It's a bit intimidating."

"Just wear your egg whites and new fragrance, and you'll be a hit."

She playfully pushed him away, but David gripped her forearm and leaned close. "You were wonderful today."

"So were you," she breathed.

"I wanted to do this today at the workhouse. I've thought about it several times since." He inched toward her face, his eyes fixed on her mouth.

Josie held her breath. Could he really be going to kiss her again after all these months? When she saw that he truly intended to, she closed her eyes and waited. His kiss was tender and sweet, just as thrilling as it had been the day they had gone ice skating. Her heart raced.

He groaned. "I can't believe I've wasted all this time. I'm so sorry."

"Sorry about the kiss?" she asked, breathless.

"No, Darling. I've pushed my feelings aside for so long. I think I'm falling in love with you," he whispered huskily. He leaned toward her, and she felt drawn forward.

A clattering sound of boots in the hall broke the enchantment. They quickly pulled apart. Josie's face was hot, and David struggled to compose his expression.

Randolph Cline soon appeared around the corner. He stopped abruptly when he saw them.

"Father, come join us." What else could she say? She sensed David's displeasure.

Randolph dropped easily into a chair and studied David.

"Looks like you're feeling well," David said.

"Yes. Your remedy has done wonders; I'll give you that." Josephine cringed at her father's rude behavior. He met her gaze. "I hear you witnessed a baby's arrival today."

"Not exactly, Father. I didn't see it. But David delivered him."

Mrs. Cline stuck her head in the room. "Randolph! Are you bothering the young people?"

"I don't know. Am I bothering you, Dr. Wheeler?"

"Of course not. We were just discussing the baby."

"How delightful. Randolph loves babies." David looked surprised. "He's an excellent father," Mrs. Cline said.

"I know Josephine thinks very highly of you, Sir."

"And I prize my daughter. I wish only the best for her."

"Father, really," Josie scolded.

"As do I," David replied. Silence loomed in the room.

"Yes. Well, it's getting late, isn't it," Randolph urged.

David stood and beseeched Josie with his gaze. "I'll be going. It has been a pleasure."

After Josephine shot her father an angry look, she followed David out of the room. Behind them they could hear Mrs. Cline reprimanding her husband for his behavior.

"I'm sorry. He'll come around," Josie said. "Please do not give up on us."

At the door, David smiled. "I'm a patient man." He caressed her cheek. "What I said earlier about my feelings toward you, think about it."

"I'll think of nothing else."

"Keep praying for your father's heart to soften toward me."

Josie nodded, and her heart leapt in anticipation of what lay ahead.

Chapter 23

March brought happy days for Josie. Days of falling deeper and deeper in love with David. April was more of the same until one day toward the end of the month when after drawing in a deep breath of air filled with the fragrance of spring flowers, Josephine livened her step. She sensed that any day now David was going to ask her to be his wife. Father's stubborn attitude was the only thing standing in their way. They had discussed that very thing the previous evening when David had left the hat she was on her way now to return.

She opened the clinic's door. The bell jingled, and she stepped inside. The stringent smells of medicine and ointments accosted her. No patients were visible, but she could hear David speaking with someone behind one of the curtained off sections of the room. Tom's head was bent over the desk. He looked up at her.

"Hello, Miss Cline."

"Why so glum, Tom?"

His heavy expression lifted, and she saw a glimmer of yearning, as if he wished to share his burden with her but then thought better of it. "Nothing for you to worry over."

She had grown fond of Tom, especially so in these last two months when she and David had been together so often. "Oh?" She glanced at the curtain again. "I have the time."

The round shoulders sagged, and Josie's heart melted, wondering what could possibly be wrong.

"My time with David is almost finished."

"Is that why you look so sad?"

"I'm glad I'll be able to start my own practice. It's what I've always dreamed of. But my future is being mapped out, and I don't like where it's taking me."

"Who's mapping it out?"

"Dr. Drake and David. They both insist that I either take over the clinic or work at the hospital. But I always dreamed of being a country doctor."

"I see." Josie felt a spark of anger. Dr. Drake was not only managing David's life—overworking him and dragging him away from the clinic and work that he loved—but had managed to control this poor fellow's life as well. And how could David treat Tom the very way he did not like to be treated? "Once you are finished here, will you have met all the requirements to start your own practice?"

"Yes, but I'll need recommendations."

"I believe you need to have courage and tell the doctors that you have your own ideas and that you expect a good recommendation for all your good work."

David's unexpected voice startled her. "Josie, are you trying to steal my right hand away?"

"I'm only suggesting that he do what he wants with his life regardless of what others try to force him to do."

"Force him? I see you do not understand anything about my plans for the clinic."

"Come now, David. No need to get angry. You've said yourself that sometimes Dr. Drake forces his opinions on you."

"Have I? I don't recall saying that."

"Well, it's what I think, that's all."

"And what credentials do you possess that you may give superior counsel over that which Dr. Drake and I have given Tom on this matter?"

Josie felt her mouth drop open at the insult. She stared at David. His face was tight and pale. His eyes flashed with anger. She felt hurt that he would take sides against her. She glared back at him. "I have the mantle of experience."

"Hah!" he exploded, placing his hands upon his hips and narrowing his eyes.

"Once I worshiped my father as you do the good Dr. Drake. But then I realized that no human is infallible and I do better to listen to my own instincts, allowing for the guidance of my Lord. It is a lesson you have yet to learn." She gave his hat a toss, and it sailed across the room while she strode toward the door. Even in her fury, a part of her hoped that he would call out her name. Tell her to stop. Apologize.

He didn't.

She walked away without looking back. Before she had reached home, her head throbbed. After all these months, she had thought that they had gotten beyond this. The same problem that had plagued their relationship from the very start still reared its ugly head. Although she had grown and become more independent, there would be no relationship with David until he did the same and broke away from his dependence upon Dr. Drake.

Friendships were good. Loyalty and dedication toward those in authority were expected. But if David continued to remain subservient to Drake, then he wasn't the man she wanted to spend her life with.

Her hopes of marriage flashed to her mind. She placed her hand against her mouth to stifle the sobs that started to come forth. Her dreams were tumbling down. David was furious with her. This time she would not be the one to apologize.

Instantly the small voice she was accustomed to listening to asked, *Is your attitude pure?*

She knew it wasn't. She was angry and jealous. She swiped away her tears and tried to get control of her emotions before she passed through the interior of the house. If she could slip unnoticed to her room, maybe she and God could figure things out. Perhaps she needed to get away, take that trip she had been planning and give herself time to cool down and pray.

David watched her go, feeling vindicated for his anger yet knowing he was in the wrong. He did not wish to push her out of his life, and even though he had been striving and planning toward it, if he was honest with himself, he did not even want Tom to take over his clinic. What she said had the ring of truth, and it was humbling. Still, she had no right to interfere in his career—and just when he had been ready to ask for her hand in marriage. But could he live with such a controlling wife? He had been so shocked at her betraying attitude that he had wanted to force her to back down from her opinion. But she hadn't. And he had pushed her right out the door, maybe right out of his life. David excused himself, walked past a pale Tom, and went home.

What he'd said about her credentials was on target. But her retort was also accurate. In fact, it was what his conscience had been telling him all along. So why had he objected so vehemently? He squeezed his eyes closed. Because he had been putting off his decision about Drake's offer to be his personal assistant. He'd transferred all his problems onto this one issue and tossed it onto her as if everything were her fault.

It was time he made the decision about becoming Drake's assistant. It was his choice. He would deal with that before he dealt with Josephine. If they were to have a life together, he needed to have in his mind what exactly he was offering her. Anyway, if he knew Josephine, she needed time to cool off.

The next day he had barely entered the clinic before his assistant confronted him. "She was right."

David stopped in surprise and turned toward Tom. "I beg your pardon?"

"Miss Cline. What she said. She was right."

"Actually I did not really hear that much of your conversation."

"She saw that I was depressed and asked me why."

"You're depressed? Why didn't you tell me?"

"Men don't talk about such things."

"Ah, but the lovely lady makes a good listener. Women are emotional, caring creatures. Men are logical. You needed her sympathy, not her advice."

"I needed her advice. You need her, too."

"What are you saying?"

"It's always been my dream to be a country doctor. I have no big ambitions. I do not want to work in a hospital. I do not want to do things the way you and Dr. Drake do things. But I do want a good recommendation. I was afraid you wouldn't give me one. She helped me to see that I deserve one."

"Of course you do. I would never hold you back from accomplishing your dream. I'm appalled that you harbored such an idea. And you've done excellent in your training."

"Miss Cline gave me the courage I needed. I can understand how this all caught you off guard, but while I'm already stretching out my neck, I'm going to add one more thing. If you let her go, you are going to regret it for the rest of your life."

David ran his hands through his hair and stared at the door. His hesitation did not last long. He approached Tom and gripped his shoulder. "Thank you." Then he hastened toward the door, pausing momentarily. "Take over things here, will you?"

"Of course," Tom said with a smile.

"And don't worry about Drake. I'll take care of him for you," David said, and added silently, *And I'm not going to let Drake run my life anymore either. I'm quitting at the hospital, regardless of what he says, and I'm staying at the clinic. If he thinks I'm stagnating, so be it.* It wasn't Drake's fault. They just weren't made out of the same stuff.

"You've never called him that before."

David frowned, trying to understand what Tom meant.

"You left off his title."

David shrugged. "Guess it went with the shackles." He grinned wide. "Josephine's doings."

He stepped outside and hurried across town. If anyone had dared to step in his pathway, he would have mowed them over. Surprisingly when he confronted Drake, his mentor took his announcement with grace and wished him the best. Savoring the euphoria over the successful outcome of his problem with Drake, he marched toward the Clines'. It was time he pleaded for Josie's forgiveness and begged her to be his wife.

At the door, he was admitted by a servant.

"I'm here to see Miss Cline. I know she won't wish to see me. We've had a spat. Please tell her that she was right. I was wrong, and I've come to apologize."

The servant's face lit, then changed into a broad smile. "I'm sure Miss Cline would be glad to hear that if she were here. But she's not."

Chapter 24

Where is Miss Josephine?" David asked the Clines' servant.

"On a trip. She booked passage on the *Moselle* this morning. I do not know how long she shall be gone. Mrs. Cline has gone to see her off."

"Thank you."

David hurried away. Josephine had been planning a trip to present her ideas about the workhouse, but this reeked of running away. And it frightened him like nothing else ever had. He could not let her go without telling her that he was sorry—that he loved her and wanted to marry her.

His steps hastened to a run. He heard the *Moselle's* whistle and instinctively knew that he was too late. Still, he couldn't stop running. If need be, he would yell it out loud enough for all those gathered on the docks to hear that he loved her. At least she would go away knowing he wasn't the stubborn fool that he appeared to be.

As he rounded the next corner, he saw the great ship pulling out of the dock. He groaned. She had promised she wouldn't take the *Moselle* but a slower, safer ship. Josie was not to be seen. Nor Mrs. Cline. He paused on the edge of the small crowd to catch his breath. A man nearby who leaned on an ivory cane acknowledged him.

"Do you know the *Moselle's* next stop?"

"Fulton. She's a beauty. The swiftest vessel. . ."

David nodded and turned to go. He didn't have time to converse.

"Doctor?"

"Mrs. Cline! I'm so glad to see you. Where's Josie?"

Her voice was stilted. She sniffed. "Josephine just left for St. Louis. I don't suppose you had anything to do with this." Her red eyes accused.

"I'm afraid I did. That's why I need to speak with her. I must go."

"But, Doctor. . ."

Without even answering, David started to jog. It was only a mile up the river to Fulton, Josie's next stop, but he needed to zigzag through the city to reach it.

An inexplicable force propelled him forward. He lost sight of the ship and knew that everything depended upon how long she would remain docked. He could only hope that he would make it in time.

He rounded the corner and saw the *Moselle* was still there. Nearly out of breath he strained to continue, but then his heart sank. She started to leave the harbor. Still, he could not give up. He pressed forward with all his might. He could see passengers crowded together on the upper deck. The people who had gathered on the shore were cheering the *Moselle* off. It looked as if she were going to participate in a race with another ship. The noise was too loud. Josie would never hear him, even if he could find her.

And then it happened. While he was still a great distance away, his chest burning from the unaccustomed exertion, the most horrible tragedy he could ever witness took place.

A deafening explosion, as if a mine of gunpowder had gone off, blew the *Moselle* apart before his very eyes. The deck of passengers was blown into the air to instant destruction. He jerked to a stop, unable to understand the magnitude of the situation and at the same time knowing he didn't want to believe what he was seeing. The sounds of the explosion and steam and destruction came first, then the screams of those witnessing the event. His own scream joined theirs as he bent over in grief and screamed "No! No! No!" again and again.

As if in a dream, he raised his head and looked toward the scene. He must find Josie. He ran to the edge of the crowd and began to push through, adding his voice to all those around him who were searching for loved ones. "Josephine. Josie. Josie."

Someone pulled on his coat and would not release him. "Help us, Doctor. Please."

As much as he wanted to hope that Josie was alive and that he would find her, he could not neglect the wounded who needed his medical attention. Working through a veil of tears in an environment that seemed surreal, and many times with trembling hands, he went from patient to patient doing what he could to revive nearly drowned individuals. He set bones, applied tourniquets, doing whatever he could without any supplies. But as he worked, he bitterly accused himself. It was all his fault. If he hadn't gotten angry, Josie never would have been on that ship. All his fault and what was he going to do without her?

Soon all of Cincinnati's citizens learned of the news. Other physicians arrived on the scene, and even those without medical training, to do what they could to help the injured, console those who lost loved ones, and to search for missing persons. His assistant found him, and once David had his medical bag, he began to treat those who had scalded skin. Yet his ears and eyes were on the alert. Where was his dear Josie? Could he bear it if he found her?

"Doctor!" David looked up. It was Randolph Cline. His face was twisted with grief. "Have you seen my Josie?"

"No. I'm just about done here. Can you help hold this? Then I'll join you to search for her."

The man assisted, but it was as if he were in a daze. Afterward, David went with him and together they started to work their way through the confusion.

It seemed forever and at the same time as if they had not gone far at all until Otis Washburn saw them. "Doctor. Can you help here?"

The reporter's woman friend had splinters in her arms. David took an instrument from his bag and began to remove them, allowing Randolph to help. As they worked, the reporter confessed his regrets.

"We were on the shore watching. It's all my fault she's hurt." The reporter started to weep unashamedly.

"Nonsense." David identified with the man, wanting to take all the blame for everything upon his own shoulders. He gripped the other's arm. "It was an accident."

"No. The newspapers' praise of the speed and power of the *Moselle* no doubt goaded the captain and owners to race against others, taking chances with the boilers. I never dreamed something like this would occur."

"Your friend is going to be fine."

"Father? David!"

At the sound of her voice, David spun round, searching the crowd for his beloved. She was alive and running toward them. She hurled herself into her father's arms. They wept and clung to each other in desperation. After a time, Randolph eased her away. "I thought I had lost you. So many things went through my mind. Your doctor has been courageous." She looked at her father, as if to ask for permission, and he nodded.

David gave Randolph a grateful look and drew Josephine close, whispering against her temple. "I came for you, but you'd already gone. How did you manage to escape harm?"

"I saw you at the port when we left, speaking to Mother. I knew I could not run away from you so I got off at Fulton. I started hurrying to find you. But when the ship exploded, I must have fainted. When I came to, I was confused."

"I know that it is selfish and weak of me to rejoice that you are alive in the midst of this tragedy. But I cannot help it. I. . ."

Josie pulled away. "I know." Her face paled. "I'm going to be sick."

David assisted her and held her until she was feeling stronger. She swiped her tears away. "You saved my life, showing up that way."

Randolph Cline, who had been listening to their private conversation and hovering ready to help his daughter, repeated, "You saved her life. How can I ever repay you?"

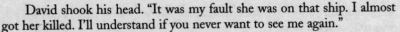

David shook his head. "It was my fault she was on that ship. I almost got her killed. I'll understand if you never want to see me again."

Randolph frowned. "It was an accident. Isn't that what you told Otis Washburn?"

Meanwhile Josie gazed helplessly about her. "We must do something to help these people."

Otis Washburn gave David a wave. He and his woman friend leaned upon each other for support. All around them were huddles of people embracing, giving aid.

"There's still much to do," David said.

"I'll help, too," Randolph offered.

Chapter 25

David and Tom worked through the night at the clinic. The door opened and David looked up with surprise. "Mr. Cline."

"May we talk?"

David glanced around the clinic. "It's full in here. Do you want to step outside?" He nodded. It seemed inappropriate to hear the birds singing at the top of their lungs after such devastation the day before. "How can I help you?"

Cline cleared his throat. "I wish to apologize for the way I've thwarted your work."

"Accepted."

"That's all?"

"I hold nothing against you, Sir. How could I? I love your daughter."

"Let me explain. When I met my wife, she was enamored of Drake. I thought I'd lose her to him. For years I had to listen to his praises from her. It had nothing to do with you."

"Drake was a happily married man. And Mrs. Cline seems very happy with you."

"I know. I've been a fool."

"Well, if it's any consolation, I've learned to let go of him also. To do a bit more thinking on my own, with the Lord's help."

"Sound advice for someone so young. Quite humbling, Doctor."

"Not at all. It's the advice your daughter gave me. She's the wise one."

Randolph beamed. "She's something, isn't she?"

David cleared his throat. "Perhaps this is the right time to ask you about her. For her hand, I mean. I know I'm not what you intended for her, but I promise to take care of her and cherish her."

Randolph Cline exhaled deeply. "I suspected this was coming."

"If it helps, be assured that even though I don't have much to offer her, I believe we're like-minded."

Randolph burst into boisterous laughter. "That's a good one. No man is like-minded with any woman. But you'll do good to listen to her. I'll give you my approval, but of course it's Josie who will have to make up her own mind. And money isn't a problem. She has her own inheritance. And I don't believe I'll have to worry about you squandering it." His eyes narrowed. "But don't be giving it all away either. I'll have to give you some lessons in business management. I believe we may make a good team." He extended his hand. "Thanks for saving my Josie."

David pumped the older man's hand. "Thank you, Sir. You won't regret it. I promise."

When Randolph departed, David felt like joining the birds in their song.

"What is it that you have to show me?" Josie asked, her expression wary. Although the weeks since the explosion had been hard for everyone in Cincinnati with the loss of loved ones, friends, and neighbors, she had been delirious with contentment now that her father and David had made peace. But today everyone had been acting peculiar—as if they were in on a secret.

Her mother's eyes had twinkled. She and her father seemed closer than ever. Josie knew that the explosion had affected many families that way. Everyone was thankful for their loved ones.

"You'll see. Close your eyes and take my hand," David urged.

She did as he suggested and allowed him to lead her from the waiting room of his clinic into one of the curtained off areas.

"You can open them now."

She did, and instantly they brimmed with tears. Looking up at him with all the love she felt, she said, "You can be so romantic."

"I know I can get in a rut. Please forgive me."

"I do."

Mrs. Schroeder peeked her head inside the curtain and winked at her.

"Please, sit down. Enjoy." David motioned Josie to a chair. She took in the table, cloth, flowers, and the dinner that Mrs. Schroeder had prepared and intended to chaperone. He seated himself across from her.

"A sleigh ride would have suited the occasion better, but I am not a magician," he said.

She clasped both of his outstretched hands across the table. "I believe with the Lord's help you can accomplish most anything."

"Your encouragement, your very presence is the one thing that has been missing in my life."

"I have not been encouraging to you?"

"That is not what I meant. But I am not to be rushed. We must take our time here and enjoy this moment."

She gazed into his emotion-filled eyes and saw the love that he held for her. "So what is the occasion?"

"The celebration of our love. I love you, Josie."

"I love you, too." She caressed his cheek. "You are a good man."

"Marry me."

She caught her breath but did not hesitate for an instant. She had waited too long for him to ask. "Yes!"

He chuckled at her eagerness and leaned across the table, and she could see that he was intent upon kissing her. She leaned forward also, but they were still lacking several inches from being able to meet. He smiled. "I see I need practice at this. Come here, *speziell Dame.*"

"*Stattlich Doktor.*" She giggled nervously.

Still holding her hand, he rose and drew her up and toward him. She slid into his arms and returned his kiss. When they drew apart, he pressed his face into her hair. "Oh, Josie. You're wearing lavender again."

She slowly drew away. "I love you so." Then she smiled. "Can we go tell Mother and Father?"

"After our dinner."

"Oops." She clamped a hand across her mouth. "I forgot."

"Let's eat, then we'll go tell your parents. And maybe after that we'll visit Tom. He's getting ready to leave soon. I'm glad we can give him the news before he moves on."

"Yes. And you'll want to tell Dr. Drake."

"He stopped in today. It was the first I'd seen him since I'd resigned from the hospital and turned down his offer of being his personal assistant. He wanted to make sure there were no hard feelings. He really is an amazing man. But he's gone now on another trip. I am eager to write about our engagement to my family."

"I hope they can all come to the wedding." They stared intently into each other's eyes. She thought about how much they had learned, how far they had come to get to this point of love and trust.

"Your father and I are agreed upon one thing."

"Oh? What is that?" she asked.

"We don't want you taking that trip to St. Louis alone."

"So now it's you *and* Father conniving together and telling me what to do."

"A nice switch, isn't it?"

"Yes. So are you going to come with me when I take the trip? Is that what you are so tactfully trying to say?"

"Maybe. We could combine it with a honeymoon."

"I believe the three of us finally agree. And I believe this calls for another kiss, Dr. Spokes."

But before they could seal their vows, the curtain moved. Mrs. Schroeder, who wore a smile of approval, quickly jerked it closed again.

A Letter to Our Readers

Dear Readers:

In order that we might better contribute to your reading enjoyment, we would appreciate you taking a few minutes to respond to the following questions. When completed, please return to the following: Fiction Editor, Barbour Publishing, Inc., P.O. Box 719, Uhrichsville, OH 44683.

1. Did you enjoy reading *Ohio?*
   - ❑ Very much—I would like to see more books like this.
   - ❑ Moderately—I would have enjoyed it more if _____
   _____
   _____

2. What influenced your decision to purchase this book?
   (Check those that apply.)
   - ❑ Cover
   - ❑ Back cover copy
   - ❑ Title
   - ❑ Price
   - ❑ Friends
   - ❑ Publicity
   - ❑ Other

3. Which story was your favorite?
   - ❑ *Proper Intentions*
   - ❑ *Ample Portions*
   - ❑ *Lofty Ambitions*
   - ❑ *Castor Oil and Lavender*

4. Please check your age range:
   - ❑ Under 18
   - ❑ 18–24
   - ❑ 25–34
   - ❑ 35–45
   - ❑ 46–55
   - ❑ Over 55

5. How many hours per week do you read? _____

Name _____

Occupation _____

Address _____

City _____ State _____ Zip _____

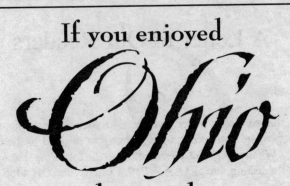